HIDDEN PRINCESS

The Rebirth of Making Mary

Dedra Lori Muhammad

Copyright © 2022 Dedra Lori Muhammad

All rights reserved

ISBN: 978-0-9766346-7-6

No part of this book may be reproduced, or stored in a retrieval system, or transmitted in any form or by any means, electronic, mechanical, photocopying, recording, or otherwise, without express written permission of the publisher.

Printed in the United States of America
Rising South Literacy School
Madison, Alabama

Dedication and Acknowledgments

To the Mothers of Civilization

And the Fathers who Uplift, Support, and Protect Them

CONTENTS

Title Page
Copyright
Dedication
Foreword
Chapter One — 1
Chapter Two — 15
Chapter Three — 30
Chapter Four — 35
Chapter Five — 53
Chapter Six — 73
Chapter Seven — 78
Chapter Eight — 98
Chapter Nine — 106
Chapter Ten — 118
Chapter Eleven — 147
Chapter Twelve — 171
Chapter Thirteen — 189
Chapter Fourteen — 200
Chapter Fifteen — 224
Chapter Sixteen — 241
Chapter Seventeen — 267
Chapter Eighteen — 303
Chapter Nineteen — 322
Chapter Twenty — 334

Chapter Twenty-One	351
Chapter Twenty-Two	372
Chapter Twenty-Three	390
Chapter Twenty-Four	418
Chapter Twenty-Five	423
About The Author	429

FOREWORD

The main question when considering a volume like the one you are about to read, is where to begin.

"Hidden Princess: The Rebirth of Making Mary" is an opus of great importance to those who seek to understand the dynamics and shadings of "The Black Experience" – and that it is not just one such experience.

As a student of history, I am reminded of the saying of The Honorable Elijah Muhammad: "History is above all our studies. The most attractive and best qualified to reward our research. As it develops the springs and motives of human actions, and displays the consequence of circumstances, which operates most powerfully on the destinies of the human being." Clearly, the events of individuals and families, neighbors and friends as written here, occurred against the backdrop of one of the most troubled and turbulent periods of all time, a period the aftershocks of which are still being felt today.

In order to weave a narrative like the one you are about to take in, a writer must have several qualifications of perspective and intellect. Such an author must be acquainted with the struggles of a people whose sojourn in America has been laden with a peculiar kind of tribulation. She must be able to empathize with and grasp the strivings and yearnings of "everyday people" to be loved and respected – to matter! This writer must be able to know, understand and contextualize the great happenings of the era under discussion, and how they affect the main characters as the apologue unfolds. The essayist who can create a full, robust read about the lives of "just plain folks" in times that are just plain apocalyptic, is the successful scribe, indeed. Author Dedra Muhammad is this kind of writer.

Dedra Muhammad is an intellectual of rare and unusual sensitivity and subtlety, possessor of the only kind of mind that could render such a work as this that places its moving account of a family's trails and triumphs (moving) into the perfect, pinpoint accurate atmospheric context.

As I write this, I reflect on the unique qualifications of Mrs. Muhammad to pen this tome. She herself is the daughter of a family of migrants from the rural South to the bustling cities of the early 20th century. She spent her college years as a star student-athlete at the prestigious University of Michigan at Ann Arbor, and today is an educator in the public school system in Alabama.

The book you are about to read is compelling, and- dare I say it? – interesting. Unlike many historic novels, there is no sacrifice of homiletics on the altar of history.

I know you are eager to begin the text of "Hidden Princess," but if you will allow, I will convey three more brief points.

First, it is my honor and pleasure to extend my greetings of peace and paradise to you, obviously a discerning and discriminating reader. I am Jamil Muhammad (no relation to the author), a Student of Islam and a Muslim Minister in the Nation of Islam for the last 41 years. I make that notation not to impress you, but to impress upon you that a life of work like mine has prepared me with a unique set of qualifications to recommend "Hidden Princess…" As an activist-servant leader in cities across America, it has been my assignment to serve communities filled with the human witness that the account you are about to take in, is true.

For anyone who cares not only to know the problems that Black people in America have faced, but also to understand solutions, this book is a must-read. The plight of Black Americans has been misrepresented, exploited, distorted, ignored, and outright historically revised, but Mrs. Muhammad's work rings true and is borne out as such by its uncanny sense of period, geography and sociological circumstance. Yes, it is a novel, but it is so much more. It is the story of an individual family and how they dealt with a tragically ubiquitous, collective reality.

Finally, "Hidden Princess…" will give even a casual reader pause, and compel him or her to reflect on the private account of their own family history. This volume that Dedra Muhammad wrote, that sits on my desk, between my pencil jar and my prized coffee mug, is like a trip back home, down the long and dusty road of time. This chronicle will move you. As I read it, her characters morphed into my own elders and ancestors. Carol and the Stranger and Beena and Casey and Vivian? Yes. But also Columbus and Herman and Golda and Leona. Not just this family, dear reader – OUR family.

So, prepare yourself. Prepare yourself and make room in your library for a cherished new addition: "Hidden Princess: The Rebirth of Making Mary".

Jamil Muhammad

Washington, DC

February, 2022

CHAPTER ONE
"The North Star"

As Vivian strolled down Woodward Avenue, in the heart of downtown Detroit, past the Hudson Department store, eight stories tall with its brilliant wide-arched bay windows trimmed with Apostle Island brownstone, she wondered if Lee would have the decency to meet her at the appointed time. She was so sick of him and his beautifully decorated bag of lies. She didn't know if she had the patience to let him continue to dog her until and unless he stumbled upon a piece of maturity one day. She wanted a rewarding life, yet each passing day with him convinced her she was being suckered down a slippery slope to hell. Peace had never existed in their household, not in Michigan, and certainly not in Florida.

This was all still so very new to her, the 1924 big city life. It was only just approaching midday, and already the streets were frenetic with vigor. Horns were honking, people were hustling to restaurants and diners for their lunch breaks, and loads of so-called Negroes from down South were getting off trains in their tattered clothes, carrying paper bags stuffed with cold chicken and pork chops, meeting their relations at the station, and so incredibly happy to have escaped the nightmare of a Jackson, Mississippi, an Athens, Alabama, or a deep-step, Georgia gone lynch-crazy. The so-called Negroes who had followed the North Star were satisfied to be in a place of opportunity where a man could do honest work like making cars and bring home a paycheck that would be strong enough to secure him and his family.

Vivian and Lee had come North for varied reasons. As she walked past Kresge's, peering into the window at the household and personal items the dime store was famous for, she feared that following her sisters up North with Lee might prove to be the biggest mistake of her life. Things had gotten worse between them. Had she been fooling herself all along about his love for her? Seeing her own sad reflection in the Kresge's window, Vivian admitted to herself that Lee found it outright easy to beat her whether they were under the Florida sun or over the pebbled roads in Pontiac. Had she not made it worse by moving in with Minnie and Henry? How in the world could she have done that, she brooded, with the overwhelming rivalry that existed between Henry and her husband?

And her knowing that Mary…

Well, at least it would be easier to keep the truth about Mary hidden because a few months earlier, Lee managed to separate the three of them from Minnie and Henry whenever he purchased a dingy room three blocks down the road from their house on California Street. She recalled how Lee had gripped her elbow while leading the tour of the new jailhouse, and how her guilt from her past culpabilities kept a forced smile on her face. No, she could not complain much as she considered the truckload of unhealthy actions she had engaged in with Henry.

Vivian's thoughts were suddenly interrupted just after she realized she was standing in front of the Fox Theater. It was two o'clock and Lee wasn't there. She checked herself in the window of the theater and was pleased with the physical mirroring. She was stylishly dressed in her flapper cloche hat and a copasetic dress that showcased her ample bosom in a tubular bodice that draped straight down to her waist, and then to a full dark green skirt that came down to her mid-calf. She had made the outfit herself from a pattern in a Sears catalog. After struggling with not knowing how to sew well all her life, Vivian finally mustered the diligence to teach herself. She had a lot of spare time these days. Lee liked the outfit a lot, but not Henry, who thought it was too revealing. She laughed to herself when she pictured Henry constantly commenting on her style of dress, and he wasn't shy about offering his disapproval ratings. However, Vivian rated Henry as not keeping up with the trends because the new American style was for women to show *more* naked flesh, not less.

Lee had promised her he would meet her at the Fox and that he would be on time. They had driven over from Pontiac that morning in Lee's new car that he'd gotten from Casey, and they had a late breakfast downtown. Afterward, Lee gave Vivian a fist full of money so she could do some shopping while he ran a few quick errands. He told her he had some business to attend to with Casey and that she wouldn't have to worry about his keeping their appointment. But she knew that business with Casey meant bootleg business, or just as likely, prostitute business. And she knew Lee had a weakness for women that neither marriage nor moving to Pontiac had cured.

"He sure runs after these hot-to-trot Detroit women," she muttered under her breath. "But has the nerve to tell me how much he loves me." She smiled faintly at the doorman as he kept an eye on her while he greeted a splattering of patrons. She could tell he was an islander.

"Are you staying for the movie, my lady?"

"No," she said with a fake beam." "I'm waiting on my husband, but I'm rather early." She would not reveal her discontent to a stranger. The Haitian left her alone.

After waiting fifteen more minutes for Lee, with her left foot on the large stone road while her right foot rested in the grass as though she couldn't figure out whether to stay or leave, Vivian eventually decided to go inside of the theater and watch the silent feature that was just starting. What's the sense in wasting this entire day, she thought. Using the fancy pocket size stationery her best friend, Madeline had given her as a wedding present, Vivian scribbled a note advising Lee that either he would find her inside of the theater, or at the Detroit Urban League. The Haitian doorman at the Fox extended his sparkling clean white gloved hand to accept the note with a gleaming smile that matched his gloves perfectly.

The movie was called *Broken Blossoms*. It was directed by D.W. Griffith and told the love story of a poor and gentle Chinese man who was addicted to opium and an illegitimate English girl from the slums who was abused by her father, a prizefighter. In the end, the father killed the girl. Vivian sat in the darkness of the theater, tears rolling down her cheeks, wondering how someone could kill the very person they loved. She was so affected by the film that she stayed seated for long moments after the final credits rolled.

Finally, she got up and went outside. Lee was still not there, and the Haitian doorman confirmed no man had inquired about her. It was three-thirty now. Vivian could feel herself getting frosty. This was just like Lee, she thought, with his trifling self. Whenever he was with Casey, he seemed to get all meek and timid like a dinky kid. With her, however, he was the big bad man who roared like a lion and knocked things around. It was scary.

The doorman made small talk with her about his arrival from Haiti a few years back, just before the United States military took up occupancy there, and how he had mixed feelings about being in America. Nonetheless, he said he liked working at the theater. Vivian discussed Florida with the Haitian while her eyes darted every time she heard a moving vehicle.

"I'll be getting along…"

"Call me Mustafa."

"Thank you, Mustafa." He nodded. "Oh! I need to cross out the part about being in the theater; may I have my note back, please?" Just as he reached for it, Vivian shook her head. "I'd best write a clean note." As she took out fresh stationery, she realized how silly she must have looked by doing so, when it was obvious by now that her husband had stood her up. Mustafa was silent while she took extra pains to show herself as proper and worthy. She handed him the revised message and muttered, "Be sure to give that note to my husband if you're still here whenever he comes." She rushed away without making eye contact. Mustafa used two fingers to sound a shrill, authoritative whistle. Startled, Vivian found herself being whisked into a streetcar.

"I don't mind walking," Vivian responded to the air as Mustafa passed the driver a nickel. Other than the name of her destination, she didn't understand the content of the Haitian dialogue shared between the streetcar driver and Mustafa.

In no time, she neared the Columbia Street Community Center. "At least I can see Mr. Gancy," she said aloud without realizing it. Gancy, the twin brother of the director of the Detroit Urban League, and the co-director had befriended Vivian and Lee whenever they first came to town. He helped them adjust to city life and even got Lee an interview at one of the automobile factories. But Lee had met Casey through Vivian's sister Robeena before the interview, and that had been the end of that. As it turned out, Lee was more interested in a quick buck, even if it was illegal, than in working hard at a sure thing.

"Baby, I'm a man who works smart," he had told her. "Not hard." What was she to do? Anyway, she liked Gancy and the people around him because they helped the poor migrants from down South who were now coming North by the tens of thousands seeking a better life. They helped people find homes and jobs; they assisted the poor with their medical needs. Under Mr. Gancy's leadership, since 1919, the center had gained a reading room, a baby clinic, and a music school. Vivian loved to go to the center whenever she could get away from all the twisted madness of her life with Lee. It was nice just to breathe the atmosphere of peace she found at the center, and to help Mr. Gancy. Of course, Lee didn't like that either. He accused her of wanting to get with Gancy. Vivian tried to explain that volunteering at the center brought balance to her life and filled her with a joy that, even though it was temporary, Vivian needed as much as she needed water and food. At the center, teaching the children how to read and listening to them as they sang and played in the music school made her feel she was near the purpose of her life, which she had never known before. Vivian accepted that she was not a top reader, given that she'd dropped out of school so early, but the children at the center, some of them had no schooling at all!

As she walked through the door, Gancy ran to greet her. "Vivian, if this ain't a surprise!" he said. "What brings my favorite volunteer out today? Some of the children were just asking about you. And where's that baby and husband of yours?" Gancy, a tall dark man with a slim mustache, reached out to hug her and she hugged him back. He was careful not to take advantage of the opportunity to squeeze her too closely--that would have to wait until he was absolutely sure she felt the flame burning in his heart.

"Now, Mr. Gancy," she said, "you know I use every opportunity I can to sneak over here. Mary is fine--she's with my sister, Minnie. And Lee's fine, too, I suppose. He was supposed to meet me at two o'clock in front of the Fox." She emitted a deep sigh of disgust. "You can guess how that went. Anyway, I thought I'd come by and check on everyone."

"And we're so glad you did," said Gancy. "It's always good to see you, darling. Besides, there's someone back in the music school who's just itching to see you." Gancy took her hand and she followed him to the far end of the music room, painted in a bright orange, with photographs of King Oliver's Creole Jazz Band, Beethoven, and Scott Joplin on the walls. There were three class sessions per day, for violin, trumpet, and piano. This was the final class.

"Good afternoon, Miss Vivian," the students said in sing-song unison, with the crisp military precision that had been instilled in them by their instructors. The martial spirit was quickly broken just as a diminutive but effusive youth from the back of the class in the piano section broke out and ran to hug Vivian.

"Hey, Miss Vivian," said the boy, gleaming. Vivian beamed with delight.

"Hey David," she said. "Are you alright?" He nodded. It was twelve-year-old David Foster. David, his parents, and seven brothers and sisters had arrived in Michigan from Mississippi at about the same time that she and Lee had. Sadly, David's mother had died during the birthing labor of her ninth child within a month of their migration. Vivian learned of his story from Gancy and thus showered special attention upon the child, who seemed to her unusually bright. They had been drawn to each other by a special magnetism.

The staff members helped the boy's father get a job and had also helped to find a house large enough to accommodate him and his eight children. As a result of the safety net provided by the staff at the center, the boy was flourishing, despite his mother's absence. The music teachers discovered that he had a unique aptitude for the piano.

"Vivian, you have to hear what David's been working on," Gancy exclaimed. David went back, took his seat at the piano, and began to play a classical piece so masterfully that tears welled up in Vivian's eyes. Then, with a devilish glint in his eyes as he looked at Vivian, David did a deft segue into Scott Joplin's "Maple Leaf Rag," his slender fingers nimbly bringing the jazz piece to life. Vivian laughed.

"You clever little boy," she cried. Gancy knew Scott Joplin was one of Vivian's favorite artists by the way she screeched whenever he had given her one of Joplin's records as a gift. Gancy laughed and walked away, pleased to see the sparkle in Vivian's eyes as she conversed with David. If music made her happy, Gancy vowed he would buy a case of records and give her one every week.

She spent the next thirty minutes with David, catching up with what he had been doing and how he'd been feeling since the last time she'd seen him, listening very carefully to both the words he shared about the loss of his mother, and the sad spirit that came from the words. Afterward, they embraced again, and he looked up at her and said: "Miss Vivian, I love you the same like I do my sisters and cousins 'nem."

"Oh, David." His innocence made Vivian want to shield him from every sad occurrence and any future pain. "You know you're my favorite," she whispered into his ear, making sure no other child heard her.

"You're my favorite, too," he said proudly. David didn't care who heard. He was content to be her favorite because all the other children had mothers. He wanted the other children to know that though his real mother had died, a new princess had chosen him to be her play son. "I'd promise that on a whole stack of Bibles."

She hugged him again, fighting back tears, wondering why she was so weepy. She taught reading to a few other students in her brief hour there, then Gancy walked her out of the center slightly before five o'clock. With her hand in his, Gancy told her he was on his way to Pontiac, too, once the center closed. His sister lived only two blocks from Vivian. Gancy offered her a ride home since she didn't know where Lee could be, but then her ears were trained to squealing tires a short way in the distance.

Suddenly, Lee drove up, screeching to a halt. Vivian walked ahead of Gancy down the steps of the center and opened the car door. Gancy knew the score. He didn't expect Vivian to wave goodbye, and he didn't bother to acknowledge Lee before he slid backward inside the center.

"Get in the car, bitch," Lee hissed. Embarrassed, she did, not sure if Gancy was still watching. Lee reached across her lap to slam the door shut. Then, he gave her a quick backhand that drew blood from her mouth. And he drove home to Pontiac.

~~~

On the inside, Lee was an emotional basket case. She had done it again. Vivian had succeeded in pissing him off to the point of no return. In the typical forecast, everything was just about her fault because today was the day he anticipated treating her like a queen. That morning, Lee got the bright idea to plan something special for Vivian, whether she deserved it or not. They would go for an outing in Detroit, and it would be fun. He needed to meet Casey, anyway, so he would kill two birds with one stone. When he announced that he had planned their day, she seemed excited about hanging out in the city with him, and for the occasion, she put on one of the halfway acceptable dresses she'd recently made.

Unfortunately, their brightly intended day turned into a stormy parade of madness when Lee suspected the worst after he arrived at the Fox Theater as planned, only to find that Vivian had trotted her fast tail down to the Columbia Street Detroit Urban League where the well-to-do and intriguing Gancy worked. Lee had given her money to shop while he took care of his business with Casey. All he asked for in return was that she meet him at the Fox. Although Lee was three hours late making their appointment, he didn't think that warranted her going down to the urban league. Consequently, after he read the theater doorman's note from Vivian stating her whereabouts, he raced over to Columbia Street in anger. He saw her prancing down the steps with Gancy, as though he was her lover. Lee guessed she was probably using her soft, sexy voice on him because that was her catchy innocent lure.

Lee glared at Gancy, but the minute he spied Lee's car, Gancy turned away, and Vivian hurried sinfully down the steps, Lee perceived. He couldn't wait to slap her silly, which he did the moment she plopped down in her seat. He noted from a sideways glance that her mouth was bleeding, and that was fine. She could deal with that and her actions that mandated his chastisement. For a long while as he drove, they didn't speak to each other. Vivian let the blood dry on her face in silent mutiny. Finally, she mustered the emotional strength to look for something to clean her face. Soon, they would arrive at her sister's house to pick up the baby, and she didn't want Ms. "I told you so" Minnie to see what Lee had done.

She found some napkins in the glove compartment. Adding a drop of spittle helped to clean the sore area, yet her lip had already begun to swell from the inside. "I'm tired of being hit on all the time, Lee," she whimpered. Lee was exceeding normal speeds as he tore down Woodward Avenue with only one hand on the steering wheel and with a gangster lean.

"I don't hit you all the time, girl. Quit exaggerating."

"Please slow down, Lee…"

"That's one thing I can say about you: You ought to be in some of the movies you be watching, 'cause you can act your stockings off." He hit the brakes just in time to avoid crossing traffic when he ignored a stop sign.

"Lee! Watch out!" He took off again, smashing his foot hard on the accelerator.

"*You* watch out…if you know what's good for you. That stop sign shouldn't even be there. So, don't tell me how to drive. Only a thoroughbred can wheel this piece. You wanna drive?" Without looking at him she shook her head. "See, you think you're slick, but you can't play a niggah that's down with the game. I created the game!"

"Just let me out of the car!" She screamed at him. "I'll walk home." She didn't want to cry, but she couldn't help herself. He was so rude. She didn't think she could stand being in his presence for another moment without exploding.

"You want me to slap you again? Then don't tell me what to do. I *told* you to meet me at the Fox. I ain't tell you to go hopping down to no Urban League. You are too burning hot for your own good."

"I stayed at the Fox waiting for you for almost three hours!"

"A woman is supposed to have patience with her man. I had a big emergency today, and that's how come I was late. You think you're too good to wait more than a few hours? All you had to do was find something to read, watch a movie, or, hell, flirt with the doorman like you probably was doing anyway."

"I watched a movie…"

"Just be obedient like a normal female. I don't want no hard-core bitch. If you are at a movie theater, then sit your ass in there and watch another damn movie and wait! You can't figure that out? Damn!"

"That's your favorite part of this marriage…if all I can do is what you say, I guess that'll be heaven for you."

He softened slightly. "Princess, I'm trying to build our marriage. Can't you see that?"

"I don't see how you think you're going to build something with me when you are with Casey doing all sorts of illegal stuff."

"Casey and me ain't as close as we used to be, baby. But ain't nothing I do ever good enough for you. I even told Casey that it wasn't a good idea for us to hang so close since me and you moved away from your family, and we are trying to be on our own. The reason I needed to see him is he promised me the title to this car, and I had to get it—-make him stick to his word, but he didn't like that. I'm trying to do this thing right, muffin." He reached under his seat for a pint of liquor that was more than half empty. "That's what took me so long. Casey was trying to convince me to be his boy, but I ain't never been nobody's boy and I ain't gonna start being a boy up here."

"Don't drink that, Lee…"

"I told him that none of his money could tie me to a life that would destroy me. Been there, done that. See, baby?" He pointed to the windshield where the title had been thrown. "I'm working things out for us. I got you this car…"

"Lee!"

He swung the jug wildly, almost hitting her in the jaw. "This ain't even a pint." He turned it up and finished it in three gulps. Vivian was concerned that he couldn't clearly see the road while he drank. She grinded her feet as though she was pressing brakes on the floorboard until her ankles ached. Lee thought about how handsome the Haitian was, then his mind darted to what Vivian might secretly think about the man's rich accent. "Right about now, you should wish I *had* another pint, and then if I drank that, maybe I would begin to see some pleasure in the fact that I married a slut like you."

Crying noiselessly, she refused to answer. She would leave him if he couldn't appreciate her. So what if people whispered behind her back or if her sisters would see her as a failure—she didn't have to take his mess. There was no way he could say he adored her and then be so disrespectful. As she slipped more into a depression, she no longer cared how reckless he was driving. She only wanted to make it to Minnie's house in one piece as soon as humanly possible so she could get out of the car and tell Lee to take a hike.

"It ain't no sense in you getting all quiet now, Vivian. You wanted to put your mouth on me…" He slowed the car relatively, realizing he was losing control. "Well, I'm now putting my mouth on you. Somebody gotta let you know that you are full of horse manure."

"Just leave me alone!" She couldn't help feeling provoked that time, but she warned herself not to utter another word to him until her anger subsided.

"I did tell Casey that. I know you ain't believing me, but that's alright." Just as he turned down Franklin Road, Vivian started straightening herself in the mirror. She whipped out some of her mother's strawberry scented oil that she'd taken from Florida and smoothed it on her wrists. "Girl, I'm trying to be a family man. I'm gonna do whatever it takes to keep my family together, you dig?" Lee glanced at her to make sure she agreed. He couldn't believe she had her make-up purse out, and that she was getting pretty when moments ago she was the queen of slop and tears. Once they reached the corner of Franklin Road and California Street, it dawned on Lee that Vivian expected to get out of the car at her sister's house. "Where in shitsmobile do you think you are going, whore?"

"I want to see my sister and just get away from you!" Swiftly, he pulled off the road and almost plunged into a ditch near the corner where the land was uncultivated. Nearing three hundred and sixty degrees, the tires spun in the dirt until the nose of the engine was facing the road again. They were two houses away from her sister's house. Lee jerked the gear to the parking mode and charged out of the car like a wrathful bull. Vivian fumbled with her door handle in her hurry to escape the vehicle before he could make it to her side. As she was tripping out of the car, he grabbed her arm, dragged her with one swooping motion and flung her over the hood. The back of her body smashed on the hard metal with a tremendous thump. Not yet feeling the sting, Vivian now hoped someone would come outside and catch him in the act, but the street was quiet.

"Do I look like some plantation slave to you? You think you can tell me where you're going without asking for my permission? I'll kick the wind out of you." Vivian rolled slowly away from him because she felt if she made any sudden movements, he would pounce on her.

She dulled her voice. "I just want to see my family." He walked away from her about six feet, only to turn around and stand within centimeters of her.

"Don't play me, Vivian. I'll slap you into next week right here and now." She glanced at her sister's house and his gaze followed hers. "You think I won't because we are in front of your sister's house? Do you *really* think I'm scared of Henry's black ass?" He moved in on her and straddled her under him. She was humiliated. He kissed her and he tasted like stale, molded cheese. She knew instantly that what he had swigged in the car wasn't his first drink of the day. She tried to shove him away, but he only budged an inch. "What's the matter? You don't want nobody to see me and you like this? Who are you hiding from, Viv?"

"Nobody."

"You used to like it. Remember the day we met?"

"Just move so I can get back in the car, Lee."

"Exactly. You finally sound like you got some sense. Don't try me today, girl." He gripped her cheeks with both of his hands, roughly turning her to face him. "Now, give me 'nother kiss." His breath was foul. "Come on and give me that kiss, baby." He took his time, even though he knew she wanted to disappear.

"Okay, so I kissed you. Can I get back inside the car now while you go get the baby?"

"What? You don't wanna come in with me? You smell all pretty—you sure you don't wanna go inside and let 'em know that we're doing just fine?" He turned her loose. "We don't need nothing from nobody, muffin pie. I can take care of you without any help from some other man. I don't want nothing from nobody!"

"I just want to go home. Please go on and get the baby, Lee, so we can go." The thought of going home sent a great surge of tears to the surface again. She didn't know where home was anymore. If she could go anywhere she liked, she didn't know in an instant where she wanted to be. The North Star had yet to fulfill its promise to her and others who had followed it chasing a dream—they seemed just as lost as she, although her people were almost sixty years up from slavery. She knew of no so-called Negro who was genuinely happy since they came up North following the same star she'd followed, and she had the inside scoop on Minnie's decaying relationship with Henry, as well as Robeena's pseudo-happiness. It was supposed to be different for her, though, Vivian thought. She was the princess over her other sisters, as people had told her all her life.

She climbed back into the car, taking a quick peek to see if Minnie or Henry had been peering at them from a window. It didn't matter. Whenever Lee made it back outside with the baby, they would go home and she would continue to lock herself in a private hell…unless someone—a knight in shining armor or a prince or a king would rescue her. It would have to be a knight or a king because it was unthinkable to suggest to herself that God would come in person to lift her to a heavenly state of being. And to Vivian, God was a ghost, not a king, a formless spirit floating in the sky, not a man who had power in his hands, not a knight. God wouldn't come to Negroes, anyway, the rejected and the despised. She had been taught in church that unfortunately, her people were cursed. Even so, Vivian reflected that according to Wali Eli, her mother's spiritual friend, God had come and addressed the prophets. Well then, she concluded, if He could show himself face to face to Moses, Abraham, and Enoch, Vivian surmised it was possible that He could come and show his face to colored folk.

Until then, she would go with the motion, make believe she was invisible, and make her thoughts mechanical to get through the chilling northern night. She looked at Lee making his way into the house to get Mary, but her survival trance would not let her count how long he was in there, or what happened during their ride home. Her thoughts were of how Michigan was a far cry from the place that Vivian had known and loved several months earlier and called home: Century, Florida. She was born there in 1905, four years after the sawmill town was founded, and it was the only place she had ever lived. The concrete Pontiac streets sometimes made her heart ache for the meandering Escambia River, along which banks she and her sisters would frolic as dainty girls. It was a place of bottomland forest and mysterious wildlife, like bears, deer, and bobcats. And, during the winter months, the music of migrant birds in nearby swamps, like the Hooded Warbler and the Parula effected the whole area. Vivian recalled that sitting outside on the porch listening to the sounds of wild birds was peaceful. For the entire ride home, she would remain on or near that familiar porch, completely shutting out Lee's verbal attack. She traveled back to the morning of her ninth birthday that was spent on the porch, daydreaming, and listening to the sounds of nature. It seemed like everyone had forgotten about her, but then her sisters surprised her with cupcakes and a song. They pulled her from the porch by her arms and raced with her to the wilderness to have a picnic. That day, Vivian and her sisters found beautiful water hyacinth near the swamps, which they learned later from their mother, was, when boiled, a delicious food, mainly the crisp and tender stolons that connected the plant to its roots.

In those dark and dank forests, suspended from the branches of the venerable cypress trees, like the graying hair of old maids, one could see the Spanish moss, a plant so supple that it could be turned into a wig, a dress, or a seat cushion. Lee was startled when Vivian giggled, even though he had just called her an unfit mother as he dumped Mary into her lap. With unseeing eyes, Vivian continued to laugh, clutching Mary to her heart. In her daydream escape, she was wearing one of the Spanish moss wigs stitched together by her grandmother, Minnie-Anne, along with her mother's high heeled shoes. While running beside the riverbed with her sisters, she stopped to kick off the heels, then paused to take in the sweetly scented air. Besides the cypress, there were the tupelos, the sweet gum, the elm, and the dogwoods, in autumn always so lush with red, crimson, and purple leaves. Flying through the trees in the summer would be red-shouldered hawks and barred owls, spying the ground for rodents and reptiles near the swamps. Not the case in Michigan: The wildlife seemed to be reduced to eerie bats and angry owls. Now, why was she thinking about angry owls? She realized one of Lee's epithets had seeped through her daydream. While Lee continued to drive and rant, Vivian creased her heart closed and traveled mindfully back to Florida.

In Florida, some fifty-nine miles to the south of Century, but at the axis of Century's universe, was the great fishing city of Pensacola and the breathtaking Bay of the same name. In 1559, a few thousand Spanish soldiers and settlers under the leadership of Don Tristan de Luna had sailed into the Bay, the first crack by a European realm to deposit firm settlement there and only the second try to forge a colony of any kind in that virgin area that would two hundred years later become the United States of America. Historians wrote that an overwhelming hurricane spoiled most of Don Tristan's ships, curtailing the gusto of the missionaries and causing them to abandon the town after two years. It is documented in history books that had this great hurricane not occurred, Pensacola would have become America's oldest city. Instead, that credit went to St. Augustine. The history of Florida was taught in the primary grades, and children of all races were expected to appreciate it. Vivian's grandmother added the history of Black people during the precious story time sessions the family enjoyed. Minnie-Anne spoke as though Black people had a rich culture somewhere in time, as though they were Black men and women before they became Negroes or colored people. She said the word Negro came from a Spanish language, and that it described black as a color, but that Black people were more than their hues. The Spaniards had a major influence in the South, despite the hurricane that devastated their settlement in the Sixteenth Century.

By third grade, Vivian learned that in 1698, the Spaniards came once again to Pensacola and settled there, as like an express train would over the next 150 years, the French, the British, the Americans, and the Confederates. Even amid her many lovers, the soothing beauty of the Bay and the infinite bounty of its waters, so full of dolphins, mackerel, snapper, grouper, and mullet remained faithful. There were also clams, shrimp, and oysters. Fishermen from around the world would come to Pensacola to fish her waters, including Nova Scotians, Germans, and Italians, as there was an ever-increasing market for red snapper and grouper. The children of Century, in their segregated schools, began to formulate ideas about the state's fish products, and possible jobs they could have. They learned about the important businessmen and who owned what, and what color the rich people were, and the jobs that seemed to be separated by class and nepotism.

Primary school instructors taught that when Mr. S.C. Cobb established the Pensacola Fish Company in 1872, it became the first recorded company for handling and shipping red snapper. The children caught on that *so-called* Negroes had the poorest jobs and did not own much of anything. It was one instructor in particular who had recently been a Sunday school teacher who pointed out to the children that they were not Negroes. Instead, he said they were *called* Negroes when they were actually Black children. However, it was difficult for the children to grasp the concept of *black* and refer to themselves as such due to the negative connotations associated with blackness. They imagined that being called a *Negro* was more glamorous. They would accept anything but *black.* The instructor pointed out that people were usually referred to based on where they originated from on the planet. However, most of the children only laughed when this new history teacher asked them to point to a place called colored people or Negro Land on the class globe. To them, their instructor was just being silly. Of course those names were not on the map! But they sounded better than *black.* Then it was settled. Given that the rules of society dictated that *black* connotated ugliness, unholiness, and all the terrible things in the world, the *so-called* Negroes and colored people would be *called* Negroes, colored, and even niggers. Indeed, it was more acceptable for some to be called *nigger* than *black* because they saw it as a color, and not their essence.

Nonetheless, the instructors always gave marvelous self-identity and history lessons. They emphasized how Cobb had the mind to bring in A.F. Warren as a partner, and he, in due course became a competitor and the owner of the Warren Fish Company, which in 1880 caught and sold 1.5 million pounds of red snapper. Enter ice plants in 1894 in the Gulf area. By 1895, ice began replacing the live wells which had been previously used to preserve the catch. Sometimes, a tough crew of fishermen would be at sea for up to a month at a time, and they would work on schooners, called "smacks" or on smaller vessels called "chings." The smacks had the capacity to carry seven to twelve men and up to 20 tons of ice. The boats weighed a whopping 50 to 60 tons and were nearly 100 feet long. Chings compensated crews of four to five fishermen who would stay out to sea for up to ten days. Most of the ching fishermen were colored, and from Century, like Vivian's Uncle Jack, before he moved to St. Augustine. The other colored men from Century mainly worked at the sawmill unless they were sharecroppers.

Reluctantly, Vivian's mind was snatched back to Pontiac and her fantasy life in the North. They had arrived at the jailhouse and Lee was still talking while Mary soaked in her sweat and his hostile voice. Vivian clinged to Mary, staring forlornly at the stars, imagining what it would feel like to be out to sea with her Uncle Jack. Any place would be better than feeling cold and lonely, waiting for Lee to drag her into the house and upstairs because she refused to walk. She was done with trying to love him. Although she tried to keep Lee shoved out of her mind by concentrating on the black, cool waves, his dirty fingernails dug into her forearm, keeping her alert in the moment. She let her head roll backward so she could frown at the North Star. "I followed you for no reason," she hissed. "What good have you been so far?" She waited, half expecting the star to answer with some astronomical sign. Mentally exhausted and emotionally drained, she placed Mary in her crib. Vivian calmed herself by imagining how peaceful it would be in the safety of a boat—even if it were filled with pounds of dead fish.

CHAPTER TWO
"The Stranger"

Vivian was the middle sister, sandwiched between Minnie, the oldest, and Robeena, who was two years younger. Their mother, Carol Johnson remained unmarried, but she received support raising the girls since they all lived together with her parents, Minnie-Anne, and Robert Johnson in a tiny cabin in Century. After her parents died, Carol maintained the girls and the cabin on her own. When Carol met her children's father, she was only thirteen years old. He was 32 and married. He was just a stranger walking by the house where Carol was out playing with her doll instead of stitching like her mother had asked her to do. When she spotted him, her whole body shivered. Carol sat there numb, wishing she didn't have that dumb doll in her hand like a five-year-old overgrown toddler.

Carol noticed the fine man staring at her, smiling. He whistled and winked his dark eyes at her. Looking shyly back at the handsome stranger, she tried not to blush. He continued walking past her all the way to the signpost before he turned around and caught her watching after him. The words "JOHNSON LANE" threatened to bleed its black ink down the metal staff of the post if a wind of relief didn't hurry along. Using his index finger, the stranger wiped a salty bead of sweat from his brow.

Carol was too stunned at being caught staring to turn away. He stood evenly under the signpost, looking her square in the face from his distance of seventy yards away. Carol wanted to appear grown-up with this high-flying, mature stranger ogling at her. She was increasingly bashful that an experienced man seemed interested in courting her. After what seemed like eternity, Carol slid the raggedy doll into the sewing basket and picked up the stitching work that sat behind her.

In and out went the needle. She kept her eyes steady on the fabric. Her fingers had become sticky and clumsy, but still, she went on like this for five minutes. Finally, her eyes lifted themselves to peep down the street after the stranger. He was still standing quietly under the streetlamp, which hovered over the signpost as though they were mother and daughter. He was unable to read JOHNSON LANE on the sign, but he could identify the words since the main road was called JOHNSON, too. He gently beckoned for her. Cautiously, she placed the needle back in its pouch and pranced stealthily over to him, hoping her mother would not notice. In her spell bound state, she supposed God must have sent him. Carol stopped after she came within three feet of the stranger.

Her appraisal of him was innocent. He seemed like someone her father would want her to marry on the grounds that he was mature, and he didn't look like a sharecropper or somebody's boy. Her dad had warned her repeatedly not to "mess around" with young boys who could do nothing for her or for her family. Robert whispered to her when Minnie-Anne wasn't around that she shouldn't do anything to worry her mother, and dirt-poor boys were worrisome. Carol weighed her father's wisdom against her mother's badgering. Minnie-Anne told her daughter it wasn't time to have males in her life, and that she should avoid all boys, as they would cause her trouble. Carol felt like she had to take a stand. She felt like whether she entered a relationship with the stranger was up to her at age thirteen. In the end, she justified making a renegade decision by using carefully selected knowledge and casting away information that was not commensurate with her secret desires. That is, she used deceptive intelligence: She deceived herself in a sophisticated way by using intelligence to make a faulty decision that if she took her dad's advice, she'd possibly make her family proud, but if she took her mother's advice, the opportunity might just pass her by. Besides, the stranger was not a boy. Her deceptive intelligence was facilitated due to minimal societal restraints and her parents' avoidance of any topics of a sexual nature. The subject was too embarrassing, so both Robert and Minnie-Anne skipped over it completely and jumped to discussions about marriage. They used slang and code words like spoiled, mess around, and ruined. Carol was expected to use her imagination to develop an understanding. She gleaned just enough to hide her movements from her parents, but not enough to scrutinize her self-worth.

"You wanted to see me, suh?" He walked closer until they were almost touching.

"Oh yeah. Oh yeah, I do," he hummed. She visibly blushed. He grinned broadly at how easily she was taken with his smooth voice alone. "What do they call you, honey?"

"Carol."

"Well, Carol, you sure is precious, you hear?" She blushed deeper, unable to look at him directly. "Come on, let's walk some, pretty girl." He shot a hasty look in her yard to make sure no one had come outside and noticed him. "You wanna go with me?"

"Yassuh." She didn't move.

"Humph! You're so fine! I wish I could take a chocolate thing like you home with me. Can you cook?" He softly snatched her hand up in his and quickly pulled her around the corner and out of the sight of her own front yard.

"Yassuh, I cook just fine."

"You live o'er yonder with your folks?" She nodded, her head barely moving. They walked in silence holding hands. The next cottage was two hundred yards away. They made it in front of there with Carol floating all the way in no time. There were three women talking loudly together and sitting under the shade of a big oak tree in the yard when they saw Carol walking with him. He knew the women knew his wife, but he didn't care. There was nothing they could do except gawk at him.

"Good afternoon, Ms. Hydie, Esther, Geraldine," Carol greeted.

"Hey there, Carol Anne." Ms. Esther and the other women scrutinized the couple suspiciously. "Where is y'all headed?" Carol's male suitor squeezed her hand impatiently, encouraging her to ignore the women. He softened promptly when she tensed.

"I was talking to you, chocolate. Do you live o'er yonder with your folks?" He increased the speed of their pace.

"Yassuh." She tossed her head back to the ladies. "I'll talk back to y'all later."

"Your mama knows where you are, Miss Carol Anne?"

"Not yet, Ms. Esther." Esther, Geraldine, and Hydie sat staring with their hands on their hips. They all smelled trouble, but neither of them felt it was their place to say anything more. Therefore, they shook their heads and exclaimed they always knew Carol was fast tailed.

"You sure are nice, Carol. Humph." Carol was still thinking about the way he shielded his face from the ladies by turning away as they passed.

"Are you married, suh?"

"What made you ask that?"

"Oh, I don't know. You're older than me, I guess is all. Seems like you could have a lady and some young ones tittering around some place." He sighed.

"Yeah. I live with my old lady. I hope this won't be the last time I see you 'cause of her! Me and her are having problems anyway. Else, I never would've stopped to talk to you. I knew God was gwine send me somebody like you. I can't explain it, Carol. Something magical made me come down this way today."

"Really?"

"Yeah. You sure are special."

"Thank you, suh."

"I'd like to take you into town. Let me spend my money on a fine thing like you, gal. Can you go with me?"

"Not today. My mama will be looking for me before long. Got me some washing to do."

"Washing? Yeah, you be somebody I can marry one day. You sound like a real woman who can take care of her man."

"If you say so." She blushed again.

"Can you make arrangements to go with me on da morrow?"

"Yassuh. I got a few more minutes, though," she said boldly. "You wanna walk some more?"

"Honey, I wanna walk with you to the ends of the earth!" He uttered more words of affection to her, telling her she was the most beautiful young lady he'd ever seen. Just as they reached the edge of the Johnson Plantation, the stranger stopped, clasped his hand together with hers, and both looked further down the dusty, country road. "I don't wanna take you back yet, Carol. I'm having me a nice time just being with you, talking 'bout nothing whatsoever. On da morrow, I wanna take you into town, show you off. Buy you some chocolate to go with your chocolate self. Would you like that?" She told him she would love that. Carol felt she had turned into a woman with his endearing words. Buy her some things, he'd said. He worked at the Florida East Coast Railway Company, for Christ's sake. He sure had to be special because colored men couldn't just walk into a job at a prestigious company like that, the stranger had told her. Therefore, her parents would *have* to approve of him!

For a while, Carol took up with him behind her parents' back. He promised her they would marry as soon as he could leave his wife. She wanted him to already be divorced before she told her daddy about him. One night, after they had been secretly seeing each other for about six months, Ms. Esther went to the shack turned into a cottage to find out if and what Minnie-Anne knew about the man who was showering Carol with attention. Minnie-Anne shared her suspicions about a mysterious boy the family had yet to meet. Ms. Esther advised Minnie-Anne that the *boy* was actually a married man.

"You mean to tell me Alma's husband has been seeing my daughter?"

Esther nodded. "Before Carol, it was a young girl named Maybelline from the Raison Plantation."

"From church? That quiet, thin mouse?" Minnie-Anne sighed. "Whatever happened to her? It seems like I haven't seen her in a spell."

"Well, they ran her out of her own church years ago. That's how come that family ever started coming to worship with us."

"My, my, my."

"I reckon by now they back down there where the Raison people worship."

"No wonder…"

"He got her in the family way. Maybelline don't do much of anything anymore. Her daughter's name is Maybelle. She's almost six months old now!"

"You don't say."

"What a pity! As my friend and neighbor, you know I had to tell you immediately. I sure hate to bring it to you, though."

"I appreciate you, Esther. I guess I need to tell my husband to dust off his shotgun."

"You're welcome, honey. That's what friends are for. We look out for one 'nother. Lord knows you don't need Carol bringing no babies home."

"My Carol is smarter than that, though. She knows better than to let that man pester her. Carol is a good girl." Minnie-Anne tried to hide her growing annoyance. An attack on Carol's decency was an attack on her as Carol's mother.

"I'm sure Maybelline was a good girl at one time, too…"

Only a tiny degree of Minnie-Anne's irritation was visible when she muttered, "I wish I could offer you 'nother cup of tea, but I reckon I need to finish my washing."

Esther stood to leave. "I'll see you at church on Sunday, Minnie-Anne."

For the next several months following Esther's proclamation, Minnie-Anne begged Robert to show more concern over the affair, but he had found a coaxing sedative to life's follies in his heavy drinking. What could he do about it? Multiple months had passed where everyone masqueraded like they did not see the relationship. Now, suddenly Carol's immodest behavior was a concern to Minnie-Anne, mainly because her nosey friend spoke the truth out of its sordid hiding place. Robert watched Minnie-Anne burst into the protective mother although he knew that she had heard Carol sneak in and out of the house night after night. Still, Minnie-Anne spent the next several weeks nagging and pleading with Robert. Minnie-Anne believed she could dissuade their courtship if she could have an audience with the stranger. Robert was kind enough to do the decent thing and not call his wife a hypocrite. Despite his analysis that Minnie-Anne and Carol were equally to blame for the affair, Robert looked up from his bottle long enough to agree to have the adulterer and child molester over for dinner. Nonetheless, the stranger refused their dinner invitations, preferring to meet Carol under the street sign so that he could haul her off to the woods.

Robert vaguely realized his role as an enabler in the grooming process of his daughter's exploitation. He would not share that deep within his soul, it ached whenever he recalled providing Carol with a mental platform which would make her susceptible to be plucked with no restrictions. Despondently, Robert resumed his heavy drinking and left the matter in the vain hands of Minnie-Anne, who was not equipped to handle an issue that was quite popular. He weighed that traditionally, under-aged girls were in various relationships with adult men, and there were no laws or community leaders who took umbrage with it. Robert recalled bitterly that his own wife had endured abuse from the plantation owner, until he rescued her. The memory of that should have been enough to make Minnie-Anne more watchful, he judged.

Although victim-blaming was a normalized function of the durable custom mounted upon some of the most vulnerable girls, like Black girls who lived in poverty and had historically been stereotyped by society to be more promiscuous than their well-to-do counterparts, Minnie-Anne did not calculate that her disappointment was directed at Carol. Even with Robert's snide remarks, off-color jokes, and passive aggressive behavior in response to the crisis, Minnie-Anne under-estimated her responsibility and that Carol was being groomed for assault. Sexual assault grooming happened on the plantation where she was raised all the time, but no one would call it that or anything similar. The mothers - the influential adults in the victim's life were not classified as psychologically, emotionally, or mentally prepped to receive and accept the assault. They were survivors, just like Minnie-Anne's mother. Minnie-Anne did not define the multitude of inviting gestures, subtle smiles from the plantation owner as abnormal, in view of it being in fact the norm. How wrong it *felt* was canceled out by the diminished alarm from the caregiver, compared to the praise from the potential perpetrator at the time that boundaries were crossed, and coupled with the punishment to be expected in the event of resistance. Consequently, both Robert and Minnie-Anne's perception of Carol's behavior was contaminated with the belief or hope that she would be capable of sophisticated rules of discernment. Ironically, they lacked the discernment that Carol knowing right from wrong did not equal being equipped with insight into the ramifications of her deeds. Moreover, her alleged participation made her feel responsible for the assault.

There were no neighborhood precedents about how to handle it, and to add insult to injury, like Robert, Minnie-Anne was convinced Carol was not guilt-free in the matter. She viewed Carol as a willing player, perhaps even a manipulator of the crime in progress. In Minnie-Anne's world, incest, rape, fornication, and adultery ran rampant. She had been a fornicator herself. Minnie-Anne desired to offer a sketch of their rich ancestry to make her adolescent daughter feel a personal high sense of dignity. Minnie-Anne didn't know her grandparents, except that her mother told her once that her grandfather, born in St. Augustine, was a Seminole, and her grandmother was an African born slave. She could share their history and feel proud.

There were four key groups of Black people living in the Florida rough country in the early nineteenth century: those born among the Seminoles, those taken into custody during raids into Georgia and Alabama, those who were runaway slaves, and those who were procured or given to the Seminoles by the British or Spanish. There were also Black people both free and enslaved living in the two Spanish cities in Florida, St. Augustine, and Pensacola. Minnie-Anne knew her grandparents and their parents were slaves who lived under adverse conditions for as long as anyone could remember. In the cotton belt plantations of central north Florida where Minnie-Anne's mother was born, many enslaved Black men and women toiled the fields under a "gang system" in which sizable assemblies of agricultural workers labored from "can't see morning" until "can't see night." Minnie-Anne's mother used to tell her she had it easy working in the big house, given that most slaves weren't even allowed to stand in the yard of the mansion. Slave stories were passed on from generation to generation, but Minnie-Anne focused on what she considered the good stuff, like having Indian blood, because she didn't want to identify with the ugliness of abuse. Instead, she developed a pattern of pretending pain in general wasn't occurring.

When Carol was fifteen, Vivian's oldest sister, Minnie was born. It was a rough pregnancy, especially the part about trying to hide it from her mama. Minnie-Anne skinned her backside with a leather strap the moment she uncovered that her suspicions were true. When she found out Carol was pregnant, she didn't want to beat her, but she felt she had to do it, since she was the young girl's mother, and all. How could Minnie-Anne face Esther? Minnie was only two years younger than Maybelle, Maybelline's bastard daughter. The whole town would see their family in a different, more degraded light because of Carol's indecency.

Carol was five months along before the stranger had the courage to step foot in her house, and when he did, he discovered he could've come months ago. Her father barely escaped his drunken stupor long enough to know what was happening. When he wasn't drinking, he'd do odd jobs around town to earn a living like shining shoes and cleaning barns. Having a man-friend was something Robert believed was inevitable in Carol's life. To Robert, Carol's "boyfriend" having a wife wasn't the most horrible thing in the world. At least he had enough money to care for her and do trivial things for the family. A young, single sharecropper wouldn't be able to afford her.

Whenever the stranger visited, he brought bootleg liquor for Robert and groceries for Minnie-Anne. He always showered Carol with flowers, perfume, and chocolate. He special ordered strawberry body oil because she said she liked it so much. The merchant he bought the body oil from said he would have five more one-ounce bottles in two weeks, and the stranger bought all of those, too. The stranger took up helping Carol's mother establish the 10 by 12 garden to extend to the edge of the wooded area behind the cottage, and across the backyard. Instead of the 10 by 12 shoe box garden, the Johnsons ended up with a half-acre farm within nine months. The stranger built the hen house; he taught Carol the magic of plants and herbs, how to use simple farming tools, and how to raise the chickens. He often brought over seeds he'd taken from his wife. Minnie-Anne grew to like the stranger and was pleased with the assistance he offered the family. She asked herself how she really felt about her daughter being pregnant, and decided, "One thing is for certain, that man Carol's taking up with certainly does a lot more for our household than anyone else." Minnie-Anne looked over at her husband with disgust. He was working less and less these days. There was no reason why he couldn't take his ass out there and help keep weeds out of the garden or chase a damn chicken occasionally, she thought. She bent over to pick up a liquor mug that was thrown near his feet as he snored softly. It was the stranger who was successful in encouraging Robert to take more pride in their farm.

The stranger continued to take care of the family as a token of his appreciation that he was allowed to frequent any room of the house at will. It was a mute understanding that if he came over, he would bring bootleg liquor for the father, and he would do and say anything to make the mother think of herself as beautiful. Two or three times, he made subtle overtures at Minnie-Anne while they were alone. She faintly slapped his advances away on each occasion. He laughed with her, ran errands for her, and never failed to spend hours cultivating their farm. The stranger knew Minnie-Anne's husband paid her curbed attention, and that was fine. He preferred the father to stay sober when the farm needed extra hands, and drunk while he was in the house calling on Carol and her mother. The farm flourished for the first five years. Everyone pitched in, including Robert to ensure they had plenty to eat and sell. The stranger did most of the work, and it seemed like his enthusiasm motivated everyone else. However, he pulled back gradually over the years as his wife was left alone to maintain their own land most of the time, and she wasn't getting any younger.

The stranger's wife found out about Carol right before Minnie was born. The small town of Century, Florida contained few secrets. Geraldine Raison waited as long as she could stand before telling Alma that her husband was on the prowl. Everyone knew about the young girl he was taking up with by now, and Geraldine didn't want her friend to find out that she'd known all along. Alma cried, scratched, and bit, begging him to stay away from the girl. He promised he would, yet they both knew he wouldn't because there was nothing and no one to stop him. His wife threatened to leave him, but she never did. To compensate for his indiscretions, the stranger became more aggressive about punishing Carol emotionally. He became unkind, mean-spirited, and he withdrew from certain charities. The stranger stopped telling Carol about the problems he was having with his wife, and he stopped buying her so many things. He started enjoying his wife more, after ignoring her for so long. Yet, he still felt the urge a few times a month to creep into Carol's private quarters and make empty promises.

About nine years and two more babies later, the stranger looked around to discover he was the sole provider for Carol and her family. Despite the phenomenal gorgeousness of Minnie, Vivian, and Robeena, and his desire to hold his precious daughters every chance he got, the stranger wasn't so "Carol crazy" anymore, and he was plain exhausted from giving the now haggish looking Minnie-Anne the attention of a queen. It was like a huge weight being lifted once he realized no one challenged him whenever he came to their house unannounced at any hour and made himself completely at home. This was the time one winter after Carol's father died right in his chair. "His heart just got tired of beating," was what his family said to anyone who asked about his death. Minnie-Anne was grief-stricken. Robert hadn't been much of a provider, but he was certainly her best friend.

When he died, her spirit died with him. It was even more crushing than when her mother passed away a few years earlier because she had been alienated from her mother since she was a young whippersnapper, still living on the Johnson Plantation. When Robert died, she refused to eat, stopped going to 2nd Century Baptist Church down the hill and around the bend, and she stopped telling plantation stories to her granddaughters. She stopped mesmerizing her granddaughters with sea stories. Lost were those tales so rich and real that they gave the water its own personality in Vivian's mind. Carol attended to her mother as best she could, even though she was wrapped up in her own personal life with her children's father, trying to make their decaying relationship endure. Nevertheless, her bright dreams about him vanished one by one, yet her innocent love did not sway. Carol swapped roles with him in expressing her never-ending love, and she also began to surprise him with affectionate notes.

In 1913, when Vivian was eight, her grandmother had a heart attack in the same chair where her grandfather had died a year earlier. Harriet Tubman, a great freedom fighter had just passed away two months before. People everywhere mourned Tubman's death and were simply tired of all the loss of lives, be it by murder, or natural causes. Everyone guessed that Minnie-Anne was tired, too. It took all the money the family had, and all that the church could offer to pay for the burial. Carol presumed the stranger would come to their rescue during this trying time, but he never did. Two weeks after the funeral, the family was almost entirely out of food. The farm had been unkempt and dry for several seasons. Carol grievously recalled making excuses over the years instead of assisting her mother with the livestock, herbs, and vegetables. It was too much work. She had the crippling thought that a Black person's freedom from gang plantations and sharecropping meant someone else should supply her food. Carol did not respect Minnie-Anne for being on all fours picking away weeds. As such, she lost the hands-on and business sense of agriculture, and therefore did not adopt the skills necessary to feed her family. Not long after Minnie-Anne's death, Carol gathered her children, dressed them smartly, and marched all three with her to the stranger's house. Her stress forced her to swallow her fear. It was the first time she'd ever dared to think about approaching the house he shared with his wife, even though she'd known where he lived for years.

Carol courageously gave the weather-beaten pinewood door multiple nonstop stern knocks. Alma rushed to the side window to peep. She knew at once who her visitors were. When she flung the door open, Carol's hand was still in the air, flying back from the force of her own pound. "Woman, how dare you come to my house. Whatchu got these bastards o'er here for?" She hastily waved at the children in dismissal.

Carol shot back, "Ma'am, I never would think to disrespect you, but these chil'ren got a daddy who lives in this rundown old ugly house." She paused to make sure Alma knew how serious she was. "I'm only asking that he does a quarter of the way right by them. I'm not here on account of me."

The stranger appeared in the doorway, half clad. He wasn't surprised to see his other family at his doorstep. A few years back, Maybelline pulled the same thing. Thankfully, Alma was not home to see Maybelline and the baby girl named Maybelle who was supposed to be his child. The stranger had envisioned Carol coming with the children some years ago. He had imagined that Carol would come to tell him how much she loved him and plead with him to make a choice between her and his wife. Of course, he would choose his wife, but the excitement would ignite a spark that could enhance his wounding relationship with Carol. He wanted Carol to be crazy about him, like she was when she was thirteen. He looked at Carol's swollen lips. Her thick limbs sprouted out through her sleeveless, tattered dress. Her hair formed a bun and was tied with a dirty ribbon in the back of her head. He could tell someone had tried to comb the children's hair, but this must have been several days ago because their hair was frizzy in the plaited cornrows. All six knees looked like a month of Sunday bathing with the absence of lanolin or oil applied to their skinny legs.

"Whatchu want around here, gal?" The stranger asked. His wife threw her arms up in the air, more displeased with her husband than Carol. She had seen the family from a distance one day from Ms. Esther's porch, but never imagined they would show up at her house to see her husband. She was ashamed that they would look so neglected, and how young the woman must have been. "My God!" Alma screeched to herself. "She must've been twelve when she started having those babies!" An eerie sensation caused a chill over Alma's body.

"You hear me talking to you, gal? Open your mouth, Carol Anne," the stranger snapped.

"We ain't got no food at the house. I'm trying to see if you can help us out."

"I come around when I come. You got no business coming o'er here talking that foolishness. I come when I come!"

"Well, we've been waiting for long enough. How come you won't get off your mean self and do something about these kids you made?" He came fully out of the house and pushed Carol away from the door. Her foot tripped beneath her, causing her to fall to the ground. The three girls rushed to help, but Carol waved them away defiantly. She scrambled to her feet, mumbling curses under her breath.

"Get on away from here, I said!" He looked behind him for his wife, but she had gone back into the house after she saw him push her. She was on Carol's side and could not watch his treatment of her, nor did she think it was her place to defend Carol. With his wife out of sight, the stranger added, "I'll be around later on . . . now get!"

Carol shamefully headed away. Minnie and Vivian followed her with their heads bowed, but Robeena stood frozen for a few long seconds, scarcely able to believe the humiliation her mother had just put her through. She instantly grew hatred for this man who was nothing but a stranger in her eyes. She picked up a rock that was half stuck in the dirt and threw it at her father. The rock hit him on the back of his thigh as he turned to go back inside. He coiled quickly to see who and what had hit him. He saw Robeena running to catch up with her mother and sisters. Carol was in a state of panic since she didn't have any money for food at all, and the cabinets at home were completely empty. She knew Reverend Washington would help if she asked. She recalled there was never a time he didn't seem to show her special favors openly and in secret. Carol wished she could be the giver sometimes, rather than the taker, though. Her pride prevented her from asking for assistance yet again, but she kept a calm ace card in the fact that she knew she could use the reverend if absolutely needed.

They came to the Anderson Fish Market and stopped. Black residents in Century, Florida operated separate grocery stores and meat markets from Caucasians. Mr. Anderson owned and ran the only Black-owned fish market in the city. He was a middle-aged man who had taken over the family's business. His half-sister was the teacher at the one school for Negro children right up the road from the store. All the Black people in Century lived and mostly worked in one section, which their area was approximately thirty-three- and one-half miles in diameter and encompassed the edges of both the Raison and the Johnson Plantations. The Florida Railway Company was zoned one mile outside of these parameters, and the Raison Plantation was just a half mile before the Railway Company. It would seem Mr. Anderson would be able to catch all the fish business from his neighbors, yet many Black people thought they were a step above if they could say they shopped on the other side of the tracks.

Mr. Anderson waved at Carol who stood hesitantly outside. Carol was undecided on whether she should enter with her family of hungry daughters. "Come inside, Ms. Carol," he called out to her. She lingered on for a moment, coming in only after Minnie pulled her along, with Vivian and Robeena making it to Mr. Anderson's arms first, as he came from behind the counter to hug everyone. Without saying anything, he went back and wrapped some red snapper together in a brown paper bag, along with other items he figured they could use.

"Thank you, Mistuh Anderson, I really . . ."

"Now hush up, Ms. Carol. I know you are having tough times with your mama dying. I'm just sorry I couldn't make it for the services and all." Mr. Anderson quickly tried to remember what he'd been doing that prevented him from attending Minnie-Anne's funeral. He used the back of his hand to wipe perspiration from his forehead. "Anytime you are needing some help, come on in. Don't be afraid to ask for nothing. I mean that, Ms. Carol."

"Yassuh."

"How are your children doing in school? My sister says she is fond of 'em."

"Suh, my girls have been reading and writing for a good spell!" Carol glanced at Vivian's pouting face. "Vivian is having some problems with her words, though. Can't get her reading like she should. Beena up there with Minnie! I don't know how she out-did Vivian. Oh well," she sighed, "I reckon she will learn what the Lord wants her to learn." Postured competitively, Vivian listened to her mother describing her poor academics. She didn't know school was important enough to discuss. Robeena didn't know, either, but the books were quite interesting--ripped and old, but colorful. The only colors Vivian noticed about the books were all the Caucasian characters that dominated the examples. In her Bible study class, there were the white prophets. In history class, the war heroes were white, brave men. Vivian vowed to find books about people who told the stories of the sharecroppers, or the ancient African people her grandmother had told her existed.

"Is that so? She speaks so well, though! My sister was telling me that Vivian is about the most proper speaking child of all!"

"Yassuh. I don't know why she be trying to talk like some li'l white gal. We don't talk like that at home."

"She'll be alright. Just keep her in school. Don't worry about her white sounding speech. Folk may tending that proper is a white thing. Naw! Proper is a proper thing." No one could've told Vivian or her sisters that that would be their last year to attend school. Two months later in July, members of the Klan burned the stuffy schoolhouse to the ground. Weeks later, Vivian visited the abandoned pile of rubbish-ashes left to blow into the air, books tarred with pages stuck together, and yet the smell of smoke was sweet to her. There were several salvageable books. Vivian carefully selected a handful of books each day until a crew came to clean away the debris. While a new meeting place was being built, Miss Anderson married Calvin Briggs and was whisked away to a life of being a housewife and making babies in Pensacola. Carol didn't really have an opinion on the matter considering her girls already had more schooling than most Negro children.

Carol thanked Mr. Anderson again before they left for home. She was grateful to her mother for teaching Minnie to cook and clean so well. Minnie was a big asset to the household that evening with her boiled fish soup, corn bread, and lemonade. She wanted to help her mother in every way she could at her young age. She wished her mama wouldn't rely on the stranger so much for everything. Minnie took pride in the fact that she was rearing her younger sisters to prepare meals, launder clothes, and keep house. Teaching them to sew was difficult because they rarely had the supplies for that.

Later that evening, the stranger came to their house and walked inside without knocking. "Hey, woman, where you at?" he called. Robeena came from a back room to greet him. She disliked him, but it made her happy when he came because that meant help for her mama. He saw her and smiled. She took one shopping bag from him into the kitchen and started unloading the contents. He followed her with the other bag he still held to help with the unloading. Carol walked in the room and stood with her hands on her hips. The stranger glanced at her briefly, and then continued taking the food items out of the bag. A long, insufferable silence filled the atmosphere. Robeena rushed through only half the groceries in her sack and stole away out the back door.

"It's time you found yourself 'nother meal ticket. Don't come 'round yonder to my house no more." He took out the last two jars of pinto beans and tossed the empty bag aside. "This here be the last meal you're getting from me, woman. How in the hell did you let the farm get so bad? You couldn't keep them chickens? You didn't think of watering the tomatoes from time to time? Your lazy daughters couldn't pull out no weeds unless I stand over y'all with a leather strap in my hand?"

"You spent more time helping me make babies than helping me learn farming. And I tried!" She started crying. "Lord knows I tried ev'ryday. Things just started spoiling and I felt like I was all by myself." The stranger thought of all the help he gave his wife with their farm and softened. He reached for Carol but she backed away and then hurried tearfully to her bedroom. She didn't mind fending for herself as far as seeing to it that her children were fed, yet it bothered her that this man could love her for so many years, and then treat her so coldly. That question drove her to continue to wait patiently for a change in him, like a drug addict hopeful of experiencing that first high all over again. She remembered how kind he was when her mama and daddy were alive. Carol decided she would never call on him for help in the future. "What other man is gwine want me and I got three half-grown girls, though?" She felt used. She sat on the bed and imagined what she must do to have greater fulfillment in her life. When the stranger saw her head to the bedroom, he took that as a sign of invitation. He followed her after a few minutes. Robeena came through the back door after finding no one to talk to in the quiet yard. She glared at his head with her fist tightly balled when she saw her mother take flight. This was the part she hated in her mama's relationship with the stranger. She was reminded of what her mama had told the girls *not* to do with "no-good boys." Just after her father disappeared into the bedroom, Robeena trotted away to find her sisters, easily forgetting the groceries lined up on the kitchen table.

Before Carol looked up, he was already standing over her with a smirk on his face. "I don't wanna see you, man," she said flatly. He had limited patience for her attempt at rejection. Nowadays, it seemed like Alma was keeping an account of every hour he spent away from home, and every penny he spent. The food and his time had price tags that he would not allow Carol to disrespect. Before he knew it, he was wringing her wrist in his hands, trying to bring her to a standing position. They tumbled together, Carol being much rougher than he. She bumped his eye with her elbow and kneed him in the belly. He kneed her back. She couldn't breathe. She turned quickly away.

"Get out," Carol panted. "You said you ain't coming back o'er here. Seems to me I can't get you to leave!" She scooted away from him, losing her scarf to his grimy fingernails. Several loose strands of hair required her attention. Annoyed, the stranger looked on as she untangled her smooth, freshly washed hair, and expertly placed a tight, silky braid where the strands had been. He wasn't in any mood to wrestle with her this afternoon, and it was clear that she intended to be a rebellious sport.

"I'll be back! He laughed. "You know I can't resist you." He turned away, his eyes steady on the wooden floor. At the doorway, he paused before journeying back through the house and out into the wilderness. He looked back at Carol until she offered him a soft smile. Although she knew he was unreliable, Carol was superfluously content with such mutterings of commitment. Far too many evenings were spent waiting in vain, hoping that his promises would burst into being. Therefore, the honeyed words would do for now.

After that first time, Carol never went back to the stranger's house. He visited her every two or three weeks for a while, then every month or so. He always brought food and household goods, however inconsistently. So when Mr. Anderson strolled by a few days later and casually offered her part-time work at his grocery, Carol was more than delighted to oblige. She cleaned fish, bagged groceries, mopped floors, and managed the store in Mr. Anderson's absence. Carol knew he couldn't pay her much. Mr. Anderson appreciated her understanding, and she appreciated everything he did for her. Inside of her heart though, Carol hoped Mr. Anderson had asked her to work there because he really needed the help and not because the whole town knew that her children's father had left her destitute. Carol always wished the stranger's wife would die, or that he would just come all the time, like he used to do. Yes: He was like a bad drug habit. Other men tried to come into her life, but she would never allow any males to cross her threshold, nor did she present herself as single. Carol felt like an old maid or a widow. Still, she feared that the stranger would pop up one day and find someone else there. She couldn't take the thought of losing him forever, so she just waited, and waited.

CHAPTER THREE
1920 "The Protecting Friend"

When Carol was thirty-two, a man by the name of Wali Eli came by her house pulling a wagon that contained fresh tomatoes, silk garments, and other goods. Earlier that morning, Carol clothed herself in a pretty cotton dress. The stranger usually came on a Saturday if he came at all, and today was Saturday, the first of the month. When the knock sounded, Carol thought she had locked the door being that the stranger never knocked. Her heart began to sing as she dashed to the door and desperately flung it open. After knocking, Wali Eli retreated to the bottom porch step and waited there. "May I help you?" He glowed like a freshly lit candle.

Carol saw a calm spirited man with straight, black hair. He could easily have been mistaken for an Asian, but then again, a closer look suggested he may even have been a stone Black man, yet his skin was exceptionally light. He looked ageless—that is, she could tell he was a mature man, but there were no marks or indentations signifying his age. She walked out onto the porch. As she browsed more closely, she marveled at his prominent African features, which were unsuccessful in hiding under his complexion. He wore a plain dark suit and a crisp white shirt with a tie. Carol stared at him impatiently; she spat on the ground, wiping her mouth with her thumb.

"Good day, ma'am. I'm passing through with some mighty fine items, and I was praying you would allow me to help *you*." His words startled Carol. She didn't quite know how to respond. She was used to more rough and gruff talk from men who cursed her regularly—not that they were trying to be mean, but conversationally speaking.

"I had enough strangers in my day. I ain't looking to see no more," she retorted. She looked down as she spoke. After she finished, she glanced at him again. Their heights were near equal from her position of three steps up on the porch. Somehow, he appeared taller than his actual physical height. His eyes were deep and dark, yet smiling. There was not the sneaky glare present as with her children's father. This man's face was gentle and responsive. He stooped down to open a crate that sat in the pinewood wagon he pulled. He took one of the smaller crates out and let it rest on the dirt ground in her yard. He lifted the top to reveal three dozen nearly round and almost bright red tomatoes, ten large pineapples, and about four dozen lemons.

"I have tomatoes, sister," he said. "And I have these mighty fine silk garments that were made by your brothers in the east." He motioned to another case covered in brocade.

"Brothers in the east? I didn't know I had no brother."

He took a large knapsack out of the brocade case and pulled one garment from it. "See how pretty they are? This is how Black people used to dress before coming over here as slaves." Inside were more silk garments folded in a cloth bag. "Have you ever touched silk so smooth that it could slip right from your palms?" Carol appeared interested, yet she hesitated to make a positive comment about the enchanting outfits. "And we certainly can talk more about your brothers in the east. I live east, too." He paused, relishing in the soft, cool breeze dancing behind and in front of him. "I've been waiting for the proper time to come to this area." Carol was extra pleased that he was talking so freely to her, yet she still was apprehensive about him. He was different from any man she'd ever seen. His speech was even different. He acted differently.

A bit unnerved, Carol looked up at the darkening afternoon sky. "We might get a li'l rain before long. You plan to be walking in it?" Her real question was from where did he come, and where was he going. Rarely did folk come through that she had never seen. Everyone knew each other, and so far, she had heard no talk about anyone who resembled him.

Wali Eli was in tune to her curiosity. "The name's Wali Eli, ma'am. I have work to do in this area. I'll be headed to Detroit soon…a place called Black Bottom. Say, do you have any tomatoes, or could you use some of these rich ones I have? And what about these pineapples and lemons I have in here? They are getting mighty heavy to pull with me much further, even with this wagon. The promising rain is telling me to leave *all* my things with you," he stated matter-of-factly, beaming.

"I ain't got no rich tomato money, Mistuh Eli." Wali Eli held his hand up, indicating his wish to bless her with some of the ripe goods, anyway.

He chuckled. "I did not say I was going to try to *sell* you my fresh goods." He looked around to see Robeena, Minnie, and Vivian running and laughing with each other on the side of the house. They all looked to be in their middle to late teens. They had been in the backyard, unaware of the presence of their visitor. "Are those your girls?" Carol nodded shyly. "You have some mighty big girls! Seems like you could use these tomatoes and things, and your daughters could help you make something nice for the family." He closed the crate, picked it up and handed it to her, although she didn't take it. "It's not as heavy as it looks," he said. Somehow he was able to balance the silk garments over his left wrist, although the cloth containing it fluttered to the ground with the pushing wind. Carol's hands were numb. No one had been so kind to her ever before. Anything that was offered to her in her life had a price tag attached to it. She did not feel as though she deserved the fruit and vegetables.

Minnie was the first of the girls to see him. She trotted over while Vivian dashed after her. Robeena stopped exactly where her feet were planted when she noticed him. She studied her mama for a minute. Robeena walked slowly to everyone, standing to the back of Wali Eli. Minnie ventured to speak.

"How you?" Minnie's greeting to Wali Eli gave Carol courage: She stepped completely off the porch.

Smiling, he turned to answer Minnie. "I'm just fine, young sister." He nodded at the other two, and then looked back at Minnie. She was the tallest, and obviously the oldest. Her unusually high cheekbones looked as though an artist sculptured them in place so that people would notice them before any of her other features. "I have a lot of walking to do. Would you mind taking these tomatoes, pineapples, and lemons in the house for your mother?"

Robeena reached from behind and snatched the crate before Minnie could respond. It was heavier than she'd anticipated, so she wasn't able to move quickly away from her sisters with it. The three girls laughed and raced past their mama into the house, Robeena with the goods, but Minnie had to give her a hand to lift the crate into the house.

Once in the kitchen, Minnie got a paring knife, and began washing and gutting the tomatoes. Vivian got a pot and another knife to slice the gutted ones. Quietly, Robeena moseyed to the far side of Minnie, and waited for her two older sisters to engage themselves in conversation before she stole a fat, juicy tomato. She ducked under Minnie's slap, moving quickly toward the back door. She sauntered around from the back yard to the front of the house. Slowly, she slipped up two porch steps and stood behind her mother.

In the kitchen, Vivian asked, "Who you think that man is, with all those goods? Did you see that silk?"

"Hush your mouth, girl. "It ain't none o' yo' business. 'Sides, that wasn't no real silk."

"You ain't pronouncing your words fittingly, Minnie," Vivian corrected, still remembering Mr. Anderson's compliment, although her mother didn't take it as one. She knew she wasn't trying to talk "white" like some of her friends and family members teased her about over the years, and although she hadn't attended school in several years, she still wanted to learn more about grammar and English, her favorite two subjects. "It's *of your* business, not *o' yo'* business." She turned her nose up at Minnie. "You sound like you're saying yo-yo or something."

"Chile, please. You talk the same way unless you're trying to be all cute." Minnie strained her neck toward the front room to see if she could hear any of what was being said.

"Dang, Minnie," Vivian expressed just as she caught Minnie stretching her neck. "Go on out there with Robeena and stick your nose in mama's business, too!" They both laughed excitedly.

Wali Eli could hear their joyful laughter from where he stood. He was pleased with the love the family seemed to share. Though obviously dirt poor, they were a cheerful bunch, all except Carol.

"Well, sister," he took a deep bow, "I'm going to head back up the road, now." He reached down to retrieve his cloth sack that had fallen. "Thanks for getting that load off of my hands," he added. Carol exhaled, happy to be relieved of the responsibility of accepting anything for free from him. Wali Eli's lip curled into a delicate smile, and then he turned on his heels and walked away, almost military style, pulling his wagon.

He took the bend around Johnson Lane and passed Ms. Geraldine's cottage. Ms. Esther was sitting on the open porch alone, enjoying the air before the storm should force her to shelter when Wali Eli approached her. Within seconds, Ms. Esther joined them. He spoke as briefly with the ladies as he had with Carol, and he left them with a crate of fruit, promising to tell them more about their brothers in the east whenever he returned. Even though the rain made good on its threat with initial splattering, Wali Eli headed away. Between Ms. Geraldine's house and the next cottage was a wide opening with an array of Mulberry trees lined neatly in two rows. Wali Eli stopped a moment to take in the beauty displayed there. Ms. Esther and Ms. Geraldine stood in the doorway to see if the man would turn back in fear of the imminent storm. After a minute, he turned away from the sight and continued his path.

Carol stared at his back, waiting for him to turn back to avoid the rain, but he didn't. She marveled at how the only conversation they'd had was about the silk and fruit, and yet it seemed he knew very much about her. She stood gazing after him until he became a tiny black dot. Stronger than before, winds blew fiercely past her. Robeena moved closer to the door, hoping her mama would hurry along.

Carol walked back up the porch steps and stood near the edge. One by one, inconsequential splattering drops of wetness landed on her head. Carol kept her eyes focused on the black dot to see if it would get bigger, seeking shelter from the rain, until she couldn't tell anymore which black dot was hers. Now the rain was shooting forward in her face, but still, she watched. She realized in layers the difference in the man who walked away--he was like no one else. It wasn't that he was merely kind--he was angelic. He was good. Carol felt a heap of blessings for no reason at all, and it was difficult to walk away. She felt like the spirit of God had visited her, and yet it was a real live man who came in the flesh. She could not put her finger on it, but she knew something extraordinary had just happened. Her dress was drenched, clinging to her petticoat, and thunder sounded in the distance. Carol closed her eyes in soothing wonder. The black dot formed again in her darkness, at first small, with a sharp reddish light in the center, and then it grew larger and larger, until everything was black. She dropped to her knees on the heavily damped front porch, keeping her eyes closed so that the blackness wouldn't disappear. Then, she found herself in full prostration, praying about everything and everyone who came to mind. It felt good to just pray, and give all her burdens to God.

CHAPTER FOUR

His hair was like twisted, wooly raisins

    The next week, Minnie met a ruggedly handsome, eye-catching young man named Henry Abiff Raison. She was nineteen years old at the time. Instantly, Minnie fell in love with Henry and all his dreams. He wanted to go North and "be somebody." His parents grew up together from childhood, she learned. They still lived on the same plantation and in their same former slave quarters household under the care of a planter by the name of James Raison. Henry's father's sister was married to his mother's brother. Henry's parents were both infants when the Emancipation Proclamation was signed. Along with his family, several other "freed slaves" continued to work as sharecroppers and live on the Raison Plantation after the signing of this great document.

    The sharecroppers who stayed on considered that Master James Raison was nice enough, which was what counted to them. When the slaves were emancipated, all he asked of his residents in his benevolence was the picking of his cotton and general sun-up until sundown labor. After a day's work, the freed slaves could do as they pleased. Although they were performing the exact tasks as before the war, the sharecroppers now felt a sense of freedom that they *could* leave, whereas they couldn't leave before. Yet, mentally, emotionally, and financially, they could not leave, were not organized to leave, and did not know how to leave. Furthermore, they didn't know if they should want to leave or if their situation would improve if they left. The older, single women like Tazra who were called "cabin mothers" stayed joyously in Master Raison's care because they were waited on by the younger girls who lived with them. They helped with the babies which offered them a continual flow of nourishment from the fountain of youth. Tazra enjoyed the prestigious position of the town's healer for Black people.

    Henry's parents were together in love since they were children. At first they fought together, until they matured into unofficial holy matrimony. His parents were one of the few Negro couples that were allowed to stay with each other without interference from the master of the plantation. This is because James Raison felt that male slaves were less productive in the fields with a steady wench challenging them every night. Henry's father was a blacksmith, though, and back bending, endless cotton-picking labor wasn't a part of his job description. He also was a good builder, and he worked well with wood. The elder Henry Raison took much pleasure in carpentry, logging, and lumbering, and he taught these skills to his son.

In parts of Escambia County, where Henry had grown up, logging and lumbering were big business. Some of his uncles had worked for old man Drucker, who built and operated the sawmill on Chumuckla Highway. The mill, which was ten miles north outside of the thirty-three-and-a-half-mile parameter, was the chief employer for over 350 mostly colored men from 1900-1927. It had its own railroad, with a track that ran from Century to Jay in Santa Rosa County and huge boilers inscribed with the name SANCHEZ BOILER COMPANY, after the man from whom old man Drucker had purchased the mill and 300,000 acres of timber.

Drucker was beloved of the former slaves and their children, as they appreciated his fairness to them as their employer. Such fairness was instrumental in convincing other Caucasian employers in the area to be more just in their dealings with Negroes. Still, during this time, all hell continued to break loose between the races in Florida, and all over America. A handful of liberal and moderate Caucasians couldn't put a dent in the hatred and resentment that their counterparts had for the now freed slaves.

Henry was born in Alabama in 1892, which was a tough year for the ex-slaves across America, especially in the South where most of the lynchings were taking place. His father was working in Alabama on the plantation of a man who was a friend of the Raison's, as skilled workers were sometimes shared. Mr. and Mrs. Raison moved back to Century after their one year stay when Henry was six months old. Henry's family almost moved away from the Raison Plantation in 1894 when a strike at the Pullman Transportation Company caused the owners to hire many Black men. Henry's father had been hired in making enough money to provide a home of his own for his family. However, some of the people who crossed the picket lines were killed by the Caucasian mobs. This scared many others like Henry's father away from employment. Henry's mother had pleaded shamelessly, falling on all four of her limbs at her husband's feet, urging him not to return there to work. She said she didn't need a new home, or a new dress, she would rather stay on at the plantation where it was safe for Negroes. Although Henry was merely a toddler at the time, he would never forget the sight of his mother clinging to his father's ankles, her dress hiked up and her tired knees dragging on the floor. Young Henry watched his parents fearfully work like dogs for Master Raison and reap rationed benefits for it. By the time he was seven, he became cognizant of status quotas and racial differences. Whenever he went into town with his mother, he saw how the Caucasians treated each other so royally, and how the Negroes were all around treated like lowly animals.

Once in a general store uptown, Henry was forced to wait with his mother until all the Caucasian people were served before they could pay for their groceries. She could have shopped at the Anderson Fish Market, but she wanted the freshest fish and fruit this time. When Henry's mother's hand accidentally grazed the grocer's sleeve, he spit on the floor and made her leave the store without her items, although she had paid for them. His twelve-year-old son kicked Henry and called him a coon as they were leaving the store. Henry moved to punch the boy in his face, but his mother stepped in front of him and spanked Henry on his rump. On the way home, Mrs. Raison wouldn't talk to Henry the whole time. He heard her tell his father that "Mistuh Lucifix Hopkins sure was behaving mighty funny this afternoon. I reckon I'll go back and get my bags later on." Henry wanted his father to question her about what really happened, but he said nothing except to nod his head.

Henry preferred shopping at the Anderson Fish Market regardless of if their red snappers were more than a day old. He liked the warm feeling he got from shopping with other Black people. The next day, Henry walked with his mother to another Caucasian owned store a few miles further than Mr. Lucifix Hopkins' store. She bought the exact things that she tried to purchase the day before. She kept her head bowed each way they passed the Hopkins's store, too.

When Henry was ten, he talked to his mother about racial injustice for the first time. The Negro population in the United States was 12%. Louis Armstrong was two years old, and Duke Ellington was three. Race riots were searing through the streets of many major cities; Black people were being lynched left and right, North and South.

Henry followed his mother into a barn. She was about to sweep up some stale chicken feed when she noticed her son. Mrs. Raison saw a hint of hostility in Henry's eyes when he asked his innocent question. What did he mean by asking her why she and his father cowered in the presence of Caucasians? Evidentially, he was saying that given the chance, he would buck against the authority of those in power.

"Just a minute, baby," she said as she casually walked briskly to her quarters to get a viable weapon.

"Mama, whatchu doing?" He looked at her with bewilderment while she danced back into the barn as though she was recoiling off a boxing ring rope. Henry was horrified that she'd tricked him into believing they would be having a mature conversation. She beat him with a leather strap until his legs and arms became raw. She told him, "Boy, you speak against white folks, they gwine kill you for sure! Master Raison has raised you. You ain't nothing but a sharecropper and that's all you ever gwine be. I'm whipping you to save your life. I appreciate Master Raison and what he's done for us. I ain't never had no cause to speak against him, and neither do you!"

"But ma, I ain't saying nothing bad . . ."

"Zip your back talking mouth!"

After her speech, she slapped Henry again as hard as she could. He fell backward and dropped to the floor. He was angry with several people at that moment: God, his father, Master Raison, and mainly his mother. Henry was angry at his mother's ignorance that had been born in him. He was angry at his father's fear of Mr. Raison, and others like his father who made him feel like a coward presently. His face was stinging as though someone had just peeled his skin away. The rage that boiled inside of him was unbearable. His body shook violently as he hugged himself to keep from exploding. His mother watched on, her hand was steady in case she needed to swat him again. Henry spun around and screamed at the wall, "Stop it!"

Mrs. Raison picked up a board with loose nails seesawing about and swung it over Henry's head. "If I hafta kill you myself, I'm your mama." She drew back to strike him again, but he ducked. Blood was coming from his nose. He ran outside of the barn and kept running for what seemed like hours. On one rotation around the fields, Henry planted himself on Tazra's stoop. He sat there, not caring that the other children saw him crying. In the afternoon, Tazra brought him a sandwich. An hour later, she patted his shoulder, then walked away to watch him from her window. The sourest feeling for Henry was that feeling of powerlessness. He didn't know how he could change a thing. He started thinking then that he had to get away from the South. Henry often heard that things were different up North.

Dusk was about to settle in, and he was still there. Tazra had finished all her day's assignments. She came out and sat next to Henry. "You reckon you gwine be fine?"

"I'm fine. Just hate it here."

"Gotta find your purpose, Henry." She had a cup in her hand of something that smelled delicious. "Want some soup?" She pulled it back as he was about to reach for it. "Nah, I'll bet your mama made something better. Probably waiting on you."

"I hate her."

"Don't say that." She gave him the soup. Filled with pride, he waited a minute before sipping it.

"One day, I'll leave this place, and I'll go to Ohio, or Chicago, or even Michigan! I'll never pick another bud of cotton, and I'll never rake another leaf," he projected. Tazra listened, nodding her head every few moments.

"You keep telling me 'bout your dreams, son from another mother. Don't mind me, I'm just gwine put some of this flaxseed to prevent tetanus from setting in where your mama whacked you. And suck up all that soup. I got some ginger in there to help with your healing. She had been there for him before, but this time was different. As young as he was, Tazra noted his determination. She shook her head. He was a good boy. It was clear to Tazra that Henry's mother didn't know how to relate to him. Tazra was never blessed with a son, but if she had been, she would want him to be like Henry. After Henry left, Tazra stayed on the stoop for a bit. So many sharecroppers spoke about going North, but they never went, and no one Henry's age had been so adamant about it. Often, Henry would discuss his plans with his cousin, Rufus, in hopes of gaining a travel partner. But Rufus was three years younger and was unreliable because he was being reared to have unconditional love for the Raison's and their Plantation.

In 1908, after Henry turned sixteen, he believed he was old enough to leave, although he didn't have the money or the wherewith-all to plan such a trip to the North. Henry began to save every penny he came across while doing odd jobs in town in what narrow spare time he had, like carrying bags of groceries for people. He didn't appreciate having to spend so much time working with his father and getting nothing, when he could go into town and earn money. His mother told him that he should be happy that Master Raison allowed him to work with his father as a blacksmith and carpenter instead of being a field hand. When he reached the age of 22, he still wanted to go, yet his experience in engaging in traveling of any sort was limited to stagnant, and he was afraid to go alone. Besides, America had already reached the Great War, and every available man over the age of eighteen was required to submit to the draft. As a Black man, Henry wasn't aware that he was required, but he wanted to leave home so badly that he begged to be a part of America's army.

In 1915, Henry found himself on a train heading to Fort McPherson in East Point, Georgia, to United States Army military grounds. Once at the fort, he, along with nearly a thousand other soldiers received basic training and then specialized training in various disciplines, such as artillery. Two months later, he walked onto a boat that would be his home for the next several months. The boat led him to Ghana, West Africa. Later, he traveled to the battlegrounds near Denmark to serve the remainder of his time in the war. His job was to carry artillery to the front lines where the Caucasians from the United States were positioned. At that time, The U.S. Government didn't think a Negro's blood was good enough to spill in heroism. Henry never considered being killed. He was conditioned to have faith that America would protect him from all harm during this Great War. Alas, after two and a half years, and plenty of money saved, he was happy to see the end of the war, which meant he could finally go home and plan for another journey. On the very day he met Minnie, Henry felt like he finally had a partner with whom to seal his dream of following the North Star.

Meeting Minnie and her sisters was fateful for Henry. The stranger and Wali Eli came on the same day, respectively casting swine and pearls into Carol's perspective. At about 6:20 a.m. that Saturday morning, Carol wiped the night from her sleepy eyes, opening them slowly to fight off the morning rays. She saw the stranger standing over her, more than likely just coming from an after-hours joint.

"I ain't seen you in a month of Sundays. Whatchu come for now?" The stranger grinned a smile that revealed crooked teeth. Those brownish cuspid fangs had always been there. Why hadn't she noticed them before now? He never understood why she tried to "pretend she didn't know" why he was there, and why he continued to come. He had been her man since she was thirteen years old. He loved his wife, but having a few girls on the side is what his father had done, and his uncles before that. It was just commonplace. Carol had given him the freedom to come and go as he pleased with no strings attached. She knew he would never leave his wife, he reckoned, no matter what lies he fed her. Why should he? Carol was not the type of woman he wanted to marry, anyway. He didn't love her for that purpose.

"I come for my woman," he answered. The sound of his words, "my woman" was like music to her ears, despite his imperfect grin. She'd always wanted to be his woman. Carol wanted the same respect she measured that he gave his wife. She wanted to be loved, and those words meant he must love her, as far as she was concerned. Carol wondered if he'd had a big fight with his wife, and perhaps she had thrown him out in the streets. She looked behind him to see if he had brought a suitcase with him. She didn't see anything, but she was still hopeful, as always. More reassurance from him would do the trick for her.

She asked, "What happened to the woman you've been keeping house with?" Leaning on one elbow, Carol allowed her hair to sweep her shoulders. Deep down inside, she knew he hadn't left his wife, thus, she didn't sincerely want to discuss it. During the times spent with him, Carol allowed herself to be convinced that he wanted only her. She closed her eyes in expectation, laced with denial about the true circumstances.

Two minutes later, Carol heard one of the girls going outside more than likely to the outhouse. She hoped whoever had awakened would get back into bed quickly without disturbing the stranger because she classified their entanglement as worthy and sanctified. Carol wasn't comfortable under his heavy arms, but she feared that if she got up, he would stir and leave her soon afterward. She simply couldn't risk the ephemeral pleasure she felt by spending even a fleeting time with him, her one and only. It was so peaceful to amuse herself by acting like he was her husband. She cuddled closer to her dreams, satisfied with the lies surrounding her pseudo-relationship. Even though her brain's natural physiological response triggered by sleeping induced a psychological mending, the daily negative programming kept her rationality tipped toward her delusions. So, while the subconscious sorting of useless fallacies from healthy sparks challenged and deleted delusions, they only temporarily revitalized Carol's senses. This is because Carol had been introduced to her dysfunctional life before the frontal cortex, the reasoning portion of her brain, was ever fully formed.

Robeena and Vivian were sitting in the only dry spot in the middle of the kitchen floor while Minnie mopped all around them when their father casually strolled out from the back of the house, straightening his shirt. Vivian had always yearned for her father's love, and seeing him had a way of making her heart race. She had seen no close-up example of a man in her life other than the stranger. The boys and men she had encountered over the years were mostly the children of sharecroppers who attended her school and church. She never made friends with any of these males, and no male relatives ever came to visit, except Uncle Jack whenever he wasn't out to sea.

When Vivian was eight, she started taking walks alone, mostly to see the Johnson Plantation with all the men and women working in the fields. She loved to watch the men and women labor joyously. She would walk for miles at a time, passing other small shacks where poor Caucasians and some Black people lived independently. Sometimes, she walked far enough to see the Johnson and the Raison Plantation together in one day. The sharecroppers worked long, hot hours six days a week for a few pennies, their meager lodgings, and food. They didn't have a lot of time to make friends with others outside of their immediate communities.

Vivian was hoping to take a long walk with her father that morning after she saw him in her house. She had never actually taken a walk with her father where they strode together side by side, but when she was six, she started following him sometimes after he would leave her mama. He fascinated Vivian. He was an appealing man, muscular and lean, almost six feet tall. His skin was dark and smooth and he had a mysteriously crooked grin.

His eyes were jet-black. Vivian had been longing to get to know him better, or at least know him period. The only time she ever really saw him, he was going into, or leaving out of her mother's private presence, and then out of the house. If the girls were visible, he did take the time to smile briefly and say, "How y'all doin'?"

This particular morning, as the stranger made his way outside of Carol's bedroom door in full view of the girls at 11:00 a.m., a pitcher of water came flying out, catching him on his left trapezoid. There was no pain associated with the pail, but the stranger was aggravated. "Hey!" He shouted at her. He walked further away, and then turned back to see what the matter was with her. Carol stuck her head through the doorway to see where the pitcher had landed. The sight of his sneering face sent her into a rage, because deep down she knew she could never have him. She rushed at him and tried to cup his face hard with her long fingernails. He gave her a hard shove back toward the bedroom and walked out of the house without acknowledging the presence of his nearly grown daughters.

"I ain't no piece of meat," she screamed after him, "I'm a human being." Her words fell on the ears of her children, and each of them derived separate interpretations related to their own dignity and self-worth.

Robeena stood up from the kitchen floor, ready to help her mother fight should the need arise. She hated her father for what he was doing to Carol; she would have the dignity to stand up to him. Minnie gave a heavy sigh and looked away in shame; her self-worth was diminished in her mind because she personally identified with and internalized the occurrence. All too often Minnie had seen and heard her mother yell and throw things at her father, and threaten him that he should not come back. Nonetheless, on those very nights, Minnie watched her mother stare out the window, longing for the stranger. She heard her mother on those nights and other nights crying herself to sleep in loneliness for him. She shared her mother's pain and understood it to be natural for women to feel that way.

Vivian didn't have the vehement dignified response of Robeena, or the diminished sense of self-worth that covered Minnie. She just accepted her father with love, simply because he was her father, and he became the example of what she envisioned a man should be. She only hoped that someone else would be the "other woman" with her man whenever she got married. Robeena planned to never marry due to witnessing the abuse Carol endured. Having a husband just wasn't worth it. And from her mother's experience, Minnie decided that a piece of man was better than no man.

Carol didn't realize that she was inadvertently teaching Vivian that it was okay for a woman to be second rated. The strongest message Vivian got was that it was more important to be the wife. In this way, she presumed, the man would always take care of her, and she would receive greater respect than the "other woman," but she learned that there could always be another woman. She saw how hard it was for her mother being the "other woman." She didn't grasp that there could be such pain in being the wife of an adulterer, or for that matter, the husband of an adulteress.

The stranger was used to Carol's temper. After their time together that morning, she had asked him if he could stay over a while for a change. He told her that falling asleep had caused him to stay too long already, and he moved to make a quick exit. Carol was exasperated with his lack of affection. She grabbed his leg good-humoredly and said, "I thought you said we would spend the day together."

"You're lucky if I ever come back to this piss spot," he'd muttered harshly. Every time he visited her, she managed to do or say something to repulse him. Today, the mere sight of her after he'd used her was too much for him. He wished she'd have more shame about her relationship with him. Where was the challenge? Her girly plumpness now heaved into a massive lump of flesh overriding her midriff. Her flabby stomach hid her belly button deep under the unattractive rolls and rolls of fat. He turned away to avoid cursing her.

He had startled her with his statement. Things never went as planned with the stranger. She wanted him to care about her, but he didn't. She knew that if he didn't come around for a couple of weeks, she would be badly yearning for him by week three, and he also knew this. She hated herself for wanting him so much, knowing he'd never leave his wife for her. Carol couldn't face this last inference. If she would admit to herself that she was only his worn-out fantasy, then that would mean to her that she had no value. His very presence near her validated her. If *he* was disgusted with her, then to her that meant *she* was disgusting. It was painful, but she began to accept the delusional angle of their relationship.

After tossing the pitcher and fussing at him, Carol turned slowly, feeling dejected by his disapproval. She went back into the bedroom, her chest heaving. Robeena took the mop from Minnie so that Minnie could do what she always did---go see about their mom. Vivian started dusting things, trying to keep busy. They were familiar with this type of depressing time for their mama. Minnie entered her mama's bedroom and started straightening in there, careful not to disturb her. Carol liked to toss her clothes on the floor after wearing them, and a pile was waiting in the corner to be put away. Minnie sat on the floor, taking clothing piece by piece, and folding them neatly, unless she placed them in another pile to be washed. Her mother had flung herself across the mattress on the floor, with her arms crossed tightly at her chest. After a while, Carol uncrossed her arms, headed for the work site, and picked up the dirty clothes from the floor in front of Minnie.

"You ain't gotta help me, mama. I'm doing this for you. You rest, hear?"

"Gal, I'm alright." Minnie shook her head.

"You shouldn't be fighting with 'im like that, mama. He ain't too friendly. If he don't wanna help, I say tell 'im to quit coming here!"

"He ain't that bad, Minnie." She stared at her mother in disbelief.

"He treats you like dirt, mama. He don't care for you."

"Don't let that man scare you into believing he don't care for me. Me and your daddy have been together for a long time. Many years. We got something special." Carol went over to sit on the bed again. "There's been plenty of times it could've ended, but the Good Lord didn't see fit for that to happen." Carol thought telling Minnie the truth would cause Minnie to judge her, so she camouflaged her pain.

"He got him a wife," Minnie said softly. "What the Good Lord be saying about that?"

"I know, Minnie. But things ain't working out between 'em. You know that. It's like I've told you. He's in this situation, see. It's hard for him to know what to do from one minute to the next. Will you put those clothes down for a minute, gal, and listen to me?" Minnie dropped the blouse she was holding and breathed hard. "When two people love each other, I mean, really love each other, it's hard when folk who don't know what they is talking about try to get in your life!" Carol stood. "Minnie." Minnie looked at her. "What if you really loved someone but you were married? You had this wife for five years and she couldn't have no babies, and then you met a pretty, fresh li'l thing like me," Carol laughed at herself. "And you fell in love? See, his wife is expecting things from 'im. He can't just leave her. It's not that easy, Minnie. Not when you married it ain't."

"But you be aching, mama. He is worse than Satan himself for doing you like that."

"I think about what if I never had met 'im. You wouldn't be here, Minnie, and neither would your sisters be. He's good, Minnie. He makes me happy."

"How could he make you happy when you're crying all the time?"

"I guess..."

"You guess what?"

"You don't know your daddy, gal. He's funny, he's thoughtful...he tries to be rough but it ain't even like that, chile."

"How can I know 'im if he won't come 'round?"

"Things would've been different if I had met 'im first. It wouldn't be so sad if I could see 'im six days outa the week and Alma could only see 'im once." Carol's laugh was sinister.

"That ain't funny, mama."

"Yes, it is! Sometimes, you hafta laugh at yourself. Life is funny." She straightened her expression. "Minnie, I guess what I'm trying to tell you is to just be happy and free with what God gives you. Don't be asking for too much, or you might end up with nothing." The possibility of ending up with nothing if one asked for justice was the resounding message for Minnie.

They both jumped at the same time as a knock came on the front door right at about 11:35 a.m. A moment later, they heard Robeena offer Wali Eli a glass of lemonade. Carol and Minnie looked at each other wide eyed at the same time.

"Go out there, mama!" Minnie whispered excitedly. "Ask 'im if that silk was real."

"I already told y'all it was real!" Carol cried.

"Mama, do we really have brothers and sisters in the east? Is that man our uncle? Can we ask 'im about it?" Minnie dipped a dirty towel that wasn't too soiled in her mother's drinking glass, soaking up the remainder of the water at the bottom so that Carol could wash her face.

Minnie felt a sense of dignity that the nice visitor, a decent person was at their house. Just then, Robeena burst into the bedroom exclaiming, "It's him! The man with the silk!" Minnie grabbed her sister's hand and the two of them bounced around, laughing, trying to be quiet. "We all want to hear what you said he told you last week. Can we?"

Vivian stood in the kitchen watching Wali Eli sip the lemonade. He felt the girl's burning eyes. He looked up from the old, worn chair and smiled. Then he stood. "You're Vivian, right?" Impressed, she nodded, staring at him blankly. For some reason, she felt safe in his presence. She looked up at him curiously, wondering if he could guarantee safety. At that moment, she thought about how vulnerable Black people were to harm. Lynchings were commonplace all over the South, Caucasians were menacing, threatening, and generally hostile, and the benevolent ones were patronizing souls who unconsciously flaunted their positions of superiority. Black men who stood up to protest ill-treatment were killed in the streets, whipped, or castrated. Black mothers shielded their sons by pacifying their young desires to stay underfoot; once the young men were old enough to venture out, the mothers found a way to keep them out of society where they could become targets. Vivian recalled how scared her great aunt was whenever her Uncle Jack announced he was leaving home to go deeper south and work in St. Augustine. Jack defied his mother's chokehold to explore the Atlantic Ocean for a living.

Even though he sent money home regularly, Jack was viewed as a departer. However, he represented peace to Vivian, the same as Wali Eli seemed to represent peace, but how could Wali Eli prevent harm? Their very lives in America were permeated by harm.

Followed by Minnie and Robeena, Carol walked into the front room with a sad smile on her face. She was wearing a colorfully flowered dress. Carol's washed face still revealed red teary eyes. The sisters silently agreed they wanted their mother to appear decent, and the presence of the stranger had an air of indecency. Therefore, even though they wanted everyone in the city to hear the uniqueness coming from Wali Eli, they all would have felt embarrassed if the stranger had been there.

"May I help you, suh?" She tried to remember the proper way of speaking. Wali Eli gave a deep bow, removing his hat.

"Yes, how was the fruit? Were the tomatoes suitable?" He studied Carol's countenance. Such a cheerless face undoubtedly accompanied a poignant life's story, he surmised. Wali Eli saw that the four of them seemed to share a bond which could help them draw strength from one another. He knew that Carol's oppression was deep, her misfortunes plentiful. Wali Eli calculated that Carol needed to take advantage of the air around her being purified by the rows of mulberry trees, the very representation of nature. They thrived in his homeland of Mount Paran, a city outside of Mecca. As silkworms suckled the mulberry leaves to miraculously upgrade and refine the production of silk, the process of photosynthesis, with its energy enhancing mechanisms could benefit Carol by alleviating her depression. He would introduce her to the magnificence of the mulberry trees that were right in her midst.

Minnie answered for her mother. "The fruit was heavenly!"

"Our mom said you are from the Middle East. We never heard of there," Robeena added. Wali Eli knew he could not explain everything at once. Much of what he could say would be foreign to them. To them, his very presence and what he represented was an anomaly. There was no one like him in the western hemisphere. There was no one like him in the world, and yet he was faced with a broken people who had been crushed for generations. This is because his love for the broken people who were considered the bottom rail by the society that rated them was unmatched. Wali Eli's father was a Black man and his mother was a Caucasian woman. At an early age, Wali Eli learned what justice looked like for both groups of people. He also had clear visions by the time he was six years old about his role in providing love and justice. Therefore, even though he was born 9,000 miles away, it was made clear to him where the people he sought to save lived. While most children thought about making sandcastles or swimming during the sizzling summer months, Wali Eli dreamed of the day when he could travel the distance to meet with the Black men and women of the Western Hemisphere. If he told them how much he, someone they were not acquainted with cared about them, they would never believe him until he could prove that it was possible for a people who were once slaves to be chosen. However, if he merely stated it, they might deem him a philosopher or a poet. Yet, they wanted to know about him, where he came from.

Indeed, Wali Eli had an incredible sense of godly love for Black people, men, and women alike. Albeit the entire nation exemplified a tilted scale, he knew the bottom rail had the potential to become the top rail and those who were illustrative of being the least would be kings in the land where they were once slaves. And like the process of producing silk required the sun's energy, enlisting a people that mainstream society deemed a sow's ear to be fertilized into their greatness would require not only the sun, but the Giver of Life to the sun. Wali Eli was motivated by the condition of Black people, especially the Black woman. He hated the way she was degraded in society. His father had raised him to honor the female, even if she didn't honor herself. He glanced over his shoulder at Vivian behind him, and then Minnie to his right. The three girls had formed a semicircle around him although they each stood about three feet away from him.

"In time, sisters. In time."

His brief explanation did not stop the sisters from pressing forward. "What does the money look like where you're from?" Minnie asked.

Laughing to himself, he reached into his pocket and retrieved five 1919 1/2 millieme coins minted in bronze with a hole centered in the middle of each one, two 5 paras and a silver qirsh. Wali Eli held the coins out to Robeena, who stood in front of him, but still a foot behind her mother. Feeling royal, Robeena took the coins. Carol said, "Don't give those coins away!" She reached into her sash and proudly gave Minnie a few dimes, knowing she could not afford to do so.

"Have you ever marveled at the sweet smell emanating from those mulberry trees all lined up like soldiers ready to fight a battle for you?" The girls giggled when Robeena snatched the money, then they headed for the door, not understanding his question at all. Minnie turned back and squeezed her mother's hand.

"We're going to go into town, mama . . . it's Saturday!" Carol smiled undetectably, her head hanging low. Minnie turned to Wali Eli and added, "Oh...and we sure don't mind getting a whiff of those mulberry trees on the way! Even the reserved Vivian was content as she held onto one of the bronze coins. They strolled up the dirt road, laughing and playing together. It was still early in the day for their purposes, and the sun beamed with the promise of a bright afternoon ahead. They passed the Johnson Plantation and saw the Negroes sweating in the fields. They were singing merrily:

> *"Swing low, sweet chariot,*
> *Coming for to carry me home!*
> *Swing low, sweet chariot*
> *I looked o'er Jordan 'n what did I see?*
> *A band of Angels coming after me,*
> *Coming for to carry me home!"*

Vivian was deeply impressed that even though the sun thumped miserably on their clammy backs, the Negroes seemed to be at peace. She quickly tuned into humming the complaisant melody, although her discouraging sisters tried to talk over her voice. Minnie didn't want to identify with the sharecroppers in any way. She concluded that the Negroes who worked the fields were of a substandard breed. Whenever Ms. Geraldine sat with Minnie to plait her hair every so often, she would warn her over and over that the plantation men behaved like paltry savage monkeys, and that the women were more like wildcats than human beings. Minnie was satisfied that Ms. Geraldine's words had aggrandized her existence and that of her sisters, and she was proud that they lived separately from these disadvantaged Black sharecroppers. "How can you be sure I'm better, Ms. Geraldine? And does this mean I might get to be invited to some of the harvest balls and whatnot that Negroes can attend when they turn 16? I'm 19 and never been to nothing."

"That's because you are dark-skinned, Minnie. You up there, but your complexion--can't nothing be done about that. Be happy with what you have."

"How do you know all this?" Geraldine shook her head and kept braiding. How did people know anything? She didn't know how she knew that, but Minnie thought she knew everything, so, she didn't want to let her down by providing no answer at all.

"Why, Willy Lynch, of course!" Ms. Geraldine said the name as though Minnie was supposed to know who Willy Lynch was, but she didn't.

"Who is that?" Minnie asked. The only thing Geraldine knew about Willy Lynch was that he was some mystery slave owner who probably never existed. Once upon a year, some Black men overheard a few planters at a tavern talking about the wisdom of Willy Lynch, and how he was teaching everyone how Negroes were to be treated in society. It seemed like this Willy Lynch guy had all the answers.

As the sisters walked, Minnie looked around at some of the people passing them on the road, wondering if any of them knew Willy Lynch. Eventually making their way to town, the girls came to the Raison Plantation, Vivian escorted them through the shortcut she used whenever she walked alone. There was a trail about a quarter of a mile behind the big house. There were unseasonably fleshy cherries growing red and wild. They stopped and picked the tangy fruit, exclaiming how unusual it was for cherries to blossom so early in the year. Then they lifted their dresses and sat on the ground to rest.

Henry Raison watched the unfamiliar young ladies walk carefree onto the Raison's land. He saw they were different, fresh. They were unlike the field hand girls he knew; these girls were wearing crisp dresses and shoes, and their heads weren't wrapped in rags. Instead, appealing bonnets brightened the entire terrain they occupied. Henry had never seen a Negro female wearing a bonnet; therefore, he didn't know that they were just as poor as he was—even poorer. He saw they were all elegant, and that they must all be sisters. They each had particularly sculpted cheekbones and spherical eyes. The tallest had the roundest face. Henry chuckled at their gay, animated features. The sisters were lean and beautiful, with confident airs.

Henry had been drawing water from a low stream when he first noticed them. He put the bucket down and followed them soundlessly to the trail behind the house. The tallest girl looked the most robust, like a wife should look, Henry reckoned. However, the sister that must have been the middle born fascinated him. She seemed so mysterious and dazzling. Her face was blemish free, aside from a delicate, tiny mole under and to the right of her mouth. Her lips were just as red as the cherries they were stealing, and just as thick. He scanned his mind, thinking about where he'd seen her before.

Just then, Vivian saw Henry looking at her out of the corner of her eye as he approached them cautiously. He was embarrassed when their gazes were synchronized. Quickly, he looked away at Minnie and then Robeena. He was still twenty feet away as he swept his eyes away from Robeena and appraised Vivian again, then back to Minnie. Henry was interested in marriage, and he concluded that Minnie looked the most suitable for that position.

Vivian was too beautiful for Henry's mental image of a faithful, lifelong wife. Besides, he couldn't imagine Vivian taking a liking to a stark ebony, burly man like himself, anyway. To him, she seemed like the type who would prefer to court a mulatto. Robeena wasn't even a consideration for him because he saw her as a mere child. She was the loudest talker, the skinniest, and the least graceful in her movements. Her face would be considered the cutest, in a child-like way, but the middle girl's beauty was ravishing. He glanced at her again to find her looking at him straight between his eyes. He found himself blushing, growing hot from head to toe as he lowered his gaze.

Although he was very dark skinned, and she preferred the lighter boys, Vivian was totally attracted to this apparent sharecropper. She could tell he was in excellent shape. She could see tightness in his arms through his loose-fitting shirt as the sun created a shadow in the soft material. His chest protruded smartly. She had seen how he looked at her admiringly, but then how his gaze had shifted in concentration on Minnie. Vivian was full force ready to plot out how she could draw his attention back to her and away from Minnie, merely because she was competitive and was emotionally handcuffed by the threat of perceived rejection. Vivian regarded her youngest sister, Robeena as the prettiest of the three, and Minnie as the homeliest.

Minnie turned suddenly, facing Henry for the first time. He was simply the most perfectly molded, striking man that she had ever laid eyes on in her life. His hair was cut short, but was all over his head in tight, twisted, wooly-like raisins. He looked to her like he could pick her up over his head with one hand, and then reposition her for a face-to-face kiss before he let her slide back to her feet. Minnie shook off her thoughts, attempting to guard herself from thinking like that about a man she'd never even seen before. He stopped advancing only for a second, then walked directly to Minnie and stood before her, shuffling his feet. "What's your name?" A voice asked from behind Minnie and Henry. Minnie turned to frown at Vivian.

Henry answered, afraid to take his eyes from Minnie, "Name be Henry. Henry Raison." He was happy his voice didn't get stuck in his throat. Minnie gave him a smile that could melt gold. Her smile convinced him that Minnie was the woman of his dreams. Robeena was the only one of her sisters who wasn't smitten by his gentleness. Vivian didn't like that he took advantage of the continuative rule with his "be" verb, but that was minor compared to his broad chest and his masculine, husky voice. Vivian had started reading books ever since Mr. Anderson's comment about her speech. After weighing it, Vivian had concluded she wanted to become an intelligent young woman. She had recently finished reading "If We Must Die" by Claude McKay, and she loved it. Vivian noticed the differences in grammar she used versus the grammar in various books.

Soon, they were all sitting together in the grove becoming acquainted. The four of them talked freely about their lives, homes, and ambitions. Henry played his pocket harmonica for them and they enjoyed listening. Robeena sucked away her craving to dance. So it was Henry who was on stage now, with his musical ability, stories about plantation life, and with his dreams about the better and free land in the North. The sisters listened to him in fascination when he talked about his adventures in the war. He told them how he had to run for his life one time because some Germans had spotted him after he had gotten lost in the brush. Miraculously, shots were fired which caused the Germans to disperse, he said.

He told them that he bore no arms since his major task was to keep the front line supplied with ammunition, food, and medical supplies as needed. Vivian could visualize the smoky haze that must have been Henry's life during the war. He seemed so brave and worthy! Vivian wanted him to become aware of her admiration for him more than ever. But to her dismay, soon, Minnie and Henry were holding hands as they walked ahead of Robeena and Vivian by the creek. Minnie had never felt so special. Henry had already said that now that he had met her, he wouldn't think of leaving for the North without her. Vivian pouted, only half listening to Robeena's chatter as they tracked the new couple for miles into town, only to turn right back around without spending their dimes or visiting any of the sidewalk shops.

Henry was undeniably aware of Vivian's wanton stares at him. He stole a couple of backward glances at her endearing face as well, mostly out of curiosity, for he was certain of the sister he preferred for his purposes. Henry was twenty-eight years old, single, and tired of it. It slowly registered to him that he had seen Vivian before, with a young man named Lee Hiram, a Negro slickster who had moved up to Century from Pensacola about ten years ago. "Hiram" was a nickname given to Lee when he was a child. Lee's father couldn't even remember who had started calling him Hiram.

Henry knew that Lee Hiram liked to gamble, and that he lived life in the fast lane. Henry had seen Lee quite a few times, even on the Raison Plantation near two or three single women's cabins. Whenever he saw Lee around Tazra's cabin at first, he imagined it could be to seek advice, and not because Maybelle lived there, as Tazra served her community's vast health needs. However, the frequency of Lee's visits caused Henry to grow weary of him. Henry considered Vivian's beauty as exceptional when he had first seen her with Lee about six months ago. He warned himself then that there was something forbidden about her if she could keep up with a man like Lee Hiram. Vivian obviously was a girl that "got around," Henry guessed. This factor also distanced his interest in her. Minnie, on the other hand, seemed motherly, and he saw her hands were rough with work. "Make me a good wife," he presumed.

By the time Henry walked the girls home that evening, Minnie's heart was filled with the dare to go away with Henry. He was a carpenter, not a sharecropper. She felt it was God who placed them together. She was in love. He was so different from her father. To Minnie's knowledge, never had her father mentioned taking her mother away just so the two of them could be together and start a new life, or to take a trip, for that matter. This was the most exciting proposition Minnie could ever imagine. She was happy he chose her, and not one of her beautiful sisters. Minnie knew Vivian would have taken Henry, had he shown an interest in her, even though Lee was her man. "Everyone seems to know 'cepting Vivian that Lee Hiram is bad news, just like the stranger," Minnie confided in Henry on their way home. Henry, being a private person, didn't volunteer any negative information he knew about Lee to Minnie.

Minnie liked talking to Henry because it seemed he really listened to her. Minnie was so excited about Henry that once they made it home, she wanted to call her mother outside to meet him then, but she didn't know if her mother would discredit her in the event that the stranger was inside. Carol wasn't home, anyway. Wali Eli had invited Carol to attend a meeting with a few other neighbors to discuss topics Carol had never engaged in like self-examination, analysis, and community development. These topics were virtually unheard of in the early 20th Century, so Carol was utterly fascinated! Robeena and Vivian went inside the house, but Minnie chose one of the mulberry trees to sit under with Henry so that he could listen to her life's story. Before he left her, they made plans to go to church together the next day. He would meet Carol at that time, they decided. When dusk settled in, Minnie reluctantly released her hand from Henry's and followed her sisters into the house.

CHAPTER FIVE
Browned Muffins

About 2:30 a.m. after the night Minnie met Henry, Lee Hiram came to the sisters' bedroom window and called inside for Vivian. For the first time, Minnie didn't scold her. Now that she had met Henry, Minnie knew how it felt to have butterflies swim in her abdomen, and therefore, she could never deny anyone that. Moreover, she saw the way Vivian had looked at Henry, coupled with Henry's brief indecision when he noticed the beauty of Vivian, so she wanted to encourage Vivian to concentrate on Lee.

"Viv. Viv!" She whispered. "Lee out there." Vivian rose slowly to her knees, wondering why Minnie had bothered to wake her. Vivian was such a hard sleeper that sometimes when Lee came, Minnie was able to chase him away by threatening to get their mother if he didn't leave before Vivian ever knew he was out there.

Carol's unhappy relationship with the stranger was caution enough for Minnie to guard her chastity and that of her sisters. There were plenty of sharecroppers from the Johnson Plantation who sniffed around the sisters. One thing Carol instilled in them was to wait for marriage, and not be smitten by smooth talking males. She wished her own mother had made that plain. Unlike Minnie, her siblings made genuine efforts not to look down on the common Negro bucks (as they were still widely called) who still worked the fields because their grandmother, Carol's mother, had lived on the plantation for years. They argued about color a lot. Minnie wondered about the division between Black people based on color. Vivian did not want to admit that she felt she stood a step above because Lee was two shades lighter than Henry, but Minnie knew she felt that way. Vivian argued to a stubborn Minnie that a Negro was a Negro, regardless of where they lived or worked. Minnie said that if she thought that way, then why did she spend so much time correcting folk like she was better or something? Vivian answered that she wanted everyone to do better, including herself. She reminded Minnie that the great Master Kent Johnson particularly favored their grandmother, Minnie-Anne. Minnie smacked her lips to inform Vivian of how distasteful it was that their grandmother served as some cheap concubine for the master.

Their grandmother, Minnie-Anne had worked in the house of the Johnsons as a handmaiden to old Master Kent Johnson's wife. After the Civil War, while most planters in the area moved away from the South because their crops had been devastated, the Johnson's had capitalized in several ways. Kent Johnson was also in the banking industry, so, when the area planters became frightened by the capture of Atlanta during the Civil War and decided to sell their land swiftly, Kent gave them small, quick cash and purchased their land. Kent's dream was to conquer the Raison Plantation, to no avail. The Raisons weren't even willing to accept that slavery was over, let alone sell their emblem of it. Many of the slaves were still on the land, and did not want to leave. The idea of being "free" intimidated them. All their lives, these slaves had depended on their masters to feed them, house them, and think for them.

During this frenzy of the aftermath of war, Kent Johnson gathered all his former slaves one evening and met with them along the side of the main cotton field. He told them they were welcome to stay on as free men and women, but that they would have to continue to work for their keep. Several slaves ventured off on their own and some went north, but several more were delighted at this safer way of life. Some of the ones who left the plantation took on the surname of Johnson because as freed men and women, they were required to have a surname when traveling, and for other identification purposes.

The native African names and tribes of Black people were long lost. Carol's parents and grandparents didn't know whether they were Hausas, Mandingos, or what. They didn't even know what a tribe was, for that matter, so, of course they had no recollection of the Black man's rich history before the divisive tools of tribes and sects interfered with their becoming one nation. What they did know was that the closer they could come to American, and in particular, Caucasian thinking and living, the more accepted they would be in society.

There were a few slaves listening to Kent's proposition who didn't give a second thought as to whether they should venture away on their own. Some of these were the ones who had not been "Negrolized" yet by systemic exploitation and dehumanization. These were some of the Black warriors who had recently been brought to North America from Africa via illegal slave importation given that importing slaves from Africa had been outlawed several years ago due to the Transatlantic Compromise between the North and the South.

On his second or third visit with Carol and some other community members, Wali Eli engaged them in a conversation about African born warriors. He told them that the difference between an African and a Negro had become so vast that most planters wanted nothing to do with the taming of the Black African warriors. However, as the years progressed, the continent called Africa became so invaded by European explorers and missionaries, that the African man in that far eastern region became brainwashed as well to inadvertently worship the slave master, chiefly because all the portraits that the missionaries, whom they trusted, brought of Jesus were presented with blond or brunette hair and of course, Caucasian. And the mixing of blood helped to further cause a racial divide within the Black population. The lighter skinned Negroes presumed they were to receive more privileges than the darker ones, especially the black-blue Africans who could scarcely speak the English language, or the Geechies who insisted on preserving their own West Indies and African cultures. Only light-skinned, mulatto and quadroon Negroes were allowed to work inside of the master's house. Only the light-skinned slaves received special assignments and entitlements.

And of course, Kent Johnson mainly chose from the light-skinned girls to have his pleasure. Even though the jet-black females exhibited unblemished, extraordinary, and exotic beauty, seeking quadroons carried the air of anti-savagery. However, Kent Johnson's illegitimate offspring were all shades of Black. It was rumored that Master Kent did not claim any of his Black children, except his lightest hued son, who could pass for a Caucasian man, and was thus given Kent's name given that he had no other male heir. Kent Jr.'s mother was one of the quadroon house servants. Fascinated with Black history, Carol repeated the triumphs and tragedies to her daughters during several suppers in a row. She included as much as she could remember about her mother's plight, vowing to instill pride in them, or at least an understanding about their kinfolk. Unfortunately, Minnie-Anne was mostly closed-mouthed when it came to the details surrounding her upbringing.

In 1875, Carol's mother, Minnie-Anne, became the blue-black woman of Kent Johnson's choice. He had watched her since she was around ten. At that time, Master Kent Johnson selected her to be his wife's handmaiden. She moved away from her mama to live in the big house and wait on Sarah Johnson, Kent's wife, hand and foot. A young lad named Robert adored Minnie-Anne, so it crushed him when she was beckoned away from the fields. Although he was only fourteen, Robert was old enough to know Master Johnson's ways with the young ex-slave girls, and he feared Minnie-Anne would be his next prospect. Her mother cried when she learned her daughter was Kent's claim while Minnie-Anne didn't understand her mother's anguish. It was a special honor for her to be favored above all the other girls by the plantation's master. He shielded her from Robert and everyone else, including himself until 1875, when she was fourteen; he was forty-five, and twenty years married.

It was difficult for Kent to have his pleasure with Minnie-Anne without his wife's knowledge, yet he refused to release the child from his conniving grip. That's why after several instances of getting away by a hair, in 1879 Kent consented to give Minnie-Anne one of his small shacks that he'd taken possession of after the Civil War. To aid in his decision moreover, she had begun to cry about wanting her "true" freedom away from the plantation, up North in Chicago or Canada.

She told him that if she must live in the shack he gave her, it would have to have her name on the deed, and only her name. For Kent, the run-down box was not a problem to release. It was nearly condemned. The place was sparsely furnished with a sturdy green sofa and an oak end table in the front room, an ice box in the kitchen as well as another one out back, two mattresses in each of the back bedrooms, an oak dressing table in the master bedroom, along with oil lamps for each bedroom. It was once lived in by his overseer and his family.

Minnie-Anne figured if she tidied up the place, planted a few vegetables and flowers, she could turn the shack into a more presentable cottage. The shack was northeast of the plantation about two miles down the road. Kent planned that in this way, Minnie-Anne could still cater to his needy wife, she could have the freedom she wanted, and he too could have the secret freedom he wanted with her. The arrangement also allowed him to set another young girl in place, as he calculated the fading of the current arrangements over time. Everyone was happy with the provisions.

However, by 1880, Minnie-Anne became once again uptight with the limited freedom she was given. She was still walking the journey five days a week to tend to her mistress, yet her own lifestyle was not improving. The excitement of living alone had worn thin and boring. She had no dreams or goals. Living alone waiting on someone to drop by was her main stay. Going shopping was a rarity because Kent Johnson didn't give her a thing except lust-filled evenings and her regular salary. Meanwhile, Robert Johnson, now a stable boy on the plantation, continued to miss Minnie-Anne terribly. One day that summer, he was summoned to travel with Kent on out-of-town business. Kent often used the trips he took as one of the few opportunities to spend a night with Minnie-Anne. During this visit, Minnie-Anne grew ashamed when Robert strode through her front door with Master Johnson.

She knew he had doubtlessly heard the rumors years ago that she was the master's paramour, but he had not seen it with his own eyes. She put on her best performance of cheerfulness when she gave them both tea to drink. Minnie-Anne acted like she didn't notice Robert's hand brush hers when she handed him his mug. Robert was crestfallen to learn that his master was still in control of such a beautiful Negro woman, a woman he himself had always wanted. Even though Minnie-Anne had never promised herself to Robert, he felt a deep sense of betrayal. That night, Robert tossed and turned, trying to drown out Minnie-Anne's high pitched, counterfeit giggles creeping through the walls from the other room.

Before Robert set out with Kent in the morning, he found time to gather some wild daisies from a nearby field. He wrapped them with a thin loose stem from a fallen branch and hid his gift on the side of the house until the coast was clear. Before mounting his horse, Kent went out back to puff his pipe. Robert and Minnie-Anne stood alone together in the kitchen during the last moments before departing each other. Robert grabbed Minnie-Anne's hands and pulled her to him for a quick kiss. Easily, she melted briefly in his grasp, remembering how they used to play together so many years ago. He left her alone with her thoughts and trotted out the front door to gather the daisies again, came back, pressed them into her arms, winked at her, and then backed away, leaving her to her blushes.

A fortnight later, he returned to her shack turned into a cottage without Kent. As it was, Kent Johnson had very sparse need for her, as his plantation was ripe with fresh fruit. Therefore, it became less and less problematic for Robert to have a secret affair with Minnie-Anne after Kent took up with a second and then a third victim. After a while, Robert became confused as to why he worked from sunup until sunset to live on the Johnson Plantation, simply to share a bunk with another man, and a small cabin with four other men. He liked to drink plenty of good liquor, and it was easy to steal it from his master—that was the only benefit he could think of for his current living arrangements.

Robert told everyone he was going out on his own, and he set out to move his personal belongings to the shack turned into a cottage of Minnie-Anne Johnson. Another stable boy ran to get the young, octoroon Master Kent Jr., who was 22 at the time, as everyone gathered around watching Robert pack. Kent Jr. came quickly to witness the uppity Negro taking leave of his sharecropping freedom.

"You still owe us two weeks' worth o' work, you grimy baboon nigger ape." Kent Jr. hissed at him.

"I plan to make that up to you, suh." Robert's brother, Jack bowed his head and pretended not to see Robert trying to make eye contact with him.

"You goddamn well better plan it, you lazy assed bastard," Kent Jr. yelled, "you be back here in the morn' before that sun comes crawling over the horizon. You'll start making it up then." He looked over at Jack. "You'd best see to it that he's here, o' you'll make up that work, Jack."

"Yassuh, Mistuh Kent." Jack was telling no one that he, too, planned to leave the plantation by nightfall, only he was headed to sea.

"Yassuh. I was planning on that anyway, suh." Bitterly, Kent Jr. figured too late that he should've told Robert he owed more time than two weeks. He wanted his father to be proud of the way he drove the niggers into the ground and generated fear in his audience. He walked venomously away. Robert was the first freed slave they'd lost other than in death in over five years. Kent's umbrage was subdued shortly when he reminded himself that his plantation had, through births, gained about thirty sharecroppers in the same length of time. And he could proudly add his biological contributions to the tally.

Because of their physical severance from the Johnson Plantation, Robert, Minnie-Anne, and now Minnie considered themselves a notch above the common sharecroppers. Master Kent had made Minnie-Anne think she was special, and Robert postulated that he was special to walk right off the plantation to a home of his own, without having to work steadily anymore. When Carol was born to them in 1888, it was the seal to their relationship for Robert. He decided he could now relax and enjoy life forever. No more worrying about trying to please people. His family was what he wanted most of all. Robert took frequent trips into town to buy bootleg liquor at the basement gambling joints. He took on drinking as much as he wanted to reward himself for being a new daddy and making it through the hard years. Robeena (named after her grandfather), Minnie (named after her grandmother), and Vivian Johnson considered themselves "freer" than those still living on the plantations. Minnie deemed Henry lucky to get a girl like her, because deep down she felt she was better than the sharecroppers' daughters.

Lee Hiram never knew plantation life. His parents never knew it, either. The only experience Lee had on the plantation was with the girls he would wrestle with who lived there. He couldn't see himself marrying any of them, though. Lee was a hard worker who enjoyed spending his money doing exciting things like gambling, drinking, and smoking. He also appreciated wild parties and lots of women. He was considered by many as more than marginally handsome—-he was absolutely stately and had the build of a young steed. At age twenty, he was a replica of his father; very experienced with juggling several women and street life. Lee wasn't sure how true it was, but it was rumored that even though he never had any brothers or sisters in his home, his old man had fathered sixteen more children between Century and Pensacola, Florida. No girl had claimed she was pregnant with Lee's baby, yet, nonetheless.

Vivian and Lee met during one of her walks. He immediately became fond of the starry-eyed, picturesque teenager, and the thing that attracted her to him was how fine he was. She saw him walking up the road on her side, undeniably focusing on her. Casually, Vivian drifted to the other side of the street when they were only fifteen yards apart so he wouldn't think he was as fascinating as he was.

"Whatchu run over there for, cutie pie?" She started to bluff like she didn't hear him, but he was too loud and obvious, and there was no one else on the road.

"I didn't run, I walked." They still hadn't paralleled each other because he stopped when she crossed the street.

"Well, walk on back o'er here, if you don't mind." She stopped, too.

"I can't find a notion to do anything of the sort."

"Yet, you found a notion to walk off, real rude like, huh?" She didn't like being called out like that. She knew it was rude, but that was supposed to be a secret. He started across to where she stood. "Do I smell, or something? It'd be a shame if you could smell me from so far away." She giggled. When he neared her, he stopped again. He stood six feet away. "Can you still smell me?" She was trying hard to control her laughter because she didn't want to seem fickle.

"I'm sorry for being rude."

"It's alright, as long as you ain't got no problem making it up to me."

"I don't suppose I know how to do that, except to express my apologies."

"You can prove to me that you're sorry by walking right alongside me and on the same side of the road."

"I'm not going that way."

"Well, where are you going, anyway?"

"I'm taking a walk."

"Where to?"

"I reckon I don't have a particular destination."

"Cutie pie, I do have a destination. I'm on my way to my job to pick up my pay envelope. I hafta be there by noon. Since you're just strolling along, what would I hafta do to get you to walk o'er yonder with me to the railway company?"

"Why would I want to do something silly like that?"

"On account of I'm begging you."

"Not for real—and even if you were…"

"I am for real." He dropped to his knees and put his face in the dirt. She couldn't believe him! His clothes were neat, pressed, and clean, yet he didn't seem to mind baptizing himself in red dirt for her, and he didn't even know her name, she considered glowingly.

"Boy, get on up out of that mud! What's wrong with you?" She walked over to him as though she wanted to scold him further, since he didn't move. "Get on up, I said!" He stood slowly, dusting himself. He had tricked her into coming closer so he wouldn't have to, she realized. Now she was standing in his personal space, only, she didn't know how she could back away from him again. She wanted him to smile, but he didn't.

"Do you care to know my name?" She definitely wanted to know his name. He had managed to put her in control over their meeting, but he seemed to be navigating her responses. He was remarkable, she thought.

"Yes, I care," she said softly.

"Not as much as I care to know yours, I'll bet."

"It's Vivian."

"Vivian, it ain't all that important that I go and pick up my pay. I can get it tomorrow. I got me some pocket change already." He patted his pockets. "So, if you don't wanna go that far, it's alright with me if we do something else. We can go wherever you want, cutie pie—but I can't let you walk out of my life after I barely got you to walk in it." This was outrageous! He was so bold, she thought.

"Um…if you need your money…"

"One thing I learned since I been in Century—I'm from Pensacola—is that money ain't everything. I live near Bridgewater with my old man. He's the one who helped me get my job at the railway. My father always tells me that a good woman is better than gold. The railway pays nice, but I ain't got no good woman." She had to back away if he insisted on talking like that. He didn't follow her.

"I'm not looking for a boyfriend, if that's what you're trying to hint."

"I definitely don't wanna be your boyfriend, either." He caught her off guard again. "I don't even know you. The woman I choose is gonna be special—with certain qualities. She's gonna know how to carry herself as my woman, see? My name is Lee Hiram. I'm all about business when it's time for business, but I don't mind having fun. It'll take a real cutie pie to walk on my arm…somebody such as yourself." She had never met a smoother talking young man. She felt that if she walked away, he wouldn't stop her again and the next girl might not be so stupid. However, she couldn't give in to him—not yet. He seemed like he knew his way around the block, and she valued her virtue.

"Look, Mr. Hiram…"

"I prefer you drop the formalities and call me Lee. Can you do that?" If only he'd smile!

"Lee..." She didn't know what to say. She had tried lying, and he stopped her at every turn. But, how could he be so sure that she liked him? Perhaps it had to do with how fine he was, she thought. Perhaps girls never said no to him. Then, did he want to add her to his list? It was clear that he could probably get just about any girl he wanted, and that he was used to everything a girl might say to guard herself against him. She decided she'd come out better if she told the truth. "I don't mean to act funny with you, Lee, but the truth is that I'm not used to all this. I never had any boyfriend or somebody talking to me like this, and I..." He took a few steps backward when she had estimated that he would come closer.

"You don't trust me."

"Well, I don't want to get in any trouble." She blushed. "I mean, I was just out walking. I wasn't trying to be fast-tailed...and I walked on the other side because I saw you were handsome, and I thought I should keep going..."

"Hey..."

"But I guess that's what you want to hear. I know girls always tell you how cute you are."

"Maybe they do say that kinda stuff to me—but it don't mean a wooden nickel." He was telling the truth. Lee knew that he had grown into an extraordinarily handsome fellow, but he was not conceited. However, he was aware that many girls came on to him because of his looks and that he was able to score because of the same reason. That was too easy for him, though, and he was looking for something different in the girl who would gain any measure of his respect.

"You sound like you have a line for everything. I guess this is routine for you, but like I said, I was simply taking a walk because I like to walk. I don't walk to find handsome boys, and if I see one, so what? Maybe I was rude because I'm trying to learn things right now about myself that'll keep me out of harm's way. My older sister says that sometimes I'll have to be mean to boys because if I don't..."

"Vivian, I really am begging you. Please don't walk off from me. I don't mean no harm to you, cutie pie. You ain't gotta worry about me getting you in no trouble, neither. I'll keep a good distance...always." He finally gave her a smile. "You think you can trust me?"

He was successful at sweeping her off her feet. This was an honorable man, she felt. Somehow, she would have to overcome her shyness and allow herself the opportunity to spend time with him, yet he wasn't helping her to slip into being with him. He wanted her to say that she trusted him.

"Yes, I think I can trust you." He walked to her so slowly that she became petrified. She recognized that his pace was to warn her that he was coming all the way! She couldn't move. He put his arms around her and kissed her in the mouth.

"You ever done that with a boy?"

"Lee!" He hugged her tightly, and then, humming, he swayed with her from side to side, as though he was lulling her to sleep. After a moment, he saw that she was comfortable in his arms.

"I think we just established something, muffin pie. I trust you, too." He released her. "I think I found what I've been searching for."

"What makes you so sure?" He started walking toward his job and she fell in step.

"You make me wanna be a right man. You make me wanna honor you. I gotta tell you the truth—all girls don't make me feel that way. Some girls make me act like a dog. But do you know what? I need me a good woman, like I said."

He won more points. He validated her. She was better than her sisters. She was better than those other girls who acted like hussies, she gathered. She was a good woman. Therefore, he earned enough points to spend more time with her so he could say those wonderful things to her all over again, and again. He was bold enough to kiss her. That was her very first kiss and it was from a confident, fine prince.

For the rest of the day, they remained together. They talked all the way to the railway company. Once there, he ordered her to stand by a Sycamore tree while he went inside to get his money. He pointed his finger in her face and warned her not to speak to anyone, and not to look at anyone in their eyes if she were approached. He was referring to the loads of employed men going in and out of the large gates, since he needed to enter through the side doors near there to pick up his envelope. Briefly, she was frightened by his demeanor, but she didn't know if he was scaring her or if she was frightened by the type of men that he was suggesting might approach her.

No one bothered her. When Lee came dashing out of the building, he raced quickly to her and led her away without asking about her experience by the Sycamore tree. He took her on the train, and they got off in Pensacola. On the way to Pensacola, she wanted him to kiss her on the train, but he sat in the chair behind her and purred in her ear the whole way, almost.

"You're so pretty," he whispered. "You know that, cutie pie?" She flushed quietly. "Yeah, you know it." Then he sat back in his seat for a while. She wanted to turn to him, but she was too embarrassed. After fifteen minutes of silence, he got back in her ear.

"You know what I think, muffin pie?"

"What?"

"I think this train is heading to heaven, and I can't wait to get there with you."

"Pensacola heaven," she added timidly.

"Yeah, baby. That's what it's gonna be."

When the train stopped, he tapped her shoulder and rushed ahead of her into the sunlight. She had never been on a train before, so she wanted to stand around for a while and look at the expressions of other people as they made their way into the crowded area to see if they thought that trains were as electrifying as she did.

"Lee, where are all these people going?"

"Who cares? Come on, cutie pie! I have a place that I know you'll like." He started trotting down the road. She was glad that he ventured at such a fast pace because her body was built for running, and too, she liked showing him that she wasn't so girly. Her long, bright summer dress with daisies printed through and through spread with the wind as she breathed down the Pensacola roads. She hadn't even broken a sweat when Lee stopped trotting sooner than she thought he would. He turned down a quiet street and then cut behind someone's shed to make it to the next street.

"Where are we going?"

"You mean where are we? Look!" Right before her was the awe-inspiring Pensacola Bay.

"Oh my God."

"That's the bay. Right on the other side of that bridge there, you can walk along the county riverbank. You wanna see that, too? I like to come in on this side because it ain't no fishing going on o'er here."

"It's so peaceful. How come they're not fishing over here?"

"On account of this is private property."

"What are we doing on it, then?"

"We're private people!" He laughed. "Come on. Let's go."

He took her way over to the bridge, which was more distant than it appeared, and larger, too. Near the dock, there were a few semi-abandoned schooners because they had mechanical problems, and two small vessel boats called chings. In addition, there was a paddle boat that seemed to have Lee's name written on it. He climbed in first and then pulled Vivian along before she could protest. And she had the mind to resist because she didn't see how she could keep her dress clean if she had to sit on the dust filled plank where he guided her. Swiftly, Lee removed his crisp creased shirt and laid it across the bench before her. He had already started paddling before she was completely in her seat. Vivian made great pains to catch herself because she knew if she toppled over, he would have to physically rescue her, and he knew it, as well.

She tried not to stare at him as he flexed his pectoral muscles every time he flushed the oars through the waves. Thirty minutes later, they were walking alongside the Escambia River. Vivian had no idea that the river was so large and spilled so beautifully into the ocean. Her eyes had never known this sort of richness. In the past, she had only frolicked besides the waters in Century. Eventually, Lee took her hand in his, but he didn't kiss her again or hug her. She wanted him to embrace her by the riverbank, but he didn't.

When they got on the train to return home, he sat behind her again, and she almost wanted to beg him to sit next to her. She turned around in her seat to face him, hoping it was okay to do so.

"You don't have to sit behind me, Lee." He was sitting all the way back with his arms crossed, and he didn't answer her. Self-doubting, she turned to face the front again after three eternal seconds of feeling like a fool. She didn't know how to take this gallant man. He acted so loving and approachable on the riverbank, but when she attempted closeness with him, he stared at her like she was unvirtuous. She bit her lip, wanting to disappear under her chair. He did like her, didn't he? Lee waited ten minutes before he answered. He moved up to speak directly in her ear.

"I gotta sit behind you on account of I can't have my leg brushing against yours, sweet, muffin pie." She crossed her legs. "I told you I would keep a good distance."

"Oh!"

"But if you want me to come up there and be with you, I will. You know that don't you?"

"I guess."

"Is that what you want, muffin pie?"

"No…no, sir."

"Good. It's not what I want, either. I adore you. You know what? I want you to be my princess."

Embarrassed, she shifted uncomfortably. Was he making fun of her? "I don't reckon I can be a princess. Princesses live in castles, and they have long, golden hair, and blue eyes."

"You know why I call you muffin pie?"

"I can't imagine."

"First thing is 'cause you act sweet as pie, and you're just as wholesome as a piece of pie. Second thing is your skin is so brown, it's like browned muffins that I remember my mama used to cook for me when I was a whippersnapper. My mama is gone now, but the mark of her will never leave me.

I ain't had none of them muffins since she left me…'til I met you—it's like I have 'em sitting right in front of me again. Baby, you would mess up them muffins if your hair was gold and your eyes was blue. See, you couldn't be my princess if you looked like that."

"I'm sorry about your mother."

"That's why I want you to be my princess. Okay?"

"Okay."

"Am I the first guy to kiss you?"

"Yes."

"Are you okay that I did that?" She couldn't say yes…not to him.

"I don't know." He knew she was lying. And he knew she expected him to kiss her when they stopped to stare at the waters.

"One day, maybe I'll kiss you again, if you let me. But you gotta be only my girl, and you can't kiss no 'nother guy. How 'bout that?"

"We'll see." He sat back and smiled all the way home. When they got off the train, it was dark. He let her lead him to her house, and he understood that she wasn't allowed to have a boyfriend, and that they would have to sneak around. He said he would come for her after church the next day, and she said yes, they could meet right there, in the shadow of the trees.

"Next time I see you, maybe I'll kiss you again, and if you let me, I'll know you're gonna let me be your man."

"We'll see."

And so, they became a couple. He took her with him to the gambling alleys in the town, proud to have such a fresh new chick on his arm that his friends had never seen before. Vivian was more than thrilled with the attention of this popular young man who didn't at all seem to mind spending so much money on her. When she told her friends, Missy and Madeline Burdeshaw about her new boyfriend, it turned out they already knew of him because he lived nearby. They agreed with her that he was sinfully fine. Vivian felt special that after seeing them, he obviously wasn't as impressed with them as he was with her, and thus supposed they were secretly jealous.

Her mother, however, was dismayed the first time she saw him for herself. It was when Lee didn't bring Vivian home until 1:00 a.m. Carol was more embarrassed than worried because Ms. Esther from down the road had a bad habit of tending to her window late at night and making public statements about what she saw lurking in the darkness. Carol looked out the window for the one-hundredth time and finally spotted the much-discussed opportunist walking her daughter freely toward their house at that unthinkable hour. Briefly, she recalled the stranger keeping her out at the same hour.

Carol recognized that her daughters were getting to be ripe young women. It scared her to think of men carrying them off to lives of wretchedness and spoil. She wished her own parents had been more forbidding with her about the stranger. A dreadful feeling came over her when she remembered how her mother flirted with the stranger, insinuating it was okay to court her vulnerable, preadolescent daughter. Carol's mostly silent concerns were inadequate to stop the relationship between Vivian and Lee, though. This is because Vivian would usually make it home before dark, and when she did, Carol didn't know how to explain to Vivian that her relationship with Lee was still improper. It never entered Carol's mind to force Vivian and Lee to be chaperoned during their courtship. She never knew where he took her child, what they did, or how Vivian even felt about him. Conversations between Carol and Vivian had been disciplinary or directive. Now that Vivian was a teenager, Carol found it awkward to discuss intimacy in anything other than a scolding tone. There were plenty of times when Vivian simply couldn't see leaving Lee just to go home, and because Carol was very inconsistent with punishing her, Vivian decided to suffer the consequences when she got home if she should stay out too late. So, Carol saw Lee Hiram for the first time when one day, after knowing each other for three months, Lee took Vivian to a birthday party held in the house of a comrade named Floyd Barnes. Lee and Floyd often hung out together, but this was the first time Floyd ever saw Vivian, and to him, a virtual princess.

Lee knew this party would last way past the night and into the morning, but he wanted his girl at his side, even though he was aware of her curfew. The evening was special for Floyd and his guests as they celebrated his twenty-fourth birthday with a big card party and gambling. Floyd threw the party for himself. He invited everyone he assumed liked and respected him. Lee was his main running partner, along with Hamilton Briggs, but there were several others that he wanted to impress with his scantily furnished home. The fact that he had a home of his own was the point.

Lee was Floyd's best friend. They met in the streets when Lee was fifteen, about five years after Lee moved to Century from Pensacola. They bonded because they both had lost their mothers when they were young, and they were both still suffering emotionally in the aftermath. Their adventures together were like none Floyd had ever experienced. Lee was the younger brother he never had. They taught each other about the birds and the bees, they tried to teach each other how to read (and they were successful); they shared their first experience with girls together. Floyd and Lee would often meet emotionally and spiritually unarmed girls who lived on the plantations and take them back to Floyd's house for wild fun. They didn't show interest in any of the girls seeking honesty and vows because they were about the business of sowing their oats and living free of commitments.

Some of the city girls were also impressed that Floyd owned his home and was single. The fact that it was a run-down, weather-beaten hovel that was left to him when his mother died didn't matter. If Lee (or Floyd) met only one girl, he would talk solicitously to her, tell her he wanted her to be his main girl, and the weaker girls might eventually end up at Floyd's place. Of course, Lee would tell the ones he met that it was his own house. Catch and conquer was the name of the game for them. The girls usually left feeling dishonored after the euphoria of Lee's (or Floyd's) words faded away and the shame of their encounter settled with them.

Before the party, Lee couldn't wait to see Floyd's mouth water at the sight of Vivian. The party was only lightly sprinkled with women that night. Most of the guests were men in their twenties and thirties who worked with Floyd. At sixteen, Vivian was by far the youngest in the house. There were cigars, liquor, beer, and marijuana available. Lee spent his first thirty minutes there watching everyone stare at Vivian while he drank and smoked. He desired the oncoming intoxication in his attempt to prove himself a man like he figured the older ones to be. When Floyd approached him about Vivian, Lee, with his freshly cleaned, overly pressed linen trousers and crisp white cotton shirt, brushed him off without even bothering to introduce them. He was wearing cufflinks again, but the other guests weren't dressed to impress. Floyd remembered telling Lee that it would be a casual affair, yet Lee always had to be the center of attention, Floyd guessed.

Several times during the party, Lee embraced Vivian in the middle of the dance floor. He was proud to be with such an innocent, youthful girl that he knew his friends would want, but couldn't have. Vivian was special. She was decent. As dazzling as Lee was, Vivian was not comfortable in that setting. During the party, Lee fell asleep in a drunken stupor in a straight chair for a full forty-five minutes. Vivian was happy he was having that opportunity to sleep off his sluggishness. By this time, it was hours past dark, and she knew she probably already had to face her mama whenever she got home. Resignedly, she sat at an empty card table with her hands clasped in a knot, not quite tight enough to contain her anxiety. She received several compliments from some of the men in the house who had purposely fed so much liquor to Lee when he seemed excessively possessive of her. She was relieved to move out of the light to a small couch after a man and a lady vacated it to play cards.

Floyd had been waiting patiently for his turn to flirt with her. He strode over and sat next to her on the couch. He put his hand on her arm, and she politely removed it, crossing her legs away from him. He smirked at what he considered to be a pretense at innocence. Any girl out with Lee at that hour knew what was next. He was sure that twenty-year-old fast lane Lee had introduced her to the world of men and intimacy, that is, if she hadn't indeed known before. The fact that she carried herself like an unchaste princess meant zilch if she was hanging on to a man like Lee's arm. Floyd perceived she obviously knew she was a good catch, so he decided on another technique.

He reached into his pocket and proudly produced two crumpled one dollar bills he'd won that evening. Vivian was looking the other way. He tapped her neck, and when she looked, he flashed the bills in her face briefly, and then reached over to touch her knee that her dress barely covered. Vivian was horrified.

"Yeah, that's right! I'm the one they call Big Money Floyd." He smiled at her. "You wanna spend the rest of the evening with the birthday boy?" She quickly surveyed the room to see who was watching. There were two men in a corner snickering at her, she suspected. She tried to move his greasy hand from her flesh, but he was determined. Floyd groped at her more forcefully. She was worth the money to him, and more. It irked him to offer her cash, but he knew he wouldn't have time to successfully seduce her otherwise, with Lee snoozing nearby. She balled her fist and punched blindly, catching him at his Adam's apple. He jumped to a stand.

"Damn it," he yelled.

"Who does this yellow eyed bastard think he is?" She muttered under her breath in disbelief. The whole room stopped. Vivian jumped up too, in defense. From the expression on her face, Floyd guessed that she was going to strike him again. He couldn't let a juvenile, fast-tailed girl disgrace him in his own home. He grabbed the front of her dress in his fist. Mutual friend Hamilton Briggs was shaking Lee awake. Lee thought he was dreaming when he saw Floyd swinging his woman around by her collar. Before he knew it, he ran over and jumped on Floyd's back.

Floyd was thrown off guard by Lee's attack. He mulled over, "What should Lee care about this one?" The seventeen or so party participants formed a crowd to watch. A stout woman slid behind Vivian to move a coffee table that looked like it could get knocked over in the scuffle. Floyd tried to flip Lee off his back. Lee hooked his elbow into a Half Nelson around Floyd's neck and under his armpit. Floyd grabbed Lee's arm, and when he couldn't pull away, he took a bite. Vivian started screaming when what she thought was Lee's blood spurt to the floor. Actually, Floyd was suffering from the middle stages of periodontal disease and had lost a front tooth with the bite.

It occurred to Vivian that she should not stand by idly while her man fought. Just as Lee voluntarily slid down off Floyd's back, Vivian punched him in the mouth. Another tooth that had been left dangling clinked to the floor. Before Floyd knew what was happening, Lee landed a fist as hard as he could on his ear. It was so painful! Floyd staggered then and dropped to his knees. Lee and Vivian looked at each other. He pulled her close. The men in the room cheered. It wasn't that they didn't like Floyd, their host, but to see treacherous Lee and his teensy-weensy girlfriend whip him was quite a show. In the middle of the wild spectators, Vivian held Lee's hand and together they left the party and walked out onto the dark street.

The only light came from the full moon on the road to Vivian's house that wee morning. Lee had newfound admiration for her. She had helped him. She proved she would stick with him through thick and thin. He draped his arm around her shoulder. They walked like that all the way to Vivian's bedroom window. Following her dates with Lee, he routinely walked her home, to her window, and she would simply climb in and go to sleep, unbeknownst to her mother.

Lee always kissed her timidly because he didn't want to scare her away. This is because she had mentioned to him early in their relationship that the men she knew seemed to only want certain things. The other reason for Lee's inhibitions was he secretly considered her as a marriage possibility, and he had strong beliefs that his wife should be pure virgin material. Lee knew himself well enough to recognize that long endured kisses created the atmosphere for more intimate relationships. Vivian kissed him timidly back, following his lead, fumbling with her hands. Lee switched between hanging his arms down by his side and crossing them behind his back. He made her melt, but she didn't want to do anything that would cause him to change the tender way he handled her. She felt that if she gave in too easily, he wouldn't marry her and she would end like her mama, who was considered the "other woman" in her most significant male-female relationship with Vivian's father.

Lee smoothed out her hair, but her tussle with Floyd had wreaked havoc on her pinned up style. "You look like a wild woman." Vivian giggled, and he smiled warmly. "But it's not your looks I'm interested in. Besides, I reckon you're the prettiest wild woman I ever saw."

Her heart raced. "Then what are you interested in, Lee Hiram?" Avoiding her question, he embraced her briefly and then led her to the edge of her bedroom window.

"I kept you out too late again, didn't I?"

"Nothing we can do about that, now. Hopefully, she's asleep."

He embraced her again and then rustled her hair all out of place. She screeched and he laughed. "Boy! Get your hands out of my hair!" He tugged at her hair while she tried to scoot away. He laughed louder.

"You're right," he said. "Nothing we can do about your mama or your hair!" That carefree moment was cherished but short-lived. Lee sighed and rested his chin on the top of her head for a moment. He didn't want her mother to think ill of him all because he insisted on being greedy with Vivian's time. Reluctantly, he gave her a boost inside the window, promised to call for her again soon, and then hurried away into the shadows. He left too quickly to see or hear Carol standing on the inside of the window, but Carol took the time to get a good, long look at him. She had been standing there watching right after she heard the carefree laughing. Carol wanted to say something when she saw this young man embrace her child, but she struggled with what she should say. Should she yell? Should she curse him? As soon as Vivian landed inside, she saw Carol standing before her in the dark. Minnie smiled in her feigned sleep. It was she who had alerted their mother that Vivian still wasn't home at 11:00 p.m. Minnie knew the laughter outside would bring Carol into their bedroom.

Carol dragged Vivian out of the room, fussing the whole time. "You wanna stay up 'til all hours of the night, gal? It's one in the morn'!" Carol pulled her daughter into her bedroom. "You can just stay in here with me since you can't be trusted. I know you think that boy is a looker, but that don't give you no reason to be carrying on like what you is." Carol plopped herself on her mattress bed and stretched. She waved her hand at a corner with a pile of clothes sitting on the floor. "That's gwine be your bed tonight, so hop to it!" Vivian went to the clothes, made herself a pillow with some items, and laid over the others. She was fine with her sleeping arrangements because she was still high from Lee's love. Once Carol stopped fussing, Vivian thought of how Lee treated her so delicately, like she really was a princess. Never before had she imagined that she was special. Black girls were not special, at least none she could name. Lee was not the way her mother or Minnie had described boys. The only thing he tugged at was her hair, and the only thing he tried to get from her was her time.

Nevertheless, Minnie and Vivian got into a huge fight the next day because Robeena identified to Vivian that Minnie was the culprit who told their mama that she'd broken curfew. Days later, when Lee found out that they were finally caught sneaking in for the first time, he felt a tinge of guilt that he often brought her home at a disrespectful hour. He admitted to himself that he intended to have her out for as long as she allowed him, as long as it was convenient for him, as well. After all, he still maintained a nightlife with his other friends. He saw little of her during the daytime because he worked sometimes twelve hours daily, the same as Floyd Barnes at the Florida East Coast Railway Company. Lee's job was to unload crates of pineapples from the freight trains and clean out both the passenger and the freight cars.

The Railroad cars had been officially segregated since 1887 in Florida, which was fine for Lee who didn't like the thought of riding together with Caucasians because of how guarded he had to be in their presence. Most of the Caucasian citizens of Century, Florida treated Black people horribly, and would not let them board any of the passenger cars. Very seldom would a car be available for Negro passengers, because if the "for whites only" cars filled to half capacity, the conductors argued that they needed to keep extra cars free to transport passengers boarding in different cities. The Negroes had to travel to Tallahassee to board if they wanted to be safe. Over fifty-nine Black men and women were known to have been lynched already that year whenever Lee and Vivian met in 1921. Because of this, Lee told Vivian he refused to celebrate Juneteenth by dancing and listening to music in the backyard of a church owned by a man who still had slaves, also known as sharecroppers working for him.

Lee had the advantage of being one of the few Black employees who was given special privileges to board the train in Century with very minute hassle, given that he was an employee. He didn't mind that the newer and plusher cars were restricted for Caucasian passengers. The Railway Company was booming in business, even with the building of the interstate highways; the company maintained the lowest rate for transporting citrus fruit to other parts of the country. The company mastered the distribution of wholesale fruit that truckers picked up in Century at comparable rates, rather than to drive all the way to Jacksonville and Miami. When Lee left work most evenings, he usually had an orange in each pocket, one that he was sure to present to Vivian whenever he would see her, and one for himself. He liked to go home, bathe, hang out with his buddies, gamble, chase women, and drink whiskey. Whenever a big event would take place in a nearby city, Lee would go back to the railway and ride into the town in one of the freight cars that was for produce only.

He would take some of his buddies like Hamilton Briggs with him when something major was taking place in one of Century's neighboring cities. That summer, Lee went with two of his friends, along with his father and his uncle Samuel from Mississippi to Pensacola on the train. Pensacola was featuring the infamous man who called himself Blind Blake. Lee's uncle still lived in a small town right outside of Biloxi, Mississippi, but visited Florida to see his brother at least once a year for weeks at a time. Samuel was a drifter—too afraid to stay in one place for long.

Samuel and Lee Sr. were born in the same town where Lee's mother's family lived. Lee Sr. was Samuel's older brother. Lee Sr. had moved to Pensacola, Florida, leaving his family behind so that he could make a better living. Things didn't go well for him with work and all at first, but since he had taken Lee's mother with him, a girl then of sixteen, he knew he had to make it work. Although he missed his family, he supposed he'd be safer in Florida because Black men were being lynched left and right in Mississippi. He learned after settling that the Caucasian Florida residents believed strongly in hanging, too.

Lee Sr. was close to all of his four brothers, but mainly Samuel who was only a year younger. It was Samuel who told his nephew that the popular new musician named Blind Blake would be touring the South. To make it better, the rising star Duke Ellington was scheduled to accompany Blake on his Southern tour. Lee had heard a lot about both young fellows, so when the opportunity arose, he made quick preparations to board that freight. He went out of his way to let Vivian know they wouldn't be together that evening, but to his dismay, no one was home at her house. This riled him tremendously because considering her cost him two hours. He spotted Carol and Wali Eli heading away from the empty house. Had his relationship with Carol been better, he would've asked her where he could find Vivian. He had the mind to wait for her, since he knew she should have been expecting him that morning of his day off. Instead, he decided to continue to head to Pensacola to see the blind man he'd admired from afar for so long.

Although he was blind, Blake would show up in rural work camps and big cities alike to play and sing, with nothing but his guitar and the clothes he had on his back. He had been in Tallahassee for over a week. It was rumored that he would be performing in the area for as long as it took him to make enough money to head to Chicago, where he was planning to relocate. Hanging out at night joints was Lee's thing. He was a lover of drinking, gambling, and womanizing, even though all these things were just for fun, including the chasing of women. However, Lee thought he deserved that kind of fun, so, even though he was falling fast for Vivian, he expected to maintain his libidinous activities in his spare time.

CHAPTER SIX
It had to be with Vivian

It was almost 2:30 in the morning when Lee got back in town from seeing Duke Ellington and "Blind Blake." Vivian had been on his mind the entire time. He half trotted and walked straight to her house from the train station, making it within thirty minutes. Now, he was being pretty bold to yell carelessly into her window. Lee, along with Vivian, was surprised when Minnie helped him in awakening her. Lee was too heated to focus on details at that moment, though. His impatience had mounted to immeasurable heights due to her absence earlier, when for the first time, no one was home to receive his calling. Never before was he unsure of his woman's whereabouts for hours at a time on a Saturday. They had a system where she would always leave a note by the Mulberry tree if she could not come outside or needed to go into town for groceries or something with her mom. There was no note. He hardly enjoyed himself by the end of the concert.

Vivian walked sleepily in her long, cotton nightgown to the window. She wanted to thank Minnie, but she didn't want to break whatever spell that had come over her sister that made her help Lee. After Vivian was able to swing both of her legs out and unto the narrow pane, Lee practically snatched her by the arm. "Hey! Watch that! You almost made me cut myself." He ignored her, pulling her roughly the rest of the way.

"Where the hell have you been?" He placed a stronger hold on her arm.

"Shush!" Vivian hushed him. She whispered, "Is your aim to wake up the whole house?" She couldn't see his pursed lips by the dim shadow of the moon. She couldn't see his eyes turn into stormy slits as they blended with the night shadows. She led him to the wide field behind the house. Vivian was becoming a bit nervous because he still had his nails dug into her arm. "Let me go, Lee," Vivian said, trying to regain control over the confrontation. He gripped her more tightly.

"I said . . . where the hell you was?" His voice was quivering. "You know damn well I come here ev'ry Saturday at the same time. I waited for you for o'er an hour. You didn't leave a note by the Mulberry tree...you was just gone!" Vivian instinctively became alarmed. Her attraction for Henry cautioned her not to speak too quickly. She imagined that Lee could see it written all over her face. She contemplated lying about meeting Henry with her sisters, but if Lee would ever find out, she would seem that much guiltier. He was making her feel awfully guilty, as it was. The rough way Lee spoke to her made her uncertain if she had done anything wrong or not. Finally, she decided she was being silly to be afraid of Lee.

"My sisters and I went walking earlier today. Mama's friend, Mr. Eli gave us some change-actually, rare coins!"

"Oh yea? What'd you buy?" Lee didn't care what she'd bought, but he felt he needed to ask something about the shopping trip. He couldn't help perceiving desertion. The iciness in his throat launched a chill through her.

"We never made it to do any shopping because we saw Henry Raison when we were cutting through the Raison Plantation, and Minnie wanted to stay with Henry the whole time, and we walked with him . . . Beena and I mainly followed Minnie and Henry . . . Wali Eli, who is a businessman and friend of my mother gave us rare coins--surely we couldn't spend those! So, we talked and ate cherries all day," she said in one breath.

Lee was enraged. His suspicions were true! He was fuming that he had blindly trusted and even loved her when she was possibly just another slut. "Who the hell is Henry Raison?" Lee was shaking her. Vivian made a more concerted effort to jerk herself free from his grip. When she did, he grabbed her by the back of her hair and twisted her so close to him that their faces were less than centimeters apart. He was frustrated because he wanted to kiss her, but his agitation made him release her violently. Vivian was boiling with acrimony.

"He's somebody we just met! Minnie liked him and I guess he liked her, Lee. He wasn't talking to me or anything like that. He saw Minnie and they're together now."

"So, the first chance you got away from me on a Saturday, you go rolling into town with your sisters, and you just so happen to meet a man and you stayed with *him* eating cherries? What do you take me for?" He remembered how desirable he thought she was whenever he met her walking that day, and imagined that whoever this Henry was, he must've felt the same way about Vivian's ravishing beauty.

"Why don't you tell me what to take you for since I obviously don't know?" She quickly stepped a few feet out of his reach. "I should ask you what you take *me* for."

"I took you for a princess, but obviously you're a slut."

"A *what*?"

"You is too new to the game to be trying to think you can out-slick me, girl." She dusted off her nightgown with the palms of her hands.

"Out-slick you?" Vivian shook her head in disgust. "I'm going back inside, you crazy sap." She took a few steps toward the house, then stopped and turned back to face Lee again, and added, "If I *was* with Henry, he wouldn't act nuts like you do, and talk all ignorant. He was raised properly by white folks, you yellow bastard." She turned and walked briskly back to the house, leaving Lee standing in the darkness as she climbed back through the window. She used to be his princess, she thought. But now, her arm was bruised and to him, she was a *slut*. Her heart pounding, she bent down feeling for the mattress with her hands, her eyes not yet adjusted to the absence of the moonlight. She liked it while she felt like his princess, and if there was any way she could get that feeling back, Vivian wanted to try. Because of Lee, she knew she was a princess, albeit a hidden princess.

She hated what she'd just said to Lee. She didn't mean any of it, but she had to take the attention away from his accusations. Now, she was sorry and was just about to run back outside and hopefully catch him before he disappeared so she could apologize, except she was distracted when she heard Minnie blow hard in disgust. Minnie lifted herself on one elbow, swishing the white sheet away from Vivian's sight and touch. Vivian followed the movement and plopped down next to her, with her legs grazing Robeena's.

"That was quick," Minnie snapped.

"Kiss my tail."

"Is that all he ever wants you for? One thing? I can't believe you, Viv. You ain't got no business out there with that boy like that. He's disrespecting mama's house and so is you. I *swear* you's a senseless child."

"We don't swear, Minnie. I'm telling mama about your filthy mouth so she can wash it out with some soap."

"If you tell mama 'bout me, then you gotta tell her you was out there doing the nasty again. So maybe she can wash that tail you is wanting me to kiss."

"You're the one who woke me up to say he was out there. I reckon if you felt that way you should have kept your big fat mouth closed."

"Next time I will, you nasty wench."

"Quit calling me nasty! I'm not nasty. Dang! All we did was talk."

"I know that boy didn't walk all the way o'er here to say hello to you in the middle o' the night. You must think your big sister is as ignorant as they come."

"Why should I have to discuss it with you, anyway? He came because he had something to tell me."

"That hustler ain't thinking 'bout you, Viv. He got a list o' women just as long as my arm is."

"You should leave me alone!" Vivian started crying. "A list *of* women," she wept.

"Leave her 'lone, Minnie," Robeena said sleepily. Minnie turned to the wall and pouted. She wanted to drill Vivian a little further, but she knew with the dramatic tears and Robeena's loving rescue, it would be impossible.

Vivian tried to fall asleep, but her mind wouldn't stop spinning the day's events into play all over again. Vivian and Lee both sulked after their first huge fight. Lee was distraught. He didn't know what to believe anymore. He pictured a husky man spending an afternoon with his woman. It *had* to be with Vivian. Lee couldn't conceive of a man choosing Minnie over Vivian, because in his eyes, Vivian was by far the most attractive and outright stunning sister. He tried to convince himself that he should never speak to her again.

"Hell. I got so many women, I don't need her no way," he reasoned. He believed her when she had said he was a fool, but that Henry was a proper gentleman. Lee felt inferior and out of control. He didn't know if he had lost her to someone else. He wanted her back. Lee mulled over surprising her and showing up at church later that morning, which never before was a consideration. "Nah. I ain't chasing that girl," he decided. He walked miserably home to bed full of worry. Little did he know, Vivian tossed and turned as well. She was sorry that Lee hadn't followed her back to the window. She wouldn't even have minded if he grabbed her arm again, just as long as he showed her he loved her. She'd rather have his crazy attention than none of his attention at all.

Vivian felt responsible. She *did* want Henry. Henry was so towering, yet gentle looking! Lee was about thirty pounds leaner, but if they weren't standing side by side, anyone would be fascinated with Lee's well-carved body. Lee possessed finer features than Henry, and would be considered more handsome by most, given that the standard of beauty was dictated by the dominant culture. As such, European features were used as a divider between right and wrong, good and bad. Vivian understood a Black person's complexion could determine privileges or the lack thereof, and the light skinned Black people were more appealing. Societal standards were that "the lighter the righter." Lee was not exactly light skinned, but he was two shades lighter than Henry. Even so, Vivian was unable to fool herself into believing Lee was more attractive. She would have to settle with pretending Lee was more handsome because Henry's features were anything but European. When people would see Vivian and Lee together, they often stopped to sigh at the couple's striking beauty. Vivian imagined that when Henry first saw her, he viewed her as attractive, as well. So, she was envious of the fact that

Henry showed no real interest in her, while he doted after her homely sister.

Vivian's magnetism toward Henry had nothing to do with her infatuation with Lee, even though she really didn't know *him*. It was the attention Lee gave her that no man had ever given her that captured her heart, and Henry didn't give her more than a glance of attention at a time. Nonetheless, all too soon she forgave herself for her cutting words, comparing Lee to Henry. Her remorse was satisfied when she told herself that she didn't mean to displease him; she was just toppling over with guilt at the time, which led her to respond defensively. Her mind drifted back to Henry. She was interested in understanding why he was more smitten with Minnie than herself. Still, she planned to make sure she looked her absolute best for church later, since Henry would be there.

CHAPTER SEVEN
Willy Lynch lives!

    The short, stubby, overweight, elderly preacher sat in his preacher chair bobbing his head in rhythm to the robust singing woman in the choir. Church had just started and already he wished he'd had enough time to finish the porridge and pancakes his wife had prepared for him. He secretly blamed her for his weight problem and his sugar condition. The veterinarian told him he had passed out recently due to elevated levels of sugar in his blood. The fancy term the vet used was "diabetes." Reverend Washington had been warned that if he did not change his diet, he could slip into a coma and die. Pork, red meat, salt, fatty foods, and pastries were his enemy, yet his wife continued to overload him with thick, greasy slices of bacon, cakes, and as much potatoes as she could fill his plate with. And what did he do? He stayed silent and consumed it because he was accustomed to eating that type of food. He could not tell her to do better because he did not want to insult her. Everyone at the church loved Mrs. Washington's cooking. There was a lemon pound cake in the church office. He wondered if anyone would notice him if he were to slip into the back and gulp it down before speaking the sermon. His eyes were searching the packed room of sixty-five regular members and approximately twenty visitors when he looked around and saw Carol, her daughters, and Henry walk into the sanctuary. The topic for the day's lecture suddenly came to mind, and thoughts of his declining health and the tinge of hunger disappeared.

    Since Carol suffered from poverty, he would speak from the book of Proverbs. Proverbs 31:6: "Give wine unto those that are of heavy hearts. Let him drink and forget his poverty and remember his misery no more." That was it: no more misery. It wasn't the way of the Lord to carry guilt and sadness over poverty and want. Reverend Washington knew Carol was a single woman, with three presently fatherless daughters. He held no liability or resentment toward the married man that fathered Carol's children because for as long as he could remember, he had seen Negro men mated with assorted Negro women for the purpose of breeding or pleasure. In the past, there had never been any responsibility placed on the breeder by the woman or her family because it was the slave master or his children who may have ordered the affairs. Marriages between Black people often took place in secret. However, the further they were removed from plantation life, the more Black couples honored marriage. Fathers and uncles of females had the freedom to protect their children, that is unless they chose to subconsciously succumb to the low standards of a society that did not believe a Nation could rise no higher than its woman.

Increasingly, Reverend Washington sensed the paternal damage that the Black man suffered throughout it all, but he didn't acknowledge his personal role and that the damage would continue for centuries. He was aware of the poverty-stricken environment that Carol's family was forced to live in, while other members of his congregation did not wonder about their next meal. These thoughts made him push the delight for his confectionery bread in the corner of his mind even further so that he could continue to prepare mentally for his lecture and responsibility to serve. Reverend Abraham Washington was a good man in the sight of America's standards. He was born in Mobile, Alabama in 1848. He was sold along with his mother to the Johnson Plantation in 1862. When he became of age, he signed his name as Washington because he had always felt a sense of devotion to his Mobile master named George Jay Washington. He had never been taught the proper standards to exemplify a man of God. He thought that Jesus, God, and all the Prophets were Caucasians, because it was what he had been taught. Consequently, since Negroes were the opposites of the biblical people, he subconsciously worshiped Caucasians, and disrespected Black people

He surmised that if one would take on characteristics of the former masters, whether physical or mental characteristics, this could only enhance the lives and features of the Negroes. Reverend Washington wasn't conscious of these thoughts: His actions and thinking had become a way of life. He didn't want to be ashamed of his identity; he didn't even understand that he was. In fact, if someone asked him if he hated being Black, he wouldn't think twice before answering emphatically "no." It didn't bother him when he saw sin because the society he lived in indicated to him that sin was a normal way of life.

It didn't occur to him to break away from the norm and be like the Jesus in the scriptures. In truth, it saddened him to preach about Jesus because he felt he could never be like that Jesus. He was the opposite of the blond haired, blue-eyed idol that was being depicted throughout the western world. This fact drove him into deeper self-hatred, non-acceptance, and disrespect of those who were Negroes, like himself. Whenever Reverend Washington encountered Caucasians, he worked to prove that he was not the typical Negro. He would speak and act just like any of them he could imitate. Abraham settled for mere association with Caucasians, since that was all he thought he could hope for in the segregated South. Still, it gave him high social status in his circle of Negroes to call out Kent Johnson's name in exaggeration as a personal friend. According to Abraham, he went way back with the Johnson family on the Caucasian side and was practically a member. Kent Jr. was more like a brother than anyone else. They grew up together after Abraham was brought over from Mobile, Alabama to the Johnson plantation in an illegal trade.

Abraham and his congregation were grateful to Kent Johnson for the use of the land and the church building. Kent had been responsible for seeing to it that Abe Washington received theological training. Actually, Kent figured that if Abraham Washington was going to use his church, he had to know the Negro purpose. He had to know that Negroes were cursed, and that's why they had been slaves. Part of this came from the European theologian's perspective of the story of Ham, a descendant of Noah. To fight slavery was consequently to fight God. That's why when the physical shackles were removed, Abraham preferred to remain attached to Kent Johnson and later, Kent Jr.

Abraham was an outsider. Master Kent assigned Abraham over the Negro church when Abraham was only seventeen because of his rich voice. Man, could Abraham sing! When he shouted the name of Jesus, it sounded like someone playing the ukulele! Kent felt positive Abraham had a decent understanding about the way things were meant to be, otherwise, he never would have given him access to his nice building as a church. Not only did Abraham receive full usage of the Negro church, but he was also endorsed as an acceptable leader in the Black community. He did not make waves, he was accountable when it came to pushing whatever agenda Kent brought to him, and he was critical in calming his parishioners after various lynchings.

Master Kent learned from the teachings of Willy Lynch that it was his job to see to it that no critical thinking, warrior-minded Black man would ever be given such lavish accommodations to expose the theology as understood by Nat Turner, or the philosophies of Marcus Garvey, or revolutionary minded men like Toussaint L'Ouverture, Dessalines, Henri Christophe, Denmark Vessey, and freedom oriented women like Harriet Tubman, Callie House, and others who threatened mainstream ideology and white supremacy. One key into the minds of the ex-slave was whether they were referring to themselves as Black, African, or Negro. For centuries to come, Willy Lynch predicted that any Black leader who would sound the trumpet, aiming at the horizontal existence of the mentally and spiritually dead Black man and woman would be considered a threat to conventional doctrines.

Only a bought and sold afflicted minded and subservient Negro would ever be allowed the furnishings to teach other Negroes. Abraham had to be able to teach Negroes that they would receive their heaven after they died, and at such time, meet Peter up in the clouds at the pearly gates. But first, they must build the kingdom of God for others right here on earth (Matthew 6:19-20).

The Negroes were comforted in their struggles to hear this. They would endure the most inhumane treatment; they believed that after they died, they would be soothed--but always and only after physical death would this be allowed. This theology continued to be taught long after Abraham graduated from his "training." Eventually, Negroes taught it *to* Negroes. The alleged mysterious slave trader by the name of Willy Lynch from the West Indies was instrumental in this programming of mental slavery. In 1712, it was said that Mr. Lynch gave a speech to plantation owners entitled *"How to control the Black man for at least 300 years."* In his speech, he said:

"Don't forget you must pit the old Black male vs. the young Black male and the young Black male vs. the old Black male. You must use the dark skin slaves vs. the light skin slaves and the light skin slaves vs. the dark skin slaves. You must use the female vs. the male, and the male vs. the female. You must also have your Caucasian servants and overseers distrust all Blacks, but it is necessary that your Black slaves trust and depend on us. They must love, respect, and trust only us."

So, Abraham was willing to accept the idea of inferiority in order to be received by a white supremacist society. He felt it was true that Negroes were inferior because God let it be so. Besides, Caucasians seemed to be doing well, and Negroes were on the bottom of the totem pole. He didn't study the scripture that said God would make the last the first and the bottom rail the top because these scriptures weren't emphasized in his training. Reverend Washington served as a mimicking puppet with a tainted doctrine, and he was instrumental in keeping the masses in compliance, coy, and unstudied.

There were no pictures of God, except the image of the Caucasian Jesus, whom many worshiped as God. His former slave masters taught whatever Abraham knew of theology to him. He could by a hair's breadth read and write for himself, and the other preachers were at war to gain the most members for their churches. He knew words like Judaism, Catholicism, and Islam, but these religions were not for his people, or anyone he knew.

Abraham had faint memories of being told about African Muslims, but his grandmother had hushed his grandfather when the conversation came up when he was a small boy in Mississippi. It was because of these utterances that he was traded away from his parents, and his grandfather was lynched. It was said that the very word, "Muslim" was forbidden in the whole of America, and a slave descendent would surely be hung if he was heard uttering the word. This is because many of the African slaves were Muslim warriors. Abraham's grandfather had referred to them as mean-spirited and stated that their spirit had to be broken down to rule them. Their religion, language, culture, and their names had to be destroyed to get them to go along with the idea of white supremacy and slavery.

Now, decades later, all Reverend Washington remembered was that it had something to do with religion. None of this mattered, anyway, because if his influential friends didn't think it was important, then why should he? And if they didn't want to hear the word, then he would shun it, too, if ever any of his congregation members had any questions about it. These thoughts flashed so briefly through Abraham's mind that he was barely conscious of only some of them. He focused on his current surroundings and the forthcoming lecture.

Carol's heart was exceptionally heavy laden that Sunday morning. During their conversation at the group meeting with a few other community members, Wali Eli had talked about everything from political issues to how Black people fit into the biblical scriptures. She wasn't like a sponge soaking up the teachings because her worries were so plentiful. Nonetheless, Wali Eli offered her courage. Carol confided in Wali Eli her fears about men taking advantage of her girls. He gave her scriptures from the Bible, mostly from the book of Proverbs that Carol could disclose with her daughters about virtue. He quoted Proverbs 14:1, "Homes are made by the wisdom of women, but are destroyed by foolishness," and then soothed her with Psalms, 46:5, "God is within her, she will not fall; God will help her at the break of day." Wali Eli explained to Carol that she should start her day before the rising of the sun with prayer and ask for God's help before attempting any tasks for that day. The explanations of the passages he shared seemed crystal clear to her all at once. No one had ever talked to her like that before, yet it made her comfortable. Presently, Carol needed advice about how Minnie had just taken up with Henry the sharecropper the day before and had even invited him to their Sunday breakfast. She would ask Reverend Washington for insight after church, and hopefully he would be able to provide wisdom and guidance.

At the breakfast table that morning, Henry had announced that he planned to move North and take Minnie with him! Carol was disturbed at how they had looked at each other longingly at the suggestion of moving away together, although there was no talk of marriage. The fact that they had just met the day before didn't seem to discourage them, either. Further uneasiness came that morning when she noticed how Vivian stole too many glances at Henry when she supposed no one was looking. Carol also observed

Henry catching Vivian's glances from time to time. She saw Henry giving Vivian questioning, curious stares in return. With all the drama at home, Carol was happy to be in the sanctuary of the church with the good reverend. It seemed to her that he was speaking directly to her—like God had put it into the reverend to watch over her. His explanation of the virtuous woman felt different from Wali Eli's, Carol noted. The music behind the reverend's voice placed Carol in somewhat of a spiritual trance.

Internally, Carol lobbied that the reverend could somehow help her with her ailing heart. When the service ended, she stood in line to shake his hand. He leaned back on his cane, joyously greeting every parishioner. Most of the women in line wanted to gain his support for their running for presidency of the Women's Club. They knew that although the women's president would be voted in, Reverend Washington had the final say. When it was Carol's turn, she mentioned her aspiration to be president, as well, and then she whispered that she wanted to seek counsel with him in his office. He smiled knowingly and told her to go there and wait. Reverend Washington's wife had already made it out of the church and on her short journey home. They had a small dwelling in the backyard of the church on Kent's property. Mrs. Washington never waited for her husband because she understood he had many souls to save.

After the service, Minnie, her sisters, and Henry walked back to the house together without Carol. Minnie knew her mother was going to seek advice from the reverend about Henry waltzing into their lives--which meant she did not approve. Without thinking about it, Minnie instinctively put up a wall in defense of anything negative Carol might try to say about her new man. Minnie wore a plain yellow cotton dress with a fading sash. Robeena was fashioned modestly in her usual soft blue cotton dress that she wore just about every Sunday. Vivian's style was a loose-fitting pink satin gown her mother had sewn for her to wear last Easter Sunday. Her discolored petticoats underneath gave her the bounce she needed to sashay heavenly before everyone. She had curled her hair tightly and pulled the bulk of it away from her face, up in a bun, and the remainder of her hair decorated the nape of her neck. In her tote bag, she carried extra strawberry body oil, gloss for her lips, a brush, and a book to read--just in case the reverend bored her silly. Vivian looked like a princess. If Minnie had known the effort Vivian was secretly going through to prepare for church that morning, she would have taken more time with her own appearance. She wanted to look her best for Henry, too. Minnie felt a tinge of jealousy before Henry arrived for breakfast when she speculated how he might look at Vivian. As it was, Minnie was already wearing her second-best dress; she just hadn't taken the additional time with her hair.

Henry was enchanted by the beauty of all three sisters, especially Vivian. Yet, he was ever more captivated by the image of his ideal wife, which Minnie fit perfectly. Henry didn't remember Minnie being so beautiful yesterday as she was standing before him, now. He was satisfied with her mere presence. Vivian and Robeena didn't fare too well after his initial examination of Vivian's sheer beauty. She was still Lee's girl and too flashy for home and making babies. He resolutely resisted the existence of Vivian while he walked with Minnie hand in hand from the church.

"Minnie?"

"Yes, Henry?" she answered in a small voice.

"I'm glad I met you. I'm gonna take care of you, you hear?"

"I'm gonna take care of you, too, Henry." He squeezed her hand. Henry wanted to make Minnie feel safe and secure, but he was the one who felt safe now. He was still living in Florida with his parents on the plantation, even though he had wanted to leave since he was ten. He had been afraid. His parents instilled the fear in him that he couldn't make it on his own. They made him believe that if he left the plantation, he would fall on his face. They told him it was wrong not to love their master who had done everything for them, and to want to leave for a silly dream.

Consequently, he had no one to trust with his dreams, and no one to believe in him. Henry never really believed in himself, yet the dream never died. Deep down, he felt if he had help, he could make his dreams come true. Now, he could make Minnie a part of his dreams. He needed her. He needed her to make his own dreams come true.

"Minnie? You really gonna go with me up North?"

"I don't want to go too soon, Henry. I ain't got any money . . . you got some?" He gave a restrained smile. He was going up North eventually. "We gotta get to know each other better, too. You don't know how long you're gonna be liking me. You might meet some other girl you like better'n me."

"You believe in love at first sight?" She looked down, smiling shyly. "Don't be scared on account of I asked you that, Minnie. I didn't believe in it either, at first." He looked back to see if her sisters were listening as they trailed behind just a few yards. Although it didn't appear they could tune in to the couple's soft voices, Vivian was glaring at him, her eyes engraved with resentment, and Robeena was chattering away. He was taken aback by Vivian's defeatist attitude. He had doubted that she would even be interested in someone rough like himself. All his life, he had compared himself to the Raison's and their standards of beauty. Therefore, his perfectly formed, well-chiseled body seemed clumsy to him. Henry regarded his full lips and his statuette ebony face as uncomely next to Vivian's delicate beauty.

Henry strained to ignore Vivian's splendid pouting image and focused on Minnie again. He stroked her face. "I sure ain't gonna rush you to do nothing. We ain't leaving this here place 'til you's ready. But, baby, please get ready fast so we can start a real life together. I've been saving the money for a long, long time, so don't you worry none about that."

"But, why me, Henry?" For a split second, he looked back involuntarily at Vivian again. After he turned away from her the second time, Vivian decided to go ahead and put on her bonnet. She had been holding it in her hands so her hair wouldn't get messy.

"When I saw you, I knew in my heart that it was meant to be between us. That's all." Minnie wished he would stop walking and kiss her in the middle of the road. She believed she was the luckiest girl in the town.

Vivian felt dejected. She never would have wasted her sleeping time to do her hair in such a fancy way if she had detected that Henry was going to play the smitten boyfriend role with Minnie. He hardly knew her! As far as Vivian was concerned, all men cheated; her mother modeled being the other woman for her since she was born. Nonetheless, Henry was acting like he didn't even want to look at her, but Vivian thrived on the admiration in Henry's eyes whenever he stole one of his glances at her. She had caught him staring and yet he continued to malinger like she wasn't even there. She got a pungent taste in her mouth when she imagined that Henry was deliberately ignoring her.

She concentrated on Lee. It was Lee she really wanted, anyway, but Henry was forcing his way into her heart, and she did not like it. She knew he was not purposely doing it, yet she blamed him. She tried to shake off her unexplained admiration for Henry by focusing on Lee. However, Vivian simply wasn't satisfied with Lee because she knew he had more women, and she wanted him all to herself. And Henry was the most *ruggedly* handsome man she'd ever seen. Vivian wanted to slap herself for allowing her mind to drift back to Henry when only seconds ago she told herself to shake away her feelings. She failed because her subconscious mind gripped the matter. Vivian thought all men were like her father, but it seemed Henry just might be different. Vivian could not suppress her competitive nature that wanted to prove Henry was the same as Lee or any other man.

She was inordinately envious to imagine that Minnie could land a faithful man, but that she could not. Vivian didn't actually know if Lee was unfaithful, but there was always some girl hanging on him at the parties where he took her, and she had seen what looked like a few hickies on his neck when they first started dating. She wanted to be certain that she was the most important person in Lee's life, something he had yet to prove.

When the foursome reached the house, they all sat in the marred, wooden chairs that Minnie and Henry pulled out from the kitchen to the front porch. Henry said, "Y'all ladies enjoy the service this morning?" Vivian ignored him. She rolled her eyes and pulled out Harriet Jacobs *Incidents in the Life of a Slave Girl* from her tote bag.

"Yeah," Minnie answered, "Reb Washington is one helluva preacher, with his old self."

"He sho 'nough is old as dirt," Robeena chimed.

"*Sure enough*," Vivian corrected, looking over her book at them. Once they all paused to stare at her, she buried her face back into her reading.

Henry made a mental note about Vivian correcting Robeena's speech, speculating that he would never pass her scrutiny. "Service was a li'l different, but I enjoyed it. On the Raison Plantation, you know we be of the Baptist faith. We worship down the alley, almost into town at Bridgewater."

"I don't mind going to your service with you sometimes, Henry."

"I know that, Minnie. Truth is I gotta do better myself 'bout going regularly."

"That's right. Ain't nothing like good preaching on a Sunday morning, Henry." Minnie grabbed Henry's hand.

"Minnie, me and you gonna always have the Lord in our lives. I know you're gonna help see to that." Vivian wanted to vomit. Henry was sickening. Vivian untied her bonnet and tossed it carelessly onto the dusty porch, but Henry didn't notice because he continued to gaze into Minnie's eyes. "He gonna help us through everything, Minnie, whether we be North or South." Vivian couldn't listen to the conversation. That's why she volunteered to go inside and make a pitcher of lemonade and a platter of pineapple pastries. She had given up on making passes at Henry. He was nearly a lost cause, yet still interesting enough for Vivian to remain in his company. She sprinkled a bit of water on her hands from the practically empty pitcher on the kitchen table. Then she peeled two lemons and saved the rind, which she cut up very finely. With cane sugar, she worked the lemon into a concentrated mixture of pulp.

"Forget him," she convinced herself. "He thinks he's something. I have no need for him. Minnie knows she doesn't want him. She hates boys. She is just jealous because I have Lee. No, I take that back. I would bet Minnie wants any man she thinks wants her. She only hates them because she never had one." Vivian let the paring knife fall on the table with a whack. "I shouldn't make a damn thing for any of them."

She went to her mother's bedroom and peeked in before entering, as though her mother was home, waiting to chase her away. Precisely the thing she needed was sitting in plain view on the old dressing table that Minnie-Anne had once used. She couldn't use the body oil in her tote bag because Henry and her sisters would see her. No. She needed her sweet scent to be applied in private. The coast being clear, she went immediately to get the oil. Her fingers massaged gingerly to rub the strawberry scented body oil smoothly on her wrists and around her neck. Then she dabbled some in the palm of her hand and smeared it on her frock. Almost as quickly as she'd entered, she exited the bedroom and made her way back to the kitchen. Her hands would need to be washed again before she could finish the mixture.

Vivian went out the back door to the icebox and fetched some more cool water. As she regulated the water in the jug spilling onto her hands, she could hear Minnie's too girlish laughter coming from the front porch. "Hussy," she muttered to herself as she went back inside with the remainder of the water to continue with the lemonade. She joined the others again a few moments later carrying a tray with four filled glasses on it. Minnie smacked her lips at the scanty goodies Vivian had prepared. Without commenting more than a few hisses, she went inside to get whatever remained in the pitcher, and to quickly finish rolling the pastry.

"It's about time you made that lemonade, girl," Robeena said. She had a petty clue that Vivian was trying to be fresh with Henry, and their mama's loud aroma didn't lessen Robeena's suspicions. There was no hint of distaste in Vivian's expression as she casually ignored Robeena altogether.

"What was that book you was reading, Miss Vivian?" Vivian stood directly in front of Henry to allow him to take the first glass from the tray. He had finally acknowledged her.

"Do you know anything about Black authors, Mr. Henry?" She hoped she smelled like a delicate strawberry blossom to him. Henry peered around her at an approaching figure, without taking the drink. Lee was coming up the street.

Lee saw his woman looking more beautiful than he had ever seen her, standing close to a thick, attractive man. "Maybe that's Henry," he guessed. His heart was thumping like crazy, but he knew he had to play it cool. He noted that Minnie, Henry's "woman" was nowhere in sight. Henry recognized Lee immediately. It was confirmed for him that Vivian's man was the same Lee that sniffed around the Raison Plantation from time to time to see the daughters of the sharecroppers. Henry also recognized Lee from a basement gambling joint in town, although he himself had never actually been inside of the joint. The gamblers would often sit outside on the porch and guzzle whiskey between games.

Henry stood as Lee advanced toward them. Vivian turned and almost dropped the glasses in surprise at seeing Lee. He was only inches away by the time she noticed him. Her heart swelled. Unlike with Henry, she didn't have to beg Lee for attention. Seeing the two men standing there together, she convinced herself that indeed, she preferred Lee, despite Henry's astonishing physique and remarkable ebony face.

"How's it going? I'm Henry Raison." Henry said this while extending his hand. Lee said nothing. He gave Henry an abrasive hand slap instead of a shake, ignoring Henry's attempt at civility. Henry tried to be accepting of Lee's gesture because he wasn't exactly sure of the greeting code for young hustlers in the city streets these days. Lee seemed perfect for Vivian, Henry thought. Lee's prince-like beauty complimented Vivian, and on a physical level, Henry could see why those two mated.

Vivian, remembering the fight earlier, shoved the tray in Robeena's direction, and put both of her arms around Lee's neck and kissed him. Not only did she want Lee to know she was incredibly happy to see him, but it was also important for Vivian to allow Henry to see her in a loving embrace with Lee. She wanted to prove to Henry that she didn't favor him at all. Lee felt uncomfortable. Vivian had never greeted him with a kiss—she was too shy, or so he had thought. In addition, she was looking exceptional and acting too saucy for his liking.

Henry blushed at Vivian's affection and bowed his head. Lee took Vivian's arms down and gently pushed her away. "You look good, girl. What's up?" Henry looked again at the couple. Lee looked at Henry although he was talking to Vivian. Henry involuntarily widened his eyes, responding to Lee's scowl with an air of innocence. Vivian tried to reply naturally to the unmistakable trepidation she heard in Lee's voice. She wanted their squabble to end. She looked at Robeena for help. Robeena shrugged and walked into the house, hoping Lee would notice that Vivian smelled like a strawberry temptress.

"Just got home from church. I'm sure glad you came by, Lee. I was just…"

"Stop talking," Lee snapped. Vivian was startled, but she kept quiet. Once Lee was certain that Henry and Vivian knew he was in charge, he added, "Let's go for a walk," Lee said offhandedly. It was unsettling for Henry to note the complacent way in which Vivian conceded. Vivian had been complaining all morning that her feet were sore and had said she wanted to change her clothes as quickly as possible after church. Now, she submitted to run off with Lee, fully clad down to her laced shoes, without thinking of her sunbonnet in the unseasonably hot, middle April heat. As the couple started away, Henry picked up Vivian's bonnet. Her name got stuck in his throat when he attempted to call her back for it. After a few moments of fumbling with the soft material, Henry stuffed it in his pocket. Minnie stood in the doorway unnoticed by Henry until Vivian and Lee disappeared past the wild vines in the field.

~~~

Vivian was happy for an excuse to be alone with Lee. Hand in hand, they walked a while in silence. About three hundred yards behind Carol's cozy circumscribed shack turned into a cottage was a large, untamed, weed-filled field. The high weeds agitated Vivian through her stockings with every swish of her gait, but to Lee it seemed he was walking through cement. It was a chore to keep silent. He could only narrowly make it to privacy with her. He was surprised but delighted to find a deserted trail leading to a wooded area that looked inviting. Vivian was all too familiar with the grounds, being as investigative as she was about nature. There was a large rock that towered above four feet near a stream. Lee released Vivian's hand to walk ahead of her until he reached the rock. He leaned back on it and crossed his arms.

Once Vivian caught up to him, he said, "Henry is mighty good looking, Viv, ain't he?" Vivian closed her eyes for a long moment in abhorrence at his choice of conversation. "Oh!" Lee continued, "I shocked that slave by coming outta nowhere, Viv. I guess you were right 'bout 'im being raised proper, 'cause proper gentlemen jump the hell up when they get caught with they hand in the cookie jar." Lee was talking very rapidly, and then he slowed after a pause. "Me? I ain't got no manners, do I Viv? I talk like an ignorant slave, don't I?"

"Of course, you have manners, Lee. Forget about our fight, alright? I'm not interested in an ugly blackie like Henry. Why would I be when I have you?"

"Because I'm a yellow bastard, remember?"

"How could you be a bastard when you know both of your parents?"

"He's so ugly that you were trying to feed 'im? Minnie couldn't serve 'im? You had to? Are you stepping out on me, Vivian?"

"No!"

"I don't believe you would've said that crap to me if you wasn't." Now, she had deep regret for the rotten things she'd said to him the night before. Lee reached for her in desperation. He believed his accusations were true, but he didn't want them to be. In apprehension of his next move, she shifted away from his contact.

"I said forget it, Lee Hiram." She turned away. "I didn't come out here with you for this."

"Come o'er yonder," he commanded. She didn't adhere. It came to his attention that her refusal to allow him to enfold her was an admission of guilt on her part. He reached out again more quickly, like a coiled snake launching after his prey, and yanked her by the ear, pulling her to him. She shrieked.

"I don't want any more fights with you, Lee! You didn't have to come around today." He was further enraged by the suggestion that she would've preferred not seeing him. Red fervor crossed his eyes as he suspected that she couldn't wait to get back to her house where Henry waited. Henry wasn't ugly at all, Lee judged, and he believed Vivian couldn't think of Henry as ugly. Even Lee credited Henry as extraordinary and enticing. So, why was Vivian lying?

Before he could think more on the matter, he flip side slapped her so hard that she fell backward onto the hard, dirt ground. The cheek of her face became instantly numb. Dust particles flew into her nose and between her teeth and gums. Vivian became disoriented after the forceful strike. It was slow to register that he had struck the cute face that he claimed to adore. She scrambled, scraping her knees until her feet found firm ground, placing her again to a stable standing position. She spit the salty blood out that she tasted oozing from under her lip. "We're through!" She cried. "It's over! We're through!" She attempted to rush away, but he pushed her, pinning her to the rock.

She didn't understand what was happening. She found herself too dizzy to speak. As hard as she tried to see, her vision had become blurry. Even though her instincts had alerted her that his fury might mean danger, she never contemplated that he would strike her without further warning. Then she realized that he had been warning her since the last time she saw him. Vivian had taken the walk with him despite his animosity because she imagined she could navigate any harmful conditions that might arise. Now, her heart was in roller coaster mode with only two speed options-anxiety and blindness. It wasn't that the slap erased her feelings, it simply confused her. She didn't believe she deserved to be hit, therefore none of it made sense to her. No one had ever hit her like that before. Even her mother had never slapped her face.

After Lee slapped her, he felt good and bad at the same time. The slap had relieved a small percentage of his hostility and tension, but it made him sad to see his knuckles printed over her pretty cheek, and the trickle of blood coming from the side of her mouth disagreed with him. He had known he was in all probability going to hit her right after he shook Henry's hand. He wanted to hit her then, but not in front of her sister and Henry. Lee had told himself that he *shouldn't* hit her, although his insides boiled when he imagined her loving someone else. Therefore, his insecurities took charge of the situation. He was consoled by reminding himself that he had tried to bypass the violence by reaching out to hug her, yet Vivian had been too stubborn to allow reconciliation.

Subconsciously, he needed to regain the control he felt he had lost over Vivian. Had she not walked away, he gradually realized he would have struck her when they were together late Saturday night or early Sunday morning in her backyard. The words she had spoken then penetrated him now. He scraped her arm from the side of the rock, and in a jerking movement, spun her around, twisting it behind her back. Her face was pressed against the rock. He hated her for not loving him in the way he wanted her to love him. Lee gritted his teeth so tightly that his words, "you whore" sounded only on the inside of his mouth.

"Stop it . . . Lee . . . Lee . . . you're hurting me," she whimpered. "You don't have to see me anymore . . . you're hurting me!" It thwarted her that she couldn't stop him because she was physically, mentally, and emotionally defenseless. Pain seared through her arm, all the way through to her abdomen. His antagonism filled his mind and clouded his ears with such smoke that he couldn't hear her cries.

"How come you say I ain't raised proper?" Bitterly, he thought about how hard it was for his father without the loving help of his mother during the critical adolescent years of his upbringing. He couldn't help it if his mother wasn't there to shape him better. How could Vivian condemn him when he was suffering already? "You thinking you so pretty, all o'er that field boy? That disgusting sharecropper? I trusted you, all for nothing! You're not a princess! You're nothing." With that, he twisted her arm up higher. One more fraction of a centimeter, and her bone was going to crack. Vivian screeched inside of anguish. She had to think fast because she saw his fury was still mounting. She was sure her arm was already broken, and that now he was going to pull it off its hinges.

"I didn't mean any of the words I said, Lee Hiram! I was just mad. I'm sorry . . . I'm so sorry, Lee. Please stop, Lee. Lee Hiram, please!" He unintentionally loosened her arm when he heard her soft words, yet he was still straining her tissues tremendously.

"You all in that man's face after you done promised yourself to *me* . . . you're nothing to me! I ought to break your arm!" He underestimated how close he was to breaking it. Lee meant to trouble her, but he had no idea how excruciating the pain was that he inflicted on her. He couldn't imagine that it could equal the pain he felt inside of his heart to have to punish her in this way, or the pain he still felt from her burning words.

"Okay, Lee! I am nothing, certainly not a princess, I'm nothing to anybody if I'm nothing to you, on account of I love you and no one else!" Her cries ultimately reached his ears. He unrestricted her slowly. She said she loved him. Never before were those words spoken between them. Vivian was groaning. The last thing she wanted was to lose Lee. Henry was just a good-looking dream, she thought—a man who didn't want her, anyway. Lee was the one who cared for her, pampered her, and took her everywhere with him because he was proud of her. She started crying, leaning against the rock for support after he let her go. She covered her face with one hand, her sore arm pulled close to her body. Lee stared at her for a minute. Her hair was disarranged, and her gown was muddled. He measured how tiny she was, even at 5'6, compared to his stocky frame. The blood from her lip came through her fingers, dripping onto her clothes.

He touched her sore arm gently. She twitched away. He moved closer and spread the palms of his hands on the rock, Vivian between his arms. Lee pressed his forehead to hers in an upward motion, lifting her face. "My angel," he said softly, "what have I done?" She didn't answer. She didn't move.

"What have I done to my sacred angel?" He asked. Despite her terror of him, his words were pacifying.

"I don't want to see you anymore Lee. I can't deal with this." Her words didn't carry the same toxin as before. He stroked her hair tenderly. Neither one said anything for a long moment. He sensed her impulse to rest under his caress.

"Did you mean what you said?" She knew exactly what he was referring to, only this was not the way she wanted to express her love. She had envisioned a more romantic setting for such words of endearment. Vivian identified, nonetheless, that telling him she loved him was what made him stop twisting her arm.

"Yes, I meant it." Vivian looked away. It shamed her to admit her love after what he had just done. Trying to leave was out of the question because she didn't want to take the gamble of underestimating his rage again. She couldn't endure or chance another physical confrontation with him.

"You meant what?" He probed.

"I do love you, Lee Hiram." She was looking at a far-off tree. Affectionately, he turned her face toward his with his index finger. She looked at him and repeated, "I love you." Slowly, he covered her cheeks, nose, and eyes with kisses. Vivian didn't move. He kept his forehead pressed against hers for a long time with his palms again spread on the rock. She was afraid to look up at him and show him her sad eyes . . . to her that would be like saying what he did was okay. He removed his hands from the rock to give her breathing room. Finally, she looked up at him.

"You mean, you love a country boy like me?" He continued staring into her eyes. "You love the way I talk—and you don't mind listening to how I say my words for the rest of your life?"

"Leave me alone," she said weakly. Lee knew she was giving in, and there was something intoxicating about her new submissiveness. It reminded him of when they first met -before rotten words had the chance to spoil their romance. He was sad to think he had to hit her to get that feeling again. He pulled her in for a hug. Vivian buried her face in his chest, emotionally devitalized.

"Muffin?" He kissed her forehead. "I done fallen in love with you, also. I'm sorry, baby. It'd kill me if you left me. I didn't mean to hurt you." Lee backed away but held her hand. "Le'me take you to my place for a while," he slurred. "Please." He made that suggestion because he didn't want her family members to see her like she was, with trickles of oval shaped bloodstains soaked on her gown. He would be ashamed if anyone would witness what he'd done to her.

"No!" She said quickly. "I need to get home."

"You still gonna be my girlfriend?"

"You don't even trust me, Lee, how am I going to be your anything?"

"I do trust you. I know I don't trust no strapping field boy 'round you. How are you gonna spend a Saturday with Henry and you don't even know if I wanna do something with you? I'm your man, he's not." With these words, he excused his act of violence as justified.

"You *must* understand, Lee . . . Henry is Minnie's man. I can't stop her from having him over to the house. What do you want me to do? Move?" He inched closer.

"You can stay with me. I want us to live together," he said without considering its impact. She looked at him in disbelief.

"Are you crazy?" He flinched at her choice of words to describe him a second time. "You can't possibly think I'm fixing to shack up with you." He took her other hand in his. They looked right at each other. She loved him, but she felt dirty and insulted.

"Muffin pie, what I'm asking you ain't nothing like that." Instantly, the dirty feeling was replaced with a fear of what she knew was coming next. I wanna know if you'd have me." He blurted, "Be my wife, Viv."

"Lee Hiram!"

"What happened today will never happen again." She wasn't all aglow as he wanted her to be.

"I don't know about all that, Lee. Your timing is off..."

"You ain't gotta answer me now. I'm gonna prove to you I'll make you a good husband." He wiped her face and dress with his shirt. "Come on, let's go to my place. I...we going through too much to leave each other so soon...then I'll take you home, I promise."

"I's...I'm tired, Lee. Let's just sit here for a spell. You've succeeded in confusing me. I can't think right now."

"I know, muffin. I know." He slid down beside her on the grass, and they both leaned against the rock. Lee began to hum an old Negro spiritual, "Steal Away." Vivian couldn't help feeling special that he had chosen her, when she figured he could have any girl he wanted given that he was so fine and creamy colored. She remembered that Madeline and Missy Burdeshaw, and some of the other girls she used to go to school with always said they wanted to marry a honey brown man that wasn't too dark at all so that they could make pretty babies. It was something about a light-skinned man, many women thought. The light complexions made men better-looking and less dangerous, she perceived. Besides, it was even bad luck to have a dark-skinned person to be the first one in a new year to come into anyone's home, her mother had taught her. The darker the person entering first on New Year's Day, the worse the luck coming to that entire household for the remainder of that year. But a fine man like Lee would be accepted into most homes at any time of the year.

Vivian was furious with Lee, but at the same time, she blamed herself for his violence. Her ego forced her to go along with his story. Not only did she want to believe he would never strike her again, but she also never wanted her family to learn of his violence. She pondered and considered, only to become more confused over the episode. Before long, she had fallen asleep on his chest. Lee listened to her even breathing, feeling her perspiration coming through his clothing. With one hand, he shuffled her head ever so lightly in order to strip down to his T-shirt. He removed the checkered shirt he was wearing and draped it over her bodice. It hid the bloody clues of their fight well enough for her to go home and quickly change from her soiled clothing, he planned.

Then he relaxed, allowing his mind to roam freely in the quietness. Lee was surprised at himself for asking her to marry him. Having a woman living with him would surely cramp his fast lifestyle. He often had women at the home he shared with his father. His mother had disappeared when he was seven. He never knew the truth about why she left because his father refused to talk about it. Lee remembered being sent on a vacation with his Uncle Samuel in Georgia one summer, and when he returned, his mother was gone. Lee decided to lose Vivian forever would be far worse than giving up his city and field pacifiers. He considered her a "good" girl, one fit to marry.

The main thing was he knew she was pure, and he knew the pretty ones were hard to come by. He didn't think he could stomach marrying a girl who was unchaste. It disturbed Lee that so many of the girls were carrying on with various men. "Things just ain't the way they used to be when a girl would save herself for her husband," Lee mused, mimicking his father's words. "Times sho is getting hard." It didn't occur to him that his wild street life was the paradigm for young sharecroppers who looked up to him, the big-time city boy, and they would follow his example of spoiling the very crop they sought.

He didn't know he would have a daughter by a field-working girl, and that his daughter would get emotionally trampled upon by half a dozen of the very same field boys who modeled after him. Lee didn't think far enough into the future to process that a whole society would come up based on the pattern set by men and women like him, and that by the year two thousand and twenty-five, finding a virgin wife would hardly be a consideration, as males and females were expected to fornicate. If a man was twenty-two and had not sown an oat, society would question his...sexuality. Marriage had nothing to do with it. The older relatives made it ritualistic that every boy should "get some." Lee's damage was so profound that generations following him would continue to be caught blindly in a web of mixed messages.

Lee was injected in an exquisitely spun web, quite symmetrical. Invisible to Lee was the piercing head or brains of the needle, but visible to him was his peers acting based on the same injected poison of classism, sexism, and the Willy Lynch doctrine. He was cool. He fit in with what was normal.

Lee, his mind dripping with the self-sustaining poison, decided he had to marry Vivian if he wanted to keep her and if he was going to ward off Henry. He sensed that Henry secretly wanted Vivian. Lee contended inwardly that he could not be fooled. He knew the look in a man's eye when he wanted a woman, and Lee insisted he saw that look from Henry. Minnie was a non-issue concerning all of this because she wasn't fine enough for a stud like Henry to favor forever, Lee interpreted. Lee intended to erase any idea Vivian may have contemplated on having Henry, thus, he had felt compelled to beat her. She was *his* prey, not Henry's. Deep down, he wished he didn't have to mar her like he did, but he deemed it necessary. Now, he felt he had to hurry up and marry her.

~~~

When Lee finally walked her home, Henry and Minnie were gone. Robeena was busy preparing supper, mumbling to herself the whole while about everyone sneaking off and leaving her to cook. Carol had recently arrived home from Reverend Washington's office and had gone straight to her bedroom and closed the door. Satisfied that Henry was gone, and that enough fear had been instilled in Vivian that she would behave, Lee finally left her.

He looked up at the afternoon sun and decided the fresh air was too nice to go home and be stuck in the house for the remainder of the day. He headed for the Raison Plantation where he knew the Negroes would be singing and working happily. Lee spotted the girl who had replaced Floyd as his best friend, Maybelle. Maybelle, a plump, reddish brown, ordinary sharecropper girl of twenty was wringing laundry to dry. She lived in a cabin with her mother, Maybelline, and her grandmother, Tazra. Tazra was also the great cabin mother and healer for all the Black people on the Raison Plantation. Maybelle looked up, saw Lee, dropped a sheet back into the bucket of water, and smiled. He winked at her. He would spend a few hours with Maybelle to rid his mind of the residual misery trapped there as a result of beating up his girlfriend. He could not talk about what he had done to Vivian with Maybelle because their relationship was...complicated. Maybelle didn't know Lee had a girlfriend. One of the reasons they hit it off as best friends was due to Maybelle's willingness to listen and laugh. Lee could talk to her and sink his sorrows into her soul because she comforted him.

"Lee, you look like you've been in a wild dog fight." She laughed, delighted that he had come today. "Where's your shirt?" Seeking to appear cheerful, Lee laughed with her as they exchanged their made-up coded handshake. Then he hugged her. "Uh, Lee," she said with a playful squirm that involved a fake attempt to get away, "young Massa Raison at home today. I can't be messing 'round with you in the middle o' the afternoon! I hafta account for twelve loads o' clothes."

"Come on, girl! You work harder and faster than any of these other folk." Lee was successful in camouflaging his distress over what had just happened with Vivian. He would not let it ruin the rest of his day. This was one of his favorite spots to visit. Maybelle was a warm hearted and humble person. She was always willing to offer smiles and good times, no strings attached. She lifted his spirits. Nonetheless, Lee didn't mind if she suffered punishment from Tazra or Mr. Raison himself in exchange for fulfilling his needs. Besides, who else could he talk to on a sordid day? His father was never home because he worked overtime often; he had lost Floyd, and Hamilton Briggs lived too far. Lee simply could not go home to an empty house. Maybelle looked around to see if anyone was watching.

Dropping her laundry in the middle of her shift to entertain Lee could cost a lot, but Lee seemed particularly agitated that day. She really liked him. She had dreams that he would end up falling in love with her and marry her one day. Although he treated her like one of his best buddies, Maybelle realized and capitalized on the advantage she had over all his other friends. She was far enough away from the sharecroppers, and everyone else nearby seemed to be minding their own business, except Liz, a nosey girl standing alone watching them with her hands on her hips. Maybelle felt like Lee needed her. Although he never acknowledged it, she provided comfort because she listened to his problems about work, agony surrounding the loss of his mother, and his general discomfort.

Lee told Maybelle things he did not bother to share with Floyd. This is because Floyd barely let Lee finish his sentences. Being best friends with Floyd had been shifting to best activities and best hanging buddy. Now that Floyd and Lee had fallen out, Maybelle was able to fill more of a void. He didn't have to tell her that something was bothering him. And whenever they were alone together, she did not badger him to tell her what was wrong. He was free to share or not share.

"Go on o'er to the barn where we usually talk. I'll be there directly." Lee was looking past her. Liz was still watching them. He made a mental note as he turned and headed for the barn.

CHAPTER EIGHT
"Take me up on a cloud somewhere"

"Henry?"

"Hmm?"

"You think we should try to leave *that* soon? You don't want to wait 'til next year this time...when we're...*right*, and have more money and things?"

"That ain't too soon. That's almost two months away, Minnie."

"One."

"What you be afraid of?"

"It's just..."

"Okay. Not May. June, then. The first week in June."

"Uh! That ain't no big difference, and you know it."

"I swear, girl. Sometimes I feel you really don't wanna go with me."

"Whatchu mean by that? Is you saying you'd go without me?" Robeena rolled her eyes. She had been trying to tune her sister and Henry out while she knitted, but Minnie made her want to vomit. She acted like she wanted to eat Henry's spit.

"Now I *know* you's hearing things. Then the second week in June. Look. I wanna be in Michigan on Juneteenth, no matter what. That's Freedom Day. We gotta make some decisions about this'n here. First, I said in a fortnight, but you didn't like that. Then I says one, two, then three months. Is you serious 'bout me, Minnie? Or is you playing games 'cause you like to see me beg?" She giggled. He smiled, taking her hand in his.

"Oh, Henry!" Minnie beamed, "I can see us now...with a church home, celebrating Juneteenth as truly free, married people!" Robeena stopped concentrating so hard on her knitting and glared at Minnie, wondering if she would bother to mention to Henry that she, too, wanted to get out of the South and live a more fascinating life.

"Juneteenth is supposed to represent the end of slavery. The only some way I'm gonna be free myself is if I go with y'all." She pouted, crossing her arms. When they didn't respond, she stormed to her bedroom and put her head back into her bonnet-making project alone-away from their stuffiness. Robeena was bored in Century and saw no real future for herself. Perhaps she would be happy to develop dreams in the North, away from southern oppression. The sun had disappeared completely from the horizon and the moon was its noble substitute. Carol would not be in for a spell. Usually, either she was home by dinnertime, or she stayed out past the time when the girls went to bed. Under the circumstances, then, Robeena knew she was over Esther's house. She certainly wasn't at a meeting with Wali Eli and other community members. When he came around, it was to teach, and that was all. Their meetings never lasted past dusk. He slipped into her mother's life representing a trusting friend. Wali Eli was a perfect example of a man, Robeena recognized. She wished his godly spirit would rub off on others, like her father. It was Wali Eli's tutelage on Juneteenth that had Carol so instilled with pride, running around repeating that despite servitude and poverty, freedom was a state of mind. Celebrations did not change conditions, just as faith without work is dead faith.

Robeena knew Henry wasn't supposed to be in the house with Minnie, just as well as Henry knew it. Wali Eli was always cornering Henry and teaching him how to be a gentleman, Robeena mused. At every opportunity, he was explaining scriptures to Henry, and urging him to study the words of God more closely. Wali Eli warned Henry in the presence of Minnie and her sisters that he should respect Carol's house in her absence. Henry wanted to share but was too shy to express that he appreciated Wali Eli's counsel.

For Robeena, as long as everyone stayed in the front room, she would keep their secrets. However, Henry always seemed extra respectful when Carol was not home, and Carol's pattern was to come home late on Sundays. Robeena knew Vivian's pattern, too. She knew Vivian should be coming home at any minute. Lee usually managed to get her back right after nightfall, cutting it close every time. Carol wanted them all inside by sunset. If they engaged in dishonorable conduct, she wanted them to at least discontinue the behavior in time to make curfew.

Robeena just wanted to have fun. That was her dream. That was all she knew, thus, fun was her idea of happiness. As dusk settled in, the crickets started their party in the fields and were even venturing close to her window, calling her. At first, Robeena did a bridled bop up and down to their music. Bop-pop. Crick-et. Bop-pop. Robeena skipped lightly on her toes, using her arms to spin her completely 360 degrees. And then, bop-pop, cricket, bop-pop. Her eyes slid closed, forcing her deeper into the trance. Henry being there was not in vain…he kept his harmonica on him always! He could play for her. He *would* play it tonight. She rose from the mattress (which was also used as a chair) and skated back out to the living room, and in front of Henry.

"Where's your harmonica, Henry?" He laughed, moving bashfully away from Minnie nominally.

"Robeena, girl, you're something else!"

"Go sit down somewhere, Beena. This ain't your party."

"Well, it ain't your party, neither, Minnie. You ain't supposed to be having no company no way." Robeena was taunting her. "Come on, Minnie, I wanna dance. Let 'im play." Henry kept laughing. Minnie tried not to grin, but Robeena was impossible! Already, she was bouncing up and down, encouraging the blow of the small instrument to take her to another planet. Inescapably, Henry stood to retrieve the harmonica from the tightly bound knapsack around his waist and immediately started playing expertly. Robeena was being fancy with a two-step despite Minnie's interruptions of thunderous outbursts.

"You ain't dancing, girl. Thought you said you wanted to dance!" Robeena concentrated on Henry's musical rhythm even more. Her body pulsated to the vivacious melody. "You're still not dancing. What's that supposed to be? You can't dance," Minnie coaxed.

"She's right, now. Come on, Robeena, show me what you got!" Henry stopped playing but continued to pat his thigh invitingly. Then he placed his mouth back on the harmonica as though he had never stopped playing. Robeena danced like never before.

As Vivian crept toward the house, she paused when she heard Henry's deep voice. Their cajoling was inspirational to her. Vivian came through the door impassioned to intertwine with the exciting spirit that permeated the atmosphere. She had just left Lee down the road, as far as he wanted to walk her, and now it seemed to be party time. With Lee, they'd argued all evening about nothing. It relieved her to be rid of him that night.

Henry nodded his head in acknowledgment of Vivian's presence, yet never missed his beat. She looked away when he nodded, afraid to look at him in his face knowing she liked him. Then she suspected that there was nothing wrong about speaking to him, so she looked at him again and mouthed her greeting. He winked at her and she blushed deeply, looking away again, this time at Robeena.

"Whyn't you show me how, Minnie," Robeena urged. She grinned at Vivian as the latter closed the door tightly, locking it since it was obvious Carol hadn't made it home yet. In an instant, Vivian was snapping her fingers and thumping her feet in tune with the rhythm.

"Yeah, Minnie," Vivian chided, "let's see what *you* can do!"

"Alright, then. Slow it down some, Henry." Immediately, Henry changed the tune to something deliberate and captivating. Minnie hurried off her shoes with a kick before joining Robeena in the middle of the floor. She was aware that she did not possess the same dancing talent as Robeena, so she decided on a measured swiveling movement to give Henry the illusion that she could dance and be foxy at the same time. Minnie would not be outdone. She worked her grind all the way to the floor until her toes popped.

"Come on, Henry, you come on and dance with me," Minnie begged.

"I'll bet you can't play *Maple Leaf Rag*!" Henry winked again at Vivian as he magnificently blew the piece she challenged. Her eyes brightened as she marveled at his talent. Minnie was now motioning more determinedly for Henry to join her for a dance. Vivian clapped and thumped louder to free Henry for the task that Minnie requested. Henry slid his harmonica back in his knap-sack on his way to the dance floor. As he passed, Robeena grabbed his forearm compellingly before he could escape. She was forced to loosen him though when he twirled her around and around. Spinning like a ballerina, Robeena never lost her ground.

"Do it, 'Beena," Vivian cheered. When Robeena recovered from Henry's spin, she merged with him in his two-step, until he left her alone en route for Minnie. Minnie's panting and sweating made Robeena decide to stop dancing. Less energy would be exerted if she could contribute to the rhythm that Vivian soloed. Not affected by his short detour, Minnie continued to summon her fiancé onward until they were one foot apart. Henry's hips gyrated while he held on to Minnie's shoulders.

"Dance, girl," Henry teased. Minnie moved harder.

"Your turn, Viv," Robeena solicited after a few moments. Minnie backed up to show everyone that she didn't mind sharing Henry in all the merriment. When Minnie joined Robeena in encouraging Vivian, Henry released Minnie's shoulders and beckoned Vivian with his eyes. As he advanced a few steps toward Vivian, Minnie joyously enlisted in the thump-thump with her youngest sister.

"Uh…I'll give up the beat, but I'll leave the dancing to you-all," Vivian stated before Henry could reach her. How dare Minnie! Vivian wanted to dance with Henry, but this was too sinister, and she expected that they all should know that. His magnificent blackness was far from ugly. In fact, he was too astounding to come too near, she imagined. She tried to certify him as unbecoming, but just the thought of him closing in on her for a dance was enough to make her knees tremble.

They all booed her until she finally halfway relented with a soft glow. After walking briskly to claim his partner, Henry wasted no time pulling her to the area they all had designated as the dance floor. His grin matriculated into a miniature chuckle as he forced her to move with him, and then Henry started laughing hard at her. She sensed he appreciated the real reason for her initial refusal to dance with him. It wasn't a matter of trying to hide her admiration for him; she feared signals were emitted right out of her and through to his skin, assisted by the closed in area. Feeling optionless, she sashayed into a two-step like the one that had Robeena hopping around, although Vivian didn't quite embody the angelic finesse of her sister.

Trapped on the dance floor, a whirlwind of emotions overcame Vivian. Her majestically revitalized attraction for Henry was gaining momentum while he held her. She thought she might faint by his electrifying touch. The connection was solid. She had to brace herself, or she would collapse. To gain control, Vivian was determined to seize the precious moments she shared dancing with Henry, and not let it control her. She wanted to talk to him about a lot of things. Ever since they met, she recognized closeness with him that had yet to be defined with words. Skeptical about how she should approach any subject with him, she took a deep breath and stared at his face until he realized she had an issue.

"Henry." He was concentrating hard on the flow of their dance.

"You say something, Viv?" She knew there was no time to waste, yet she couldn't produce the words to describe the roller coaster inside of her soul. She didn't want to expose herself too much or give the wrong impression, but at the same time, she recognized that she had only seconds to talk to him.

"Have you ever felt like you were drowning?"

"Huh?"

"Like you were suffocating? Swallowed up by the ocean? And it felt good to be in the ocean, but at the same time, you were drowning? You were in the water, but you would rather be on a cloud…floating? I mean, it felt awful sometimes because of who you were out there with, but the water felt good. But then at other times, it didn't feel good at all. You just knew you would die if it didn't stop. But it depended on if you had help out there you could trust whether you could survive. If somebody you didn't trust took you out there, you would die. But you stopped knowing who you could trust because the people you thought loved you started hurting you." He slowed his movement to hear her better.

"I guess so."

"Sometimes I feel like I need somebody to help me out of the water to keep me from drowning. Take me up on a cloud somewhere and just let me be. Don't take anything from me, just let me be who I am…" Vivian ceased expressing her situation because she could almost swear that Robeena was reading her lips as she tried to explain things to Henry. Robeena could tell the dancers were losing their inspiration. She wanted another turn herself to twirl Henry, but Minnie wasn't keeping up her part of the music, either.

"Y'all ain't dancing! Viv, you ain't working like I know you could work!" Then, Minnie interfered with Robeena's cheering by something she said to her in a muffled voice.

"Wait a minute, Minnie! You need to be stomping your feet, anyway. Can't you see your sister needs some help out there?"

"Dance, Viv," Minnie challenged.

"I told you-all I couldn't dance," Vivian offered more to Henry.

"You doing just fine, baby girl," Henry whispered in the midst of Robeena's and Minnie's hooting. Vivian heard him, but more, she abided his breath hot in her ear, which caused remarkable caginess. As though that wasn't enough, Henry put his arms around her waist, moving steadily to the clapping and thumping. Unsure of herself, Vivian two-stepped faster. The faster, the freer, she speculated. She was panicky. The thought of Lee doubling back tonight was enough to send quakes throughout her body. What if he had forgotten to tell her something, or what if he figured out that Carol wasn't home, or worse than that, what if Lee suspected that Henry was in the house alone with the girls and dancing with her at this very moment? And what was Minnie thinking about Henry's hands on her waist?

In his effort to slow her movements, Henry grasped her tighter, all the while trying to lead her in the two-step. There was no way she could ever pick up their conversation again. She had made a fool out of herself! She felt his hands on her. She felt every one of his fingers clutching her side, pulling her into his rhythm. He hadn't held Minnie as close as he was holding her when they danced—and he was pulling her closer! It frightened her when she could hear no more clapping ringing in her ears. The thump-thump faded into crisp silence. How could she possibly dance with his body smashed against hers—or was it hers smashed against his? Her quadriceps had turned into magnetic strips of putty. Shamefully, Vivian managed to steal a glance at her sisters standing off to the side. There they were, Minnie and Robeena sinking into a hazy cloud. The whole room seemed to be engulfed. Stuffy. Robeena was saying something to Minnie that made Minnie cover her mouth and laugh. Minnie turned around to allow Robeena to fix her cummerbund, which had come undone during all her thrashing about. They appeared to be moving in slow motion.

Vivian looked down at her feet and discovered with amazement that they were still moving in time, back and forth, right along with Henry's feet. She glanced up again to find Henry staring straight at her. No more giggling. No more counterfeit smiles to convey a false reality. It terrified Vivian to chance looking back down at her feet to check again for movement. She was sure now that the two of them were standing stark still. Yet, she could still feel those hands of his holding her waist!

Then, as though he touched a hot coal stove, Henry abruptly dropped his hands from her waist and backed away. He knows, Vivian sensed. "I wasn't dreaming, and neither was he," she said to herself. When she saw Robeena straightening Minnie's dress, Vivian comprehended that the episode that seemed like an eternity to her had only lasted a few seconds. She would have to reconfirm if Henry knew of her longing or if the whole ordeal had been a revealing dream.

Henry was walking away from her already. He approached Minnie just as Robeena moved over. Carelessly, he stroked a loose braid at the nape of Minnie's neck until it unraveled. Minnie turned back to strike him playfully. Vivian slipped away to her bedroom, overcome with uncertainty.

"Hey!" Henry was acting like a small child, dashing about, trying to take another tug at a braid in Minnie's hair. She reached again to pinch him.

"Cut your mess out, boy." Minnie thought too late to talk more properly like Vivian, and maybe she could impress Henry further. "You know you need to cut out your mess!"

"I'm sorry. I'm just having a li'l fun." He turned to Robeena. "Beena, girl, you dance mighty fine!"

"Humph."

"I mean it. Don't she dance good, Minnie?" Minnie shrugged.

"I reckon."

"Do y'all really think so?"

"Yeah, girl. We said yeah..." Minnie conceded.

"On account of that's what I wanna do—dance. I wanna move North, like I told Minnie." Robeena looked hopefully at Minnie. Minnie didn't say anything. Secretly, she felt she *needed* Robeena to go with her if they moved away. In this way it wouldn't be so unnerving for her. Henry observed Minnie's expression at her sister's claim. It wouldn't bother him if Robeena tagged along if that's what Minnie proposed.

"I believe I could hit it big in Michigan, y'all. I could take me some lessons and everything!"

"Beena, I ain't certain mama would even let you go with me and Henry. I hope she will, though."

"Oh! I know! I wish she could just trust me."

"I do too," Henry said. "I been talking to my cousin, Rufus 'bout tagging along, but he ain't said nothing. If we had another man, Ms. Carol might feel better—and maybe that way Minnie won't be so scared to leave." Minnie gave him a scowl.

"Child, please. That'd be the last thing my mama wants is a whippersnapper traveling up the road with Beena. She ain't hardly want me going with you since we ain't yet legal." Henry quickly looked away.

"Henry. When is y'all truly leaving here?" Robeena asked. Henry looked at Minnie again. She gave a deep sigh.

"I guess he's waiting on *me* to answer that one. Supposed to be the first or second weekend in June," she conceded. Henry treaded closer to Minnie. After all his weeks of begging, she had finally agreed openly to the relocation. He wanted to encircle her within his hold, but something choked him to a halt. Still, he took a step forward only to stop again. An ocean of waves surged between them, causing a great fog amidst his judgment. Instinctively, he looked around for Vivian only to discover that she'd left the room.

The haze swarming in the room became thicker with each enduring second. Robeena was saying, "Yeah, Minnie, let's do it…" and Minnie agreed again that they'd leave in June. Sparks weren't flying everywhere as he'd expected. Due to the decision they had just made jointly, the trio experienced separate emotions. Nonetheless, a commitment was formed that neither felt they could break. Minnie had promised Robeena that she should travel with them. Robeena vowed that she would partner with them. Henry promised Minnie that he would go.

The dancing seemed a distant memory. They were all different people floating on separate clouds in the haze, and Henry couldn't touch any of them. It seemed one of the clouds belonged to Vivian, but she wasn't there, and they *were* there. He was on his cloud, near them, but he was alone.

While in Century, there were no commitments—just promises that could grow or die with the wind. In three months, his promise would transform into a commitment, and he would have to do it. And he *could* do it, blend in with the thump-thump, but he could not embrace it. Now, the haze suffocated him because he could not embrace it.

CHAPTER NINE
June 1921

The next few months were less exciting for some, yet quite eventful for others; Lee and Vivian lived in partial bliss and in a partial war zone, Carol waited in vain for the stranger, Maybelle missed her third menses in a row, and Robeena joined Henry and Minnie whenever she could. She had already convinced Carol to grant her permission to leave with her sister.

Carol and her daughters didn't miss a Sunday from church, and Henry was always right at Minnie's side during the services. The first Sunday in June 1921, Lee accompanied them to church. Vivian had finally said yes to Lee's almost daily marriage proposals. Carol wasn't pleased about Vivian's choice, but the excitement of a marriage was enough to send her flying around like a peacock to make sure the church would recognize the event. There was no date planned yet, but Carol was sure it would be in the next couple of months. Regrettably, Minnie and Robeena wouldn't be there for their sister's wedding because they would be leaving for Michigan with Henry on Saturday, less than a week away.

They all went to church together to celebrate the pending nuptials. Lee had invited his father and his friend, Hamilton Briggs to the occasion. Lee didn't know if his father would make it to the service, or not. He also hoped his Uncle Samuel would still be hanging around when he won Vivian's promise to marry him. Unfortunately, his uncle was drifting in another city, and Hamilton told him he was never stepping foot in any more churches ever in life because Reverend Washington had silenced the church members after Hamilton's father was lynched when Hamilton was only twelve. There had been an uprising brewing after Mr. Briggs was murdered in cold blood. The congregation wanted to organize a protest, even fight the injustice by marching with signs, as they were hopeful that the heartless, cold-blooded lynchers would read them and feel sorry for them. The killers had been identified. It was up to the sheriff to have them arrested. When Hamilton and his mother arrived early at the church for the protest meeting, he saw Reverend Washington shaking Kent Johnson Jr.'s hand. Smoking a pipe, Kent Jr. dipped out of the side door. The reverend canceled the protest meeting, but in church the next morning, the congregation was told that Mr. Briggs had been guilty of a crime, and the lynchers were acting on behalf of the sheriff's department. Hamilton remembered the duplicity like it was yesterday and thought that someone ought to have Reverend Washington removed, yet his mother's complaints fell on deaf ears. After just a few weeks, the community lost the zeal to fight for justice for Mr. Briggs. Lee was hoping Hamilton would be able to put his personal feelings aside and celebrate his pending nuptials.

Minnie was envious that Lee was so romantic to beg for Vivian's hand in marriage. Henry sometimes talked about marriage, but he always made it seem like something that might happen in the future. Minnie's pride wouldn't let her force Henry to pinpoint a date. It bothered her enormously, though, that he would talk so much about going to Michigan, but so non indulgently about formulating a binding commitment. She didn't dare air the ultimatum that perhaps they shouldn't move to Michigan unless they were married first because she felt that would be like taking a chance of losing the infinitesimal piece of him she held. Nonetheless, she hoped some of Lee's determination and passion that Sunday would graze Henry.

No one in Vivian's family had any idea that Lee's passion included a raging temper whenever they evaluated him. Henry, however, was becoming ever more concerned about Vivian. She simply didn't seem to be the same bouncy, flirtatious girl as when he first met her. He wondered if his observation was merely his rejection of her that caused her to decrease her subtle advances. Then, he weighed if her advances were not all in his head. Had she really done anything out of the way? Henry figured that Vivian had been unsullied until she met Lee. Minnie had confided in him regarding her concern about Vivian getting pregnant with no husband. She also told him how Lee would come to the window late at night for Vivian. Seeing the way Vivian behaved in church with Lee that Sunday caused even more skepticism for Henry. He noticed before the church meeting, Vivian hadn't mingled with her two friends, Madeline, and Missy Burdeshaw as she usually did. The first few times Henry accompanied the sisters and Carol to church, Vivian and her friends were inseparable. According to Minnie, Vivian rarely got the opportunity to see the sisters outside of church, although they were best friends. This Sunday, Henry spotted Vivian trailing behind Lee as he laughed and socialized with several of his buddies for twenty-five minutes before church officially started.

Henry further scrutinized that Vivian didn't take the opportunity to spend time with her friends even when they took the time to approach her. Madeline and Missy lived only two blocks from Lee, and being best friends with Vivian meant they already had the inside scoop on the engagement announcement that was to take place today. The sisters knew of Lee's unrestrained haphazard life, but trying to discourage Vivian was next to impossible. Early in their relationship, when it was clear Vivian was serious about Lee, Missy casually mentioned that Lee "got around," and it nearly started a fight between the girl friends. Vivian misunderstood their sentiment because she estimated that she had the most handsome man in all the South, and she knew they knew this. Both Madeline and Missy had exclaimed about Lee's debonair appearance when they first learned from Vivian that she was his choice. Obviously, they were secretly jealous, according to Vivian.

Henry continued to look around. He surveyed that no one else in their small party seemed to react to Vivian's behavior. Therefore, he became ill at ease for apparently paying too much attention to her. He turned away shortly. Minnie perceived his preoccupation, so she glided his hand in hers on their way inside the church. She hoped Henry was preoccupied with how *he* could propose to *her*.

~~~

Overall, the church trip was a disaster. Maybelle was almost four months pregnant that June. Two weeks before, near the end of May, she tried to tell Lee about her condition when they convened together in the same beat down barn on the plantation where they always met. A few chickens lived there, but it was mostly abandoned, except to store hay. She had seen him another time since she believed she might be pregnant, but she didn't want to say anything until she was certain. She waited to tell him in the aftermath of their togetherness. He was about to go to sleep when she made tiny circles with her fingers under his chin and commenced to tell him of her condition. He hadn't so much as opened his eyes at the news before he simply said, "Well, I'm happy for you, but don't you go telling people *I* had anything to do with it..."

She removed her finger from his chin in a snapping motion. Maybelle had vague comprehension of Lee's life off the plantation. She knew she couldn't possibly be Lee's only woman, but she did think she was his main one because of their strong bond. She took for granted that he knew how she felt and would never hurt her. Why else would she risk so much to appease him whenever he felt the notion to quickly visit--usually in the middle of her shift? Did he not know how rude and selfish that was? She had been considerate and respectful enough not to chastise him or act possessive those times whenever she saw Lee walking along the sides of the field with Liz. In fact, the day she wanted to tell him about her condition, she spotted him standing at the edge of the plantation with Liz. That day with Liz, Lee had seen Maybelle stop in her tracks, but he chose to leave without speaking to or acknowledging her. Maybelle showed him respect by honoring his privacy and obvious desire for distance, even though the announcement she wanted to share with Lee was heavy-laden on her heart.

Of course, he returned to smooth things over the very next week. That's when she revealed her pregnancy to him. After talking about it for a half minute, Lee lifted himself up from the hay and told her they could finish discussing it tomorrow. He didn't want to be held accountable. Although he had never fathered any children, he always knew somebody would tell him eventually that she was with his child. Now, Lee certainly did have a burst of pride bubbling inside of him at the revelation that he had made something, but still, he didn't want Maybelle to get any inkling of including him in her plans. Tazra, her cabin mother grandmother, would tell her how to get rid of it, he guessed. He understood that he would have to stay away from her for a good while until she healed. And if she wanted to keep it, that would be alright, too, as long as she kept quiet about it so that Vivian would not learn of it. When Lee left, promising to come back the next day, Maybelle did not openly pout because she thought that would turn him off. Instead, she agreed with him that he needed a day to clear his head.

Maybelle waited vainly for Lee to return. A week went by, then two, then three, and still there was no sign of Lee. Maybelle became excessively worried because she was sure Lee would marry her if she could prove to him that this was indeed his child. He had told her he loved her numerous times, and she loved him as well. Eventually, she mustered up the courage to go into town in search of her man. As far as she was concerned, there must be a dependable explanation as to why he didn't come again, and she intended to be supportive rather than selfish.

Maybelle was dazed to fathom that she knew little about Lee. She had no idea of where he even lived. She did know Floyd Barnes was a friend of Lee's, since she had been Floyd's girl first. In fact, it was at Floyd's house where she'd met Lee. She made her way hurriedly past the west side of the Raison Plantation and around the bend, to the road. With her head hanging low, Maybelle tried to whistle a familiar tune to remain calm. It had been over a year since she last visited Floyd Barnes.

Long, dry roads spilled into wide, dry, endless roads. The closer she came to his house, the more she slowed her stride--almost to a crawl pace when she approached his hard dirt walkway. Maybelle stared with uncertainty at the dwarfish brown wooden house. There were three lawn chairs in the front, tiny yard, and empty beer bottles scattered about in the dying patches of grass nearby. An abandoned dog was eating from a garbage bag that was spilled over onto his porch. The house's only window facing the street was curtained with yellowed newspaper. Maybelle didn't remember Floyd's home being so unkempt. Feeling more confident and pretty since his house was more raggedy than she had remembered, she finally went to the door and tapped sternly.

Her knock awakened him, although it was 2:00 in the afternoon. He shuffled on out to the porch to greet his visitor. Floyd was ecstatic that she had come to him for help with finding Lee. He couldn't wait for the opportunity to verbally blast Lee. He wanted revenge on his forsaken friend for beating him up in his own house. Floyd had yet to live down the humiliation of what Vivian and his former buddy had done to him in front of a room full of mostly men. Things hadn't been the same for Floyd since that day. Floyd had lost the respect of some of those who were his friends, and the word spread quickly to the ladies that he had gotten whipped.

Floyd also felt a tinge of jealousy that Maybelle hadn't come specifically to take him out of his gloom. Therefore, he enjoyed telling her that Lee was strutting around town like a spectacle spreading the news that he was to be married to Vivian. Maybelle's heart sank. Who was Vivian? Floyd told her everyone knew Lee was going to make his big debut in church on Sunday to announce the news. When the tears flowed freely down Maybelle's cheeks, Floyd encouraged Maybelle to fight for her man. He insisted that Vivian had cast some voodoo spell on Lee to make him marry her. Floyd volunteered to escort Maybelle to the church on Sunday so she could have the opportunity to confront Lee face to face. After she left, Floyd brightened and grinned a toothless smile. He shooed away the dog sniffing in his garbage and picked up a few beer bottles in the yard before going back inside.

Maybelle wiped her tear stained face the Sunday morning of Lee's engagement announcement. Tazra had twisted and brushed her hair to perfection. She didn't waste time asking Maybelle what the occasion was. Her granddaughter was a sweet and sour mass of sneakiness. Maybelle had a beautiful dress made for the crashing affair, at Floyd's expense. She was ready. Floyd was waiting behind the curtains of a two-horse pulled surrey that came right on the plantation to escort her. Tazra watched curiously. The mysterious man behind the curtain was not gallant enough to appear long enough to help her into the wagon, and Maybelle didn't have the self-respect to wait until he did. Instead, she hopped up like a tomboy and they rolled away.

They arrived at the church early as planned. Floyd quickly paid the driver so the horses could gallop down the road instead of pawing around, drawing attention to himself and his guest. He told the driver to come back in two hours and wait outside, and then he walked with Maybelle into the empty church. They took the last two chairs in the back row. Other members began to arrive just five minutes after he did. He had forgotten how early the members always came to congregate amongst themselves before service, since he hadn't been to church in a few years.

Floyd saw Lee enter the church and walk to the second row of chairs, followed by Vivian who was on his heels. He looked down at the floor for several minutes to hide himself until the last in Lee's party, Robeena, took her seat. Lee didn't notice Maybelle under her wide brim, low casted straw hat when he waltzed into the sanctuary and went by her chair.

Shortly, Reverend Washington was preaching from First Peter; 2:18-20: "Servants, be subject to your masters with all fear; can I get an amen?"

"Amen!" The members said in unison. Reverend Washington repeated that the men should not fight, but should suffer what was put on them. He was speaking about the recent lynching that had taken place in Century. The whole town was disillusioned by the loss of four Black businessmen who had been accused of stealing pencils and stationery. Carol knew the reverend would be providing guidance to soothe her soul. Black people were outraged. They felt they did everything to appease the idea of white supremacy: They worked for delimited pay, they suffered racism, and they moved aside to let Caucasian people pass them by on the road, stepping in puddles of muddy water if necessary to provide enough passing space to make white citizens comfortable and satisfied. No matter how much the Black community submitted to second class citizenry, they could expect to be lynch, taunted, spit on, and raped with no consequences. They could not see the end to the humiliation and tyranny because even Caucasian children were disrespectful. Church was a place where feelings could be expressed, where peace existed, and where they could organize to defeat their problems.

Kent Johnson Jr. had met with Reverend Washington on Friday to discuss the appropriate scriptures due to the ugly aftermath of the recent lynching climate. There was fear among some of the Caucasian Protestants that an uprising was inevitable if a Negro leader did not work to quell the violence brewing in the souls of the bereaved survivors. Rioting would be met with more deaths, Kent explained to Reverend Washington. He reminded Washington of what people were now calling the Red Summer of 1919: Instead of bearing patiently like the scripture suggested, Black people in Chicago had started a protest about the loss of Eugene Williams, a 17-year-old Black youth. On July 27, 1919, Williams drowned in Lake Michigan after being attacked with stones by white men who deemed his black body unfit to be immersed where Caucasian people were unofficially sanctioned to swim. Master Johnson reiterated that Williams had arrogated to himself the unmitigated audacity to go swimming in an unofficially *designated* whites only swimming section. The police's unwillingness to arrest the concerned Caucasian men who were trying to protect their area in the Eugene Williams case, Kent Jr. said, should be a warning that hostile Negroes would bring only death and destruction to Century. Next, Master Johnson made the connection by suggesting that no one knew if the colored businessmen in Florida had *not* stolen the pencils. It was the reverend's key role to not only provide an air of calm, but to report the names of any uppity members of the congregation who appeared to have the potential for mischief. There was a subtle warning that the reverend would be held responsible if any troublemaking Negroes were found to be members of Washington's congregation at 2nd Century Baptist Church. Reverend Washington wished his members could understand the pressure he was under. He also felt the sting associated with the climate. He was not insensitive to the cries of his own people.

Reverend Washington continued, "Be patient not only to the good and gentle, but also to the forward. For this is thanks worthy . . . for what glory is, is, if, when ye be buffeted for your faults, ye take it patiently? But if, when ye do well, and suffer for it, ye take it patiently, this is acceptable to God."

The reverend said since God wanted it this way, then so be it. He said the men in his church should fear those in charge, and do their biddings quietly . . . but, when the Lord cometh, after they die and go to heaven, the Negro will receive his reward for suffering on earth.

Lee sat through the lecture feeling uncomfortable. Subconsciously, he knew something was wrong, but he couldn't put his finger on exactly what it was that bothered him about what the reverend was saying. He *knew* Negroes were inferior, and he *knew* God had made it that way because Reverend Washington had gone over the scriptural story of Ham multiple times. As soon as Lee and his father moved into town from Bridgewater, Lee was enrolled in Sunday school, and he was a faithful attendee until he turned sixteen. In Sunday school, the children were told that Noah had cursed his son, Ham, to be black in hue, and Ham's lineage was cursed to take on his blackness. One Sunday school instructor said the curse was because Ham uncovered his father, making him naked. Another Sunday school teacher argued with the first teacher that it was Ham's grandson who saw Noah naked, and that no one uncovered him, yet Ham's older brothers covered him. Lee recalled their disagreement was a huge deal--so much so that it was taken to the reverend for discernment. The reverend received clarification from Master Kent that indeed, Ham was cursed to turn black, and Negroes were colored black as a punishment from God. Moreover, blackly colored people were made slaves because of this curse, and should always serve Caucasians as long as they both lived on Earth. After that, Lee was made to memorize the Biblical references about his inferiority before he could pass from one Sunday school class to the next. In unison whenever prompted, the children would shout the verse from Joshua 9:23, *"Now therefore we are cursed, and there shall none of us be freed from being slaves, and hewers of wood and drawers of water for the house of my God."*

In other realms, Lee had been fed inferiority information since he was in the cradle. He recalled his parents would not allow a dark-skinned family member to be the first person to enter their house after the first day of a new year. To do so would mean their household would be cursed for that entire year. And the light-skinned girls were the prettiest. Even if she were ugly, she was the prettiest because her skin was lighter. Buried deep within, Lee contested the idea of white superiority, but he didn't want to be cursed further by questioning God. He looked behind the reverend at the big picture of Jesus hanging on the wall. His piercing, blue eyes stared back at Lee lovingly and protectively, Lee perceived.

Reverend Washington's wife took her position at the lectern to deliver the announcements after the sermon. She mentioned the tribute dinner to Old Master Kent Johnson, who was turning 86, for all that he'd done for the preacher. Of course, Old Master Kent Johnson wouldn't be attending the ceremony, but the Negroes would glorify him in his absence, and the money they collected would be presented to Kent Jr. She told the congregation of the upcoming bacon eating contest...all proceeds from the entry fees would be donated to the Johnson Missionary School where Reverend Washington received continual theological training, at Old Master Kent's bequest. The school was closed for the summer because the missionaries who ran it were busy in Ghana, Nigeria, and throughout Western Africa spreading the Word.

"...And now we have a special announcement. Y'all know Carol Johnson. She's been a devoted member of our church since she was a teeny-weeny girl. You see her daughters, Robeena, Minnie, and Vivian always with their mama, too. What am I saying? Y'all know 'em!" Members of the congregation laughed good naturedly, enjoying the light mood. "Well, I would like for Vivian Johnson and someone you may not know, Lee Hiram, to come up front and complete the morning announcements."

The church was filled with several words of "amen." Lee bravely led Vivian to the lectern. Mrs. Washington pranced out of the way, smiling brightly as though she was responsible for the couple's engagement. Lee looked around the church before speaking, cocksure that he had the most beautiful young woman in the building. His eyes stopped at a radiant ebony girl whose skin looked like it had been polished with black-blue paint. No matter how many points were given to the lighter skinned Negroes, the exquisitely black complexions always kept everyone in awe. The voice of his Sunday school teacher who had been fired as a result of claiming the story of Ham was a false teaching rang loudly in Lee's ears, *"Gotdammit! Quit telling these children that black is ugly! Black is not a color! It's the essence of God, and there's no such thing as a Negro! How can we be colored black when black does the coloring for all other colors, including white? Teach these children to use a lower-case b when referring to a color, and an uppercase B when speaking of their ethnicity. You always use a lowercase w because white is a color that describes the Caucasian people!"*

The other teacher had answered, *"You don't need to be a Sunday school teacher, what you be is a rebel! These children can't understand all that shit. Let's take it to the reverend."* Lee cleared his throat, attempting to remain in the present day.

Maybelle stood slowly, feeling numbness throughout her body. She made her way to the center aisle in the back. None noticed her at first. Everyone was laughing at Lee's witty opening remarks about being nervous since he hadn't been in a church in so long, but not too nervous to claim what Jesus had given him. Vivian was the second person to notice her. Reverend Washington was the first to behold Maybelle's frame curving out of place through the rows. The emotion on Maybelle's face expressed torment. At last, Lee saw her. He paused for a moment, but decided to continue, inclined to think surely she wasn't walking straight to the lectern. However, he hesitated to make the clear announcement.

"Lee . . . tell me it ain't so!" Maybelle had made it three quarters the way to interrupt Lee. Vivian became afraid when she spotted the strange girl approaching them. She claimed Lee's hand. The church members were too excited to move. Reverend Washington was on the edge of his seat. Lee looked around to see which deacon would come to his rescue, at least so that the matter could be discussed quietly. The church was filled with silence. Lee could hear the gurgling noise of the steady breathing of Reverend Washington twenty feet behind him.

"Girl, go sit your behind down, or get the hell out of here," Lee whispered coarsely, even though those seated in the rear heard every word.

"Where she gonna go, Lee? Being that she's with child?" The voice came from Floyd Barnes, who was now standing. Lee jerked his head promptly in Floyd's direction. Vivian was leaning on Lee for the inspiration to remain standing. Robeena covered her face with her hands in disgust. Carol sat in the second row of chairs with her mouth hanging open, her main thought being the predicament this was causing her. Two years struggling to become the president of the Women's Club at the church, and now this. She'd never get the presidency! Moreover, she'd be the laughingstock of the entire town. However, Maybelle was just another pregnant girl. They popped up everywhere. Esther shook her head, laughing inwardly. Minnie sympathized with her sister, but she was relieved to discern that Vivian didn't have the best man. Minnie brushed this last thought aside and tried to feel more empathy for her sister.

Henry was absolutely mortified by what Lee was putting Vivian through. He sat in heartfelt shock. He wasn't pleased when he learned of their engagement, anyway. Lee was a poor role model for Vivian, according to what he knew of Lee's nightlife and Minnie's testimonies. Without intending to do so, Minnie helped to change Henry's perspective about Vivian all together. This is because she often shared personal information with Henry about Vivian that only served to widen his sense of compassion for Vivian. Minnie had hoped to make Henry think Vivian was a fast-tailed slut. Nonetheless, Henry's heart was soft for Vivian now, and hard for Lee.

"Oh. It's you, Floyd. I was wondering what all this was about, but now I see." He turned to Vivian, who was visibly dissuaded. "See, muffin? There's Floyd in the back. They's playing games." He turned back to Floyd. "You still mad about that li'l incident . . . and now you wanna play games, you and your girlfriend?" Lee didn't sound too convincing because the crowd preferred the former scandal. Lee appealed, "Can one of you deacons walk these two outta here?" The deacons became irritated that Lee should pick on them to save the day. They both ignored him.

Something about Maybelle's countenance told Vivian that Floyd was telling the truth. However, to believe him meant throwing her dreams out the window. Maybelle wanted to cry. She hardly looked at Vivian.

"Whatchu saying, Lee? You gwine leave me like this?" She nodded her head toward Vivian. "She put some sort of voodoo on you to make you leave me and your child?" Vivian was flabbergasted that this undomesticated girl doubted Lee's love for her. Maybelle answered Vivian's startled look by smoothing her hands over the front of her dress, making the small bulge apparent.

"I don't know you." Lee had resolved to use whatever tactics he deemed necessary in the church to abolish the situation, since it was clear by now no one would be coming to his aid. With these words from Lee, the fight in Maybelle was gone. This was a different Lee. Maybelle didn't know how to deal with this phantom, so she creased her mouth together unassertively. Henry stood up with his fists clenched when the first tear dropped from Vivian's eye. Minnie snatched his hand and tried to pull him back to his seat, but he stood paralyzed. Carol stood, too, then Robeena, then other members.

Maybelle started crying. "I'm your best friend, Lee!" Lee shook his head in denial.

"You's a dirty niggah!" Floyd volunteered loudly.

"Watch your language in God's house," Reverend Washington offered, more to himself. Few people heard him clearly.

It suddenly dawned on Lee that he didn't have to stand there and take such discomposure. Surprising everyone with his sudden shift, he whisked by Maybelle, pulling Vivian behind him, and bolted out of the church. Reverend Washington hurried to the pulpit and began preaching furiously to provide a calm. He knew his words would fall on the hearts of those who were rushing away, and by golly, he would have the last word in the house of the Lord.

"Vivian!" Henry yelled. Minnie gritted her teeth at Henry's cry. Vivian didn't turn around to look at anyone. She wanted this escape. Robeena and Henry looked at each other, then they both started after Vivian and Lee, leaving Carol and Minnie in the chairs. Yet, the congregation bustled out into the lobby before them and began to form a mob, blocking Henry in the aisle. Since they were blocked in, Robeena decided that it was Maybelle who needed her assistance more than Vivian, anyway. She squeezed herself back inside and went to a quivering Maybelle who was standing alone. The two girls sat together. Robeena wrapped Maybelle in her arms and patted her back while Maybelle sobbed. The congregation moved about full of animated chatter as they followed Lee and Vivian outside. Floyd was outside, entangled in the mob, trying to figure out if he had been successful in destroying Lee's relationship. He and the other members hoped someone would stop Lee, but Lee never looked back as he trotted up the road, pulling Vivian with him. Eventually, Floyd boarded the surrey and waited impatiently for Maybelle.

Minnie recklessly elbowed an elderly man as she chased after Henry. She caught up to him and grabbed his arm. "It's crazy in here!"

"Lee was wrong for that, Minnie" He wanted to continue after the troubled couple, but Minnie was still holding his arm, pulling him back.

"The girl might be lying, Henry. We don't know." She could see he was not accepting her take on it.

"We better keep moving before somebody steps on my foot again," Henry said.

"I know. Some old man just elbowed me in my chest trying to get outta here." She expected Henry to ask her if her chest was okay, but he continued to stare past her. By the time Henry and Minnie made it outside, Lee and Vivian were nowhere in sight. Carol made it out a moment later, still visibly shaken.

Reverend Washington paused preaching when he digested that in the chaos, the charity buckets hadn't even been presented for the second giving. He stumbled over to the money containers and threw them like horseshoes to the two deacons who had remained inside to say 'amen' while the reverend preached. They jumped in the air to catch the buckets, and then raced to the door, chasing the tithers. A flash crossed Reverend Washington's mind of the large crowd his church was sure to receive on next Sunday. He knew he had to get a good sermon together. Many souls would need comforting and meaning making after this scandal. He *would* have the last word from the pulpit.

CHAPTER TEN
The mellow smell of fresh strawberries

After escaping the accusing questions and stares from the congregation, Carol dashed home with Minnie and Henry to console Vivian, only she wasn't there. Robeena took another route, too. She entered the surrey behind Maybelle and in front of Floyd. Besides the reverend and deacons, they were the last ones to leave the church. Maybelle felt secure as Robeena began to placate her. Robeena was Vivian's sister . . . the closest thing to Lee that Maybelle could touch besides her unborn child. Robeena looked around the murky space and smiled. This was the first time she'd ever been in a carriage that she could remember. Floyd was as delighted as Maybelle was to give Vivian's sister a lift home. Maybelle hoped Lee was there, even if it meant seeing him with Vivian. Floyd took the scenic route, hoping to see Lee walking with Vivian. When he didn't, he dropped Robeena off at home. Henry and Minnie were sitting on the porch.

Carol, along with Minnie and Henry, was concerned that Vivian hadn't made it back to the house yet. By the time evening came, the mother in Carol surfaced. She never liked Lee, so for Vivian to disappear with him after such a traumatic morning at the church nauseated her. Lee reminded her of the stranger. "Minnie," Carol murmured when Minnie came back into the house with Henry. The couple had been sitting on the porch until Henry said that they should go back inside and check on Carol. Everyone was still dressed smartly in their Sunday outfits. Henry wore a thick overcoat that was cut like a long suit jacket. He fashioned a ruffled hand-me-down shirt and a dark blue bow tie. The last few times he had gone to church with them, he was underdressed. However, he was resourceful enough to collect clothing items one by one until he had a completely decent outfit. "You know where 'bout Lee lives . . . or where Viv might be?"

"No, mama," Minnie said, increasingly agitated. Vivian was bad about walking off on her own, finding secret hiding places. Even when she went the distance to visit the Burdeshaw sisters who lived near Lee, she went alone, and she usually did not tell anyone of her plans.

"Well," Carol started, "I can't go to sleep 'til I know she's all right." She crossed her arms and sat back in her chair. Carol looked at Henry questioningly. He shrugged his shoulders.

"I don't know where Lee lives, either ma'am. I think if we just be patient, she'll come home soon, Miz Carol."

"Lord! Did you see what he put my baby through? He insulted this whole family. I'm afraid he's convincing my poor child not to believe what her own eyes done told her. You know she's half outta her mind when it comes to that yellow son-of-a...."

"Yeah, I reckon he got her going to and fro, Ms. Carol. Vivian is just gonna hafta find out for herself, though. You can talk with her when she comes home, try to see where her head is…"

"That's right, mama. I can't tell you the number of times I tried to get her to do right and leave that thug alone. Once Viv makes her mind up about something, it's hard for her to listen to logic. She's just loose, mama, like you said."

"Well, whatever. But I still need to know where she is before I can just fall asleep. What kinda mother would I be if I didn't try?"

"There's nothing you can do, Ms. Carol, 'cept wait."

"Wait? Naw. I can't handle that. I wish I knew where 'bout Lee lives. We could find out though if we headed out."

"Vivian is so trifling: She won't let nobody know nothing. I reckon we should just wait like Henry said. Madeline and Missy live near him—that's all I know. I don't even know what road it is, 'cause they're just chil'ren…"

"Which is probably best. I think y'all is looking for trouble. Women don't go wandering aimlessly, especially when nighttime be approaching."

Carol shrugged. "Did they say that girl's name was Maybelle?"

Ignoring Carol's question to underscore Vivian's poor character, Minnie responded to Henry's comment. "Vivian does. But she ain't no real woman. She's just a dippy, savage brat. Wild is all."

"Yes, Ms. Carol. Her name is Maybelle. She lives on the Raison Plantation. Her mama is Maybelline, and her grandmother is Tazra, the healer."

"Maybelle ain't the only one. Just ask Missy and Madeline…"

"Henry, you don't know where you could find Lee?"

"Not really, Ms. Carol."

"Now, how's he supposed to know, mama? Him and Lee ain't friendly. Henry don't be within six miles of the likes of Lee."

"I just figured by you being a man and all that you maybe would have some idea of where to look, that's all," she challenged subtlety.

"All I can say is I do know a couple of the places where he lays his hat. I've seen 'em. But I'm afraid Minnie is right: I don't take the same paths Lee takes." Henry said this as a matter of fact, but he remained sitting. In truth, it was killing him to think that Vivian was off somewhere with Lee after he'd publicly shamed her. He cautioned himself not to appear overly anxious. When he noticed Carol continuing to stare at him expectantly, he added, "I can go and look for her, if that'll stop y'all worrying some."

"You find her, Henry," Carol cried, "you find my baby!" He stood resignedly. Minnie sucked her teeth.

"I will, Ms. Carol. Promise I will. Everything's gonna be fine. Y'all get some rest. It's been a long day, and it's only getting later." He looked at Minnie. "It's all right. She's with her man. They are probably somewhere making up together. Maybe they need this time alone . . . but I'll find her." He kissed Minnie on her forehead and left quickly. Minnie secretly hoped they *were* somewhere making up so everyone could stop paying so much attention to "poor Vivian." She sulked as Henry lifted from his kiss.

Henry was ten times more apprehensive than he revealed. He didn't trust Lee for one minute. He didn't like the way Lee had yanked Vivian out of the church in the first place. Henry wasn't at all surprised at Maybelle's predicament—he was just stunned that she advertised it in church on the day of Lee's engagement celebration. Henry deliberated on how Vivian appeared so disheartened these days and about how he had ignored her wounds. He felt sick. Finding her was imperative. He charged himself for letting her down in the church by not doing anything. "I messed up...and I'm supposed to be a man," Henry scolded himself, "Lee's not no man, but I am. For Minnie's sake," he rationalized, "I should've done something at that church. She told me she was drowning...and I let him take her under. Damn!"

He walked aimlessly for about two hours, searching here and there, yet no one seemed willing or able to help him find Lee. After a while, his feet were saturated in his own sweat, his leg muscles a mass of cramps. Henry checked in the gambling alleys, stores, and bars. He finally got his success when he went to a nightspot and saw Hamilton Briggs, a man he had seen with Lee before. Henry told him that he owed Lee money but wasn't going to look for him all night to give it to him. Hamilton quickly told him where Lee lived. As it turned out, Henry was only a half of a mile away from Lee's house by that time. He walked briskly to the address. Approximately seventy yards away from Lee's address, several men were drinking and shooting dice by the light of a lantern. They saw Henry and ignored him, suspecting that he was a salesman or something, since he was still wearing his church clothing.

Henry knew it was going to be awkward showing up at Lee's house, but more importantly, he knew he had to see Vivian and assure her safety. As he approached the house, his veins pounded fiery blood that poured from his arteries like hot lava. His heart churned like molten bricks in his chest. He could see a candle burning in the front room. The bright moon lit everything else. Henry was walking scrupulously up the porch incline to the front door when he heard a whimper. He jumped.

"Who is that?" He asked. There was no answer, and he didn't hear anything else. He searched in the darkness for a puppy, perhaps. Henry saw a form crouched in a ball in the corner of the porch. His heart raced. "Vivian?" There was silence. He lurched closer to touch the heaving figure and recognized Vivian's dress. Henry squatted down next to the lump of the body and lifted the face of it.

"My God!" Henry gasped. One of Vivian's eyes was shut and swollen. There was a knot on her forehead. Vivian was clutching her side in pain. "Where is he?" Henry asked intolerantly, balling his fists. He stood erect, moving toward the screen door to enter the house.

"He's not here, Henry. He's out drunk. You'd better leave." He gulped.

"Leave you out here on the porch? Vivian," he whispered, "you know I can't do that." Henry squeezed his eyes closed tightly for a moment and gritted his teeth. "Whatchu doing out here like this, Vivian? Did Lee do this to you?"

"Me? What are *you* doing here?"

"I've been looking for you...for hours. Ms. Carol sent me to check on you."

"I know I shouldn't be on the porch so late. But I had to come out here on account of I can't stay in there by myself." She tried to stand as she spoke, but her legs wouldn't allow it. He rushed back over and kneeled beside her.

"Of course you can't." He couldn't look at her. She couldn't look at him. He stole painful glances at her from time to time. "You're coming with me. I'm gonna take you home to your mama. Ms. Carol is worried to death about you."

"No! Vivian almost yelled, contorting with pain because of a bruised rib. "I'm not about to let my mama and sisters see me like this. I reckon I'll stay here. I'm all right. Lee's just drunk. He's not going to hit me anymore."

"What?"

"It's all right, Henry, really. He . . . we had an argument, and. . . ."

"Viv, stop that ridiculous talk. Do you understand what happened today? Lee...your so-called *boyfriend* done beat you half dead." Henry had to hold himself from appearing angry. He did not want to add to her injuries by chastising her, but he was furious with her for a fleeting moment. Why would she let Lee do that to her and then stay at his house? "Girl, you must be mad to be hanging around his house after what he did—like hell if you ain't coming with me!"

"You can't *make* me go home," she screamed. He looked around to see if anyone heard her yell. She started crying. "They'll think I'm stupid," she asserted, convincing herself of the importance to hide the domestic violence. I don't want my mom to see me like this!"

Henry simply didn't understand. He spit in an attempt to get the acidic taste out of his mouth. "I would never call you stupid, but you really are crazy. You should let your mom see you even if you had to crawl home. You can't be too smart to stay somewhere after somebody just whipped your ass."

"Shut up!" She screamed. "Please shut the hell up! You have no right to judge me! I'm not having this conversation with you!"

"Quiet down, girl," he said rather loudly. "You think I came all this way just to see you and not do nothing but leave you in danger?"

She quieted her voice but continued to plead with him. "Just leave, Henry. I'm begging you. Lee will be back any minute."

"Leave you with *him*? Sweetheart, you don't know nothing about me, I reckon. That's what Lee did-he left you like this." Henry switched from his kneeling position to sitting next to her, stretching his legs out in front of him. He tried to pass off the air of being relaxed, but his heart was pounding so hard in his chest that he felt like his whole body might blow up and crumble into a million pieces. "I'm not going nowhere." He had a brief flashback of being in the military with bullets flying over his head. There were so many hurt soldiers on both sides. He recalled wanting to save anyone. No one should have been left behind. His commander forced him to leave the dead bodies behind. Maybe some weren't dead! He thought he should at least try to save them, or at least one person…one of the friends he'd made. Just leave?

"I didn't ask you to come!" Vivian was out of control, Henry realized, and yet she somehow thought she was wise enough to make decisions. She was not listening to him. He had to figure out how to make her listen and not allow her to handle him.

"Yeah, whatever you say, baby," he said more soothingly, patronizing her all the same. "I know you ain't thinking clearly. If I could let you know how much your mama just wanna see you…she loves you, darling. She would never blame you for getting caught up…you didn't know!"

"Don't you understand anything? They wouldn't…they'd never forgive Lee if they saw me now. My mother already thinks he's no good."

They accidentally caught each other's eyes. "I feel like crying, Vivian. Look at you all bruised up. You can't even open your other eye, can you?" She looked down in humiliation. He lifted her face again with his index finger. "You're beautiful to me, no matter what he did." Lightly, he touched her bruised cheek with the backside of his hand. She attempted a small smile.

Henry became very conscious of the mellow smell of fresh strawberries emanating from her essence. He stood. "Then you'll go to Ms. Esther's home to get cleaned up before you face your mama—but like hell if I leave you here."

Vivian knew Ms. Esther would help her, and she also knew she was in bad shape. Either she could stay on the porch arguing with Henry and risk Lee seeing him, or she could submit to his reasonable request. "Fine, Henry," she said, too proud to acknowledge she needed help. Of all the times Lee had beaten her, this one was the most debilitating. Henry pulled her to her feet by her arms. She winced in pain. He saw that her dress was torn badly, and there was blood on it.

"My God, Vivian! What the . . . ?" Henry let her arms go to touch her dress, but he had to catch her from falling back down. He cursed silently, lifted her effortlessly and tossed her over his shoulder. Vivian wanted to speak. She wanted to explain things to Henry about the way things were with Lee. She wanted to tell him how nice Lee really was, but she was so tired and emotionally spent. Vivian took a deep breath of relief, and then she passed out for a few minutes, feeling safe in her unconsciousness as long as he supported her with the weight of his concern. Henry was not aware that she drifted in and out of consciousness.

Henry hoped to God he didn't see Lee as he made his way down the now deserted road with Vivian. He knew he would have no problem breaking Lee's neck if he tried to stop him from taking her. He wanted to confront Lee, but more than that, he wanted to get Vivian away from there as quickly as possible. How could Lee think he could get away with beating a female so terribly? Henry was sweating by the time they came to Johnson Road. It would be another quarter mile before they would reach Johnson Lane, and Ms. Esther's house was near the corner. While lost in thought, Henry almost missed the sound of a disturbing commotion somewhere near the edge of Johnson Road. Just in time, he caught the view of a near lynching, causing him to dip back into the shadows. His sudden move brought awareness to Vivian. He let her slide off his shoulder to a sitting position. She felt much better.

"What's happening, Henry?" He didn't know, but multiple flashlights were pointing to a Black man on the ground.

A horseman said, "We hear you were making trouble at 2nd Century Nigger Baptist Church this morning. Well, we don't take too kindly to Negroes moving here, spiteful troublemakers." One of the men started swinging a bullwhip at the sprawling man on the ground.

"I ain't done nothing at no church, boss, I swear!" he pleaded.

"Henry, oh, God!" Henry slapped his hand over Vivian's mouth.

"Not a word," he whispered. Half of him wanted to rush out and help the brother, and the other half wanted to stay hidden. Henry felt castrated because he knew if he did nothing, the Black man was surely going to be lynched. And just like that, he was in the war again--World War One reincarnated to the fight in his own country. If he got involved, he would be putting Vivian's life in danger, yet he would regret not helping a fellow soldier for the rest of his life if the man died while Henry was fifty feet away. Without thinking, Henry stepped out of the shadows. Before the men could see him, Vivian leaped forward and threw her arms around his ankles. "Stay back," he warned her in a hoarse whisper. Reluctantly, she released him. She instinctively knew they were going to kill the Black man, then, they would kill Henry, and probably kill her, too. In a flash, the tables turned: The man with the bullwhip got two good licks in before the Black man squirmed away.

"Get back here, nigger." The running Black man did not look back as he sprinted like a lightning bolt down the road. Instead of chasing him, the Caucasian men laughed. They were drinking whiskey and causing mischief, Henry noted. The Black man had not been at the church that morning. There was the possibility that if Henry made a sound, he would be noticed, and they would profess they thought *he* was a trouble making one. He realized it was senseless to place Vivian in danger. They would have to retreat the way they came if they could do so safely. Henry was thankful Vivian was intelligent enough to hold her breath and remain stark still on this occasion, because her day-to-day conflict resolution skills were remarkably skewed, he observed. He would give his life, but Vivian's life was to be protected. The men were not paying attention to Henry and Vivian in the shadows. Once that crystallized, he silently backed away, grabbing Vivian's hand. They would have to walk in the opposite direction, and run if they were discovered.

Henry liked the fact that Vivian behaved like a trooper through it all. He watched her limp without complaining as they vanished back up the road. Once they were far enough away, Henry stopped. "Wait, girl."

"We can't wait!" Without stopping, she grunted with every step. Henry shook his head in pity and easily swooped her up again.

"You're hurt, Vivian. We can move faster if I carry you some."

"We wouldn't have to move fast if it wasn't for what they were doing to that man."

"Don't worry none. Our suffering is for a divine purpose," Henry said, copying the words spoken a few weeks ago by Wali Eli. "If I had a wagon, I would put you in it, but since I don't, I reckon I'll still carry you as far as I can." Once she was back over his shoulder, she realized she had used every ounce of energy she had and was glad to have Henry's help.

The closer he came to the main road, the clearer he heard the distant sound of drums beating against the night. He knew the drummers had to belong to a group of African protesters called the Marooners. Since the explosion of the Ku Klux Klan in Escambia County, a growing number of Black men formed a coalition which had the purpose of reminding the ex-slaves of their rich history, and they used drums to communicate awareness. The Ku Klux Klan was a cloak-and-dagger terrorist association that originated in Pulaski, Tennessee during the period of Reconstruction following the American Civil War. It was rumored that the Klan was responsible for some gruesome crimes against Black people.

There was an accelerated exigency in the beat that stirred a dread in Henry. He heard the cry, "Allah-U-Akbar" encoded with the calculated pattering of the drums. Another Black man had been found dead, lynched up on a tree somewhere between Century and Pensacola. He squeezed Vivian's fingers together, but she didn't flinch. People were on edge all over the country. Riots that involved mass murder were the order of the day in America. Henry's heart ached when he considered the recent massacre of a Black community in Tulsa, Oklahoma less than one year ago, and the Red Summer of 1919 just before that.

"It's not enough that the pale-faced man is killing our people left and right. Seems we's starting in on each other. This crap is too much. Hang in there, Viv, because I gotta hang in there, too. I gotta be a Black man that makes it outta here without losing my dignity. I wanna be able to work where I please and for who I please. I don't wanna shine nobody's shoes or fix no other man's bath water. I wanna work side by side with 'em if my skills be the same.

"I just don't see why we can't stick together. Them dogs was able to get us in Tulsa. We need unity," he said, repeating Wali Eli again. "I understand disagreements, but why would a man hit his own woman? That's how you make it so others can do terrible things--on account of us showing we don't care. Might as well be siding with the Klan. This place is liable to be another Tulsa the way these whip crackers carry on."

The Tulsa, Oklahoma riot of 1921 was ghastly. Henry discussed it privately with his cousin, Rufus so that he would not appear militant. A vicious gang of over 10,000 Caucasians assaulted the Black division of the city, annihilating more than thirty-five square blocks, and killing more than 300 people. The Caucasians had machine guns! The mob used at least eight airplanes in their efforts to obtain local information that could prove beneficial in their attack. It was reported that some of the planes were used as bombing tools during the riot.

This frightened Henry more than he wanted to say. To Rufus, he only hinted the riot was one reason he wanted to move north. The brutal, senseless attack on a people because of the color of their skin sickened him. Henry wanted to fade inside the night, and simply listen to the splattering of the drums as confirmation that there was *some* unity and love between Black people. He found comfort when he thought about God's hand in all of this. It was hard for Henry to shake off a puzzling air of blessedness permeating Vivian's suffering. Although he hated what Lee did, he was motivated that he was the one to find her, and now, he was protecting her from a storm. There was no way he would have allowed the Caucasian men on Johnson Road to harm her. No one would harm her, he vowed.

The drums sounded again, startling Henry. The reality of the lynching era sank into his soul. As he had told Rufus, the foremost reason for his decision to leave Florida was fear of the Caucasian led mobs and just the general disdain that existed for Black people in Florida and throughout the South.

"That's how come I'm leaving, Viv. I don't want nobody to lynch *me* 'cause I walk outta these thin boundaries to the other side of the railroad tracks. Lynch me 'cause some conniving woman looking at me, and mad on account of me ain't interested. I tell you; an honest man can get set up down here. If I stay too much longer, I won't last, darling," he continued, as though Vivian had asked him these things. "Ever since I can remember, I wanted outta here. Well, this weekend will be my chance...might be the only chance I'm gonna have since it took this long at all!" Ignoring the cramping of his muscles, Henry carried her on his shoulders for the two miles back to the Raison Plantation. He stopped to rest a few times; whenever he started again, he merely shifted her to the other shoulder to overcome being overwrought with fatigue.

"It's okay, my precious darling. It's okay," he kept saying. Vivian stirred, then passed out, then stirred again multiple times before they made it to Henry's cabin at 10:30 p.m. He carried her inside and to his bunk, where he deposited her gently. By the time she opened her eyes, fully aware again, he already had a candle lit.

"Where are we?"

Without answering, he dropped his head in shame, making her know they were in his cabin on the Raison Plantation. Vivian preferred his cabin over home, but she thought he would have dropped her off at Tazra's cabin, which would have been more appropriate.

"For some reason, I feel like Tazra lives nearby." They both knew he was out of order.

"Vivian, I don't think you know who Tazra is."

"I do, too. She's the healer. I thought you might take me there if we're on the Raison Plantation."

"Tazra is Maybelle's grandmother. They live together, along with Maybelle's mama. I couldn't---that's why you're here, Vivian.

"You knew about Maybelle and Lee all along?"

He shook his head. "Of course not. You want some water?" She accepted a large jug from him and chugged the water nonstop. "I'm sorry for bringing you here." He kept his head lowered. "I just needed a chance and a place to think." Vivian let out a huge breath of satisfaction after finishing the water. He watched her for a moment when she didn't respond, then he left the cabin without saying anything. A feeling of coziness swept over her in the potency of his room. An open polished trunk revealed his carefully folded clothes. His soldier uniform was folded snugly inside in plain view. His room was larger than the one she shared with her sisters, yet there were no signs of any other occupants. On a wide tin shelf there were rows and rows of bottles and jugs filled with liquids she couldn't identify. Vivian heard some bustling about outside the thick, straw-built door. She sat up on the cot, wanting to protest her strength to him.

Henry came back shortly with more water and several damp rags. He noticed Vivian trying to exhibit her strength, but he was unimpressed due to what he deemed her exhibition of weakness in the matter with Lee. "Vivian, I want to be the one to help you get cleaned up. If I send you to one of the house mothers, I'm just gonna worry about you and hang around and wait outside."

"Wait outside? You don't have to wait at all."

"I can't leave you after what happened to you."

"I'm not your responsibility, Henry."

"I'm troubled, Vivian. Ain't nothing else going on tonight for me except to see for myself that you're safe. Nothing else fits well with my soul. It took a lot for me to say that...you know. Be honest with you, so I hope you understand."

"Thank you for being honest, Henry. I can be honest, too." She sucked in her breath, feeling vulnerable. "I think you are just like the others because you do think I'm stupid."

"Fair enough. I won't lie to you. I'm disappointed. But I'm here to help you, no matter what."

She continued. "I also admit I don't want anyone else involved, and I'm ashamed that you have to see me like this."

"Don't be ashamed in front of me. When I look at you, what I see ain't from judging eyes or for my purpose. It's for yours. If I didn't see you, I couldn't help you, and you ain't got nobody's help but mine right now." Henry crossed his arms over his chest as though he thought she would challenge him. "Your turn," he added. She smiled up at him.

"My turn again? I have already said my piece. I don't want anyone to see me like this." She didn't care what he thought or anything about his advice. There was no way she could let Minnie or Carol see what Lee had done.

"I'll help you get cleaned up back fresh and pretty like you were before Lee got his hands on you. If you want to protect Lee, then I won't be the one to tell Ms. Carol about it, either." She decided not to comment on his sarcasm. He motioned toward her dress. "I hope you know that odds are that dress is ruined. But I can take it to the dress shop for you and see if them women can get it all fixed back up again."

"That's right kind of you, Henry, but I know how to make that dress over myself."

"My, my, my. I sure wasn't trying to…"

"It's alright."

"No, it's not. I haven't been seeing you for who you are. I keep putting on like you don't amount to nothing. That's why I… but I ain't never took time to get to know you, and what you can do. It's just that…well, you looked so pretty at church today in that dress that I…I guess…"

"Thank you, Henry." She liked the fact that he was blushing. It made her feel he really meant it when he said she was pretty.

"Shame on me for assuming you couldn't sew that dress back. Anyway, I got some clothes you can wear…let me find something in a minute…won't be in here, though, I gotta check with my family." She smiled inwardly that she'd surprised Henry with her miniature sewing talent. She would need Minnie, or most likely Carol to help her with such a complicated project of repairing a garment that was ripped from the middle, but that was none of Henry's business.

"Like you told *me*; there's no need for shame, Henry. Most girls wouldn't know how to fix that dress, you know."

"I can try to get some of them stains outta it, though. You give me that dress before the blood dries on it and soaks through any more than what it already has. I reckon you don't have too many dresses like that. It looks like it cost a fortune to make." He groaned in disgust. "You chose to be at your finest for Lee today."

He held the damp cloth up and waited. He enjoyed stubbornly showering Vivian with jealousy about her inclination to please Lee, but Vivian perceived that Henry was judging her. She felt a bit uneasy as she started on the first few buttons down the front of her dress. Even though she was relieved now that she'd chosen her ruffled shoulder to ankle petticoat as well as a laced, full-length slip with the itchy trim, it was something about the process of unbuttoning that made her shy. She was moving at a snail's pace, and she was unmistakably visibly rigid. Henry laughed. "Girl, gimme that dress. I'm not your man, I'm your doctor tonight."

He walked over to her, put the washcloth in the pail and touched her hand over the next button. "Let me..."

He bent over to help her. "Henry." Her face burned every time his hands that were so careful not to touch her offhandedly slipped and touched her. What did he think he was doing? His declaration which was supposed to signify emotional distance was lost in interpretation and vibrations. This is because the instant his words were sounded, his next thought--that he dared not utter-- was that he *wanted* to be her man. Thus, his voice, his trembling, and the spirit emanating from his aura, communicated his ardent desire to Vivian. Because of this, it was hard to detect if he was being brotherly and if she was getting tense for no reason. She became numb in every place where his hands brushed. He ignored her call of his name, continuing cautiously with his chore. Vivian watched his eyes as he gently pulled the soiled dress away from her shoulders.

"I promise I won't eat you." Her uneasiness subsided since he was gentle enough to add humor. Henry's mouth fell open when he saw the many cuts and bruises on her arms and neck that her outer garment had hidden from him. He sat next to her with a defeated gasp and tightened his jaw. He envisaged what weapon Lee used to hammer her up so badly all the way down to her wrists. He looked over and noticed there was a bruise the size of a quarter under her right ear. Henry imagined the pain she must have been in from that sore spot alone rubbing against his back when he'd carried her for over two miles. A flash of serving in the war crept back into his consciousness. He could not help everyone, even as fellow soldiers were wounded. Helplessness was the worst feeling for Henry. He turned angrily toward the flat timber plank wall and punched it with great force. Startled, she gazed at him with restlessness in her eyes.

Rubbing his aching knuckles, he was captured by the breeze of her anxiety swishing past his heart when she recoiled. He softened. "Sweetheart, I didn't mean to make you jump." Then, he narrowed his eyes, peering at her. "But why did you? Have I ever done anything to make you think you can't trust me?"

"Let me think, Henry. Maybe because you just hit a wall for no reason." She exhaled. "I didn't even know that I jumped." Henry could only slowly come to terms with how fragile her experience had been.

"I'm sorry. It's just that I'm upset that that two-bit punk did this to you. He don't have no right..." He choked on his words. She was so priceless! How could Lee wound such a first-class jewel like this? "If you was mine, I would cherish you, honey." She inhaled deeply. The uneasiness washed over her again with his closeness.

"Henry..." He took the cloth again and dabbed at her bruised arms. When he dabbed her swollen eye, she cringed.

"Take it easy, doll, I got you," he reached over and kissed her eye softly, then he tried to dab it again, but she still flinched. "Aw, Vivian! Look at what he did to you!" Vivian pretended that his kiss was innocent. She couldn't face that he had brushed her with his lips. His nearness was making her head spin.

"I know, Henry. Quit saying it over and over. I know what he did. I was there, remember?"

"Lean up on this pillow." He dipped the rag in the water again. "He don't deserve you..."

"Don't say that. I'm nothing for anyone to have to go and deserve." Although she didn't want to hear anything negative about Lee, she readily met his direction. After he put a straw pillow under her head, he dabbed her injured body that he could reach without embarrassing her by having her remove anything else. Her long petticoat made it difficult to measure the extent of the damage, but he noticed signs that made it obvious that Lee hadn't just slapped her around--he had stomped her. Why else would dirt in the shape of a shoe be on several parts of her gown, and indentations of shoe prints be on her petticoat? Vivian stayed contorted in pain. Clearly, Henry had underestimated Lee's audacity. Damn! He thought. He needed to take her to Tazra for help. He could only hope there was no internal bleeding. With the wetted cloth, he rubbed peanut oil from one of the jars Vivian had noticed earlier over some of the bruised areas.

The love he felt for her was overwhelming. It was hard for him to focus on doing what was best. Henry found himself taking several deep breaths, suppressing his feelings, and answering to reason. He shook his head. What good was peanut oil? He was only fooling himself. She needed a real doctor or someone who knew what they were doing, not someone who wanted to play doctor as an excuse to be near her. "We hafta go see Mother Tazra, Vivian." She didn't say anything. "I'm selfish to try to keep you here. This ain't protecting you."

"I just want it all to disappear, and seeing Maybelle would make the pain increase."

"Girl, your mama sent me out after you because she trusted that I would get you safe. Your emotions--I can't do nothing about that, but if I'm a man then I hafta make sure your life is not in danger."

"I'm okay..."

"But Lee stomped you, didn't he?" A visual image of Lee kicking Vivian flashed in Henry's mind, causing him to become nauseated. He doubled over for a minute until the feeling subsided. Vivian saw him double over in agony.

"Are you okay, Henry?" Composing himself, he lifted himself and resignedly went over to the far wall where he got a lantern and a blanket that was folded on a bottom shelf.

"I see you don't know how precious you are, baby," he said as he extended his hand out to her. She didn't know what to do. His very words covered her with goose bumps. "I wish I could show you how precious you really are."

"You're so silly, boy." She tried to joke and hoped it worked to downgrade his openly expressed sentiment. She *had* to joke if she were going to accept his hand. Gently, he pulled her to her feet and wrapped the blanket around her.

"Let's go, baby." He wasn't giving her a choice. She really did prefer disappearing, running away to a far-off land as opposed to letting Maybelle know that Lee had beaten her. As though Henry could read her mind, he added, "I'll keep you in the shadows. I'm just gonna tap on their door and ask Tazra to come out. That's how it's done." When they stepped outside, Henry reached over to lift her in his arms, but she resisted.

"I'm strong enough to walk."

"Alright." Still, he kept her close with his arm draped over her shoulder. Minutes later, they were standing on the side of Tazra's cabin where there was no window. True to his word, Henry went to the door by himself. The tap tap, wait, and tap tap tap was the rescue code that the Black citizens used whenever they needed healing. Tazra woke up immediately and automatically grabbed her medicine bag which was always right next to her. No one else in the cabin moved since the routine was familiar. Tazra loved being needed and respected by everyone. There was always a new face, always a different situation. She knew Henry, but the last time he was there for help was when he was barely ten years old after his mother had embedded his backside with rusty nails. Tazra allowed Henry to lead her to his patient.

"Ms. Tazra, this young lady don't want her mama to know she went horse riding without permission. She only agreed to come here if it could be kept a secret."

"What happened to her?"

"She got trampled by a horse." Tazra held the lamp up to see Vivian's face.

"You belong to Carol Anne...that's your mama?" Vivian nodded. "Then that means you and my Maybelle are sisters." Confused, Vivian stopped nodding her head.

"You might have her mixed up with someone else, Ms. Tazra."

"That sure was a big horse, wasn't he?" Tazra asked as she examined Vivian's ribs.

"Yes, ma'am," Henry answered for Vivian, knowing she did not want to speak. "I was using peanut oil on these bruises, but I don't know if it was helpful."

"Did the peanut oil burn you, gal?" Vivian shook her head. Referring to Henry, Tazra asked her, "How did *this* horse find you after the other one trampled you?"

"Ms. Tazra..." Henry tried to respond for Vivian again, but Tazra cut him off.

"Even if the peanut oil starts to sting, keep using it. It'll keep the blood circulating. You done good, Henry."

Tazra stared at him until he dropped his head. Then she turned back to Vivian. "Gal, I'd take a switch to you if you told me he's the one who did this to you."

"It was a horse!" Vivian exclaimed. Tazra finished up quietly.

Hushing Vivian, Henry answered, "No, ma'am. I would never hurt her and then bring her to you."

Tazra stared at him up and down again. She concluded that she didn't believe Henry was the abuser. "She'll live. Just need to stay away from horse pastures." Henry slipped a few coins into Tazra's open palm. A look of satisfaction swept across Tazra's face once she counted the money. "Do you need a pallet for her?"

"No, ma'am. I'm taking her on home." Henry paused for a moment to see if Tazra would object. Finally, he grabbed Vivian's hand and led her away. Once they turned slightly, and she realized the ordeal with Tazra was over, Vivian snatched her hand back. Tazra stayed outside and watched them make it through the dark passageway next to her cabin.

Once they were out of sight, Vivian said, "She didn't believe your ridiculous horse story."

"It doesn't matter. She won't talk. She told me all I needed to know. My peanut oil is magic," he said with a grin. "Can I do that for you?"

"No," she replied quickly. "And you told her you were taking me home, but you're not doing that either, are you?" Henry took her hand again. A strange, but warm feeling washed over her, but she would not divulge that she felt safe with him. He led her back to his cabin in silence.

"Stay here. I'm gonna find you something decent to wear." He was gone in a flash. Vivian sat back down on the cot. She didn't know what to do. Something had happened between them where he had asserted himself into a position of authority, but it felt different from Lee's authority. A wave of anxiety filled her insides. What would she do whenever he brought the clothes back? Vivian checked the strength of her arms by stretching them in front of her. She had used them to guard herself from Lee's flying fists and feet. She was filled with emotional fatigue and muscle weakness. What she really wanted was to succumb to her foggy, sleepy head. It was nearing midnight, and she hadn't had a full night's sleep in days. Henry came back with a ghastly looking dress and on the other arm, a pair of men's trousers. He held up the dress as though it would be her first choice.

"I'm not wearing that."

Henry smiled. "You don't hafta. Once I saturate those bruises with the peanut oil, you can choose which one you want."

"Didn't you hear me? I hate the way that peanut oil smells, so, no." She pouted. Henry put the clothes down and picked up the peanut oil. On the cot, Vivian sat fidgeting, twiddling her thumbs. Henry approached her with the peanut oil despite her indecision.

"Now, you don't want those bruises to turn ugly and leave marks, do you?" Leering at her reddish marred arms, she shook her head. "Besides, I think it's best that you let me cover up that fresh smell of natural strawberries you got going on." He picked up a sore arm and started gently. "There we go," he said tenderly, pushing her backward. "You can relax. You ain't in a cabin with some wild dog."

"Henry…"

"I see you like to say my name." He grunted in a miniature laugh. "Say it again. You make my name sound…important." She kept quiet, wishing she knew how to respond. He could feel her tense up whenever he pressed a sore area too much. It was easier to do small sections. Henry started on her other arm, trying not to gawk at the bruises. None of it made sense to him. What could she have done to deserve a beating that left her mangled?

"I would go crazy if something happened to you." The oil felt warm under his careful massage. Some of the bruises soon were relieved of the burning pressure, but the pressure of his verbal caress continued to thicken. "You know, there's a way a man should treat a woman. Seems to me Lee ain't fit to have you."

Vivian finally relaxed, not minding the muggy air over her head, or his constant speech. Subsequently, she closed her eyes. Henry calculated that Minnie and Carol had retired for the night with hopes that Vivian was safe. He would tell them what happened in the morning, yet he knew it was going to be difficult to explain to Minnie that Vivian had been on his cot for even a moment, although he had already decided in his mind that they'd have to remain together until just before daybreak. Next, he rationalized to himself that he certainly couldn't get on the tarnished floor. Soon, the darkness under Vivian's lids became dimmer. It was the shadow of Henry's head coming down next to her head that added the overcast. Without contemplating any longer, he lowered himself next to her and took her loosely in his arms, boldly responding to the miracle he didn't think was possible.

"Henry..." She wanted to kick herself for calling out his name again.

"Am I hurting you?"

"No...but my ribs are sore."

"But your arms feel better, right?" He was careful that only their upper torsos touched slightly, except his arms that held her determinedly. "It's time for us both to get a li'l rest." He held his breath for a few seconds. "Do you want me to get on the dirty floor?" He rocked her gently. "What about that tiny chair? Should I sleep there? Or do you want me to leave altogether, maybe go build me a treehouse to sleep in?" He was funny, she thought. She became carefree even more, letting her head rest naturally on his chest.

"I don't know..." She confessed to herself that this was exactly what she wanted. She had daydreamed about him defending her, holding her, and saying soft things to her. Henry was surprised at himself for embracing her. He wished Lee could see him right now with her, mending her after his brutality.

Then Henry felt cheated. The one he had fallen in love with by accident belonged to another man who sullied and brutalized her. She was not letting him hold her because she liked him; he was merely a substitute for challenging times. Henry believed Lee knew he cared about Vivian--in fact, Lee knew before he did, Henry thought. He blurted, "Your boyfriend thinks he can go around beating you up?"

"It's not the way it seems..."

"He mutilated you like a coyote would snatch the life outta a puppy. That's your man?" The stance appeared very personal to Henry, so that it became an assault on him rather than simply on Vivian.

"That's what you think? I'm a little dog?" Vivian said, trying to change the subject.

"I can't let 'im get away with this, Vivian." He loosened her and bowed his head in his hands for a second. Then sharply, he looked at her. "Has he ever hit you before?" She remained silent, causing his fury to surmount again. "I want an answer!" He demanded thunderously. She involuntarily cowered once more. Henry retreated, reminding himself not to allow his emotions to continue to manifest with such agitation. This was a wounded dove that rested beside him, and he had to remember that while she appeared normal, Lee had sliced her up in places he could never see with the naked eye. Yelling and cursing was undoubtedly what Lee gave her, and he shouldn't behave in the same fashion. He tried to control his aggravation, but his voice remained strained, and she could feel marginal shuddering. She wished he would drop the subject. He searched her face. "He *has*! Hasn't he?" Vivian nodded her head, refusing to look at him.

"Never like this, though, Henry."

"I'll be damned." His shudder was unmistakable now.

"Henry, I don't intend to go over this with you. This stuff is private for me. My life is no open book whereas you're supposed to know *any* of this." At that moment, he thought he could kill Lee with his bare hands had he walked through the door. Henry cursed himself for not doing something sooner. He reflected on all the days Vivian had been withdrawn, and how those days went by without any vocal concern from anyone. Henry felt personally responsible since he seemed to be the only person who suspected something was wrong, yet he'd said and done nothing. It sickened him now to think that he neglected to help her because he had been so afraid that someone might detect his undercover longing for her. Hastily, he pushed those suggestions away. He had done a terrific job suppressing that longing, and he felt he needed to continue doing that. Somehow, he had to get her home fast, but he couldn't see how that was possible, and Lee was to blame.

"He ain't right. I'll bet don't nobody know nothing about this mess."

"It's not what you think."

"You don't know *what* I think, princess."

Henry reached over to the small table near the cot and blew out the candle. Then he sat up briefly to take his overcoat off in the privacy of the dark, but he dared not remove his shirt and necktie, as confining as they were. His body strained, he finally loosened his tie and unbuttoned his shirt at the cuffs. To hell with Lee. He'd have to figure things out later, but one thing was certain: Now that he'd shown such tenacity in getting on the cot at all, Minnie would only find out about this partaking if Vivian told her. Henry offered his overcoat to her since he did not have a quilt. That and his tattered blanket would have to do, if he could find the words to tell her that her elbow was pinning it. For now, all words were stuck in his mind and throat.

Vivian was immobilized where she was, one forearm under her head, legs crossed at the ankle, facing Henry. He remained perfectly still in an attempt to ease the tension belonging to both of them away. How satisfied he was just to know she was safe and to have her so close to him! He didn't want to think about tomorrow, he wanted to simply bask in the moment of her nearness. He wanted her next to him, and he said it to himself now, instead of claiming falsely that there was no other place he could've taken her.

In the dark, in the quiet, he could hold her, and she would have to deal with him. Whatever Vivian did, he vowed to make sure if he had to face his feelings, she would have to face hers. If it was Lee she truly loved, he would challenge her. Henry relied on holding her in silence, empowering her heartbeat to speak to him. By the time of the rising sun, he hoped their hearts would beat as one. He held her tighter against his chest. Vivian thought she should say *something* more to make light of the situation. There was an unmistakable, striking firmness about his actions. "I can't wait until this stupid bruise clears up."

"You reckon it's just one bruise?"

Ignoring his sarcasm again, she said, "I'm not going to let them see me like this. Now, I'm not asking to stay here, but I'm not going home…they'll laugh at me and say that they told me so . . .I can't stay here. I shouldn't be here, Henry. It was a mistake to leave Lee's house because I can assure you, he wasn't going to hit me anymore…" Henry hushed her by putting his finger to her mouth.

Startled, she stopped in mid-sentence. Vivian remembered that Sunday afternoon when Lee had struck her for the first time. She remembered how she only *thought* she had control over the circumstances, but in reality, Lee was in total control and ready to manipulate her. A flash of fear spread across her as she suddenly considered the vulnerability of her current situation. Although she wanted to be right where she was in Henry's strapping arms, she didn't want the feeling of powerlessness with the experience.

With a deliberate downward motion, he removed his finger. He wanted the two of them to fall asleep together in peace, and he did not want their last thoughts to be about her leaving him.

"I don't see how you can lie there and defend 'im, if he would do that to you, sweetheart. You plan on going back o'er to Lee's place after all that?" He asked gruffly. "That's whatchu trying to tell me?" He regretted the question as soon as it came out. He wished he had said, "I love you," instead. Then he accepted he was being careless.

"I'm in the middle of a fight with Lee that has to be finished whether you think I'm stupid or not for what I got myself into."

"No, Vivian. You're wrong. I think the world of you. But I can't let you go back o'er there with Lee."

She released an abrupt, counterfeit laugh. "Can't be too much more he could do."

"That's not it…"

"All I'm saying is I have to face Lee sooner or later. He's my boyfriend." Henry shook his head in denial.

"Not anymore, he ain't. I don't want you with 'im, Vivian. Not after this, unless you wanna get me or him killed."

She gasped. "It wasn't my idea to involve you, and I certainly don't want you to get hurt or bothered by something that's not your fault."

"I didn't know what he did would bother me so much, either."

"You can't treat me like I need somebody to control my life and make decisions for me. People must make their own mistakes—isn't that how we grow? Just on account of you helping me doesn't mean growth for me—I'm the one who has to grow myself and see what there is to see—if there's anything to see!" Her voice was raised. He didn't *really* care about her. If he did, he never would've chosen Minnie when he *knew* she had a crush on him, she thought. After all of that, he now thought he could tell her who could be her boyfriend and who couldn't. Henry tried to silence her by placing his finger back over her mouth, but she talked around it. She seemed delirious. Reality was settling in. She had never stayed out all night before. She became frightened, but to cope, she took on an air of hypervigilance.

"Shhh." Henry noted that Vivian refused to stop being combative. He had to stay in control of himself and not let her continue her challenge to handle him with her provocative words.

"There's no sense in you coming *now* trying to act all like you are supposed to be so concerned—and at the same time getting all deep in my business…you probably can't wait to tell my folks about how you found me. Minnie's hero saves the day. Have you even figured out what I want? Or does that matter?" He discarded his useless finger from her chattering lips, placed it under her waist again instead in a tender hold, and found her mouth with his tongue and pressed it closed. It was only natural for him to come down then with his lips.

At first, he wasn't kissing her at all; his mouth was only crushing her mouth closed to silence her. The kiss started slowly, as he used his tongue to spy on her lips. It did occur to him at once that he was kissing his fiancé's younger sister, but he couldn't stop. He wouldn't stop. He didn't want to think about it. He was in love with her. Vivian. He was in love with Vivian. Or was he? He closed his eyes tightly at the realization of what was happening. He half expected her to push him away, but she remained stock-still. Henry tried to envision it as Minnie he held so devotedly, but it didn't work because he wanted Vivian in his dreams. He would let himself dream tonight.

"It's okay, honey," he whispered hoarsely in acknowledgment of the lifeless gesture she adopted after a few seconds. He imagined that she was contemplating squirming away. He kissed her again before finishing. "There's not gonna be no more talk about you going nowhere . . . least ways not tonight. I just wanna keep you safe. If you'll just let me hold you close to myself, I don't plan to say nothing else tonight about you going nowhere, and I'm not gonna to let you say it, either. Is that a deal?" She swallowed until her mouth was almost dry. He forced himself to detach from her so that he could stand. He walked a few feet away to hide himself in the darkness.

"Henry, maybe I *should* leave," she said faintly. "I...I don't know why I'm taking you through all of this. I guess I was too ashamed to go home, but..." He stood still, almost afraid to breathe.

"Please, Vivian. Don't."

"I don't know, Henry. I think I'd better..."

"Hold on, baby. It's not all your decision no more, sweetheart. You waited about an hour too late to say that. I'm not taking you home at this time of night, and I think you know I ain't letting you leave by yourself. It's too late, sweet girl." He heard her sigh. "I'm not trying to be harsh with you, neither, but it wouldn't be safe walking around this late with all that's going on---colored folk getting snatched up by them blood thirsty devils...that'll be the day I die because I ain't going behind no bush with no whip crackers. Either they'll kill me on the road, or they'll get dead themselves if they so much as stop to ask me for a match when I know they ain't up to no good. Then again, suppose we run into Lee? You gonna stand in the night and watch me twist his neck off his head and then toss his ass in a ditch? You *know* he would try to take you away from me, and after what he did? I can't allow that —not tonight."

"But...if I don't go home...Minnie..." She looked around and marveled at the hugeness and the neatness of his dwelling that she could see from the moonlight seeping into his window. "Minnie might come over here for you and find me here..."

"No, Vivian. Don't say that...and what the hell would Minnie be doing o'er here at this time of night? You figure that I'd allow that kinda foolishness?" She shook her head. "Vivian, you *know* it's too late. 'Sides, Minnie ain't never been in my cabin—I swear ain't nobody been in here."

"You mean you got this gigantic room and no one has been in it but you? Never mind. You don't have to explain anything to me. And what are all of those jars over on that wall?" She could ask about the jars and buy time to think.

"Mostly my mama's stuff. She thinks I got demons in me for not loving these white folk more. I guess she got this stuff in here so some fumes might cure my brain." He laughed. "Some of them jars got good stuff inside, though. Like that peanut oil I put on you."

"Oh."

"Don't think I got me some woman I keep. For a long, long time, I've been all by myself. Ain't no reason to lie to you. I wouldn't do you like that, princess. I never even thought to ask Minnie to come here—and I don't know how *you* got in here with me, but I want you here…"

"What's happening to us, Henry?" He bit his bottom lip because he didn't know how to answer her.

"All I know is that I can't let you go…I can't let you go. I might lose my mind if you try to walk out on me, now." She rolled herself nearer to the edge of the bed and sat up in preparation to stand. He took a step forward in her direction and then stopped when she stopped. "Stay with me. I ain't gonna do nothing to hurt you. I just wanna be with you, Vivian, tonight, just to hold you and care for you. Please stay here. I won't say anything. Just let my heart talk to your heart." She was totally consumed by the life he breathed into her, yet she was weakened by the life he'd just sucked out of her with his compassionate words.

Henry held his breath, moving around silently. Vivian heard the whisper of his raiment drift aloof, although her eyes refused to follow the sound. The evening they danced together sprang to life in his mind's eye. The haze was thick then as it was now, only now he felt they rode the same cloud. She waited a few seconds, and then she glanced upward. The light from the moon blazed on his rippling brawn, causing his upper body to illuminate. She looked away quickly, unprepared for the breathtaking assembly. She became so instantly weak with the yearning to experience his heart smashed against hers that it made her light-headed. His frame advanced toward the cot with the moon following him, unshadowing him.

"Vivian," he breathed, "please look at me." She rested her eyes luxuriously on his glistening face. "I ache to love you the way I do. But you love *him*. So I hide my love every time I see you."

"I'm confused right now, but I know Lee, and he would never…"

"Girl, don't you know that love ain't supposed to hurt? With me, sweetheart, I couldn't ever again hurt you." Vivian didn't know how to define what was happening inside of her. The moment had crept upon her surreptitiously, allowing her no earthly formula of resolution or guard. Vivian let herself sink into the moment, soaking in his attentiveness and husbandry.

"I can't think..." He took the last step to the cot and kneeled slowly so that one knee rested on the floor.

"Don't think."

"Henry..."

He picked up her hand and kissed it several times, with each kiss becoming ever more penetrating. "You *wanted* me to take you on this cloud, and guard you from the storm, 'cause you trust me. That's what you said to me." His affection traveled through her skin and to her soul. She marveled at his ability to produce enthusiasm within her.

"How do I know who I can trust?" She started to stand. He placed his hands on her shoulders and pressed her back into a sitting position. He grazed her throat under her chin, to her cheeks. Then he moved closer to her, bumping her side. She winced when he accidentally pressed her injury.

"I'm sorry," he soothed. "I'm not gonna hurt you. There's no way I wouldn't be so incredibly careful with you..."

"You're getting too..." she attempted.

"You can trust me, Vivian." The sensation of his heart beating with her heart was disarming to them both. He maneuvered about brazenly responding to his own foray. "Damn. I just wanna be here for you," he murmured. "Will you let me do that?"

"You *were* there for me, Henry. I was out there alone, and then you came..."

"Yeah. And if it would've taken all night, I was gonna find you 'cause I couldn't take it no more, baby. I couldn't take what he did to you and Maybelle at the church, but mainly you 'cause of what I feel for you."

"Henry, you say things that make me feel so special."

"That's on account of you *being* special. You're so sweet." He kissed the back of her hand again. "You're so soft." He kissed the back of her other hand. "Lee don't know what to do with a sweet princess like you, but I do..." He was kissing her neck. She gasped in both panic and exhilaration. Lee had never been as near to her as Henry was now. Not even close...no way. Was there more? She knew there must be, but it was inconceivable. Her rationality was escaping her.

"If he finds us here like this...I don't want anyone to think the worst, Henry."

"Ain't nobody getting in here, girl. I ain't doubtful 'bout what to do with you. I imagine myself being the one to care for you. For me, caring for you would be easier than riding a bicycle, which I learned how to do when I was six years old."

"Things are so messed up, though."

"It's all right, Vivian," he said softly, "give me your heart." Every time he moved it was deliberate and in slow motion, Vivian thought. She was floating, heeding to his unhurried, yet constant beckoning. He clasped her arms. "If you was my girl, your vines would never wither because you would always be cultivated. You know them cherries y'all was stealing that day when I met you was so delicious on account of how I prune them trees. Something that's growing up pretty needs proper treatment and love. And under my care, *you* would always be tended to and nourished."

"Do you really care about me all that much? You…you feel like you want to look after me? But, why me?"

"I've always thought of you like a special, beautiful flower that needs just the right kinda watering and heat. If I was your man. . ." She wished he would stop referring to himself as "her man." It reminded her of Lee, then Minnie. She was sad that her "real" man was out getting drunk somewhere, perchance with another woman.

Vivian wanted to bring Lee down with all her might for what he did to her, and for what she blamed him for making her do right now. Rather than submitting to her self-accusing voice of reason, she used her deceptive intelligence to interpret God, taking on His attribute as an Avenger. This was easier than acknowledging to herself that she was still with Henry because *she* wanted to be. She could blame it on Lee because the disrepute he caused her was ten times greater than the physical abuse for Vivian. He had humiliated her, and now she would humiliate him. Minnie, on the other hand, had done nothing to deserve this.

She distanced herself as much as she could. "You chose Minnie." Henry kept trying to convince her, pulling her deeper into a sticky web.

"Don't say that. I didn't choose her. I care about you so much that I can't think about her or nobody else right now, just how I must've let you down by not doing nothing sooner. I feel like I *let* this happen." He held her close, rocking her devotedly. "I mean that, Viv."

"There was nothing you could do."

"I could've told you that he wasn't no good for you."

"You're not God, Henry. Therefore you can't say who's good for me and who isn't so good, either."

"I know that God can make it be that a man can lose a good woman. If Lee has you and don't know what to do with you and won't allow himself to be taught how to care for you properly, he can lose you to someone who does."

"You didn't want me when you met us three together," she pressed.

"You don't know that. I wanted you months ago when I first laid eyes on you."

"My Lord! How can you say that?"

"I was afraid to choose you. Why would you want me? I thought you was with who you needed to be with. If I had known then that he...." Using his finger, he traced the outline of her face, stopping at her most bruised eye. "It's not my obligation to allow you to die of thirst and to wither away because a marriage ceremony might or might not take place. You have a special assignment," he added. He gently stroked the side of her face. Vivian shifted nervously.

"I don't know what kind of assignment you mean, Henry. I'm just a plain old country girl."

"Being as lovely as you is must be one of your assignments. You're a real live strawberry and you's so ripe and red that your smile can light up the whole of Florida. I reckon your assignment is to light up somebody's—the right somebody's life."

"I know what you're trying to say. And you're right—I reckon you think I can't light up Lee's life."

"Leave 'im, then. Walk away and don't look back. You could light up his life if he wasn't so stupid, but he can't attend to you properly. Ain't even no need to ask what he hit you for..." He grimaced. "I want you to light up *my* life. Say yes to me, Vivian."

"It's not that simple."

"It's as simple or as hard as you make it." He kissed her. "You already is a light for me."

She started to correct his verb-subject disagreement, but thought better of it. Missy pointed out *her* poor speech enough for Vivian to realize how irritating it was, and she remembered how her constant critiques continued to get her in trouble with Lee. Besides, she thought, the sensuousness of his words outweighed his improper verb usage. She noted how he was advancing rapidly, yet seemingly in such slow motion that she could hardly keep up with what was taking place. "My princess! I care for you so much..."

"Oh, Henry!"

"Sweet, precious, African doll Vivian...I know I disappointed you once by my...choices, but..."

"You didn't...you didn't disappoint me, Henry."

"I was foolish. I'm tired of trying to hide what I feel even when I see you."

"How...can you say that when...Minnie..."

"I know what I'm saying...and I ain't gonna stop...'cause you keep saying her name. You let *me* handle that!" She wished they didn't have to discuss Minnie because it made her feel quite lacking in virtue. Now, she was sorry she mentioned her name. Yet, Vivian had a burning passion for Henry to know that she did care about Lee and Minnie.

"Lee and I are having problems, Henry, but that doesn't mean . . ."

"What it means is that he's not good enough for you. It means you need to let 'im go. No girl needs a man like that, Vivian." His articulation was boosted above the quiet tone he'd been using since their first hug that evening. She wished she could believe him. Perhaps she would leave Lee if she had someone like Henry who would love her and be faithful to her and not hurt her, she thought, yet Henry was untouchable. And how could she even consider leaving Lee when, even according to her friends, he was the finest man they'd ever seen? Yet, as Henry had her pinned in his room, she let herself savor *his* absolute beauty, which ironically and directly contrasted Lee's physical finery.

Henry was past listening to any voices inside of him that told him his advances were wrong. His shrewd aspirations told him that Vivian being with him was predestined. The enchantment of Henry's caress washed away her doubts. This wonderful feeling was too accessible to deny. The world he offered even as a fantasy overtook Vivian's power to reason. Therefore, Vivian resolved against rejecting his overtures. She didn't know if she'd ever feel this congenial again with him or anyone else. He was scheduled to leave her behind in less than a week. She considered the strong liking she'd taken for Henry since the beginning of knowing him, yet Minnie would be the one he whisked away forever. Embittered, Vivian wanted to draw Henry into her own web. Although she wasn't emotionally ready to be estranged from Lee, her flattened pride intrigued her objective to cause uncertainty in Henry about his own plans.

Henry continued to pry until he met substantial and durable resistance. "Don't you like me just a li'l, honey?" he teased. Her conflict was only registering bit by bit with him. Henry kissed her cheeks, nose, and eyes. "Tell me how much you like me," he urged more seriously. "Even if you don't mean it, Viv, please say you do..."

"Oh! Henry, I can't tell you how I feel—that I like you...this is too much for me right now!" He followed her until his eyes fixed in on hers.

"Okay, sweetheart. I know. But I need you to say it. Say it to me, princess, please...even if you don't mean it...yeah, it'll hurt me to know you don't mean it—that you don't like me..."

"You *know* I mean it...yes I do," she surrendered, now willing to participate more in the sea of fallacious warmth that tasted like sugar coated blueberries, but still, she involuntarily constricted. "I like you a whole lot

Henry…a whole bunch…I know you know that I like you."

"Me, too, darling…relax, darling . . ." She buried her head in his chest, forcing away all residual thoughts about Minnie. After a minute, he released her from his embrace and grasped her face, pulling her head up to face him. "You okay?" He searched for her expression in the darkness. He knew with his unending determination, he could make a foul move, and he didn't want that. He guarded himself by inhaling deeply. "Now, why did you stop hugging me, my precious darling?"

"Because!"

"Because what?" He took her fists from his chest and guided her arms back around his neck.

"You *are* mighty, you're charming—everything about you is pleasant… *too* great for me to behold!"

"When are you gonna stop fearing me? You could hardly dance with me."

"Yes…I…"

"I never told you how happy I was that night, just like tonight…because you ran away. I didn't want you to run away, and I was lost when you left the room. Do you believe me?"

"I believe you."

"I wanna take care of you—make sure you ain't needing nothing. I want you to be my woman. Do you believe that, too? Please, please say yes."

"I feel safe with you, yes."

"Say yes to me!"

"I believe you…"

"You stopped hugging me again, darling."

"Henry, I . . ." He could hardly hear her. It was difficult for him to comprehend at first because all he could think of was that she was "fast" Lee's girl.

"Wow, Vivian," he said soothingly, "I didn't know. I swear I didn't know."

"How could you not know?"

"I just…"

"I feel like I'm in a whirlwind. I'm spinning fast, Henry!" He finally wanted to be totally honest with her about everything he was feeling, from day one. He sized up what he could do or say to make her unafraid of him. It felt like heaven when she confessed that she liked him, but she was shaking like a leaf. He could feel her intense desire to kiss him back when he kissed her, but her lips would only tremble their sentiment…and now she seemed to be pulling away, pushing his heart back with her knuckles. He had to concentrate on pulling her back.

"That doesn't change anything, honey. Everything is fine…it's all right, I promise," he pressed, flattening her knuckles under his chest. "You're in good, gentle hands, sweetheart, I swear. It was no slip-up that I found you tonight. I didn't plan this—but I thought that Lee…?"

"Obviously, I'm not like how you imagined me to be, Henry."

"I imagined you to be sweeter than sweet, too good for words to say. And you are sweeter than sweetness can ever be." His heart sailed in her palms; his mind was no longer functioning on a conscious plane. He swam, pulling her with him into the waves, parting the silk water with his fingertips so that she could glide.

"Someone might…."

"I told you already—it's just the two of us, honey. Vivian, I was *always* afraid to tell you how I feel about you, too. But not now, I'm not. Don't be afraid of me. Sweet girl, you're sweeter than the sweetest strawberry—so sweet…when I first met you face to face, it was love at first sight, Viv. I care for you so much."

"Uh!"

"I love you, darling."

"I don't think you love me!" Easily, Henry detected that her words did not reflect her manifest pining.

"You don't mean that. Don't tell me I don't love you, baby. I told myself I didn't for too long when I knew deep down that I did. I didn't want to face what it would mean to love you when you might not love me. But see, love is patient. Yes, I do love you. See how much patience I have with you? Can't you tell how much I love you, sweet angel? Can't you tell? Since day one I've loved you."

Henry preferred this state of euphoria. He pushed all interfering thoughts aside while he placed more emphasis on winning over Vivian's affection. Anxiously, he kissed her endlessly, until he deliberately forced her quivering lips into submissive numbness. And at the same time, he prodded more aggressively, as if to find a hidden door to her soul. Vivian floated away with Henry at the oars. Eventually, she was out of the safety of the boat, hanging on by the sides, gradually depending more and more upon Henry to lead her to the shore. Suddenly, Vivian blinked her eyelids rapidly as though she was drowning.

"Henry!"

"Say yes…" Miles from the shore, she welcomed the pacifying command of his voice. "You ain't gotta worry 'bout nothing. Just hug me. Tell me you want me to take you to the shore."

"The shore?"

"That's right…I'm not gonna let you drown out here. I know how you feel about being alone but not alone…"

"You don't know…"

"Yes, I do, Vivian. I remember what you told me when we danced. You thought I wasn't listening to you, but I always listen to your every word. I like to, too. I look at you all the time. I feel you when you're sad. I can even taste your tears when you don't know that I know you're crying. You ain't alone. Pinch me and see . . . I'm real . . . do whatever— just don't ask me to leave you all alone no more. Ask me to stay, Viv, and I won't go off to Michigan this weekend. Tell me you love me and mean it, and I won't go, I swear on my life!"

"Henry, wait…"

"Say yes to me, darling."

"You know how I feel…"

"Tell me…"

"I can't tell you to stay."

"Yes, you can. Yes, you can."

CHAPTER ELEVEN
"I hate your mouth"

Lee pulled Vivian out of the church hurriedly, ignoring the shouting voices behind them. He wished she would stop crying, drawing attention to themselves as he moved double time down the southern roads with her. "Quit crying, muffin, I'm gonna explain ev'rything once we get to my house where we can talk." Vivian followed him blindly, tears streaming down her face. She, too, wanted to get there quickly so she wouldn't have to stand the stares of all the passing citizens on the road. Lee didn't say anything else until they made it to his house a mile and a half away. As soon as they entered, he went straight through the house to the kitchen. Lee finally let Vivian's hand go at the kitchen threshold so he could rush to the cabinet and get a bottle of whiskey and two cups. He poured a shot for Vivian, and then placed her cup on the ice box. He turned to look at her.

"You want a chaser?" She shook her head, wanting to tell him that she didn't want anything except an explanation However, she decided she'd wait before she said anything to him at all because she was past angry, and she knew her words would slice him to pieces if she told him the truth about what a low-down asshole she rated him as. She was still standing in the doorway sniffling, looking at a smeared spot on the wall. Next, he filled his cup to the brim, and then carried both cups to the table. He knew he wouldn't be comfortable unless he had the whiskey bottle right in front of him, so he treaded back to the ice box where he left it and took it back to the table. Lee pulled out a chair for her before pulling up a chair right beside it. She labored over to the table and plopped down in her seat.

"Muffin, that ain't my baby," he said, sitting slowly. She smirked at him in reproach. He didn't return her snare. Weakly, she marveled at how fine he was, yet unfortunately, she couldn't help seeing him with Maybelle in her mind's eye. "I'm sorry all this happened, but it shouldn't stop our plans, girl. Skip Floyd." He drank his liquor in one long gulp. Immediately, he refilled his cup. She took a sip of her drink, and almost spit it out because it tasted like gasoline. Vivian replaced her anguish with opposition.

"Lee, I know you are messing around. I believe that *is* your child."

"What? Are you accusing me of something?"

"No. But there's no way I'm talking to you about a wedding."

"Then you *are* accusing me," he shouted, "I can accuse you, too."

"I can't believe you put me through that kind of embarrassment, Lee. If you want to mess around, you can continue! I don't need this crap. Besides, I don't need to accuse you. Everybody knows you're nothing but a gamer."

"Your mouth is your biggest enemy, girl. See, Vivian, whyn't you listen sometimes? You always tune out the voice of reason. There's no telling what other li'l ideas you got in your head. The whole thing was a set-up. You just is too blind to smell a rat trap."

"Whatever, Lee. I'm fixing to go home. I shouldn't have let you drag me over here." She left her seat in the middle of her sentence. Before Lee knew what was happening, she'd made it to the front door. He ran to catch up with her, still holding on to his second cup of corn whiskey.

"They's lying, muffin! Don't believe 'em." He had her by the arm. He took a couple of swigs so his liquor wouldn't spill as he juggled it and Vivian.

"Look, Lee. I need some time away from you, okay? I just want to go home now." Her voice was very level in her attempt to contain her fury. His insecurities and his own guilt caused a big green monster to emerge within himself.

"You seen all them men up at the corner . . . whatchu rushing off down there for? Are you trying to prove some point?"

"What? I have to go that way to get home! I'm not studying any men." She marched toward the door again, but Lee tracked in front of her, blocking her path.

"If you'd just wait a damn minute, I'll walk you home."

"That's not necessary, Lee. Look. I'm upset, okay?"

"Who you gonna trust? Me? Or Floyd and some vagabond?" He took his time finishing the drink. Vivian observed that he was losing all rationality, but her frustration motivated her responses. She couldn't think of a safe way to get past him, yet she had no intentions of staying.

"Move out the way, Lee! I don't want to see you right now. Can't you hear?" The big green monster grew. Inescapably, it shoved her down to the floor. Scooting, he pushed her back toward the kitchen, all the time mumbling under his breath. She caught herself and tried to run back past him, to the door. He put his foot out in front of her, causing her to trip. Vivian scattered about until she found herself in a corner, with Lee standing over her.

"You's the hypocrite that was all over Henry." He kicked her forcefully in her side with a great deal of his weight. "Now, you trying to play like this here thing is *my* fault."

"Ahhhh!" She screamed. "You ape!" He kicked her again, this time harder because the monster in him now closely resembled an ape as it grew. On her belly, she tried to force her way past him to the front door. He crawled after her, straddled her and socked her in her eye twice, and then he punched her in the jaw and about her head. Vivian lost consciousness. Her face hit the floor with the last impact. When she came to, he was still punching her. She realized he didn't acknowledge that she was not fighting back anymore. Then, she drifted back into unconsciousness. Lee closed his eyes and swung and bit and scratched her everywhere he could and as fast as he could until he was out of breath. Panting, he rested on top of her for a few moments, and then he got up and casually walked back into the kitchen to fill his cup. He sipped slowly for a few moments, as though in deep thought. Suddenly, he hurried back to her. He swigged the rest of his liquor, and then bounced the cup off her forehead. The jolt of the cup caused her to return to reality. She clutched her head as she miraculously made her way to a standing position. She felt a hot wetness on her fingers. He waited until she had gathered her bearings before he back-hand slapped her across the left side of her face.

"Who you calling an ape?" Vivian could not remember saying that. "Is you trying to play me, woman?" He slapped her again. Vivian threw herself back on the floor, seeking refuge in the corner again, but Lee continued to kick her for a few more minutes, until some of his rage had dissipated. He watched her sprawled out in the corner, whimpering. Given that she didn't appear eager to move, he left her to get another cup of whiskey. After he poured himself a triple shot, he pulled one of the chairs out from the kitchen into the front room, just inches from her, so that he could finish talking with her about the issue at hand.

"See there, Vivian. It's your mouth. I hate your mouth. Do you think I be wanting to fight you? I had promised myself we won't gonna fight no more, but you don't trust me. If you trusted me, nothing Maybelle or Floyd could say would make you blink. You know why you don't trust me? 'Cause *you* are guilty." He shook his head inflexibly. Vivian remained perfectly still. She had misread him. She thought he'd never beat her like *that* because she felt certain he wanted to marry her. Surely, a man who wanted to marry a girl would not kick her like a dog! Vivian wished she could comprehend how he could see her sprawled out on the floor like that, and not want to lift her to him. She felt unloved, which fed her insecurities and low self-esteem, thus she felt invoked to accept the current chain of events. Distantly, she heard him continue to speak about the situation, yet she was afraid to disagree with him, or say the wrong thing.

More than the actual blows, Vivian was offended by the fact that Lee didn't ask her how she felt, nor had he apologized for hitting her. She *wanted* to accept his excuse for why he said he'd hit her. He said she was threatening their relationship with trust issues, and that he was doing everything in his power to keep their relationship from tearing apart. He told her he'd hit her because of his frustration due to her constant threats to end the relationship.

Wasn't it Lee who wanted to talk following the incident in the church? And wasn't she aware of Floyd's animosity toward them both? Lee tried to convince her that of course Floyd would lie. Vivian attempted to make sense out of the ordeal. She needed to figure out what she was doing wrong to keep her man so vicious toward her. She heard Lee go back to the kitchen table with his cup once more.

"I gotta drink to be able to deal with your evil ass," he said after taking a gigantic gulp, "on account of I gave up everything to be with you . . . my friends…it's your fault me and Floyd broke off, anyway . . . not you personally but you as a woman. Then you're gonna tell me you don't know if you want the marriage just 'cause some wench tells you something. Muffin?" She attempted to open her swollen eyes in a gesture of good faith. "Is we gonna do this thing, or what?" He was standing over her, staggering drunk. She didn't answer.

"Well, I'm gonna go out for a spell to think for myself. Hell. I sure can't think in here! But I know one thing: You is lucky to have a stud like me. Why the hell should I be begging your narrow behind? I know what your problem is. You're very unappreciative. It don't seem like what I do matters at all. You complain about every goddamn thing in the world. You finally find a man like me who's working, and you're hollering about all kinds of petty bullshit.

"Sometimes, I feel like you just ain't worth the effort. Yeah. I best get on up outta here 'cause you's the type of woman that'll make a decent man beat your ass. I need to be around some civilized people. People who ain't with their butts on their shoulders all the time. You think you're too good for me? I'll bet Minnie's ugly self got you thinking like that. I buy you all kinds of stuff. I spend all my money on you, girl. I see I'm gonna hafta put this on hold for a minute. I'll be back to deal with you." He shook his head. "You ain't right. You know that don't you?" She held her breath. "Get on up and go to the bedroom and wait for me." She kept still. "Get, niggah!"

She struggled to her knees, and then crawled in the direction that he'd shown, refusing to inflame him further. "Viv, don't think I's playing with you. Don't leave this house 'cause I'll be to get you if you do. See, I can't talk to you now, 'cause I'm liable to whip your behind…you sitting 'round talking that foolishness to me. You better be ready to talk when I get back," he roared on his way to the streets.

Ensuing his departure, she let herself crumple in the middle of the floor. After a few minutes, she half crawled out the front door for fresh air. She wanted to go home, but she was afraid to make him angrier, and she was in too much pain to consider walking right away. She needed rest. The main thing that kept her there, however, was embarrassment. Vivian didn't want her family to know that her fiancé was brutal and oppressing. She wanted her family to admire him as she did. Vivian slumped down in a corner of the porch, gathered her knees in the crook of her arms, rocking back and forth, until Henry came for her.

When Lee returned at about 3:00 a.m., he was ready to apologize to Vivian and ask her again for her hand in marriage, although he was still intoxicated. He was crushed to find that she had gone, but in his drunken state, he forgot his promise and instead took immediately to his bed. Lee slept with the vision that Vivian had rushed home after he'd left, and her family was thus sheltering her from him.

The next afternoon following their fight, Lee wanted to go to Vivian. He started drinking as soon as he returned from work. Because of his sheer depression, he requested and was granted two days off without penalty or pay. All he could think of was that he couldn't lose her. He knew he had beaten her badly this time. He wondered what her mama and sisters were now saying about her probably swollen eye. "They probably think I ain't nothing," he brooded. Lee took another swig of the whiskey. He half expected Vivian to show up at his door, given that he knew she loved him. He hoped and prayed for the next three days that Vivian would come because he was too ashamed to go to her and face her entire family. Furthermore, it would seem as though his discipline had been in order if he waited it out until she came. It was certainly a gamble because if he waited too long and she never came, he could risk losing her.

By Thursday, Lee looked ashen. His body was filled with liquor, and he had hardly eaten in the days that he lived distressfully alone in his father's house. It was almost six in the morning when he clambered out of bed. Minutes later, he fumbled with his shirt buttons, brushed his hair, and had a cup of coffee. It was necessary that he report to work today, otherwise, he could lose his job. He carefully drafted a note to Vivian and posted it on the outside door before leaving, with miserably high hopes that today would be the day that she would come.

At the railroad station where they both worked, Lee saw his father at lunchtime. Lee saw Floyd, too, but Floyd quickly turned his back to him. Lee paused only faintly before he inched his way toward his father. They were usually so busy and many at the railroad that sometimes Lee Sr. and his son didn't see each other all day, including at lunchtime. During lunch, all the Negroes were congregated together in a large area for "colored only." They stood, sat on the ground, or found one of the few weather-beaten benches where they could enjoy a few moments with refreshments and socialization.

Lee's father had been looking for him since he hadn't seen his son at work all week. Lee Sr. hadn't been home in several days because he had taken up house with Charmin, a high-yellow plump woman of about forty-five years old. It wasn't an unusual occurrence for Lee Sr. or for Lee to stay away from home for days at a time, but the father and son team regularly saw each other at work a few times in the week.

Charmin liked to bring his lunch to the station for him. It didn't bother her that only sweaty men worked in the area because they clearly admired her brief but daily presence. She proudly walked over to the lunch area to find Lee Sr., and when she did, she gave him a sloppy kiss and a plate of food that was wrapped in waxed paper. All eyes of the men in the area followed the woman when she came in, including Lee's eyes, and that's how he spotted his father. Charmin only stayed for a minute or so, as she had to get back to the children she kept during the day. Lee Sr. thought the railroad yard was no place for a woman. He agreed with her against his better judgment that she should bring him his lunch hot. His greed was the deciding point of whether to have Charmin leave the house full of children she supervised unattended for fifty minutes so that he could receive some smoking fried scavenger flesh. Lee walked past Charmin to greet his father as she was leaving.

Lee Sr. reached up and slapped his son on the back. "Boy, where the devil you been? I was coming home today to see 'bout you."

"My luck don't seem to be as good as yours, pop," Lee said, nodding in the direction of the woman walking away. "I done had a big, huge fight with my woman. I been there at the house by myself mostly all week, drinking and carrying on."

"Uh oh. You done had a tit for tat with one of your vagabonds . . ."

"Don't call her no vagabond, pop. Her name's Vivian. Man, I been with her 'bout eight months. I told you 'bout her already. Told you we was having an engagement party at her church. Expected you to show up, too," Lee said with a lingering drip of disappointment. His father nodded, urging him to continue. He did not want to be reminded that he hadn't been able to make it because he had been having a lazy time with Charmin. Besides, how could he take Lee seriously about getting married when he was hardly an inch past boyhood? Lee squeezed next to his father, making a space on the bench. There was an older gentleman sitting next to Lee Sr. who generously gave

Lee some space. Lee Sr. opened the paper plate containing the greasy, divinely forbidden pork and gnawed the diseased, worm filled fatty tissue free from the bone.

"The problem is she won't mind me. She's not tamed. I tell her to do one thing, and she tells *me* what she's gonna do. She be trying to change me, pops. Always correcting my speech—sometimes I feel like she don't want me to be myself."

"Womens always try to talk better than us mens. Don't figure on her trying to change you, son that just be their ways. I'm sure she don't mean nothing by it."

"Sometimes when she gets to talking that mess, I be wanting to smack her, man. She can't hear what I be trying to say on account of she be listening to how I say it. I'm tired of trying to be all proper just to please her. And I ain't fixing to keep doing it, neither."

"Some of these gals coming along mayhap is a li'l wilder than what they used to be."

"She's too pretty for me to just let her run wild. Some pecker is liable to get to her and spoil her."

"Oh yeah? How you reckon you gwine tame her?" Lee didn't answer. Lee Sr. searched his son's face. Yes, the "boy" Lee was almost gone. His son resembled a stocky and cocky full-grown man, but Lee Sr. wisely recalled whenever he was that age. He recalled thinking he knew things he had never been taught, and then, boom! He was the father of children who needed guidance that he could not give. Nonetheless, Lee Sr. was touched that Lee seemed to be experiencing true love. He didn't know what the problem was in his son's relationship, but he assumed it to be minor. He remembered the fights he had when he was Lee's age. Lee Sr. was too conscience-stricken ever to discuss with anyone the profoundly stupid things he had done that caused the waste of his beautiful relationship with Lee's mother. He proclaimed now that he would never stop loving her. Lee Sr. couldn't stop the bitterness that ran through his veins whenever he reminisced. He thought moving from Pensacola to Century would help ease the pain of her loss, but it didn't. Lee Sr. was about to drift back into some painful memories of some horrible mistakes he'd made with Lee's mother, but he caught himself in time to quickly push the sordid recollections to the back of his mind.

"Boy, don't you put your foot in her back-side. I'm telling you now 'cause I can see it with my eyes."

"Too late, pops. I reckon she naturally won't let me come around no more." Lee Sr. shook his head. Lee used the base of his palm to smack his forehead, and he kept his palm pressed, his fingers digging into his scalp. "I hate what she makes me do." He removed his hand and smiled faintly at his father. "You should see her, pops. She's…she's really nice."

"Oh, yeah?"

"Yeah." Lee thought about the five inches he towered over her and the seventy plus pounds he packed above her weight. "I know I ain't got no business hitting…but I ain't never done nothing like this to no girl! I don't know why she…"

"Boy, keep your hands to yourself. You's getting to be too willful. You gwine hafta settle down right and find you a family. So, I hope your engagement party means wedding bells and she don't back away from you 'cause of your silliness. You that age where you be needing a wife to see 'bout your needs."

"What 'bout you, pops? Do you ever think you'll marry again? I mean, I know you must miss mama . . ."

"Nope. I mean, I miss her, but I'm not looking to marry right soon." He tried to laugh at himself but his son was too serious-minded. Lee Sr. suggested he was finished with the discussion by picking up his trash and cleaning around his lunch area.

"Pops?" Lee stood up when his father stood to leave.

"What, Lee?" Lee Sr. answered harshly.

"You know I've been wondering for a long time why you and my mama started hating each other."

"Quiet yourself, Lee Hiram. I never hated your mama . . ."

"Didn't she care nothing 'bout me? I mean, what made her leave *me*, daddy? She had to hate *you*."

"She didn't leave you, boy, she left me. Anyway, I'm to blame—and I don't wanna talk 'bout your mama—you leave it be." Lee Sr. turned away from Lee in dismissal. Lee stared at the back of his father's head as he left him standing in the middle of the lunch yard. He left Lee to suppose all sorts of fantasies about his mother. Lee's most prevalent thought was that his mother had shamed the family, thus was asked to leave quietly. His father had always told him that his mother was a decent woman, though. Lee contemplated why his father took all responsibility over the destroyed relationship.

He knew his mother was from Mississippi. Her family that still lived there wanted nothing to do with his father, but they ended up cutting Lee off, as well. Years ago, Lee overheard his father's brother, Samuel tell someone that his mother ran away after her husband beat her; Lee Sr. let her go, thinking she would come back in a few days. Although Lee didn't believe the rumors, it bothered him to hear them, even from his uncle. Lee preferred his father to tell him the truth about what happened rather than hearing bits and pieces of the story from this or that relative. Uncle Samuel said that her pride kept her out of doors with no food, until she got sick with pneumonia and died in the streets.

The sound of a shrill bell interrupted Lee's thoughts. He stirred back toward his crew with his head hanging down. "That's it. I can't take no more of this. I'm going after her tonight," Lee mumbled bitterly to himself. "I'm gonna win her back," he encouraged himself. "Vivian's got plenty of that pride like my mother had. She won't come back unless I go and get her. I won't leave her out there alone. I'm gonna win her back. I gotta."

Way past dawn, when the birds finished their feast of worms on the surface of damp terrains, and way past the time sprouting flowers had spread their petals for swarming bees, Henry opened his eyes to see a sleeping Vivian on his arm. She was beautiful to him, more mysterious than Minnie. He accepted that he had been preoccupied with Vivian for several weeks. He hadn't let himself think about it much in his devotion to Minnie but seeing Vivian all beat up merely ignited and manifested his pining for her. Henry didn't want to cause Minnie to agonize. As it was, he didn't know how he was going to face her. However, he wasn't willing to trade those precious hours with Vivian for a pot of gold. He had lived out a fantasy, and he wanted to prolong the sordid affair, even if only in his mind. The idea of repenting was as remote to him as wishing the experience never took place. His heart skipped a beat to think of not seeing Vivian again, but he knew he had to hurry and put some distance between them if his relationship with Minnie was going to survive. Vivian opened her eyes to see Henry staring at her mournfully.

"Viv?"

"Hmm?" He pulled her closer to him, warmly.

"Are you okay?"

"Yes."

"You still like me a whole bunch?" He grinned at her.

"You still think I'm sweeter than sweet?" He nodded, still with his grin.

"How do you feel, darling? You want some water or something?"

"Yeah...yes, please." He positioned her so that her head rested on his cheek, and he held a tin cup for her, allowing her a sip. When she finished, he gulped the remaining contents before letting her head slip back on the bed, his arm still under her. He poured more water into the cup from the jug Vivian used the night before.

"I need to know how you feel, Vivian. I want the truth, too." He knew she had to be in a great deal of pain. Her face was swollen under both eyes, and last night he figured out also that Lee must've struck her around her rib cage. He prayed that he hadn't added to her suffering. "Girl, Lee did a job on you—so don't tell me you feel fine 'cause I might not believe you."

"Well, I do feel fine." He reached for the cloth with peanut oil on it from last night and gently washed her face with it. "I like the way you make me feel, Henry. Maybe I'm floating or something because of how tender you are. Maybe in a minute when I get up to go home, I'll be in pain again…sore. But right now, I feel like you're an angel or a dove and I'm wrapped up in your wings…and I'm feeling pretty, I'm feeling special, and I'm feeling like I'm your girl dove, protected by your wings. Whatever Lee did to me, you took it and threw it away. It's outside somewhere, but it's not here with us." He kissed her forehead.

"Thank you."

"I have you to thank."

"Last night was the best night of my life."

"What made it so best?"

"On account of I ain't never spent no night with somebody I love."

"You chose *her*. You met us at the same time, but you chose her instead. That's not love for me."

"If I *had* chosen you, it wouldn't have made no difference seeing that you're tied up."

"Oh yeah? Well, you chose me last night, it seems. I wasn't any more tied up when I first met you than I was last night, you know. I guess you'll be choosing Minnie tomorrow."

"I'm sorry, baby." He sighed. She sighed, too, smiling. There was no need to argue with him after such a glorious evening.

"You didn't do anything wrong."

"I know," he lied.

"It's okay, really. There's no sense in talking about all that, anyhow."

"Was you able to get some sleep with me here, taking up all of the room?" She shook her head.

"I slept. I just kept waking up every thirty minutes, it seemed. But then I'd go right back to sleep, though. This whole thing seems like a dream," she said weakly.

"I kinda wish it *was* a dream," he replied, "'cause then I could still have you, but not the real life heart ache that comes with having you." He brushed her eyes with kisses.

"Can you believe it, Henry?" Her eyes were dancing merrily. He wasn't sure if he liked her gay, fickle attitude about what he considered to be a very serious transaction.

"I believe it, but I didn't plan it, princess. All I wanted was to be near you and keep you from him. The closer you got to me... I couldn't help myself, darling. Now, I gotta go see Minnie 'nem. I gotta be in a world of fudging to face Minnie."

"We should probably get going, then."

"You ain't going nowhere. I'll go."

"Are you sure?"

"Yeah."

"Why?"

"Because you need your rest. I believe that'll be a bit too much for you right now. Just wait for me, okay?" He gave her two quick kisses on both cheeks, and then he kissed her with more fervor. After a few seconds, he moved only a centimeter away. "Okay, darling?"

"Okay. Thank you. I truly don't want to see everybody yet."

"I know you don't. And I ain't ready for you to leave me, neither."

"I'll bet they are waiting to hear something from you concerning my whereabouts."

"I wish I didn't hafta go yet."

"The longer you wait, the worse off it might be, with them being curious, and all."

"Don't move." He went to his knapsack that was sitting on the floor by his pants. When he kneeled over, he quickly looked at her with a sly grin, knowing she was watching him. Bashfully, she turned away. In an instant, he was back in her arms, happy that she felt comfortable enough to embrace him, first.

"What do you have, Henry?" He pulled a wad of cash from his knapsack and tossed it back on the floor.

"Here, baby."

"I can't take your money!" He pressed it into her palm.

"Right now, I can't think of nothing I can do to make you happy. But I can give you some of my money, which I know it'll help you with things you need." She thought about how she could really use the cash, and she was thankful.

"I don't know..."

"Hey, baby...that ain't no money. I got a whole bunch more that I've been saving."

She closed her fingers down on the bills. "Well, maybe I can buy my mama some of that perfume she likes so much, on account of I've been taking her oils and what not."

"Sweetheart, you smell so lovely— I pray I don't smell like fresh strawberries like you do."

She cringed. "Uh…I smell like medicine. Like a ghastly peanut plant."

"No you don't!"

"Henry?" He was kissing her face again.

"Hmm?"

"I'm glad things happened the way they did. I mean, I'm glad you were here for me yesterday and now, too." He stopped kissing her to smile brightly at her.

"And not Lee?"

"You made me forget my pain. Lee caused that pain. I knew I was safe when I saw you last night. I knew nobody else would do anything to me. I was happy you found me and not anyone else--I feel the safest with you."

"Good, because I would lay down my life for you," he breathed. Vivian drifted to another orbit where big, Black angels presented themselves passionately to do the biddings of their princesses. She could travel along this sphere, and Lee was not invited.

"Lee would simply die if he knew about this. The way he is, he says he wants to marry me before long. Whenever we do get married, which won't be too soon at all considering I'm ill with him about what he did---but as you know, I'll hold this memory of *you* for the rest of my life." Henry stopped breathing for a moment. She was talking about "when" with Lee. Didn't she know he didn't want to hear that? Even though Henry planned to stay with Minnie, it burned him that Vivian would speak of a future with Lee. Besides, he was only staying with Minnie because it was the right thing to do—not because he didn't want Vivian. Henry didn't think real romance was a benefit of marriage—marriage had other benefits. He never expected to achieve the level of romance with his wife that he did with Vivian. He had lived out a dream, and now it was time to go back to reality.

"I guess me and you hafta forget 'bout what happened between us, huh?"

"Guess so," she said. Vivian smiled, satisfied with how things had evolved. She couldn't help liking Henry. He was big and clumsy, yet extremely cautious and refined when it came to how he treated her. He was clumsy when he proposed to Minnie that she go with him to the North, Vivian regarded, but he was unhurried when he kissed the sadness away from her face last night.

"Maybe I don't wanna forget about it, sweet girl." In feigned horseplay, Henry lifted her off the cot.

"Put me down, man!" She loved the way she felt light as a feather in his arms. Henry carried her, spinning around and around until they both were laughing and dizzy. They ended up at the window. The bright sun identified the hour as 6:30 a.m. Almost exhausted, Henry placed her on the top crate that contained his clothes. She faced him. He held her face within his hands, resting his forehead on hers.

"Baby, I can't be with you like I want, and you're telling me to just *forget* about what happened?"

"*You* said forget about it…"

"I was on that cloud with you. *I* brought you to the shore, Vivian, not this man you say you still wanna marry. You were drowning, remember? We share something that you could *never* share with Lee, now. It's too late for Lee, you hear?" She nodded half-heartedly, knowing he didn't believe she was ready to abandon Lee. "Right now, you're wide awake, and I don't want you figuring that last night was no dream. It was real, my precious, precious darling. It was real."

At 11:00 a.m., Henry left her in his cabin while he went out and washed himself. Then he brought a large bucket and rag in for her, with warm, soapy water. Without informing her, he left again, this time to go to her house. As he walked along the dirt road, he was oblivious to the children scattered about, playing, and waving at him. He thought of the beautiful time he'd just spent with Vivian. Henry tried not to think of leaving her, but he knew he must. He had promised Minnie a life with him, and he knew she desperately wanted that life. She was mesmerized by him and Vivian wasn't. How could she even consider marrying Lee after what he did to her? There was no way he could witness a hypocritical ceremony like that. He would be the first to stand with a list of reasons as to why the marriage shouldn't take place, and the number one reason submitted would be that after what Lee had done to her, Henry estimated Lee had no rights anymore. But then, it was clear that Lee thought he owned her, and there would have to be bloodshed. And for what? For Vivian to choose Lee after all would be a slap in his face. Minnie would be devastated that he took such a stand, even if Vivian said no. The closer he came to Minnie's house, the more he tried to block out Vivian's soft voice, her precious hands, and her tiny mole from his mind.

Minnie ran out of the house and burst more vividly into his thoughts to welcome him after she'd heard some of the children who were playing nearby shouting greetings to him. "You seen Viv, Henry? Is she still with 'im?" Carol and Robeena followed the voices out to the front yard.

"I found her," he said simply to Minnie. He turned and repeated to Robeena and Carol, "I found her."

"Is she okay?" Carol asked of Vivian's spirits. She never suspected that

Lee would have hit her.

"Now, ev'rybody, don't get excited. I found her at Lee's house last night. It took me a spell to figure out where he lives, but I found her. He beat her up pretty badly . . ." They all gasped.

"He *beat* her?" Robeena echoed. Carol clutched Minnie's hand.

"She is on the Raison Plantation now. I took her there late last night on account of Kent Jr.'s men patrolling the roads, preventing decent folk from passing by. I had her on her way to get cleaned up at Ms. Esther's house if it wasn't for them racist cowards. She has said she's not coming home on account of she's too ashamed." He looked away. "So, I took her to Mother Tazra last night. I mean, Lee got her all bruised up, Ms. Carol. Viv don't wanna hear no 'I told you so" from nobody."

"Well, I'm gonna go and talk to her," Robeena said. "She hasn't got no cause to be shamed."

"What is he beating on her for?" Seems to me like he'd be trying to make up with her," Minnie explored out loud.

"Now look, I done talked to her, and she's not in no state of mind to be questioned and what not. I didn't ask her what the fight was about, on account of it don't matter. He don't got no business fighting no lady like that." He frowned. "I told her to come on home. I'm gonna tell her again when I get back. I just didn't wanna rush her 'cause she said if I made her leave the Raison Plantation, she'd go somewhere . . . mayhap o'er to Lee's, but she ain't ready to come home." Minnie nodded her head, seemingly in agreement to his decisions, but Carol eyed him with open mistrust. She wanted to ask him if Vivian had slept at Tazra's place last night, but she surmised that the question would be too forward, especially with Minnie standing there looking at him as though he was the saving angel. Carol immediately regretted her ill perception in suggesting that Henry go off to find Vivian in the first place.

Minnie said, "I hope she leaves that man alone and comes on to Michigan with us, when we go." Henry took Minnie's hand.

"Ain't no sense in us trying to get ev'rybody to go with us. We gonna scarcely be able to take care of ourselves." Henry wanted to quickly end all gestures to invite Vivian with them up North. He knew his attraction to Vivian would not have the likelihood to disappear unless he could put some distance between them. "I'm planning on seeing about the coach today. Plan on leaving Friday morning, not Saturday, y'all. Gotta leave on Friday if we's to make that train on time." Minnie shrieked and jumped in his arms. He caught her and swung her around in the air. Robeena ran over excitedly, waiting for her turn in the air.

"It's for real, ain't it Henry? We really are leaving by the weekend?"

"What about me? I'm going with y'all." Henry and Minnie laughed. Carol smiled, too. She brooded over her earlier suspicions and decided it was a great idea for them to leave Vivian behind right away. She was also relieved that Henry didn't seem to want Vivian tagging along. If he was sweet on her, wouldn't he make up some excuse for her to go with them? In truth, Carol was distraught with the idea of her children moving away. She never had the dream or the inclination to travel so far away, yet the happiness of her children meant a great deal to her. Carol was sure Henry could make a good husband for Minnie, but it worried her that marriage did not seem to be a part of his plans.

Vivian didn't return home until late on Tuesday. On Monday, Henry confessed to her that he'd already informed her family that Lee had beaten her. She feigned displeasure, but agreed that hiding from them was fruitless. She was secretly undisturbed about the opportunity to go home to her own bed. Vivian was depleted. Almost two days with Henry, coupled with the mental and physical fatigue associated with being battered had taken its toll on her. By Tuesday, Henry was insistent that she stay in his private confines until he left town. It saddened her on her departure day to reflect on Minnie, and the love out of which she was being cheated.

When Vivian finally resolved to go home, she was overcome with guilt because Henry held her in his arms, crying real tears. She had never seen a man cry like that before. Vivian stood limp, yet patiently in his arms, patting his back aimlessly. She was wearing one of his shirts and some trousers he found somewhere that fit her. She held her church shoes in her hand, determined to walk home barefoot.

During the final moments of his deep rousing display, she couldn't help it to think of Lee. It was killing her to guess whether Lee had been looking for her in vain. Henry emitted a muffled, sobbing statement that he would be leaving for Michigan right away, but that he would rather not abandon her. He begged her to ask him to stay, but she didn't think he meant it—he was simply being polite and he was confused. Not only that, but she didn't want to give Minnie the satisfaction that she wanted her man. He truly didn't think she wanted him forever because in his estimation, he was not as handsome as Lee, and he was too dark for her to prefer him. She would have to prove to him that she wanted him, in which case he would marry her instantly, he told himself.

"Miss Carol is gonna give us a going away party on Thursday. If I come, I'd be torn to see you and hafta say goodbye." He said he knew from the moment of their first embrace that he must leave immediately. He said he couldn't stand seeing her any longer, hiding his love, while his love grew. Henry told her he knew now that he loved her. He wanted her to love him back. Vivian felt tactless during his testimony because she would not admit to herself or him that she loved him, too. She only knew that she did not regret their stolen passion one iota.

She felt what had arisen between them was an act of inevitable energy. Furthermore, she gauged his words were merely the result of the beautiful fervor they'd shared. She thought that his love for her was only for while they had been together. Vivian decided for the delicacy of the circumstances that it would be curt to tell him he was under an illusion about this whole "love" thing. It was true that he *was* just like any other cheating man. She figured he would snap out of it in the coming hours or minutes.

Moments later, Henry was walking closely beside her, carrying a potato sack packed with her personal belongings, and brushing into her whenever the wind blew him nearer. He self-effacingly ended his chaperone service once they reached the lamppost at the corner by her house. Henry wanted desperately to hold her, but he didn't have the courage to so much as look at her still lovely though swollen face. He certainly couldn't face Minnie in Vivian's presence. Therefore, he left word with her for Minnie that he had many things to do, so he wouldn't be able to see her until the night before their departure, at the party. Henry instructed Vivian to inform Minnie that the coach would come for her on Friday morning. He squeezed his hand over hers when he gave her the sack. She looked up at him, but he kept his eyes cast away. Following his last statement, he dipped into a bow, and then turned quickly away.

Vivian watched him hurry down the street. She waited to wave at him, but he never turned back to offer a glance. It took her five long minutes to point her feet in another direction. She exhaled, then inhaled heavily with every inch she covered on the way to her house. She was satisfied that her street was deserted. Whenever passing folk looked at them on the way home, she imagined that they could see right through her, and that they somehow knew that she was...different. She wanted to spy her mother and sisters before they, too, could look through her.

Much to Vivian's approval, her family members became experts in making her feel comfortable, and not saying, "I told you so." Carol was pained that Vivian didn't feel she could come home and talk with her sooner, but now that she was home, Carol felt a sense of urgency to "be there" for her daughter. They all hugged and told her how happy they were that she'd come home. They didn't even say anything about the strange clothes she was wearing. Soon, Vivian let some of her defenses down, picking up her normal routine about the house. As soon as she thought she could do so discreetly, she stowed away and changed her clothes. Everyone was excited about the party scheduled for Thursday, and her mother and sisters were already busy with the preparations. Therefore, the fight with Lee went un-discussed. Even though Vivian was made to feel sheltered by her family, her inner pain was something she would have to deal with alone.

~~~

Her daughters helped tremendously, but overall, it was Carol who put together a fantastic feast on Thursday for everyone. Carol made sure there was ample food for the party, in addition to the extra preparation that guaranteed the trio would have plenty of snacks with them on the road. She made rice cake, banana bread, smoked grouper and red snapper, green beans, iced tea, and more.

The guests all brought nicely wrapped gifts with them. The Reverend and Mrs. Washington came . . . not for the party, of course, but they wanted to pray over the family during this special time of pending nuptials. Minnie told everyone that a private wedding ceremony was planned for the day they would arrive in Michigan.

Only a few members from the church had been invited, but with the excitement of last Sunday's drama, unsolicited members couldn't wait to enter Carol's household. They peered openly at Vivian, who sat through the party with a piece of cloth taped over her eye. She told anyone who asked that she had an infection. No one from the church was bold enough to ask her of Lee's whereabouts, although their noses itched with the appetite to know the truth about what was happening. Certainly, they didn't believe her "infection" story for one second.

Carol had forgotten all about the community meeting planned to take place at her house that evening. It didn't occur to her until Wali Eli came to the door just as the party was roaring. Carol didn't have to apologize to Wali Eli-he waved his hand at her and took a seat, pleased to meet the guests whom he had never seen, and pleased to fellowship with others like Mr. Anderson, Geraldine, and Esther. He spent a good portion of the evening in a religious discussion with Reverend Washington. It appeared to Reverend Washington that he and Wali Eli were the only ones in the room. The reverend was trying to convince him that he should worship Jesus, whom he said was actually God. "Yes, *and* Jesus said in the scriptures: 'Why callest thou *me* good? There's none good save the Father," Wali Eli stated, looking around for Minnie. And he wanted to talk to Henry.

Reverend Washington had never heard anyone add more to what he had been taught in Old Master Kent's school. This fair man who knew the scriptures inside and out, and who had more knowledge in general, disturbed him. "No man can enter into heaven except through the name of Jesus," Reverend Washington shouted, sweat dripping from his brow, and foam building up in the crevices of his mouth.

"You are right, my friend. *And* Jesus asked us to pick up our cross and *follow* him (through that door). When his disciples asked him how to pray, he said pray to *our Father*, hallowed be *Thy* name. He said: 'These things you see *me* do, *you* can also do'..." Reverend Washington scooted closer, in hopes that Wali Eli could better hear his point. Wali Eli continued with a smile. "*And* none knows interpretation but God."

"Say, man, are you a Christian? You don't sound like a Christian..."

"It's something how the name 'Christian' originated. Christian means one who is crystallized into oneness with God, using Jesus Christ as the example. Jesus wasn't born "the Christ." Christ is a title that was given to him. Christ means one who crushes evil. I am a Christian because I mean to crush evil wherever I see it. You can't find anywhere in the Bible, though, where Jesus is calling his followers 'Christians.' It was at Antioch, three hundred and twenty-five years after his crucifixion that the *enemies* of Jesus identified his followers as Christians. We read Acts in the Bible to learn more."

"Well, that ain't what I was *taught*."

"You should read the book for yourself, brother. It's yours to read."

Reverend Abe Washington had not been taught anything about this at Kent's school. Abe looked around to see if anyone from his congregation was hearing this discussion. He was beginning to feel hostile toward Wali Eli for reasons he couldn't categorize. "Whatchu is, a revolutionist or something? You a rebel, boy?" He called him a boy because he knew that was exactly what white folk would call him if they could hear him talk like he did. "Talking like that could get Negroes killed." He looked around the room while he spoke loudly. "Get all of us in here killed with that talk."

Wali Eli narrowed his eyes and said, "If I would be a revolutionary, I would only revolt against what is wrong."

"Look here. I don't like wrong, neither. None of us do. We's just trying to make it, Mr. Eli, without causing waves. They ain't got no problem lynching Black people for the kinda talk you's doing. I don't want no harm to come to Carol and the girls..."

"Are you sure that's it?" Reverend Washington folded his arms in defense.

"We just don't know you, suh. It ain't right for a salesman to tell us things we haven't heard from Mistuh Johnson. Yes, suh! Mistuh Johnson will have questions 'bout who you are!"

"Who do you see me as?"

"Only God knows who you is. I'm trying to save your life. All I can do is put Jesus on you. Tell you about my Jesus. You better pray he don't come on down out that sky and deal with this." Reverend Washington wanted to say something positive, but there was murmuring regarding a stately newcomer, and this was Reverend Washington's chance to remind everyone that *he* was the Black Leader in the community, not Wali Eli.

"You see Jesus coming as some formless spirit floating in the sky. Well, Matthew saw a Son of Man coming out of the east. The Son of Man is not coming from the sky except that you will see a great one coming through the clouds of heaven, if you only understood. The Book says that 'As lightning shines from the east even unto the west, so shall the coming of the Son of Man be.' It never said the son of a spirit. The book says that 'Wherever the eagles are gathered together, there shall be the carcass.' And now God is coming out of the east to breathe life into a dead people who live in the west… America…under the symbol of an eagle. That's what a carcass is—something dead, but was once alive. We were once a great people! And the Jesus that you've been looking for is not the man that lived 2,000 years ago. He was great and he pre-figured the Jesus that would deliver you from death. But the Jesus that would deliver you would himself be dead. And he would be the first begotten of the dead. For the Son of Man when he comes, He will raise him from the dead and give him power to raise you—a nation of dead people and put you on top of civilization."

Suddenly, he wanted Wali Eli to share more things with him, but his ego resisted having a perceived salesman teach him anything. Just then, Ms. Esther motioned for them to join the other guests. She was telling everyone about the community meetings she had been attending with Wali Eli, and she was inviting others. Shaking his head all the while, Reverend Washington tried to separate what was real and what was imagined. He had a binary responsibility where moral fortitude sometimes conflicted with duplicity. It was easier to be instructed by the designated leaders like Kent Jr. Johnson than to make unpopular decisions. He had already heard that some of the lynchings were being discussed at the community meetings, and though he cared deeply, it was too risky to discuss it and call himself a man of the cloth. When the two large circles of guests merged into one, Reverend Washington left his seat and walked outside to take a puff from his pipe without muttering another word.

The church members were taking turns watching Vivian and spying on Minnie, too. Henry hadn't appeared, and the party was over. Minnie's disappointment was written all over her every fake smile, hug, and handshake.

She was distraught that he'd walked so far to bring Vivian home on Tuesday, but that he didn't ask to see her. Minnie wanted to see him every day, as she was consumed with loving him. She had wanted to dash outside after him when she saw them together on the corner, but something in the way he hurried off halted her. Something in the way Vivian watched after him made Minnie take in that Henry did not desire to be detained.

At the very moment during the party that Minnie thought those thoughts, Henry rested on his cot staring at the ceiling with his hands under his head. He knew the party was taking place now; however it didn't seem particularly important at all. What was important was whether Vivian had made up with Lee. He couldn't help wondering if Lee was there with a leash on her. Henry considered the possibility of Lee daring to kiss her, even after having the unmitigated audacity to beat her--and if so, would Vivian be too blind to see the betrayal in Lee's actions? Would Vivian think of him? Henry got up from the cot, his shoulders slumped, and went over to the crate containing his clothes that sat neatly under the window. He leaned on the crate, envisioning Vivian's bright smile and gay laughter. If Vivian had said she wanted to stay on with him, he would have let her, he confessed to himself. How could he send her away after taking her most precious gift if she wanted to stay?

Only, she'd made it painstakingly clear that she wasn't interested in the risk they both would have to take to be together. Henry granted to himself that leaving would be easier on everyone. He wasn't a dramatic person, had never been involved in any domestic scandals, and he didn't want to cause pain to Minnie or anyone else. Indeed, he resolved, it was best that things turned out the way they did. He reached down, picked up the crate for a moment, and then he dropped it back to the floor with a crushing thud. Henry decided miserably that he didn't want to do anything regarding preparation for his journey. He wasn't interested in taking most of his meager belongings with him, therefore it took him under two hours to pack some sentimental items on top of his clothes. There was no one who wanted to hear his goodbyes. His father didn't want to discuss the trip, had refused the invitation to the party, and thus refused to take the time out to even meet Minnie. Furthermore, he decisively wasn't speaking to Henry on this last day. The only thing he wanted to hear was that Henry had changed his mind about leaving.

Henry's mother simply covered her face and cried when she knew for sure that Henry was serious about leaving on Friday. She left it to her husband to try and change Henry's mind. Mrs. Raison imagined Henry was punishing her for something she had done years ago. But she hadn't thought he could be extreme enough to really move so far away. Both of Henry's parents had been invited to the party, yet it would have been better that Henry never extended the invitation, considering its utter lack of appreciation.

Lee knew about the party, too. It didn't take long for Madeline to check on Vivian after her dear friend's sheer dishonor at the church. She came to call on Monday, the day before Vivian returned home. Henry had just left an hour earlier after bringing the news concerning Vivian's whereabouts. Robeena told her that Vivian was away with a friend, sorting things out, and should return home soon. Although she didn't say it, Robeena alluded that the friend Vivian was with was Lee. Robeena looked at Minnie for a sign of gratitude, but Minnie broke the subject to tell Madeline about their forthcoming departure. Robeena knew Minnie was secretly embarrassed that Henry was caring for her sister, regardless of the circumstances or Ms. Tazra's involvement. In truth, she wanted Madeline to know, too, so that together they could shame Minnie to her senses. Like Carol, Robeena judged it to be improper to have Vivian over all night on the Raison Plantation, even if she was at Tazra's place, when Minnie was his girl. Whatever help Tazra was providing, she was reporting to Henry. Why was Henry her patron? Minnie kept the truth private because she didn't want Madeline to think the wrong thing about her fiancé's relationship with her sister.

Minnie was all too eager to drop the subject about Vivian and announce the going away party, whereas Madeline felt it befitting to relay the information to Lee, who lived just up the road from her. She figured the news about the party would be a great excuse to see Vivian at Lee's house, had she been there. When Madeline saw Lee Monday evening, sloppy and drunk, she thought it was a shame that he should waste his good looks by behaving like a savage.

Lee wanted to attend the party but figured his presence would merely cause a scene. He was apprehensive about what Vivian must have told her family and too spineless to face any of them right away. Yet, he intended on seeing her later, just as soon as the gathering of people dispersed. On Thursday after work, he bathed, and then stalled time until he believed it was safe to go to Vivian. Lee was not a praying man, but that day he got down on his knees, begging God to see him through the upcoming endeavors. He promised God that if he could get Vivian back, he would never mishandle her again. He'd simply have to find some other way to make her obedient.

Falling prostrate, Lee bargained that he would appear at church regularly and keep up prayer. Lee knew there was a God somewhere, but he didn't have a relationship with Him. He knew God was real because of the evidence that he could see in the birds, the trees, and the sun. On this day, he called on the God who created the heavens and the earth, the fowl of the air, the fish of the sea, and every creeping thing that crawls. He begged God that if Vivian was returned to him, he would honor her, treat her like a princess, protect her, stay away from his ladies who served as bed warmers, glorify her by making her his wife, and he would stand as a principled man with high character, credit, and distinctive morals.

In his communion with God, Lee interpreted that ironically, the umbrella of the cynical community in which he lived mocked his attempt to ascribe to himself decent morals, given that fornication, drinking, and gambling were all good, and suitable just two steps away from church doors. However acceptable his lifestyle was in society, it still didn't jive with his nature because after tarrying out of bounds however slightly, Lee's self-accusing spirit hinted at whispered admonitions. It was a hard struggle because his self-accusing spirit was buried under the rubbish of a corrupt society where right was made to be seen as wrong, and wrong was accepted as right. But society was like a strong-willed person who would be accepted. Society represented the culmination of power, force, and the standard of the mighty. In his position of prostration, Lee rejected the standard, vowing to increase his personal integrity.

It unfolded to Lee that when he engaged in eccentric, loose behavior, his father, and all his friends openly applauded him. Yet deep under the debris where the self-accusing spirit was buried, Lee knew faintly that he was stinging people—that some of his female partners were developing romantic feelings for him... feelings he could not, or would not return. The society in the South and in America at large allowed man to seek pleasure first, and then suffer the consequences later, if any.

Although God said no fornication, society decided it was okay. Lee admitted that he was overly accepting of sexual norms, while God's rule on killing should be followed, given that the so-called freed slaves were murdered at whim based on the color of their skin. After the abolition of slavery, pockets of conditions improved, yet the trembles from the aftermath would effect centuries and generations to come, and the consequences would be so severe that Negroes would even refuse reparations for their suffering and the suffering of their people because the internal damage was not even detected by them. The damage was soaked into the seams of the mighty society who did not want to deal with the Negro problem. As such, the damage would be like an infectious disease, a silent killer of ambitions, self-love, and self-respect. Other pockets revealed an air of hostility toward "uppity Negroes" who dared to scowl at the sovereign efforts of the southern planters.

As far as the trembles of the aftermath of slavery, one impact was the absence of shame. Whereas during slavery, women practiced discretion and modesty, a hundred and fifty years up from slavery, for sheer amusement, it was not unheard of for a so-called African American woman to allow a man to swipe a credit card between her buttocks indicating that she's for sale, and have this filmed musical video captioned as entertainment for the world to see on un-censored television right when unsuspecting adolescent latch key children were bursting in their homes unsupervised and plopping down in front of the stupid box, and the music video would play again right at prime time, yet few would cry out against the behavior, while others would watch and cheer. The internal and structural damage of a whole people would go ignored in the minds of 85% of the poor, rejected, and despised. Since societal norms dictated that her standards were the best choices, more and more men would be honored and respected by their material wealth rather than moral substance.

In most of America, democracy was the voice of the people, not the voice of morality. If most of the people wanted to defile their bodies, murder, rape, and commit adultery, then these things were done, and justified with deceptive intelligence. If most of the people wanted to gamble, then laws were passed to make it legal. Those who suffered death, destruction, and mayhem because of becoming addicted to gambling were left to fend for themselves. If they lost their jobs, stole from their families, wreaked havoc on the community, so what. Even in America's courts, the majority ruled. It was okay to rape a woman, as long as she was a Negro. After all, she was considered to be only three-fifths of a human being. Although the three-fifths rule was made to control property and influence elections, the common citizen viewed Negroes as being substandard, and not fully human.

Lee's former slave masters were the gods of his world, rather than the True and Living God, with Whom Lee had no acquaintance. This is because he honored, worshiped, and obeyed *them* as he should have honored, worshiped, and obeyed God. His nature, however, rejected Satan's hold, yet Lee had not the foundation of morality to sustain himself as an upright man. Since Lee couldn't please both the world and his self-accusing spirit, it came to be that the spirit remained buried and gauche animal instincts governed his direction. Nevertheless, when challenges emanated (such as the possibility of losing Vivian), Lee knew inherently that he had to recognize the True and Living God.

On his knees in submission, Lee acknowledged the Beneficent, the Merciful God. Now, Lee appealed to the God of his nature with sincere intentions to begin listening to his self-accusing spirit rather than his lower, earthly appetite. All too soon, Lee stood up from his bent knees, changed into a fresh, crisp shirt, and sat at the kitchen table to wait.

He gazed at the half empty bottle of whiskey, tempted to take a swig. "I better not," he cerebrated. "God is sufficient for me." Then, another voice crept in as he mulled over how he was going to face Vivian sober. Already, the self-accusing spirit was being buried away when Lee decided he needed an external source of reinforcement rather than looking to the God within for strength. He snatched the whiskey bottle up, tilted it, gulping its contents until he could feel the tension leaving his body.

CHAPTER TWELVE
"I done learned my lesson"

As Vivian sat by herself at the party, indifferent to the visitors gawking at her, she began to lose her strength of resistance for Lee. She estimated that surely he should have come over to apologize by now. She sighted Robeena having a glorious time, laughing, and chattering, making her long for Lee even more. Maybelle crept up into her thoughts. "You ruined everything," Vivian judged. She entertained the suspicion that Maybelle was indeed lying. However, considering Lee's reputation, she noted that that was a very unlikely notion. Consequently, she rationalized that it mattered not if Maybelle was pregnant by her man…it was clear that Lee didn't want her. "I'm the one he wants," she hypothesized with a smile.

With amazing distortion, Vivian pictured the way Lee had rushed her out of the church to shield her. She remembered how he had begged her at his house to marry him, and not to allow other people to come between them. "He only hit me because I threatened to leave him," she defended. She ended up scolding herself for being so dogmatic on Sunday during their argument. "Or rather, when I argued, and he talked," she suggested to herself. She warily looked at some of the single, more mature women from the church who were also looking at her. Vivian smiled partially, her one semi-good eye shifting from their faces to their slumped postures and gloomy countenance. "Lee wants to *marry* me. Me. I'm better than some old maid who doesn't have a man," she convinced herself.

Lee's absence shook her firm resolution a bit, though, while she wondered where he was. "Then why hasn't he come for me?" she hissed. Vivian decided at that moment to return to his house as soon as she could. With a sickening fear, she pictured him with his arms wrapped around Maybelle. "Have I given my man away? No! She can't have him. I'm letting her win . . . she knew I'd get cross if she came to the church! I let that heifer put me in a fix," she blamed. "I should've kept Lee when I had him." Vivian breathed heavily. Her tongue flickered in and out in anxious anticipation. "And Floyd! How could I believe that hobo over Lee? Floyd is surely jealous of Lee. Likely, Lee *was* with Maybelle once—but that doesn't mean he's the father! No one can tell me a wench like that doesn't have at least a few men hopping, whooping, and calling!" Vivian glanced at Minnie's sunken countenance as she was mulling over her predicament. She didn't want to think about how Henry had made her feel so beautiful and special after Lee publicly shamed her. Unlike with her and Lee, Minnie and Henry seemed to have a trouble-free relationship, except she had just ruined that for her sister. Nonetheless, Vivian felt that somehow if Lee would come, everything would snap back to normal.

Carol almost had to jerk Vivian's audience away one by one as she helped to usher the well-wishers out of her modest house because of the lateness of the hour. Fulfilled, they all left with plenty to report to their loved ones and friends who didn't come: Minnie's fiancé never even showed up to at least thank everyone for the gifts; A preacher man of sorts by the name of Mr. Eli, who knew the Bible inside out, even better than the reverend was there; and lastly, Vivian's face was all bandaged and taped. The general whispered consensus was that she was wearing a purple eye that Lee (who also didn't show up) gave her.

Wali Eli left with the guests, walking out with a parishioner who had questions about being raised to a higher level of consciousness. After giving the parishioner information on their next community meeting, Wali Eli moved down the road in silence, concentrating on his goal of finding one person to teach, then perhaps that person could help do something to save the Vivian's, Minnie's, and even the reverends from the mental graves that their lives had become since and before their servitude in the wilderness of North America.

A tired Vivian was happy to see everyone leave, at last, even though it was too late to venture the journey to Lee's place. Not only that, but Vivian had no idea what she was going to say to Lee whenever they would meet again. Her family seemed thoroughly convinced that the relationship between them was over. They, too, had expected Lee to show up by Tuesday night. When he didn't come by Wednesday, Carol was relieved. In the face of her family, Vivian deluded them into believing she also disapproved of Lee. Too many other things were going on in the home for them to notice how Vivian jumped at the sound of every noise that could signify that Lee was at the door or window.

That night, Minnie wasn't interested at all in Vivian's social life with Lee, or whether Vivian jumped at the sound of a bird landing on the roof. Minnie's concern involved Henry and the dishonor his absence had caused her. Had he decided to cancel their traveling plans? She was completely packed already, and so was Robeena. Minnie wanted to go straight to bed and dive in headfirst onto the mattress after the guests had all gone, but Carol was feeling sentimental. She gathered her three daughters together in the front room. Carol sat in the chair where her mother died while her daughters curled up next to her on the floor.

"Whatever happens after this point . . . we's a family. It don't make no never mind where each other lives, we gotta stay in touch with each other. I loves y'all equal, y'all hear?"

"Yes, mama," Robeena answered, followed by the chiming of both of her preoccupied sisters. She glanced at all the dishes that had yet to be washed tonight. Sometimes, Robeena liked being the helper. Just as she had stayed behind and counseled the heart-stricken Maybelle who needed her services, now, she could clearly see that Minnie's disappointment about Henry not coming and Vivian's pain made them both poor candidates for housekeeping. Whether she mumbled about it or not, she wouldn't dream of going to bed without cleaning up for her mama and sisters.

"...Remember the Lord in ev'rything you do, chil'ren. Don't let a day go by without you giving thanks to Jesus." She looked at Vivian. "On account of you staying here with your poor mama, you *know you* ain't excused from your daily prayers."

"Yes'm," Vivian responded mechanically. Carol paid attention to Vivian's short reply only vaguely, as a more pressing issue captured her attention.

"Robeena! Look at you, gal! You is nothing but a child! Why you wanna go to some ole Michigan? A place you don't know nothing 'bout? Minnie can't take care of you proper . . . she gwine be running up behind a man the whole time." Carol rolled her eyes at Minnie, who cringed at the reminder that Henry was not her husband. Robeena panicked. Had her mother picked this time to tell her she couldn't go?

"I got dreams, mama," she pitched. "I got big dreams for that new land up North."

"That land ain't new, gal." Carol wasn't the least bit curious about what she considered Robeena's nonsense dreams. She had no idea Robeena could dance so well, or that she even liked to dance.

"But mama..."

"I know, Robeena." Vivian and Minnie seemed preoccupied, and neither did Robeena appear to recognize her mother's attempt at closeness. Carol felt dejected about the fact that her daughters were willing to leave without wanting to spend quality time with her.

"Who's going to wash the dishes?" Vivian asked, looking over at Robeena.

"That all you care 'bout?" Carol knew Vivian was taking Robeena for granted.

"I'm sleepy, mama. We are still up this late all because they are supposed to be leaving town. If they're leaving so early, then we should go on to bed, it seems."

"Then go to sleep, dummy. You big loser."

"Why are you calling me a loser, Minnie? You're going to see who the loser is when you get way up the highway with no money." She diffidently thought of the wad of dollars hidden in her shoes that Henry had given her. She knew that had to be trip money and that she'd cut her sister short by accepting money meant for her trip. Oh well, she thought, it seemed like he had plenty more, anyway. Embittered, she measured that Lee had never broken her off so lavishly.

"Y'all cut out that fighting."

"Henry got money. We wouldn't be leaving if he didn't. You's just jealous 'cause you can't go. You gotta stay down here and let Lee beat on you."

"Leave me alone!" Jumping up, Vivian yelled at the top of her lungs. "Whatever money Henry has isn't yours. You're not his wife—maybe you never will be!"

"No, we will get married, and it'll be good. If you're stupid enough to marry Lee, it'll never be good. You know why? It's on account of you've been a nasty wench. Won't no real man want a ruined ally-cat like you!"

"That's a lie! Leave me alone!" Vivian tried to slap Minnie, but Robeena grabbed her hand." Minnie saw that she wouldn't have had time to move away from Vivian's slap had Robeena not intervened.

"Vivian! Calm down!" Carol stood, gathering Vivian in a rocking squeeze. Vivian became rigid.

"Leave her alone, Minnie. That wasn't nice."

"*You* stay outta it, squirt."

"I hate her, mama."

"That's not true." Carol rolled her eyes at Minnie. "Minnie...you's a wicked something." Minnie turned her nose up and away.

"Yeah, Minnie, that was a cruel thing to say. Henry ain't ev'rything, you know. Just because he don't beat on you yet don't give you no cause to jump on Viv like that. Henry still ain't asked you to marry him, did he?"

"We *are* getting married, you li'l donkey."

"Alright! That's enough! Minnie, you're too ornery." Carol was pointing her finger at both of them, holding the stiff daughter tightly. She felt Vivian's stiffness, but anticipated if she held her long enough it would go away. Vivian didn't want her mother's touch. She smelled stale to her. Vivian felt that closeness between them was too late.

"Let go, mama." Sullenly, Carol loosened her, giving Minnie another threatening look. Robeena and Minnie kept quiet, respecting their mother's command, but the back-and-forth glares continued until they both heard their mother in the background of their thoughts, lecturing them again.

"I reckon we *would* be fighting, knowing our lives is about to change forever. We should learn how to find joy in that. That's what I hafta do. Y'all know I ain't too keen on no moving outta state like you's doing. I suppose if you got your mind set on it, I gotta support you. Never said I agreed." She shook her head. "Never said that."

"Are you still sleepy, Viv?" Vivian looked at Minnie before answering. When she perceived the fight was gone, she answered.

"Yes."

"Me, too," Minnie said apologetically.

"I'll wash the dishes, then. Later." Robeena closed her eyes and leaned her head against the back of the chair, stretching her legs out in front of her.

"I'd like to stay like this for the rest of the night with y'all."

"Don't worry, mama, I ain't even trying to move," Minnie piped. As tense as the moments before and even the days past had been, they all felt they could exhale. They each had a chance to release pent up emotions, only to find they were still there for each other. Carol and her daughters rarely spent close moments together, filled with sharing, expression, and tears. Tonight would be like a sleepover between friends. They all needed each other. Somehow, being there together in the front room wiped away fears and loneliness, and replaced those dreadful feelings with harmony and peace. Carol hummed "Swing Low, Sweet Chariot" in a delicate quiet whisper until the girls were lulled into a light sleep.

Then suddenly, everyone was unbounded from their placid states when they heard the front doorknob turn a few minutes later. It was locked. A knock came shortly. No one moved. Vivian's heart did somersaults at the anticipation of Lee. She put on her "how dare you come here" face. Minnie was frozen with optimism. "Better late than never," she thought, regarding Henry. Robeena and Carol awaited the audacity of Lee. The knock became more urgent. At last, Robeena went to the door and opened it. She stood blocking the passageway, gawking at the visitor. The stranger shoved her aside impatiently, hardly looking at her. He only glanced at the other two girls briefly. He didn't notice the cloth covering Vivian's eye. "Watch out, now, gal! Where's your mama at?" Carol stood, postponing her precious farewell moments with her daughters, and went to greet the stranger. Carol didn't see Robeena staring at her with mixed emotions.

The way Robeena saw it, having a relationship with a married man was not the problem; she was raised to believe it was sometimes inevitable and therefore acceptable. The problem as Robeena calculated was when her mother had been loyal solely to the stranger. Robeena was determined that when she got older, she would not rely on one single man to bring her a life of grief. She aimed to be a defender of women by causing pain to men, given that the man she knew as a father was conspicuously worthless. The stroke of her father's nonchalance over her existence caused Robeena to downplay the decency of her Uncle Jack, Mr. Anderson, even the polite, well-mannered sharecroppers whom she was taught to judge erringly. She missed the goodness of the Black angels who were called niggers and coons; the very men who did all they could to protect their communities--and clumped all men in the same sack as her father. Wali Eli was the one exception she could think of, perhaps because he was very light, and she was taught to have a distaste and distrust for those who were with dark complexions.

Robeena was the last to go to bed as she wrapped herself in glorious suppositions of how exciting a new life would be in Michigan. She finished the dishes with joy. Minnie and Vivian retired for the night not long after they watched on apathetically as their mother dragged the stranger in an emotionally starving grip to receive validation. The two twin sized mattresses pushed together on the floor gave each girl the leverage needed for maximum comfort, if they shared evenly. Sometimes, one of them used the mattress only as a pillow, while at other times it was used to cushion one's whole body. Usually, two of the girls would stretch vertically across the bed on opposite ends, forming a vee with their outstretched arms, making it difficult for the last retiree to find a clear space on the pad. The breeze coming from the slightly opened window offered a steady, calming whistle accompanied with the fresh seeping air.

After cleaning the kitchen, which took all of thirteen minutes, Robeena joined her sisters. "Move over, Minnie," Robeena urged as she forced her way on the edge.

"I'll be glad when we get to Michigan. I won't hafta share no bed with y'all. I'm gonna be sleeping with my husband. Yes!"

"You ain't got no husband, Minnie, now move over some more." Minnie didn't move, so Robeena threw her leg over her sister's waist. "I ain't sleeping on the floor after I just got done cleaning them stinking dishes while y'all laying out, talking 'bout sleeping with some man. You need to learn, Minnie, that you ain't got no husband."

"Shut-up, Beena. We's just as good as married. Soon as we get to Michigan, we gonna have a private ceremony, then we's gonna find a house and settle down."

"Girl, please. He's gonna spoil you first if he ain't already."

"You must be talking 'bout Viv and Lee, 'cause Henry ain't like that."

"Hey! Leave me out of it."

"He never asked you?"

"Asked me what?"

"You know." Minnie bubbled with pride and chastity, allowing Robeena more of the mattress.

"Naw. Henry's a gentleman. You see mama likes him."

"No she don't."

"Mama loves Henry. It's Lee she can't stand because she knows he ain't up to no good. He's done made a tramp outta you, Viv, and you too stupid to care. I don't be saying these things to fight with you. I'm trying to let you know how boys are!"

"Lee has never done anything nasty to me, either."

"Liar."

"Least he wants to marry me."

"Yeah. To treat you like daddy treats mama. That girl was ugly, too. That means Lee would sleep with a calf and marry you at the same time."

"Henry's the darkie monkey slave living in the field with animals. You wish he was fine like Lee, but he's not, on account of he's too crispy black like some burnt bacon. And that's sad because he's not too ugly for you, even though you're an animal yourself."

"Y'all shouldn't talk like that to each other."

"She shouldn't talk about Henry at all. He let her stay on the plantation that she likes to talk about so bad after Lee busted her face all up. You's stupid, Viv. I would never let a man beat me like that. Would you, Beena?"

"Girl, please. I'd cut 'im up first."

"I didn't ask your funky boyfriend to let me stay on that funky farm."

"That's right, trash. 'Cause if you go back over there again, I'll scratch your eyes out. Henry is so clean, he be smelling like soap. Your sorry man works with dirt and be coming o'er here all stank with some rotten oranges that he be buying you for. Yeah, I said it right, tramp. You keep your claws in that sneaky dog that was made for you."

"Your mama's a tramp, and so is your daddy. Now, you evil witch. I can talk like a slave, too. Whyn't you put some o' Henry's soap on yo' tongue and wash *that* out."

"Mmm, mmm, mmm. I wish folk could hear how trifling you really is. When you get 'round boys you be thinking you so hot, trying to talk all proper. But now look at you. Talking like a prostitute and then marching your tail up in church like you's so holy. You ain't the princess you try to make out to be by a long shot.

"Come on, y'all, go to sleep. It's late."

"I walk in church the same way my mama and my sisters walk in. I reckon we all cut from the same cloth."

"You o'er there talking 'bout your own mama."

"Minnie! Please!" They fought all the time. Robeena hated it.

"Okay. Viv ain't worth saving, no way. Good-night, Beena."

"Good-night. Good-night, Viv."

"Good-night, only to Robeena."

In the Johnson's house that night, sleep came easy for no one except the stranger. Everyone else heard Lee in the front yard thirty minutes after Robeena finished the dishes when he crept through the tall weeds, whistling softly all the way to the girls' bedroom window on the side. His black patent leather shoes that had waltzed brilliantly into the church, and spun in circles to the music of Blind Blake's guitar now sank in the moist dirt as he staggered closer. Lee swallowed his pride in one big gulp before calling Vivian's name gruffly. Although Carol only heard muffled voices, she was able to discern from the caller's intensity that it was Lee. Vivian's sisters heard how Lee pleaded with Vivian to come outside with him.

"Vivian!" He called. Robeena turned on her side to view the full effect of Vivian's response. "Vivian!" He called again, louder. Vivian crawled underneath the window, poking her head in his view before ducking back below the pane. She wanted him to receive the clue that she was close enough that there was no need for him to yell.

"What do you want, boy?" Vivian finally answered, trying to disguise the gaiety in her voice. She was well aware that her sisters were listening to every word, and that Minnie would undoubtedly report her response to all other interested parties not currently in earshot.

"I be needing to talk with you 'bout something important." She didn't respond. "Viv…come on outside for a spell," he begged.

"I'm not coming out there, Lee. It's over between us."

"Muffin, I'm sorry. Come on out here and see me, girl. I got something for you. I need to see you!" He cried desperately. She considered what spectacular, shiny trinket he might have gotten for her. "Well, if you're not coming out here, I'm coming in after you." He waited for her rebuff. Nothing. Vivian felt a rush of exhilaration after his last words. She hoped he begged well so she could give in to him dramatically. When he made his way through the window, she leaped erect with an air of disbelief, as though shocked that he had entered. She stood stock-still as he walked cautiously to her. Minnie and Robeena ceased feigning sleep, they now stared openly at the couple standing in the shadows. Minnie was in such a foul mood because of Henry's absence that she would have alerted their mother right away, were it not for the presence of the stranger in their home. She knew their mother acted like her daughters were invisible when the stranger came. Minnie knew the routine. With unusual animosity, she watched uninterrupted by the darkness as Lee took Vivian's hand in his, attempting to pull her outside.

"I'm not climbing out that window. Are you trying to wake up everybody? You know you're not supposed to be around here."

"Fine, Vivian. We can talk in here," he gestured toward the bedroom door. "Out there, I mean. I only need five minutes." He switched directions, heading for the front room of the tiny dwelling. She easily let herself be led away by him. Lee knew Vivian's mother didn't care much for him, however, his hopelessness prevented him from worrying much about the chance he was taking by being in their house at that hour.

"I'm only going to talk to you for five minutes," Vivian reminded him. She hurried him past the only other bedroom in the small cottage, to the couch. Vivian knew, too, that the stranger's presence meant her sisters would not be disturbing Carol.

"Hey, cutie," he said, sitting as close to her as he could manage without being overly distracting from his verbal ploy. "I don't know what happened. One minute, you and I was all right. My life stopped these last few days without you. I've made some mistakes, muffin, I admit that. I don't wanna talk 'bout Floyd and Maybelle. They's mad we're together and gonna get married." He clutched her hand tightly.

Vivian didn't want to talk about Maybelle, either. She felt things would be easier that way. Her intentions were to erase Maybelle and the unborn child out of her mind, and that Lee would do the same. Forever. She knew it could be done because she had experienced firsthand information. She witnessed the works of the stranger while he fiddled with her mother and danced with his wife, ignoring the three girls the whole time.

It didn't bother Vivian that her motives, though not ulterior, would help in depriving a child-to-be of his father. The jealousy contained in the idea that this unborn one should have a father when she never did unbalanced her rationality. She was acting primarily out of frustration rather than hostility. Vengeance was her second motive since indeed she was the widow of a pure relationship gone sour. Vivian charged Lee and Maybelle equally for that rape. In her mind, the soon to be fatherless child was a small price for Maybelle and Lee to pay compared to the suffering she'd endured by their unthinkable acts.

"You want me to accept Maybelle and that baby. Well, I'm not doing it, Lee." How was Vivian to know that she had just spoken similar words that the stranger's wife had spoken, approximately fifteen years ago when she learned that her husband had seeded three misbegotten children? As with the stranger's wife, Vivian would prefer that if anyone at all suffered from her fiancé's infidelities, it should be the children first, and the mistress second because the mistress would also suffer first through her children's agony. It never occurred to Vivian to encourage Lee to take responsibility for his actions. That would place too much risk on her own emotional and financial welfare, she philosophized.

"Naw, cutie pie. I done learned my lesson for kidding 'round with Floyd 'nem. They like to get me involved in a whole lotta stuff that's not right. When I first met you, I was still running 'round with Floyd, and yeah…we knew girls. But that was then," he minimized. I don't wanna see Maybelle or none of 'em. That's my past, Viv. Can't we leave the past where it belongs…in the past?"

Vivian wasn't satisfied. She wanted a direct and concise statement from Lee that he wouldn't have anything to do with the child, regardless of whether he was proven to be the father. They both secretly felt that if he denounced the child, Vivian might be convinced that she unequivocally was the most important person in the world to him. As far as Vivian was concerned, her emotional security with him could only come if he worshipped her over his parents, any unborn children, certainly over any other woman, and God, too.

"Now, that baby will be your excuse to be over there with her," Vivian insisted.

"Hell naw, muffin!" Inside, Lee was bubbling with joy. The way Vivian was talking made it appear as though there might be a chance that she'd take him back as long as he agreed with her on a few frivolous particulars. By then, Lee would've promised anything if he thought it could restore their relationship. "I'm not gonna have nothing to do with Maybelle. Besides, I ain't never said that was none of my child." Lee's self-accusing spirit advanced unexpectedly to the surface of his consciousness. It said in Lee's own voice in his mind: "You know that chances are ninety-nine to one that you most likely are the father of that baby. You need to take on the responsibility. Be honest with Vivian . . . no matter what."

"Promise?" Vivian asked. Lee shook away his integrity by promising himself that he'd deal with the truth one day, soon, but right now, Vivian needed something else from him.

"I promise." Neither of them dared to mention the beating Lee had given her. They both felt inwardly that to discuss the physical attack would take too much effort. Lee carried on like he didn't see the wound dressing that was not secured well over her eye. Vivian believed there were acceptable extenuating circumstances as to why he had resorted to violence. She said to herself, "If my man is going to beat me, it'd be better be because he thinks he's fixing to lose me." These thoughts guarded her. Then, Vivian thought about her two straight days with Henry. Their time together touched her so exceptionally that she had to forcibly shove him out of her mind and heart. She told herself that if Lee had not beaten her, Henry never would have had the opportunity to claim her soul. She rationalized that her nights and days with Henry were the untold price Lee had to pay for his acts of corruption and fraud.

Lee omitted apologizing for the beating because once before, he had promised never to hit her again, yet he had recently broken that promise. He figured if he brought it up now, it would be like opening a complex issue, especially since Vivian hadn't demanded an apology. He stretched back on the sofa in a sitting position, with Vivian's head resting on his chest. They were both tired, but they didn't want to leave each other yet. They knew they couldn't spread out together on her mother's couch, so they slept like that, sitting, until dawn. If anyone saw them, no one could accuse them of doing anything wrong. Certainly now, sitting in Lee's arms in plain view in the front room wasn't as distasteful as being tucked away behind a locked door like her mother. Carol simply wasn't a positive role model in this aspect for her children, and she knew this left her weak to speak against their wrongs.

The first person to discover them was the stranger. He left Carol to go home at 4:30 a.m. His wife considered 4:30 still to be nighttime. If he got home while it was still dark, she didn't fuss too much. The stranger saw two people tangled together confidentially on the sofa. It took a moment for his eyes to focus on the face of his daughter with a man. She wore a contented, soft smile. The stranger was disgusted to think that his daughter was allowed to entertain a man at home, and at that hour! He marched closer to get a better look at the man nestling his daughter. He knew him! Even though he worked on the other side of the tracks, they both worked at the railway company. In addition, the stranger had gambled with Lee Sr. as well as young Lee Hiram. In fact, the stranger considered Lee Sr. his friend. He had seen young Lee at some of the town's wildest parties since whenever Lee was only fifteen years old. His father had been with him, then, and had bought prostitutes for Lee.

The stranger never had paid much attention to his daughters. He was trying to figure out if Vivian was the youngest or the middle child. He would have to see them together to remember. And it was easy for him not to know her because in all her sixteen, soon to be seventeen years, the stranger never had one personal conversation with her, and he had never once looked her in the eyes. He saw now that Vivian was beautiful—much more so indeed than her mother had been at her age.

The eye bandage had slipped halfway off sometime during the night. The stranger pulled a matchbook out of his pocket. Hastily, he swiped one stick, using the flame from it to find a candle. He discovered a night lamp that had lost its blaze, so he carried his fire over to light it. He could see that Vivian had certainly been hit. The stranger saw her healing, yet swollen eye. He looked at Lee's tall, more than semi-muscular frame with his arm draped sloppily over Vivian while he snored moderately. It was evident to him that Lee was more than likely the one who had given her the purple eye. He considered Carol and her hard mouth that had caused him to slap *her* a few times, but his daughter was different, he reasoned. No man had the right to beat one of his natural flesh and blood children.

"Hey," he yelled. Both Vivian and Lee jumped awake. The stranger held the lamp close, as though he was still trying to decide who the parties were.

"Hey, yourself," Lee said easily, not bothering to remove his arm from around Vivian's shoulder, or to sit up straight. Lee instantly recognized the stranger from the nightlife. Lee knew of his wife, and he also knew of the stranger's prominence in the prostitution houses, but he did not know he was Vivian's father. "How you been, player?" Lee asked in an overly friendly manner.

"You don't got no business in here, boy," he spit back at Lee. Lee squinted at him, taken aback. He expected if anyone would question his presence, it would be Carol or Minnie.

"Daddy!" Vivian looked around. Lee straightened himself to erectness when Vivian confirmed paternity. "Be quiet lest you start waking folk. This is Lee, and he has just as much right to be here as you do." Lee was ecstatic that she would defend him.

"I don't give a skip who I wake up," he said louder than before, "I wanna know how you end up with a bruised eye?" The stranger paced closer so that he peered directly into Vivian's face. Carol and Vivian's sisters came quickly to the front room when they heard the stranger's interference. Carol was too tired to be bothered with all of this. She knew Lee was there--the thin walls did not conceal his verbal reconciliation mutterings--but she had hoped Vivian was sensible enough to get him out of the house before she might be required to address it.

"It's not your concern!" Vivian screeched. She was annoyed that the stranger had reminded them that Lee had physically abused her.

"I'm yo' daddy. Whether you like it or not, I'm yo' daddy. And dat's disgracing as hell to have a child ev'rybody knows is mine laying up and carrying on . . ."

Robeena laughed in the background. Startled, the stranger turned to see what was so funny.

"Her *father*?" Robeena emphasized. "You got some nerve coming o'er here trying to tell somebody what to do or who to be! We don't even know you. You're not *really* our daddy."

"Now hold it. I know I ain't always here . . ."

"Please!" Robeena cut him off. "We don't even know you. You don't know us, neither. You've never been interested in anything o'er here but disgraceful things." Carol covered her mouth with her hand. "You know what you are to me?" Robeena asked, "You know what the first thing is I see in my head when I think of you? You's a stranger. That's what I'm fixing to call you from now on." Lee felt sorry for their father at that moment. His self-accusing spirit tried to tell him that he could be in the same predicament as a nameless father if he didn't do right by Maybelle. Yet, Lee became exasperated with his self-accusing spirit for always putting pressure on him, so he quickly buried it back into his sub-consciousness.

"Y'all's mama evidently didn't teach y'all no respect," he invoked. It was hard to tell the amount of emotion he felt due to his aura of indifference. When Robeena perceived he wanted a fight, she braced her small feet on the floor, tightened her jaw, and prepared to give him a sound piece of her mind.

"Mayhap if you'd been around, *you* could've taught us some." If it were not for the sound of an approaching surrey to alarm the stranger, Robeena would have gotten that fight she wanted with her last words. The stranger walked to the front door and opened it.

"Lord, have mercy! Who dat is, comin' o'er here dis time o' morning in a horse drawn carriage?" Minnie's heart raced. Robeena jumped up and down. The sisters and Carol forgot about the stranger completely in their excitement that Henry had arrived with the coach.

"He's here! He's here!" Minnie cried. "Beena, is you ready?" Robeena rushed past the stranger out the front door and onto the damp, muddy lawn to greet Henry, but as he grew nearer still, she ran back inside to report that it actually was Henry who had come at last. Minnie's rubbery legs didn't dare take her outside. She turned to her mother who was standing now by the stranger, peering out the front door at Henry as he strolled out of the coach. Carol was explaining to the stranger about the move when Minnie interrupted with, "Oh mama! Bye, mama." Robeena and Minnie went to give their mother a hug and a kiss each, and then they wandered away a few feet

—both feeling too uncomfortable to remain close to the stranger for more than a second. The stranger gathered the main points of what was happening quickly, and then he turned to Carol with more blame.

Henry could see the discontent of the stranger at the doorway. He paced himself slowly to where the unhappy couple stood. "What kinda loose house is you running, Carol?" You got one of my daughters playing house with a known hustler," he shot Lee a look filled with venom. Lee knew when to keep quiet. He had already concluded from the stranger's conversation with Robeena that he was just briefing through, blowing off steam. The stranger continued, "And the other two fixin' to run off with a fellow who none of 'em married to." Henry moved like he didn't hear all that was being said as he reached Carol and the stranger. He greeted the stranger shortly, without bothering to extend his hand, nodded at Carol, giving her a brief hug, and then kissed Minnie on the cheek. Robeena smiled at him and then ran to take a quick bath.

The stranger knew he was defeated. He suddenly wanted to know this alluring man coming for his daughter, yet Robeena's words stung in his ears. Carol had turned away from him to get the baskets of food for the trip, leaving him standing alone to look on at the family moving about.

For the absolute first time, he acknowledged he had missed out on his children's life. It was way too late. He'd been so busy trying to pretend they didn't exist when the whole town knew that they did anyway. The children he'd always wanted—he got them years ago and he slapped his gift from God to the ground as though his daughters were not worthy of his gratitude or time. He knew he had betrayed his covenant with God, so how could he accept his children as a gift *from* God? The stranger swayed away from the house into the dark dawn of the morning. He looked back to wave at whoever cared, but no one noticed his departure.

Henry surveyed the room. His eyes stopped on Lee, who had managed to usher Vivian to the far side of the kitchen where he felt they could privately seal their continued relationship contract. Lee wasn't sure if Carol would be putting him out shortly. Way from the kitchen, Lee immediately caught Henry's glare.

The two men communicated silently. Henry didn't give Lee the same questioning, sedated look he had given him whenever they first met each other face to face. Instead, Henry pierced his eyes and openly frowned. Lee wasn't expecting such antagonism. He knew Henry had seen him before messing with the girls on the Raison Plantation, and supposed Henry's disdain resulted from that. Henry was a main reason Lee decreased his visits with Maybelle. However, just a week after Maybelle showed up at the church,

Lee rushed to see her again. He explained to her that he didn't mean to disturb her like that in the church, but it was all because she had surprised him with her visit.

Lee snapped himself away from the image of Maybelle when he discovered Henry was still scowling at him. Just as Lee was about to shoot daggers back at him, Henry turned away.

"Minnie," Henry said quietly.

"Yes, Henry?" Carol stared at him.

"I need to talk to you in private." He nodded his head in the direction of the outside. Minnie licked her lips, unsure of herself.

"Now? Can't it wait, Henry? We can talk all the way to Michigan if we like." Carol crossed her arms over her chest and shook her head. She glanced sharply at Vivian. Lee and Vivian weren't in hearing distance, nor were they paying attention to Henry. Lee was asking Vivian if she would let him come back later that day to see her.

"Come on, Minnie," he said, turning around. He walked ahead of her, not waiting to see if she would follow. Minnie wouldn't look at anyone as she rushed out after Henry. Carol stood stark still, staring at the door Minnie closed behind her.

"What is it? You're embarrassing me, Henry." He kept his back to her.

"Minnie. I just want us to be sure, that's all."

"I am, I am!" She touched his arm. When he didn't move, she gently urged him to face her. She gave him a weak smile when he finally turned to her. "And why talk about this now?" He started to speak, but Minnie cut him off. "Look. Robeena is ready, too. You're just being silly, Henry. Let's go back in so they won't be thinking the worst."

"Wait, Minnie." He forced himself to look her in the eyes. "We're talking about a lifetime here. I think I was wrong for pressuring you to leave your family like this. We ain't gotta do it just because people is expecting us to."

"Henry, when you asked me to be your girl, you didn't do it because people expected you to---you did it because you wanted to. And I said yes because I wanted to. There was a reason you came o'er with the coach this morning. God led you to do that because you didn't hafta come."

"I know that..."

"Look at us! We all nervous and stuff. Come on, Henry, you're finally gonna get the dream that was always yours. Don't let your fear get in your way. There ain't no pressure. I'll love you forever. I'll be a good wife to you one day. Henry, I'll see to it that your dreams all will come true."

"You is making me 'shamed, girl. I'm the one supposed to be saying them things to you."

"It don't make no never mind 'bout who say it. Long as we both believe in it."

"Maybe you're right."

"Of course I'm right." She looked away. "Let's go back in, Henry." He stood silent with his head hanging down. He knew he would be out of place to ask what Lee was doing in their house at that hour. Staring at the ground, Henry pursed his lips tightly, aware that he cared more about Lee's business than he did about whatever Minnie was saying. It was stupid of him to come with the coach, only to tell her he had a change of plans. Minnie started to say something else, but she couldn't afford to take that risk, so she simply pressed her eyes closed and went back inside. Carol backed up just in time to avoid being smacked by the door.

"Is ev'rything okay? Where's Henry?"

"What do you mean, mama?"

"Nothing. I just thought it was odd that he called you outside, and he hasn't come back in yet."

"How dare you!"

"Wait a minute with that tone, Minnie."

"I was outside talking to my fiancé about something personal regarding us eloping. You wouldn't understand, mama. I just don't like it when you invade my privacy." Henry walked back inside with his head still hanging low. "I hafta go, mama. Never mind."

"Don't act sour on your last night, Minnie."

"Oh there you are, Henry. Let me go get Robeena. This is the most joyous day of my life," she shrieked. Carol walked away, too.

During his short visit that morning, Henry failed in his attempt to hide his feelings for Vivian. He gave himself away to both Carol and Lee because he refused to so much as look at Vivian when it was obvious that he should. He didn't speak to her at all for the full hour he was there. He hugged Carol goodbye, and even shook Lee's hand half-heartedly. Lee saw Vivian slide up to Henry to offer a goodbye, but Henry responded like she wasn't there. Lee knew Henry secretly wanted to squeeze a pretty girl like Vivian on his way out of town, knowing it would be his only opportunity to do so. Therefore, Lee supposed that Henry was trying to throw him off the scent, to no avail.

Henry couldn't say the things he wanted to say, and he didn't know if he'd ever have an occasion to explain things to Vivian again. It was too deep for a mere goodbye hug to seal it for him. Henry was a recluse. World War One and his travels served to strip him of his innocence and confidence. There were things that happened to him that he could never share with anyone. After being hunted like a dog by bullets and nooses on both sides of the world and hunted by two vastly different but conniving, exceptionally well to do Caucasian women, Henry went into himself and lost general trust in people.

The first woman wasn't even supposed to be there. In Germany, his opening assignment was to secure the captain's wife who traveled with the crew, along with about ten other women for "special" purposes. He felt like the biblical Joseph as he drew inner strength to resist her satanic devices, only, he didn't feel anyone would take too kindly about that high class woman's desire and simply jail him and then make him king—he knew he would be hung if the word got out that she favored him. And it was clear to him that she wanted revenge for his unexpected refusals.

Alas, he escaped with his life. But when he returned home, it was like the captain's wife was reincarnated through a rich Raison girl. Henry didn't even trust his mother because she had been fighting for the enemy all her life. Henry believed she would sell him out if it pleased her white gods. So, when he came home from the war and one of the female Raison offspring tried to place him in yet another compromising situation, he knew he couldn't alert his parents of her misconduct. However, he was successful in politely denying her and keeping totally to himself because he thought it would be better. He didn't think he could trust another female, and so he became a recluse. He knew Vivian would never believe him if he told her that he hadn't had a woman in years. And what was she thinking about him and the love he'd made to her, only to witness him leave with her sister four days later?

The hardest thing Henry ever had to do was walk out of that door, leaving Vivian behind. It ached worse than the endless punishments from his mother, worse than the sound of bullets just over his head, thousands of miles from home. In his mind, he knew for sure now that he loved her. The love he felt was stronger than the love he had for her when he watched her limp behind him a few nights ago. It was stronger than the day she passed him lemonade on the porch, or the day she walked into his arms for a dance and confided in him. If there was a hint during any of those previous times that she loved him back, it would not have been too late for him to cross sides and leave Minnie with dignity. In Henry's view, now, he had already made his choice, and evidently Vivian had made hers. His heart was noble, even as he resisted the itch in his neck that beckoned him to turn back and give Vivian a farewell glance when he walked out of the door with Minnie in tow. His soul yearned for Vivian right then and there, yet he shook the vision of Vivian's smiling face in his arms just days ago from his mind.

Minnie and Robeena were laughing and chattering excitedly about their journey. He walked silently beside them, dropping Minnie's hand as he helped them one at a time into the coach. Vivian and Lee followed the trio to the yard quietly behind Carol and watched them board. Henry trotted past Vivian with his head bowed, back to the porch to fetch the bags that the girls had lugged there. On his second trip back to the porch, he remembered he meant to return her bonnet that he had stuffed in his knap-sack. Henry tried to recall what his reasoning was for not simply giving it to Minnie that day a lifetime ago after Vivian had dropped it on the porch. One thing was for sure; there was no way he could return it now with Lee smothering her, Henry decided. Henry climbed in after giving Carol another hug, and sat next to Minnie.

"We gonna board the train in Tallahassee, Ms. Carol. We got a pretty long ways to go like this." She nodded absently, silent tears forming behind her eyelids. There were two Negro drivers talking together in the front of the coach. They glanced around between comments to find that the party was ready for the journey. Snap! Went the reigns securing the two-horse team. The horses started away, slowly at first. Minnie and Robeena pushed their hands out through the curtains. Carol grasped both of their hands and ran along beside the coach. Soon, the horses graduated into a gallop, and Carol was forced to let go. She looked back at the house, thirty yards away, where Vivian and Lee stood together in the yard. She jerked her head back around, refusing to face Lee's unwelcome presence at her home.

CHAPTER THIRTEEN
As a So-called Negro

Soon after arriving in Pontiac, Henry worked odd jobs, but then he landed employment doing construction work for the city of Pontiac. He was an errand boy by title, although he engaged in most of the same activities as the other construction workers. His supervisor refused to give a Negro what he deemed the esteemed title of a "construction worker," so Henry gave himself the title. He was extra happy with the pay—it was more than he ever could have expected to receive in Florida for doing similar work. The foreman responsible for hiring him was pleased with Henry. Henry started looking for a house for his family, and was blessed enough to be successful very early in the process. But in the meantime, they crammed themselves into a small boarding room. With the excitement of finally getting away from Florida to start a new life, Henry and Minnie were happy despite their meager dwellings, never complaining about the space or lack thereof. However, Robeena became impatient with the arrangements after the first night of having to change her clothes in the dark. Her complaints led to the beginning of her nightlife. She found more joy in hanging out until the wee hours of the morning than in being cramped in a room with Minnie and Henry, watching her sister make a sucker out of herself.

Robeena pretended along with Henry that she didn't see Minnie hoping Henry would look at her whenever she changed her clothes. That's how Robeena was able to establish a habit of staying out late without Minnie saying something sooner. Minnie appreciated the alone time with Henry. She resolved in her mind way back in Florida that she would not stress him into marriage, but she needed to be close to him. She didn't know what to feel about the fact that he never tried to create the right place and time for them, and he didn't seem to mind that it hadn't happened. Was it because he honored her? If so, she wasn't interested in his honor.

During their first sister to sister outing in Detroit, Robeena wasn't fooled at all concerning Minnie's motive behind buying a spectacular peach, lace nightgown at the Hudson's department store. They had taken a streetcar down Woodward Avenue to do some minor shopping and browsing. She shook her head and selected a gold bracelet and necklace set for herself. It matched the navy blue and tan dress she would be wearing to the bar later. Minnie thought Robeena shouldn't go to a place like that alone, but she didn't care because tonight would be special if Robeena stayed gone, Minnie planned.

When Henry got home from work late that evening, Robeena had already stepped out, and Minnie was sleeping. Fully dressed and dusty, he tried to creep into the bed without waking her, but Minnie was ready. She awakened as soon as he came within six inches of the bed because she smelled his soft sweat and the soap he used thirteen hours ago.

"Henry?" He turned his back to her and dimmed the kerosene lamp light off that she'd left burning.

"I'm sorry for waking you, Minnie. Go back to sleep."

"I want you to see what I bought today, though." He didn't say anything. "Henry. Did you hear me?" He faced her.

"I'm glad you went shopping, Minnie, and that you got something that makes you happy. 'Cause you know that's what I want…you to be happy."

"Make a light on so you can see me, Henry." He paused, but not long enough to upset her, he hoped. He followed her orders, and then turned slowly back to her. She had done her hair nicely, and the silk negligee made her look ever more inviting. The peach color set well with her smooth dark complexion. It left little to the imagination. He blushed.

"You're incredible, Minnie."

"Really? I sure was wishing you'd like it." He looked around.

"Where's Robeena?" He shook his head. "She went out, anyway, didn't she? I told her to stay her ass here tonight. Did she tell you where she was going?"

"Nope. She don't need to be carrying on like this up here. She don't even know a lot of folks."

"Man!"

"Don't worry, Henry. She'll be home directly."

"I know. But I wish she was here where she belongs. I don't wanna be getting on to her real rough, but she ain't gonna be able to behave like that under my watch." She nodded her head. "Minnie, you need to say something to her. It's hard for me to watch her if I'm gone all day working. If I hafta talk to her myself, it ain't gonna be pretty."

"What about me, Henry? I'm here, where *I* belong. And *you're* here…it seeming we got ev'rybody we need for tonight." He smiled and it made her more comfortable. "I'm glad to be here with you, Henry."

"Yeah, but I'm still wondering 'bout Robeena, though." She bit her lip and took his hands.

"Will you please be quiet about her?" He withdrew and got out of bed and paced the floor. Minnie wanted to cry. She knew this wasn't about Robeena. "What's the matter, Henry?" He treaded near the middle of the floor.

"You don't need to do this, Minnie." She started crying silently.

"Please tell me what's wrong with me!" He quickly went to soothe her. She flung her arms around his shoulders in desperation.

"Nothing is wrong with you." He emitted a long breath. Then he hugged her back and kissed her. "You're fine, you're fine," he whispered, kissing her tears. "I was just hoping you'd wait on me."

"That's what I've been doing, Henry—waiting, waiting, waiting."

"There just ain't been no time for all this. You know that. Come on, Minnie." She was weeping now. "You know how I feel about you. Rushing things ain't never been my style." He continued to kiss her tears away. "Now, what am I supposed to do with you carrying on like this? You know I don't want you to be sad. Stop it, girl. Stop it."

"If you don't want me…

"I do want you! You're incredible."

"It makes me feel good to hear you say that to me. I'm so glad you brought me with you. I know you love me, Henry. And I love you, too. Very, very much, I do." He grasped her tightly before letting her go.

"We're gonna be okay, Minnie."

"Yes, we are. I'm happier than I've ever been in my life, being here with you."

"Florida wasn't real—that was someone else's life. I had to get out of there."

"You were right to do so, Henry. You were right. I'm gonna do everything for you. You don't hafta do nothing no more but be happy. I love you. I would kiss the ground you walk on." Slightly, he recalled his mother on her tired knees at his father's feet, clinging desperately to his ankles as her face and body got dirty. More vividly, he envisioned his mother kissing up to Lucifix Hopkins while he disrespected her and didn't value her. Then, he pictured Minnie on all fours kissing the pissy grass where some sweaty man had just spit, all because she thought he was her knight in shining armor. Vivian wouldn't kiss the ground for any man, he imagined. She was too precious to even think about doing something so silly and degrading.

"Don't say that."

"How would you know it if I don't say nothing?" She started massaging his back.

"Minnie, you gotta hold it a minute." He moved away from her and covered his head in his hands. She sat next to him, feeling stronger, feeling as though she could help him through whatever it was, now that he had told her that he was glad to get away from Florida and be with her. "I need some air."

"You're not gonna leave, are you?" She panicked. He didn't answer her. Instead, he flopped back on the bed with his hands under his head for a minute. Then, he rolled over, pressing his elbows into the mattress.

"I hafta be ready, Minnie. It can't be because you think of something in your head and pull my strings like I'm some puppet." He got up and paced again. "That's a trap."

"Whatchu talking about? I don't understand you saying you ain't ready, and all that. I got sense, Henry. You've been all over the world, probably getting ready and doing things. Why are you saying this stuff about me pulling your strings? I would never..."

"All my life crackers have been trying to control me and my family, and I can't stand that kinda thinking. So, you think I'm gonna let you take over me like that, woman? I ain't weak like that. That's what I mean by not being ready. Don't nobody make choices for me no more. I don't give a damn what it is. I ain't never take nothing from no kinda body on account of what they offering. I take 'cause I want to. I've been way across the world fighting for my life, and you can lose your life falling in bed with every which and not. I'm too strong to lose my dignity 'cause somebody offers me something—if that's the case, I woulda been hung several times over. I learned that game years ago." Drifting back into a scary place, Henry continued. "They can't trap me. I knew what they wanted before they could get their game right, and I knew how to say no to the best of 'em."

"What?"

Henry snapped his head as though she had just walked into the room. "Minnie, it hurts me to see *you* coming on to me like that. This is serious. You don't use tears for that kinda stuff. You make a man do something he don't wanna do because you crying. That's not right."

"My tears were real," she screamed at him. She felt like a slut. He stood over her.

"Don't raise your voice to me ever again, woman."

"I hate you," she sobbed quietly. He grabbed his shoes and sat back next to her. After fastening the buckles snuggly over his feet, he turned back to her.

"No, you don't." He patted her head. "How you know what I got planned for us? I may want us to have a nice wedding, and do things the right way, but you throwing yourself at me like this ain't lady-like. This ain't how I planned things to be."

"I feel stupid."

"We *are* gonna get married, Minnie. I promise you."

"It's just that I love you so much, Henry. I didn't mean to be like that with you. I'm so ashamed of myself..."

"I know."

"Get back in bed, Henry, okay? Please just put your arms around me!"

"It's not right, now. I'll be back in a bit. I'm just going so I can think for a minute. I'll be right back." She jumped up and followed him to the door.

"Henry?" He didn't turn around, but he stopped for a second. "Are you truly happy you came up here with me?"

"You wait and see, Minnie. It's gonna be just like I told you. I'm gonna make you my wife when the time is right. You'll see."

That September, Minnie got the much yearned for marriage proposal. Henry had saved enough money from his inferior paying job to finally take Minnie on as a wife, without needing her financial support. It was important for Henry to avow to himself that no woman would wear the pants in his house. Henry needed to feel in control, and even though he was treated like a boy instead of a man at work, he knew how to stay detached and pleasant at the same time. Henry shucked and jived like he was happy to be happy there, and as long as he remained aloof, no one cared enough to scrutinize his emotions. At home, he was already suffocating enough because he had left the girl he loved in exchange for following another dream and a job. The detached method of existing at work would spillover to home because marrying Minnie would mean that he would have to pretend again, and he could do that so well! Henry would pretend to be in love with her for the rest of his life to avoid hurting her feelings.

To some degree, it was a blessing to the northern American society when in 1921, more and more Negroes migrated from the South to work. The freed slaves had been trained expertly in the endeavors of physical prowess and subscribed mental deficiency. Negroes could be hired at less than half the pay that Caucasians received and one could expect double the work from them. All that most of the Negroes seemed to want to do was work for anyone they trusted to give them security and be accepted in that society. In return for the pseudo-acceptance, the Negroes were willing to be puppeteers and caterers to the needs of their supervisors. Henry had been taught to place Caucasians first, above his needs and the needs of his family. Internally, naturally, he rebelled, but the rebellion was foreign to the nature of the society in which he lived.

He could only protest the opposition he experienced while he was at home with his family. Unlike Lee, Henry was not such a physically violent man. The injury he inflicted on Minnie was a withdrawal from gaiety. Henry never set out to make his wife suffer; it was the throbbing and dissatisfaction that filled him inside that caused his lethargic attitude. Henry wanted to be a man, yet his blackness, the essence of his being, was a stumbling block to acceptance of true manhood by the society that rated him. He couldn't use the same restroom as his co-workers; he couldn't eat at the same lunch table, and he was always sent on the most strenuous errands. Henry noted if he didn't smile, buck and dance at work all day, his co-workers considered him insolent.

He thought his ethnicity would only be rejected in the South, but he learned miserably that the racism in the North was barely overt. To Henry, the northern styled rejection he experienced surpassed by far the dehumanization he was subject to in Florida. Yet, he still felt a sense of high esteem to be only one of two Negro men working for the company. The other brother made Henry sick. Freeman Price. He proved his gratitude for being hired at half the pay as his counterparts much like a dog does for its master; Freeman wagged and barked in joy whenever he was near his supervisors. He laughed at things that were not funny, he scratched nervously in places that did not itch, and he made jokes about his condition and the condition of his people. As such, he was accepted as one who stayed in his place.

The supervisor and fellow workers made it clear every day where Henry's place was as a Negro. Therefore, he kept to himself, mostly. Freeman preferred to buck dance in front of the other workers, and he rarely spoke to Henry—except whenever they were alone. However, they laughed at Freeman's attempts to be friends and called him a "dumb nigger" to his face. From time to time, Henry found himself smiling when he wanted to spit, and laughing when he wanted to cry, but he refused to be the Sambo figure Freeman posed as. By the time he got home on most days, he couldn't wait to take the stupid grin off his face and drop into a more somber mood. Church was a place Henry felt he could go for relief from feeling like a secondhand citizen. Everyone was always laughing and singing so that his spirits gained momentum during the segregated church hours. There, he could hide from his fears, and beg the Lord's forgiveness for his sins.

He promised God that he would be a good husband to Minnie, and thanked Him for her. Henry, like all the other Negroes from the Raison Plantation, was a Baptist. Minnie, like all the other Negroes from the Johnson Plantation, was a Methodist. Of course this was because Old Master Kent Johnson was a Methodist and the late master Raison was a Baptist. Henry and Minnie were comfortable with going to two different churches to serve their religious needs and for spiritual food. Minnie did make a point to go to church with Henry about once a month or so, and he would attend with her the same.

The Black people who came from the South brought the religion and their way of worship that was given to them by their slave masters to the North with them. Of course, they added a soulful touch to the service that no one could give them. They were filled with pride at the way they could feel the presence of the Lord through the music and songs they sang. The scriptural references in the pages of the Bible were confusing to the illiterate, the semi-literate, and even the well-educated ex-slaves. The major theme emphasized was forgiveness for the racism, rape, and injustices they endured.

Their religious lives worked out well at first for both of them, on the surface. Minnie prayed to God that she could be the perfect wife. She felt as though Henry never loved her deeply enough, and she wondered if something was wrong with her. She reflected on how fond of her he'd been whenever they first met. Now that she thought about it, she remembered that he never tried to really know her—he was always more interested in having a companion with whom to share his own dreams. Sure, he listened to her when she talked, but he never asked her anything or initiated anything regarding the upliftment of their relationship. She could not deny that he loved her, but it was more of a brotherly-sisterly love than that crazy kind of romantic feeling a man gets when he loves his wife, she felt. Inwardly, she ceased her romantic feelings about him, settling with the idea of "loving" him, but not being "in love" with him. She *wanted* to be "in love" with him if he'd let her.

Minnie knew what her responsibilities were as Henry's wife, and she knew exactly what he expected from her. She felt compelled to honor his perspective as it brought the feeling of peace and contentment throughout their household. It was easy for her to accept Henry's despondency because she understood that no man had ever really loved her mama, either, thus Henry's behavior was at least familiar.

That's why she jumped for joy when Henry asked her to marry him that middle of September, sunny day. Minnie had resorted to living with Henry since they left Florida, disregarding their marital status because she felt like it was what he wanted and he was all she thought she had. Henry knew he couldn't put the marriage off any longer. She had been relentless until she finally conquered him and he didn't appreciate the way it went down, either. He was remorseful about using her, yet she was the one he chose. It didn't make sense to drag her so far from home and refuse to dignify her with the legalities. The truth was that from day one, he viewed her as some sort of traveling partner. He never knew love, so he didn't know what to expect from it. He had never been anxious to marry her—he was only anxious to get away from the South. It was great for her that they were to be married in a private setting by the Justice of the Peace in downtown Pontiac. In this way, they both could save their reputations since neither Henry nor Minnie had corrected their fellow church members on the status of their relationship. Hence, everyone assumed they had been married in Florida.

None of these things excited Robeena. She stood by the table looking on with preoccupation as Minnie chased Henry around the kitchen with excited chirps about the wedding plans. Robeena wasn't interested in the Baptist or the Methodist church, or in her sister's dull relationship. She was, however, interested and delighted in the time Henry and Minnie spent away from home. Robeena had friends she liked to entertain, and she knew Henry would not allow males to call on her in his home. The last straw was when Henry tried to give her a curfew. She told him that he wasn't her daddy, and he walked in her face and said he was her daddy until further notice. Robeena made a smirk at how religious Henry acted when correcting her behavior, although he had been committing fornication with Minnie until he decided it was convenient to marry her at last. Nonetheless, she knew she'd best find a room of her own to rent.

She didn't know how pretty she was until she got to Michigan. Boys and even men whistled at her every time she went anywhere. It's amazing the effect even a few months away from home can have on a young, blossoming girl when she is emotionally and spiritually ill-equipped to handle what life in a fast track city like Detroit offered.

Once she settled in Pontiac, Robeena concentrated heavily on her appearance because she enjoyed the attention she received. She was always picking up the latest fashion magazines; she loved window shopping outside of the plush boutiques that Detroit showcased. Minnie was too busy trying to build a life with Henry to chaperone her baby sister. Therefore, Robeena ran as loose as a runaway chicken from the time she arrived in Michigan. She was thrilled to find how inspiring life could be as a single female, and she vowed never to be locked down like her mother, pining away over any man for any reason. Although Robeena was grateful that her mother seemed to be coming away from the stranger's grip, still, her life seemed so colorless and fragmented. Robeena was also fairly disenchanted by the lack of zeal in her sister's relationship. The only subject that seemed to come up at the boarding house where they shared one bedroom was what happened at church. Minnie would constantly ask, "When are you coming to church, Beena?"

Robeena stared out the window in deep thought. She reflected on her new life that she spent at the local bars on the weekends, and dating the men she'd met there during the week. Robeena had learned quickly how to talk to the men, and get things from them. She remembered her mother's constant struggles, and decided to take a different route. She made sure in procedure that the men she spent time with were financially secure regardless of how they obtained that status. Financial security for her meant they were able to wine and dine her. Robeena also accepted money, gifts, and opportunities in advance of spending personal time with a man. On rare occasions, she accepted direct monetary gifts in return for the immediate rendezvous the men requested.

Her relationships were short-lived. Robeena was afraid to let herself love a man like her sisters and mother because she associated men with pain and heartaches. She resented men because of all the negative experiences they brought to her life, but it was impossible for her to hate what she was drawn to naturally, therefore she developed a sick obsession for them. Robeena was insatiable. Entertaining men became her life. She used and abused the men she met first, to prevent them from doing the same to her, instead. She believed it was inevitable that any man would abuse a woman if he were given the opportunity to do so. When she was the abuser, she convinced herself that it was for the sake of vengeance for her mother's pain. And Minnie's pain. And Vivian's pain. And her grandmother's pain that she'd heard about from her mama.

She was inspired by the notion that all men, regardless of ethnicity, were dogs. It was a Caucasian dog, her mother had told her, who had given them their house. Robeena gathered that this dog had made a victim out of her grandmother, Minnie-Anne, and that her grandfather, a Negro dog named Robert, had capitalized on Minnie-Anne's whoredom. She figured from her subjective experiences that Caucasian dogs didn't just *give* a colored person *any*thing. Therefore, her grandmother must've suffered the loss of her dignity so that there could be a roof over her grandfather's head and her mother's head. How then, could she respect the man who made all this possible for Minnie-Anne?

Robeena knew that dog to be Old Master Kent Johnson. Her heart pounded when she reflected on how Caucasians treated Black people as though they were animals, and forced them to live in degraded conditions. How could Minnie-Anne be so proud of the scanty cottage Kent gave her, when he was sitting on top of a mansion that was built in large part by her ancestors? And she didn't enjoy the way Negroes were herded into tight, impoverished areas in the South as well as the North. So, her dissatisfaction surmounted: All men were dogs, and she lived in a racist society which meant more dogs and less opportunities and justice for her. The fact that she was being unreasonable--speaking from personal pain didn't matter. The ones who tried to be good would pay dearly to prevent them from defying her irrationality. She was clearly aware that she could count more good Black men than so-called bad ones, but so what. The hand she had been dealt meant men would pay. Black men would pay because those were the ones she could reach.

There were no Caucasians who lived in their section of town in Pontiac, yet they came there to sell the Negroes things, and to cause problems, as far as Robeena was concerned. In 1910, the City Council of Baltimore, the northernmost city in the South, 50 miles south of the Mason-Dixon Line--approved the first city ordinance designating the boundaries of Black and Caucasian neighborhoods. This ordinance was followed by comparable ones in Dallas, Texas, Greensboro, North Carolina, Louisville, Kentucky, Norfolk, Virginia, Oklahoma City, Oklahoma, Richmond, Virginia, Roanoke, Virginia, and St. Louis, Missouri. The Supreme Court declared the Louisville ordinance to be unconstitutional in 1917, yet, in the 1920's, Robeena reflected, Michigan had the same unspoken ordinance which formed covert racism. She faced racial injustice heavily for the first time early that September. This was when Antoine, a hip barber from New York who had recently moved to Detroit told her he'd pay for the modern dance classes Robeena wanted to take. True to his word, they went together to a small place on Telegraph Road to enroll her in the school she had found by reading the newspaper, only to discover that the school was not taking applications from Negroes. The Caucasian woman behind the desk appeared amused that the couple had ventured into the establishment.

Robeena bounced back from her dejected feelings due to her denied application after another dream popped in her head that she should own a nightclub. She pictured a fancy cabaret with a great big dance floor where she could have dance shows herself. She decided to be nice to Antoine at least until she could sort out her plans. Robeena managed to save much of the money she earned via her regular nightlife. She was very calculating and business minded. She was determined to make it on her own. Robeena weighed the idea of Vivian coming to join her.

Minnie was such a dud to her, but Vivian would be willing to attend the parties and keep her company. Vivian could leave Lee, Robeena planned, and find a new man in Detroit, if she needed one. Robeena worked extra hard that week to save even more money so that she could send for Vivian as soon as possible. Little did she know that in the same week Henry and Minnie were making their wedding plans, Vivian had also decided to reconsider Lee's proposal and marry him at once.

CHAPTER FOURTEEN
"Swing Low, Sweet Chariot"

Since Vivian's reunion with Lee, he had been the perfect gentleman. When he wasn't hanging out at sleazy bars, seeing Liz or Maybelle on the Raison Plantation, (once Henry left, Lee resumed his regular visits there), or out gambling, he was waiting on Vivian hand and foot. He faithfully gave her a tiny fraction of his earnings, enabling her to buy new shoes, dresses, nice toiletries, and help her mama. Lee took her for long walks in the woods and down the dirt roads. He often walked with her through the tree-lined trail, to the rock where he had pushed, slapped, and entrapped her in what seemed like an eternity ago. He always paused their walk at the rock to kiss her, and murmur endearing things to her. Because of this, she became classically conditioned to associate tenderness and abuse as though they were natural pairs.

Early in September 1921, Lee kissed Vivian's nose and backed her into the rock. Vivian was quite expecting his usual petting maneuvers. He planted several routine kisses on her forehead. "I love you, muffin," he said. Vivian knew that if she didn't do something quickly, they would soon be leaving and he would walk her home. She almost tripped over several pebbles covering the uneven slope where she stood. Vivian moved away so that she could reach the bottom hem of her skirt which was getting tangled in the twigs. Then she grabbed his hands in hers.

"We belong together, Lee," she said seductively. She surprised him with a kiss of her own, and then another. Lee was startled by her boldness. Fair maidens and princesses did not initiate kisses.

"Vivian! What is you doing?" Embarrassed, he looked around to see if anyone had entered the deserted path. He wanted the townsmen to know for certain that his future wife's chastity was guarded. Lee snatched his hands away. She became thoroughly self-conscious at his rebuff.

"What's the matter, Lee?"

"Wait, muffin . . ." He pushed her gently away. Lee felt strange resisting a woman. He didn't know what to do with his hands. He valued that this might be his opportunity to make her commit herself to him again by specifying a marriage date, like before Maybelle came to the church. "I've been trying to get you to marry me for the longest, but I reckon you haven't forgiven me yet. I want to respect you and do the right thing by marrying you."

"Yes, Lee. I'll marry you." Lee was not yet affected.

"When?"

"Let's do it tomorrow!" Lee laughed at her with uncertainty. He thought she was joking. His laugh got stuck in his throat when he saw she was serious.

"You saying you're ready to marry me, muffin? Right now? As soon as we can?" He held his breath.

"I love you, Lee. I really want to be your wife tonight, not tomorrow." Lee was happy. He held her to his heart, vowing silently to do right by her.

Six days later they were married.

Even until her wedding day, Vivian hadn't told anyone about the baby growing inside of her, not even Missy or Madeline. She attempted to wish it away, but every morning that her body felt heavy, she knew the "thing" was still there. Vivian looked down at her still fairly flat stomach as she prepared her hair for the small ceremony. Vivian refused the help of her friends and mother in getting ready. This was one time she insisted on being alone. She imagined her friends and mother preparing her hair, and suddenly having to vomit right in front of them. There was no way she could let anyone witness something like that. She had made it this far carrying the lie—she couldn't let anything get in her way. Vivian tried to remember when it was that Henry and Minnie had left town. Sometime in June.

"Lee must never know," she said to herself. She figured that she would undeniably be showing in a fortnight and prayed that Lee wouldn't notice that she was unchaste. Vivian knew how much her purity meant to him, and that it would destroy his ego if he ever found out that she was going to have Henry's child. "Damn. It's all Lee's fault," she rationalized, "if he had just kept his brutal hands off me, Henry wouldn't have been there to pick me up. Now look at me! I'm about to marry a lie, *and* live one. Oh Jesus! Help me, please!" Tears streamed down her face. She dropped the brush on the vanity table and covered her eyes with her hands. Faintly, she heard her mother approach her room door.

"Viv?" Carol knocked. "Come on, now, you're already late. You need help in there?"

"No ma'am." She was wearing the same dress she wore when Lee last beat her. She ended up taking it over to a dressmaker. She had kept it balled up in the potato sack Henry had stuffed it in over three months ago. Besides, she had changed her mind about letting her family examine her dress before it was back in mint condition. "Here I come, mama." Vivian gloomily wiped her face, picked up the brush, and rushed herself ready, pushing the "thing" out of her mind.

The wedding was held at the church. Reverend Washington accepted the honor of marrying the couple with several well-wishers and witnesses in the audience. Carol invited the stranger, but he declined. There were the Burdeshaw sisters, Carol, the two deacons, and Lee's father. The most special guest for Vivian was her Uncle Jack whom she hadn't seen in so long. Uncle Jack got lucky because he had arrived in town for a surprise visit, and it happened to be in time for Vivian's wedding. The other attendees were mostly church members who were super eager to attend the ceremony, despite Carol's very charming and stern request to have (what she said was) her daughter's wish to have a private ceremony.

Floyd, who had immediately been informed of the wedding by one of the gossip committee members at the church, tried unsuccessfully to get Maybelle to crash the party. Maybelle knew Lee would distance himself from her again if she tried another stunt like the first time she came to the church. The way she saw it, a piece of Lee was better than no Lee.

Maybelle rose early to the thrust of kicks coming from within on the day of Lee's wedding. "You sure gwine be something, boy or gal," she chuckled, rubbing her abdomen. "You gwine be wild just like your daddy." At seven months pregnant, Maybelle felt unsightly and insecure. Even though Lee still visited her often, she knew now that he didn't love her. Of course, they never talked about Vivian. He merely came, indulged her, slept, talked about nothing that meant anything, and went on his way. She was crippled by her obsession with Lee, powerless to control her compulsions. Somehow, she felt she belonged to Lee and him to her; she just needed the opportunity to show him that she was the best woman for him.

Maybelle was naturally drawn to an inner desire to please and comfort Lee. More than others, she was attracted to his strength, the god sparks in him, and his kindness, even when he acted sourly. It happened that circumstances were causing Lee's god sparks to flicker instead of shine. Maybelle also had sparks, many of them impacted by Lee whom she relied on to offer life and light. In his current state, Lee wasn't qualified to give light to another while he attempted to find his way out of his own blindness. Lee had been nearly destroyed--trying to hang on between the balance of hope and shots of liquor. Much of the credit for the destruction was due to Lee's own submission to traditions and his failure to adhere to the self-accusing spirit within him. Maybelle gave him hope and she also provided stolen tin cups of liquor which also seemed to calm Lee and soothe his spirits. Maybelle appreciated Lee's attention and accepted his detached position. Because of this, she was not motivated or inclined to teach her unborn male child *not to* impregnate unsuspecting women and then leave them—or to use them for selfish purposes alone. She didn't have the where-withal to teach her unborn daughter to guard herself from men who had no idea of the will of God in their relationship with women. How could she? She was the granddaughter of a slave that had been trained under the *idea* of moral inferiority and indecency. Under Maybelle's examination, it was whatever. Who would dare to judge her? Who would turn up their noses at her when she was just trying to keep her head above water and stay out of the way of trouble? If she were treated like an animal, then certainly she wasn't bothering anyone. Her grandmother had been trained like she was an animal the same as Vivian's grandmother.

Her grandparents had been trained to breed babies only to watch those babies be sold or otherwise discarded or misused. A slave woman had to be tough to survive that kind of lunacy. A slave woman had to be either thoroughly abused or internally psyched out to model such ruthless behaviors in the presence of her children. Vivian and Robeena were the grandchildren of women who were raised like lowly beasts—only their grandparents weren't typically allowed in the master's house like the beasts were. At that time, there was no available teaching to disengage them from their roles as degenerates. Unshackling the chains did not loosen the mental servitude and feelings of inferiority. The babies saw the role of the Black woman, and thus learned their own places.

Slavery certainly wasn't the only institution responsible for the mental condition of Black people, but slavery was the main institution in America that perpetuated the spiritual, educational, and economical deficiencies for centuries at a time. Centuries of the slavery lifestyle placed the continuation of unshackled slavery in momentum for centuries to come. Black people were castrated on all levels. They were stripped even of their names, their language, their religion, culture, and their God. Missionaries brought the image of Jesus as a Caucasian to the African continent and placed that image as the door to heaven in the minds of Robeena's grandparents and all generations to come. Defiance was synonymous with outcasts, troublemakers, and insolent, uppity Negroes. No other group suffered such an inclusive dehumanizing experience where they ended up with a deep self-hatred that cursed their children generations over – a self-hatred that led them to hate their blackness 300 years later. Other castrated groups were left with their cultures, names, religion, and identities intact.

The girls' Sunday school teacher insisted that *Six hundred million* Black people died from the middle passage through to the Civil War, and after the affliction (that was barely whispered over in textbooks), Robeena's anger would always be toward Black men. They were to blame for everything. Although articulation barriers, societal norms, conformity, the teachings of Willy Lynch, Jim Crow laws, and centuries invested in making a "Negro" from a Black man and woman prevented the Johnsons' from developing the potential to change their own reality, they knew something internally was wrong. Robeena knew. The nature of her self-accusing spirit or God's Will that was born inside the soul of the oppressed citizens revealed it.

Maybelle's grandmother had been instructed in an ordered sequence necessary to make her a fit slave. Maybelle's mother had been instructed by the same ordered sequence, to such an extent that even her grandchildren's grandchildren did not detect consciously the psychological, emotional, and even physiological damage that slavery entrusted to a whole nation of people. How then, could Maybelle know when she didn't know the true and living God that though buried, lived inside of her? Yes, she went to church, but the preachers of religion were taught under the same slave-making tradition and system. Oh, the mastery of it all! The subconscious was further weakened by the trance created whenever the stimuli of vibrating music, closeness, the name of Jesus, and that warm coziness that family time affected, expressly when accompanied by a hearty meal. Yes, happiness meant burying sorrows and any voice that reminded them of pain.

Maybelle was in such a state of degradation that she didn't recognize her own voice that accused her. Her mental shackles told her it was "cute" sixteen years later when her son, Lee's child, went hopping around the neighborhood visiting strange women. "Boy, don't bring me no babies," she would say playfully. Actually, a grandbaby would comfort her in her loneliness, as did a baby of her own, when her son was born.

Maybelle was tolerant of her condition. She saw that Lee would continue to come by, she believed, because she was carrying his child. She measured how long it would take him to visit her now that he would marry today. Maybelle figured on at least a fortnight's wait. "I'll be ready to have this baby before that hussy will let Lee outta her sight," she speculated. Her frustration subsided when it settled in her that there might be an extended delay before she could be with Lee again. She spent half of the day pacing the floor, already feeding her unborn child with negative thoughts, stress, and unrest.

Vivian's child certainly was no better off, living in the water of confusion, physical aggression, fornication, and lies. It didn't occur to Maybelle or Vivian that their mood produced a chemical release that fed the child. On this wedding day, Vivian's unborn child was suffering from a too tight girdle, and the anxiety of being submerged mentally, emotionally, and physically.

Even though she wasn't showing yet, Vivian wanted to make sure the wise, older women who might come by the church after the ceremony didn't detect anything. They were always the first to know.

The wedding went on without chaos. Several members of the church were kind enough to shower Vivian with presents all wrapped and bowed. Carol saw to it that all gifts were brought over to Lee's house prior to the wedding by one of the deacons. Lee took Vivian back to the house that he shared with his father for their "honeymoon." Lee Sr., meeting Vivian for the first time that day, accompanied them proudly home in a horse-drawn carriage. The three of them played cards, drank wine, and laughed together. They opened the wedding gifts; Vivian's favorite being a circular, puffed short sleeved evening gown with a high waist, and a round low neckline, practically off-the-shoulders. The muslin-lined dress was outfitted with a padded, double silk rouleaux trim at the skirt's bottom. Vivian loved the hand stitching and the broad band at the sleeve cuff. So what if it was tight fitting, and several inches too short? It hardly covered her knees, but Madeline must have spent a fortune for it. Vivian liked having nice things, though, so the fact that it was solicitous and daring didn't bother her much. She examined it closely, already challenging herself that she could make something nice like that for herself. Lee took one look at it and told Vivian that she should only wear the dress when she was with him, and even then, such an enticing dress might still pose a problem. Vivian thought to herself that she wouldn't dare wear it without him, anyway.

Early in the evening, Lee Sr. mildly tried to excuse himself, but was urged to stay by both Vivian and Lee. After they finished together the third bottle of grape wine, however, the joy of seeing his son happy, and the presence of a new daughter became exceptionally pleasing to Lee Sr., and then it would take a team of mules to pull him away from their company. Lee Sr. teased them, gave fatherly advice, and wore the posture of a licensed therapist with a specialty in marriage and family. Lee was drunkenly delighted that they all were getting along so well.

Seeing his father talking cheerfully with Vivian sparked a vision of his own mother in Lee's mind. Depression came over him when he was forced to remember that his mother had abandoned them. He recalled that his mother was often gay, just like Vivian was right then. Lee shuffled the cards and placed them before his bride. She looked at him with a smile.

"Oh, are you ready to lose again?" She asked mockingly.

"As long as I don't lose you, it doesn't matter." Lee Sr. became agitated at Lee's attempt to get intimate in the middle of his getting to know his daughter-in-law.

"Well, we're married now! You're stuck with me, Lee Hiram." She giggled.

"That ain't necessarily for certain," he glanced at his father. "You can always lose somebody you love." Lee Sr. was unaccepting of the hinted reminder of his wife.

"Naw, boy," he answered his son, "you do right by your wife, then don't worry 'bout losing her." Lee Sr. was excited that a pretty woman was going to be sharing their abode. He was not going to allow Lee's reminders to shake his mood. Furthermore, he hoped his son wouldn't do anything stupid again to scare the girl away.

"But . . . my mama . . . why'd my mama run off and leave us to fend for ourselves, daddy?" There was the boy Lee again, coming to the surface. Lee Sr. felt a rush of pain at what this boy must have gone through to suddenly be without his mother and to never hear from her again. A sickening feeling settled in his heart to absorb that no matter how much Lee tried to be a strong man, a part of his life had been stripped away from him. There would always be an empty vessel of pain and curiosity.

"Don't you remember that my mama left us . . . she didn't even say 'bye,' neither," Lee pushed in his intoxicated state. Lee Sr.'s chair screeched as he stood abruptly.

"Now, you listen to me, boy. Your mama's gone and there ain't nothing neither you nor I can do to change that. Don't let me ever hear you say one ugly word 'bout your mama. If you gotta hate somebody—hate me!"

"Pops, I didn't say . . ."

"Look, boy! You got yourself a wife now. You take care of her. Now. That's it." He was drunk, too. "What the hell am I doing at home tonight, anyway?" He laughed at himself, mumbled a few things, and then stumbled off into his bedroom.

"Don't get too drunk, Lee, like your daddy," Vivian said smiling, trying to make light of his condition. Lee had mentioned his mother to her, but had always been unwilling to discuss details about her absence. With the wine she was helping the men consume, Vivian wasn't in full possession of all her sensitive faculties. As such, she was virtually unaware of the measure of pain her husband was facing at this moment.

Lee wished he had someone he could talk to about his loss, like Maybelle. For years, he had been forced to live alone with the pain. Other than Maybelle, there was no one close enough to him that he felt he could confide in, without being looked upon as weak. He only talked about it with Floyd, but he had never told Floyd about the void in his heart, or the sleepless nights he endured from time to time. And now his new bride was laughing at him, yet she had made it clear that he wasn't supposed to have Maybelle even as a friend. Vivian was a princess and could not know about his deep pain, but Maybelle was a girl who knew suffering and was thus more emotionally compatible. He needed her in his sadness. Lee was comforted, however, by the level sound of Vivian's voice, and the fact that he really didn't want to talk about it with her yet, anyway.

"Why?" He teased. "Something I'm supposed to be alert for?"

"On account of I don't want you to get sick, Lee Hiram," she responded. He laughed merrily, overjoyed by the fact that he had been lucky enough to marry the girl he loved. He stood up and reached for her hand.

"Let's go," he said. Vivian followed her new husband to their quarters, although she had visited his bedroom on social occasions a few times. As much as she tried to prevent it, the vision of the solid Henry crept into her mind just as Lee was approaching her. Vivian diffused her disparaging expression, wanting to kick herself for thinking of Henry on her wedding night. She moved further into the room and sat on the bed, with Lee following her, jumping in beside her. The affection Henry had smothered her with was absent in Lee's expeditious route, she measured. Lee had grown accustomed to brisk encounters, as he was used to meeting his mates behind barns or beside a scratchy tree.

"Ouch," Vivian wheezed. He looked at her, unaware that his thumb was pinching her skin at the waist. "Lee, remember how understanding you used to be when we'd take our walks? Keep that in mind, now," she begged. Impatiently, he followed her instructions for about twenty seconds. Vivian was at least relieved to discover that he didn't seem aware that he had a predecessor. Just when she decided she might as well make the best out of it, Lee collapsed, forcing her to carry the burden of all his weight.

"Whew!" He sounded, before falling into a deep sleep. A moment later, she managed to dump him aside. Then she held onto her pillow for a bit, thinking of the mess she was making out of her life—wondering what to do about her pregnancy. There were no answers, she thought. Trying to get rid of it was out of the question. Her mother often expressed to her that one of the beauties that stemmed from the stranger's presence was her daughters, whom she wouldn't trade for the world. So, the lie would continue and she would simply try to be happy together with her new family. She pictured holding her unborn child and Lee holding it, loving it, and being the perfect father. Her exhaustion from the long week caused her to slip quickly into a fitful sleep with these dreams.

The next day, Lee left for work at the crack of dawn. At lunchtime, he told his father his version of the wonderful late night spent with Vivian. They were both happy that the conversation about Lee's mother leaving them was apparently forgotten to the other. Charmin, the high-yellow woman came with Lee Sr.'s lunch as usual, but even she wasn't enough to erase the preciousness of Vivian out of his father's mind. He wanted nothing to happen to destroy his son's relationship with Vivian, the princess.

Lee Sr. befriended Vivian over the next several months. When she needed someone to talk to about her husband's absenteeism (Lee maintained a highly active nightlife), Lee Sr. was there. Whenever the baby kicked inside of her, Lee Sr. rubbed his colossal, baked hands over the heartbeat. The times she cried, like a pregnant woman so often does, it was Lee Sr. who had to stand in Lee's absence. Vivian valued her father-in-law's attention because she felt desolate. Notwithstanding, Lee Sr. did not appreciate the markedly muddy direction he could distinctly see his son was taking by not paying attention to Vivian.

Vivian told Lee that she must've gotten pregnant their first night together, and he instantly believed her. He felt he was debonair, and her quick pregnancy only proved it for him. However, the idea of starting a family with Vivian did nothing to keep him away from the streets and other women. Lee hardly ever stayed at home; he gambled and lost a good deal of his money every week, and Vivian was suspicious that he was still involved with Maybelle. She was sure of it one evening whenever Lee came home accompanied by Maybelle and Leland, the baby. She knew the child must have been born, but had heard no word about it or Maybelle from Lee. Vivian was beside herself with rage over how her marriage was progressing. She was big and pregnant, and feeling quite ugly.

Vivian looked out the window for the fiftieth time that evening in January. Then, instead of the empty cold roads, she saw Lee and Maybelle coming up the street huddled together to ward off the brisk and misty wind. In Lee's arm was a bundle of something wrapped in a short, blue quilt. Vivian could see that the two of them were deep in conversation . . . they didn't even notice her standing in the open doorway when they walked into the yard.

"Lee!" Vivian yelled. "Why have you brought this adulteress here?" Vivian vaguely remembered an experience like this that occurred when she was a small child, but she couldn't remember any of the details, and she didn't know whether it had been a dream or not. Lee handed the baby to Maybelle.

"Now, hold on, Viv. I got my child with me. Maybelle done got herself involved in family scuffling. Her and the baby was cold, so I brought 'em on home for a minute, 'til we can figure things out." Maybelle shot Lee a riled glance, yet avoided Vivian's eyes.

"You brought her here for a *minute!*" Vivian shot back. "That rhinoceros isn't coming into my house for a *second*!" Lee shook his head and brushed past Vivian, beckoning for Maybelle to follow him into the house, as though his wife had not spoken. With some things he let her have her way, but Lee had already made up his mind that Maybelle would stay until he could help her. He felt it was his obligation to help her and the child. He was delighted that he could answer what he deemed to be his self-accusing spirit this time with responsibility.

"You better stop all that damn yelling at the top of your lungs, woman," Lee said casually. Maybelle sidestepped to follow Lee so as not to touch Vivian. She wished Lee would've taken her by the hand and had led her in the house rather than to assume that she would follow him, leaving her behind with Vivian. Maybelle could only imagine how awkward the arrangement was, and how terrible Vivian must have felt, but she desperately wanted to spend time with Lee. When he'd come by to see her earlier, she exaggerated the circumstances of an argument she'd had with her mother and Tazra. Now, she basked in the joy that Lee would be there for her and Leland, despite what his princess bride might think.

Vivian blocked her as she approached and shoved her back. Dramatically, Maybelle let out a shriek, with a look of terror on her face. "Don't hurt my baby!" She screamed. Lee turned back to see Vivian with her fist drawn, and Maybelle still stumbling backward, miraculously catching Leland, who looked like he had just been tossed in the air. Before he could think about what he was doing, Lee slapped Vivian so hard that blood spurted from her nose.

Out of all the past times Lee had hit her, this was the most mortifying episode. Before, Vivian romanticized his beatings to mean he loved her. She had always convinced herself that his frustration over the suggestion of losing her drove him to aggressive insanity. Like the first couple of times he hit or roughed her, it was because he was jealous of Henry, and he thought she wanted Henry. Another time, he hit her because she told him she wouldn't marry him. Vivian conveniently erased from her mind the fact that Maybelle was a present factor that time, too.

Vivian couldn't twist the truth this time and rationalize the violence. It was clear that he had just slapped her to defend Maybelle! Anguished, she looked at Maybelle only to see a returned cast of triumph on her face. As an emotional survival mechanism, Vivian justified that Lee had hit her because he thought the baby was in danger.

"You spoiled brat," Lee's harsh tone snapped her out of mere humiliation to sheer desecration. "You touch my child and I'll stomp you so hard 'til I break your neck," he barked. Vivian scraped up her smeared heart and held it tenderly in her hand, wanting to give it back to him even if he would smash it again.

"Oh yeah? Well, what about your child growing in me? Will you stomp him too?" Vivian was outdone. She was exasperated that her father-in-law was not home to come to her aid. Fortunately for her ego, Lee read the torment in her sagged shoulders. He softened his tone, but first, he motioned for Maybelle to pass him and enter the house, which she did happily.

"I'm sorry, muffin. You know I love you and the baby. But you gotta trust me. See, trust was always a problem with you. I saw her on the street with my baby and she told me Tazra done put her out. The baby is dirty and hungry. What was I 'posed to do, muffin?" She searched his eyes that noted the partial truth and decided the sincerity of his love outweighed any discrepancies in his story. Besides, it seemed to her that her back was against the wall, anyway, given that he was so adamant about helping Maybelle. Vivian didn't know what else to say without appearing to attack her husband's child, and she saw what results that would bring. She resolved that Maybelle had tricked Lee into believing she had nowhere to go. Vivian was crushed. She knew Lee intended to have Maybelle over for as long as he saw fit, at least until he could find a proper place for them to stay. That could take hours!

"Where is she to go, Lee?" Vivian yelped. "I don't want her here." Lee hugged her soothingly. She let herself receive the affection she thought she needed lest she die in that moment.

"Me neither, muffin. I'll think of something, okay?" He cupped her chin with the palm of his hand. Vivian was sorry that Maybelle was not able to view Lee's show of endearment toward her.

"But…why do you have to help her—is it your child, Lee?"

"Shhh. I can't see how it could possibly be mine, but for some odd reason, she thinks it is, and I don't want *no* baby to be out in the cold."

Reluctantly, Vivian followed Lee into the house. She stood back obediently while he and Maybelle talked in low voices. Vivian's stomach turned when she saw Lee take the baby from Maybelle's arms and carry him to the bedroom. Vivian pretended she didn't see Maybelle pursue them. She decided it would be in her best interest to wait patiently at least for five minutes until the trio returned to the front. At that time, she would eagerly help search for shelter for Maybelle before it got too late. She figured she could have Maybelle out within two hours.

Vivian smiled to herself. She was on to Maybelle and her trickery. If all else failed, Vivian would offer her own mother's place to Maybelle. "One thing is for sure," she chewed over, "that heifer is forbidden to stay here—if that's her plan." Ten minutes passed. Then fifteen more elapsed. Vivian was glued to her chair. Finally, Lee walked out of the bedroom to a hallway closet. He took out sheets and a blanket, and carried them back into the bedroom. Vivian almost fell out of her chair.

"Lee?" She called with feigned calmness, after catching herself. He stuck his head out of the doorway, as though he was too busy to attend to whatever trivial thing she might have to say.

"Come on back, Viv. We just back here trying to get things situated." He disappeared back into the room. Vivian was not ready for the sight that greeted her in her bedroom. Lee had given Maybelle one of her nightgowns and Maybelle had already changed into it. It was red with fluffy lace around the low neckline. Missy had given her that negligee as a wedding present. Maybelle's grapefruit figure protruded and jutted out more than Vivian's did whenever she wore it. Maybelle had made a perfect compact bed out of sheets for Leland in one corner of the room, and now she was straightening her own bunk right next to it. She innocently strutted to her area as soon as Vivian entered the room.

"Lee," Vivian cried, "I thought we were about to find a place for her!" Lee shot her a weird look.

"Come on now, Viv! You know how cold it is out there tonight. Ev'rybody tired." Vivian was horror-struck. Certainly, Lee didn't mean Maybelle and Leland were going to sleep in the bedroom with them? She was afraid to ask him, remembering the slap he had given her earlier. She calculated that she was willing to take another slap, but what she didn't want was the dishonor that would come with it if Maybelle was there to witness it. There was no way she could leave and go crying to her friends or her mother. What would everyone think? Maybe she was making a big deal out of nothing. Also, she thought, hadn't he held her? Hadn't he told her he loved her, and promised her that things would be okay?

"Viv, you know she can't sleep out in the front room with my pops coming through in the middle of the night and crap. Hell. I know I'm sleeping in my own bed, too." Vivian didn't want to gamble shaking Lee's mood. He seemed so content and peaceful. Maybelle knew they were married, she reasoned. Surely she had nothing serious to worry about. She weighed the effects of shaking his mood, which caused her to go along with the setting for now.

Lee was pleased with Vivian's compliance. In the back of his mind, he knew she only obeyed him because of fear of what he might say, feel, or do, but her fear of him didn't disturb him, as obedience was obedience to him. He never said to himself that if she would not obey, he would slap her. In fact, he hated it when he deemed it necessary to physically subdue her. He resolved that it would be so much simpler for all if she would just let him lead in their relationship without challenging and bucking him as though she wore the pants.

He rewarded her compliance by playing with her tummy, and then pushing her playfully on their bed once she was caught off guard. Next, he dived beside her, tickling her, while Maybelle watched. Vivian was satisfied with the exchange of her obedience for the two hundred seconds of affection. Receiving attention wasn't something she was accustomed to taking lightly. It was a rarity as it had been all her life. Lee used to be very intimate, but it seemed that once she married him, he started taking her more for granted. The small degree of warmth she attained now was like a delicate petal being waved around her heart.

Two hours later, all was quiet. Leland had fallen asleep, Vivian rested on her back, comfortable under Lee's arm, and Maybelle was propped up on one elbow, with disappointment dripping from her loins. Vivian drifted off to sleep, unaware of Maybelle's continued plotting. Maybelle rose from her bed, careful not to trip over Leland as she advanced. She glided into her hand made tree bark shoes, feeling in the darkness. She took a place about two feet from the head of the bed.

"Lee," she whispered, "Lee!" Abruptly, he sat up sleepily. "Take me so I can go to the outhouse." He didn't say anything for a moment. Then he stretched back out, now on his side with his back toward Maybelle, and facing Vivian, falling asleep again. "Lee!" He turned his body tiredly toward the sound of the intrusion to his rest. She slithered closer. "Lee! Come on and take me outside," she said again in his ear. Mechanically, he eased out of bed and led her away, fighting his annoyance. Vivian never acted so helpless, he thought. Vivian wasn't afraid to go to the outhouse by herself. Lee's chest was bare, but wore a pair of loose fitting short trousers. He grabbed an overcoat left on the back of a chair as they passed through the house. He ignored his shoes by the door. Maybelle had hoped Lee would make a move on her when they were alone, but he didn't. He walked lethargically over the pebbles, through the damp grass with her to the outhouse.

When they returned just outside of the room, Maybelle reached for his hand and squeezed it. He ignored her ploy at first, however, he stood still for an extra moment, straddling the line of integrity. In the instant of his indecision, the battle was lost. The night crickets hollered at each other while a faraway owl hooted. The mosquitoes balanced on the screen sensed the hot blood running through the veins of the twisted couple. Lee decided to delight in the night breeze coming through the window and the gentle smell of honeysuckle seeping nearby. Maybelle savored the taste of her victory when

Lee crept behind her shadow, expectant of the mystery belonging to this outrageous exploitation.

Vivian had been sleeping comfortably until she heard low murmurings coming from the next room. Vainly, she groped the sheet next to her, not expecting, but hoping to touch Lee and wake up from a bad dream. Vivian was too scared to move. What would he do if she confronted him now? What would happen to their relationship? She decided that if she challenged him, she had better be ready to end their short-lived non-bliss at the very moment. There was no way she could stay married to him with the shared knowledge of his current encounter—the contempt would drive her crazy. It would be difficult enough to sustain the injury from within. Vivian contorted her face in sorrow. Somehow, she had to keep it together, not lose it. She envisioned the sharecroppers on the Johnson Plantation singing cheerfully in the blistering heat. Her roots were from there, and although she had escaped, the kindred connection she felt to her people there was firm. Now Vivian sang her favorite spiritual song just under a whisper to the baby inside of her.

"*Swing low, sweet chariot . . .*" She hoped Lee would assume she was still asleep whenever he returned. Lee was barely distraught as he momentarily anticipated Vivian's response to his absurdity. However, he knew her well enough to conclude that if she in fact was awake, she wouldn't dare interfere during his frolicking.

In the following moments, he could not withstand the urge to have Vivian know that he would do anything he damned well pleased. He was the man in the relationship. He remembered how she had flirted with Henry, and how magnificent Henry looked when he stood slowly from his seat that Sunday, so many months ago, ready to shake his hand. Lee cringed as he remembered the nightmarish big, rough hand sprouting out to him. He pictured Henry's solid, finely toned and sculpted face smiling at his wife, causing his present savagery to become more spiteful.

Ensuing his adventure, he stared at Maybelle for five minutes, wishing he did not have to make the hard choices life required of him. Finally, he tore away from her desperate clutch, crept back into the room and under the covers. Maybelle crept in behind him, satisfied that he loved her more than he wanted to say. Lee had never been happier. He had everything he wanted. He knew his wife was going to have a baby soon, although he never kept up with the dates or anything like that. He figured that the time would come when the time came. Now that he had a boy, he hoped Vivian would have a girl.

It was easy for him to never question her fidelity based on her innocent countenance and his mental image of what she represented. Her flirtatious ways didn't soothe him into these thoughts, although Lee felt they only served to mislead the libidinous Henry. Vivian was his wife. He loved and respected her for that position. No man had held a position so high in her life. He reached out to pull her close to him in the darkness. Vivian automatically answered his snuggling with rigidity. Blood rushed through to his head when he sensed her retreat. Without words, she openly opposed him when he only wanted to warm up to her and provide comfort. And she had the nerve to question why he slapped her around so much, Lee thought. If he wanted to be mean, he could have left her by herself for the rest of the night.

He was moderately appeased when he considered that Maybelle had the practice in the tenderness department. The way Lee saw it, there was no connection between Vivian's rebuff and his behavior. Once he returned to her with open arms, he decided it was time for a new chapter. Whatever he did five minutes ago was in the past. Sure, he cared about Maybelle, but Vivian's breed of a woman was different; she carried herself as the girl any man would be proud to marry. She was always trying to better herself by taking on new projects like sewing, collecting books, creating new dishes to cook, and she was fun. Vivian was a decent girl, and he liked her smile, her high cheekbones, and her long legs. He hoped Vivian could understand that women like Maybelle were made for one thing. He wrapped his arms tighter around Vivian's ice block waist.

Restless and stiff in his musty arms, Vivian waddled in self-pity. She continued to feign sleep. Vivian was panicky about the chain of events. The relationship was out of control. She didn't want to lose Lee because she didn't want to end up like her mother. Vivian started focusing on the things she could do to make the relationship stronger and better, and of ways she could change herself to control the actions of her husband. She premeditated about the baby inside of her and exclaimed to herself, "Lee must never know this isn't his child!" The idea of being trapped into telling lies as a way of life caused her heart to viciously pump away the innocent, fresh love she had for Lee, which was replaced with anguish, trickery, and despair.

Lee's obstructive behavior was God's wrath on her, Vivian decided bitterly, so there was no way out. If this was God's chastisement, as she believed it was, then walking out on Lee would be like trying to escape a chastisement that God had ordained. She truly didn't want to leave him; she just wanted things to be better. She longed to receive the entire breadth of his undivided love.

She imagined Maybelle had Lee wrapped around her baby finger, and that she was using the baby to keep him. She remembered how the stranger had strung her mother along all those years, and how her mother accepted it since he was the father of her children. When she reflected on her mother, Vivian marveled at the chances of Maybelle sitting, waiting stupidly for Lee like her mother did with the stranger for almost twenty years, to no avail, yet undoubtedly wreaking havoc on his own marriage. It was then that she decided to take Lee and move to the North. This plan helped her to sleep that tense filled night next to her snoring husband.

And then one by one, sleepy eyes were wiped, each person with different visions and goals for the budding day. By the rise of the morning sun, Lee decided he wasn't thrilled with the responsibility associated with having Maybelle around. His impression was that she was too possessive. His intentions were not to antagonize his wife, although he perceived the immense pain he must have taken her through already with his selfishness. After everyone dawdled out of bed, Leland began to fuss at Maybelle, begging to be fondled. Maybelle picked him up and handed him to Lee.

"Whatchu giving 'im to me for? I ain't got nothing to give 'im." Lee refused to extend his arms for the wailing child. "He wanna suckle, girl, can't you see that?" He glanced at Vivian's sulking, tear-stained cheeks. Then he looked at Maybelle, who saw fit to boss him around, but Lee wasn't having it. He gazed back at the pained emotion on his wife's face, even though she tried to appear leveled. Lee admired Vivian for this. He didn't want or need to upset her beyond what he already had, especially to satisfy insignificant Maybelle. The arrangement was for Maybelle to serve *his* needs, and not the other way around.

Maybelle didn't think too much about his sentiment when he did not accept the child in his arms. The morning was young, she felt, and she had plenty of time to let Leland's father hold and bond with him. She clumsily propped the baby up to her breast and sat on the edge of Lee's bed. Vivian's eyes bulged out of her head as she cocked her neck vigorously to get a better glimpse of Maybelle's nerve. Lee knew without having to look at Vivian again that he'd better hurry and usher Maybelle out of their house. Even he had boundaries that he deemed necessary to respect. Wasn't there a blanket or some other simple covering nearby that Maybelle could use for privacy?

It wasn't long before the trio departed, leaving Vivian to reminisce on the occurrences of just a few hours ago. The minute they walked out of the house, tears rushed to the surface and streamed freely down her cheeks. She didn't know where Lee would take them, and she didn't care. She mostly blamed Maybelle for what took place the night before because it was well known (she had been taught) that a man would have a woman if she was a free-for-all breed.

Vivian busied herself by cooking a hearty meal and scrubbing the kitchen floor. But as the strong odor of bleach made her eyes water and her nostrils flare, she dumped more of the liquid onto the floor. Crying freely, she let her palms get soaked with the bleach, and then she collapsed face forward, a nervous wreck. She wondered how long she would have to stay in the poison before her unborn child would die along with her. And she wanted to die at that moment. The bleach made her cough violently and it stinged her eyes. Involuntarily, she lifted herself away from the poison, frustrated at her own weakness. She tried to inhale it again, but she knew the bleach would have to be swallowed, though, and she wasn't willing to taste it. She kept her lips positioned to the right, her head tilted back. Reluctantly, she got up and pulled herself together. She was willing to take her life, but not with a gun. Vivian searched for pills--any pills at all. In her search for death, she recalled the life-giving words of Wali Eli whenever he spoke about the necessity of struggles. Quoting something, he had asked her mom and sisters if they thought men would be left alone on saying they believed in God, and would not be tried on that belief. Abruptly, Vivian turned away from a cabinet next to Lee Sr.'s bed that may have contained pills. "I'm a believer," she said to herself.

Before Lee returned alone four hours later, she managed to launder her clothes and all his trousers, as well as a few items belonging to her father-in-law. She changed into Henry's shirt that she wore whenever Lee pissed her off or if she was just feeling lonely. When Lee walked in, Vivian tried not to watch him or appear too interested in where he'd taken Maybelle. Maybelle represented discouragement to her mood and relationship security. Vivian knew she had to work fast to save her marriage, yet, she had nowhere to turn. She was far too ashamed to divulge to her friends that her marriage was sour. Given that her mere belief was not carried into the practice of asking God for guidance, she was on her own. Once she thought she had a plan, she acted without consultation, prayer, or vision.

Lee Sr. came home right after Lee got back. He was disappointed when he saw his son there. He wanted the opportunity to spend some quiet time with his daughter-in-law before he and Lee went out gambling later. There hadn't been such a pure, good-natured woman in the house since his wife lived there. He loved the smell of melted butter entering his nostrils that early afternoon. Vivian quickly handed her father-in-law some of her freshly baked cream of wheat muffins--made using one of Wali Eli's brilliant recipes-as soon as she saw his arm pushing the door open. She had been sitting on the sofa, away from Lee, who had been walking around the house looking guilty. Lee and his father exchanged formalities. When his father sat down with his biscuits, Lee took that opportunity to eat and bathe in peace, knowing that his dad would occupy Vivian while he relaxed. Now, Lee Sr. sat next to her on the sofa, basking in the flavor of the juices dripping from the browned dough. She watched helplessly as Lee took his supper to the bedroom for a silent meal. Then, he came back out to get a pail of bath water, which said that he would be leaving the house for some party.

Vivian had observed the pattern that Lee hardly ever bathed in the afternoon on the days that he didn't work, except to get ready for a night of gambling and partying. She was also aware that her father-in-law would be joining her husband, and when she asked him, he affirmed that he had made plans to go out with his son for Saturday night gambling on Orange Road. She sat back on the couch, dejected. He scooted closer beside her, taking her small, delicate hands into his own. Vivian was comforted by his presence—she only wished he had come earlier to be that rock upon which she could cry. She was in search of a god, someone in whom to seek refuge amid her suffering. Lee was not being the god she wanted him to be. Her quest was to worship him as a god besides God, but his behavior prohibited this. It was not that Vivian manifestly attempted to place Lee in that high status of God Almighty! In fact, she said to herself that she believed in only one God. But wasn't it God who gave her Lee? And she imagined that the gifts she deemed were from God had the power of God. She believed God was too far away to physically reach, and yet here was Lee, slacking in his representation.

"Papa," she started, "things aren't working fine with me and Lee." Her eyes surged with tears. He used his free hand to wipe them.

"Whatchu so upset for, gal?" She could only make hints of the reprehensible particulars of the previous night that Maybelle stayed. She burst into uncontrollable sobs. Lee Sr. waited, patting, and squeezing her hand from time to time.

"I baked the bread to remind him of what he used to think of me," she wailed. "He used to tell me I was his princess, and that I reminded him of how happy he was when his mom was alive. He said I was warm and brown like a princess and that I was special. If I am a princess, I'm a dirty, raggedy one hidden from the world. If I'm a princess, nobody can tell because everyone treats me like dirt!"

"Shhh."

"He's been taking up with Maybelle—I knew it all along, but I'm surer than ever," she wept. He shook his head. She wept harder. "I'm not about to share him with anybody. I'll leave him first, papa." At that moment, Vivian was self-conscious about her mother's lifestyle with the stranger. She thought somehow that others expected her to accept Lee's behavior because of her mother's example.

"Gal, you just better get a hold on yourself," he warned. "You is married. That ain't none of your boyfriend for you to be talking like that…"

"But it isn't fair! We're about to have a baby but he doesn't like the sight of me pregnant, I don't reckon. Ever since I gained weight, he has been staying out more."

"You're not fat…"

Her weeping remained uncontrollable. Lee had decided to take a nap after his food and bath, which prevented him from hearing all the poignant commotion. Lee Sr. wanted her under constraint before his son would come back out to join them and notice her pessimism. He wanted to have a fun filled and peaceful evening. If only Vivian could accept the fact that Lee was a regular man, he felt, everything would eventually work out well. Lee Sr. considered her rebellion would only make the air worse. He shook her.

"Gal, Lee is a man. You know the kinda things men like to do. Shouldn't be any surprise to you that he be wanting to play a li'l bit with other women sometimes . . . you ain't no baby. You know that's just be how mens are. Now you listen, ain't a man out there gonna be with only you. A Negro's sexual nature is stronger than what white men have, and white men like to stick there peckers every which a way, too, so what that tell you 'bout a shine?" He made a mental note to talk to Lee about discretion, however, in these delicate matters.

"That's not true, papa. Besides, Mr. Wali Eli taught us that we are not animals, yet here you are excusing Lee's rotten behavior by blaming it on God."

"It ain't decent for you to speak to me that way, gal. I'm not on Lee's side." He shook his head. "Yeah, I heard about this Mr. Wali Eli."

"Papa, all the good Black men we have around here, but you reduced every one of them because we're not supposed to be good. By the way, the whole town knows Hamilton Briggs' father was good, but they ran him out for being good. My Uncle Jack, Mr. Anderson…so what about Lee?"

"What about 'im?" Lee Sr. asked defensively.

"I want my husband to be an upstanding, faithful citizen- One who doesn't beat me, cheat on me, and one others look up to for leadership. Is that wrong?"

"You hafta accept Lee for what and who he is," he said weakly.

Vivian had her mind made up that she wanted a man all to herself, or she wanted no man at all. Her frustration mounted when she confronted her status as a recently married girl to an abusive, gambling adulterer. Not only that, but she was pregnant, which she felt further entrapped her. These facts did nothing to stop the love she felt for him, but who here would respect her? She knew she must be the laughingstock at church and of her dear friends, the Burdeshaw sisters. She supposed they all were too embarrassed for her to say anything about her disaster.

"Papa, I'm going to tell Lee I want to move up North like my sisters did. It's the only way I see fit to save our marriage. Maybelle has devices to use that baby to keep him, yet I don't plan to go through what my mama went through all her life. We must move," she said with conviction. If Lee Sr. had believed for one minute that Lee would follow her up North, he would have taken great pains to alter their plans from the time he heard them. As much as he had grown fond of Vivian, he wanted his own life to be filled with the love of his unborn grandchild and them there with him. The fact that he had no relationship with any of his other children, coupled with images of growing older and being all alone in this life was scary enough for him to sabotage his son's future before he'd be left alone.

If push came to shove, Vivian indeed could leave his son, but he wouldn't dare let her take Lee with her away from him. He wanted her to know that since Maybelle was not the only girl in Lee's stable, chances were that if Lee did move away, he would continue his lifestyle in the new place. Lee Sr. assumed the obligation of explaining to Vivian just what life was all about. It would be up to her to come to terms with the good as well as the bad in being married. She needed to stop the nonsensical talk about Black leaders and what not. He wondered how Lee married this fiery, rebellious girl. Lee Sr. was sure Vivian had too much spirit to sit back and demand nothing from Lee other than a pay envelope. He beheld that she intended to fight back, primarily to keep her man, but also to defend herself against Lee's lifestyle. He briefly mulled over how serious she might be about moving away, remembering that her sisters had no qualms about leaving. He wondered what Vivian would do if Lee absolutely refused to move up North.

"Don't risk your marriage o'er it, gal," he said feebly.

"Shucks! Why not?" She stopped crying, but her eyes were bloodshot from exhaustion and worry. "I have my baby to think about, papa. And he hasn't stopped jumping on me, either," she lamented.

"What?"

"Can you imagine that, papa? I'm about to have a baby and he slapped me up just the other day in front of . . . her." She couldn't say her name. Lee Sr. was beside himself. Although he knew his son had been violent before, he didn't consider that it was still happening, or rather, he hadn't faced that possibility. Lee Sr. was well enough aware that their relationship *was* going to go to hell if something wasn't done. This girl his son married was not an ordinary, passive person who'd sit idly by and allow him to physically abuse her on top of all the other garbage he put her through, and not retaliate in some form, before long, Lee Sr. recognized. He could not defend Lee's behavior and expect Vivian to swallow it wholesale.

"I didn't know, Vivian. He needs to cut out the foolishness. I'm sure gwine tell 'im 'bout that mess." She felt better with her father-in-law on her side. He offered to play her a game of cards to bring her cheer. Albeit with disinclination, she let him pull her to her feet and lead her to the table. They ended up playing and having fun together for three full hours before Lee got out of bed. That's when Lee Sr. dipped away from his special babysitting duties.

An hour later, father and son stood next to each other, both handsome and ready to hit the streets. Vivian felt trapped. One way she supposed she could show Lee her disapproval was by hitting the streets herself, but her protruding stomach made that almost impossible, she reasoned. She vowed to herself that one day, she would pay him back, that is, if they lasted that long. "I'll be as wild as he is," she said to herself. She harked back on how good it felt when she had been entangled in Henry's arms—how Henry had made her feel strong enough to face another day in her darkest hour.

Her comfort tonight came from the reliance that her father-in-law was going to try to make Lee see things from her perspective while they were out gambling. Lee Sr. was awfully easy to talk to—much unlike Lee, Vivian evaluated. Lee was only easy to talk to when she was agreeing with him. It occurred to her that she would have to make Lee think it was his idea that they move away, or else it might not work. Vivian practiced her introductory speech on the topic of Michigan after the father and son team left the house. She figured they could talk about it upon his return. Vivian stayed up trying to sew herself a skirt until 2:00 a.m., although Lee did not return until well after 4:00 a.m.

Lee and Lee Sr. went to a new gambling joint on Orange Road that everyone had been talking about. The "casino" was actually in the basement of a house turned into a club. It was the opening night for the clubroom upstairs. Lee Sr. remembered his promise to Vivian, but he really didn't want to talk to Lee about Vivian when they were on their way to have fun. When they arrived, the party was in full blast. Flashing lights bounced off the walls and twinkled on the hardwood floor. Shoes slid and pivoted in dancing moves to the spellbinding beat of the musical band. Lee shielded his eyes, not yet accustomed to the great ball of light twirling from the ceiling. He noticed a man in the corner of the room trying to get his attention. It was Hamilton Briggs.

Seated next to Hamilton was Floyd Barnes. Lee hesitated in the middle of the room. His father was not aware of the friction between Lee and Floyd, so he walked ahead to greet Hamilton. When they were a few years younger, Hamilton used to come over to their house quite often with Floyd to play cards and drink. But now, the boys liked to go out more to clubs and casinos. Lee Sr. always had a fun time with the boys—all three of them, and he welcomed the chance to have a few drinks with them. Lee put forth much effort to successfully follow his father. Slowly, Floyd nodded his head in a greeting to Lee. Lee sighed, giving off a breath of relief before nodding back.

The blaring music was not the scene that night for Hamilton and Lee Sr. who wanted to try their hands at cards, so they headed to the basement, leaving Floyd and Lee to face each other after their friendship had been smeared. "Hey, man," Floyd apologized, "that night me and you fell out...I didn't know Vivian was so special to you, man."

"I know, man," Lee answered.

"I mean, you ain't never brought no broad around that you was serious 'bout."

"Yeah, man. But that's just me. Things happen like that sometimes, man. We can put all that behind us, though. Hell, we's married now."

"Congrats, too, niggah."

"Thanks, Floyd."

"You is luckier than luck itself. She's one hot bi..."

"Yeah," Lee quickly cut him off. "She's hot," Lee said, disguising his discomfort. He wasn't sure if he liked Floyd complimenting Vivian. "Tell me something, Barnes...why on earth did you bring Maybelle to the church?" They both laughed hard. Lee got serious first. "I'm telling you, man, you almost made me lose her o'er that crap."

"I'm sorry, man," Floyd answered. Floyd *was* sorry. He was sorry about a lot of things. First, he was sorry Lee had found a beautiful woman before he did. He was sorry Vivian had turned him down as though he was dirt. He was sorry Lee had fathered a baby with one woman, and now he learned that his wife would give him a baby as well. In short, Floyd envied him. His envy matriculated into heartfelt hatred stemming from disappointment with the perception that God didn't bless him the way He blessed Lee. In the dark crevices of Floyd's imagination, he disagreed with the hand he was dealt. Sucking his teeth between sips of liquor, Floyd made a silent, subtle charge that God was unjust because he viewed that Lee constantly possessed what God should have given *him* instead. The only way Floyd knew how to respond was by embracing Lee as one of his best friends, keeping his envy hidden. Floyd gained life from the flesh of the secrets he gained about Lee's blessings. However, the life he gained was brief, and could only endure if he consumed what he coveted, even if his consumption led to destruction. Floyd calculated that he would have to buffer some of his obvious hatred. He wasn't proud that he had openly fought with Lee twice over a woman that didn't belong to him.

"I'm sorry, too, man." They were both relieved to be able to spend time together again. Since they had been the best of friends for so many years, it didn't make sense for a woman to come between them, Lee reasoned. The two of them toasted with drink after drink to their renewed friendship. Lee was almost drunk when a short, well-rounded lady meandered over to him and pulled him onto the dance floor. He spent the rest of the time at the club with her, never once making it to the casino part. This was too much for Floyd. If there really was a God, how could he be so unjust as to allow Lee to possess a pretty lady like Vivian and still have plenty of women who were willing to eat out of his hand? He hadn't scored a point with a woman all evening, and he'd been there since six-thirty. What did Lee have that he didn't have? True, Lee was good-looking, but as far as Floyd was concerned, money mattered more than looks, and it wasn't as though Lee had more money than other trying men, either, Floyd pondered. Lee was too cute to be considered a true stud, according to Floyd, and he wasn't dark enough to be fully trusted. Floyd was disturbed by the women who fell all over Lee simply because he was debonair and so stocky. He thought those women deserved whatever they got for preferring a man based solely on his looks and physique.

Floyd spent the rest of the evening drinking, and listening to the music. It was 3:30 a.m. when Lee Sr. came upstairs, ensuing winning a pocket full of money. He found his son in a corner of the room locked in a fervent grapple with the woman. He hated to interrupt Lee, his protégé,' but he wasn't sure if he had seen this woman come into the club with a man that had been downstairs gambling. He figured if they waited, they'd find out soon enough since the gambling downstairs was winding down. Lee Sr. pulled his son away from the woman like one would take a radiant toy from a baby.

When they finally made it home, Lee fell drunk on the couch, next to his father who hit the floor as soon as he walked in the house. Lee Sr. wasn't drunk, he was just too lazy and tired to go to bed. When Vivian saw them in the morning, she was relieved that Lee had decided to come home at all. She could think of many nights when Lee had better things to do than to come home to her. She sighed as her hand unconsciously roamed over her protruding stomach. For the sake of her unborn child, at least, Vivian resolved to fight for her relationship, but at the same time, she was determined not to let Lee get away with treating her badly, humiliating her.

CHAPTER FIFTEEN
Making Mary

Things picked up at least financially for Henry and Minnie. Since they both were working, Henry was quickly able to buy a house for them on California Street at the corner of Harvey in a quiet Black neighborhood. Robeena was not asked to contribute anything. The only jobs available for a Black girl during that time was cleaning houses or keeping children. Henry had a hard time with allowing Robeena to clean a Caucasian woman's house, although he felt Minnie and her sturdy back could handle it fine. Secretly, he wanted Minnie to take up something, anything that would remove her from his sight occasionally. She crowded him. He liked *some* of her attention, but he didn't want her looking in his face every time he sat down to a meal. He could get his own bath water. He didn't want to talk to her as soon as he made it home from work. If she worked, she would be too tired to bother him every day and night. Yes. A job would help her to lay off him. They both wanted Robeena to just keep growing up slowly and without worry. The monthly payments were reasonable enough for Henry to manage more than comfortably. Although he didn't need her nickels, he also wanted her to have plenty of money to do all the shopping she wanted and for as long as she wanted. Saying it politely, Henry gave Minnie advanced permission to stay gone for as long as the streets could hold her.

Across from their house was a field of weeds growing wild. It reminded Minnie of Florida where the crickets had their own playground. They had two neighboring homes to the left of them, and another small field after that. Also, to the left, down the block and across the dirt street was a white house that was made into a storefront. Its backyard was an open field which went all the way back on the opposite side of the street to their house on the corner. The area was cozy. It definitely made Robeena feel a whole lot better. Henry and Minnie needed much more than a house to fulfill their dreams, though.

They both felt a child would do their relationship well. Neither Henry or Minnie wanted to admit their love was escaping them. Minnie was too unfulfilled with Henry to offer him one hundred percent of her love again.

He had failed in his promise to bring her happiness. All she felt was emptiness. Where was the urgency in his kisses? A child would bring excitement to their dull relationship, they both privately thought. Church was their only exhilaration, and even that had its limitations. There was a lot of singing, clapping, and temporary spirit boosting in church, but negligible application regarding the spiritual resurrection needed for self and community improvement. They both inwardly felt they needed someone like Wali Eli to help them place things into perspective, remove the conjecture, and explain the allegorical content of the Bible and hymn books that read like a fairytale. If Minnie was saved by the blood of Christ, deep down, she wanted to know what that meant in unadulterated truth. If Jesus died for his sins, Henry wanted to know if he was forgiven or if loving Vivian was a sin.

Henry did not believe that at the *end of the world*, his spirit would fly out of his body and up to heaven. He felt his spirit had escaped from his body whenever he left Vivian behind, and that his soul was a hollow vessel. In church, they learned that a man would come who would be the antichrist and he would rule the world with evil. He would have horns coming out of his head. God would burn the world up with fire and that is when the souls of the people would fly out of their bodies up to heaven. Master Kent Johnson was not the only one who taught that at one time, snakes could talk, had legs, and could walk around. Henry secretly did not believe a real snake talked to Eve, but he thought he would be committing a sin to ask Minnie her thoughts on the matter. The church lectures focused on what Jesus of two thousand years ago did, what Moses did four thousand years ago, and how happy a life Jesus led until he died for the sins of the people. However, they were ill-equipped to apply the scriptures to their current struggles. Unlike Minnie, Henry did not want to dance and sing about what life would be like after physical death. When Minnie went to church, she expected and enjoyed going into a spiritual trance, jumping, and shouting her love for God, and she hoped her high would last until the next visit, carrying her through the pain. Although Robeena believed in God, she stopped attending church.

By February, Robeena's new lifestyle heightened, but Minnie and Henry's monotonous lives activated a degree of frustration for them that a baby was not yet conceived. Nonetheless, Henry seldom talked openly about his dream for a girl, and Minnie mostly silently allowed herself to wish for a boy. Henry never initiated conversations of such intimacy. He whispered softly to Minnie when she expressed her futility, yet refused to burden her with his own.

Robeena, true to her word, found a place of her own, not a half-mile away from Minnie. It was only a tiny room in a house with other boarders, smaller even than the one she had previously shared with her sister and brother-in-law, but it was her own. She did befriend a lady who lived in the house by the name of Connie. Connie was divorced, and as far as she knew, her ex-husband was away with the army since he never came home from the war. Connie wasn't up with what was going on across the waters with the government. Her main concern was that the United States Army had sucked her husband up before she had the chance to work things out with him. She was willing to get back with him if he'd just come home. Often, she told Robeena stories about her life with her husband, and how things had changed for the worse just before his departure.

Robeena empathized with Connie, but another downhill relationship was an all too familiar story she'd witnessed time after time in her young life. She told Connie that the best advice she could offer was that it was never good to settle down with a man simply to get hurt. Subsequently, the stories were too boring for Robeena to continue listening to, so Connie started watching how exciting Robeena's life was becoming.

Robeena galloped into living a full-blown nightlife that often ran into the next day. Men were for the expressed purpose of receiving monetary gains. She was tired of the drawn out charades with men--she felt she could see their hands before they presented their cards. Robeena grew steadily into the hustling community. There was a time that she would date a man for an entire week before obtaining some tangible fulfillment. But now, she would come to terms seven times sooner as opposed to investing time only to have it wasted. She imagined how pleasant things would be if Vivian would join her. Lee was the only problem, Robeena judged. She moped whenever the idea of troublesome men crept into her mind.

She knew her other sister, Minnie, was trying frantically to have a baby with one of those "low down jack-asses." She thought this idea was insane, considering the lack of zest in their relationship. Robeena feared a baby would drive Minnie and Henry further away from each other because instead of focusing on each other, she envisioned that they both would dote on the new baby. She calculated that Minnie would just let herself go totally with a new child. She would pity Henry if that happened. Robeena stated her concerns to her sister during one of her visits when Henry was at work.

"Girl, why for you wanna get pregnant? You're gonna be stuck with a bunch of babies and can't do nothing no more."

"Having a baby don't make you stuck, Beena."

"...And then Henry gonna say you're fat and ugly. He don't pay no special attention to you no how . . . what is a baby gonna do?" Minnie's heart dropped. Robeena regretted her words as soon as she tasted the acidic toxin on her tongue after saying them.

"Can't nobody tell me my man don't love me. I don't care what you say," Minnie said, trying to convince herself.

"Did I say that or did you just think it?" Although Robeena didn't mean to insult her sister, she couldn't stop herself from saying what she felt.

"Well, whatchu saying then? You trying to say Henry don't treat me like he should?" Minnie was ready to fight. Robeena wasn't armed to explain that it wasn't the kind way he treated her, but the anesthetized way he acted. How could Robeena propose to Minnie that she (Robeena) could tell that Henry wasn't the portrayal of a doting husband? "At least I got a man," Minnie stabbed. "Don't no man even want no fast floozy like you." Robeena threw up her hands in defeat.

"It ain't about me, Minnie. You always gotta be so dagnabbit defensive for nothing."

"I ain't defensive."

"Never mind. Go have a baby." Minnie folded her arms across her chest. "Minnie, all I'm saying is I think you should be trying to go on a honeymoon with 'im. You know? Some place special where it's just y'all. Be romantic. That's what y'all need."

"Beena, I don't know what's wrong! He loves me, I know he does." Robeena looked away. "He just ain't never have nothing to say. It's like he wants me to be his wife, and not for me no more. Like, who I am inside don't matter to 'im—as long as I can cook, clean, bring in some money, and give 'im a baby. I guess that's all he is supposed to care about. It could be worse. Least he's here. Oh Beena! I don't know what I'd do without 'im."

"But Minnie, you always trying to tell me and Viv something, but you were never supposed to move in with 'im without making 'im marry you. In fact, he was supposed to be begging for marriage, not for you to travel with 'im as his mistress. What kinda girl would move in with a man who ain't none of her husband?"

"Lots of girls is doing that sort of thing nowadays, Beena. If you be thinking about staying with someone for the rest of your life—how you gonna know if you don't try living together first? I mean, forever is a mighty long time…"

"You talk like you is one of them automobiles that folk be driving around town, testing out the goods before they'll sign. You didn't offer him no challenge, so what makes you think you can give him one now?"

"None of that even matters, Beena. I mean, as long as we is finally married—what difference does it make when we got that way?"

"You don't get it, do you? If he had begged, then you would've known that you was worth a dime to him. Henry ain't hafta go through no effort to have you. He decided to take you, like you was a piece of fruit dangling from a tree, and he just plucked you off and you fell limp in his arms. Now, how can a man enjoy a meal like that? A man is a hunter. He wants to find a buried treasure, not have one to fall down on him." Minnie burst with laughter.

"Is that what them mens be doing at those bars you go to? They be hunting the womens?"

"Something like that."

"Pitiful girl. You being at the bar is the clearest sign of a piece of fruit dangling there could be!"

"Not if I'm the hunter."

Minnie stopped laughing when she determined that the joke was on her. Robeena did not possess an ounce of lady likeness. She sighed. "If I could go back in time, I would, Beena. But for now, I gotta give 'im what he wants."

"You mean you trying to have a baby 'cause it's the wifely thing to do? That ain't no love, Minnie."

"No, Beena, that's not it. I wanna have a baby to love it. I need somebody to love strongly. Henry only takes so much of my love. I got so much more to give." Minnie desperately wanted to talk about something, anything else. "Beena, you realize we ain't written mama 'nem yet? Let's write 'em tonight. I gotta go o'er to Mrs. Miller's house for a spell. I'll write to Vivian when I get settled o'er there." Robeena nodded her head in agreement. "I'm so busy thinking about myself and having a baby that I forgot about what you know we gotta do."

"I hope you get one real soon, Minnie. Really. I know it must mean a lot to you. You go to that church of yours and pray that this February blesses you with the family you want so much. And Minnie, I'll be praying with you."

February was quite a different story in Florida concerning babies. Vivian went into labor at night on February 21, 1922. Lee happened to be home that evening when Vivian's water broke. They were sitting at the kitchen table engaged in separate activities when Vivian started feeling queasy. Before she could brace herself, a sharp pain cut across her back causing her to arch forward from her chair and grit her teeth. She dropped her head in her sewing basket, and then pushed the basket violently off her knees and onto the floor. Lee looked up from his girly magazine that was concealed by the *Century Weekly Press* newspaper.

"You okay, muffin?" She remained in her arched position for another few seconds until the pain subsided.

"I think this is it, Lee! This baby is on his way out!" Lee hopped out of his chair and trotted to Vivian's side, making sure he folded the newspaper over securely before he dropped it in his chair.

"Whatchu want me to do, Viv?" He asked frantically. She laughed at his anxiety, but then another sharp pain knocked the grin right off her face. He slipped his arm around her and helped her to the sofa.

"Lee, listen to me. Go fetch Madeline and Missy. Tell one to get my mama and Tazra or Pixie, the midwife. Tell the other one to come quickly!" Lee stood still with Vivian in his arms, his mouth gaped open.

"Hurry, man!" She commanded.

"I can't leave you here by yourself like this, muffin! Something might happen to you, and it'd be my entire fault." She tried to conceal her fear so that he would have the courage to leave for help. She didn't dare want to be left alone with him to manage the task. She hadn't planned on going into labor in this way. She thought she'd get symptoms for a while so that she could prepare.

"Yes, you can, Lee. I'm fine. Go on, now! Hurry back. It'll only take you ten minutes away from me. Nothing will happen in ten minutes. Quit wasting time," she encouraged. He helped her down on the couch and kneeled beside her. He wanted her to pray together with him. She let him begin the prayer. After a minute, another contraction caught her from under her belly button. She broke into his prayer, "Move it," she yelled. Startled, he almost fell over her trying to stand. He ran out on his errand that instant. Less than ten minutes later, he was back with Missy. However, it took two hours for Tazra to arrive. Madeline got back with Carol and Pixie after only an hour.

Following a quick examination, Pixie told everyone that Vivian wasn't quite ready to have the baby, but that she would by morning.

"Vivian's body gave off a few false alarms, y'all. I knew better. That's how come I didn't rush. I was just here yesterday."

"It sure feels like the time has come," Vivian said weakly.

"Oh, it's real, honey. Your water erupted, so I hafta give you something to make you have the baby if it doesn't come by morning." Tazra stood back, monitoring the situation. She considered herself the authority; she would only speak if it seemed like Pixie didn't know what she was doing.

Carol said, "I'll stay with her." Vivian was frightened to death. What if the baby looked exactly like Henry?"

Without waiting for Lee's approval, Madeline announced, "We'll all stay."

"Good," Pixie responded. "I'm just up the road. I'll be back at dawn. In the meantime, make sure she gets plenty of water and rest!" With that, Pixie wrapped her shawl around her shoulders, glanced at Tazra for approval, and was out the door.

Tazra said, "Clear out." Glancing at Lee, she added, "You, too. I need to examine her in private." With only the two of them in the room, Vivian avoided Tazra's eyes while Tazra quietly started her examination. Then, like a cougar paying close attention to the patterns of fish swimming close to a riverbank, Tazra zoned in on Vivian's guardedness: Vivian showed Tazra her eyes whenever she peeped up at her. Tazra knew the truth was somewhere behind those eyes, and would come from them as opposed to any words Vivian may have spoken. "I figure it's been nine months since I last seen you, gal."

As expected, Vivian gasped, trying to quickly dart her eyes in another direction. "No, Ma'am. I've never met you."

"That's a mighty fine horse you got, gal. It seems like it went mad for a spell. Is it better, now?" Vivian snorted, dismissing her. Never once had Tazra snitched on anyone. And Vivian surmised there was no way Tazra really knew the truth.

"You don't know anything, Mother Tazra. You're making a mistake."

Finishing up, Tazra said, "Lawdy, I hope that horse is better. You got a mess on your hands." Just then, Carol tapped lightly, peeping in before entering. Tazra motioned for her to come all the way inside the room. "She's yours, now. I can't clean all this mess up. Can't fix ev'rything." Without hesitation, Carol went to work cleaning the room.

Tazra waited an additional hour before leaving. Carol busied herself by cleaning the house from top to bottom, mumbling the entire time about how unkempt everything was. Madeline and Missy helped Carol, and took turns making sure Vivian had water and that she remained comfortable. Lee held Vivian's hand all night. He refused to allow Madeline or Missy much time to comfort his wife in his stead. At 6:00 a.m., he sent Missy to tell his supervisor at the railroad yard about the pending birth of his child. In addition to passing on that message, she saw Lee's father as he was about to enter the gate on the colored men's side. She knew he'd want to know, too, and she was right. At lunchtime, Lee Sr. clocked out and rushed to Vivian's side. He made it just in time to hear the baby's first cry.

One hundred minutes after the baby was born, Pixie had everything cleaned up, including the baby. While Pixie and Missy sanitized the birthing area, Lee carried his wife to the freshly laundered pallet that Carol, assisted by Madeline, had made for her in the front room. Pixie checked the baby from head to toe. Vivian was able to rest comfortably, and she was happy everyone was making a huge fuss over her and the baby. Lee didn't seem to notice anything odd about the brand new little girl who was supposed to be his daughter, and no one else gave any strange looks. After Pixie finally placed her stamp of approval on everything, she left, but promised to come back soon to help Vivian write down what happened. Lee carried Vivian back to their bedroom and laid her on the freshly made bed. As he gently scooted her away from the edge, he was embarrassed at how easily he could lift her. Even during her "big" stage before the baby was born, he sometimes played with her and picked her up so that their heights could be equal. How then, could he smack her around when she only weighed 117 pounds compared to his 190 pounds?

Lee reflected on how Carol treated him like she despised the sight of him. Even now that they were married, he knew Carol was not comfortable in his presence, and she didn't trust him. During the time of their courtship, she never confronted him or told him she disapproved of him, yet Vivian let him know that Carol never really wanted him hanging around. He wished Carol could know how sorry he was for not being a better man; he desperately wanted her to know how much he really loved Vivian.

Carol placed a bundle of towels in the bedroom. Lee smiled faintly at her when she glanced over at him. She gave him a fragile smile in return before she left the room. Lee knew her message was that she would accept him if he made Vivian happy. Madeline brought in the baby, leaving immediately so the couple could be alone. Lee sat at the foot of the bed and rubbed Vivian's feet.

"I love you, muffin. I love you more than anything in this world. You hear me?" She smiled weakly. "I mean it, Viv! I'm gonna give you everything. Anything you and the baby want."

"Lee?" He made sure her legs were covered down to her toes with a freshly laundered sheet.

"Hmm?"

"What I want is to move to Michigan with my sisters. And not just on account of them, but I want a new life with you."

"Now Vivian, you know I can't . . ." Vivian jerked her head toward the wall. "Come on, now, girl," he pleaded. She focused on the cooing baby.

Lee was inflexible in his insistence about having a love filled day with his wife and new baby. He continued to rub her feet under the sheet until finally she looked back at him and smiled. He smiled, too. They looked at each other for a long moment.

"I love you, my beautiful wife."

"I love you, my dear husband. Thanks for being so good to me today." They spoke of nothing other than their love and the precious baby that afternoon. Vivian did not want to nag him about Michigan, although she had her mind made up. One way or another, she would be leaving the South. Missy and Madeline finally went home around four, once they were convinced Lee could manage without them. Lee Sr. became acquainted with Carol for the remainder of the evening. And Carol forgot to think she was missing out on something by not being at home waiting for the stranger. She basked in a joy that was her own in having a new family. Carol found a bed on the sofa, but she was not needed because Lee stayed up half the night waiting on Vivian and the baby. Carol ended up staying for over a week before going back home. She smiled to herself, reflecting on the significant occurrences: She had a new family in Lee Sr. as well as her first grandchild.

Lee was great that entire week, and the next. What with Lee's smothering, Lee Sr. could barely squeeze himself in to spend time alone with his beautiful daughter-in-law. After Lee put in over a month of pampering, his father did manage to steal him away for a night to hang out on Orange Road again. Lee Sr. wanted nothing more than for his son to be happily married, but it certainly goaded him that Lee was indulging in an overabundance of "womanly" duties. And to make matters worse, he did these girlish chores with exuberance! Lee Sr. didn't want Vivian to lose her soft, ladylike manner. He didn't want her to forget who wore the pants in the house, or it could mean doom for his son. Vivian had already threatened to leave Lee if he didn't do like she wanted, Lee Sr. recalled. He didn't want her to forget that it was her sole responsibility to care for the child.

It wasn't a complicated task to talk his son into going out with him when Mary, named after the mother of Jesus, was just over four weeks old. Lee missed being out in the lust of the darkness, so with the strength of his father pressuring him, Lee estimated he'd been at home under Vivian for long enough. He didn't see how he could miss the event the new club was having called "Lady's Night."

Hamilton and Floyd were there again, and this time, the stranger was there. Hamilton and Floyd joined Lee and his father who arrived first, at a table in the center of the room. By 9:00 p.m., the latter two had guzzled all the beer they'd brought with them, while the former two were well into their whiskey stashes. Floyd put his arm around Lee's back.

"Man," Floyd slurred, "it's cool we are hanging again."

"Yeah, man," Lee said, "we've been through some stuff."

"I don't know why, man! Look how long we've been tight. How are we gonna fall out like that?" Lee hesitated to answer, recognizing that Floyd was drunk. He smiled a little and looked away from Floyd. His smile, as faint as it was, quickly faded when he noticed the stranger walking over to them. Lee Sr. followed his son's gaze, and stood as the stranger approached. The stranger wore a grim face. He was holding a fifth of scotch, with a cigar dangling from his teeth.

"Well if it ain't my son-in-law," he muttered bitterly. Lee Sr. was quite surprised by the stranger's tone. He had known years ago that the stranger had fathered children, but he hadn't recognized Vivian as his daughter. Lee Sr. ignored the sarcasm and shook the stranger's hand.

"Hey man, what's your problem?" Floyd asked the stranger.

"Oh, he got a really big problem, my man. He got a problem with me being married to his daughter." Lee Sr. smelled trouble coming. The stranger shifted.

"Naw, baby!" The stranger said too loudly. "What I got a problem with is your pimpish ways, hustler." Lee Sr. instinctively swayed closer to the stranger.

"You's the pimp, home boy," Lee said lazily. Lee Sr. was now standing directly between them. Floyd jumped up and stood next to Lee Sr. Then Hamilton stood slowly, with a blank expression on his face. Lee felt smug, thus decided to stay in his chair and relax. He was touched that Floyd, of all people, had his back. The stranger did not want a physical confrontation as a measure to make his point; his frustration and guilt had led him to Lee's table. He pleaded with Lee Sr., whom he had known casually for many years from the nightlife scenes and the railway company.

"Lee, man, me and you goes back a long way. You know your son ain't gwine do right. What is he doing out here with all these fine ladies when he got a wife at home? He showing disrespect to one of my daughters."

"Aw man. Why you wanna say it like that, man? You got a wife at home, too! Ain't no cause to jump all o'er my son." The stranger looked at Lee Sr. as though he had no right to bring in *his* personal life. The stranger thought it was understood that it was okay that he cheated on his own wife because his wife wasn't related to anyone at the table. Everyone read his sentiment at the same time, and they all laughed at him. Lee Sr. was trying to remain diplomatic since he was the oldest of his posse. He attempted to keep his laughter muffled. Floyd laughed even harder when he looked over at Lee Sr.'s puffy cheeks and tight lips. Tears began to roll out of Lee Sr.'s eyes. Finally, he couldn't hold back any longer, so he burst out laughing with the others.

The stranger boiled with hatred. They were making a fool out of him, he thought, and there was nothing he could do. He hated Carol for raising Vivian stupid enough to marry a player like Lee. He hated Vivian for giving him what he considered to be a bad reputation by marrying a street hustler.

"Man, you oughta come by and see Mary sometimes," Lee said seriously.

"Who?" The stranger asked gingerly. The men's laughter was exchanged for disgusting sighs.

"Oh! You didn't know?" Lee asked. "My pretty wife done gave you a grand-baby." The stranger was awestruck. He hadn't seen much of Vivian since the night he saw her sitting on the couch with Lee, and he hadn't seen her at all since her wedding. On a few occasions when he visited Carol after the wedding, Vivian would be there sitting with her mother, but he hadn't taken the time to look at her closely or give her more than a greeting.

"Naw. I ain't heard."

"Yeah, pops. Can I call you pops?" The stranger was too sheepish to speak. He mumbled promises to visit them, and then hurried away from their table. Lee Sr. remembered Carol speaking to him about Vivian's "no good" father, but she hadn't mentioned his name. He felt that Carol should have at least told Vivian's father about having a new granddaughter, despite whatever personal problems she had with him. Lee Sr. passed his empty liquor pouch over to Floyd and followed the stranger.

Floyd was having an exciting time. Drama was his forte. He drank himself into a stupor, losing all sense of direction by the time the night ended. Lee and his father had to half carry him home with them because they were both tired and Floyd lived much farther away from the club than they. Hamilton was no help because he was just sober enough to get himself and only himself home. They dropped Floyd on the floor in the front room, and Lee and his father went straight to bed.

Morning came all too soon. Lee Sr. was happy to spend more time with his son, even if they were on their way to work. He hurried him along because Lee had the habit of dragging behind and making them both late. Lee Sr. chuckled to himself when he guessed Lee must have gotten that characteristic from his mother -she used to be late for everything! Floyd woke up when he heard the two men talking to each other. He watched sleepily for a moment while they didn't know he was awake. Floyd thought how nice it must be to have a father to share things with and to talk with from time to time.

"Hey," Floyd called, "what if I get hungry?"

"Don't worry, man, it's plenty to eat in here," Lee said as he rushed out behind his father. He stepped over Floyd in his haste. Floyd was still for a moment in the quiet of the morning. He wanted Vivian to fix him some eggs and toast with honey, except he was too tired and hung over to demand it of her. Before long, he slipped back off to sleep.

Mary slept soundly in the crook of her mother's arm, and Vivian was content. She didn't know Floyd was there until 10:00 a.m., when he woke her up to tell her to fix him a bite to eat. She gasped at his nerve to enter her bedroom with the impudence that he expected her to cook for him. He explained to her puzzled look that he had been in their front room all night after hanging out with Lee. Vivian didn't want to hear it.

"I will fix you nothing, boy." She leaped out of bed, happy now that the chill from the dawn had cautioned her to wear her robe to bed after her husband had gone. "The nerve of my husband to leave you here in my house without my knowledge."

"Bitch, this ain't your house," he said viciously, catching her off guard. She placed the still sleeping Mary gently in the center of the bed. Walking past him, she smiled as though she took his words to be in good humor. All she knew is she couldn't be in a back bedroom with that savage. He followed her with uncertainty, not able to read her. Floyd recalled his bare cabinets at home. Instead of buying bread, he had recently filled his shopping bag with liquor and soda. He watched her grab the last biscuit from a basket on the kitchen table and topple it down her throat in practically one gulp. She also slurped the remains of what was in the cooler in a pitcher that smelled like lemonade, not bothering to get a cup. She looked at Floyd, smiling passively at him. Then, she stretched her arms out and yawned.

"Your husband has plenty more manners than you."

"I'm demonstrating to you how to simply get something to eat. I know Lee didn't tell you to treat me like your maid."

"I guess by you being a woman and all, you might not have wanted me in your kitchen. That's why I politely asked."

On her way out of the kitchen, she said, "If it's not my house, then it's not my kitchen."

He blocked the doorway. "I said fix me a sandwich." Vivian simply couldn't stomach doing anything nice for him. He gave her goose bumps by his mere presence.

"You tried to wreck my engagement party. I did tell you to help yourself. Why you think I'm a slave woman to bake for you, I will never know."

"You gotta come up off that old story. Lee and I are cool now."

"I don't care if Lee is supposed to be your friend…you don't mean a thing to me, therefore I'm not making you a sandwich. Everything you need is in the icebox!" She didn't understand why they were having the conversation. They glared at each other.

"Vivian, why you always gotta treat me like I's some low down dog?" He begged.

"I'm not wasting my breath on you anymore," she hissed with raised eyebrows.

"What? You think you better than me or something?" She looked at him with disapproval from head to toe, and then she turned her nose up and sniffed at him. She tried again to go through the narrow passageway that he blocked, but still, he grabbed her arm and pulled her up into him.

"Ugh!" Vivian screeched. "If you don't get your dirty, funky, crusty hands off of me, you better!" He backed her into the wall and came against her. Right away, she went into a panic when she recognized a wild look in his eyes. The rush of her blood throttled her as she felt herself sinking to the floor. Everything turned dark in the whirlwind that encompassed her. She tried to escape but something clutched at her legs, pulling her back into the spinning river. She tried to scream, yet she could not find her breath. She was drowning. Searing pain raced with intensity until it tore into her. She felt the urge to shriek at the top of her lungs, yet she could not, would not allow herself to be discovered in such a position.

"What you got . . . to . . . say . . . now, what you gotta . . . say, princess?" She cried silently. Everyone was always treating her like she thought she was some sort of princess when she didn't feel that way about herself. She wanted the ordeal to be over as quickly as possible. Defeated, Vivian gave up the fight and let the tears roll down her face. She felt as though she was suffocating. He was practically cutting off her airways with his flabby, sweaty body. Damned if he cared, though. He would teach her a lesson for rejecting him in her siditty and uppity manner. He loved the feel of the power he had over her now, as he violated her. Never again could she look down on him or sneer at him as though he was nothing. He would make certain that she knew *she* was nothing. He groped and clawed at her mercilessly.

Vivian's cries were inaudible, but her body shook loudly. Mary's wails came from the bedroom once she awakened to find herself in an empty bed. Mary sensed that something was amuck in her home. She had a keen sense of awareness of the times her mama and papa fought, as those times created such anxiety in her. Crashing voices and tension-filled tones constantly agitated her in her budding infancy. She could tell the difference from the times her parents fought between their loving whispers, and the soft tender words murmured near her or to her.

She sensed now that there was a stranger in the house; another man who was hurting her mama. She knew it was of the male persuasion, like her daddy, and she had it formulated in her mind that males always win, and that males liked to fight. A male was a deep, stern voice that was heard last, after her mother's voice. It moved harder, louder. It was filled with thunder and fighting. What *was* fighting? Those ear-splitting voices and shrill screams. Fighting was the pounding of fists, the separation of bodies, the forceful joining of bodies, and the rapid heartbeat that echoed in her ear when she cuddled on her mother's chest. Fighting was muteness, crying, and sleepless nights.

Fighting was now. Mary could discern her mother's muffled cries because her anguish shook the house. She wanted to be fed and comforted by her mother's breast. She wanted to consume her mother's pain. Mary liked the soft way her mother smiled at her, and her kindly hands, how they reached for her, cuddled her, loved her. She screamed for her mother and hollered when she didn't get a response. This was abandonment to Mary. She had no confirmation that her mother would *ever* come for her. She cried for the relief a kiss or a hug could give. Vivian's greatest pain now came from the inability to go to her daughter. She closed her eyes tightly and imagined that in a few moments, she'd be able to hold her screaming baby and ease both of their pain.

Vivian didn't know she was already feeding her child the ingredients of psychological pain and torment that Mary would have for the rest of her life. Every time she yelled at Lee, or Lee yelled at her, every time she was sorrowful, Mary recognized the despair in her mother's shaking arms, and she tasted the suffering in the chemical produced by that despair in her milk. Since she was a baby when these ingredients came to her, she would never know or understand from whence they came, or that these ingredients of her make-up were even there.

Without being audited at the cellular level, Mary would live her life repressing her psychological trauma. She would never seek help for her hardship because she would learn to sweep things under the rug, to mask the horrors of her life as if they didn't exist. Ignoring the problems would become progressively easy as the years passed and as the damage took on the "snowball" effect, increasing in intensity and frequency. Yet, soon, the time would come when Mary no longer noticed the dysfunction, and she would no longer cry during arguments. Violence, gambling, drinking, fornication and adultery, and overall mental anguish would be the norm for Mary. And for her children, And for her children's children.

"I have to get my baby," Vivian begged. Floyd was behaving ferociously in his fit of rage. He grunted and panted like a wild, stray dog in her ear. "Let me go now, Floyd," she pleaded tearfully. He was triumphant. He gnawed at her flesh repeatedly until he tasted her peeling skin. Contemptuously, he rolled onto his side. She was afraid to move, lest he notice her and attack again. He reached over and squeezed her hand in what he believed to be a tender gesture before standing to put his pants back on.

"Thanks for the meal, princess." He looked around the room to make sure he wouldn't leave anything behind, and then he left.

Vivian laid there frozen cold in indignity for what seemed like an eternity. Mary had stopped crying because she was simply too exhausted. Her wails had become scratchy and breathless. Vivian wanted to see about her, yet she was anesthetized. Everyone thought she was a slut, including Floyd. Minnie called her a slut, a woman ruined. They knew the truth about her. Floyd viewed her as trash and that's why he did it, she thought. Vivian closed her eyes and accepted death-hoped for death. The thing that made her finally stand was her paranoia that Lee might walk in unexpectedly. She wasn't sure what Lee would think about her if he saw her like this. She imagined his accusing glare, his unsympathetic arms crossed over his chest, the profanities flying from between his teeth. If her father-in-law would come, she would want to throw herself in his arms and lament. He would understand and know that it wasn't *entirely* her fault. Yet, she was too ashamed to tell anyone because she believed everyone thought she was unvirtuous, anyway. Her mother, she believed, thought she had been spoiled years ago. How could she explain to her mother that no one had touched her before Henry? Henry! Even he was surprised to learn that he was her first. She felt dirty to think of what she'd *volunteered* to do with him, knowing that her sister loved him.

    The words to describe what had just happened tasted like sewage on her tongue. Vivian was sure that if she uttered such words, her mother would never believe her. Fornication and adultery were both played out in her house, making them acceptable examples of lifestyles. Her self-accusing spirit told her fornication was wrong, nevertheless, she loved and respected her mother, who had been her main teacher. Carol role modeled adultery for her three budding daughters, thus, the environment Carol provided challenged the core of Vivian's moral being.

    Vivian was confused about her identity. She pictured herself as cheap and undeserving because she used men as the measuring stick to her self-worth. Before Wali Eli came around, no decent men had ever given her, her sisters, or her mother the time of day, except to display to them how to take abuse and live in unhealthy relationships. Mr. Anderson was decent, but he was busy with his store and his own personal life, so Carol and her family were merely a backdrop in his life. Uncle Jack spent his life out at sea, loving the fish and the water as Vivian wished he would have loved them.

    The fact that Carol showed Vivian how one could commit adultery with a married man for all the years of her life was proof to Vivian of her own lack of virtue. Carol showed her daughters how to disobey God without so much as a conscience about doing so. They went to church every Sunday, but Satan reigned from the pulpit because the preacher spoke the biddings of the men who controlled him. Before and after church, Satan ruled their lives. When the stranger would creep in and out of Carol's bedroom, she came out behind him to face her daughters as though everything was normal. Vivian saw how her father took advantage of her mother, yet her mother continued to live in the relationship. How then, could she tell her mother or anyone that someone had violated her against her will? Those types of things didn't happen to decent people.

Vivian didn't have the emotional fearlessness to tell anyone about what crime Floyd had just committed. Deep down, she felt she deserved to have her body contaminated by Floyd's rape because she shouldn't have acted like she was too good for him. She knew she wasn't doing right by God, so she felt it was God's punishment that Floyd had just raped her. That is why it was easy for her to suffocate inside of the affliction, all alone. Vivian concluded that telling Lee was out of the question because he would view her as dirty, spoiled. Lee had never protected her from anything, but Henry had, she rationalized.

"If Henry could come today, he would comfort me," Vivian whispered to herself, clutching her heart. Vivian believed Henry wouldn't let anyone defeat her, including Floyd. All Henry had to do was show up and embrace her tightly, and everything would be okay. She rubbed her arm that ached from Floyd's roughness. "Oh, Henry!" She mourned. Holding on to the walls for support, she made her way to Mary and lifted the child gently in her arms. Mary rested her head on her mother's chest and sighed. At that moment, Vivian decided in her time of duress that the only comforter who would do was Henry. She wanted to be held tenderly and reassuringly, yet what she pined for would feel too weird coming from her father-in-law...but Henry could hold her and his tenderness would heal her. She sank in her seat when she finally considered that she loved him. "Oh, God! I've always loved him, but I can't love him! He—it was always wrong. But I need him so much." Mary looked curiously at her.

"I'm going to give you a middle name, child," she said in a shaking voice. "I'm going to call you 'Henri-Anna.' We're going to put that down in writing for Pixie when she comes to make me sign the papers. You will be my comfort, and I'll be yours." Mary Henri-Anna Johnson smiled up at her mama. Her lovely child gave her the strength to wash herself, get dressed, and get on with the day. Her main concern about what happened to her was what she would do if her husband got too close to her tonight. If necessary, Vivian planned to cover up the crime by telling him it was still too soon after the baby had been born.

There was no time for Vivian to wallow in self-pity. As a defense mechanism, she repressed the horrifying details of her injury. She could never forget what happened, but she could camouflage the memories or "pretend" it never happened. She borrowed a piece of her heart and stored the bereavement there. Still, she didn't know how to prepare to combat the internal injuries sustained or how to prevent it from recurring. She didn't delve into how the tragedy made her feel as a woman. She didn't stop to consider that she would never be the same because she had been viciously raped. It just added to her low self-esteem and negative self-worth. She told herself that it was her fault for being too careless, and that Lee would be right to blame her if he ever found out what happened.

The words Wali Eli had spoken to a group of all women finally registered with her. Wali Eli had told the women that raping a woman was like raping a nation, for women have the capacity from their wombs to give birth to pain and suffering, or peace and quiet of mind. It was a woman who nurtured Jesus. He said, "Imagine if Mary, the mother of Jesus had been brutalized, mishandled, and assaulted? Could she then produce Jesus? A woman nurtured all the great men and women of the world. To inflict pain on a woman is to inflict pain on the nation, for the woman carries the torment in her breast and feeds it to her children—the children who could have turned out to be the world leaders." Vivian had tuned him out because he was talking about respect for women, treasures from God -but his talk came near a time whenever Lee had recently slapped her, and after she had behaved immodestly with Henry. Therefore, she did not see herself as a treasure or a princess. This negative self-talk helped in silencing her. She thought she could handle it on her own, and she could—on the surface. When she scraped herself off the ground with the support of the wall, she packed her catastrophe in a bag, and carried the luggage with her for the rest of her life.

CHAPTER SIXTEEN
Two dimes

Lee didn't even know Liz had a father until the rumors began to circulate around town that he was looking for him. Lee's co-workers were beginning to harass him daily because they knew Big Earlton was serious about having a talk with Lee. Lee had been avoiding him for three weeks, but Big Earlton's persistence never wavered. Big Earlton was well liked by many because of his reputation as one who would help anybody, and his overall good-natured attitude about most things. He never bothered anyone, but he was extreme when he had to brawl. There was only one brawl to speak about, and that was five years ago when a man cheated him out of two dimes.

Big Earlton had purchased a fine toasted chestnut brown stallion from a passing cowboy, only to learn that the horse was stolen. He sought the man out before he could leave town to confront him. The man concealed that the horse was stolen. However, he said if Big Earlton insisted, he would return his money—and he did, all except two dimes. The entire episode ended in mass chaos because Big Earlton wouldn't let it go. Several people heard the disagreement, but none saw Big Earlton lay a hand on the cowboy. Two days later, the horse-seller was found dead by the Escambia riverbank, strangled. No charges were ever brought against the suspected Big Earlton, and no one ever messed with him afterward, that is, until Lee messed with him by messing over his daughter.

Liz's father arranged a meeting with Lee down on Orange Road near the railway station for either Friday or Saturday afternoon at four. Lee's father couldn't provide refuge from this inevitable encounter. Lee's co-workers gave him Big Earlton's final messages and told Lee that he requested a return response this time. So Lee picked a Saturday afternoon to meet him on Orange Road. He went alone to spare himself the embarrassment that could come from the meeting. There was no way he could allow Floyd or Hamilton Briggs the satisfaction of witnessing Big Earlton making demands concerning his life. Lee felt certain Big Earlton would try to force him to marry Liz, unless he'd discovered that he was already married. Big Earlton might even try to injure him, Lee thought, but still, he went alone.

Music was blaring and people were coming out of the small places of business on the crowded road. Merchants were outside selling their goods, calling out to the passing crowds of people with enthusiasm. The two meeting men paid no attention to the hollering traders or the goods displayed. Lee recalled the description he was given of Big Earlton as he saw the large frame approaching him now. Big Earlton saw a sneaky hustler with his hands stuck down in his pockets sliding up to him with game. Sure his daughter would fall for this handsome hoodlum, he thought. There would be no way she could escape his grasp, being as young and innocent as she was. No one spoke right away. The mockery was obvious.

"Are you Lee Hiram?"

"I am." They ducked into a deserted doorway, away from the hustle and bustle of the busy crowd. Big Earlton took out a pack of cigarettes, lit one, and offered Lee one from the pack.

"You smoking?" Lee silently accepted a cigarette, waiting for Big Earlton to hand him a matchstick.

"Thanks." They both dragged heavily, neither taking the opportunity to look again at the other.

"I guess you know she's in the family way, my man." Lee wanted to suggest the possibility of another violator, but somehow he didn't consider it plausible to accuse her of being loose in the face of her father.

"I suspected it." They both waited for the other to speak. "You know what she's planning to do?"

"Do you know what *you's* planning to do?"

"Not really," Lee answered truthfully.

"You know, I hear tell you's making a lot of enemies 'round town. You like messing over people, don't you?" Lee looked at him, not surprised at how fast the conversation had escalated. Still, his goal was to make it home in one piece.

"Hey, man…"

"Well look here, boy. You's gwine hafta do what's right or somebody is gwine hafta put a stop to you."

"Look, Big, I didn't come down here to argue with you. Man, I'm married. Liz didn't tell you that?" Lee took an extra long drag off his cigarette, with Big Earlton following suit.

"I reckon she don't know nothing about your other women, but *I* was told that, yeah. My concern has nothing to do with that, though. See, that's my precious daughter, man. She's my princess." Lee's disagreement was concealed by his poker face. The only princess he knew was Vivian. "I ain't gwine let you shame her." Lee laughed and wished he hadn't.

"What you wanting me to do, Big Earlton? Leave my wife and marry

Liz?" Big Earlton dug his shoe into the dirt and spit in the hole.

"Not for long," he answered. "I want you to do right by her 'til she has the baby so her name won't be tainted. You know what I mean?"

"I'll hafta think about that, my man."

"You have a better idea?" Lee shrugged his shoulders. "I'll tell you what. I ain't afraid to make this a threat. When she has that baby, she's gwine be a married woman or a widower. When people starting to *see* she's with child, she's gwine be married. Now, Liz told me that you's the only man she's *ever* been with, so you know I ain't playing with your sorry butt. You got that, niggah?" He took out another cigarette after only half smoking the last one and lit it.

"Whoa, my man! I know I gotta do something. Just level down, level down. You act like you think I don't care about her or something. I love that girl, man. She's the best. I just need to figure out what I'm gonna tell my wife. That's all."

"Well, what you gwine do?"

"Like you say. I love her, Big Earlton. I don't mind if we have us a wedding with all our friends and family. But you know I already have a wife. It ain't working out 'tween us, no way, on account of she knows I love Liz. Me and Liz, we could have a small ceremony, with just a few people. Hell. This is just the break I need. Mayhap Liz will have me for real. Mayhap I *never will* hafta go back to my old life."

"She's a good girl, Lee. Too good for you."

"With my baby, I gots to just try to do better, that's all."

"I never gave her nothing in her whole life. She's a good girl. Never had nothing good. I wanna do right by her."

"My friend Hamilton's preacher would be a good one to perform the ceremony. I need time to set this thing up." He hoped Big Earlton wouldn't ask for the preacher's name because Lee was too tense to think of one.

"Tell you what. I don't know if you's trying to run a game, see? We need to meet again once I see some action. Whatever you say to her, this needs to be locked down in a fortnight. We need to meet again, right here. What you say to that?"

"I say it's swell, my man. I ain't bulling you. I'll be right here with Liz at my side."

"Dig that."

"Dig that."

~~~

Over the next few weeks, Lee noticed a difference in his wife. Vivian had been unusually quiet. She had stopped complaining about the night hours he kept. He figured she was sullen because he'd denied her request to relocate to Michigan. Although Vivian didn't discuss it much, she made a point to mention it during his most vulnerable times. This pained Lee because he genuinely loved his wife. He loved her as much as possible since he didn't have self-love. That is, Lee did not have that magical sense of wonder about himself or curiosity that would take him to insurmountable levels of self-love or personal achievement and investment. He was numb to overall self-actualization and progress. Even so, somewhere buried within, he knew there was more to him than his every day, mundane life. He knew he was someone worthwhile who could be admired, yet Lee was not acquainted with that buried version of himself. Therefore, he projected his anger and internal suffocation away from focusing on himself. Instead, Vivian became the object of scrutiny. Seeing her downtrodden spirit over a period saddened him. He re-evaluated his disapproving response to her biggest dream. The foremost element he feared about moving away was quitting his job without the reassurance that he could find another one up North. Lee didn't know if he could rely on Henry to look out for him up there, or if he even wanted to put himself in a position like that.

One day in April, Lee decided to approach the point again with his wife. The major factor in his decision-making involved his coworkers spreading rumors and threats again about Big Earlton looking for him. Lee had failed to meet Big Earlton at the designated time that they'd planned two weeks earlier, and now he knew he must avoid him. Lee felt that Big Earlton would try to kill him for dishonoring his daughter. He was feeling a bit guilty for placing his family in such a predicament. What if Big Earlton handled the situation no better than Maybelle did down at the church? Vivian surely didn't need another heartache like that.

Optionless, Lee felt his luck was getting better after a letter arrived from Minnie. At first, Lee decided not to let Vivian know that a letter had come from her sister over a week ago. However, after reading its contents and reviewing what he was facing with Liz's father, Lee wanted to share the invitation Minnie extended. Vivian was sitting on the sofa nursing Mary when he walked in casually.

"Why you wanna go to Michigan so bad, anyhow, muffin?" Vivian smiled inwardly at the fact that he volunteered to talk about moving without her prompting. She knew she had to handle this conversation delicately since Lee had already stated that he was dead set against going.

"I want to go so badly to make a clean start with you and Mary. They have more opportunities up North for Negroes. I could help out, too."

"Naw, you can't. You ain't never gotta work. I'm always gonna take care of you," he said, taking a seat. "You're my wife. I ain't fixing to let you scrub nobody's floor. But we ain't got no lot of money, Viv. What if we went up there and I can't find no work? See, you gotta understand what it's like for a man who got a family to feed . . . he can't be running hither and thereabouts all crazy like." Vivian bowed her head and nodded vaguely in counterfeit agreement with her husband's words. This is because she wanted to urge his point forth. She knew there must be some purpose to the fact that Lee himself had mentioned this topic tonight. She secretly planned that they could stay with Henry and Minnie until they were able to get on their feet, but she didn't dare mention Henry's name to Lee—not yet.

"You're right, Lee. You know, that's one thing I love about you. You're always looking to care for me. Even though you know my biggest dream is to go up North, you're thinking about how we're gonna make it." Lee wanted to show her other ways he cared, like giving in to her dreams. He appreciated the way she responded to him just now with such meekness. He decided it was time to present her with the letter he had been stashing. Lee stood up just enough to reach into his back pocket, retrieved the opened letter, and handed it to his wife.

"What's this, Lee?"

"It's a letter that came not too long ago." He waited for her to explode since he'd opened it. Nothing happened. "It's from Minnie," he ended. Vivian could feel the heat of her blood inside of her skin. She held herself back from screaming profanities at him and showing him her disapproval for a time. She was more enraged at the fact that he had opened it than that he had kept it for so long. Outwardly, she smiled amicably at him and batted her eyes.

"Now Lee, why would you open something that is for me, and your name is no place on it?" She said, gritting her teeth softly. She closed her eyes as the memory of what Floyd took when his name was nowhere on *her* crept into her consciousness. As much as she tried, she simply couldn't shake the ordeal. Daily, something would remind her of his brutal attack, and it would send her flying into a state of depression or a mess of tears if she were alone.

"Cause I ain't want to hear no talk from them, yet." He raised his voice, convinced that his answer was sufficient. "I wanna know what they's saying to you," he added for clarity. "Mayhap they's saying you should be gone up there without me. Since they can't say it in my face, I'll read their letters!" Vivian was already disinterested in what he was saying. As far as she was concerned, there was no reason in the world for his blatant disregard for her privacy. By her facial expressions, she refused to continue hiding her air of indignation. Finally, she began to read the contents.

Minnie sent the first letter on March 1, 1922:

Dear Vivian,

I miss y'all so much! It's been quite lonely here without mama, that's all I can say that's bad about this place. Henry has been good to me. We's married now . . . legally. Henry and I went to a Justice of the Peace who done married us off! Tell mama she ain't gotta hide her face in no more shame about me, on account of me and my man finally done it right. We got a house that's big and nice. Can you believe that, Vivian? A house! It's way bigger than our house down South, too. This one is two stories, and has a separate dining room. It's two other houses on our road. Well, there's more than that, but from our house to the field is two other houses.

We found some decent hand me down furniture for each room, but most of the stuff in our house, Henry made it by hand! He made our chest of drawers, a boxboard for our bed, and he still making stuff for our house. Got two other bedrooms besides our own. Beena was supposed to be in one of them 'til she went on 'bout her way. We both be working good jobs, too. Henry got him a job helping some folks with building all sorts of things. There's this place called the Detroit Urban League, and a Negro man named Gancy and his twin brother runs that whole center. Can you believe that? He found Henry a job on account of that's what they do down here. Henry's part of a crew that's building a big building right downtown. Girl, he learning a lot. He even built us some cabinets in our house. We trying for a baby.

The good Lord has been with us all this time. Oh yea. I do washing for two families! Ones, I keep her child while she runs errands and be with her husband, and you know, she rests a lot and she is needing me to look after her boy. I believe I got hired on account of I can read and write so well. Mrs. Miller is thinking I'd be good for her boy. She a fragile woman, Mrs. Miller is. The other family I just do the washing for. I might not be with them too much longer, though. Beena doing fine, too, except she likes to hang out in the streets too much.

Vivian, tell mama to think about coming out here and getting a life going on. Ain't no white person gonna give you nothing in the South. They don't too much bother us up here, they just leave us be. And the type of work we do up here and the money we make is better than what we would make down in Florida. Take this $10.00 and give most of it to mama. Kiss mama for me, too. Tell her I'll write her when I can sit and get a good letter going. I just finished reading her letter. This the address mama gave me for you. Said you was married to Lee! I can't wait to tell Henry. Maybe now y'all can come on up here. You can stay with us 'til you find a place, too. Well, Viv, I just wanted to write you as soon as I heard the news. Little William Miller is tugging on my dress, child! I love you, and may God bless you. Write back soon.

Mrs. Minnie Raison 409 California Street Pontiac, Michigan 48053

"Well, I guess if you're wanting to go up North so badly, we can go," Lee blurted. A startled Vivian dropped the letter and stared at him. She only glanced at the ten-dollar bill as it fluttered out of the pages to the floor. Then, she placed Mary on the sofa and jumped in his lap.

"Oh, Lee, thank you!" She planted a series of kisses on his face. He laughed, squeezing her.

Two weeks later, Mr. Anderson at the Anderson Fish Market sent word to Lee that he had another letter waiting there for his wife. It was from Robeena. In good faith, Lee decided not to open it before retrieving it and giving it to Vivian immediately. He could tell from the postage date that the letter had been written sometime in March. From this, he knew Minnie had not yet received Vivian's return letter stating that the two of them were coming up North (Mary would be a surprise).

Dear Viv,

Hey girl, what you doing still down there in hot Florida? You ain't packed yourself and mama up yet? I know you all ain't mad with us on account of we got out of that jungle, are you? How mama doing? Is that Wali Eli still coming by to teach? Ain't no needing me asking 'bout daddy, 'cause I know that sorry hustler ain't doing nothing for you or mama. This is real living up here, Viv. I'm thinking 'bout leaving Pontiac and going to Detroit, girl! They got fine men all the ways from New York what be in Detroit, too. I don't stay with Minnie no more. Her and Henry too boring for me. But they do have a big, nice house. In their yard they got a green apple tree, a pear tree, AND a grapevine. They got two big trees in the front yard, too. Henry gave them all his money and they say them ain't got no problem selling no house to a colored boy, long as he pays. Henry had us three to take a fine portrait together. Says he gonna put it in his new house. Minnie told me that you was married now to Lee. I know that's a fat lie. Girl, you better write me and tell me what's going on! Take care of mama for me, and write me back.

Love you,

Beena

Vivian folded Robeena's letter over and tucked it away, super glad Lee hadn't read it. How stupid of Robeena to write such an unwise letter, knowing how nosey and controlling Lee was. Lee was busy making last minute preparations for their move. He had several challenges to meet in the coming weeks. For example, his father knew Lee was trying to save money for the move, but Lee Sr. started asking for more money for the house and things. Lee Sr. was openly bitter about them leaving, as well. He was privy to the real reason Lee was adamant about skipping town, but was still against it. Running was never Lee Sr.'s style. Considering the situation, he figured Big Earlton was being quite reasonable. If Lee was conniving, his father estimated, Vivian would only suffer for a few months, and he would be there for his daughter-in-law in his son's absence.

But for Lee, it was more complicated than that. His father's advice didn't include the issue of Maybelle pressing him a lot more these days for money, too. He didn't bother telling Maybelle he was leaving because he knew she'd go running her mouth. Lee advised Vivian not to mention the move to the Burdeshaw sisters, either, because he said he didn't want the word to get to Maybelle. He said she should wait until the last minute to tell anyone of the date of their move, if at all, so that Maybelle wouldn't find out and pull any tricks out of her voodoo bag. The move would be a secret to Floyd, Liz, and even to Hamilton Briggs.

Lee cunningly sent word to Big Earlton that he was willing and ready to uphold his end of the bargain, and that they should meet as soon as possible. Lee knew that Big Earlton might recognize his message as a cop-out given that no definite meeting time was provided, and because he didn't show up for their last scheduled meeting. But for further cushioning, Lee had been purposely misleading Liz in hopes that she would repeat his empty promises to her father, buying time for Lee. He wanted to leave town before any of the rumors got to Vivian. He watched Vivian's face as she rocked Mary and read Robeena's letter. Lee knew that his father would be home from working overtime in a matter of forty-five minutes, and they were going gambling tonight. It would be the last night he spent hanging out in Florida, so it meant a lot. He figured that now was the time to pet his wife so she wouldn't get too wired up that he was leaving for the evening. He had become a master at controlling her emotions. He knelt beside her and kissed her. Then he took Mary from her, and walked her around the room. Vivian looked on dearly at her small family while she stretched her tired legs out in front of her.

"Mary, Mary . . . you are very very . . . my merry Mary," Lee sang over and over playfully in her ear. Before long, her endearing head was sweating with sleep on his shirt. He took her to the bedroom and laid her down in the middle of the bed, just like Vivian had taught him to do. When he went back into the front room, he sat in the chair across from his wife.

"Come here, princess," he said. She knew he didn't know that she knew he must be going out tonight. Vivian had observed the pattern long ago with her husband. She could tell by the timing of his affection whether he was using it as a means for a gain. The fact that he would be going out later didn't matter that moment, however, when he wrapped her in his arms.

She needed to be held, to feel loved and cherished. Her soul was empty and her heart ached. She wanted to let it all go—all her pain and the lies she stored—she wanted to cry them onto her husband's shoulders. Ever since Floyd's attack a few weeks ago, no one had gathered her in a long, tender hold. She needed him to do it now. She was confused and lost. Lee's arms around her told her that everything was going to be okay. He was holding her and it had nothing to do with sexual intimacy. He was squeezing her and it felt good that he cared about her enough to take the time to hold her for no reason other than that he wanted her to feel loved. Even if he wanted to party later, right now mattered. For that moment she didn't care that her mother would be broken-hearted to learn that her last daughter would leave town. Vivian forgot the vicious attack Floyd had made on her. She forgot the times Lee's hands were used to slap her around and how slimy Floyd's hands felt; the only hands she felt now were the ones of her husband's as he held her tightly. She wished he knew that all he had to do was hold her tenderly day and night, and not ask anything of her. He didn't have to say a word. If he would just hold her quietly for as long as possible and as often as possible, she would be healed.

The main thing that concerned Carol about Vivian moving to Michigan was she strongly suspected that Henry had a crush on her. Furthermore, she feared the possibility that Henry could be the true father of Vivian's child. While Lee wasn't counting the months, Carol was. That's why Carol was stunned when Madeline Burdeshaw came bursting into her house to tell Carol to hurry to Vivian's side. Lee had bragged practically to the whole town that his wife was a virgin until their wedding night. It was the one thing that made her not too embarrassed when Ms. Esther or one of the other ladies reported what people were saying about her daughter. That special virtue was getting harder and harder to find in the stock of available marriage partners.

Yet, Vivian delivered a healthy eight-pound baby girl after being married for only six months. Carol repeatedly did the math in her head, praying to find herself in error. She weighed the possibility of Lee lying about intimacy with Vivian, too, before she settled it in her mind to "leave it be." If the town's women were not gossiping, she would let sleeping dogs lie. However, she could not push her math away if Vivian planned on following Henry to Michigan. Carol paced the floor, finally sitting down to sip a cup of coffee. Her mind was frazzled with mixed emotions. For every calm thought she had, a disastrous one would follow. It bothered Carol to think that if her suspicions were true, Minnie could very well find out the truth. She was besieged to imagine her two daughters becoming enemies for life about this. Then, she decided she was simply catastrophizing, but then her thoughts drifted to what Henry would do if he ever found out about this. Carol remembered Henry's pained look as he walked away from Vivian the morning of his departure. He couldn't even look at her. Carol was comforted by the belief that Vivian would more than likely hoard all skeletons in the closet. The family members were experts at keeping secrets and living a lie. Carol knew the shame of this would keep everyone's mouth shut, including her own. Nevertheless, she figured it would be easier for all if Vivian and Lee stayed in Florida where they belonged. But then Carol guessed Lee wouldn't let Henry anywhere near Vivian, anyway. Carol chewed over who the baby would look like whenever it got bigger.

"Silly me," Carol thought, "I'm making a mountain out of a molehill. Can't be Henry's child. It'd be too awful. Just can't be!" Carol busied herself around her small house that she now had all to herself. Wali Eli was having another meeting for a close-knit group of community members. This time, they would be meeting at Carol's house. Because of Wali Eli, she had made friends with neighbors she had never spoken with before. She saw a different side of Mr. Anderson, too. At the meetings, it seemed like everyone came alive. Wali Eli had become an important person in Carol's spiritual life. He talked with her about God, and how He could live inside of a person, if the person would just let Him. Carol decided to let her guard down and accept him as her one true protecting friend.

"How do you let God live in you? I mean, what would God be doing inside of me, Mistuh Eli?" Geraldine shook her head, as though she knew the answer. The other guests, around seven of them, waited eagerly for the answer.

"God moves in the flesh, Sister Carol. His spirit must be contained by flesh, just like there must be a conduit for electricity. You cannot see electricity, but you can see the effects of it. You cannot see God's spirit, but you can see the effects of it. You can see man working with the spirit. That's why we say a tree is known by the fruit it bears. If a tree bears rotten fruit, the tree is no good. But when God lives in a man, you can tell by the works, the fruit of that man." Carol was puzzled by this. She had always been taught that God was a formless spirit that floated in the sky. She remained quiet, staring at him curiously.

Wali Eli made sense to her, but this was a strange teaching that she had never heard before. However, her programming made her feel as though she was sinning by the mere fact that she was having this talk with a man who was not a member of her church congregation. She wanted to break the subject. "Well, Mistuh Eli, my girls are all gone up North now. I would've been too scared to make a move like that by myself when I was their age. This here be the only land I ever knowed," she said to him. "My girls! They's up in Michigan. Vivian mayhap done made it up there, too, by now." Vivian had left for Michigan five days earlier with Lee and Mary. Carol and Lee Sr. saw them off early in the morning—the same way Minnie had left.

"Yes, I sure hope Vivian has made it safely to Michigan with her husband and the baby, Sister Carol," he responded. "Is she going to send a letter back stating she made it all right?"

"If she doesn't, Minnie is sure to write to me and let me know what's happening. We've been writing back and forth. Vivian says she wrote and told Minnie to meet her at the train depot in Detroit. I pray tell Minnie got her letter in time to know Vivian is coming so's she and the baby won't hafta wait too long in the wilderness for they's family to come for 'em." Her omission of Lee's welfare was unconscious and unintentional. "Minnie wrote to her and told her 'bout the waiting area where they stayed 'til they could figure out which way to turn. Vivian knows a Negro family could wait for a spell if necessary. If they run out of room, the Negroes will hafta get off the train and let the white folks board. Could be anywhere between Atlanta and Toledo where they might hafta get off for a day or two, 'til another train comes through."

Wali Eli said, "I asked a few brothers I know to circulate at the train stations, and be helpful to their brothers and sisters coming up there from the South. Maybe they will see Vivian and give her a hand if she needs one." Carol accepted the pleasure moment and relief from anxiety, albeit she felt it was unlikely that anyone Wali Eli knew would be able to find Vivian.

Carol went out to the kitchen and came back with tea. She poured everyone a cup.

"Whatchu gonna to do with yourself now that your girls are gone?" Mr. Anderson asked.

"I ain't trying to get in nobody's way. My girls are grown now. I'll be happy to get to see the sun set most evenings. Them be my goals. Work out in my garden and make sure I gots food to eat every day. Hell, I don't need nothing else. I gots plenty of nothing, and nothing is plenty for me!"

"You hafta believe in more than plenty of nothing," Geraldine piped, thinking she was taking the words out of Wali Eli's mouth.

"Rev Washington said we Negroes would have our culture in heaven! We will all live together in the land of milk and honey in the hereafter. That don't sound like nothing--that sounds like something!" Esther answered, wanting to be a part of the conversation. They all looked at Wali Eli, letting him know they were ready for his vision. He often waited for their subtle invitations to speak before saying anything at all.

"When you talk about heaven, you look up. When you talk about hell, you look down. Yet the earth rotates at the terrific speed of 1,037 and 1/3 miles per hour, so what is up at noon will be down at midnight. And if it's a *land* of milk and honey, you know you must have it on earth to have land, with grass to feed the cows to make the milk…and flowers growing from the ground—not out of the sky—for the bees to make the honey! Jesus didn't talk about the thereafter, he said the hereafter."

"Well…that couldn't be…something ain't right. Ain't heaven up through the clouds up there? I mean, heaven can't be in this world, on this earth—that don't make no sense…" Ms. Esther said.

"Doesn't the Emancipation Proclamation mean anything to you? We was freed," Carol said desperately, hoping to sound intelligent.

"The condition of your mind frees you, not the signing of a document. If you don't free yourself, you're not free. Isn't it interesting to say your mother didn't free you from the womb? You were the instrument of your own freedom by developing in the womb, by the Grace of God. Your mother's choice was to give you up or die. If you don't free yourself, you're not free. That's why they call Black men freed men, never free men. Freed is the past participle of the verb to free. When someone acts on your behalf and frees you, I would say you then have a responsibility. Let's say someone opens the gate, or unlocks it for you."

"You mean like Lincoln…"

"The compromises between the North and the South weren't meant to free you—Lincoln freed the slaves in the rebel states, not the slaves in Massachusetts and out east. Mind you, there were political goals behind freeing any Black person. You can read a transcript of the Lincoln-Douglas debate."

"You be having that kinda stuff?" Geraldine asked.

He chuckled softly, nodding his head. "Sister Carol has a copy of it. I brought it here several weeks ago. I have another copy." Carol sat up abruptly. He had given her a copy of the magazine containing the Debate and some other jewels. Vivian must have taken it, she guessed.

Carol asked, "You want me to go to school and be a lawyer? "What kinda goals do you want me to have? I only went to grade school for two years, Mistuh Anderson," she whispered with embarrassment. "Negroes ain't got nothing. 'Cerning Mistuh Lincoln, ev'rybody saying he was a good white man," she said triumphantly.

"Sister Carol." He looked at her soothingly. "Lincoln's aim wasn't to free us. He never saw us as his equal."

"He must've wanted us to be equals! I mean, what you is saying I ain't never heard nothing like this before. Seems like Reverend Washington would've said something."

"Lincoln begrudgingly affirmed slavery was wrong, but he was against giving the so-called Negroes social and political equality. Even during the War, there were Union commanders under Lincoln's watch who returned fugitive slaves to deep-seated rebels."

"Hey! Wait a minute—there were Negroes who fought for both sides!" She remembered Reverend Washington boasting about this fact from the pulpit one Sunday.

"The North and the South needed black bodies before long to fight for their causes," Wali Eli explained.

"My body is not as black as Mr. Anderson's is!" Rufus said, causing the ladies to chuckle.

"Why for we have so many names? Nigger, Negro…and you saying Black?" Geraldine had been wanting to know this for a long time.

Esther took a stab at it before anyone else could say anything. "Negro is the modern way. It's more proper among respectful people to use that term. White people who respect us call us Negroes instead of Niggers." Esther kept her face turned toward Geraldine instead of looking to Wali Eli for confirmation so that she could appear wise and confident.

"Calling us colored is better. Y'all need to stay with the times," Mr. Anderson clarified. "But it don't matter if they is dead bodies. A colored dead body is just as dead as a Nigger's."

"At first, Lincoln refused to free the slaves and give them guns to kill the Caucasian soldiers, although it ended up happening anyway whenever he forced so many into the army. He straddled the fence on so many issues. He didn't want to deal with the so-called 'Negro problem,' so today, we must deal with ourselves. We have to do it for ourselves as Black men and women."

Geraldine asked, "That's why you say so-called Negro?"

"What! Carol sat up, focusing on Wali Eli, and ignoring Geraldine. "Ain't nobody doing nothing for me." Carol averted her eyes from Mr. Anderson, wishing she could snatch her words back.

Mr. Anderson answered Geraldine with, "It might as well be so-called colored people if our names keep changing." Carol was relieved that he didn't take it the wrong way when she said no one had done anything for her. She was thoroughly grateful for everything Mr. Anderson had done, and never wanted to offend him.

"Aha!" Wali Eli smiled. "But your blackness, your essence never changes.

Every group except Black people are called by their names based on where they originated from on the planet. As a Black man and woman, you can't be colored people because Black is the essence from whence all other colors are derived. Black isn't a color, it's original. There are many ways to describe you, but, given that you were the first people on the planet, there is no land mass to describe you. You were before Africa, so you are not Africans. You were before Europe, America, and South America, Australia...the Black man--not the Negro--the Black man is the original man."

"Damn," Rufus breathed. Five long minutes passed in silence. Everyone wanted time to drink it in, and they all hoped no one would interrupt their processing. They were Black people. No matter how many times names to describe them changed, they were the original people. They had been lied to about black being ugly. Black was more than beautiful: It was powerful.

Wali Eli finally continued. "Yes, I'm saying dream big! Have faith, but your faith without work is dead."

"I dream all I want to, don't mean it gwine get me nowhere."

"Faith without work is..." Before Wali Eli could end, the group members finished for him.

"Dead," Everyone said together, smiling at each other.

"It'd get you somewhere if you'd stick to it, Sister Carol," Mr. Anderson offered. Carol ignored him and kept facing Wali Eli.

"You telling me to have dreams? I do! I do have dreams, Mistuh Eli." She stood. "I dream I could start a nursery right here in the house. The girl's bedroom could be a play area, and I would use the front room, too, depending on how many kids I got to come." Her smile began to fade once she realized everyone was staring at her.

"I would . . . could . . . be a better mama . . . than what I was to my girls. I could be a better example. I dream I could wake up, see the sun rise and be happy."

"You can do it, Sister Carol!" Wali Eli stood, too. She stopped smiling all together.

"I can't. It's too late." She plopped back into her seat.

"Yes you can. Come on, Sister Carol, believe in yourself!" Why was Mr. Anderson saying so much? He was a guest! Now, it felt like everyone in the room was ganging up on her. What they were pushing her to do seemed so far away and advanced. She didn't have the tools to start a nursery in her home. It was only a dream. She thought they were making fun of her. Carol had no idea of how she could start a nursery. Wali Eli sat back down in the chair. She looked away, covering her eyes with her arm.

"I am here as your friend. A protecting friend."

"I know. It's just…nobody came before just to be my friend. I guess that's a sad thing."

"You've been impaired. I understand that. But now, Sister Carol, I want you to listen to the things I tell you. Sometimes it might seem like I'm pushing you, but really I'm just concerned about you." She wished her mother had had more concern about her relationship with the stranger. This is because Carol felt that her life would've been different—better—if she hadn't started having babies so young. She had spent so many years trying to shield her daughters from the truth that she was unhappy with the way things were.

"I don't know," she sobbed. "I just ain't never had nobody to treat me like a human being. I keep expecting you not to."

"Let's meet again next week." Wali Eli looked at everyone. They all nodded and chatted together. Finally, Carol refilled Mr. Anderson's water glass and even offered him some muffins. He wrapped it tightly in the napkin it came in and prepared to leave, touched that Carol had given the one muffin to him when it was clear that was all she had to eat in the house. Rather than embarrassing her, he decided to bring her plenty of food from his market the next morning. Wali Eli left ahead of the other guests. The ladies barely wanted to leave, but were escorted home by Mr. Anderson and Rufus, the other male guest. Everyone seemed well fed, even though they had only consumed words and beverages.

The next morning, Carol went walking jubilantly down the road to the well to fill her water bucket. She came back and doused her tomato plants with water, then dug a few more rows of earth, and started planting. She sighed heavily and said out loud, "You reap what you sow." She dropped the hoe, knelt on her knees, and tenderly parted the soil with her fingertips. That evening, Carol was able to watch the beautiful sun set in peace.

When the sun set a couple of hours earlier in Michigan, however, Vivian and Lee were hardly interested in its magnificence. It was colder and much less green in Detroit, a city forty miles from Pontiac. There had been a thunderstorm that lasted for almost two days that caused the May temperature to drop to a windy thirty-eight degrees.

Vivian and Lee waited at the Detroit train depot, watching the passengers un-board the Five O'clock p.m. Southern. Minnie didn't know for sure what day they would arrive, so Vivian hoped she would come by the train depot today to check. Ever since the start of the war, the Six O'clock a.m. Southern came up through Detroit daily unless there was a layover in another town. Lee, Mary, and Vivian had been waiting outside like statues since 6:00 a.m., and now all three were exhausted and bothered.

"This don't make any sense, muffin. We got the damn address. Let's just hire a driver and go!"

"Oh yeah?" She whispered hoarsely. "What cars do you see around here picking up niggers?" Lee began pacing back and forth, wringing his hands nervously. There were so many strange things, so many diverse types of people together all at once. The so-called Negroes behaved like they were forbidden to speak or nod to one another, passing as strangers rather than as brothers. He knew there were streetcars that could drive them into Pontiac, but he didn't know how to get to them, or who to ask. And too, he only saw Caucasians getting into some of the nearby cabs.

Several uniformed Caucasian soldiers departed the train, all laughing and happy to see their families who greeted them. A prissy young Caucasian girl in a frilly tan colored dress revealed by an unbuttoned long blue trench coat ran two inches in front of Lee. As she sprinted past him, he had to lean back on the balls of his feet to avoid physical contact with the child. Lee's heartbeat increased with fear when a gold ribbon in her hair came unraveled and blew in his face. He caught it before it twirled to the ground. The girl's father was coming around the corner with another soldier when he saw her stop and turn back to Lee.

"Gimme back my ribbon, you black monkey!" She said crossly, over, and over. Lee stood frozen, afraid to reach his hand out to the girl. Vivian looked over when she heard the privileged girl and saw the pretty lace in her husband's hand. The girl's father came nearer until he could touch his daughter's coat. He wore a brass name tag on his uniform.

"You got a problem, boy?" He asked Lee.

"Naw, suh." Lee still held the ribbon, standing as straight as a board. The father shook his head, turning away.

"Little Karen, you can't wear that bow anymore. A darky's done touched it. It's contaminated."

"But, daddy!" She yanked her arm back toward Lee. Vivian, who was only standing a few feet away, hurried closer to her husband's side. Mary was asleep over her shoulder. Vivian read that his name was Lucifix Hopkins, Jr. She took Lee's free hand in hers to show support.

"But daddy, nothing. Now come on and let's get away from these dirty animals. Haven't you noticed that they smell? What will your mother say if I bring you home smelling like a coon all because you wanted some nickel and dime hair bow?" He said to Lee, "That's ten cents you owe me. Give it to me, now, nigger." Vivian quickly reached for her change pouch, thankful that she had separated the dollar bills, just in case the soldier wanted to rob them further. She counted ten pennies, and rushed them into the girl's eager, elitist, outstretched hand. "Here you are, Mr. Hopkins." He ignored her attempt at graciousness.

"Some things just aren't worth having," her father ended, leading her away. Vivian had to practically shove Lee to get him to move after that. He cringed at the way she behaved as though the episode never took place, while he became sickened by it.

"The ribbon is contaminated, but our money isn't. Muffin, let's get the hell out of here."

Wishing the episode away, Vivian spotted a sign over a side door that read "COLORED WAITING AREA." She assumed segregation was only in the South. What was that sign doing up? Jadedly, she led her family to the door and peeped cautiously inside. It was a room about the size of four large bedrooms. Vivian knew there were waiting areas nearby, but she didn't want to go earlier because she was afraid to consider that they would have to wait for any extended length of time. She wanted at any moment that her family would come with fleeting joy and escort them to a haven.

There were twenty metal chairs dispersed about, but the thirty or so occupants mostly were sitting or lying on the floor. There were some Caucasians that occupied the rest area for the Negroes. Vivian noticed instantly that these Caucasians in the waiting area were not clean and fresh like Karen and her father. This fact gave Vivian the strength to enter the room, leading her husband. She avoided eye contact with anyone who might have looked her way, until she claimed a small area of the room. She ordered Lee back outside to retrieve the rest of their luggage. He walked mechanically away. When he got back, he didn't sit before she pulled him down beside her on the blanket she had spread. After making a pallet for Mary, Vivian went into their food storage and pulled out some jarred smoked fish. She also found some rice cakes that were left, which she added to the meal she placed before her husband. Vivian then walked out of the waiting area to the front of the train depot, purchased two cups of steaming hot coffee, then returned to sit beside her anxious husband. It was just safer for her to do everything considering the hostility present in Detroit because women were less intimidating than Black men.

As she began to feed her husband, she hummed *"Swing Low, Sweet Chariot"* to sooth him. The last thing she needed was unrest at a time like this! Knowing Lee, he would make good on his promise to board the next train going back to Florida if he became too unnerved.

Henry didn't let himself believe Vivian was coming. He wanted her to come, and he didn't want her to come. Each day for the last two days when Minnie and Robeena returned from the train depot without Vivian, Henry's heart dropped. Each day when they left for the train depot to see if Vivian had indeed come, his heart raced. There was nothing he could do to change things, he decided. Vivian was coming and that was that. He knew Lee would be with her, which both pained and calmed him. He hadn't truly lived after they arrived in Pontiac until the day Minnie received a letter from Vivian stating she was moving to Michigan. The day that letter came, Henry became a new man. Outwardly, he put up much effort to appear normal, but inside, his muscles were like putty, and his blood kept rushing with heat to his cheeks.

On the day Lee and Vivian arrived in Detroit, Robeena and Minnie decided not to take the trip to check on them. Henry wanted them to go and check so badly. He thought he could feel Vivian's presence. He wanted to tell Minnie to go to Detroit and find Vivian, and that she should not return without her. He was sure Minnie was able to see his heart coming through his shirt. It took all his might to bluff like it didn't bother him either way if they waited until tomorrow to fetch Vivian.

That night, in bed with his wife, Henry was under duress because he perceived that Vivian needed him. It was all he could do to not get up in the middle of the night himself, catch a car to the train depot, and remain until Vivian came. But no one asked for his assistance, and he couldn't bring himself to volunteer to run such a personal errand, not again.

Neither Henry nor Minnie knew that Robeena had stayed all night in Detroit with her newest boyfriend, Casey. His plush apartment he shared with his brother, Tim was more than Robeena could've imagined. She was sure the two of them would get along just splendidly. Robeena believed her mother should've sought more riches instead of settling for the stranger who gave them nothing.

Tim, who worked at Ford Motor Company, was Casey's older and only brother. His job at Ford Motors helped his family to stay off public assistance once they moved to Detroit. If Casey loved anybody in the whole wide world other than his mother, it was his brother, Tim. Casey never developed a close friendship with any other person. Even in grade school, he was a private person, never attending the birthday parties of his peers, and never inviting other students to his one room flat. Although there were dozens of children living in the same projects, he always imagined he was the poorest child of all. He couldn't perceive that the clean, well-dressed students could also dwell in roach infested, rat frolicking dumps. It didn't occur to him that their roaches crawled through the walls and became his roaches before he ever moved there. He was ashamed. Although his mother told him he was being ungrateful, his brother never judged Casey.

Tim was twelve years older than Casey. He was born to his parents in 1885 in Athens, Georgia. Tim never knew his father. Their mother, Fannie met Casey's father when Tim was four years old. He migrated with her to New York, where Casey was born. Their family was so poor that they had to hang their food on clothes lines to prevent the rats from eating it. They tried their luck in Canada, but Casey's mother was unhappy because she was alone all the time, except for being with her children all day. When Fannie's mother moved from Athens to Detroit, Michigan, Fannie moved away from Canada to follow her mother to Detroit, with only her sons. By this time, Tim was able to make small money and help support the family.

Black migrants did gain entry to new jobs in northern manufacturing plants. As in southern manufacturing, pay differences between Black men and Caucasians working similar jobs at the same plant were small, in most cases, but there were several undercover instances where the pay was absolutely unequal. Unfortunately, Black laborers were limited to the types of jobs they could get, too. Black men like Tim remained forcefully concentrated in unskilled laboring positions. For instance, in the auto industry, the Ford Motor Company hired a tremendous number of Black workers, while other automakers in Detroit normally disqualified these workers. Because their choices were few, Black men could be worked very exceedingly and could also be used in obnoxious and precarious venues, like in the foundry of auto plants, and blast furnaces in steel plants.

Throughout the 1920s, Black men did not regularly have the support of unions to protect their working rights and conditions. Many unions in the North had overt policies excluding membership by Black employees. Tim didn't see the need to become part of any union when he was hired to work in the foundry. In fact, he was not optimistic that the Caucasian and Jewish led unions would protect his interest as a Black worker. A weekly pay envelope was what concerned Tim.

Tim also wasn't interested in participating in any of the strikes that were beginning to occur more and more because he considered that he was able to land his job due to Caucasians walking out on their good paying jobs. It wouldn't be until the Great Depression that Tim would appreciate the efforts of the union, and why some felt that striking was necessary.

Casey and his mother relied on Tim to keep a straight head. Someone had to pay the bills, Casey learned early. Nevertheless, despite his respect for Tim, Casey couldn't see himself working in such dangerous conditions, coming home so dirty and rusty, only to be faced with more dirt once inside of their crowded neighborhood. Casey wanted to do something fancy and clean. He wanted to dress up on his way to work, and still be clean whenever he came home.

When Casey was still an adolescent, Fannie fell in love with an ordinary fellow who made a decent living and decided she wanted to spend the rest of her life with this new guy. Her sons were happy for her and happy to be free from her constantly watchful eyes. This ordinary fellow moved in with them, and not long after that, they moved to a better home of their own. However, the ordinary fellow had a problem with Tim acting like he was the man of the house. To prove that things were going to be different, he often beat Casey in Tim's presence, daring Tim to interfere. Within six months, Tim moved out and took Casey with him to that expensive, plush apartment on Detroit's west side.

Henry had just about given up on Robeena when she first introduced him to Casey. What a thug, Henry thought. It grieved him that Robeena had moved out of his house where he could look out for her. He had promised Carol that he'd be her patron, but now, Robeena was making poor choices and she refused to listen to his advice. She laughed at him when he tried to give her a curfew and be the father figure to her that she'd never had. Henry had the mind to write Carol himself to let her know about Robeena's behavior, but he became distracted when he learned that Vivian was coming. Carol didn't need the extra headache, he thought. Besides, he figured Carol could do nothing to get Robeena to return home.

Henry witnessed the bright rays of the morning sun before he could close his eyes in sleep. He had just over an hour before he'd have to get up and get ready for work. It depressed him not to know if Vivian was okay. He was impatient with Minnie as the night grew deeper. Henry took more cover than he needed because he wanted her to feel the cold so that she would get up, and get Vivian. He practically pushed her out of the bed to encourage her to hurry on her way when he got up to prepare for work. On three days a week, she got up with him to head to work herself, at the Miller's house. However, she told Mrs. Miller that she needed a vacation this week to prepare her house for her sister's arrival. Minnie was still unaware that Robeena planned to look for Vivian as soon as possible in the morning. Therefore, she waited for Robeena to arrive that morning. Minnie walked over to Robeena's house later that morning, only to find her absent. Oh, well, Minnie thought. Vivian would just have to wait another day.

Robeena agreed to go to Detroit with Casey instead of taking him to her home so that she could earn bragging rights for finding Vivian. She waited until she saw the sun creeping over Casey's peaceful face before she nudged him from his sleep. She couldn't wait to impress Vivian with the polished Ford automobile that Casey drove.

Robeena found Vivian, Lee, and Mary all sleeping in the waiting area when she and Casey arrived at the bus depot the next morning. She excitedly hugged and kissed Vivian, and exclaimed over the baby once she stirred. "This sure puts a damper on everything," Robeena mumbled under her breath about Mary. How in the world was Vivian going to hang out with her when she had not only Lee to contend with, but now a crumb-snatching infant as well? With a deep sigh, Robeena blew out all the air she could gather from her lungs. She'd deal with it later, but for now, she had to hurry along because she didn't want Minnie or Henry to come for Vivian, not knowing she was already on the job.

Robeena and Casey escorted Vivian and her family straight to Minnie's house. She knew she'd have a chance to talk to Vivian alone in time. When they arrived in Pontiac, Minnie was just getting supper prepared at 1:00 p.m. She had gotten back in bed to steal a two-hour nap after getting back home from Robeena's house. Minnie was outdone when she saw the baby. She walked right past Vivian to Robeena, who was holding Mary. Robeena felt important holding such a precious baby, and standing next to the dazzling Casey, whom she didn't know was a pimp. She was happy to show this man off to both of her sisters, and especially to Lee. Robeena wanted Lee to feel like a nothing country boy next to Casey. She reluctantly conceded that Lee was better looking, but he wasn't as smooth as Casey, and Lee didn't have a car. And Casey had this sexy gap between his front teeth, plus he was bow-legged, and he wasn't skinny and he wasn't heavy. He dressed better, with more classy taste. He was darker than Lee and his skin was smoother. His nose was just the right size, his eyes were clear, and he was almost just as tall as Lee. Casey was about two years older and he looked two years more mature, according to Robeena's judgment.

Lee was immediately influenced by Casey. He could tell Casey was only about 23 or 24, but he carried himself like there was never anything that he didn't know. Casey was the one to move their luggage without asking anyone if he was doing the right thing, or for anyone's help, Lee recognized. He fell in step behind Casey, wanting him to believe that he was on his way back out to get their things from the car, anyway.

Robeena watched with her sisters as Lee and Casey got all the bags upstairs to the bedroom Robeena once occupied. When they came back downstairs, Casey took Robeena in his arms and swayed her back and forth. Lee, not wanting to be outdone, slipped his arm around Vivian's waist. Minnie was moderately embarrassed at the open affection these men displayed, and was glad Henry wasn't there to make her feel lonely and undesirable. She ducked away before anyone could gain clues through her hollow eyes.

"Casey," Robeena said, "Lee here ain't never been out of the South. His grandparents be straight from the African jungles." She laughed, playfully hitting Lee on his arm as though everything she said was out of fun. "Why don't you tell him how life is in Canada, Casey?" Robeena lifted her eyes at Vivian, making sure she was taking a good look at the type of men the North had to offer. Casey was ahead of Robeena, but he had already surveyed Lee and decided that he appeared nice enough. He wasn't interested in Robeena's grudge-bearing games. He was on a mission to wine and dine her, spend a mountain of money on her, and romance her for weeks straight before he turned her out. Casey had been watching her work men at the clubs. He felt sure if he could have a few weeks of private time with her, she would be totally his.

"Lee is your name, right, son?" Lee nodded yes. "Well, maybe I can tell you about some of my adventures if you and I go out for a drink together. You know, once you get settled in." Lee beamed.

"And me and you can go out, too, Viv," Robeena said, shooting Lee a hateful look. "As soon as Lee gets to figuring he's settled enough that he can go out shaking that thing, we shaking, too, you dig?" Lee got dizzy for a second at the mention of his wife out doing some of the things he did when he was out there.

"You can wait one minute, Beena. My baby ain't gonna be in no streets with you shaking a damn thing that belongs to me. You got that, girl? That ain't what we came up here for." Robeena offered Lee an evil smile and pranced back into Casey's arms. "Look at her, muffin," Lee sucked his top right teeth, "Beena done got buck-wild."

"Whatever." Robeena didn't want to take it too far, and she became self-conscious about Casey hearing Lee talk to her like she was a tramp. Casey liked Lee's spirit in dealing with Robeena with regards to his wife. He noticed that Lee didn't have much respect for Robeena, which meant he could talk openly with Lee about things, if they were going to hang together.

The vibes he got from Lee were very opposite from the ones he got from Henry. Casey wouldn't dare discuss his lifestyle with Henry. He saw how virtuous Minnie acted, and he sensed Henry valued that characteristic in a woman, thus would never tolerate Casey's indiscretions. He looked around for verification, and sure enough, Minnie seemed to be the only tamed one. Minnie had taken Mary into the kitchen and had given her a piece of a peach to suck, while Vivian and Robeena argued with the men about who would stay out in the streets the longest. Casey wanted to get to know Vivian better just so that he could see if she was more like Minnie, or Robeena.

"Viv," Minnie called, "you and Lee ate anything?"

"Yeah, we're fine," Lee lied. The small meal Vivian had prepared for him at the train depot was stale and unfulfilling. Robeena propped her eyes at him and laughed. She and Casey had only crackers to offer on the way to Pontiac, and she knew they must be tired of eating the scraps they brought up from so many miles and days ago, as she had experienced the same thing when she'd come. Robeena had promised them that they would get a huge meal at Minnie's house.

"Girl," Robeena said to Vivian, "I know you's gotta be starving!

"Beena, you know I am, girl!" Robeena took Vivian's hand and led her to the kitchen. Minnie returned to the living room to unload Mary in Lee's startled arms, and then she followed her sisters back into the kitchen. They talked and laughed together like old times. In the front room, Mary was a quiet baby as she listened to Lee's conversation with Casey. Casey revealed a pint of liquor that was once stashed in his pouch. The more whiskey Casey chugged, the more he talked.

Lee was fascinated with Casey's tales about life in the big cities, hardcore basement gambling, and his fame with women. Casey was everything that Lee aspired to be. Casey liked Lee because Lee was well-built and dashing—the kind of man women would instantly be attracted to upon first glance. With the right clothes and a smidgen of polishing, Lee could make women from all classes fall at his feet. He could really use Lee to build his illegal kingdom. Casey told Lee that he could play poker in his sleep. He confessed that women like Robeena admired him because of his fat bankroll. He said the women who lasted with him were the ones who were willing to do their parts to insure his bankroll. He winked at Lee when he said this. Casey agreed with Lee that love was important in life, but he explained love had nothing to do with business. They talked for a great while, both becoming increasingly comfortable with the other. It wasn't long before Casey gambled, saying much to Lee about his lifestyle.

"Man, you mean to tell me you get down with five or six women in one week?"

"Naw, son, you ain't listening. I never wear myself thin like that. I stick with one woman for at least two to four weeks at a time." He glanced in Robeena's direction. "I give her everything she could dream of having. I take her to fine restaurants, I rub her feet," a sick feeling came over Lee when he involuntarily imagined Casey, instead of himself rubbing Vivian's feet. "...And I make her feel like she's the most important woman in the world. You don't hear me, baby." Lee nodded, seriously listening, and trying to learn. "It's like a drug. I'm like a drug that she's gotta have. I listen to her - I hold her, let her cry, I become better than her best friend. She starts to depend on me for everything -money- Then, I suddenly leave her alone. By this time, the woman is so desperate because she already done figured ain't no other man gonna treat her like I did, and she's right! But what she don't know is that it's all a game to get her hooked on me. Now, don't you go out and try this, man, you gotta have serious bank to pull something like this off. Once she's hooked, the chick will do anything I damn tell her to do..." Casey paused, giving Lee a curious stare. Then he half asked, "Son, you ain't really interested in what I do. You don't want to hang with me."

"Come on, man," Lee pleaded, "I was lucky to meet you. When my ole lady dragged me up here, I didn't know what to expect, but it sounds like this place maybe got some life to it!" Lee really didn't know what to make of Casey's tales. Surely, the type of game Casey was claiming was unthinkable. Casey could tell Lee was a quick thinker, and more than likely a good gambler. He could use a man like Lee to help him in his all-around game. After pondering briefly over this, Casey immediately decided it would be unwise to hip Lee to the *real* science of making a prostitute out of a woman (or a man). Though already inebriated, he was aware that he needed to halt his liquor intake unless he had a chaser.

Casey observed that the only hindrance to Lee's future role as a hustler was the fact that he lived in the house with Henry. Vivian could be controlled, and certainly, Robeena *would* be controlled. Casey fantasized about training Lee privately to shape him up for the games, like the way he trained his women, and then using Lee to make big money. He needed someone new around him that he could trust. He laughed to himself at how the Negroes came from the South with big dreams, yet they were so ham-fisted and funny talking.

Casey took pride in the fact that he was born in the North. He never had to suffer in the South, like his mother did. He figured he could say whatever he wanted to Lee about his game and Lee still wouldn't be able to pull it off on his own, even if he had the desire to do so. He thought he had a jump-start on Negroes like Lee. Casey even talked with more confidence. This is because his brother kept him sheltered most of his life. Tim couldn't stand it whenever Casey came home from grade school crying because he was the poorest child of all, and the dirtiest. He decided to make sure Casey had the finest of everything, even if he had to work two jobs to provide for him.

Casey recognized that all Lee needed was a couple of years in a big city, and a good teacher to achieve a reputation in the streets. More and more, Casey viewed Lee as a future competition. He changed his conversational pace. "My new friend, Lee." They laughed and shook hands. Lee placed Mary down on the couch next to him, while he poured himself more of the liquor

Casey had brought in with him. Mary tried to reach the fascinating bottle when her father held it in his hand, but Lee kept blocking her way. He wasn't aware that just by having her in that environment where she could see and smell the fire water was enough to send certain signals to her brain that could pose problems for her in future years.

Casey wanted to tell Robeena to get them a chaser for their drinks, but, true to his game, he was the provider of everything at this stage in their relationship. He excused himself from Lee to fetch what he needed for the liquor. Right on top of the ice box were several bottles of cola. "Hey, baby," he said to Minnie as he grabbed two colas, "I hope you don't mind if I grab two of these to mix with our whiskey."

"I could've gotten that for you," Robeena said helplessly from her sitting position at the kitchen table. Vivian sat in front of her, and Minnie was up preparing the food. Without realizing it, Robeena had already allowed herself to want to please him. He stopped with the colas in one hand to stand behind her chair. He reached down, took her hand, and squeezed it, lifting her petite fingers to his lips.

"You're doing enough right now, sugar. Just being here with you is all I need." Casey turned to Minnie. "Whatever you're cooking smells mighty good." All the while looking at Minnie, he slowly released his hand, untwining Robeena's fingers one by one. "You need some help, baby?" He was careful not to turn away until he heard the refusal he knew was coming.

Shivers shot up through Minnie when she considered that this man thought she was lovely enough to call her baby. She tried to act natural, like she was used to being caressed by the words of men. "Ain't nothing to it, Casey. I'm only stirring up some pork back, Lima Beans, and some greens. Y'all go on and have a good time." Vivian felt conscience-stricken at that moment to be sitting there aimlessly and not helping Minnie fix dinner. She found herself wanting to seem better than that to Robeena's fine man.

"Don't even think about trying to help me . . . none of y'all," Minnie said, letting Vivian and everyone off the hook. "I got this. You just be careful not to let Henry know y'all is drinking in his house. You know he don't allow that in here." Casey found her weakness. She was deceptive. She would lie to her husband, disrespect him, and allow others to not respect him in his absence. A smile slyly crept across his face with the realization that Minnie wasn't so virtuous. However, he was vexed that Minnie was willing to defy her own husband's house rules for the sake of wanting to please her guests. Any house is weak where there is no unity between husband and wife.

Women like Minnie made Casey appreciate his line of work. He couldn't figure out why a woman would betray a man who loved her to please another man. Unless of course they didn't love each other, he thought briefly. Casey had never met a woman he could trust; a woman who was totally loyal to her man. That's why he felt he had to be hard on the women in his stable. He felt that most women were dishonest and disloyal, including Minnie and Vivian.

"We'll keep our glasses down, sugar," he said simply, and went back to sit with Lee. The sisters excitedly tittered while Minnie now put extra care into the feast.

CHAPTER SEVENTEEN
"Priceless"

By the time Henry got home, they were all having a marvelous time together. Minnie was tired out from cooking, talking about old times with her sisters, and doting after Mary all day, and Mary finally exhausted herself after trying to stay awake to enjoy all the excitement. Minnie waved at Henry coming through the door on her way to take Mary upstairs. She placed the sleeping baby in the double bed she shared with her husband.

Henry was quite cheerful when he walked in the house and saw the party taking place. He was proud to have the accommodations to provide for the comfort of all his guests. He heard Vivian's gay laughter coming from the kitchen and his heart melted. He wasn't sure whose baby his wife was holding, nor did it dawn on him that it could be Vivian's.

When Casey and Lee got up from their seats to shake his hand, Henry heard it grow quiet in the kitchen. She knows I'm home! We're gonna have to face each other, he thought. Lee was thanking him for letting them stay there for a spell. I'm letting your *wife* stay here, Henry said to himself, unless you've changed, I want you out!

Minnie rushed back downstairs in time to greet him before anyone else would have the chance to tell him about the surprise Vivian and Lee had brought with them. She had a strong tinge of jealousy that there was no way Henry would be able to tell that Vivian had recently had a baby simply by looking at her, since she was still model thin and shapely. Minnie had put on about twenty-five pounds during her short stay in Michigan, and she wondered if Henry noticed.

Vivian, led by Robeena, started out of the kitchen to greet Henry, but before Vivian could make it to the living room, Minnie rushed back downstairs and managed to pull Henry away in the middle of Lee's sentence. "He'll be right back, Lee. I wanna show 'im the surprise!"

"Oh, yeah." Lee turned to Casey again and they picked up their conversation as though Henry had never interrupted by coming home.

Minnie led him upstairs to show him Mary while he followed cautiously behind her. Halfway up, he could hear the baby cooing. There was a creak with each of his footsteps on the old, hollow, wooden stairs. Minnie made the creaking sound natural as she ascended, but the noise Henry generated sounded accusing. It was as though he was sneaking up to see the baby.

Before approaching Mary, Henry leaned on the wall near the closet located right across from the bed and changed from his one pair of shoes to his slippers. Laboriously, he heaved his way over to where Minnie stood. His heart pounded massively in his chest when he saw the perfect, adorable child sleeping soundly in his bed. He could hardly breathe. Minnie was standing directly behind him, as though she was a correctional officer waiting to cuff him if he made the wrong move. The delightful baby smelled so refreshing! Her blameless, round face and unusually high cheekbones did not stop Henry from eyeing Mary suspiciously in the first sentimental moment he saw her sleeping so soundly.

"I didn't know they had 'em a baby," he said quietly.

"Me neither." Henry wanted to dissipate into thin air. Was Minnie waiting to see what he had to say about the baby? Why couldn't they just go back downstairs with everyone else? He'd seen the baby. Why was she just standing there, waiting for him to speak?

"She's a beauty."

"Yeah. She is." There was a long pause.

"Well, we better head back down so's we don't wake her."

"I know, Henry. I just like looking at her. Vivian sure did surprise us with this one! She ain't said nothing in her letter about this."

"Yeah."

"Henry?"

"Yes?" His hands were clasped together.

"We just hafta be patient. I know God will bless us with a child one day."

"That's right, Minnie."

"You believe that, don't you?"

"I believe that if God Blesses us with a child, then it was meant for us to have one, and if He don't Bless us with one, we should always continue to count our Blessings for the things He *has* given us."

"I wanna make you happy, Henry. I wanna give you a baby." He rubbed her back with the palm of one hand.

"Don't you worry none, Minnie. Just rely on the Lord. Listen to your own advice about patience. The Lord knows what He's doing."

"I reckon so."

"I *know* so."

"Me, too. I know so."

"Man!" Henry shook his head. "I guess I need to take off work for a couple of days---run Lee down to that new center, the Detroit Urban League as quick as lightning."

"That's right. Looks like he's gonna be needing a job sooner than we thought."

"Yeah. Gancy is sharp—he'll help 'im." He turned away from the baby. "You ready to go back down?"

"Yes," she said sadly.

"Come on." He took her hand in his and faced her as she turned toward the door. He hugged her tightly. "Come on, Minnie." She forced a tear to roll back under her eyelid, wiping the residue of it on his shirt. "Now, don't you go and let nobody see you been crying when we supposed to be happy." She gave a weak smile, which was sufficient for Henry.

Minnie and Henry returned to their guests together, without saying much about Mary to anyone. He socialized with Lee warmly and welcomed him again into his home for as long as he needed it. His emotions were to the point that he graciously accepted Lee into his home because it seemed the right thing to do. He had hoped Vivian would have been sensible enough to leave Lee behind, unless of course he'd changed his ways.

However, one look at Vivian when she came to greet him covered Henry with goose bumps. She was as lovely as he'd ever seen her. Henry couldn't keep his eyes from trying to penetrate Vivian's soul when he thought no one noticed, and there was no way he could stop his heart from racing when they gave each other a greeting embrace, initiated by Vivian—but only after Henry gave Lee a quick hug, first. Once Lee lowered his wings to Henry, admitting that he needed help in caring for his family, Henry decided to give him a brotherly embrace. And then Vivian stepped right into his arms and thanked him, too. He stared at the floor while Lee stared at him.

Lee had acquired a very acute sensitivity to social cues that could suggest a need to be extra watchful over his wife. Spending just a few hours in Michigan, he discovered that there was something about Henry that still made him nervous. Lee did suspect that Henry wanted to have his wife, and, moreover, there was an uncanny fierceness and intensity about Henry's relationship with Vivian. He shook his head in disbelief at his own thoughts. "Hell, he's married to Vivian's sister! He don't wanna do nothing with me," Lee judged.

Notwithstanding, over the following few days, Lee made sure Henry did not have one opportunity alone with Vivian for over a second. Lee had already threatened Vivian that she should stay clear of Henry. When Vivian had argued back that he was overreacting, Lee slapped her. Following that, Vivian was dramatic in her efforts to avoid Henry. She wanted to call attention to, and display how ridiculous Lee was being. Whenever Lee left the house, Vivian would stay in their bedroom, unless Minnie called her out for something. And Lee made Vivian provide every detail of her activities whenever he came back home. To avoid facing the fact that she was a battered woman, she focused on making a point to her husband that he was being ridiculous to suspect Henry. Therefore, with silent defiance, she let the whole house know she was under house arrest with hopes that her sister might give Lee the frown he needed to drop this nonsense.

Nonetheless, Minnie and Henry were not clear on why Vivian was acting so bizarre. They didn't associate her behavior to any threats Lee might've made because he was kind and gentle in their presence for a long while. Henry could never seem to get alone with Vivian long enough to have a private conversation with her about their past relationship, and whether her present distancing was a result of their former romance. Although he moved to Michigan with the hopes of avoiding all such future conversations with her, seeing her again only worked to fan the flames of his passion. As hard as he tried, Henry couldn't detect if she was happy in the relationship with Lee.

She seemed happy when she was with her sisters. They would go shopping in Detroit, and Vivian would get off the city bus at the Urban League where she volunteered her time to help the children there. Many parents were able to drop off their children and be certain there were several educational programs and even food for the children during the day. Minnie and Robeena would come back after shopping and Vivian was content with whatever they might have picked up for her, as long as she could spend a few hours at that center. And Mary would be right with her the whole time.

One week, Henry decided to start working on a bed for Mary using some of the fine wood he'd taken from his job. He would present it to Vivian as a token of his affection and love for her, but of course the bed would be a gift to Lee as well. Lee discovered from Minnie that he was making the bed. On the last day of labor, Lee stood around until Henry finished. Then he thanked him, and the two of them rolled the beautiful work to Lee's bedroom where Mary slept, also. It was of dark-brown pinewood with five bars on either side of it. It had four wheels on it so Vivian could roll the heavy crib if she wanted to. Vivian was only allowed to mutter a quick thank you for his efforts, because Lee was always there—always watching.

She exemplified her fear of Lee in the form of drama to paint a picture to herself. In her picture, she depicted Lee as over wrought; someone she would appease for the sake of synchronization. In this way, she didn't have to face his physical aggression because she rationalized it was her job to keep the peace. Whenever she dwelled on the imprisonment in which Lee held her, she would remember the love filled days she'd spent with Henry, and her guilt would keep her accepting his continued abuse.

They had already had a few big arguments about Henry, and Lee had slapped her each time. During one fight, Lee had slapped her because she poured Henry a glass of orange juice. The first time they fought, it was about pouring coffee while Henry was present. Lee had come downstairs to find Vivian and Henry alone in the kitchen together. Lee was too tense to postpone the discussion until later. He also wanted to send a clear message once and for all to Henry that he was on to his secret lust for Vivian.

"Viv, get your ass upstairs up off from under that man! The minute I take my eyes off you, you go acting fast-tailed." Henry turned away in startled shame because he didn't even know Lee was home, but he did know Minnie was at work. Henry was just contemplating on trying to take Vivian into his arms after she came into the kitchen to make coffee. They had only been alone in the kitchen together for under two minutes when Lee came bolting in. Henry had almost reached for her, but despite his pining to catch her alone, he wasn't totally prepared for such a time. Lee's words cut into his thoughts like a butcher knife.

"Your language ain't necessary, son," Henry stated conscientiously, "you ain't got no business talking like that at your woman no way." Lee was furious with Henry for having the nerve to speak up in defense of Vivian. His suspicions were right that Henry would defend her. Henry's outspokenness contributed enormously to Lee's uneasiness about him. Vivian stood perfectly still, wishing Henry would shut up. She knew if he angered Lee, *she* would have to pay for it later.

"Lee, I just came into the kitchen to fetch you some coffee like you asked," Vivian reminded him softly. Henry looked at Vivian in astonishment at her tolerance for Lee's rudeness. It was instantly confirmed for him why he hadn't seen much of Vivian.

"Man," Lee said, ignoring Vivian's response, "I know you ain't involving yourself in my marital affairs, is you?" Henry deliberated silently if he was stepping out of line. Lee continued, "I mean, she is my wife, not yours. She's my wife." The declaration of vows was a momentary block for Henry. How could he defend his entanglement in a marital affair? However, Henry charged himself with a lights out, foul on the play move for slipping up by referring to Vivian as Lee's "woman." Henry wanted Vivian to think of herself as *his* woman, who happened to be married to Lee. What was marriage, except for a piece of paper drawn up by their enemies for stupid legalities? He married Minnie when Vivian was his woman, he felt. When Henry didn't answer right away, Lee snatched Vivian's hand and pulled her upstairs.

"Hold it, Lee! You're making a big deal outta nothing." He slapped her when they were at the top of the stairs before pushing her into their room.

"Hussy, I told you I better not catch you up under that niggah, didn't I?" This was his way of explaining to her why he'd just slapped her.

"Be quiet, Lee, unless you want to wake up Mary," Vivian whimpered. She walked into the bedroom only pausing for a second. She tried to pretend the slap never happened. He had only just grazed her face—she hardly felt it. Lee lowered his voice. He knew Saturday was rolling around, and he had promised Casey they would spend the whole afternoon together, just chatting casually and going over gambling techniques. Since Minnie worked all day on some Saturdays, that would leave Vivian and Henry in the house alone for hours. Lee didn't want to antagonize her, which would only serve to heighten his insecurities.

"Come here, cutie pie." He took her hand and sat with her on the bed. "Look, Viv, I ain't mad with you. But I asked you to stay away from that man!"

"Lee, we all live in the same house. How am I not going to end up in the same room with him from time to time?" He knew she was right. He also knew she was happy to live with her sister, especially since he wasn't working yet.

"See, that's why I didn't want to move up here and stay with them. This ain't working out, muffin." She, as he expected, panicked. She sat in his lap.

"Lee, baby...you're my man. Sometimes I feel you think I want somebody else. Henry doesn't mean anything to me . . . you don't have to watch me like a hawk. Even if you're not home and I'm in the same room with Henry, you have nothing to worry about." She thought about her time shared with Henry in Florida, yet, how after a few days, he still came to get Minnie, and how he never looked back. She thought that had she not ended up in Michigan, she could have rotted in hell as far as Henry was concerned. He could have sneaked a letter for her to her mother's house—a simple note stating that he missed her...but nothing. She kissed Lee and he kissed her back, easily pushing Henry out of his mind, while she cried silent tears.

Downstairs, Henry sat in the dining room wondering what was happening upstairs. He wrung his hands together in exasperation, remembering how Lee had pulled Vivian roughly away. "I ain't gonna have him whipping her in this house," he convinced himself. However, Henry was disappointed when he didn't hear any battle noises coming through the walls. If the couple fought, it could mean Henry mattered to them.

He thought about the baby Mary, as he always did ever since he saw her. Henry, like Robeena and Minnie, was quite surprised to discover Vivian had given birth. Robeena just assumed that Vivian was not the genuine virgin girl everyone thought she was. Robeena was tickled at the remembrance of

Lee's constant boasts that he would marry a virgin, yet, now it appeared he had canceled his dream out of his own greed and lust. Henry, on the other hand, had been frantically trying to learn the mathematics involved in child gestation. He casually asked women in the neighborhood questions like "What's the shortest time a baby can stay in your stomach and come out healthy?" And, "Can a woman get pregnant the first time she ever has been with a man?"

Mrs. Brown, a middle-aged widow, loved answering his questions. She just wished he would tell her more about why he was asking. "If that's my baby, I need to know," he said, looking up at the ceiling which was the floor of Vivian's bedroom.

These questions continued to haunt him until the next Saturday morning. On Saturday, Casey came around noon to pick up Lee. Vivian was upset that Lee hardly wanted her to do anything without him, even with her own sisters, yet he was on his way to spend the day with a man he'd practically just met. Lee had told Vivian that he was going out with Casey to handle some business, and Vivian said that was fine because she was going down to the urban league.

"You ain't going to no urban league. You're gonna stay right here and get some of this laundry done."

"There's only a few clothes left to be washed, Lee, and besides, we don't have any soap. You could buy some, you know, instead of making me ask Minnie for those types of personal items all the time."

"You ain't gotta announce it to her every time you borrow a cup of sugar. That's your excuse for not doing what I say, which I'm getting tired of begging you to obey me."

"I don't want to argue, either, Lee, but it's not right for me not to get to do the things I want, yet you can go anywhere and do anything you please. I don't think it's fair just because you're the man…"

"You damn right I'm the man. I don't hear Minnie arguing with Henry over this type of mess. When he leaves to go out and do his thing, it's as peaceful as it could be. Did you hear 'em arguing when Henry left? Of course you didn't." Lee saw Henry leave the house about 7:30 a.m., while Minnie was still getting ready for work. Henry had gone out for his exercise including a morning run, but when he came home, Lee didn't hear him. Lee saw him leave with a bag, and figured he would be gone for a while working on someone's house or something, but Henry only carried a towel, two ten-pound dumb bells, and shea butter for his muscles.

Casey heard a portion of their argument given that Vivian followed Lee downstairs to the door with her complaints. Casey noted that Lee was oblivious to the heightened frustration in Vivian's voice and actions.

"Lee, aren't you planning on listening to me?" Lee slammed the door on Vivian's words. She dropped down angrily on the sofa with her arms folded tightly across her chest. Thoughtfully, she picked up the carefully typed carbon copy of the Lincoln-Douglas debate that Wali Eli had left at her home in Florida for reading material. It was one of many documents and books she had brought with her whenever she packed for her Michigan move. She felt like her mother wouldn't mind if she came over and ravaged her old bedroom and the house, claiming all the bottles of strawberry body oil, books no one ever read, and some of the clothes her sisters left behind. When she wanted instant peace, reading was the thing that allowed her to travel out of her life and misery into another existence. Casey silently interpreted that Vivian's unhappiness with her husband would make her easy prey to anyone who wished to come between their marriage.

Henry finished rubbing shea butter on his chest, and then he tip-toed out of his bedroom so that he could monitor Lee's departure. He held his shirt in his hand for a few seconds before pulling it over his head. He couldn't wait to trot downstairs and finally corner Vivian, but he took in several deep breaths to calm his nerves. He hesitated until everything was totally quiet before creeping slowly down the stairs. Vivian jumped slightly when out of her peripheral vision, she saw Henry descending the stairs to stand by the edge of the sofa, next to her. She didn't realize that he was even home, either, just as Lee thought Henry was gone because he'd been quiet with his door shut all morning long after he came home from exercising at 8:52 a.m. Minnie had to be at work at 9:30, and he needed to catch her so he could give her his shoes which needed to be repaired.

Lee didn't hear one indication that Henry had entered the house again, or else he would have minded his temper with Vivian with more restraint. Henry's feet were sore from running in his hard shoes, so he removed them the moment he came back home, which caused him the ability to creep like a cat back up to his room, although he wasn't trying to be surreptitious. Even as her fury with Lee occupied her mind, Vivian was very aware that they were alone together for the first time since she arrived.

"Vivian?" Henry looked at her questioningly when he called her name. He walked closer to her, cautiously, as though she might get up and run away at any second. When he reached her, he bent forward, placing his hands on her wrists, and gently pulled her to her feet. She was still clutching the article. "What's this?" He asked, taking the article from her. She froze in indecision. "Aha! You're reading about our friend, Abe." He chuckled.

"He's not my friend, but he might be yours," she shot back, as he knew she would. "I'm nobody's tool for political gain," she continued, happy to focus on something other than the obvious. Tossing the article back onto the coffee table, he pulled her to him, and wrapped her in his arms. He refused to open his eyes or loosen his grip. This might be his only opportunity to ever hold her. Long seconds lapsed in total stillness. After that eternity, he kissed her cheeks one at a time, yet she remained aloof. She turned her face away. He pulled her closer, causing her feet to involuntarily leave the ground.

"Henry…" Vivian whispered, trying to find the floor with her toes.

"Will you read the Great Debate to me later, sweet girl?"

"I left it on the table for anybody who wants to look at it."

"You're still sassy, hunh?" She didn't answer. "I've been waiting for this moment." He took a deep breath. I finally have you alone—all to myself."

"This isn't real."

"Shhh. It's been so long since I held you!" He murmured some other soft things.

"But Henry," she looked down at his thick arms around her, "please don't touch me like this." He unclasped his hands that were met together behind her back and rubbed her arms up and down. Her feet sank quietly into the floor. Henry smoothed her hair down and away from her ears, holding the bunch of it in his fists, causing her neck to tilt.

"You're hurting me…" She thought he would automatically loosen her, but he didn't.

"Of course I'm not hurting you. If you're scared, that doesn't mean I'm hurting you."

"This isn't real," she repeated.

"I miss you so much, my beautiful, priceless love." She felt her throat tighten when he kissed it. Priceless, he'd called her. Floyd had tried to give her a price tag. She blushed. Gently, he let her hair go and put his arms back around her. She tried to make herself stiff ever more. "I've died inside not having you. I just wanna talk to you, Vivian." She was uneasy with her response to the way he was holding her. Her ardor for him surfaced reflexively.

Vivian kept her eyes trained on her feet. "Truly, I'm late for my appointment at the urban league, Henry. Mary is upstairs sleeping still. I have to get her and me changed so we can hurry along. I just don't have time to talk…"

"Are you sure your appointment is today? The center is only open for a few hours on the weekends. Gancy was at my church last week giving a talk about the center. I spoke with him, and he told me he was coming down *here* Sunday to carry Lee that Pontiac Motors application. He said he would be in Pontiac today, too, though. What business have you got up there today?"

"Oh. Yes, Gancy did say he was coming to Pontiac to see his sister, and that he was stopping by here on his way home from church." She tried to shrug her shoulders. "I guess he meant this week. But I met some other friends at the center, also, Henry. They like to play their music for me, and such." Henry continued to hold her while she looked away as she spoke.

"Hope you ain't got no man friend you met up there. Gancy sure seems to have a lot to say to you." He squeezed her lightly while he placed his mouth on her neck again. She backed away sufficiently enough to make him stop, but he still held her near. Henry pressed, "When he was helping *me* to find a job, he never made any personal house visits, and I have a tough time believing he's coming all the way down here to see Lee…"

"It's little David, one of the children. I told him I was going to try to get up there today." Henry's breathing was labored. When he didn't say anything, Vivian continued, "I should hurry because you are right about them closing early on Saturdays…we read together, you know…and…I want to make a good impression. Gancy is supposed to be working closely with Lee, to find him a job. I volunteer down there not because he's helping Lee, either. I like it down there." He knew she was nervous, but more than subtlety, he continued to urge her.

"Definitely, we gotta talk. Right now, Viv," he said as softly as he could. "You ain't gonna make it to no center before two, 'cause that's when they close, doll."

"Well, what do you want to talk about?"

"Mary. I wanna talk to you about that baby." He could feel her body constrict next to his. He moved closer to her, still, locking her firmly against him. She wriggled violently as she lost her footing again.

"Let me go, Henry!" She felt as though she was being smothered. Henry had caught her completely off guard. She hadn't prepared a speech for this moment. Her plan was to conceal Mary's paternity forever. She wasn't ready to be confronted.

"I ain't letting you go 'til you can tell me how you got that baby so fast when you married Lee five months ago." He was trying to remain calm, but he felt himself growing saucy.

"I married him six months ago."

"I don't give a damn!" He pressed his eyes into slits. "Vivian." He raised his voice significantly at her, then lowered it by the time he murmured her name. "Is that my baby?" She attempted to squirm away. He kept her in his grip, shaking her gently. "Is it?" Her hesitancy convinced him that there might be some legitimacy to his suspicions. He bubbled with joy at the mere possibility that he had fathered a child. He was beginning to question his fertility since Minnie hadn't gotten pregnant. Minnie! What if she knew?

Henry panicked right along with Vivian. Never once did he predict that Vivian would get pregnant even after their two days together.

"It isn't your baby," she answered dimly.

"I think it might be. How can you say for sure that she ain't mine?"

"Just like I said it."

"I need you to convince me that I'm wrong."

"What you think has nothing to do with me, Henry. If that's your opinion, it's not my job to change it. I said what I had to say, now let me…"

"Hell yeah it's your job to change my mind! Ain't nobody else gonna do it. And if you can't change my mind, then we need to investigate this thing, 'cause if that's my baby…"

"Leave well enough alone. I'm a married woman." He was looking at her with disdain. She was rebuffed by his apparent disapproval, thus felt the need to defend her position. "What's your problem, Henry? You act like I wasn't supposed to have a baby with my husband. Lee was the one who wanted to marry me . . . not you."

Henry's heart was heavy as he held her now at arm's length, ready to shake the truth out of her if necessary. He considered her words and tried to imagine how awful it must be for her if Mary indeed was his child. How could he have been so stupid? Vivian was terrified and he regretted that it was because of him. She felt his fingernails digging angrily into her arms and she imagined that Henry was about to throw her to the ground and stomp her because…that's how men behaved whenever they were angry. He looked down at her frightened face and pulled her close to him again instead of shaking her. Vivian emitted a heavy sigh.

"Honey, I don't want you to be scared. I know I'm a li'l rugged and clumsy, but I'm not gonna hurt you." He noted she relaxed slightly and cautiously rested her head on his chest when he acknowledged her emotional pulse. "I need to know. You know I do. Mary has my features. Don't be like that, baby, *please!* Ain't no way in the world I'll let anything happen to you, Viv. If I'm Mary's father, I'll do whatever you want me to, you can believe that." He kissed her forehead.

She regained her composure and lifted away from him. "She isn't yours. I already told you. And there's not a doggone thing I want you to do but live your life the way you've been doing without me. Imagine! Henry, how could you even mention this?" She shook her head in disgust. "It's improper. If you don't want to hurt me, let it go."

"I can't let it go, and I can't let *you* go." Henry stared into her shifty, misty eyes. Then he kissed her mouth coarsely in his impatience to touch her lips. She broke away from the kiss, but Henry was still clutching her desperately. She didn't want to feel this way with him. She had promised Lee she would stay clear away from him. "I think you are lying to me, Viv, though, and I'm gonna find out."

"Stop it, Henry."

"I can't."

"You won't."

"You know I can't. Not 'til you tell me the truth."

"Seems like you're going to believe whatever you want."

"No, I'll listen to you, I promise."

"Well then!"

"It's just that a seed must've been planted right around the time you were with me. That's all I'm trying to figure out."

"And?"

"What the hell do you mean by 'and'?"

"I'm just saying it wasn't necessarily *your* seed, as you want to put it." He let her go abruptly.

"What did you do? Leave my bed and crawl into his?"

"Maybe I left his and crawled into yours." For sure, he would slap her after that, she thought. Not only did she expect him to, but she also wanted him to slap her because then, she would be standing on familiar ground. Still, she backed away. He stepped closer and grabbed her wrists.

"You better watch your mouth, Vivian. I don't ever want you talking to me like that no more."

"I'm done talking."

"Naw, Vivian. You ain't done 'til *I* say we're done."

"Let go of me, Henry!" He loosened her, not sure if he was being too aggressive or if she was handling him, controlling him.

"I'm not gonna let you talk shit at me." His voice was slightly raised again.

"But you insulted me, Henry. You might as well have called me a whore."

"That's a lie, and you know it."

"Just leave it alone."

He seemed to back down, but he grabbed her wrists again. For the next minute, he simply stared at her. "Come on, doll, let's go upstairs and just talk about it, okay?" She wanted to reach up and touch his black, tight hair, but she didn't dare let him know of her desire.

"That's not a good idea, Henry, please..." He was walking backward, dragging her with him.

"It *is* a good idea. We can't be discussing something like this standing at the front door! This is too important, right? And we got a whole lot to talk about, baby." He pulled her back into him, placing the crook of his arm behind her neck so he could tilt her head back and kiss her from shoulder to shoulder. Electricity shot through Vivian's entire body like a bolt of lightning rushing down from the sky. She negotiated with her self-accusing spirit that she would only surrender for a transient moment or two to this bellowing ball of combustion.

Vivian fell limp in his grasp with her eyes closed, deciding to make the best of the limited seconds she had allotted herself. He was almost forced to catch her, and when he did, he lifted her in a cradle position and carried her up the stairs. She considered waiving the traveling time during her lustful countdown to make things fair for her starving soul. Reality gripped her like an iron clamp when they passed a portrait of Henry, Robeena, and Minnie on the wall by the stairs.

"I don't want to talk *upstairs*, Henry. Somebody might catch us and think the worst. It's too dangerous. That's why I always say leave the past where it belongs. Where are you taking me? To my room? To your room? Just put me down!" When they got to the staircase landing, he put her down, letting her legs dangle on the stairs. He tried to kiss her again, yet she turned away.

"What did you come up here for? Knowing what I feel for you, and you gonna move in with me, and bring another niggah to my house? What the hell is wrong with you?"

"I thought we were invited. I have my life, and you have yours, so what difference does it make if I brought two niggers and a cowboy? You went on with your life and you told me to forget about what took place between us....and that's exactly what I did!"

"Don't act like you didn't know what would happen if I saw you again… in my house. I see you at nighttime on your way to be with him, I see you when your hair is wet, I see you laughing, and I see you sad…"

"Please…Henry…"

"I've been so sad, Vivian, sweetheart," he muttered breathlessly, as though a river of fire was rushing to break an internally built dam in his throat. "I'm sorry for what I did to you. I swear to God I was trying to figure out how I could go back down South to get you! What story to tell, how to leave my job…every second I can't reach you is like an hour to me, and every hour is like a day. The way your husband keeps you locked up, I hafta be mindful of the few minutes I have with you, which is now, and only now." Before she could start the clock, he lifted her again and carried her the rest of the way upstairs to the bedroom he shared with her sister. She stopped fighting him.

"You know I shouldn't be in here, Henry."

"Why not, Viv?" She looked away. "I just wanna talk. I *need* to talk with you." He led her to a seat in the rocking chair he'd constructed out of scrap wood. Henry was the builder of just about everything in the room. Vivian knew this and was proud of his abilities. Everything was as he desired about the atmosphere. The temperature was snug; the shade from the trees blocked away the light-giving sun. Henry got down on one knee, holding one of her hands in his. She resented Lee for leaving her wanton, which she rationalized made Henry's nearness more enticing.

The closest she came to weathering the oncoming storm was earlier when she had promised herself that she'd only entertain his fancy for two minutes. In Vivian's mind, she felt she was "supposed" to have Henry's comfort, given that he knew things about her that no one else knew. She felt the need to respond only to her emotional nature, which she deemed the most important. Henry would safeguard her from Minnie and Lee.

"You oughta let me take care of you, and Mary, too. I don't care if I'm *not* the father, Viv."

"That's impossible."

He pleaded, despite her now inaudible protests. "I love you, sweet girl, I always have," he whispered. It felt good to her when he said that, although she didn't fully believe it. "You oughta know that I would do anything for you!"

"Henry, stop this! You're pressing…we can't…"

"How come we can't? You know you're supposed to be with me, anyway. But I made a mistake. When we danced that night, I wanted to ask you to be my girl. I wish I had, baby."

"With your girlfriend in the front room?" He ignored her sarcasm.

"Honey," he said, "is Mary my child?" She couldn't talk about it. "Listen, Viv, don't ever be scared to tell me nothing." She slid back into a dark tunnel as she silently savored his energy pulsating somewhere deep inside of her soul.

Henry contemplated the possibility that Vivian didn't know if he was the father or not, but still, he pushed onwards. Vivian knew he was incensed, yet he handled her so gently. His tenderness made her want to confide in him. She felt safe with him—so different from an infuriated Lee.

"What do you want me to say, Henry?" When she finally spoke, he encouraged, caressed, and held her. Neither of them said anything for a few minutes, although Henry expected her to make some sort of explanation.

"I do love you, Vivian. All I ask is you to tell me the truth. I ain't mad at you. Princess, don't you know I think you're the most refreshing, priceless and precious thing in the world?" He paused. "I got the right to know." Vivian tossed his hands away, and stood up from the chair turning her back to him. He stood with her. "You think I'm gonna say something to jeopardize you...or my child?" He placed his hands on her shoulders and turned her around again.

"Do you always get your way, Henry?"

"Don't seem like I do."

"My answers won't satisfy you."

"Ev'rything you are satisfies me. No one else can or has ever done that for me. Your smile and that pretty mole of yours satisfies me."

"You don't know what it's like, Henry. I ...I...I'm all grown up, now." Painfully, she grieved over Floyd's abuse. She shook her head. "Things are not the same anymore. I'm not priceless, and I am surely no princess. I have things inside of me that need to stay buried."

"I reckon if it's buried, that makes you a hidden princess." He smiled at her. "Open up to me, sweet girl," he insisted. "There ain't nothing you hafta bury. Can't you see that my shoulders are broad enough to carry whatever burden you got?" She opened her mouth to speak but no words matured into sound. Effortlessly, he pushed her back down in the chair, and returned to his position on one knee.

"I can't live without you, Viv. I missed you terribly when I came up here. I tried to run away from it, but I see that it ain't just gonna go away, sweetheart! Every day, I wake up thinking about you. Every night I go to bed wishing I could be holding you. I want us to be together, Viv, as man and wife." She gasped at how swiftly he'd maneuvered himself once again. Before she could catch up with her thoughts, he was kissing her like his very life depended on whatever oxygen he could suction from her, and he had to do it fast because he was dying since he hadn't seen her since before time. Miraculously, she managed to turn away and catch her breath.

"Where do you think you're going?" He turned with her.

Despite his visible frustration etched over his eyebrows in sweaty wrinkles, she said, "I can't do this!"

"Quit trying to push me away," he remarked, trying to swallow his agitation.

"I should have pushed you away nine months ago."

She finally hurt him. The emptiness that washed over him was one of the coldest moments he'd ever experienced. He felt lost, rejected, and momentarily powerless. However, walking away from her wasn't something he could do. He wanted to sob, but he had to hold it together. "I know what you're trying to do. It won't work with me."

"What's that?"

"You're looking for a fight, and anger, and yelling."

"Why would you say...?"

"Because you did push me away nine months ago. But I laid the law down then, and I'll lay it down today if I have to, and you know it. Yet, here you are, coming against this brick." Speechless, she gasped involuntarily. He shook his head. "I'm not Lee, Vivian, so stop comparing me to him."

"I already told you..."

"And I told *you.* It won't work, Vivian. If I have a child in this world, I wanna be able to love it like it's mine. Please don't take *that* away from me. Please don't make me spend the rest of my life wondering if it's mine!" He reached for her arms, using his hands to coax her into relaxation. "Do you know who Mary's father is? If you don't know for sure, then tell me *that*, Viv, but tell me the truth—I'm begging you." Now his hands were roaming over her back soothingly. His words brought regret to Vivian's heart. She wanted Henry to know she had kept their love sacred, and there was no possibility that the baby was Lee's.

She never weighed how important this was to him. Men she knew had babies all the time, and they hardly cared to know or offer support. His words were strange. She tried fruitlessly to imagine her father uttering similar words to her mother. "Yeah, right," she said to herself. Vivian mused over how Henry truly could love Minnie, yet be so passionate with her. She thought about her own situation with Lee, and although she loved Lee, she quietly avowed that she wished Henry was her husband. Lee hurt her too much with his nightlife. She wanted a man to stay with her and covet only her. Lee was not that man. And Henry was now showing her that he desired her over Minnie. Vivian liked that.

She didn't want to damage Minnie or her own husband with the truth about Mary, but she decided she was cramping Henry more by withholding the truth from him. She brooded like her life was beginning to come apart at the seams. She was overcome with disorientation. Tears strolled uncontrollably out of her eyes.

"Go ahead and cry, my sweet, sweet love," he urged. She slumped further into the chair, wishing she could disappear under it. He pulled her up, kissed her tears, and took her back up in his arms. He remembered having to kiss Minnie's tears when she failed at seducing him. He only wanted her to stop crying, but with Vivian, he didn't really want her to stop crying because he didn't want to stop kissing her. Where there were no tears, he still kissed her, and he wished her cries would continue so he could give her all his comfort and security. Cautiously, he pressed closer. His gentleness only made her release her burden even more. "That's right, honey. I'm here for you, baby. Just tell me what you need and I'll give it to you. Anything, Vivian." He kissed her mole, her chin, and wiped her runny nose with his shirt.

"I don't want anything..."

"You want to lash out at me and hurt me like I hurt you? Tell me you hate me?"

"No!"

"You want some of my money? Baby, I'll give you everything I got. You want this house? I'll get another job—I'll work two jobs and you can have all that. It's like I told you—you ain't gotta worry 'bout nothing! All you gotta do is put that jive time hustler out—or just tell me that you *want* 'im out and I'll do the rest..."

"Henry," she attempted. Again, she recalled Floyd's brutal hands. She wanted to tell him of her humiliation. Finally, there was someone right in front of her who would listen. Henry made her feel like no other person had the ability to make her feel. "A lot of things—dreadful things have happened to me since I last saw you. I'm not the same person I was. You left me alone to deal with everything by myself. I don't want your money. I'm spoiled goods. I needed *you.* You weren't there for me, Henry. My life is all wrong, now. People have turned me into trash, someone that no one would want to marry, but you left me by myself. I'm ruined, Henry. And now, you expect me to think you don't care that I'm truly not a princess unless I'm a hidden princess buried under my own rubbish? Well, I can't do that. You told me I could trust you, and then you turned around and left me, Henry, so I've had to hurt people too, to survive."

"Who made you feel like trash? Who ruined you?"

Vivian sighed, waiting for Henry to say something else or ask another question. The only sound were birds chirping and leaves being brushed by the wind. Henry vividly recalled the night a lifetime ago whenever he danced with Vivian for the first time. She had told him she needed somebody to help her out of the water -keep her from drowning. They had connected in a space of air between them without hardly ever speaking directly to each other. Electrical currents had joined them albeit he lowered his gaze whenever he came near her -keeping his eyes steady only on Minnie. Not out of his peripheral vision, but out of his spiritual eye, Vivian was there. He had fallen in love with her while openly trying to avoid her. Dancing with her pushed her into his real space, but even then, he only talked to her when she talked to him out of nowhere, except that magical space they shared between them that was filled with the fire of their unexpressed love. It was within that magical space that Vivian asked him and no one else to take her up on a cloud somewhere and just let her be. Now, Henry understood that someone ruined her in his absence, and yet, he was asking her to trust him again, when clearly, she could not trust him after she risked everything by relying on the magic in their unspoken space. He could interrogate her, but a question was already on the table. *"Who made you feel like trash? Who ruined you?"*

He had to hold her and just let her be. He had to wait for her to say what she wanted and do what she wanted without too much pressure so that she would feel safe. If she was not ready to talk about Mary, then so be it. Perhaps someone had violated her, and that's what she meant by ruined. Perhaps Lee was her knight after another man had violated her. Perhaps Lee had violated her. Or was she talking about him? Maybe she weighed their relationship as the one that ruined her. Henry made his chest her cloud; he pressed her head into it and rocked her there. "I'm right here, sweetheart. Right here, and I ain't never leaving you. I know you're hurting all because of me. I wanna make it right. I wanna make it better. Damn. I know I never should have left with her. I was weak minded. It wasn't 'til I got here that I realized I had left my whole life behind!"

"It's okay."

"I need *you*. And you need *me right now*, too." He looked down. "Viv, I had to marry her. You know that."

"No, I don't know anything."

"I'll leave her. And the only pain it'll cause me to walk out on her is the hurt it will cause her—but I wanna be with you…not her. Do I need to prove that to you?"

"No…"

"You want me, baby? I mean, you want me to be your only man?" He grabbed her shoulders. "If you do, we can stop these games and I'll take you and Mary away. I swear I will do it tonight…"

"You didn't do it then, so don't say you'll take me anywhere…"

"Tell me, Vivian. Say you want me. Once you tell me you'll be mine forever, *then* you can call me on what you think I won't do." She kept quiet. "Why won't you say it? Is it my imagination when I kiss you—what I feel?"

"No. Things are just different, now."

"You're not ruined. Whatever someone did to you is what they did, and it only makes me want to protect you, the woman I love, and regret not being there in the past. If you feel like I ruined you, then I want you to know how much I admire you, then and now. Nothing has changed about that. What's different is that I realize now that I'm in love with you, and I always will be. What's different is maybe me and you got us a li'l baby together."

"Now, wait one minute…"

"Look at me and tell me it ain't so about Mary. Straight in my eyes, Vivian." She kept quiet. "Don't do me like this, sweet girl. Please don't shut me out. If you don't wanna talk about it, then fine. But don't lie to me."

"Okay!"

"Okay, what?" He saw her bury her face in her hands in grief. He placed his hands on her hands, but did not uncover her eyes. "Here I am, Vivian. Just like I was before, I'm here again."

"Yes," she whispered.

"Yes, what?" He rubbed her fingertips for a long moment, holding his breath.

"I got pregnant . . . that night . . . the days with you." He exhaled.

"Well, I'll be damned," he said as a matter of fact, as though he knew he was holding the trump card, but could finally slam it on the table.

"That's why I married Lee so fast . . . on account of the baby. No soul knows about this. Oh Henry! I made a mess of my life! I don't want anyone to know . . . please don't tell Minnie," she cried.

"Shhh. You don't hafta say nothing no more. I know, honey. I knowed it when I first seen y'all." He moved closer to her. "Thank you for my baby, honey." Henry almost squeezed the breath out of her first, then Vivian turned to hold on to him for dear life, it seemed. Neither of them dared to move for several moments.

"What am I going to do, Henry? I never meant for you to find out this way!" He fought extremely hard to keep his emotions calm so that he could be there for her, but tears rushed to his eyes and down his cheeks anyway at the revelation. His body shuddered so violently that he had to move away so as not to smother her with his heaving. Vivian was enthralled by the warmth, sensitivity, and kindness he was showing her.

"You mean what are *we* gonna do…I'm with you, darling. Me and you—we gotta work together to make this thing right."

"I didn't want to tell you."

"I'm glad you trusted me enough to tell me, honey."

"I just don't want it to get out…"

"Ain't nobody here but us." He noted that when she smiled, it was with the absence of confidence. "Darling, I want you to know that not one day has gone by without me thinking about you. Damn, I missed you! Now, here you are with my baby."

"But I feel like I'm messing up your life!"

"Sweetheart, there's no greater love that you could've shown me."

She thought he would tell her she was too deceptive to stay in his company, and then possibly he would push her down the stairs and throw a few bags at her, telling her to get the hell out of his house. And he could do it, too, she judged. She had lied to everyone and then she brought the lie to his new family to make them all suffer. She thought he would be traumatized if he knew the truth, but his tears were of joy! It took a few minutes for him to gather his composure, but when he did, he gave her a bright, tear stained smile. She smiled back at him. This was the second time she'd seen a man cry, and Henry was that man both times. She chortled good-naturedly, kissing his tears the same way he'd kissed hers moments before. He didn't want to let her go, nor did she. So they stayed together, each receiving comforting hugs and words of encouragement. When his knees got too numb, he resorted to the floor, supported by his elbow, pulling Vivian with him. He patted her head on his chest, her ankles over his shins.

The exhilaration shared between them was intoxicating. Vivian giggled for no reason and Henry tickled her when she was already laughing. Vivian gazed at his forehead and told him she loved him. More than Lee? Yes, more, better, and stronger than Lee, she breathed. He kissed her before she could finish uttering Lee's name. Then he grabbed her cheeks in his hand, forcing her to look directly at him and he told her he loved her more than she loved him, and more than Minnie. Always more than Minnie. Always more than any other woman he'd ever known. He told her that he'd always thought she was too good to be true, but that he wanted to touch his dream today because it was so close to him.

He took her hand and led her to the many clouds and asked her which one she wanted. She pressed his fingers and told him that he could pick the cloud this time, or the moon, or the sun—would he dare want to touch the sun? Yes, he told her. Of course he wanted to touch every ray. He would brave it. Whatever she wanted, he would happily brave it. She smiled, relieved that he wouldn't judge her, and everything she said and did was okay with him. She was still special, still priceless, still the sweetest person he ever loved. And she drifted away, dreaming, and he drifted away, dreaming: Dreams so lyrical and rich that they're unbearable. Henry considered Vivian had *always* been unbearable, untouchable, priceless, and too good to be true. He could no longer think about the unbearable future, the unreachable star, the impossible dream. She was here with him. He had come to Michigan chasing a dream and his dream was left behind in Florida. But that was then. His dream had followed him, and he was thankful. Whatever the future held would be dealt with when it came, but for now, she was here. Breathlessly, he basked in the moment of her sweeter than honeysuckle nearness.

If Lee or Minnie had come home early, Henry and Vivian would have been observed in their carelessness. No one had locked the door after Lee left with Casey. The person who came unexpectedly was Robeena. They both became alert when they heard her on the porch, which was right beneath Henry's bedroom window. She was chatting loudly with a neighbor. When Vivian heard her sister's voice, she nudged Henry frantically.

"Wake up, Henry! Beena is outside!" She rose on her arms, swinging her legs away from him, escaping his love hold. His arm went immediately around her lower waist as he wrestled her back down on the floor. He propelled her to lie flat on her back, entrapping her under him. Vivian wondered if she had imagined Robeena's voice because surely Henry wouldn't behave this way if he knew Robeena was right outside! Henry's plan was to let Robeena's knocks go unanswered, which she continued to bang only for a moment, but she also tried the door.

Vivian was hysterical that he would attempt to remain together, despite the presence of their visitor. She tried, but was unable to loosen herself from his insistent hold. "Where are you going, doll? She can't get in here."

"Why not? She used to live here, so I'm sure she can still get in!" Robeena knocked again upon entering. Vivian thrashed about to make him aware that she was serious this time. He laughed at her.

"Naw, baby. She got so mad at me for telling her what time to come in that she slammed her keys at me before she moved." She was beside herself with torn emotions; first there was fear that if he thought this whole thing was so funny and didn't move away from her, Robeena was going to catch them together. Then, too, she was disturbed because she figured his selfishness paralleled and even surpassed hers.

As soon as he rolled partially away, she scurried off. Robeena was already in the house by this time, calling Vivian's name. "You left the door unlocked," Vivian blindly accused Henry. She didn't wait for an answer before she dashed forward. He grabbed her arm, pulling her back. He guessed that Robeena would stay downstairs if she thought no one was home.

"I said where are you going so fast?" Vivian shook her head. "Get rid of her, doll, and then come on back to me," he hummed. He frowned at her, holding her arm toward him until she nodded "yes," that she'd be right back once Robeena left.

This meant Robeena was halfway up the stairs when Vivian came running out of Henry's bedroom wearing rumpled clothing. She pretended like she was coming out of the tiny room facing the stairs when she saw Robeena turn the corner on the staircase landing. They met eyes.

"Ahhhh!"

"Vivian!" Robeena glanced suspiciously at Henry's bedroom, knowing Minnie was at work. "Where is ev'rybody?" Vivian stuck herself in her own bedroom doorway, speaking to Robeena from behind it.

"Henry went somewhere early this morning, and Minnie left for work early, too," she answered, with the full understanding that Robeena was asking specifically about Henry. "I thought I was in the house by myself. Somebody must've left the door unlocked downstairs . . . is that how you got in?" Robeena nodded silently. She was relieved to learn that Henry was not at home. She was only marginally skeptical about Vivian's jumpy attitude because it was an absurd suggestion for Robeena to deduce that Vivian had just been in a bedroom alone with Henry. Robeena quickly suggested to herself that if Vivian *had* been alone with Henry, it would have been in innocence, of course.

"I'll be down in a minute," Vivian said, trying to sound normal.

"Hurry up." Robeena skipped back down the stairs to wait. She went to their kitchen and found herself an apple to eat. Henry went to his bed and rested on one elbow, sweat dripping from his brow. Given that Vivian had decided to say he wasn't home, he hoped she'd get rid of Robeena quickly so he wouldn't have to hide in his own house.

"I have a flesh and blood baby!" He smiled broadly as the news sank in. He wanted to leave his bedroom and tell the world about it. Henry considered the possibility of more children with Vivian, and concluded he didn't want to take any precautions to make sure that didn't happen. He told himself he must take Vivian away with him as soon as possible because he didn't want Lee raising his children. Having a family with Vivian locked her in and harnessed them together tighter than Lee's hold on her, he assessed. He put his hands under his head and laid on his back, thinking about Robeena's untimely visit.

Vivian changed clothes and went downstairs to join Robeena, whom she had only kept waiting for a few minutes. They both sat in the dining room. Robeena was beside herself when Vivian told her Lee had gone somewhere with Casey. She was beginning to suspect that her weeks of fun, romantic filled days with Casey were over because he had never stood her up before today.

"We gotta do something fun together, too, Viv. Them mens think they can just hit it while we remain behind. Hell naw! Let's do a jig tonight."

"I know you're not talking about hanging out at a bar!" Robeena looked at her as though going to a bar was the most natural thing in the world for them to do. "Girl, you know I can't hang out like that with you," Vivian continued, answering her sister's expression.

"Why not?" Robeena asked. Your husband ain't got no qualms about hanging out all the time." Vivian didn't know what to say to this truth. The only time she had experienced any resemblance to a club was when Lee had taken her to a house party, or two. Never had she ventured out on her own, or with any other person.

"I don't know, Beena." Although Vivian had meditated about hanging out on him before, she didn't think the opportunity would ever present itself.

"Girl, how is you gonna say that? You ain't allowed to hang out with your own sister? That man dogging you out, girl. Lee does what the hell he wants, and he don't never ask for your opinion about squat. But you gotta find out whether it's okay with 'im for you to have a li'l bit of fun." Vivian still didn't look convinced. "You know he'll tell you that you can't go nowhere. Come on, girl. It's Saturday, too! Even Henry done gone out this morning, with his boring self," she reminded her, "and you gonna deny yourself?" Robeena thought for a fleeting second of how much livelier Henry had become since Vivian's emergence.

Vivian thought about how jealous Lee used to get whenever they went out together where other men were. She knew he'd go berserk if she mentioned that the thought crossed her mind to even consider going out with Robeena. She knew the only way she could dream of going was if he wasn't home whenever she left. She wanted to defy him, but she had never done something so bold before, hence, she wasn't certain of the effect it would have on him. Vivian hated herself for being so cowardly, given that she knew he would stay out all night if the urge beseeched him. Why wouldn't he? Lee hadn't experienced any speakable repercussions for his behavior to prevent him from doing exactly as he pleased. He decided that if Vivian was going to leave him, she would have done so a long time ago.

"I just don't want to get in any fights, Beena."

"You shouldn't let him beat you like that, Viv." Lee had already slapped her three or four times since their arrival. Robeena knew about some of his harsh treatment from Minnie, but it was hard to get Vivian to discuss the details. The worst fight since they'd come to Michigan was when she had poured Minnie, as well as Henry a glass of freshly squeezed orange juice.

After she had served the two of them, she got a glass for Lee. Lee didn't say anything about it. In fact, he laughed and joked with everyone for an hour before expressing his longing to exit with his wife. Once they arrived in their bedroom, however, he let Vivian have it for pouring his juice last. Vivian was so ashamed of being struck physically by her husband that she remained in the bedroom for the remainder of the evening. That was the start of Vivian becoming so withdrawn, even whenever Lee left the house. Since then, Vivian resorted to remaining in the bedroom whenever he left so as not to arouse his cynicism, or just to keep the peace.

Vivian could have hibernated in their bedroom all winter, and Lee still would've suspected something was amuck. This is because he knew deep down, where his self-accusing spirit was buried, that there was a season coming when he would have to pay for his own infidelities. He thought if he could control Vivian, he could avoid God's chastisement. She was the only person or thing, he believed, who could cause him pain because his heart was in her hands. Still, since there were no immediate repercussions that he could measure, he decided to take his chances at living his life worry free.

It was midafternoon, and Lee was exhausted from taking gambling tips from Casey all day long. His lovely wife was on his mind. Casey invited him to hang out with him later at a club on Woodward Avenue. Lee presently had the mind to leave Casey and return home to his wife. He savored going home not because he loved or respected Vivian, but for an instant, Lee pictured the well-toned, 6"2, 225 pounds of solid muscle named Henry all alone with Vivian; he knew Minnie was at work today, and he didn't know what time Henry might make it back home. The image of Henry looking at Vivian with lust sent chills up and down Lee's spine.

Lee was unnerved by the fact that he knew he couldn't treat Vivian any kind of way in Henry's presence. Not only would Henry disapprove, but he would also have the overconfidence to speak out openly against it. Lee remembered with uneasiness the way Henry had glared at him when he'd grabbed Vivian by the arm. "She belongs to me," Lee consoled himself, "ain't no 'nother man gonna tell me what I can and can't do with my wife." With that thought, Lee decided he was being silly to worry about Vivian right now. He knew if push came to shove, he would simply take Vivian to their bedroom and slap her around for a while -that always had an effect on her disobedience problem. If he hadn't learned anything else at church, he learned a woman was supposed to obey her husband.

No matter how many times he physically abused her, he never wanted to get used to doing it, though, because it sometimes nauseated him to even think of knocking her down. He wished things wouldn't have to come to that, but he knew of no other way to get his point across at times. Lee was saddened to conclude that he would have to deal with Vivian when he got home because of the probability that *maybe* Vivian hadn't stayed in the bedroom all day as was expected of her when he wasn't home. This was not something he could simply ignore. What about the possibility that she may have looked back at Henry with the yearning Lee knew Henry had for her?

"Nah, he ain't got the balls to take up with my wife," Lee said to himself, shrugging off his caginess once again.

"He got some balls to leave me here with his wife," Henry mumbled as he heard Robeena preparing to leave. He listened for the sound of Vivian's soft steps coming back up the stairs, but they never came. After ten minutes, Henry got up to go downstairs after her. He called her name, looking out the front door, with his body well hidden behind the old wood. He could see Robeena standing on the corner talking to a man and a lady. Quickly, he stuck his head back inside, honoring the lie Vivian had told concerning his whereabouts.

Henry searched the rooms downstairs without finding Vivian. He even looked in the closets for her. He figured maybe she had stepped into the back yard, but the back door was still chained. Shortly, he heard noises in the basement, but he doubted if he would find her in that cold place, yet, he went down to the lower level, anyway, searching behind boxes and baskets of clothes. Henry looked beyond the stairs to spot her feet sticking purposefully out from behind the furnace.

"Vivian! Come from 'round yonder! I see you o'er yonder." He wasn't sure what to make of her hide and seek game.

"I'm not coming," she answered solemnly. He stopped short, wondering what Robeena and she had talked about that made her so upset that she behaved like a small child. He walked closer to her.

"What's wrong, honey? What did you and Beena talk about?"

"What's wrong is I told you earlier to stay away from me. You aren't listening to me. Beena doesn't know, but people are going to find out about Mary if you don't cut it out."

"I'm sorry," he said simply. Henry took a seat next to her on the floor, but when he experienced how cold and dusty the floor was, he got back up immediately.

"You didn't even take heed when Beena came, either! She could've caught us together, you know," Vivian said, trying to hide her passion.

"Caught us what? We wasn't doing nothing wrong, Viv."

"How can you say that? You know it was wrong."

"What? Falling asleep with you in my arms? Loving you will never be wrong in my eyes."

"If it's not right, then it's wrong," she confessed.

"Being there for you *is* right."

"My clothes looked like I had just gotten into a fight with somebody. That's how Beena saw me when I came out of your room."

"Sorry, honey." He stroked her face with the back of his hand.

"How did we end up like this today, Henry? I mean, we haven't seen each other in months!" She put her head down. "I thought it was over between us."

"We have a family."

"You don't mind having a child?"

"I guess seeing how lovely Mary is, I wouldn't mind us having two beautiful babies…or three, or four if you act right." He made a smirk at her.

"This isn't a game, Henry. If others were to find out about Mary, they'd know what they can never know. Babies don't just fall out of the sky, Henry. I told you I was trying to put all that behind me. But you keep stirring up the past. I told you I didn't want to go upstairs, but you took me, anyway. I told you to leave me alone, but you kept at it! And I told you down South, too." Her objective was to excuse her own part in all wrong doings.

She wanted Henry more than she would even admit to herself. As such, she aimed to make him think that the whole thing was his fault, not hers. She set out to convince them both that what had taken place between them was like rape of sorts. He had forced her. Thus, she rationalized the truth so that the sin in which she was partaking would be more acceptable to God. This was easier than wrestling with the weakness of her flesh. In this way as well, she could partially live out what Floyd had done to her without facing it.

"You're right, honey," he submitted. "Come here. Let's get out of this dusty basement." She hoped by his saying that she was right, he didn't mean he would stop his advances. Therefore, she stood up at his command, letting him know nonverbally that she would indeed heed his requests of her. She waited patiently for him to make another demand. Henry took her hand and led her up out of the basement, through the front room, and back up the stairs. He led her to where Mary was sleeping soundly in the small, exquisitely carved bed he had made for her. Henry proceeded as though casually entering Lee's bedroom with Vivian was normal. He was with his child and the woman he loved. His aura caused a serene calm over Vivian, also, as she leaned over Mary, pointing to her tiny fingers and toes as though Henry had never seen the baby before.

"Isn't she beautiful, Henry?"

"Yes. Vivian?"

"Hmm?"

"This here is my child? Really?" He squeezed her hand, hoping what she spoke earlier wouldn't disappear.

"Yeah, she's yours." She smiled at him warmly, squeezing his hand back.

"Why did you have *my* child, Vivian?"

"What do you mean by that?"

"I mean, didn't you ever think about trying to get rid of it?" She pouted.

"I mean, since you was gonna marry Lee and all."

"That thought never crossed my mind, Henry." She turned sideways to face him. They embraced each other for a long while, each engaged in their own private thoughts. Vivian pondered on how she could continue to enjoy Henry's attention and love without causing a problem for Minnie and Lee. She liked the way Henry loved her. Where Lee was abrasive and inconsiderate, Henry was soothing and thoughtful. While Lee was hasty, Henry forced patience in himself and in her. When Lee would strike her, she wished for the warm arms and the comfort of Henry. Still, she was tied to Lee because he was familiar to her, thus she let herself love him. In addition, she noted his potential to be a great man and a devoted husband, one day.

Vivian allowed herself to trust Henry more because he showed her an example of kindness, although it was foreign to her. She was afraid of her love for Henry. He thought as he held her how he was afraid of her, too. At least, he used to be afraid of her. When he first saw her, he was afraid of her beauty, afraid to love such a delicate, wildflower. Now, though, he was willing to settle for having a lifelong affair with her, under the circumstances. He wanted more children with her, he wanted regular intimacy, and he wanted to be a father to their children, and a husband figure to her. Henry was frustrated with how subservient he thought Vivian was to Lee. He rated himself as caring more for her than her own husband, and willing to do more to make her happy. He felt inferior that perhaps Vivian did not share the same view about him. Resentment formed heavily in him when he faced that he was married to a woman whom he didn't truly passionately love, and moreover, the woman he thought he loved was already married. This suffocated Henry whenever he dwelled on it.

Before Vivian moved to Michigan with Lee, Henry lived in a zombie world, doing only those things he deemed necessary for day-to-day existence. He was prepared to continue in this matter for the rest of his life because of his idea of commitment to marriage and family. He held no hope that life would ever offer more to him than what he currently was receiving. God had given him a wonderful wife. He considered his blessings the opportunity of a lifetime when he'd moved away from the oppressive South to the pseudo-progressive North in pursuit of his dreams. He dreamed of the day he could go back down South without Minnie to visit his parents and to find Vivian again, but the chance to do that had never materialized beyond a silent prayer.

Now that Vivian had arrived, a glimpse of happiness shot before his eyes. Unfortunately, Lee was quick to remind Henry that his forged happiness belonged to another man. Henry's feelings of carnage were thus directed at Lee. Henry found himself looking for excuses to throttle Lee. Oh, how he hated him! He envisioned Lee walking in the house with a smug look on his face, and the smell of some whore's perfume on his shirt. He despised how Lee expected Vivian to be in their bedroom waiting for him whenever he returned home from exploring the deviant women in the neighborhood and throughout Pontiac.

Henry wanted to injure Lee. That's why deep down, he didn't mind if Robeena *would* have caught him holding Vivian—he wanted others to know he was not trapped in a private hell, but that his life was exciting and filled with dreams, too. The only thing that held him back was Minnie. He had no reason or motive to slight her in any way, specifically after he'd promised her a lifetime of joy, even though deep down he felt she had forced him to marry her. She had to know he didn't love her. His hunger to feel whole and to defeat Lee overshadowed his conscious thoughts of whether he was crushing Minnie already. Now, Henry saw that the zenith destruction for Lee would be the discovery that the baby he thought was his belonged to another man. Henry calculated Lee's physical prowess to be subordinate to his own.

What difference would it make, then, if Lee himself witnessed Henry and Vivian together locked in an intimate clasp? What could he do? He fantasized about his pinnacle high: Lee tied to a chair, mouth gagged while Henry held her under his tight grasp. He would tell Lee that she was *his* woman, and that he would break him in half if he came near her again. Then he would look at Lee while he held Vivian and tell Lee the truth about Mary's paternity. When Lee would struggle fiercely to get loose, Minnie would come bursting through the door. Henry would tell Minnie that she had nothing to do with his love for Vivian, and that he loved Vivian before he ever knew her name. Yes: He could blame Minnie and make her pay, too, in the apex of his fantasies because how could she not know that he loved Vivian? They could put on forever, but a woman knows, he thought.

He contemplated his religious upbringing that was so strict under his mother's watch. Based on her truths, he theorized that surely God would forgive him if he continued to commit adultery because Jesus had already died for his sins. And, he did love Vivian.

"Vivian?" Mary stirred this time at the sound of her father's voice. They tiptoed backward out of the room, keeping their eyes on her to make sure she didn't become restless. Once they reached Henry's bedroom, Henry asked, "What if Lee caught us together like this? Me holding you?" She laughed factually, as if Henry should know the answer to that question.

"I'd be dead meat, that's what," she answered.

"I wouldn't let 'im hurt you none, honey, no matter what." She smiled weakly, shaking her head hastily. "I wouldn't! Long as I'm here, you ain't never gotta worry 'bout 'im. Even if he finds out about Mary, I'll stand up for you, and I'll tell the world—even Minnie—that she is my child." He cupped her chin as if to force her to believe him. "I'll be there for you, Vivian."

"He'll never find out the truth, Henry. I never want him to know about Mary."

"What if I tell 'im myself?"

"You wouldn't do that." He smiled mischievously. "Stop saying that. Henry, don't even joke about it. Promise me right now that you'll keep…"

"Why should I make a promise like that? That's my baby and you're my woman."

"Henry!"

He shrugged. "The truth is gonna come out *one* day. You want me to lie to my own daughter like she ain't mine? You think I'm gonna watch her calling another niggah 'daddy' for the rest of my life while I know?"

"You need to be careful, Henry. You wanted to know so badly, and now you are saying things about what we did that was supposed to be private. And you're saying stuff out of selfishness. You're not thinking about me, Minnie, or how your words can hurt other people."

"I know, baby. All I'm saying is one day—or one year—could be years from now, but we may not be able to hide something like this forever. *You may want to tell Mary the truth one day.*"

"Well, I don't need this to get back to Lee. You make me nervous with that kind of talk, honey."

"I'll tell you what—he'll never lay another hand on you as long as I'm alive."

"You can't stop him from . . ." He waited expectantly for her to finish. After a few seconds, he realized he could finish the sentence for her.

"Beating you?" He asked. She shifted and pretended to listen to Mary's cooing. Henry cupped her face with both of his hands. "Don't tell me that blockhead is still beating on you." Henry prayed she would answer in the negative, notwithstanding Lee's foolhardiness would bring him one step closer to being able to take Vivian from Lee, Henry thought. Certainly, Lee didn't have the impudence to hit Vivian while he was there. Gradually, his mouth dropped. Idiot, idiot, idiot! Henry chided himself. Of course Lee was still physically abusive! All the signs were there the same as before. Why else would Vivian change so completely from the high-spirited girl he'd met on the plantation to such a dastardly, agitated creature? And what did he *think* Lee would do next, after he viciously grabbed Vivian's arms?

Vivian couldn't wait to reveal Lee's violence to Henry. She wanted to finally get it off her chest, and to know it was not her fault. She knew Henry would make her feel better about things. He would marvelously heal her self-esteem. Henry moved stiffly to his bed holding one of her hands. Slumped over, he sat, and pulled her down with him. She rested her mind in his strong hold.

Everything was okay for her, now. Henry knew about it. He was her savior. He was her god, for he was the only one in whom she sought refuge. What Henry said was right was what she accepted. She depended on the belief that Henry could make everything better. Even if she drifted to sleep next to Henry right in her sister's bed, somehow, she figured, Henry would take care of everything. He would prevent her sins from reaching another god.

"I don't like this, Vivian," he said quietly, cupping her chin again, "if I see you with one scratch on your face, I'm coming after him."

"Henry! That's not . . ."

"No, I mean it. Don't you dare expect me to stand idly by and watch no mess like that." He caressed her chin using his two middle fingers. "I oughta whip him anyway. Baby, you just say the word, and I'll beat his narrow ass."

"Henry, I don't want anything like that, do you hear?" He looked on like a neglected puppy being deprived of a bone.

"Yeah, whatever." Goosebumps covered her body at the notion of Henry wanting to fight over her. How special! She didn't want Henry and Lee to fight over her, but the thought that he would be willing to go through such lengths on her behalf was spine-tingling. She never wanted to leave him—he made her feel like she was on top of the world—as though *he* could prepare a table for her in the presence of her enemies.

Nonetheless, she knew her time left with him was short due to the other intruders who lived in their home, she mused to herself with a silent laugh. She glanced past him out the window at the bright afternoon sky. She could see the leaves waving from the big oak tree in the front yard. The sun was moving across the horizon, shadowed by the branches.

"It's around four o: clock, Henry. Won't Minnie be here at five?" He nodded reluctantly, allowing her to untie herself from his enfold and walk away from the bed. He got up and followed her to the bedroom door. "Beena is supposed to be coming later so that the two of us can go somewhere. He'll have a fit if I'm gone when he gets back, especially if I go to a nightspot like Beena wants to do."

"A club ain't no place for you, girl. Single, loose women are what be there." He caught her from behind, pulling her to a halt while he made his statements. "Lots of drinking and carrying on up in them places. I know you don't drink and do all that clowning. Whatchu wanna be around that stuff for?" He kissed her hair. Henry couldn't help himself from thinking about how delightful it would be if Vivian was in fact gone to a social club when Lee got back, though. "And I don't care if you ever provoke him, whether it be by going out or anything else, I'm gonna whip 'im if he lay a hand on you, Vivian." Although Henry wasn't keen at all on the idea of Vivian going out with Robeena, under the circumstances, he decided the results would be worth it.

"Henry, you don't think I should go?" She asked hopefully.

"I guess just this one time will be alright, Vivian." She was disappointed by Henry's permissiveness. She wanted Henry to tell her no, that he would not allow the woman he loved in such a sordid place. Vivian felt cheated when she surmised that Henry would never permit Minnie to go club hopping. She pouted as he embraced her once again before she left him. As she prepared herself to receive Robeena, she could hear Henry washing himself and singing at the same time. Then, he went downstairs and started dinner for his wife.

Vivian was thoroughly daunted. The green monster of envy had completely taken over her. Minnie came into the house at 5:10, and found her husband humming to himself in the kitchen. At that time, Vivian needed more reassurance from the man she worshiped as a god besides God. She wanted Henry to pay special attention to her in the presence of Minnie—not so that Minnie could detect anything, but a secret wink would suffice. She walked stealthily into the kitchen to greet Minnie. To her dismay, however, Henry failed to glance in her direction, even when Minnie left the kitchen for a minute. Henry was afraid to look because he felt his love for her would be written all over his face for Minnie to see. Even when Minnie stepped out of the kitchen, Henry didn't believe he would have enough time to smile at Vivian and have the sentiment and desire vanished by the time Minnie might appear again.

Nevertheless, a dejected Vivian retreated to her bedroom. She decided she would fix Lee and Henry both. Vivian took special care in bathing herself for the second time that day. She used Madam Walker's Wonderful Hair Grower to oil her scalp, and then she brushed her hair over and over, until it shined like soft silk. She went to her closet to retrieve the daring dress Madeline had given her as a wedding present, and wriggled into it. She took two hours to perfect herself to her liking, but when she was ready, she looked very appetizing for the nightlife scene.

Vivian stayed in her room until she heard Robeena come over at seven. She strolled downstairs, pretending not to notice Henry's gaping stare out of the corner of her eye as she sashayed past him in the front room, on her way to the kitchen. Minnie and Robeena were sipping some Indonesian tea that Minnie had stolen from her employer, Mrs. Miller. They stopped their conversation immediately when they saw their middle sister shimmering seductively.

"Girl, girl, girl, girl, girl! Are you trying to make a statement or something?" Robeena asked excitedly. Vivian took two paces toward them, then spun around and took a deep curtsy. She could see Henry's knees leveled with her eyes from her bowed position after he came following her to the doorway of the kitchen. He stood in the archway with one of his hands on his hip, and the other one perched high on the doorway wall.

"No statement, I just want to look my best for my first night out on the town," she said, spinning again, laughing.

"Well, you are so accomplishing that, my sister," Robeena piped. "Ain't she fine, Henry? What's the man's perspective?" She asked teasingly, looking enthusiastically at Henry. Because Robeena had caught him off guard, he did a lousy job of hiding the disapproval on his face and in his voice.

"Depends on what she's trying to represent," he blurted. Minnie looked at him and shook her head in a silent warning that he should not insult her sister, but secretly, she was happy for Henry to show displeasure in Vivian.

Vivian couldn't resist smiling slyly at him. "What's the matter, Henry, you don't like my dress?" Vivian asked mockingly. He rolled his eyes at her and left the room. He wanted her to go out and show Lee a thing or two, but he didn't know she was going to dress so immodestly. He couldn't believe how tight her dress was! He reminded himself of why he hadn't wanted her to be his girl in the first place. He wished he and Vivian were alone together so he could rip that dress right off her.

"Whoa! What's his problem, Minnie?"

"I don't know. I think he's just bored, me being at work all day, leaving him at home doing nothing on a nice Saturday like this," Minnie speculated. "He ain't used to going nowhere, so I reckon he can't expect nobody else to get dressed and go nowhere, either. It sure would be nice if we could join y'all." Robeena looked thoughtful. "But ain't no sense in asking him 'cause Henry don't like that type of atmosphere with all that drinking and carrying on. Me, neither."

"He can't be too bored, 'cause he didn't stay home today," Robeena offered.

"Humph. I don't know why you say that. Henry only got one pair of shoes, which I took to work with me to have Mrs. Miller's husband repair 'em at his shoe store for church tomorrow. Henry ain't been nowhere today. Why you think he was gone?" Robeena looked at Vivian with uncertainty. Vivian seemed preoccupied playing with a small flower on the sleeve of her dress.

"I just reckoned he was gone this morning." Robeena glanced back and forth from Minnie to Vivian, expecting further explanation from either of them . . . preferably from Vivian. Henry came back into the kitchen from the front room where he had stowed himself away momentarily, and without looking at anyone, grabbed a pear, only to leave again. This time, he went stomping upstairs.

"Well, Beena, we need to leave before Lee gets back," Vivian suggested. Minnie was a bit uneasy at the open mention of Lee coming home to an empty room. Vivian saw the concerned look on her face, but chose to ignore it so as not to cause any further delays. "Mary should be waking up shortly, Minnie, and when she does, she's going to be hungry. I left some milk over there on the ice." Minnie stared for a moment.

"Where am I 'posed to tell Lee you at when he gets here?"

Vivian contemplated silently. "Tell him I went out looking for him." She giggled, grabbing her soft Cashmere sweater that was a present from Gancy, even though she'd told Lee that she'd gotten it on sale at Hudson's. She knew Lee wouldn't understand that Gancy was just nice like that. "Yes. Tell him I was troubled because I haven't heard from him all day, so I got worried and went on to the clubs and all to see if anybody heard from or seen him." Robeena and Vivian laughed wildly and headed out into the awaiting lust of the night.

By 2:00 a.m., Lee wasn't sure he hadn't bit off more than he could chew. It was clear to him then that Casey was in fact a pimp, not just some street hustler or player. Pimping was how Casey sustained himself. Earlier, when 10:00 p.m. came, Casey and Lee were sitting at the bar inside of a lounge on Woodward Avenue having light conversation. A tall, slender, dark-skinned woman wearing a blond wig came in, sat two stools down from them and lit a cigarette. It was the first time Lee had ever seen a woman smoke in public. He was repulsed. Lee studied that the woman was obviously a streetwalker, based on her sleazy clothing. Shawl in hand, she wore a short gold glittering dress that clung to her body like a pair of stockings.

Lee imagined his wife's nice clean breath as he watched the woman blow circles with the smoke. He thought that Vivian was surely sleeping soundly by now. He was happy to think she would never put a cigarette to her mouth, and never would she wear such bewitched clothing. Lee didn't connect that the woman wearing the blonde wig had anything at all to do with Casey. Fifteen minutes later, another slim woman with a high styled hairdo took up the stool next to the first woman. The man who occupied the seat she needed vacated it promptly. Lee watched the hookers in fascination.

After a few minutes, Casey, who had remained nonchalant during the entire entrance of the prostitutes, excused himself quietly and walked casually to the women. Lee saw them pull a wad of money from their bosoms and hand it to Casey, who counted every bill carefully. Then, the two women left together, switching their behinds in the air. Casey walked back over to where Lee sat and continued their conversation as though the episode with the prostitutes had never taken place.

An hour later at 11:00, a half-breed woman came in and stood in Casey's view, but like the first women, did not approach him. In an apparent show of power and control, Lee guessed, Casey ignored her for twenty minutes before calling her over to him. She walked casually to her pimp, looking from side to side at who might be watching her in the club, wanting her services. Again, he took money and sent her back out into the night. Lee became frightened. What if a police officer saw this very fair skinned women whoring for a Negro? Casey was surely walking death.

It wasn't like Lee was so innocent, but the prostitutes he was familiar with usually hid themselves in a house and locked themselves in a bedroom until they got that special knock. These women were parading publicly down America's streets like harlots. Lee felt intimidated when he desperately tried to figure out what his wife's sister was doing with a man like this. Lee knew he was way out of his league and suddenly felt like a small boy. However, Casey didn't volunteer any information to Lee about his transactions with the women, so Lee was able to slowly digest everything without vomiting.

At 12:00 a.m., the women returned together, including another bright skinned, pretty, small boned woman Lee had never seen before. Lee followed helplessly as Casey led his stable from the bar, all of them climbing into Casey's Ford. The small boned woman forced Lee to scoot next to Casey when she followed him into the front seat. Casey drove south on Woodward Avenue to a motel a short way down the road. A room was already registered to one of the ladies. They all claimed an area inside--Casey sat in a comfortable lounge chair, Lee took a desk chair, and all the women tossed themselves onto the bed.

Before long, Lee's feelings of intimidation turned to that of importance in the company of Casey and the women. Casey laughed and patted him on the back several times on the way to the motel, contributing to Lee's replaced emotions. He told the ladies to be "nice" to Lee. They smiled knowingly, each one taking long cigarette drags. Casey put his cigarette out in an ashtray on the old, over-used wooden end table on the left side of the bed. Then, he went over to the chest of drawers and pulled the bottom drawer out all the way. Folded neatly in a pillowcase was a long, sharp-edged knife in a brown leather holster. Casey swiftly removed the knife from the holster and held it up for all to admire. Lee licked his lips at the beauty of the souvenir. Casey walked slowly to Lee for effect, carrying the knife in both hands. When he reached him, he extended the gift to Lee, who gladly accepted it.

"I'm giving you this, man, 'cause I trust you. I'm gonna teach you how to fight right and good one day, okay? If I ever leave you with my stash, you'll need to know how to lay down the law."

"Wow!" Lee exclaimed. "This is the first time I ever done had something this nice. You can trust me with it, Case! I mean, I ain't no dummy. I'm a hard-core southern man." He nodded his head toward the ladies, "I know to look after everything that needs looking after." The ladies all giggled, but Casey gave him a stern look, appraising him all the while.

"That's right, man. You take care of me, and I'll take care of you." They looked each other in the eyes for a good minute. Lee felt an unfamiliar surge of power rush through his veins as he held the weapon. His adrenalin almost rushed through his pores. With the knife, he felt he was the man. He was in control now. All his life he had been searching for some sense of control, only, he didn't know where to find it. Now, he knew. With this weapon, he could subdue people and dominate them. He idolized Casey for showing him the way. Many of his apprehensions flew out the window as he held the power in his hand. Casey didn't know the thought processes that were going on inside of Lee, but he could read the appreciation in Lee's eyes. He looked at Sandra, nodding her in the direction of Lee. The small, pretty woman sauntered over to Lee, and took his hand.

"Can I have this toy, daddy?" she asked Casey, teasingly. Lee was intimidated again, but this time by a woman for the first time. Forgetting about the power he'd just felt earlier, he removed her hand quickly, but not roughly, afraid to enrage Casey. The other women looked on with gaiety.

Casey said, "I guess you can, Sandra, if the toy needs someone to play with it." He looked at Lee with a cunning smile. "Go 'head, man! That's one of my best ladies!" Everyone laughed at Lee's uneasy expression. The tallest woman, Barbara, took a small pipe out of her purse and deposited a moderate portion of dry, small leaves from a plastic bag which was also in her purse into the pipe. Two pipes of the marijuana were now going around after the half-breed woman started one, along with the bottle of whiskey Casey whipped out of his suit coat inside pocket. Everyone participated gladly. Lee had smoked marijuana before in Florida with his father at times, and with Floyd and Hamilton, too, but those times were rare. Sandra, after noticing Lee's newfound ease, slithered back to him. This time, he was much more receptive. He laid his gift down on the table and balled his fists tightly at his side, enjoying the presence of the strange woman, without yet taking a more active role. Casey clicked the lamplight off, and left with two of the women. "You owe me, man!" At that moment, Lee didn't care what price he had to pay.

CHAPTER EIGHTEEN
Robeena and Casey

By midnight, Vivian was begging Robeena to leave the music joint. There was a local music group who kept the patrons entertained, and Vivian danced several times with men who asked her, but she visualized her poor husband pacing the floor at home, wondering where his wife had gone. She figured Lee must have learned his lesson by now, and she didn't want to overdo it by staying out too late. There was an intriguing, bearded man named Bruno who had been watching Vivian all evening. He had spoken to her a few times, even danced with her, but she seemed distant in her demeanor toward him, so he backed off his advances to give her space. After Vivian had danced to three songs in a row with Bruno, she hurried off to be with Robeena, who had just made it back to their seating area.

"Do you think he's cute?" Robeena asked as Vivian removed her shawl and sat next to her. The sisters had to raise their voices slightly to hear each other.

"Who?" Vivian asked innocently.

"That man you were dancing with." Robeena smirked. "You know who I mean. What's his name?"

"Bruno. Girl, no!" They both laughed. "But he does have a puppy dog look...more dog than puppy. He ain't nearby as fine as Lee."

"Screw Lee."

"You talk like a middle-aged, drunk man, Robeena." They both stared at the men and women on the dance floor.

"Viv, why do you let him treat you like that?"

Vivian sighed. "I don't know."

"I mean, you never seemed like the type to let a man beat on you, Viv. That seems more like something Minnie would do." They both laughed.

"It's not as bad as you're trying to make it seem. He doesn't hit me all the time like you think. I only told Minnie about one time since we've been up here that we got in a fight."

"Please. The *first* time a man puts his hands on me will be the last. I can guarantee you that much." Robeena took the last swig of her rum and ordered another one. "He can't love and respect you if he's gotta do all that,

Viv."

"It's deeper than what you can ever imagine."

"So, why'd he beat you like that down South? *He* was the one that got caught sleeping around!"

"You're not a li'l kid, Beena. Daddy hit mama, and I don't see you questioning her like you're questioning me."

"I was never a kid. A kid is a goat. You should know that with your fake, proper talking ass."

"I'm not fake. You know daddy has hit mama."

"Get real."

"*You* get real."

"Are you that dumb?" She wiped her drooling mouth with her thumb. "You'd better do something about that fool. Henry can't save you forever."

"What?"

"Don't even try it, Viv."

"Henry has never saved me from anything."

"You went running to him down South after Lee whipped you. You stayed o'er with him for two days. Say you didn't."

"I did no such thing. Henry took *me* to his place." Vivian put her hand up to stop Robeena from interrupting. "But that was only because Master Kent Johnson's son and his gang of hillbillies were making mischief, preventing us from passing on Johnson Lane."

"Damn."

"Yeah." Vivian decided it was necessary to sip from her wine glass. "Then he took me to see Tazra."

"I hope you know how that looked, though," Robeena commented.

"That time…it was crazy, Beena. I felt like I could talk to Henry, and he was the only one there. It only made matters worse, anyway. I just needed some time to myself after what Lee did to me. He's jealous of Henry, you know. When we got to Lee's house after church, he tried to twist the whole thing, too, like Henry was involved. He thinks Henry's sweet on me. I could never tell him that I stayed over at his place. You don't need to be bringing that up, either."

"How do you think Minnie felt about you being at Henry's all that time?"

"She never said. Besides, I told you I was at Tazra's place."

"That's a lie. Plus, Minnie told you to your face that you better not chase after her man again."

"I never chased after a man. Why would you ask what Minnie thought if you already had the answer?"

"I was just trying to jar your memory, 'cause it seems like you forgot.

Was he home earlier today or not?"

"What's wrong with you, Beena? Here I am out here trying to have a suitable time, and you're trying to start some shit. All I was saying is that Minnie and I never had any real conversation about it, 'cause it was a non-issue. You have no cause to bring up the past."

"It was a scandal, Viv. As many times as you and her used to fuss about boys, what makes you think she would want her man taking care of you all because you let yourself get beat up? Get real."

"Well, she never said. It was no big deal, Beena, so stop trying to make it into one."

"Girl, you better wake up. You're gonna find out that Henry's more trouble than he's worth." Robeena was speaking with a drunken slur.

"Why would you keep harping about Henry when he has nothing to do with this? Never mind. Don't answer. I see you're just picking at straws, trying to find out stuff that is none of your concern. You have always been like that, Beena."

"All right, Viv," she said, smashing her drink down on the bar.

"Robeena! You're fixing to get all of us put out of here! You are acting all drunk and carrying on."

"Trust me—I've held down more liquor than this before…"

"You're about to get the owner in trouble with the law! We're in a non-drinking establishment, and you're getting wasted. If the police are outside whenever we leave, they could take you to jail!"

Robeena ordered another rum and coke. "I ain't gonna say nothing else about it, since you're so stubborn."

"That's best, Beena. I didn't come out here for this, no how. I told you I was ready to leave."

"It's not even one o'clock yet. I got you out here to help you, Viv. You just might can't be helped, like Minnie been trying to say." Vivian wanted to leave Robeena right there on the stool getting drunk, but she didn't want to walk home alone, nor did she want to leave Robeena in the condition she was making for herself.

Robeena, having minimal solace for Lee, finally relented at 1:15 a.m. "I ain't going nowhere else with you no more, bitch," Robeena sneered.

Vivian hissed at her sister. "You are one to talk! Keeping me up in that place all this time," she whimpered. "You know I need to get home!" Vivian was almost in tears.

"Aw, girl. Be quiet," Robeena said unsympathetically, "it ain't even 2:00 yet. Thought you were 'posed to be letting Lee know how it feels when his wife hangs out like he does. So don't go home acting like you ain't have no good time, neither." Vivian pouted. She could never face Lee as though she was jubilant about hanging out in a place where other men were. She now felt that going out with Robeena was a grave mistake. Bruno saw Vivian was leaving with her sister with no escort or protection. He shook his head at how careless they were, knowing the racial climate given that a second, huge wave of the Ku Klux Klan had been the constant talk among Black citizens in the nearby counties. Robeena, oblivious to the world outside of her own desires, did not fear walking home alone. She felt invincible and ready to conquer her dreams. She could have easily obtained a paying companion, but her mission on that night was to show Vivian a good time.

Bruno caught up with the sisters just before they made it outside. He walked step in step on Vivian's right side. The semi-moist, warm July wind was whistling harshly at the trio. Gently, he took Vivian's shawl from her arm and placed it over her shoulders. He motioned his jacket to Robeena, but she wasn't paying attention. Right away, Robeena noticed his Salvatore Ferragamo platform shoes were created from leather and the soles were of sound rubber. Vivian giggled unrestrained, inebriated from all the wine she had drank that evening. He slipped his arm around Vivian's waist at her apparent invitation. Robeena was perfectly comfortable with the atmosphere, given that this scene was all too familiar to her. However, Vivian spun around, unwinding his arm from her side, and danced to walk on the other side of Robeena.

"Men actually touch women they don't know up here, Beena?" She brushed her clothes off where he had touched her, as though swatting away nasty flies. An image of the little Caucasian girl at the train depot flashed before Vivian. She wanted to seem prim, white, and proper to Bruno. Robeena was sorry for Bruno that her sister was so lacking in her social skills.

"Vivian, don't be so stuck-up if we're gonna hang together." Bruno appreciated Robeena's comment, but was wary about touching Vivian again. He felt remorseful and concluded that she had every right to respond in such a manner. Bruno was out trying to have an enjoyable time and also to find a decent lady friend. He didn't hang out much at all, and he didn't really know where he could find a mate. He wasn't picky. He wanted someone whom he could love, and who would love him back. Putting his arm around Vivian's waist was what he thought was the appropriate thing to do upon meeting a nice lady at a club, although he was shy about doing it, anyway.

Vivian was startled that Robeena could say what she deemed such encouraging words to the man when Robeena knew Vivian wasn't attracted to him, as they had discussed this in the club. At least Robeena's winks gave Bruno the courage to try again, this time without touching her. He tipped his hat to Vivian, grinning broadly.

"May I have the pleasure of escorting you home? I think I told you my name earlier. It's Bruno." Vivian was flattered by Bruno's offer, but she feared Lee might be waiting outside in the shadows, and she certainly didn't want to risk Lee seeing her with Bruno. Robeena was concentrating on the old-fashioned "John Bull" straw top hat Bruno wore that must have cost a fortune. Then her eyes were trained to the sparkly light glowing in the darkness illuminating from the diamond ring on his pinky finger. Robeena calculated that this man would best suit her purposes, rather than Vivian's, anyway. Casey was flashy, but too flamboyant with a ghetto style that took a distant second to Bruno's polished class.

"She's too shy," Robeena replied, answering for Vivian. "'Sides, she got a husband at home she's trying to rush to, right, Viv?" Although she was annoyed by Robeena's declaration, nonetheless, she was relieved that Bruno now knew she was married.

"Afraid so, Bruno..." Vivian was interrupted by her disturbance at the fact that Robeena had grabbed Bruno's hand. He glanced at Vivian only for a fraction of a second before clutching Robeena's hand in return.

"But you can still walk with us, Bruno," Robeena said, insensitive to Vivian's mid-sentence halt. Vivian walked ahead of the two of them, sulking. However, she was glad that he was clearly walking with Robeena, just in case Lee was somewhere watching, waiting.

"What's a pretty lady like you doing without an escort," Bruno asked Robeena.

"Had a man just last night, but I guess he don't want me no more," Robeena said, looking boldly into Bruno's eyes. They stared at each other for a moment, until Bruno lowered his gaze. He was disappointed in himself for being the first to drop his eyes, but there was something so daring about Robeena that he couldn't help himself. Robeena was satisfied that gaining control over Bruno came so easily. The "eye stare" was a mere game she played with the various men she encountered.

She resolved to teach Casey a lesson. She knew Casey was sure to drop by her house first thing in the morning after standing her up earlier. This is because whenever they weren't together on a Saturday night, he was the first sight she saw on Sunday morning. "If he thinks I'm one of his everyday floozies, he got another thing coming," she muttered silently, unaware that those were Casey's thoughts precisely. Had she known Casey was a pimp, she wouldn't have felt so disgraced by his missed appointment with her. She would have been willing to view the relationship as business. Had she known he was a pimp, she would have politely refused his offer to pimp her.

As it stood, though, Robeena felt degraded that Casey had plainly stood her up on their morning date for no apparent reason, except that he chose to go out with Lee, instead. Robeena did not know she was not a tough, hardcore street walker, like some of the girls who grew up on drugs, without parents, and homeless. According to Robeena, she was just as smart as any of the girls she met in the nightlife.

As she walked with Bruno, the feeling of triumph swept over her to imagine Casey's wide-eyed look when he would see them together in the morning, providing that he would come by her house, and that things worked out with Bruno. They dumped Vivian off at her front door. Robeena was anxious to quickly retreat to a resting place of her own. "You want me to come in with you?" Robeena asked, already turning away. Vivian genuinely wanted Robeena to come in because she didn't want to face Lee alone, but Bruno's presence made it easy for her to decline her sister's half-baked gesture.

"No. I'll see you later," Vivian said, disappearing into the house. Robeena started away, but Bruno grabbed her hand so they could watch Vivian close her front door safely behind her.

"Henry Raison is her husband?" Bruno asked.

"Nope. Henry is my other sister's husband. Minnie. Vivian is married to Lee Hiram. He ain't no good. Lee is just as rotten as they come. Why? You know Henry?"

"I reckon I know him fine. We go to the same church. Never seen his wife, though. I come by this way from time to time and I see him hanging around his yard. Heard he was mighty good with his hands…a master builder. Mayhap he can help me to build a den onto my house."

"He's good, but he ain't the master." Robeena was pleased to learn he had a house of his own. She discovered during their conversation that he had a degree in accounting. They made it to Robeena's place in no time at all as they talked easily together.

Once Vivian closed the front door behind her, she stood for a moment, listening for any noise in the house. She heard no one stirring. After the eternity of another minute, she ventured toward the stairwell and stopped right beneath it to listen again. Suddenly, she felt dirty and cheap in the tight dress she wore. It would demean her if Lee came charging down the stairs to see her dressed so scantily. She unbuttoned the dress, pulled it off over her head, and balled it, tucking it under her arm.

In her petticoat, Vivian crept surreptitiously up the stairs on her hands and knees. When she reached her bedroom, she tried to gauge how lightly or heavily Lee might be sleeping. Finally, she concluded that he would undoubtedly awaken, no matter how hard he was sleeping, in his expectation of her return. Vivian took a deep breath and turned the knob steadily, pushing the door open in one motion. Upon entering, she quickly tossed the dress into the darkness, causing it to land in a pile of clothes on the chair. The room was quiet. Mary was in the bedroom with Minnie and Henry. She snatched up her robe that was hanging on a hook on the back of the door and put it on. Vivian let her eyes become adjusted to the darkness. She wheezed when she saw the bed made exactly the way she'd left it with the pillows still fluffed neatly. She looked in the corner of the room at the straight chair that was Lee's favorite place to sit. It was empty.

At that point, Vivian didn't feel she could avoid awakening her sister to find out if Lee had been home. Surely, all her efforts to teach him a lesson were not in vain! She inched as quietly as a spider across the narrow hallway, and opened Minnie's door. She thought she heard Mary moving around uncomfortably, undoubtedly wondering where her mama was. Vivian slipped into the room and headed for the wooden crib Henry had made for her. When she reached there, she saw that Mary was sleeping soundly. Vivian let her eyes grow accustomed to the dark, once more. What she really wanted was to confide in Henry about her horrible evening. Whenever she focused, she noticed two heads and upper torsos were completely covered by a blanket, leaving the night air to surround their lower limbs. It didn't take long for Vivian to recognize by his breathing that Henry was awake, yet trying to remain as still as a statue. She regretfully concluded that Henry was trying to hide himself from her. Henry was too completely embarrassed to move.

Vivian felt used, cheapened, and depressed. Her husband was loafing in the wilderness, and her man was too busy to care. There. She said it. Henry was her man in her dreams. Vivian hit an all-time harrowing low while she stood immobile in the sweat-filled room. She remembered the night her husband permitted Maybelle to stay over and appraised which scene troubled her the most. Vivian couldn't imagine anything stinging as much as the torment she was experiencing right now.

Henry was her god, her confidant, and her comforter. Vivian needed him to help her through the indignation that Lee caused her to experience. Then, sheer frustration came over her with the realization that she was not the most important person in anyone's life. Her emotional degeneracy wouldn't let her consider her importance to Mary. Before she married Lee, she had forced him to promise her that she would come before every other person. In his goal to marry her, Lee had inevitably made that promise, but then, tonight, where was he?

Henry had previously succeeded in making her feel as though she was the most beautiful and special lady in the world. Because of his charm and expert caress, Vivian assumed that he would always be there for her whenever she needed him. Even though she knew he was moving to Michigan before he romanced her, he told her that all she had to do was ask, and he would stay for her. Henry did not comprehend how attached she could become to what he represented to her. That first night together, she had asked him, "What about Minnie?" And he had answered, "My heart is with you." Vivian interpreted that to mean she possessed Henry's heart always, and over Minnie. This position in Henry's heart was essential to her emotional survival. Vivian needed someone to validate her as a person, and both Lee and Henry had failed her.

Vivian wished she could simply go to bed, but in her depressed state, that was not possible for her at all. She felt as though her whole life was useless, and she had to make sense out of it before she could sleep. Someone had to support her before morning or she thought she'd simply die. She considered her options. She would be too afraid because of the late hour to go for one of her relaxing, long walks, even though she felt that was what she needed. The comfort of Mary would have to do.

"Ooooh! Is my baby asleep?" she asked, noting that even Henry's breathing became stark still at the sound of her voice. Vivian listened sadistically to their fake snoring. Neither Minnie nor Henry moved, but instead they waited patiently for Vivian to leave the room. After several minutes of talking to Mary, who was still asleep, Vivian finally walked morosely out of the room, rolling the crib in one hand, and clutching Mary in the other. She couldn't believe how uneventful her night had been while everyone else had given her not a second thought as they plunged their way into a night filled with pleasure.

Vivian reminisced on what a coward she had been at the party—afraid to talk to any of the fine, northern men. She snorted at the memory of how Robeena was able to snatch Bruno right from under her fingertips, all because she wanted to rush home to a husband who hadn't considered her enough to come home himself. Vivian knew if the tables were turned, Lee would not tolerate such behavior from her. He would never take his clothes off at the bottom of the stairs to prevent her from seeing his attire, no matter how inappropriately dressed he may have been. He would never sneak into the house to avoid awakening her.

Vivian's resentment for Lee was greater than her respect for him, and the disappointment in herself for putting up with him superseded the respect she had for herself. She felt everything she said or did to him was what he earned. Even when she made apologies to him for her part in their tearing marriage, she had no real remorse for her cutting words or adulteress affair because of him. He deserved it.

She placed the still sleeping Mary back in her crib and went downstairs to look out of the windows for Lee. She didn't spot him coming up the front street, so she moved to the side window and glanced down Harvey Street. Overwhelmed with frustration, she wrapped her robe around her, and trudged out onto the porch to stare at the stars in the night.

"Why isn't this working out?" She asked the brightest star of all. Vivian suffered through a brief image of Lee with another woman as she stared up at the sky, but the agony that accompanied that image was too intense, so she toyed with the notion that something deadly had happened to her husband, and that was the reason he did not come home. She spied the North Star. "I followed you all the way up here to make a better life for me and my family. This is not the picture of better."

The sound of unknown animal chatter sent her hurriedly back inside, locking the door quickly behind her. A glutton for punishment in her depression, she went stubbornly right back to staring out the first window. After forty-five minutes of watching the empty roads, Vivian succeeded in exhausting herself. She concluded that something indeed must have happened beyond Lee's control which prevented him from coming home. She walked doggedly back up the stairs, comforted by the latter, less painful suggestion.

Her soul was captivated by the somber mood of her emotions, her heart unable to pump purely the blood flowing through her veins. The negative chemistry produced by her self-hatred, depression, emotional fatigue, and mental exhaustion spurted through her arteries, swelled her hollow heart, and deposited into her limbs, muscle tissue, and breast milk. By now, though, Mary was used to the bittersweet taste of the psychological poison she packed a punch suctioned daily from her mother. Vivian slept in her hell as best as she could, holding Mary under her breast.

Lee opened his groggy eyes at 6:00 a.m., preceded by his nostrils flaring alive when he involuntarily sniffed the sweaty, stale perfumed musk of the women on either side of him. He wanted to enfold his wife in his arms because her smell was fruity and her touch was soft to him, which made her flowery. But since she wasn't there, he tried Sandra. She was comfortable enough to hold, yet Lee simply didn't enjoy cuddling with her. He removed his arms from her and turned his back to face Chelsea's back. Lee believed this was one way he'd always remain faithful to his wife—Vivian was the only one he wanted to "make-love to," and hold. The other women were simply good for savage pleasure. There was no woman he could say he'd made love to since he was married. With this stance, Lee felt he had made some sort of a connection with Vivian, which allowed him to ease back to a sleep filled with dreams of beautiful women, money, and gleaming new automobiles.

Casey was in his dream driving his stately car, wearing a wide brim hat, with a saliva moist cigar in his mouth. He stopped in front of the bar where Lee stood, and three women got out of the car. Lee smiled when he saw the women were holding twenty-dollar bills, waving them at him. He noticed, however, that one woman stayed in the car with Casey, only she was in the back, and Casey was behind the wheel. There was something familiar about the woman's gay, cheerful mannerisms. She tossed her head back, turning her face toward Lee, and he saw that it was his mother! Lee ran back inside the bar and stood behind the door to hide from Casey and his mother. Casey got out of the car and banged on the bar door.

"Lee! Open up," Casey yelled repeatedly. Sandra shoved Lee awake since Casey was calling for him, and she didn't feel like getting up to answer the door. Lee stumbled sleepily to the door, troubled by his dream, and not certain where he was. With every step toward the door, his dream traveled back into his sub-consciousness.

"Damn, man! What took you so long to open up that door?" Casey snapped when Lee stood hung over before him.

"Man, I was knocked out," Lee said shortly, trying to remember his dream. Casey walked in saying something to the girls. Lee sat on the edge of the chair near the door and crossed his arms over his chest. He tried to shake himself awake. It was 7:15 in the morning. He knew there was a certain important woman in his dream in the car with Casey, but he couldn't remember who. The image of his mother soared like a racehorse billions of miles and light years away into the deep vesicles of his cortex. A current and modern version of a woman he loved surfaced on his brain . . . "It was Vivian!" He said just above a whisper to no one in particular. He was disturbed at what he interpreted his dream might be suggesting in placing Vivian in such a foul rank. He felt immediately that it was time for him to go home to his wife. An odd sense of isolation and desperation came over him.

Casey walked over to Lee to repeat his last point, as Lee seemed to be floating in another world. "Did you hear me, Lee? I said today is a big gambling day. A lot of men drop their wives off at church, and come on to gamble at the Big Pointe with whatever money they have left on Sunday, baby. They open the doors at noon. Remember all those tricks I taught you? Well, today is the day to put 'em to use. Today, and every Sunday is card day." Casey planned on making at least ninety dollars that afternoon and evening by cheating in poker and dice. This is not to say he wasn't a decent player on his own without the use of deceit and lies, but cheating gave him his gain more rapidly. He had enough confidence in Lee's ability to pull off the operation that he felt it was probable to make a pretty mint if they started early enough.

"Yeah man," Lee said, still boggled down with the need to see his wife at once, "I need to get on home for a minute right now, but we going at noon, right?"

"Right," Casey answered, "but I wanna *be* there at noon," he emphasized. Lee nodded his head impatiently, already moving to gather his things. Sandra was unraveled at the way Lee completely ignored her as he prepared to leave. Even the most ruthless tricks at least grunted their thanks to her, especially if she spent the whole night with them. She decided that "freebies" just weren't worth the trouble, and that men appreciated her company more when they had to pay for it.

Bruno spent hours talking and laughing with Robeena in her front room. She learned he was an accountant—the only Negro accountant at the downtown bank. He had no children, had never been married, and was twenty-six years old. He came from a very close-knit family, and his siblings were successful, too. His older brother was a doctor who happened to own the only Black clinic in Highland Park, Michigan. It was clear how proud Bruno was of his brother. He said his brother inspired him to take his accounting knowledge to another level.

Bruno talked a lot about opening his own accounting business. Robeena listened with sincere interest to Bruno's philosophies about life. He felt that Black people should pull their resources and unite economically. He possessed a respect for women that only Wali Eli seemed to surpass. He didn't touch her, gaze at her too long, or make any underhanded suggestions to her. He told her he enjoyed her company, but when 3:30 a.m. rolled around, he said he should leave. Robeena urged him into further conversation, refusing to even consider permitting him to leave her abode. She explained that she would worry immensely if he ventured home at such a late hour.

At 4:30 a.m., Robeena convinced Bruno to rest his hat until the sun rose. Dog-tired, he leaned his head back on her sofa and covered his eyes with his wide brim. All was quiet in the boarding house after Robeena retired to her bedroom to catch a quick nap herself. Robeena had been successful in sharing the entire night with Bruno, and she desperately wanted to acquaint Casey with this exaggerated information.

Awakening to the sun creeping over the horizon, Robeena curled up in a fetal position and sucked her thumb. She waited patiently for Casey, with the confidence that if he didn't show up today, he'd certainly show up on Monday. At any rate, Robeena contrived to have Bruno nearby for Casey to meet. She vowed not to weaken like Vivian did, but she was going to teach Casey a lesson. She promised herself that no man would subdue her. All the suffering her mother went through would be avenged through her craftiness in dealing with "these no-good men." Robeena wanted to get a taste of Casey's response when he saw Bruno relaxing comfortably in her tiny, cozy room.

Even though it appeared Bruno was a square, he clearly was a man with expensive taste. Bruno's upmarket shoes and suit were proof of that. Robeena knew, too, because she kept her head in the latest fashion magazines and she went to plenty of places in Detroit where the best dressed Negroes dwelled. Bruno's presence was twofold; Robeena's first purpose for him was that she counted on Casey seeing Bruno as serious competition, and hopefully, this would cause Casey to revert to the caring ways he exhibited when he'd first met her. Robeena didn't love Casey, but she saw some goodness in him in his providing ways, and she'd always hoped that *maybe* a chance existed that there was someone out there who could love and respect her. But if he was going to abuse her like the others, she was now willing to play the game with him and teach him a sound lesson. Therefore, she jumped into the inferno of game playing, killing herself by virtue in her attack on all men.

Robeena also wanted to use Bruno to take her mind off Casey to enable her to avert the feelings growing inside of her for Casey. She recognized that to love him was to risk her heart. As it was, Casey's charisma had seeped through some of the wire fencing surrounding Robeena's heart. He handled her like no man could—he was her soul mate to the limit of her experience. All he had to do was look at her and she'd blush. She had to disregard her attraction and neutralize her predicament. Robeena sat back calm and cold, formulating negative opinions about Casey as a defense mechanism against any grief he had the potential to cause her. She repaired the old wires Casey had bent by going through the holes to reach her heart. She put up extra wiring to make it more difficult for unpleasant things to seep through.

Bruno and Casey were unaware of the wiring surrounding Robeena's heart. After Casey dropped Lee off at home, he went straight over to Robeena's nearby abode to assess his progress. He only intended to stay with Robeena for the few hours Lee needed to recuperate before going out on the strenuous gambling spree they had planned. In fact, had Lee not been so insistent about going home, Casey would have waited another day to visit Robeena.

When Casey arrived, Robeena and Bruno were having coffee and bread in the kitchen. Connie, the divorced border, came out of her bedroom and pretended to do some dusting so she could witness the drama that was sure to come. With no place to go, Robeena had dressed in a casual cotton dress, stockings, and laced shoes by 8:15 a.m. This was in her foresight and preparation to receive Casey. Bruno held his hat in his lap and was willing to properly greet Casey, but Casey refused to dignify his presence. It was impossible for Casey to tell what events had transpired in his absence. Robeena was truly calculating. It made no difference to her if Casey came or not, she would have prepared for his coming for as long as she had a trickle of emotion for him in her heart.

Casey had never seen Bruno before at the nightspots or in the streets, nor had Bruno seen him, so they each took the opportunity when Casey first entered under the threshold of the narrow door to size up the other opponent. It was difficult for Casey to tell much about Bruno because, although brilliantly dressed, his special taste brought a fresh style altogether to the scene. Robeena innocently batted her eyes at Casey after she offered him a seat in the front room of the boarding house. Casey glanced at Robeena's boarding mate. The short, robust woman of about thirty had stopped dusting to pay more attention to the trio. Bruno listened on from the kitchen.

"Casey! Whatchu doing here?" Robeena asked quickly, needing to take control of the conversation from the start. "I was so disappointed yesterday when it appeared you dropped me like a hot rock—it's such a surprise to see you at my place today!" If she had been one of his whores, he would have slapped her to the ground for trying to play "mind games" with him. He knew for certain that his visit obviously was no surprise to her, and she really hadn't forgotten about him as easily as she now alleged. Nevertheless, he indeed had stood her up, so he begrudgingly had to go along with her game, for the moment.

"I couldn't make it back yesterday morning because I was involved in a business deal, and then I got tied up with Lee all day." They both knew it was a lame excuse because he had to come all the way from Detroit to get "tied up" with Lee. Besides, Robeena lived just a few blocks from Lee. Casey was forced to concede: Robeena now had the upper hand. He knew she had to know he and Lee had gone out to a party or something. And seeing the suave man sitting at the kitchen table made Casey wonder if Robeena, too, had gone out last night. Oh, he knew she had, but how far had she gone was his concern.

Casey found himself becoming livid with Robeena's amusement. This country woman had succeeded in catching him off his professional guard. Being from Florida did not make her slow. Southern women and men had endured more overt hardships and were accustomed to surviving in more hostile environments. He was at a greater disadvantage still, since Robeena neglected so much as to introduce him to the man seated at the table. Maybe he was there for the other border? Casey decided that was too unlikely based on how Bruno kept glancing over at Robeena, although the other girl was right before him. Casey was annoyed at how much more auspiciously groomed Bruno was than he, even though he didn't deem him as handsome.

"Well, I'm sorry you couldn't make it by yesterday," she said cheerfully. He wanted to ask her who Bruno was, but he did not want to place the tiniest degree of significance to the man. Casey could have simply walked out the door and out of her life, but he would certainly be the loser then for sure, he calculated, because he had an invested interest in this woman. Casey couldn't ever see himself marrying any woman before he turned at least 50, and Robeena's type wouldn't be in the consideration line, but he did appreciate her as a companion. Other than Chelsea, Robeena was the only one of his women that his family had met. He liked Robeena enough to have her in his car when he went to his mother's house for dinner one Sunday.

"Whatchu doing Saturday?" She asked. Casey almost hit the roof at her insinuation that he should call on her again in a whole week away. She was used to seeing him every day and night. Casey feared it wasn't a game. He entertained that Bruno was someone she'd known from the past—not someone she'd just met, but someone who held enough significance in her life to conflict with his own relationship with her. Was this strange man from Florida? This wasn't something that he'd figured when he met Robeena, though. He had courted her better than any other girl because he presumed that by her being from the slow down South, she would undoubtedly become one of his most loyal girls. He panicked at the notion that he might not be able to add this beautiful, young, sultry woman to his stable.

Casey hadn't selected Robeena for her looks alone. He admired the way she worked the clubs night after night on her own. His mind raced. One thing was for sure; she wouldn't be allowed to frequent where his ladies did business if she wouldn't belong to him in his establishment. He could feel himself getting frosty.

"Look, Beena," he said, raising his voice and glancing in the direction of Bruno, "we need to talk. Get rid of him. And make it quick. I'm going outside for a smoke. I'll be back in ten minutes," he dictated. Out of the corner of his eye, he saw Bruno give him a sharp glimpse, but Casey took two long strides and he was out the door before anyone could oppose his demand. "Damn!" He muttered to himself once outside. Robeena smiled brightly like a schoolgirl at the slammed door, pleased at how ingeniously she was able to complete the first phase of getting even with Casey. Before she turned politely to walk back into the kitchen, her smile was engineered to vanish. Robeena engaged herself in a troubled look, instead, and poured Bruno another cup of coffee. Connie frowned and retreated to her room.

"I'd like another cup, pretty lady, but it looks like your man is upset. I'm not sure I want to be around for the fireworks," Bruno said, standing to leave. "Don't forget to tell your brother-in-law that I'd be interested if he could help me build a den at my place." Robeena was relieved that Bruno was leaving with no further prompting. However, she detected he expected her to ask him to stay.

"Aw, come on, Bruno! You 'member that sometime-y man I told you about last night. Well, that's the one." She was sure she'd need Bruno again. "He won't be long, I promise. Can't you come back and see me later?" She gave him a hug and a kiss before he could answer. Bruno was delighted with the prospect of seeing her again. He believed her when she said Casey was insignificant. They both agreed he would come back on Tuesday, his day off from work. Robeena promised to tell Henry about the side job Bruno offered. Finally he left, hurried out the door by his hostess who was looking over his shoulders for any signs of Casey.

Casey didn't bother knocking when he returned to the boarding house twenty minutes later. He hoped the man had not come all the way up from Florida, and that he'd given her enough time to get the man out of her house. He knew Robeena would be waiting for him, and he was right. Only, she wasn't sitting on the sofa or waiting by the door as he expected. Instead, she was busy washing the coffee cups and saucers.

"Oh! You're back," she called nonchalantly from the kitchen. "Have a seat anywhere you like," she added. It was exceedingly difficult for Casey to play the "nice guy" routine. He regretted that he was going to have to spend more money and time with her to get her completely in his clutches. He resented her for this and thus promised himself that he would treat her cruelly once she was his established whore.

It crossed Casey's mind that the man who sat in the kitchen was not an old acquaintance but a gentleman caller. If so, then why would she be totally dressed already by 8:30 a.m.? Casey was thoroughly confused. He believed if that were so, he deserved a portion of the money, nevertheless. He estimated he had spent approximately $280.00 on Robeena thus far. He had bought her the finest clothes, shoes, an emerald ring, other jewelry including a 20-karat gold necklace and bracelet set, groceries, and other decorous items whenever she expressed a desire for something. He had been paying her rent steadily ever since they met. Casey had been wining and dining her since day one, and he also was the one who paid for all her hair and nail jobs. He'd even given her cash when she told him of her dreams about being a dancer and owning a club.

Robeena assessed she had hit the jackpot when she met Casey. She intended to never let him go, as long as he was treating her so lavishly. The struggle today was how she was going to keep Casey and his money all for herself, away from Lee and clubs where other women frolicked. At the same time, she had to stay emotionally and psychologically detached from him, which would require dating other men. She was so deep in deliberation that she didn't hear Casey stealthily enter the kitchen. She jumped when he circled her waist from behind.

"Ahhhh! Casey! You scared me." He wondered what evil thoughts she was thinking about him to cause her to jump at his touch.

"Who was that man in here, Beena?"

"Who? Bruno?" She didn't say anything else. Robeena finished all the dishes, including the ones left on the kitchen table by the other boarders. Now, she was drying them, not responding again to Casey's touch.

"Yeah, Beena. Bruno. You really disappointed me. I mean, I reckoned *I* was your man. I take care of you, don't I? I buy you things, give you money... did I deserve that, baby? All because I missed one tiny date?"

Robeena administered a silent lecture to herself about how all men were dogs, and about why she shouldn't feel sorry for him. "But, see, Casey, you probably went to a cabaret last night with Lee, and your brother probably went, too. What woman were you buying things for, then?" She turned to face him so he could see the blaze in her eyes. He saw the fire, but it didn't represent the flaming rage she was trying to depict, but from it he understood right away her attempt to smokescreen a degree of her pain and jealousy. It was instantly clear to him why Bruno was in the house: Robeena knew his pattern. She was aware Casey would certainly come by after not seeing her all night, and when he did, she knew he would be sure to see Bruno in the early morning. He recognized Robeena was more of a rebellious lot than he had originally anticipated, and not suitable for a pimp. He wanted to swoop the glittering emerald ring he'd bought for her right off her finger so he could give it to the hard-working Chelsea, instead. His better judgment told him to cut his losses and immediately dump this non-profitable woman, but his stubbornness and love for excitement caused his proclivity to challenge her stance.

"Yeah. I took Lee to show him around. I thought about you the whole time." She turned away in disbelief. He turned her back around to face him. "Baby, look. I'm a hustler. I have to go out at night to handle my business. That's how I make my money to buy you nice things." Casey was breathtaking and confident. Even the way he said "baby" sent shivers all over Robeena. She knew women would want him whenever they met him, and truly she preferred that he spend more time with her because he was as good as he looked. Yes, she wanted to be his number one and only. Robeena discerned that if he did spend all his time with her, he couldn't make money. She knew he had a hustle, although she wasn't privy to the intricate details of his job description. Casey could see her face untighten at the mention of buying wonderful things for her. She was greedy like all the rest of the prostituting women he knew.

"Well, I think you might have messed around on me is why you ain't showed up all day, yesterday," she declared, letting her defenses down with the security his warm arms provided. Casey had already determined that he had won her back. He released her and sat down in a kitchen chair. He was just beginning to realize how tired he was. Well, now, he could rest. As it was, he only had a couple of hours left before he had to go back and get Lee, and he wanted to spend his time sleeping. He didn't see the benefit in lying to her, or explaining anything to her about his chain of events last night.

"I was too busy doing my job to mess around on you, girl. Then I come over here, and you got some man in here—don't play me cheap."

"Seems like all you know is women. Ev'rywhere we go, they always gotta have private time with you…all this 'can I see you for a minute' crap I gotta deal with at ev'ry turn. So I guess I can feel like you might be playing around."

"It's about respect, sugar. Respect comes in knowing when your man is tired…knowing when to talk and when to cool it. That's what I need from you. I expect you to show consideration when it comes to my business. Like I said, don't play me cheap. I ain't no choir boy, all cute and ready to sing to your tune, sugar."

"I think we should respect each other. It shouldn't be a one-way thing."

"The only thing left for me to do is stand on my head. Gotdamnit, Robeena! I told you what happened. Now, I'd appreciate a place where I can rest myself for a minute before I have to go back out on my hustle." He kicked off his shoes, pushed them under the chair and stole a glimpse at her. "Well?" He asked. Robeena nodded her head in agreement and rushed to change the sheets with Casey right on her heels.

"I didn't say you could come in my room, yet, Case," she said. She gathered her evening dress, spiked heeled shoes, and tossed them casually aside. Casey stood silently about ten feet away, humored by her fidgety behavior and nervousness. She avoided his eyes while she put clean sheets on the bed, and made the bed over neatly. She prayed Casey didn't think she was changing her week-old sheets due to Bruno's visit. She wouldn't have taken the old ones off had she known Casey was going to barge in her room so soon and uninvited. She shoved her glittering purse behind the headboard. It agitated her to acknowledge she cared about his opinion regarding her reckless behavior.

Robeena was disappointed in herself that though he seemed to like her a great deal, she was presenting herself so horribly. It was true Robeena planned to never allow herself to indulge in affecting attachment to any man, but this was because she didn't feel she could trust men on that level due to the agony brought to her family by men. Nevertheless, if there would come a man who was different from all the rest, she would certainly venture cautiously to explore her options. Casey was beginning to seem like a worthwhile investment, so it was important to Robeena how she handled him.

She could feel his eyes cutting through her flesh as she made the bed. Robeena couldn't help feeling sorry for offending him deeply by throwing Bruno in his face. When the bed was made and the covers turned back, Casey walked past her and climbed under the sheets, fully dressed except for his shoes, hiding his eyes from the brilliant waves of the sun. He turned his back on her to face the wall. Robeena stared at him for a moment. He looked so innocent and placid to her that even though she had work to do around the house, she decided to suspend her duties and squeeze close to him. When she slipped in bed beside him two minutes later and hugged his back, he had already fallen into a deep sleep.

~~~

Lee had fallen asleep on the couch after he entered the house with the decision not to hear Vivian's mouth. He was having so many strange feelings, coupled with his dream that he didn't want to see Vivian right away. Lee couldn't get the picture of her with Casey out of his mind. He hoped if he got some rest, he'd feel better by noontime. He was dissatisfied with Vivian for not providing him with the confidence that she would never be with another man. When they first met, he thought she was so timid, reserved and refined, but now, he deliberated more and more about how far she would go with another man. Had Gancy made a pass at her? If so, did she giggle in *his* face and coax him further with her soft voice?

Lee was also still puzzled by Robeena's relationship with Casey, and he knew how close Vivian and Robeena were. He knew Robeena relished trying to persuade Vivian into her dishonorable lifestyle, whatever it was. "Not if I can help it," he reassured himself.

Vivian did hear Lee when he came home, but by then she was just turning over, too tired to move. Soon after, morning was in full swing, and she didn't have the strength to fight with him. Instead, she opted for additional sleep. She slept for two more hours, awakening at about the same time Henry awakened, both thinking about the other. Vivian was fed up with Lee; she didn't care anymore whether he was still downstairs or not, given that he hadn't bothered coming upstairs whenever he got home. She wanted to feel Henry's big arms around her and Mary. "Damn you, Lee," she sighed. A tear came to her eye when she remembered Henry with his wife last night. She had laid the claim for too long that his devotion was reserved solely for her.

CHAPTER NINETEEN
Vivian's prison

Henry bit his bottom lip, enough to draw blood. He moved slightly away from Minnie who was sleeping snuggly beside him. He was self-conscious about Vivian coming into his bedroom the night before. He intended to soothe her feelings about what she might have seen. Henry hoped Lee would go out this afternoon, whereas he knew Minnie would be at church. He wouldn't even tell Minnie he wasn't going to church—he would simply leave and then come back home after Minnie left for her own church. He vowed to do whatever it took to avail himself the opportunity to spend time talking with Vivian alone. Henry scolded himself for being so selfish in his craving to simply be near Vivian that he'd hardly talked seriously with her about anything except the baby. But, this afternoon, he promised himself he would cater to her every need.

When he went downstairs to start coffee for everyone a little later while Minnie was getting prepared for church, he inhaled stale smoke and perfume reeking from the area of the couch where Lee snored. He stood over Lee with his fists clenched, wondering how it would feel to pummel his face into a bloody mask. He hadn't gone to bed until well after midnight, therefore, he knew from reasonable deductions that Vivian had come home to an empty bed. It wasn't the first time Lee had stayed out all night partying, leaving his wife all alone since they'd been up North.

Lee opened his eyes after a minute and looked into the brazen stare of what resembled a raging, oversized bear. Lee jumped, alarmed. He shook himself awake and breathed his dislike for Henry. "Man, I wish you'd put some clothes on," Lee hissed, referring to Henry's great bare chest that intimidated him. "You ain't the only one who got a wife in this house."

"If you think you got a wife, why don't you act like you do? But if you think she's interested in my bare chest, I guess you would want me to put a shirt on. You can take your shirt off, and no one would give a damn," Henry dared to say. Lee had the notion that clearly he misunderstood Henry, for surely he wasn't implying in any way, shape, or form that there was a remote possibility that he could tell him how to act, or to implicate Vivian.

Nevertheless, Lee sat up defensively when Henry refused to cease sneering at him. "Come again, my man?" Henry looked on, unruffled by Lee's defense. If Lee had anticipated he could physically subdue him and still live under his roof, he would have throttled Henry right there in the front room. The whole situation dismayed Lee to unimaginable heights. Lee suspected Henry was merely teasing him, yet something deep down in the back of his mind warned him of a truth to Henry's suggestion. He knew Henry disliked him immensely, but he didn't know *why*. If Henry had a crush on Vivian, it would seem he would be humbler. At any rate, Lee was determined to keep a closer eye on Vivian, and he vowed to get a new home for his small family as soon as possible.

Henry knew Lee wanted to physically assault him, as he saw him vainly size up his opponent. He snickered softly at Lee's apparent apprehension of him, and was delighted he was able to generate a similar fear in Lee as Lee instilled in Vivian. Henry rated Lee as a coward. He wanted to tell Lee that he knew about the beatings because Vivian had collapsed in his arms and confided in him.

"Henry," Minnie called from their bedroom, "come zip my dress." He glanced backward at the staircase. Before turning to retreat up the stairs, he gave Lee a look that promised this wasn't the end of the subject.

"I asked you a question, man," Lee yelled at Henry's back. Henry ignored him and went on to aid Minnie. Momentarily, Lee followed him up the stairs and almost banged on his brother-in-law's closed door. Instead, however, his better judgment forced him to shift his manifest opposition so that he entered his own bedroom. He found Vivian sitting up in the bed playing with Mary.

"You know what, bitch? If I find out you've been messing around on me, I'm gonna kick the wind outta you." The vehemence inside of Vivian soared. She was torn that he hadn't come home all night, yet had the boldness to accuse her of something before granting her the respect of a simple greeting. She hated his guts. "You hear me, wench? Answer me when I talk to you, you goddamn prostitute," he jeered, heedlessly referring back to his dream.

Although it wasn't clear if Vivian was listening anymore, Mary heard him. Vivian knew how to tune him out, but Mary felt the tension of his presence through her mother. At first, loving arms held her, but they were traded with the clinch of uncertainty and rigidity. Although she wasn't yet one year old, Mary didn't like herself. She was hardly able to separate herself from that of her mother and father. The realization that she was not actually a physical extension of her mother is a developmental stage for infants.

In this sense, Mary was developmentally delayed because she didn't feel secure enough within herself to accept her individuality. She always awaited the compassionate part of herself (her mother) that held her after the loud voices and screams. The part of herself (her father) that could be so brutal and loud frightened her, yet she couldn't control it. But compassion wasn't always guaranteed with her mother's hold, and her father was often gentle and responsive. Mary's confusion over all of this caused some emotional and developmental retardation, and future adverse susceptibility.

Lee went back downstairs to gather the socks and shoes he'd kicked off under the couch, then he raced back upstairs. Next, he tossed the testimonial evidence which placed him at home sleeping downstairs in front of his wife. She continued to rock back and forth with unseeing eyes. This satisfied Lee because he wasn't enthusiastic about hearing any back talk that would undoubtedly cause him to beat her. He preferred to climb in bed and go back to sleep until at least 11:30 a.m., when Casey was sure to return. He knew Henry should be long gone to church by then, and so should Minnie.

Lee walked in front of Vivian and went straight to the bed. He jerked to himself the portion of the blanket that was under Vivian and pulled it over his face, leaving only his eyes exposed. Henry's words rang in Lee's ear, causing him to shiver underneath the warm blanket. Trying to detect any hint of truth to Henry's implications, he stared prudently at Vivian. Before he knew it, though, he had fallen into a fitful sleep, tossing, and turning every time his self-accusing spirit tried to sneak up through a dream.

When Lee tired of trying to sleep at about 10:40, he opened his eyes only to discover that Vivian had escaped the prison of their bedroom, leaving Mary behind asleep next to him. Lee dashed about frantically, found his slippers, and hurried to stop her from whatever fun she might be having without him. Lee feared if he allowed Vivian to have too much enjoyment with anyone other than himself, she might decide she didn't need him anymore.

Minnie and Vivian were in the kitchen. Henry, still bare-chested, was sitting on the sofa reading the newspaper, the Pontiac Press. As Lee rushed past after the chattering voices of the women, he had to force himself not to give Henry a second glance. Animosity and tension built inside of him to see Vivian's even white teeth talking and laughing confidently with Minnie, not concerned that Lee had entered the kitchen. She was wearing a cozy, thick, velvety robe that he didn't buy and that she didn't have down South. Lee wanted to pull her by her hair and slam her head over the icebox. How dare she stay downstairs with Henry half-clad just a few feet away! And why didn't Minnie suggest to her husband that he wear a shirt in the house?

The sisters went to the dining room with biscuits and tea, narrowly noticing Lee's presence. When they both plopped down in two of the chairs, Henry joined them, commissioned by the aromatic flavor that scented the area. He also ignored Lee, smiling inside all the time at what Lee must be feeling to see him with no shirt on in front of Vivian. Minnie was certainly not a part of any scheme to "get" Lee; she simply didn't find his presence interesting enough to stop what she was doing to acknowledge him. Minnie felt that as long as others were present, there was no need for concern about her husband not having a shirt on in front of her sister. It certainly wasn't an uncommon practice for a man to go bare-chested indoors or even outdoors in the warmth of the season, regardless of what ladies, visitors or little girls were present.

Nevertheless, Lee's paranoia caused him to believe all three of them were conspiring against him. The savagery of Henry's actions was subconsciously recognized by Lee's spirit, which superseded American customs. Sagging heavily, he traced his steps back out of the kitchen and slouched helplessly in the dining room, uncertain if he should take the last chair or not. Minnie laughed when she reached for the same biscuit Vivian grasped. Henry's arm went into the basket, too, grazing Vivian's elbow to possess the fluffiest of the butter rich baked goods. Lee saw immediately that he had to keep the reins tight on his wife at this bewitched breakfast party.

Just as Vivian turned to see what eyes were burning through her flesh, taunting her, Lee was startled to an upright position when he heard Casey at the door so soon. Knocking briefly, Casey called out to Lee. The trio looked up at Lee standing in the corner as though seeing him for the first time, and waited for him to answer the door. Meanwhile, Casey called out again, impatiently. When Lee refused to quit his post, Henry got up jubilantly to unlatch the chained screen, and returned shortly with Casey. Henry gave up his chair to Casey and walked to the other side of the table where he could stand against the wall facing Vivian.

Casey only planned on sitting to appear sociable for a few seconds, then he started to urge Lee to hurry along, but the dynamics in the room caught his attention immediately, intriguing him to hush his polite, small talk. Casey was amazed at Minnie's apathetic regard for her husband's open admiration of Vivian, and he marveled at Henry's aggressiveness. He looked over at Lee to see his reaction, and was surprised at how worried, discouraged, and slighted Lee appeared. Because Vivian virtually ignored Henry as well as Lee, it was difficult for Casey to uncover what was going on. He realized Lee had hardly greeted him because, Casey noted, he focused on Vivian's reaction to Henry—it was as if Lee was trying to find some hidden meaning to Vivian's avoidance of Henry's deference. It was at times like these that Casey deeply appreciated his expertise at studying people. A good pimp must know people and be aware of the workings in social interactions.

Minnie chattered away about her delicate, sleeping Mary and how perfectly plump she was. To Casey, she behaved like she had carried Mary for nine months. Vivian smiled graciously, nodding her head occasionally, seemingly in tune with the conversation. Casey caught Henry cautiously, yet defiantly stealing long glances at Lee here and there. Vivian surprised Casey when she turned abruptly to him, although with a very warm smile, and offered him a cup of iced tea. He tipped his hat, and stood to give her a deep bow for effect. "I'm sure your tea is the best in the North, South, East and West, my lady, but me and Lee got some place we need to be right now." Lee had almost forgotten why Casey was there. He knew he would have to renegotiate his plans with him, at least until Henry left for church, yet it didn't look like he was trying to get dressed too fast.

"Aw man," Lee said to Casey, "I forgot I have that appointment with that Detroit Urban League man today, that Gancy guy. I'm having problems with getting a job, so he's gonna show me what's what. I ain't never heard nothing from them car peoples when I filled out the application a long time ago. He is supposed to be finding me a job at Ford Motors or somewhere. I don't know."

"Man, you can't be serious about that shit." Henry squinted at Casey. "For real, though. On a Sunday, man? You playing it real straight, ain't you?"

"Plus I'm tired as hell. He yawned for emphasis. "I wasn't able to get no sleep this morning. Think I'm gonna stay on, and in another thirty minutes it'll be time to go down to that stupid ass center." Everyone was infuriated at Lee's announcement except Minnie, who couldn't care less. Casey silently cursed Lee as he mentally subtracted the dollars he had counted on making with Lee's presence at the gambling institutions. It began to formulate in Casey's mind that Henry's presence might be the real cause of Lee's change of plans.

"What, man?" Casey glared at Lee. Lee took on a helpless expression, casting his eyes down from Casey's glare. Even though Lee didn't want to disappoint his new friend, he found he had no other choice. Casey grew hostile when he saw Lee didn't intend to discuss it further. "Man! We gotta go make that money!" He looked at Lee's wife at the mention of money, certain that she'd perk right up and order her husband to the task. Yet, Vivian had stopped paying attention to the conversation, it seemed, and was twirling her spoon in her iced tea. Lee looked quickly at Henry in short-lived indecision. Casey followed his eyes and confirmed the suspected source of the problem in Henry's smug, pursed lips.

Minnie finally began to take an interest in the social circumstances surrounding her, but by this time, she knew she had to hurry if she wasn't going to be late for church. She stood and faced her handsome husband, remembering the beautiful night they'd shared, hoping they could go to church together, even if it meant going to his church.

"Honey, we're gonna be late for church. You coming, ain't you?" Casey knew Henry's answer before the question was completely out of Minnie's mouth, and so did Lee.

"Naw," he started to call her 'baby,' but it seemed too awkward with Vivian sitting there, "Minnie." Casey watched Lee's jaw tighten. "I got a lot of things to do today." Henry looked away from Minnie, closing the subject in the same tone Lee had used earlier to close the subject with Casey. Minnie was too disappointed to notice any similarities in the battle. She dragged away from the table, focusing on the contentment of the previous night to carry her through this indignation. She didn't like it when he disagreed with her desires in public. Henry had decided he didn't want to go through with the charades of pretending he was going to church just to mislead Lee. Instead, he wanted Lee to suffer with his presence regardless of whether Lee decided to go on with Casey.

With Minnie absent from the table, Vivian could see no reason to stay, given that Lee and Henry were both in the doghouse as far as she was concerned. Henry was cognizant of the grief he'd caused Vivian by being careless last night, and now that she was walking away before they could atone, he didn't know when he'd get the chance to talk with her again. Lee staying home meant Henry might not see his lover for the rest of the day or night! For a moment, he couldn't breathe.

"Don't go," Henry called after Vivian, who had already gotten out of her seat to leave. Overcome with surprise, she stopped dead in her tracks. Lee had no intention of tolerating such open disrespect from Henry, and not in front of Casey. Given that Lee wasn't sure how much, if at all, Vivian was a part of Henry's efforts, he strategically didn't want to alert Vivian to the fact that he was overwhelmed with Henry's obsession. However, Lee sensed Henry was merely provoking him, thus he decided not to take the bait. To call Henry's bluff, he grinded hard on his tongue and forced himself not to speak. Lee knew if there was no bluff, there would have to be a fight.

When Vivian turned to read any astonishment in Lee's expression at Henry's awkward request, Lee shrugged his shoulders ever so lightly, looking fiercely at her, and square in the eyes. She faced Henry.

"Don't go?" There was revulsion in her voice that Lee mistook for bewilderment, but Casey studied what had transpired between Vivian and Henry to cause her to speak to him with an air of animosity. Henry tried to convey to her with his eyes that he was sorry. She looked away, still seething. Casey now wanted to see more fireworks at Lee's expense, considering Lee's rebellion toward his agenda. He folded his arms across his chest, and sat back in his chair. Neither Henry, Lee, or Vivian noticed him. Henry had to shake himself to get a grip on what he was doing. He had no idea what he meant by telling her not to go. He sounded crazy saying that to her with Lee standing there, and they all knew it. He had to think quickly because the silence in the room, coupled with his bare chest was beginning to feel uncouth.

"You ain't even finished your tea." He smiled. "I guess there are too many hard legs in here, but I for one is leaving." Henry picked up the newspaper off the table and walked past Vivian without looking at her, through the front room and up the stairs. He grunted to himself. Henry's expedient departure didn't convince Casey of innocence in his relationship with Vivian. What puzzled Casey was Lee's apparent lack of influence over his own wife. Casey was accustomed to controlling women, as well as men, so he couldn't understand how Henry could make such innuendos and get away with it.

Vivian took Henry's advice and sat back down to her tea, without giving Lee so much as a sideways glance. A high degree of respect Casey had for Lee flew out the window like a scattering bat. "Man," Casey said, "it's hard to tell who wears the pants in this house!" Lee balled his fist and hulked on the hardwood floor. Vivian rejected both of their ploys to provoke a response from her.

"She don't wear no pants in here," Lee retorted. Casey laughed in disbelief, but stopped shortly when he focused again on the time being wasted. He stood and stuck his hands in his pockets.

"Alright, Lee, man, you coming?"

"Naw," he said grimly, "I got something to do. Gancy supposed to be coming by here to drop me off another application and to help me fill it out the way them white folks want it."

Casey laughed resentfully. "Man, you just a lying son-of-a..." he looked at Vivian and took a thoughtful bow. "Excuse me, lady." She ignored him. He didn't appreciate her funky attitude, but he knew he had no choice except to feign like her snobbishness did not affect him. He turned back to Lee. "You just stood there and said you was *going* to the center, and now all of a sudden you is *waiting* on somebody. What's up?" He walked toward the door and Lee fell in stride with him. Lee didn't feel like explaining that he really didn't know what Gancy's plans were, because the point was simply that he needed to stay back and keep an eye on Vivian. So, he said nothing. Before Casey dipped fully from the threshold, he turned to shake Lee's hand. "Remember what I told you, right?" Lee didn't remember. "I said 'you owe me,' baby." Lee vaguely recalled hearing those words, but before he could think of a response, Casey was halfway down the walkway.

Vivian wanted to be far away from Lee, so she sneaked upstairs to their bedroom, almost crouching past him as he stood at the door, saying his goodbyes to Casey. She hoped he would stay downstairs, and he would decide to leave. When Lee closed the door behind Casey, he saw the tail of Vivian's robe sweep a turn high on the stairs. He heard her stop to say something to Minnie who was in the hallway, and then Minnie came down alone.

"Vivian told me to tell you that she wants some privacy, so if you is willing, please stay down here for a spell." Lee was ill at ease by Minnie's impudence, and he was teed off that his wife would involve her on such a personal errand.

"Oh yeah? Well you'd best be going on to church, and not concern yourself with the business of me and my wife. You do have a husband you need to tend to," Lee answered, trying to talk properly like Casey did from time to time. Minnie pointed her nose at the ceiling, also copying her claimed mentor, Mrs. Miller.

Despite the invitation she had previously extended, she now wished Lee and Vivian hadn't come up to Michigan at all. It seemed like every room Vivian entered, all the men in sight flocked in after her. And as far as Minnie could tell, Lee was not serious about finding a real job. Gancy constantly went out of his way to help Lee, yet Lee acted like he couldn't even complete the damn application. Lee had been in town for weeks, yet had mentioned nothing about contributing financially to the expenses, even though he had shamelessly revealed his wad on a few social occasions. She left for church wishing there was some way to criticize Lee's lack of enterprise without making him seem like the victim—all alone with no family except Vivian's folk—she could hear it now. Minnie counted her blessings when she added that Henry was so much more stable and mature than Lee. She thoughtfully hummed an old Negro hymn all the way to Reverend Foote's church.

Henry hid behind his door after Minnie left and surveyed Vivian in the hallway until she disappeared into her room. A moment later, he saw Lee's lanky legs go shrewdly in behind Vivian. He felt himself shivering and imagined he was coming down with the flu. Then, he recognized his low spirits were causing him to become physically sick. It was too much to handle. He was lying to his wife, loving her sister, and his demons were anxious to come up for air. He didn't want to live his life in such a way, but he would have no less than every moment with Vivian that he could get. She was surprisingly sassy. She challenged him -she wasn't easy to handle. She kept him on his toes. She had a voice, her own opinions, and she was bursting into her own freedom like a magnificent butterfly. He liked watching her emerge so exotically. Henry walked heavily to his bed and climbed under the covers. Overcome with gloom, he tried to think about positive things. The image of the perfect baby Mary instantly entered his mind. She had smiled at him the night before whenever Henry had taken her from Minnie. He had rocked her until a sweat broke out on her tiny forehead, and then he fanned her.

"My baby girl," he said, his heart bubbling with joy. Henry rolled over on his side, fighting the urge to go knock on Lee's door and ask for Mary.

Mary was not asleep in their bed when her parents entered the room one after the other. She stiffened when Vivian lifted her. She was curious about a toy block with colorful numbers and pictures situated next to her head, but her stress wouldn't allow her to continue to play with it and learn from it the way normal babies do. Mary sat retarded in her mother's arms, awaiting the distressing battle she sensed through the thickness in the air she breathed.

"Why this room ain't clean?" Lee kicked a shirt that was crumpled on the floor in the middle of the room.

"I'm not your dog, Lee," she answered, placing Mary in her crib.

"You ain't did shit all day." In the midst of his profanity, he went on casually to disrobe himself and come at her. Vivian was in the perfect mood to respond to his snide remarks and what she deemed to be his animalistic treatment of her. The antagonism she had for him was so inexorable that she found it impossible to contain her contemptuous comments. His brutality and utter lack of sensitivity as he approached such physical and intimate matters compared no less than Floyd's behavior, in her estimation.

He grabbed her around her waist, and when she twisted away, he pushed her onto the bed. She rolled to the left and stood again. "Leave me alone, nigger," she sizzled. She was looking for a fight because she knew that was exactly what she would get if she should remark back to Lee when he was as enkindled as he was. "I thought you wanted me to clean up this nasty room." She moved to pick up one of his dirty shirts. He came behind her and grabbed the side of her robe, using it to fling her forward into the dresser with a thud. Mary cringed. Her little toes pointed wide apart and straight out in anticipation. Vivian spun back around insubordinately. He pushed her back on the bed.

"Tramp," he spat, "don't you ever tell me to leave you alone. I do what I damn well please. You don't wear no pants… I'm the man!"

She sprang forward and went around him. "You mean you're a two-legged beast!" He popped her in the eye. Vivian didn't know what came over her after that. Her fury sent her at him wildly, with her claws stretched out eagerly. After he assaulted her, he turned and walked away in disgust. He heard her scream, but before he could turn around, she pounced on him. Her fingernails dug gingerly into the flesh of his cheeks, attempting unsuccessfully to break the skin with every nail.

"Ungrateful street bitch!" At that moment, she *was* a prostitute to him. She was the one in the car with Casey in his dream—it *had* to be her. He suspected everyone was prodding at him today, including her. No one respected him. His mind was racing. It was during these times of feeling isolated that he worried that he'd never see his son again unless he got his own life together. He figured he'd never see his mother again, and wouldn't recognize her perhaps if he did see her. Lee felt his mother couldn't have loved him to have left him without a word. His heart wouldn't let him accept his uncle's suggestions about his mother having died in the cold. And now, Vivian was trying to take his mother's place as the only woman he loved, yet she didn't qualify for that position in her worldliness, Lee decided.

He drew his hand back, made a tight ball of it, and sent it pummeling into the side of his wife's face, catching her other eye this time. She dropped to the floor on impact. A bone in her cheek almost snapped when he reached down and sucker-punched her. However, Lee didn't think that was quite enough. He went to the straight chair, picked it up as high as he could, and dropped it on her. It landed on her back and arms. Mary wailed, desperate for the armor of her mother.

Henry ignored them when he heard muffled arguing coming through the walls, but when Henry heard a loud thud, he sat up with a jolt. He listened for a few seconds, and then he leaned back, with his palms clasped together. Henry heard Lee yell, and he pulled the covers over his head in denial. Then, he heard the straight chair crash to the floor, followed by the baby crying. He finally went quickly to the sound and rapped edgily on their door.

"Viv?" Lee, with his foot in midair aimed at his wife's abdomen, jumped to his senses at the sound of the knock.

"Don't bother us man, we busy," Lee called impatiently. Mary continued to cry. Lee looked at Vivian to see her response to Henry's knock, and discovered she was only able to whimper in pain. He lifted her, half dragging her to the bed where he deposited her. Henry ignored Lee's order. He tapped on the door again, this time more loudly than the first time.

"Viv! You all right?" Lee hurried to cover her with the blanket, and quickly crawled under with her. Vivian, welcoming the comfort of her bed, put up no resistance. She hoped Lee would hurry before Henry would see that she had been beaten. She preferred that Henry learned about her beatings after the fact, instead of witnessing her looking sloppy and disheveled. Henry turned the knob and walked slowly into the room. He spotted the overturned chair, but then he saw Vivian and Lee in bed together. He wondered how Vivian could let Mary cry so frantically without tending to her. Lee looked up as though Henry's presence had caused a big disturbance.

"Get outta my room, coon," Lee barked, propping half up on his elbow. Henry wanted Vivian to look at him, see his agony, suffering, and predicament. He wanted her to know that he would be there for her, like he promised her he would. Henry wanted her to understand that he had stayed home from church in hopes of spending time with her. He walked over to get Mary who was yelling at the top of her lungs while Vivian remained still. He quieted the baby, and took her out of the room, leaving the bedroom door wide open.

A second later, he reentered the room, grabbed her blanket, a cloth diaper, her booties, and retreated again. Lee remained leaning on one elbow, staring at the door in confusion. Henry had just entered their bedroom at his own will, and he knew exactly where to find Mary's belongings. If Henry would do that in his presence, how many times had he entered the bedroom when Vivian was alone? Lee's senses became rattled.

Back in his room, Henry sat Mary on his lap while he pulled her socks on, and then changed her diaper. He tied the old one as tight as he could, and then tossed it in the dirty clothes hamper in his room in the closet. He knew Minnie would have a fit when she found the soiled diaper—she always rinsed them right away. After wrapping the blanket securely around her, he carried her outside and strolled down the street. Before he could make it a block, he saw Gancy climb out of his polished Ford, but Henry didn't bother to retreat. He knew he was being rude because it was obvious that Gancy saw them, but Henry didn't feel like watching Gancy fuss over Mary as though he was a part of their family. Vivian's relationship with Lee was falling apart, and perhaps Gancy sensed this, too, Henry thought. Well, Gancy had another thing coming if *he* wanted to be the one to move in on her after Lee was finished.

Henry's behavior only served to put Gancy on point. He knew before he knocked that he would get no answer. Gancy was aware that the only way Lee would let Henry anywhere near Mary was if Vivian was 100% occupied. Therefore, he easily concluded that Lee did not want to be disturbed. And if Lee wasn't inside of the house totally occupying Vivian, why was Henry walking with Mary by himself? No. Lee wasn't going to give Gancy the time of day concerning a job that he didn't want, anyway. He slid the application under the door after a couple of knocks and left.

~~~

"Your daddy is here, child. I'm always gonna be here, so don't you worry none about that crazy man back there." Mrs. Brown, the lady who had given

Henry so much information about gestation, saw him and the bundle coming up the road.

"My word, Mr. Raison. Is that the baby you were asking so much about?" Henry swallowed his pride in a giant gulp. He wanted Mrs. Brown to admire his lovely child, but instead, he walked on by.

"No Ma'am. I wasn't talking about no child in particular. This one belongs to my wife's sister. Have a good day, Mrs. Brown." Henry walked down four more blocks, singing, and talking to Mary until he calmed her into total relaxation. Henry made her happy. She felt her breathing come out in spurts, and her heart was tickled. Mary had never felt this strange, delightful way before...she was laughing for the first time in her life.

CHAPTER TWENTY
I'm dreaming about you Nadine

By the time Henry made it back around to the house, Casey had also made it to Robeena's house, and to her bed with his shoes still on his feet. He had decided it would be senseless to go to the gambling joint without Lee since he had no other partner. Sometimes, Sarah Mae would go with him, but he hadn't told her in advance, and this was the first Sunday of the month, her day off. Casey's irritation had subsided because he was plum drained. He concluded that had he and Lee gone gambling after all, it was highly likely that it would have proven to be a dangerous arrangement. Any mistakes he or Lee would make due to inattention could result in their being caught in their cheating. Therefore, Casey decided to get some good sleep in town at Robeena's. Later, he would pick up the money from the two girls who were working this Sunday.

Robeena entered the room carrying a box of crackers and two glasses of lemonade. Casey sat up just enough to receive and taste the refreshments, and then he slid back down on the pillow. She made herself believe his insecurities were the real reason he'd come back so soon. Robeena took the glass out of his hand and sat it on the nightstand. She figured Bruno's presence had made an impact on her relationship with Casey, and that she could expect more attention and gifts. In return, she would offer him peace and quiet of mind.

"I'm happy you came back, Case, but as I recall, you're supposed to be going somewhere with Lee, right?"

"Sure 'nough, but they're some odd folks 'round yonder!"

"Humph." Robeena thought so, also, but she didn't want to say too much since they were her family. Nevertheless, the wish to boost her own ego ratified her to elaborate. "I'm surprised Lee even up here, the way he used to carry on down South!" She gained Casey's interest.

"How do you mean?"

"They used to fight all the time, Lee and Viv. Lee's crazy!"

"What way do they fight? You mean physically?"

"Shoot yeah! Lee used to smack her around—over dumb stuff, too." Casey sat up again. "Vivian came crying to me a few times after he roughed her up, begging me not to tell mama. She was always so scared! I tried telling her to leave him, and she would. But they'd get back together after a few hours, it seemed like."

"You're jiving." Robeena folded her arms and pouted, looking away from him to show her seriousness. "How do you know, then?" He asked. She turned back to face him.

"Cause I used to be there!" Casey looked at her in disbelief. She corrected herself. "Not there when he used to hit her, but, you know, I would be there afterward, when she would come home and all. I don't see how she put up with that."

"What about Minnie and Henry," Casey eased into the subject, "Henry beat his wife, too?" He asked as though he disagreed with this notion.

"Hah! Not a chance. Henry's a big teddy bear. Minnie ain't gotta worry none about him." For a fleeting second, Robeena recalled how hostile Henry had grown about the late hours she kept. She remembered how he had taunted her and how he tried to force her into submission by towering over her. However, she determined she could distinguish between Henry's care and Lee's control because Henry never had that wild look - he behaved like her father might have, had he been around.

Casey was mindful not to seem too excited about this helpful information concerning their family dynamics. Robeena was revealing family secrets and treasures to him, and Casey intended to use all information for a profit. He was a hustler in his every endeavor. Everything Casey indulged in was for his personal gain. Very rarely would one find him sitting idly with another human being unless he had just finished eating or something.

"Well, Henry sure seems to pay a lot of attention to Vivian," Casey was careful not to peep around at Robeena's face. "He probably knows about Lee beating on her."

Robeena curled up on the bed. She rested her head on his chest, and threw her legs over his legs. "Yeah. He knows." Casey didn't dare speak because he refused to interrupt her train of thought. A minute later, Robeena decided Casey was someone she could confide in about all of this. "Henry *is* funny acting around Viv," she began. Casey held his breath. He knew he was going to have to reward Robeena for this. He draped his arm around her shoulder lovingly.

"How do you mean," he feigned concern.

"I don't know. I'm not sure."

"Come on! You know," Casey said mischievously, in order to encourage her further, "because you *might* be talking about what *I'm* talking about," he bargained. Now, Robeena's own curiosity was sparked. She would exchange with him, then. She'd tell first.

"I went over there the other day, right?" Casey nodded his head vigorously. "I walked on in the house, and I saw Vivian in the hallway by Henry's door. She was really nervous, too." She checked Casey's response. He didn't appear excited about her broadcast, so she added the rest quickly. "She was stammering and all, then she told me that no one was home but her. But later, when I saw Minnie, she said Henry hadn't gone nowhere all day on account of he didn't have any shoes!" Casey gasped loudly, imitating his prostitute, Sarah Mae, to seem like a good girlfriend to Robeena.

"You mean . . ."

"That's exactly what I mean."

"You think it just happened that one time? Or was it going on down South?" Robeena had indeed considered that possibility before, but it was hard for her to imagine *it* happening at all, for that matter. Her heart skipped a beat. Although she felt it was in bad taste that Vivian had slept on the Raison Plantation under Henry's care, she never wanted to assume that she'd had a romantic affair with Henry. Robeena viewed Vivian as highly flirtatious, but not as a homewrecker.

"No...that's not what I mean."

Impatiently, Casey remarked, "You just said..."

"I just meant that they seem to be awfully good friends, but nothing..." Suddenly, she sat upright, her mouth flew open, and her eyes bucked.

Casey played the hypnotist. "What do you remember, Beena?" He urged.

"Aw, man! One time down South, Lee beat Viv up pretty bad. My mama 'nem was worried about her because she didn't come home, so they sent Henry to find her. He didn't show back up 'til the next day, and when he did, Viv wasn't with him. He told us she'd spent the night on his plantation with a healer on account of she was scared to go home. I wanted to go see her, but Henry said Viv didn't want to see nobody. She came home like a day later than that!"

"Whew!" Casey exclaimed. His nosey, backbiting appetite heightened. "Nobody said nothing about that?"

"Nope."

"Does Lee know?"

"I'm not sure. I don't think so. He acts like he knows, though. He don't let nobody come near her when he ain't around—at least he tries. Even when he is around, he still acts like he don't even want us to talk to our own sister. And don't *let* Henry say *nothing* to her."

"Well, what I saw today was Henry looking at her too hard, and Lee was pissed as hell, but he let it go," Casey volunteered as a token of his good faith for receiving private details of their family's secrets.

"That's hard to believe, Case." She shook her head, not wanting to admit to Casey or herself how she had been bothered by Henry and Vivian's relationship for months. "It's too crazy. I ain't got no proof of none of this." Casey didn't care what Robeena thought now that he had gotten an ear full. He was tired of talking about it for the time being. He showed this by turning over on his side with his back to her, allowing her head to gently come down on the bed with the assistance of his hands.

"You want some more lemonade?" Robeena asked, trying to maintain the closeness they had just shared. He shook his head. Robeena picked up her glass, taking one last gulp. Then she cuddled next to him where they both went fast to sleep, both still exhausted from their separate parties of the previous night.

Vivian opened her eyes slowly. She felt dizzy. The light in the room caused tears to swell behind her lids. Lee was looking at her with a frightened facial cast. She tried to speak, but her mouth felt heavy and puffy. The feel of his sweaty thigh against her leg produced a friction inside of her. She was irritated by the smell of his breath and its heat on her face. Lee was overjoyed that she seemed to be gaining her senses. She had blacked out for a moment.

"Princess!" He scooted closer to her and hugged her. "Muffin, you scared me half to death." He had overcome his temper with her that had caused him to beat her. She had two swollen eyes and a knot on her forehead. Vivian used the blanket to cover herself in darkness, and to seal off his hot breath. She evaded him for ten minutes. He couldn't say anything because he needed to know where her mind was before he made his next move.

"It's the same ole stuff, Lee," she said dryly. "I'm sick of you hitting me. You stay out all night, then you come home like I done did something wrong. I's—I'm tired of you, and I'm tired of this stupid marriage." She was ready for Lee's usual apologies, nevertheless, she was disinterested in hearing them repeatedly. She braced herself for his routine repentance when she heard a short series of sniffs. Slowly, she removed the blanket to sneak a look at the hated beast disguised as her husband.

A single, oversized tear made the pilgrimage down one cheek, pausing at the crook beside his nose. This was truly an unusual sight to see. If home version cameras were readily available in that year for poor Negroes, Vivian would have taken a picture. She had not conceived of this act in his reparations. Nevertheless, she was highly pleased with his dedication and effort. She showed empathy for his display of emotions by removing the contempt in her expression. Seeing that his plan was working, he released another huge tear from underneath his eyelid.

"Muffin, I don't know what the hell's wrong with me," he divulged truthfully. "Sometimes, I just feel out of control." He touched her shoulder lightly before continuing. "You're my princess, baby...I know I got a lot of faults, and I know you see 'em. I'm thinking you done turned against me for my faults. But if I can't change 'em, what right is you got to hate me?"

"You can change them, Lee. You just don't want to. You want me to sit here and wait on you while you go out and play. I knew you had women down South, and now you have them up here. There's no sense in us being married to torture one another." He shifted uncomfortably.

"Don't leave me, muffin pie! Please don't. I ain't got no life without you. I'll talk to a preacher if that's what you think is best. Mayhap I do need some help, 'cause Lord knows I want us to be happy together."

"I can't trust you, though, Lee. I can't count the number of times you beat me. I suppose you're going to keep doing it, too, if I let you." No one said anything for a long while.

"Help me, princess. I married you 'cause I love you." It had been a great while since he had uttered those words to her. She was grateful. "That's why I told Casey to go on—I wanted to be with you, but I was stupid. Me and you should do more together, baby. That's our problem—we don't spend enough time together. How would you like it if we go to Detroit and just be together, shopping, eating—you know?" Vivian instinctively glanced over to check on Mary.

"Where's Mary?"

"Henry got her," he said reluctantly. "He took her when you were asleep."

"I wasn't asleep, Lee. You knocked me out," she said bitterly. She felt better to think of Mary in her strong daddy's arms. A picture of Leland flashed past her mind's eye. She empathized with the toddler's circumstances; however, her marital expectations superseded the importance of Leland. If she could trust Lee to behave around Maybelle, then perhaps Leland could be a part of their lives.

As much as she tried, she could not shake the image of Lee's bestial countenance preceding the force of his blow crashing against her facial structure. Presently, he didn't resemble a beast at all—he had shifted back into a kind, loving man. Vivian looked beside her and saw the majestic Lee, the man who had swept her off her feet almost three years ago. This was the man who had begged her to marry him. He had refused to dishonor her with fornication. He insisted that they make their union legal in the eyesight of Almighty God. This chivalrous person offered her a life with the promise of more fulfillment than her mother had enjoyed in her own degrading pseudo-romance. Then, what was the meaning of his violence? The suffering it took for Vivian to acknowledge that just moments ago she had drifted into unconsciousness, no matter how briefly, was more severe than the actual blows.

Lee was suffering, too. He loved his wife and child, and he wanted the three to be a family forever. Somehow, though, he was unable to stop his resentment from mounting at times. It was Henry's fault. Lee confessed to himself that he frequently allowed Henry to get under his skin, and his anxiety sent him fleeing to beat his wife. Once again, he not only had struck her, but he was responsible for blackening her eye, and swelling the other one, which could blacken, too. The id fury that had precipitated his passion fled the scene. Now, he was left with his rational self to deal with the state of affairs, and the truth was that he had no proof or reason to connect Vivian with un-holiness. Surely, his princess bride wouldn't dream of committing the sordid acts he connected in his mind. He remembered the fight with Floyd at his birthday party. It all started when Floyd got fresh with Vivian, Lee learned from Hamilton. Vivian was obviously so sure of herself that she never found it necessary to even tell Lee what Floyd's aim was that night, Lee thought. He had to learn how to trust her before he lost her.

He was in a state of panic that for the first time since they were married, Vivian had threatened to leave him in a profoundly serious tone. When he'd forced his two tears earlier, it was to say to his wife that he cared about her and their relationship. He was willing to cry even more tears if necessary to prove the validity of his love. Lee rationalized that Henry was married to her sister, and therefore could not, would not commit adultery with Vivian. The question that lingered on Lee's mind was "why was Henry so opposing?" He wondered what Henry's motive was in alienating him, and what views Henry carried about him that triggered this disdain.

Mary's voice cried from the hallway, proceeding Henry's knock. "Hello in there," he called. "Mary wants her mama." Vivian, without having been directed by Lee, automatically pulled the blanket over her face to hide her bumps and bruises from the awaiting visitor. She positioned herself to face the wall away from their guest. Vivian created a back door because she preferred to hide in her private hell. Henry was the only one welcome to witness her hell, but he was accepted only when she decided it would benefit her. In her hell, Henry had front row seasonal tickets by the fiery furnace; she could torture him for not choosing her over Minnie.

When Lee slapped her or knocked her down, she was knocked down emotionally and spiritually, as well. Yet, when she regained her posture physically, her psychological posture remained in a horizontal position. Even though she had mentioned the fights to her sisters and Henry before, she mentioned them confidentially, and under circumstances that made her family members powerless to help her. She didn't want to be helped if that meant removing Lee from her life. She preferred to be pitied. Help to her was when Henry told her she was beautiful and didn't deserve such treatment. She received emotional courage if (she interpreted that) her sisters silently acknowledged how much Lee *had* to love her to go to such extremes.

Lee returned to his smug self at her quiet concealment. He jumped out of bed--happy to let Henry see *his* bare chest for a change, walked with agility to the door, and flung it open. For Lee, Vivian's refusal to acknowledge Henry relieved a great deal of apprehension, and it made him appreciate her for her discernible devotion and obedience. The first thing Henry noticed when he looked immediately past Lee was Vivian sagging over under the covers. Even though she hid her physical being, her heartwarming self in which she connected with Henry spoke loudly. Lee trudged directly in front of his view and attempted to take Mary. Henry sidestepped forward to the left, entering the room with Mary held close to his chest.

"Vivian," he called loudly enough to awaken her had she been sleeping, "Mary wants *you*!" Lee caught up with him and reached for Mary again.

"Hey man! I'll take my baby." Henry allowed Mary to slip into the arms of Lee, who went to put her in her crib, fully expecting Henry to be gone by the time he turned back around. He heard Henry call Vivian's name again, and when he looked around, Henry had already made it to the bedside.

"Vivian?" He called again. Henry had to decide. Either he could walk away like he did earlier and pretend the knocking around he'd heard was normal, or he could investigate what was more probable. If he made another step, he might make a fool out of himself. Was he to wake her up for no reason? How could he explain himself if he pressed forward? Yet, if he walked away, he would be denying the fight he'd heard. So what? They could fight and it was none of his business. Oh, well, Henry thought. It was now or never.

It took Lee a few seconds to regain the ability to move after the initial shock at the temerity of Henry to approach Vivian while she was in bed. Henry finally snatched the protective shield away from her face when she didn't answer the second time. When he saw her, it was like a stick of dynamite being ignited in his gut. He stood perfectly still, as if attempting to avoid the flames from spreading. Nevertheless, the fire from the dynamite flooded his intestines, moving through his limbs, and, the flames reached his heart. There was an internal explosion that manifested externally with

Henry's body visibly shaking. Vivian opened her eyes to figure out why the covers had been pulled away from her face. A flash of Vivian sitting crumpled and beat up on Lee's porch entered his mind. This time was different. She was the mother of his only child and another man had dogged his family right while he was twenty feet away in the same house.

"Vivian!"

"Go on, Henry...please go on out..." She sat up abruptly.

As though he had just found the missing piece of a crime puzzle, Henry nodded thoughtfully and said quietly, "Well, I'll be damned."

"Niggah, you better get the hell out of here like she said before I..."

"Please, Henry!" He looked over at Mary and shook his head. Then sharply, he shot a few daggers in Vivian's direction.

"Ain't this a bitch?" Vivian had never seen the look in Henry's eyes. He was angry with *her*! "Vivian, are you okay?"

"Yes, of course I am," she muttered, jumping to her feet. She knew she had messed up this time because Henry doted after Mary so. He was ill with her for having his baby in a hostile environment. Vivian didn't know what Henry might do or say. His demeanor frightened her, and her fear of him outweighed her fear of Lee.

"So Mary was in here screaming earlier..." He glared at Lee. "Y'all couldn't see about her because you were beating up your wife instead?" Henry appraised Vivian with disgust. "Get Mary and take her to my room..."

"Niggah you don't give orders to my wife. I do that."

"It's okay, Lee—I'll go!" Henry clenched his fist. Vivian briskly complied without looking at Lee, who was thinking diligently of a way to save face since Vivian had just blatantly disrespected him. He searched for something smart to say as an excuse for his wife's condition when he was left alone to face Henry. He knew Henry cared too much about Vivian to let this incident pass.

"This is a sad damn sight. Man, you *know* you's a sorry assed faggot, don't you?"

"Look, Henry...I'm trying to be calm about this, but you know you ain't got no business in here."

"Why don't you make it my business and put your hands on me like you did her? I would like that a lot, Lee." Lee didn't see how a fight could be avoided. It was evident Henry meant to have a showdown or else why send Vivian away with Mary? Lee hoped Vivian would hurry back and act as an intercessor to any impending violence. In the meantime, he took a step toward Henry in a display of fearlessness, and to save face, but that was the wrong move. When Henry saw him coming, he charged at him with a drop-kick, sending him flying halfway into the hallway, through the wide-open door. Vivian screamed at the top of her lungs on her way back to the scene. Henry chased the flying body, and viciously kicked Lee in his temple and chest, putting great might behind each blow. Lee did all he could with his arms to prevent the power from smashing him to pieces.

"Henry! Stop it!" Mary let out a yelp. Henry spun around at his daughter's wail, tightening his jaw. He faced Vivian.

"Go tend to her." He spoke with an apparent calm that contradicted his shimmering, blazing heart. Vivian quickly made it back to Mary, and scooped her up with one arm. She kissed her, patted her head, placed her back in the bed, and then ran back to the scene, shutting the door behind her. Mary was too bewildered to cry out again.

When Vivian got back out into the hallway, Lee had stopped trying to make it up off the floor. His head was bleeding. Henry hesitated under the threshold as if in indecision about whether to kick him once more. When he saw Vivian again, the same flame re-ignited wrath in his heart, causing him to put extra weight behind his foot that visited Lee's abdomen this time. Vomiting, Lee slipped immediately into a state of oblivion. What seemed like hours later, Lee heard some words uttered by his assailant.

"Damn you, Lee, that ain't no way to treat her!" He looked at Vivian and shook his head. "Fetch me some water so I can pour it on this moron's head and then I'll use his head like a mop to mop up that stinking mess in my hallway." Vivian started away to get a towel and water bucket, praying Henry really wouldn't hit Lee again or use his body as a mop. He grabbed her arm. "Naw, don't go nowhere yet, sweetheart. I'll clean it up directly. We need to talk."

"I…she…uhhgh," Lee muttered, not realizing he was incoherent.

"I swear I just want her to be happy, man. You not gonna be able to beat her like this while I'm here, niggah. Vivian, stop crying. He's all right—he ain't gonna die. Why are you crying o'er him? You should be crying o'er yourself."

"*She started the fight…*" Lee still did not realize his words only sounded in his head.

"I do cry over myself, Henry."

"Get out…"

"Vivian, you've been beaten badly. Your face is torn up, baby." She walked back into the bedroom, and Henry followed her.

"*Baby?*"

"Stop crying. I'm sorry for talking to you like this, but it's the truth. Just stop crying. I'm sorry."

"Why are you in my room? Make him get out, Vivian!" From his position halfway in the hallway, Lee thought he saw Henry take Vivian around her waist, and hold her close with trembling arms. Vivian was shuddering uncontrollably.

"You ought not have done that, Henry!" As Lee slipped out of consciousness, he considered that Vivian had felt as helpless as he did currently when she herself had been unconscious earlier. Henry's frenzied voice thundered through, waking him briefly.

"How long are you gonna let 'im beat you, woman?" Lee wanted this man away from his wife so enormously that he could taste it in the blood oozing from his lips and forehead. "What kinda relationship is it when a woman gets whipped all the time?"

"I'm not letting him do anything!" She felt weak and pitiful. Henry knowing about what she was going through with Lee was not as romantic as she originally had pictured it. He was repulsed by it.

"I hate this shit," Henry spat. She could tell he thought she should be able to control what happened to her. Maybe he was right, she thought.

"Please don't be mad at me, Henry," she cried.

"What? Come on, baby, sit down. There's no way I could get mad at you."

"Don't look at me like that, Henry. I prefer to stand."

"No. Sit. Vivian, you ain't the only one involved here. Mary is a part of this foolish behavior, too."

"I know, Henry. I need a moment to think…"

"Damn!"

"Stop looking at me…I know I'm a mess…"

"Honey, I hate to say that I have seen you worse off at the hands of your so-called husband."

"*Honey?*"

"Yeah, but…"

"I don't want Mary having to see this happening to you. See there—I told you before, Vivian. Now I'm acting like Lee with all this violence. I don't wanna be an example like that in front of Mary. I wanna know everything! If you can't handle it, Viv, then it seems somebody gots to handle it, see?" He still had her encircled in his hold.

"Let go, Henry. Don't do that. I can walk." He easily led her to a seat on the bed. After picking it up from the floor, he pulled Lee's favorite chair up close to her. Henry was asking her to tell him what it was like with Lee. He wanted to know how things had come to this.

Lee heard Vivian tell him about the time he twisted her arm in the woods, near the rock. "Are you talking 'bout that day after church?" He heard

Henry's voice ask.

"The day you met him."

"I didn't want you to go with him, even then."

"I knew it!"

"You sure hid your feelings well."

"I guess so. But not no more."

"Shhh!"

"Had he hit you before you met me?"

"Henry, we talked about this. You asked me about this already, and I admitted it way back in Florida."

"But, I should have asked more questions. I wasn't listening good enough."

"It was the first time he hit me, I mean like, struck me. You don't have nothing—anything to do with it, Henry."

"This ain't you, Vivian. I mean, you like to sew, read, and someday, maybe you can be a teacher. You don't need stuff in your life that'll bring you down."

"I haven't stopped sewing and reading…"

"Good for you, but what he's doing is still wrong." He held her hand loosely in his. She closed her eyes, thinking of how Lee insisted that she was carrying on in front of Henry, even before she wanted Henry to know that she had a crush on him. "No, I mean it. It ain't normal for a man to do you like that. Now, you tell me how long you're willing to let 'im jump on you."

Lee opened an eye and saw his wife's hand in Henry's hand. He couldn't stop his eyes from closing back again as he thought, *"Yes, this is the first time anybody has ever hit me, except my daddy when I was a young boy."* He remembered that time his father whipped him for tracking mud in the house. His mother let him beat him, and later, he saw his father buttoning the back of his mother's dress. She swung her head back, with her eyes closed, and used her small, dexterous fingers to put on her jewelry. They were going out together, as though his whipping and sadness from it didn't matter.

"You make it seem like I want this, Henry."

"No, but you gotta hate it just a li'l bit more, baby. Don't you know you don't deserve to have no man do you like that? You truly, truly don't know how precious you are, darling…you hear me?" She thought of how she cheated on Lee with Henry, and decided inwardly that she deserved whatever she got from Lee.

"Yes."

"It don't make no sense."

"We just get to arguing all the time. I don't know."

"So, you have a disagreement, and then he decides to put his hands on you?"

"I'm not dumb, Henry. Sooner or later, all men beat their wives over something."

"What happened to you, Vivian? Why do you think that's normal?"

"You tell me. You're a man."

"Look at all the lynching and carrying on we suffer. Why would it be normal for us to hurt each other? Ain't we had enough? Ain't *you* had enough?

"I'm dreaming," Lee mouthed. He tried to open his eyes again, but this time, too much strength was required. He vaguely heard Vivian describing a couple of their fights. Henry kept asking her for details. *"I'm not crazy! I know I ain't the first man that beat his girl, and I ain't gonna be the last..."*

"Come on, Henry! Don't focus on bad stuff."

"That's why he's still beating on you. You need to open your mouth and bear witness to what's happening. The longer you hide in this hell of a marriage, the worse he gonna get."

"It's not like I don't know, but it's so shameful to me—what my life is like."

"I can't believe you put up with it. What all did he do to you, girl?" Henry's voice urged onwards. Lee lost track of the time. He managed to squint one eye open to see Vivian's hand still trembling. He couldn't tell if the skin he saw was a big blur of Vivian's hand or Henry's hand over her hand. She was weeping quite a bit.

"A lot of things—they don't matter anymore."

"I don't matter."

"Honey, you can talk to me. Don't cry. They do matter—everything that makes you unhappy matters to me. It ain't your fault what he did. Don't hold it inside no more...this is the only way you're gonna be able to do something about it. You gotta face it. You married him, but, he's the worst thing in your life."

"The worst thing in my life?" She blew a heavy breath, sticking out her bottom lip. "I could think of something worse."

"Tell me!" His voice had become ever more caressing. She whimpered. Lee hopelessly wanted to shout out to her but his words were floating in his brain. He desperately wanted to silence Vivian. *Too much talking in the house about nonsense made his daddy crazy. What was that his mother had told him? No, that was his father who used to always say there was too much talking going on in the house. Lee remembered his mother used to laugh at his father and say he was too serious. Then, she would call for him, her only child, and ask him if he wanted to go out and play. Next, she would kindly shove him out the front door so that she and daddy could "talk." Lee remembered how calm his mother had acted when she rushed him outside, making sure his sweater was tied, and his hat fastened. His father would impatiently pace the floor, obviously aggravated with, what was his mother's name? Nadine! He had forgotten for years. It was Nadine!*

"The worst thing? You don't want that information." She wished she could tell him what happened to her, but not now-unless he could guess on his own. "Lee---his friends are just as bad as — worse than him."

"He's a trifling thing, and ev'rybody he hangs out with. You's the only sunshine that man got, and he's stupid enough to hurt you."

"Henry, there are things I let happen to me that weren't all Lee's fault, either."

"How come things ain't his fault? He's supposed to be your husband. Hell. I want a shot at that job so I can show you how a man is supposed to love and protect a woman."

"I'm just saying I know I play a role in all of this."

"It's not your fault, sweetie. You can't grow him up."

"We all make mistakes, Henry." She wondered if Lee could hear them. It didn't seem like he could, but she needed to shut Henry up, because he was getting too emotional, and Lee, her husband, was sprawled out on the floor a few feet away while Henry discussed how he wanted a shot at being her man.

"But why would you marry him? After what he did to you down South… how could you let him be your husband? See, I can't understand that. Vivian, if you let me see—just what the hell do you take me for? You know how I feel about you…"

"Shhh! He'll hear you!"

"Come closer to me, then." He whispered hoarsely in her ear, "I told you down South I wasn't gonna let 'im get away with this. You'd better do something, baby. Mayhap you need to come on to church with me and Minnie so as you can tell the pastor. Get some papers drawn up to end this thing, Vivian."

"What?"

"You heard me."

"Well, maybe I don't want to be all alone in this life. You have Minnie… and as I can clearly *see*…you seem to be loving her fine," Vivian said just above a whisper.

"Don't say that."

"That hurt me more than somebody pounding me in my face."

"I wish you would leave that alone for now. You is going through too much to be bringing that up. I know what you saw when you came into my room last night, and we can talk about that in a minute…"

"Henry…"

"Come here…" *Lee saw his father reach for his mother and swing her around as though they were dancing, only her calm, serene look had been replaced with one of stricken terror. Lee saw his mother through the curtains allowing herself to be subdued. He ran away down the street feeling ashamed. He hated her for her cowardice with his father, yet loved her softness. Young Lee loved his mother immensely. She was pure, rich, beautiful, his first teacher, and his first doctor. Therefore, young Lee would look to marry a woman who possessed similar characteristics as his mother. He listened for his mother's low, familiar voice, now, but suddenly, there was a great silence in the room. Lee opened his eyes and saw he was still parallel to the chipped painted ceiling. His whole body ached. Comprehension poured over him.*

It was true! Had Henry held her while she wept? He looked up quickly at the bed. Vivian was there with Mary. There was no sign of Henry. It had to be a dream, yet his pounding head negated the possibility of all the recent events being in a dream. He forced the image of Henry tenderly embracing his timid, battered wife, and the picture of her hand clutching Henry's out of his mind. It simply couldn't be. It exasperated him to even suggest such a thing to himself as Henry touching Vivian in any manner for any reason.

"Vivian?" Her countenance was gloomy when she looked at him in silent contempt. Scooting into the bedroom, he dragged himself successfully from the floor, over to their bed to be near her. She moved over to allow him a cozy space beside her, only, she didn't truly welcome his presence. She needed one of her walks- one of the few things she'd never let him take away from her. She found the streets of Pontiac just as calming as the roads in Florida for her walks, even without the numerous trees and wide, green fields. The fresh, snug air was suitable when she was all alone with Mary, walking and thinking. "What happened?" He beseeched.

"You got in a fight with Henry," she replied flatly. He held his breath.

"I saw 'im hold you, Viv."

"My hands were shaking. I was trembling. He held my hands until I stopped trembling."

"You don't know how that made me feel, to see 'im touch you."

"It wasn't like that, Lee. He was just trying to calm me after…"

"You let 'im hold your hand. I saw your hand on the sheet, and his hand —the hand of another man's was o'er yours."

"Stop it, Lee."

"What else happened here?" Her expression was that of disinterest.

"Nothing," she said quietly, "except you-all act like children when you-all fight like that. So, what are you fixing to do *now*, start another fight?"

"No!" Lee said quickly, nestling closer to her to let her know he was through battling. "I should, though. Henry ain't have no right to jump on me, 'specially without me looking. Did you see how he jumped me from behind? Double-dealer can't even fight fair."

"Well, you can't either, because you are a man and I am a lady. Yet, you jump on me from behind, sideways, or anyway you see fit." Lee tightened his face.

"See, your mouth is why you get jumped on. We were doing fine 'til he came to the door with Mary. You were speaking to me nicely, and I was speaking nicely to you. We were even talking about going on us a li'l date to Detroit. I wanna take you shopping and stuff." Vivian wondered if he remembered what led to Henry taking Mary in the first place, given that he conveniently omitted those intricate details in his report. But then again, Lee always seemed capable of pointing out the faults in others, excluding himself from all wrong doings, she thought. "Now, for some reason all of a sudden you act like you on *his* side."

"You know better than that."

"Humph."

"I was not involved in any way, except for getting jumped on after you stayed out all night."

"All I know is we're getting outta here. Hell. I ain't staying nowhere I ain't wanted. I would go get with that boy right now and put my foot in his behind, but then where are we gonna stay?" Vivian gave a wide-eyed look in pretense that she believed Lee had the capabilities to subdue Henry. Lee chortled grimly, to discredit the occurrence. "Man, Viv, I was out like a light when he came at me from behind!" Lee mulled over how he was going to show his face again around Henry, after it had been proven that Henry meant serious business about his unspoken mission.

Lee vowed to never again beat his wife—not because he was afraid of Henry, but he knew Henry couldn't be a germ of a threat if Vivian was happy in her marriage. He wanted to improve his relationship with her if she'd only do what he wanted! He didn't want to declare that he didn't know how to make her happy. The meaningless trinkets and the money he gave her only influenced her for so long. After they ran out, he recognized that he didn't even know what to say to her at times. There were no substantial conversations or anything to stimulate her mind. He didn't read the same books, or at all, except for girlie magazines. He didn't want to go shopping with her, he didn't want her to go anywhere with him, either. Furthermore, he bitterly accepted he was not excelling at anything that would make her want to follow him anywhere. The only thing that seemed to work was to feed her emotionally. This is because she had been emotionally starved all her life, therefore, any nutrition that fed this need was accepted by Vivian.

Lee chose Vivian as the woman he would love forever—not so that he could beat her or humiliate her by chasing other women, either. He chose her because she reminded him of his mother whom he loved with all his heart. He had a certain image of his mother that was never tarnished in the vessels of his soul. The complications came because Lee didn't know how to love anyone else, as he was a victim of self-hatred.

Lee did everything to place himself in harm's way. Anxiety and depression drove him to booze, drugs, and loose sex. Ignorance drove him to swine and greasy, fried beef burgers weighted down in salt and fat, even though the physical manifestation of the poisons was visible in his neighbors, family members, and friends. Whenever he was at his optimum, he ate fruit, fish, and grains -very conscious about his body and skin shine. When Lee was a small boy, he would ask his mother, "What is self-love?" She told him it was learning to read, play musical instruments, and working harder to 'be somebody' than anyone else around him. However, the spiritual tone was not emphasized in a way Lee could comprehend, so, as he got older, the major thing Lee worked hard at was figuring out how to juggle his time between the streets and home so that he could possess his cake while eating it. Lee deliberated on how he could live the street life like Casey, but at the same time, he wanted to be home enough to stand guard over his wife.

Lee's grandparents on his father's side had told him stories to humor him about the ways of life on the plantation, but the stories did more than that for Lee. Even as his grandparents told him that the slave masters always wanted to know how they could control the slave, Lee calculated how he could control Vivian, so that she would be devoted only to him. His love drove him to lock her up to build trust. Lee had to devise a plan which would allow him to continue his street life and keep his wife in love with him. Although Lee would never fathom the depth of injury that his former slave masters committed, he knew he could never trust them. Thus, he was able to discern that because of his own wicked ways, he could never hope that Vivian would trust him fully. He wanted to trust her at home alone with Henry while he would go out to fornicate and smoke. His guilt made him lash out at her because he *expected* her to rebel against him. This immensely obstructed Lee as he knew not a way out of this condition.

He didn't know how to use the keys to get inside of his own mind and figure things out because he kept the keys buried under the rubbish that he was making of his life. His insecurities wouldn't let him find the keys— wouldn't let him know that he could make a better reality for himself and his family. Moving away without changing the condition of one's heart is like taking a trip with nothing but garbage in the suitcases. Lee discovered how impossible it was to open the door to a new life using old keys.

The keys Lee used were to help him keep Vivian under control. He knew he had to use the key of affection, which he recognized she craved as it provided instant gratification. Endurance and tolerance of one another as a means to long-term satisfaction was foreign to both Vivian and Lee. That is why they each settled on every moment of happiness in exchange for hours and years of bitterness. They only used the keys as pacifiers to unlock momentary pleasures that would not open the door to long-lasting trust and bonding, as they should hope.

CHAPTER TWENTY-ONE
Casey at the bat

Lee and Vivian entered the "kiss-kiss" stage in the cycle of violence that permeated their relationship. Affectionate behavior, promises to never distress each other again, renewal of vows, lovemaking, and long, romantic evenings characterized this stage. The "kiss-kiss" period would last roughly two weeks. Vivian wanted to look sexy for Lee. She ditched some of her long skirts that she'd struggled to make and started buying more of the seductive clothing she found at Sears department store. When she got the hang of it, she made several blouses and skirts that were "in style" nowadays--her favorite being a dark green, tight-fitting skirt that narrowly covered her knees past one inch.

Lee's enduring appraisal and nods were the applause Vivian received for her short skirts that were scarcely beyond, and sometimes just above the knees. Vivian was torn between taking the time to sew as much, or to enjoy shopping trips where she could purchase the latest fashions with the wad of money Henry had given her last June. Her indecision was part of an entire movement called "Women's Liberation" that germinated in the 20's and would later explode in the sixties. When the Women's Liberation Movement hit the scene, women marched down the streets holding up signs saying they wanted equal economic advances as men were given. They said they didn't want to sew and cook as much, because they needed jobs to rear their families. They said they refused to be discriminated against, and they wanted the same pay as men. By this time, several major wars had already impacted the labor pool of men.

The Movement was possible because disgruntled America and her wars left hundreds of thousands of women to fend for themselves. With World War II, many women lost their husbands for a few years, and some of the husbands left never to return. Many women didn't have time to sew because they had to go out and work in their husbands' absence. Eventually, sewing, mending, and even cooking were not encouraged practices. Sarah Lee would do the baking, and Chef Boyardee (who wasn't a real chef) would blend the sauces for the pasta. School aged children wanted their clothing bought from the store, in order that they would "fit in" with the other students. For many, it was more acceptable to shop at J.C. Penny's and Sears & Roebuck for new attire.

Big businesses and those who owned them could not become rich if women were sewing their own clothes. Eventually, the long, pretty cotton dresses Vivian used to wear were redefined in some of the modern communities as "mammy made." This phrase came as a derogatory title for the clothing that mothers used to make for their children when mothers knew how to sew. When mothers and neighborhood seamstresses no longer dominated the clothes making industry, the long sleeves and high ruffled collars went out and hip huggers came in.

Vivian knew nothing of Women's Liberation, but she knew she wasn't experiencing freedom, justice, and equality in her relationship with Lee. She knew she was ready to stand up and fight for that justice, to ensure peace in her household. What she didn't know or accept was her own role in the destruction of her marriage, and life. The kiss-kiss stage made it ever so easy to ignore undercurrents and brewing storms. What Vivian wanted was deep emotional fulfillment that would erase any thoughts of future planning, accountability, and self-control. Vivian wasn't willing to accept any personal liability for Mary's upbringing and emotional retardation. She was satisfied to be able to blame Lee for all mishaps, and use him or any other available person to feed her starving soul in any way possible.

Both Robeena and Minnie pulled Vivian to the side during this kiss-kiss period to counsel her. They thought it was absurd that she should walk around with two purple eyes and still act like Lee was the prince of all times. The fact that Lee had bumps and bruises all over his face, too, only proved to Robeena and Minnie how dysfunctional the whole relationship was. Henry never revealed to Minnie that he had taken more than a couple of punches at Lee.

It wasn't until eight o'clock in the evening that Lee came face to face with Henry for the first time since that morning after Henry had throttled Lee. Lee was standing on the front porch enjoying the breeze when he spotted Henry turning the corner at Franklin Road with a brown paper sack in his hand. Henry had found a nearby variety shop that sold strawberry body oil, and he had also purchased some peppermint candy hearts for Vivian. Henry stopped approaching his house to look at something on the ground. There was a small stake planted in the field near the walkway with a sign attached which read: GETHSEMANE CHURCH. There had been much talk, but it looked like a new church was going to be built two houses away. Smiling, Henry moved forward, anxious to get home, bathe, and eat again—alone. The events of earlier troubled him so much that it was a strain to spend time with Minnie. He had beat Vivian's *husband* to the ground because Lee messed over sweet, precious princess Vivian. He couldn't bear the lies of his own silence in Minnie's presence.

Henry slowed his pace when he noticed Lee standing on the porch. Lee had a chance to disappear inside the doorway before Henry got too close, but he stood staring at Henry's shirt until he made it all the way to the porch. It became obvious to Henry that Lee wanted an audience with him.

"Hey, son, sorry 'bout what happened upstairs," Henry lied. "I'm just a defender of women and I saw you damaged one pretty badly." He walked all the way onto the wide porch and stood about two feet from Lee.

"Oh yea?" Lee meant to deal with the issue head on, finally. "But you seem to forget that that's my wife, man." Henry was moderately startled by Lee's abruptness.

"What?" Henry looked Lee square in the eyes. Lee shuffled his feet, but then stopped, remembering to stand upright in the face of fear like Casey had taught him. Lee's fear wasn't that Henry could physically subdue him — that was already apparent—it was the fear of truth in Henry's suggestion made earlier before breakfast that morning.

"I said that's *my* wife." Henry snorted, half turning away from him, trying hard to dismiss Lee's words as trivial.

"Humph."

"Man, if you got something to say to me, why don't you spit it out?" Lee felt his voice getting louder. His bruised ribs and swollen temple would not stop him from confronting Henry. "Man to man, just say it!" With clenched fists, Lee waited for Henry's reply. Henry put his hands on his hips while his fingers smashed his bag close, and spread his legs shoulder length apart.

"All right! Yeah, man. I do got something to say." Lee braced himself for what Henry could say next. Henry frowned at him. "I don't like the way you treat her." Lee became instantly inflamed. How dare he speak so intimately about Vivian! The way he *treated* her? And *baby*, and *honey*? What compassion! Lee's heart skipped a beat when he suddenly realized that never once could he recall Henry referring to Minnie as anything but Minnie. No pet name at all, and yet he would call *his* wife honey? "You don't deserve her, Lee," Henry continued. Lee swallowed deeply. This was too much! What was Henry saying? Henry stood his ground.

"When I first met her, she was lively. You took all that, son. That girl had spirit. You don't give a damn about her. You always running the streets, chasing skirts." Lee's fists came un-balled. Clearly, Henry was taking it and *had taken* it to another level and something had to be done immediately or his marriage would be in danger, Lee thought. "I saw you down South on the Raison Plantation with women and girls. I knowed you before you ever saw me. You ain't no good for her." There was a short pause, but Lee was too stunned to say anything. He mulled over whether Henry had mentioned his visits on the plantation to Minnie. That would explain her sour attitude toward him. In fact, Minnie acted like she wanted him out of her house. "At first, I thought she was wild like you, but turns out she was decent, *and innocent,*" he said, placing great emphasis on his last word.

"You don't know what she was at first or nothing about her. You only wanna know. Well, I'm the man who's in your way, right?" Henry ignored his question and Lee knew he ignored him on purpose.

"Can't you see how miserable you make her? If you don't want her—if you got all these other women 'cause you's a damn playboy, whyn't you leave her alone?" Henry pleaded vainly.

Just then, Minnie came to the door and spoke, making both men jump. "Henry, you still be wanting something else to eat like you said before you left? I kept the food out for you." She would have asked Lee, except she was still agitated with him from that morning.

"Naw, Minnie. Changed my mind. I done had all I can stomach for one day." Henry knew he could eat some other time, but Lee had to be dealt with this moment. Minnie, seeing that the two men were heavily absorbed in conversation, quickly vanished back into the house, hoping they'd hurry it up so Henry could come back inside and be with her. She was fed up with all the fighting going on in her house. Vivian was all bruised up, and it looked like she had gotten a few licks in of her own, according to Lee's face, Minnie thought. She didn't want Henry in the middle of it. She felt if Vivian was stupid enough to let Lee kick her ass that was her business.

When he was certain Minnie was gone, Henry went to the door and closed it to ensure more privacy. Lee was ready to continue with Henry. "Leave her alone? That's deep, man. You're right on that line, Henry. You think you wanna cross it?" Henry clutched his bag of stashed away goodies for his lover as though holding the candy hearts made him closer to Vivian.

"Naw, son. *You're* right on the line. In fact, you done crossed it too many times. That's why I'm involved. What would Ms. Carol say if she knew how you..."

"Involved?"

"I mean...you and I, we fought..."

"So you think getting physical with me is gonna win you points with my woman? She ain't thrilled by that."

"I didn't say she..."

Lee cut him off again. "You know, Vivian is in love with me, you got that?"

"I just don't think you treat her how a lady deserves to be treated. I ain't gonna lie about that so you can be happy. You dogging her…in front of ev'rybody." Lee shrugged his shoulders in exaggerated mockery.

"I mean, that's all well and good, man, that you have that opinion of me—but I can't see where *you* fit in. So far, everything you said gots to do with me and *my* wife." A long sixty seconds passed without a word. The tension was so thick on the porch that a passing dog turned, and went the other way. "But I know you might like her more than you wanted to say," Lee forced, silently pleading for a denial to his statement. Henry was serene and unruffled, provoking Lee's impatient mood. Henry wanted terribly to inform Lee about Mary at that moment. He wanted to confess everything, but he knew that would destroy Minnie and possibly Vivian, too. He wanted to risk it all, though, just for the gamble that he could get back at Lee.

Nonetheless, as he considered his affection for Vivian, he felt sorry for Lee who would never know her as he did. Henry did not believe Vivian was in love with Lee, and he believed he loved Vivian more than Lee. If Lee would be kind to her, Henry promised himself he'd stand back without interfering in their affairs. He rationalized to himself that seeing her happy would give him the strength to put more effort into his own marriage. He loved her enough to let her go, but he loved her too much to let her go.

Henry wanted to tell Lee if he couldn't treat her right, then he planned to pursue Vivian to the end because he was in love with her, not Minnie. And still, if Vivian would accept him, Henry would search Planet Earth for a way to relieve himself of his duties to Minnie, and receive the full responsibility of taking care of his child and his child's mother. Sure, he was stupid to let her go when he possessed her in Florida, but now he would correct the wrong and make her his wife, if only she'd let him.

But Henry knew Vivian's interest was not in leaving her husband to go away with him. To be with him would mean she would risk her relationship with her whole family. No. There was too much at stake for Vivian, too many lives would be damaged because of their passion. Henry knew he could never ask Vivian to make such a move—that would have to be her decision.

Thus, he stared speechlessly at Lee, and Lee stared back at him until he won the staring contest. Henry simply turned on his heels and headed inside the house, slamming the screen door behind him. Lee sighed heavily in relief. Although he was not fully aware of Henry's position, Lee was thankful Henry avoided making a clear and concise statement regarding his aspirations. This is because Lee wasn't exactly ready to deal with the response he very much feared would come from Henry if pressed.

From that moment, Lee decided to make Vivian as happy as possible. Lee was always deciding to change his ways, and be more of a husband to Vivian, but things kept coming up to make him forget his promise to himself and God. As he stared at Henry's broad back going inside the house, Lee felt he needed explicit assurance that she would not leave him, particularly for another man.

So, the kiss-kiss period was prolonged. During the next couple of weeks, Henry saw very little of Vivian or Lee. Everything Vivian needed from the kitchen, Lee was happy to display his devotion by fetching it for her. He even managed to go out with Casey a few times (when Minnie was home), while Vivian waited for him in their bedroom. He started to bring more money home to help with their expenses. Lee hoped Minnie would appreciate this gesture a great deal. He hoped she could become more tolerant of him. When he would go out with Casey, Lee made certain to return home some time before daybreak (like the stranger did with his wife).

Each time Lee would leave, Henry attempted to catch Vivian alone so that he could speak to her just to make sure she was okay, he told himself. The three bedrooms, three story house never felt so large to him before. He wasn't convinced that Lee hadn't coerced her to remain in her quarters. Henry couldn't comprehend that Vivian didn't need him during this time of her honeymoon with Lee. A few times, the two of them would manage to sit together on the porch by themselves, or with Robeena. Henry liked to watch Vivian's mouth curve into laughter at his humor, but she avoided his eyes. If Robeena left them, it wouldn't take Vivian more than ten minutes to head back inside the house. Henry would rush to open the door for her, and recklessly kissed her hair a few times whenever he thought he could get away with it. She never told him to stop. Like Henry, Vivian hoped no one saw his overtures. There were times during the honeymoon period where the two of them had dinner together before Minnie got home from Mrs. Miller's house. At other times, they all ate together, including Robeena whenever she visited. They discussed politics, and it was like no one else was in the room. However, if Lee gave a certain sigh, Vivian would shut up altogether, and then Minnie would try to contribute to the conversation by asking questions, sincerely trying to learn about whatever the topic was. Boldly, Henry reached for Vivian's hand under the table a few times, hoping he didn't accidentally touch Lee.

At one point, during the second week of only catching a glimpse of Vivian here and there, Henry was ready to send Minnie off on an errand into town after Lee had left with Casey. Robeena came over to visit that day during Henry's despair and mentioned that she was on her way to Detroit for a bridal show. Henry insisted that Minnie go as well. Robeena wasn't particularly interested in Minnie's company because she wasn't sure if she would be returning to Pontiac after the event ended. When Minnie declined, he became visibly agitated. He had to have Vivian again. To wrap himself in her soft, smooth presence was his vision of joy. From the smirk on Robeena's face when she agreed with Minnie that she'd rather go alone, Henry swore to himself that Robeena knew he wanted Vivian.

"Where's Viv?" Robeena asked, "She may want to come as well."

"She's tending to Mary," Henry answered, looking straight at Robeena. She did feel somehow that Henry was asking her to take Minnie away so he could be alone with Vivian. Robeena felt trapped. She wished Minnie could see through him. "Go on, Minnie," Henry insisted, "go have some fun. Do it for me." That extra urging convinced Minnie it was a task that would please her husband, therefore she finally conceded. Minnie wanted Henry to know she would do *anything* to make him happy.

After they left, (with Robeena sulking the whole time), Henry stood in the middle of the room, electrified at what awaited him upstairs. He wasn't interested in whether his wife and Robeena suspected anything unusual about his demeanor. They were gone and Vivian was upstairs, and they could only speculate. If Minnie confronted him, it would be like heavy weights being lifted from his chest. Henry chained and bolted the doors, clasped the windows, and hurried upstairs.

When Lee told her he was going to play cards with Casey to make a little bit of money, Vivian decided she would spend the time alone in her bedroom sewing. However, a depression swept over her that she couldn't explain. She let out a deep sigh and plopped down in the bed. Mary was playing quietly by herself. In her solitude, Vivian concluded that what she truly wanted was to bury herself away from her life and the lies she had made of it. Even though she knew she had to, how could she go on forever professing Lee was Mary's father? It was killing her that Lee was being so nice to her, yet she was so deceitful. She closed her eyes, moaning softly.

Vivian turned her back to the sound of the knock on her bedroom door. "Vivian, can I come in, please? It's me, Henry," he begged.

"Go away, Henry," she said weakly. Mary looked up from the toy block she was sticking in her mouth. Henry entered, anyway, heading straight to the floor to play with Mary. This was one area where Lee was still lacking, Vivian judged—he didn't take much time to see about Mary. Lee seldom rocked Mary unless he needed something from Vivian, they were just making up, or when he knew he would be hanging out all night. After a moment, Henry got up and walked over to the bed to sit beside Vivian. He rubbed her back.

"I know you've been avoiding me, honey," he said quietly, "but I really need you right now." She heard the despondency in his voice, which was disheartening to her. Vivian understood that she needed to elude him, but contributing to his unhappiness was not part of her plan, she convinced herself. Vivian sat up in bed, wringing the sheets tightly. She pivoted her feet away from her sewing basket which sat nearby.

"Where's Minnie?"

"She went to a bridal something with Robeena."

Vivian let out a sigh. "They didn't invite me. I guess my luggage wasn't desired on their outing," she said, referring to Mary.

"Whatchu making?"

"A skirt."

"I'm proud of you and the way you've been making clothes for yourself. When is it finished?"

"I have to hem it." She glanced into his eyes and he tightened his lips together, unsure of himself a bit.

"Don't hem it too high, Vivian. I also been noticing you wearing your clothes extra tight these days, baby. Don't do that."

"I'm just trying to stay in style."

"Try that skirt on for me."

"I wouldn't dare!" He picked it up and examined it. "Put that down, Henry. It's not ready."

"Girl, I can tell this is gonna be too tight for you." She snatched it away and tossed it back into the basket.

"Okay! I can loosen it some."

"Loosen it about this much." He stretched his arms out wide, jokingly.

"I said okay, Henry," she said sheepishly. She cared about what he thought and she valued his opinion concerning how she looked. She didn't want him to think she was fast tailed whenever he might see her in the skirt, yet she wasn't going to be able to loosen it all that much, either.

"Why are you in bed in the middle of the day, Vivian? How come you're not sewing? Are you sad? 'Cause I do that too when I'm feeling empty inside."

"You don't have to worry about my sadness or my happiness anymore."

"Oh. I see you thought I was lying when I told you I want you to give me your hurt so I can bear it for you."

"Henry, you shouldn't be in here," she groaned, "you're a married man, and I'm married, too." Contradicting her words, she placed one of her hands in his, which he gladly accepted. "I know you love my sister…you don't want to hurt her, do you?"

"I don't want to hurt or cheat you, neither, sweet girl, and I ain't gonna let nobody else do you like that," he said, scooting closer to her. "Besides, there ain't a woman alive that I've ever loved more than I love you."

"Henry. You can't be in my bedroom like this. What if Lee comes home and sees you sitting on his bed?" He pulled his hand away and reached for Mary who had crawled near his feet. He lifted the child to sit on his knees and rocked her.

"It ain't his bed," he retorted childishly. Mary wasn't interested in being cuddled in her father's lap, which was still a strange feeling to her since Henry didn't get the opportunity to have that kind of quality time with her much. Even though she needed affection like all children do, she was used to loud commotions and madness in the place of loving care. This caused her to not consciously crave intimacy much from her current sources anymore. She struggled to break away from his hold until he got the message and placed her back down on the floor.

"Henry..."

"Don't call me that," he said, begging for her warmth. She took his hand back.

"Well, sweetheart. You know what we've been doing isn't right. I'm gonna--going to put a stop to it if you won't." It was not her self-accusing spirit that surfaced with her self-righteous words, but rather her low self-esteem and multi-needy personality that requested whichever man suited her for a specific purpose. Since Lee was doing well for the time being with supplying her heartwarming needs, she had decided she would reward him by not being intimate with Henry for as long as possible. Vivian felt confident that she could suspend Henry and regain his affection later. Although she felt she loved him, she wanted to be happily married to *somebody*, and Henry couldn't fulfill that right now, but Lee could. She was so confused and upside down -she hoped Henry could understand.

"I've missed you." Her hand felt cold. "Honey," he nearly wept, "don't just leave me alone. Don't you know that I love you more than life? Baby, you *are* my life!"

"If you loved me, you wouldn't have married my sister," she almost snapped.

"Come on, Vivian! You know how that went down. I'm paying for that decision every day and night."

"Leave it be, Henry." Carefully, he inched closer to her, not realizing she had already begun to beckon him. "You seem to be getting along just fine with Minnie, far as I can see!"

"I know you saw me that night you came home," he cried. "I hate it happened like that 'cause I never planned on you ever seeing nothing like that. I'm sorry, honey." While they talked, Mary crawled out of the room, into the hallway, and neared the stairwell.

"Mary!" Vivian called instinctively. Henry automatically jumped up to fetch Mary. She heard his footsteps and turned to shine her bright eyes on him, helping him to lift her by clinging to his t-shirt. Shutting the bedroom door behind them, he rubbed Mary's nose with his nose before placing her in the middle of the floor. When he returned to Vivian, he noticed that she was watching him patiently with a petite smile in her same half sitting, half slouching position. Henry liked the fact that he could please her by proudly caring for Mary, and he wished his compassion would win him points with her, now.

He turned back to Mary. "You wanna take a nap, beautiful? Here, let daddy put you in your crib and lay you down for a nap while I talk to your lovely mama." He rolled her in the crib to his bedroom. "You'll have quietness in here, my darling one." Mary looked at him curiously while she enjoyed the ride. He picked her up and kissed her forehead. "There you are, precious," he said, placing her back in the crib. He went back to Vivian's bedroom, hoping Mary wouldn't holler.

"You can't be referring to her as 'daddy.' What is your problem? If she repeats you in front of Lee…"

"I only want the absolute best for you and Mary, honey. Sometimes, when you love someone, it's difficult not to disgrace that person."

"Thanks for saying that, Henry. I feel like you really mean well."

"Don't play games with me, Vivian. You know quite well I mean every word of it."

"Fine. But tell me how I'm supposed to feel when I catch you like *that*? There's nothing I can do but be miserable. See, I tried to leave it at what happened down South, but you're the person bringing emotions to the table, and then you let me *see* you."

"I don't hafta see *you*, Vivian. All I hafta do is think about it, and it tears me apart."

She giggled. "And quit touching me under the dinner table!"

"I touch you to remind you who you belong to." She laughed again.

"You're so nuts, Henry!"

"Am I?"

"Yes, you are. What happens when you grab Lee's knee, thinking it's mine?"

"I'm thinking I'm tired of sneaking around. I hate that the only way I can feel you is to crawl under a table. Maybe I'll just take you from him."

"Okay, now you're going too far…"

"The way you let that man beat on you, only to sleep in his arms later in the night is sick. Is he that good-looking to you? That it don't matter how he treats you, if people can say you got that half-baked joke? What do you think be running through my head when your so-called loving husband shuts your bedroom door for the night? Then when I come in to console you, all you can say is for me to stay away."

"At least we're trying."

"He don't love you the way I do, sweetheart." Henry shook his head. "What do you even talk about with him? He doesn't understand you…what moves you."

"So, you and Minnie have a lot to talk about? She's an airhead."

"I never said that. And you kiss him? See, I don't kiss Minnie like that, I swear I don't. Not no more—not since you've been here. Damn some papers, baby—we belong together and you know it. I'm asking you how many more nights do you really think I can stand knowing he has you, and I don't? How can you expect me to live like this? I don't want 'im touching you, kissing you, or nothing. When I know y'all is in here together, I hafta think about something—anything so I can block that picture out of my head. That's the damn truth."

"It's just lonely, Henry. Sometimes, I get sad. I wish you were here for me all the time, but I know you can't be because of someone else. I wish you had chosen me, Henry, but you didn't. So now, I must try to make it work with Lee. He is really trying to do better nowadays." Henry wasn't sure if he could contain his anger. He had given her his heart and his soul, and she still wanted to try with Lee. Even if she didn't want him because of Minnie, he wished she would leave Lee for good.

"You know, I used to tell myself that as long as you were happy with Lee, I would leave you alone. True love, which is what I have for you, is knowing the other person is happy. But I don't think like that no more because I can't trust 'im with you, the love of my life. I'm not giving up so that he can *try*."

"But…"

He stood and paced back and forth in front of her with his fists clenched. "Don't fall for it, Vivian. He's the same li'l boy that kicked your tail for some wench, and the same li'l boy coming home at two and three in the morning with lipstick on his shirt. Just because he ain't brought no prostitutes home *this* week don't mean shit…"

"But he…"

"I'm not gonna let him keep you from me, Vivian. I'm not ever leaving you alone. You hear me?"

"Well, how can I ever make my marriage work if you feel like that? You know how I feel about you, too. So when you talk like that…"

He stopped two inches from her. "Your so-called marriage and my dry marriage never had a chance in any way. So don't throw that out there in my face—not today. I don't wanna hear that shit. Every time the mood hits you, I gotta hear about how I married Minnie. I think I paid for that long enough, don't you think?"

"I'm not trying to make you pay for anything."

"Good. Maybe it's time you make a decision about who you really want to be married to."

She laughed. "Boy, you are acting so jealous right now." He smiled at her, but didn't laugh.

"Oh…is that what it is? I'm jealous?"

"Yeah."

"I can't let you go." She laughed again. "What's so funny, Vivian?" He smiled some more and started tickling her, causing her to laugh harder. "Be quiet, girl…you gonna disturb Mary." He stopped tickling her, and pressed his forehead against hers. Her laughing subsided.

"You still have to stay away, Henry."

"I choose you for me. I can't change the past, but it's you I want in my life, Vivian.

"You have to stay away, Henry."

"I would if I thought you truly wanted me to, but I know you choose me, also."

Vivian couldn't help it when her mind drifted to that day, so many months ago, when her husband's friend insisted she was his choice and insisted he would be hers even if only for that morning. In Floyd's mind, Vivian wanted him, but acted like she was too proud to acknowledge it. Floyd resented her for treating him like dirt when he thought she was nothing but a high-class floozy. Floyd would never be convinced that Lee cared much about Vivian. He knew the "real" Lee. Floyd considered that Lee never would have met Maybelle were it not for him. Lee had not dared to enter onto the Raison Plantation until Floyd escorted him first, one day. Maybelle was a girl Floyd had dealings with on a regular basis. One day, Floyd had brought Lee with him to see her, and Maybelle took a fine liking to Lee and his creamy complexion. Over time, Maybelle began to favor Lee. Eventually, she thought of herself as Lee's "woman," and she would no longer allow Floyd the privilege of intimate encounters.

Although he never openly complained, Floyd had not at all forgiven Lee for taking Maybelle away from him. Even after Lee told Floyd that he had stopped his regular visits to her place, Maybelle still contended she only wanted to be "friends" with Floyd now. He weighed that one night with Vivian would even the score. When Floyd saw Vivian at the party, of course he was willing to pay her a few dollars. She was different and alluring. Floyd didn't think Lee was justified to have a girl specifically for him, anyway. He had no remorse for raping her—she deserved it, and so did Lee, he judged. Besides, they couldn't be any more humiliated than he was, he rationalized.

After Floyd left Vivian's house that sordid day, he felt better about himself and more in control for finally taking a stand. Floyd believed Vivian would never tell Lee because she was guilty, too. Wasn't it she who had tried to squeeze past him through a space that would require full body contact between them when he had blocked her in the kitchen? Did not her breast land softly on his chest as she made her way out of the kitchen? Hadn't she been sassy with him when he merely asked her for a bite to eat, when she could have easily fixed the food without provoking him? If push came to shove, he would tell Lee how Vivian knowingly seduced him, practically dared him. He would tell everyone about her involvement in their love entanglement.

Henry wasn't a blamer like Floyd, Vivian thought. Henry would never inwardly or outwardly blame Vivian for any of their ignoble acts. Given that she had not healed from Floyd's attack, she applied emotional ointment by transferring his affliction into a comparable affection provided by her ally. If Minnie would catch them together, Vivian and Henry both knew he would stand in front of Vivian, accepting full responsibility for the entire proviso. He made it so easy to love him, she thought. Vivian wrapped herself in indecision regarding her relationship with Henry. He made it so easy to fall right back into his arms after she told herself she wouldn't. Now, as he leaned over her, staring longingly at her richly blushed, bronzed cheeks and the thin smile she wore, he sensed her pain burning thickly in the small space between them. It was intoxicating. Space never mattered to their spirits. He held his breath, hoping she wouldn't reject his consolation.

~~~

"Hey, man," Lee started, "you know of any places down here that have rooms for Negroes to board in?"

"Not off hand, baby," Casey answered, "why?" They were sitting on a stoop outside of a motel on Telegraph Road, smoking marijuana and drinking corn whiskey out of plastic cups. The half-breed girl came with more whiskey and a wad of money. Lee watched Casey spank her on her fanny, then he sent her back out into the wilderness.

"Man, I gotta get the hell up outta there, man. I ain't keen on my wife's sister *or* that jive time player she be married to." Lee put the smoke out under his foot.

"Yeah, man," Casey agreed, "I don't see how you could live with 'im anyway, with 'im being all in your wife's face and shit." Casey was extremely delicate with his tone of voice while emitting this unsolicited observation. However, his delicacy didn't prevent Lee from blowing half of his high instantly upon hearing Casey's feedback.

"I didn't say that, Case . . . what the hell do you mean by *that*?" Casey looked absolutely surprised at Lee.

"Aw, come on, son! A blind man can see how sweet that man is on your wife—I was trying to see how long you were gonna take that bull from..." Casey paused to let his next word sink in, "...a square."

"Hell. I ain't taking nothing off 'im. He can like her all he wants, don't mean a damn thing, long as he don't touch her or say nothing to her 'bout nothing." A bemused cast came over Casey. He shook his head.

"What, man? Why are you looking at me like that?" Lee asked with exasperation. Casey became serious.

"Look, baby," he said quietly, "whatever's going on in your house is your business. You handle it." He got up and started walking away, but Lee half stood, reached out, and grabbed his arm.

"You know something 'bout my wife? If you do, you better tell me." Lee felt his chest growing extremely hot. He let go of Casey's arm and sat back down. He drank more of his whiskey, inviting more hotness to run through his veins to numb himself from what could sprinkle forth from Casey's crooked toothed mouth.

"Hey, son," Casey started, regaining control over his limb, "I don't know no more than you do. I mean, it started down South, right?" More than his hankering to be plum cruel, Casey judged that every man needed to know if their woman was cheating on them. It was like a code of honor for men to inform each other of disloyalty in women.

"I know he *liked* her." Shame prevented Lee from acknowledging his concern that Vivian had been flirtatious with Henry during that time, as well.

"*Liked* her?" Casey echoed. "What you think they were doing all night together on his plantation?" Lee smashed his drink down on the cement at Casey's words. "You *do* know about that, Lee, don't you?" Lee glared at him. "Beena said you knew," Casey muttered apologetically. Casey motioned for Lee to follow him inside of the motel room out of the September wind to finish the conversation. Lee walked in and over to the window where the sun was shining through bitterly. He looked up into the nearby trees with the leaves sitting frivolously, sucking up the warmth of the sun. He remembered the gorgeous orange-red sun from Florida compared to this blazing yellow, unfriendly one. Lee left the window, walked back over to the bed, and stood in front of it, too agitated to sit.

"Beena said this?" Casey nodded his head. Lee plopped himself on the edge of the bed. Casey followed him, standing a few feet away.

"You beat her up one night down South, right?" Lee looked up at him sharply. "Beena told me their mama sent Henry to find her. He found her in *your house,* man, and snatched her away from you and took her to his place. Like he came in and dogged you out, baby boy! What's that all about?"

"Ain't nothing to that, Casey. Henry ain't never been to my house to get my woman. Straight up."

"Beena says Vivian didn't show back up for two days." Lights flashed from everywhere inside of Lee's head, blinding him. He remembered not seeing Vivian for days after the church incident with Maybelle. "Beena said they's doing it up here, too," Casey added for emphasis. Almost nothing else Casey could have said would have the ability to penetrate Lee's heart more deeply than the bloody daggers that were already causing him to shiver inwardly.

"This my first time hearing anything like this, man," Lee said melancholically. "I don't know what to believe." Lee wasn't willing to throw his dreams of a cozy future with Vivian away just yet. Surely, there must be an explanation for all of Casey's reprehensible words.

"I shouldn't have told you," Casey tested. Lee attempted to take on a perky mood to show his appreciation at being told the gruesome tales about his wife.

"Yeah, you should've told me." Lee got up and shuffled over to where Casey was standing and touched his shoulder in brotherly love. Casey bowed his head shamefully, imagining the disgrace and gloom he had caused Lee in the guise of true friendship. Yet, he forced himself to recall the hundreds of dollars Lee's inconsistencies had cost him, and by that, relieving himself of all fault. His monetary loss, coupled with Casey's hatred of women who cheated on their men, and the sorry men who allowed it, directed Casey's animosity again toward attacking Lee.

"Come on, son. It's time to head on back down the road. Our ladies are waiting on us." Although Casey wanted to get to Robeena before it got too late, he became ill with Lee at how quickly he moved at the mention of rushing home to Vivian. Had he not heard what was just stated about his adulterous wife? Lee was almost pulling Casey by his shoulder. Somehow, Casey was able to blame Lee for all the money that had been wasted on Robeena, too. He resented Lee for being married to Vivian, Robeena's appealing sister. Casey guessed he would have had a great friend in Lee if it were not for Vivian's demanding presence. He felt she had too much control over Lee.

"Son?"

"What, Case?" Lee felt sort of strange holding on to Casey's shoulder. It seemed that negative currents were being transmitted through him. Once he dropped his hand from Casey's arm, Casey's words held the same ignition from whence he was running.

"Nah, it's too terrible. Never mind," Casey baited.

"Talk, Case. Ain't nothing too terrible no more," Lee said solemnly.

"Well, it's just something Beena said . . . I'm sure it don't mean nothing." Lee had already gathered that Casey was eager to drop a few more bombs, but he didn't think Casey had any more power to shame him after what he had just heard.

"Let me be the judge over what means something 'cerning my wife," Lee stated with authority.

"It's about your child." Sickness overtook Lee until he clutched his stomach. He wished Casey would shut up right now. Lee almost bolted out the door. "Beena be thinking it's Henry's."

"What?"

"Son, I told Beena I was gonna talk to you about this, 'cause I ain't want her to be telling no gossip to me about people's private affairs."

"My baby?"

"Well, 'course she don't know for sure. She just saying that on account of she said the baby was born 'bout nine months after Henry left from down there. Heard tell he left right quick, too, I did. Like he was running from something."

Lee didn't hear anything else Casey said on the way home. Before he knew it, he was standing by the front door, shaking like a loose grape on a vine on a windy day. He wasn't quite sure how to handle this whole thing. He could beat her, but that wouldn't solve a thing, he reasoned. He didn't dare assume the allegations were all factual, anyway. His main objective was to separate Vivian from Henry. He knew he had to move away with his wife at once.

Lee focused his eyes on the shimmering doorknob to keep everything from spinning too fast. Still, he felt himself becoming very dizzy as the knob illuminated its metal strikingly before his eyes. He tried closing his eyes, but that made it worse. He staggered to the door and seized the knob for support. Lee believed he could deal with the possibility that his wife had slept with his enemy long ago, down South, if they were able to move away, and if she would promise to never have contact with him or even Minnie, ever again. Nonetheless, the suggestion that Mary was the child of another man was unbearable. It wasn't that Lee was the doting father, or that the paternal loss would be very substantial, but rather the sheer corruption over the whole ordeal was shuddering.

It wasn't true. Couldn't be. Casey was envious of him and wanted to degrade him. Lee remembered his dream where Casey possessed Vivian. He rationalized that his dream was a derivative of Casey's jealousies and desires. None of Casey's whores could hold a candle to Vivian, Lee judged. Vivian was a gem. Henry knew this, Gancy knew this, and evidentially, Casey knew it, too. What did Robeena have to do with all of this? Lee decided that she was bitter over Vivian's ability to land a man. Robeena never could keep a man, Lee recalled. She was jealous of both of her sisters, in fact. He tried laughing at how reckless Casey had been in telling him the harmful rumors. "He thinks he can confound me? Never," Lee said to the doorknob.

"I'll see you later, baby," Henry whispered to Vivian, although he remained with his head resting on her shoulder. She moved over as gently as possible, allowing him to kiss her fingertips before she slid away. She kept her hand outreached to him, backing away, until he reached out his long fingers to her, rising to follow her.

"Go on, now, Henry," she urged. He advanced closer and gathered her in his arms. A miniature smile crept on their faces until they were beaming at each other.

"You gonna let me see you sometimes? You ain't gonna shoo me away next time I call on you?" She filmed her fingers through his short hair, which was like soft, dried raisins.

"No, Henry. I know I have to consider your feelings." He caught her hand and held it where it was in his hair.

"And I meant what I said. After this, I don't want you sleeping with him no more, either. Sweet girl, you ain't gotta worry 'bout me touching Minnie—it won't happen. She just be there. I wake up in the middle of the night...but I want us to start meeting at 2:00 in the morning downstairs so I can hold *you*, baby."

"That's impossible!" He used both of his hands to lift her swiftly off her feet while he held her at his height.

"It's possible. You can tell time, can't you? I'll leave at 1:50 and wait for you in the kitchen. If someone comes, I'll hide in the basement like I'm gone, and you can say you wanted something to drink and you couldn't sleep." He put her down but held her close. "Do it. 'Cause I ain't fixing to wait two and three weeks before I can hold you again. I want you down there every night."

"I'll try, Henry, but I'm scared we'll get caught trying something like that."

"If it's too dangerous one night, and you don't come, I'll understand. But the next night, I know you'll be there, right? I'm not talking about when he's home, but you know he's never home before four…and I want to start tonight."

"Tonight?"

"You're my woman, ain't you?"

"But, Henry…"

"You know what I'm saying? You ain't gonna be going back and forth like that, 'and I ain't, either." She shook her head. "Did I say something wrong?"

"How is that going to look, Henry?"

"What? You wanna be with him…still?"

"Can't you see how crazy this is?"

"You gotta know by now that Lee ain't about to do right. He may be treating you fine today, but what does tomorrow promise with a clown like that? He ain't what you need—he belongs in the wild with some alley cat. He ain't fit to have a hidden princess like you." He kissed her passionately. She broke away when he didn't stop.

"Oh, Henry…"

"I love you, honey."

"I love you so much, too. I never knew what love was before, until you. But it seems like Lee is trying harder these days…I'm so confused."

"I told you, princess. You ain't got time in your life for that niggah to be trying. If you ain't happy all the time with him, and you're crying half the time—I don't see why you would make yourself and our baby miserable, Vivian."

"Henry, my lover, I think I *would* be so fulfilled if we were a family."

"Baby, what good it would do my heart if I thought you were half serious."

"I sit in my room sometimes, and I am so unhappy. It's a big empty hole in my soul, and I just know you're the only man who can fill it…well, so far in my life it seems like that…"

"Baby, let me tell you something. The cards are in your hands. I ain't afraid to fill that void you talking 'bout. I been telling you that. Is it that you don't believe me?"

"Shhh…did you hear something?" He listened with her.

"I'm not sure…"

"Go on back now," she insisted. He squeezed her closer, giving her one last peck on the cheek before walking away. Mary whined when she saw him. She had not gone to sleep in Henry's bedroom at all. She had merely waited patiently for him to come back for her. A few seconds later, he rolled Mary back in, a sheepish grin on his face. She gathered his things that he'd left behind and shoved them into his arms. His eyes bulged with a dancing smile that he'd almost forgotten to retrieve his personal belongings. Silently, he waved at Vivian and crept away.

Vivian stared at the closed door for a moment once he left. Then, she started picking up things around the room, preoccupied with all sorts of emotions ranging from frustration to glory. She made the bed over, changing the sheets and fluffing the pillows, and then she went to prepare the washtub for her bath. She took Mary with her, feeling more of the frustration. Vivian tried to concentrate on Mary's round, precious face, but instead, Henry's smile filled her mind and her recent forbidden encounter with him.

She took the washrag between her fingers and let Mary grab at it merrily, splashing water. Vivian imagined what life would be like if she were Henry's wife. "Mama would never speak to me again if I were to go away with that man. Besides, Lee and I are getting along much better these days, anyhow...but if he messes up one more time..." Mary kept playing, trying to answer her mother with gurgling noises. Vivian experienced an insecure feeling; perhaps Henry didn't truly want to go away with her. He really didn't do all that much talking on the subject. Sure, during the heat or aftermath of passion he'd say anything, but when he was sober minded, where were the plans to take her away? With Minnie, he took the pains to plan their entire trip. Besides, just as easily as he had whisked Minnie away in the darkness, he could have come for her. There was something that kept him from her, she pondered.

With Lee, however, her future was secure. Notwithstanding, the next time she could get to be alone with Henry, they would discuss it further. She would discover once and for all why the words that flew out of his mouth contradicted his behavior. She finished bathing and straightening the room as quickly as she could, since Lee had been coming home early lately, ever since his physical brawl with Henry. Vivian felt it was his insecurities that led him home early. It bothered her that his love for her did not have the power to do what his need to control her could do. Just then, she heard the familiar sound of his footsteps coming into the house and shuffling around downstairs. Her heart racing, Vivian wrung her hands tightly together. Then, she made a dive for the bed with her sewing basket and quickly took out some material to cut. Mary heard Lee climbing the stairs, too. She turned her back to the door and continued to play as if content on ignoring both for a time, but Vivian retreated to pick her up and took her to the bed as well.

Lee gathered his strength and trotted up the stairs, half expecting in his uncertainty to find Henry and Vivian together. Henry had quite purposely made certain his bedroom door was ajar when he heard Lee enter the house. Excitement stirred in him whenever he held Vivian in his arms just moments before someone came home. Upon ascending the stairs, Lee risked a glance into Henry's bedroom to find Henry disposed of in his bed looking at him! Lee quickly turned away, pretending not to see him. He knew Henry was taunting him because it was evident that Minnie wasn't home. He struggled with his fear for just a moment before he was able to enter the room and face his wife after the drastic news Casey had just told him. The sight of Vivian in bed sewing with Mary on her lap reassured him. Mary tensed when she saw him, eager to continue playing alone so that she wouldn't have to be amid any war zones. Vivian held onto Mary and her sewing so that she'd have some things to occupy her eyes in the face of her dishonor. Lee didn't notice.

He resignedly wanted to have peace with his wife. He greeted her with a kiss, and then he took Mary from her and placed her in her crib. His movements had become awkward. "I've missed you, baby," he said, trying to relax himself. He made his way back over to her, forcing the image of Casey and Henry from his path. He would give his marriage the chance it deserved. He could not lose the love of his life to a sick rumor. They would have to work out their differences soon before some hateful, envious person was able to take advantage of their misfortunes.

Vivian was relieved that he seemed to be in a good mood. She pursed her lips in shame at the sordid way she was rewarding his noble efforts. No matter what Henry meant to her, she could never leave her family forever. Even if Henry would do it, wasn't it too late? The only thing she could do was be his mistress—but for how long? Lee looked pitiful on this day, she identified. She was robbing him of true love. If it were not for Henry, Lee would be so happy. She repeated her vows to herself to treat him better and become his wife again.

What occupied Lee's mind was getting out of Henry's house as fast as possible. He started taking Vivian with him more, whenever he wasn't with Casey. And he almost totally suspended his activities at night to chaperone Vivian. Lee wouldn't let him have her, so he could either lose his family, or spend more time at home. Henry had sent too many signals for Lee to ignore. He wasn't a fool. He didn't know what was going on, but whatever it was would stop.

It was crystal clear to Henry what Lee was doing. Smart move, Henry thought. There was nothing he could do but look forward to getting Vivian alone again and for longer. Holding her hand under the table or reading a newspaper together was not enough. He hoped Lee wasn't winning her heart, which was what mattered. Henry noted with miserable concern that Lee started coming home before midnight, whenever he left at all. And Minnie hardly went to bed before eleven.

Casey didn't have a wife—someone he really cared about or loved. Thus, Lee felt he could no longer put his marriage on the line to run around like a teenager with an insensitive playboy like Casey. Those days were finished. He had the girl of his dreams, yet he was throwing her away by trying to live life in the fast lane. Lee was losing his desire for loose sex because the wanton women perpetually left him empty inside. His heart ached for his wife, even before he could roll away from any of the various free-for-all women who wound up in bed with him. He realized it would be daring to go on assuming Vivian would never leave him when the handwriting was on the wall and in Henry's countenance. Secretly, he admired Henry's stability and his maturity, and decided it would be smart to take distant lessons from him, instead of Casey.

One afternoon, Minnie talked about how pleased she was that Lee was looking so hard for a room of their own. Henry's heart sank. He couldn't let him take her away! He didn't know what to do if he couldn't talk to Vivian, though. Henry didn't know Lee was capable of keeping such close grips on Vivian. What had happened? Even on Saturdays, Lee was with Vivian and Mary, and sometimes, the three of them left for the entire day. This behavior was unheard of for the troubled couple.

Minnie couldn't be happier. Henry could no longer shy away from her affection and longings. He also needed someone, and Minnie was his wife. Could he love her if he lost Vivian to Lee? Henry had to catch himself. He had already lost Vivian to Lee.

CHAPTER TWENTY-TWO
"I was a boy, then, but now I'm a man!"

Within three weeks, Lee was lucky enough to find a room for his little family a few blocks down from Robeena. It was on Bloomfield Street in a chestnut brown wooden house. It was not too small with three bedrooms, a front room, and a kitchen area. Grass grew in assorted patches where the neighborhood children didn't run too often. The front door was usually kept unlocked, while the three boarding families kept their bedroom doors locked at nighttime. There was Yetta Evans, Mr. and Mrs. Cook, and now, Lee and Vivian sharing in the quarters. Yetta and Vivian quickly became friends, although Lee only mumbled greetings to his new housemates. Yet, under Lee's unfriendly exterior, he was satisfied to have a place to call home for his family.

He got a job as a bellboy in a hotel downtown, and didn't mind walking to work every day, as long as Vivian stayed in their new snug home with Mary. For Lee, it was truly belittling to work as an invisible servant. He was accustomed to making big money with Casey and down South, too. Notwithstanding, he was trying to quietly wean himself from Casey's grip and influence, as hard as it was to do so. So, taking a job as a bellboy when he was qualified to do something more skillful was something he was willing to do for his family.

Being so wise, Casey venomously peeped that Lee was trying to dump him. The feeble excuse Lee tossed Casey was that moving took so much of his time and energy, but he assured Casey he would fall through to see him as soon as he got settled in his new place with Vivian—only he didn't have a car yet, so it would be hard. Casey understood what Lee really meant was he owed Lee a car for all the hustling Lee did for him, and Casey also assumed Lee was negotiating getting financially squared away sufficiently before he would continue working undercover for him. Since Casey had recently bought a brand new car, he loaned his Ford to Lee whenever Lee wanted to drive it. Lee kept the car parked in front of his house, and started driving it to work and everywhere else, and Casey never asked him for it back.

Lee was so in love with Vivian, he was willing to do whatever was necessary to make their relationship work. Lee was more determined than ever not to allow Henry, Casey, or Robeena and her wagging tongue to ruin his marriage. He knew Vivian much better than all three of them put together, thus he refused to believe Vivian would commit those acts of which they were accusing her. Robeena's lifestyle fit that description more perfectly than Vivian's, Lee judged.

Henry was just a bad dream. Lee resolved that the things Casey had said were all lies, pure speculation based on the attraction Henry had for Vivian. Lee knew Casey wanted to use him as a pawn and a flunky just like he used his prostitutes, only Lee demanded a fair cut from the profits. He knew Casey didn't want to give him another dime since they weren't hanging tough anymore, and that Casey was continuing to try to buy him with the car, but still, Lee demanded money in hopes that Casey would decide on his own to cut the umbilical cord of their rundown relationship. After all, Lee had a family to support.

Casey had been indignant, he reasoned, and speaking against Vivian was simply part of his retaliation. Lee decided to keep quiet about Casey's slack talk. He worked hard to forget the ugly rumors he'd heard about his wife. Even if they *were* true, Vivian's relationship with Henry was in the past. He realized that his love for her outweighed whether she'd made a sexual mistake with a dazzling womanizer, and he could always contend she hadn't made such a mistake. Lee would make certain she never saw Henry again. If she ever complained about not seeing Minnie, then Minnie could come to *their* house. And if necessary, he would remind her that he never complained about not seeing Leland. He would save his money, and in a few months, he would take his family out west or something. Wherever he pleased, and her family would learn about it whenever he pleased. His father had done the same thing with his mother, Lee recalled. He now saw how some things were inevitable.

Meanwhile, Vivian was bored stiff. Her only joy came from visiting the Detroit Urban League and sewing —which there was not enough space in her room to sew like she wanted, and Lee always copped an attitude to learn of her visits to Detroit, unaccompanied by him. Lee didn't want Robeena to visit, Minnie was too busy, and Vivian hadn't made any friends, except for Yetta. Yetta hardly liked to do anything fun; she preferred to either visit at Vivian's or have Vivian come to her room to gossip all the time. Lee promised her he'd take her out more, but that turned out to be a lie. True, near the end of their tenure on California Street, Lee took her with him to many places to ward off Henry, but she felt now that he had her imprisoned, he no longer found it necessary to court her. Every blue moon, he would take her to Detroit and let her do a little shopping, but she complained that they didn't go often enough. Vivian was tired of staying home with Mary all day, every day, with no relief. She wanted someone to cater after her, to cook for *her* for a change. Lee didn't pay enough attention to her, like Henry.

She missed being held in awe by Henry and loved so tenderly. She missed his kissing and his concern. Lee was a big disappointment all around. All he did was work, come home, and want sex or something to eat. And his sex sucked. They never had anything to talk about because the books he read were soaked with the colorful ink of naked women on the covers, and he never read the newspaper. He didn't like her taste in music, he didn't like politics, and he wasn't interested in her opinions. Now that he had her in jail, he'd started hanging out with Casey again. She had to admit he only went out with Casey when Casey came over unannounced on some weekends, but if Lee was too tired to go, she felt he needed to tell Casey the truth. Sometimes, it didn't matter anyway, because she wanted Casey or anyone to come and get Lee out of her sight.

Although he seemed to be trying more than ever, the glass that contained her love for him, which had been filled with him, now had a chip in it, and her love was floating mildly at the bottom. Vivian still wished she could fall into Henry's arms whenever Lee left with Casey, but she couldn't because Lee had managed to isolate her from her lover. And he never wanted her to leave the house unless she was with him because of his extreme jealousy.

At first Vivian didn't mind his jealousy. She thought it was a sign that he worshiped her, and would die if another man came near her. Now, however, Vivian saw his behavior as keeping her in a prison in her own home. Lee was disenchanted by Vivian's lack of appreciation over all the sacrifices he had recently made for her -not to mention the sacrifice he had made to move to Michigan against his better judgment in the first place, he told himself. They could've moved to Chicago or Canada if they had wanted. After working sometimes for ten hours, he expected the house to be clean when he got home, but if it wasn't, he at least wanted some peace and quiet of mind. However, Vivian was forever cranky about everything—it was as though she was purposely trying to make him miserable.

~~~

"Get off my back, slut!" He shouted at her one day after an outing in Detroit when they were walking back inside their room. *She* was angry because when they went to pick up Mary from Minnie's house, he made her stay in the car, and she knew it was so she couldn't catch sight of Henry. She wanted Henry to see unhappiness written all over her face in hopes that he would finally do something meaningful to help her. *He* was angry because she was still nagging him about the fact that he'd stood her up in front of the Fox

Theater. She complained that she could've gone to Detroit by herself, and she would've had a better time, but he refused to leave her with enough money to have fun on her own. Vivian tried to avoid a fight by daydreaming about Black, cool waves in a far off ocean, but Lee was incorrigible. She was done letting him get away with attacking her. Therefore, 30 minutes after they got home, they were yelling at each other at the top of their lungs.

"I hate this nasty jailhouse you say is my home!"

"Your raggedy ass better be happy I put you up in anything with a roof and a loaf of bread. I ain't your pimp…you want a pimp?"

"Good for you and your wood and wheat. That's all you've ever been able to offer me, because compassion and love are not your gifts."

"And what would you consider a gift is that you got? Nagging all the goddamn time?"

"I wouldn't have to nag if I were able to get out of this hell hole every once in a cotton-picking blue moon."

"The last time somebody gave you money to go to town, you ended up in the woods with Henry Raison! Who will it be next? Gancy? I saw the way he was looking at your legs when I drove up, with that tight ass dress on!"

"Oh? So now it's tight? I thought you said you liked it on me. I guess you'd like me in anything, including a burlap bag—as long as I'm locked away in some closet somewhere."

"Always running down to that center talking 'bout teaching somebody to read when you can't half read yourself. You think I'm an idiot? I can't trust you. If I could trust you, things would be different."

"I like to read about society, fashion, and politics. The only thing you can read is the label on a beer bottle."

"Yeah? If you could read, then why do you talk so damn much?"

"When I'm not reading, I listen to the finest music to drown you out!"

"Never in my life did I think I would end up with a dishonest, fast-tailed woman. What I thought you was, you ain't the half of it."

Passive-aggressively, she casually walked over to the record player that Gancy said the center was throwing out—so he gave it to her about a month ago, along with some records. She put the needle on Scott Joplin's *Maple Leaf Rag*. Earlier that day, when little David played the piece so masterfully, it placed her at peace. She wished for that same inner feeling, now, but she was too emotionally imbalanced to gain refuge in the music. She turned the volume a notch above Lee's yelling. "You are one fine, smooth talking hypocrite, Lee," she screamed. You're the biggest two-timing, jive time hustler I know. You *never could* be trusted. Far's I know, you could be out with women every time you leave here. That's why you don't trust me, on account of you are as guilty as Satan."

"I wear the pants in this house, Miss High Tootin' Bitch, and don't ever forget that." He took her by the collar of her tubular bodice and pushed her down in a chair. "Don't talk to me just any kinda way," he barked. Vivian was ready for him this time. She bounced out of the chair like a jumping jack, taking a standing position directly in Lee's face. Quickly, she tossed her flapper cloche hat on the floor.

"And who are *you*?" She asked. He shoved her out of his way. Vivian laughed an illegitimate bellow as she regained her balance. "What will you do? Beat me like you always do? I guess that's the only thing you know, besides running around with Casey, making out with all kinds of women you pick up in the back seat of that trashy, smelly car you-all think is so grand." She was yelling hysterically. Lee was in awe at the temerity of her to fuss at him when, in his estimation, he had always treated her like a queen.

"You tramp!" He slapped her with all the force behind his left hand. Had her adrenalin not been flowing so sporadically, she would have hit the floor with a thud. Instead, Vivian caught herself. Just when she did, he slapped her the opposite way with his other hand. Lee wanted to see her crumble at his fist, but first, he wanted her to hear what a whore he thought she was. "You talking 'bout *my* women? You knew about my women before you married me. I ain't never kept no secrets from you," he lied, "but when did you start letting Henry touch you?" Vivian was caught off guard with his second slap, coupled with the slap of his words. She stumbled, but maintained her ground. Still, she loaded both barrels and fired back at him.

"When did *you* start with that fat gorilla, Maybelle?" Lee had wanted her to scream that *he* was the player, and that *she* certainly had not been with Henry or any other man. Any form of a denial to his question would have been sufficient. He needed clarification on the meaning of her point addressed in the form of a question. He charged at her, growling like a lowly creature, and vowed that this would "be the best ass kicking you ever got."

In his attack, he tramped on one of Mary's fingers as she was scrambling away. Her cry annoyed him. There was too much noise, too many distractions keeping him from the truth of the matter. He knew suddenly that he did not want to know the truth, but he couldn't stop it from coming. His blood rushed to his head. It seemed as though his mind was separate from the rest of his body—he wasn't positive if his mind was telling the rest of his body what to do, or if his body was controlling his mind. A few months had gone by with Lee determined to push the past away forever, but now, he was ready to get it all out in the open. He tried to punch her in the face, but this time, she bent under, grabbing him around his waist, and wrestled with him until he broke away. She wished her not too long, dark green skirt wasn't so tight, now. She couldn't fight Lee like she really wanted to let him have it with the skirt restricting her movements, but she was at least glad that she had loosened it an inch at Henry's suggestion.

Mary was petrified in these new surroundings. There was no Henry or Minnie to fetch her during the fight, and she had an eminently keen sense of awareness of being alone in a struggle. She crawled to the farthest corner of the room and fastened her eyes on the only two earthly beings who were her legal guardians and champions.

"He spoiled you, didn't he?" Lee asked, sinking into a lower position of control. He raised his fist at her, shaking it in the air. As it was, though, Vivian was just as infuriated as he was. She was tired of his double standards, his lies, and his extremely chauvinistic attitudes.

"No! He didn't spoil me!" Lee relaxed instantly upon hearing such relieving words. "He *loved* me," she added spitefully. He paused for a brief second, uncertain as to how he should punish her. There was no question that he must beat her now. He took his belt off and whooped her across her face and neck about a dozen times until his arm tired. She fell to the floor, kicking up at him with one foot, and using the other foot to pivot her body around to face him.

Lee imagined a smirk on her face that he intended on slapping away. He would smack away the smirks of all of them—Robeena, Casey, and Minnie, too. He pledged never to let her or them laugh at him again. If her words were true, then she had made a fool out of him in front of everyone. Henry had been laughing at him inwardly all that time. Henry kept the secret that he had been bedding Vivian down for months on end, however, he was generous enough to give Lee all the data he needed to figure it out all by himself, had he really wanted the truth.

Vivian was appalled that Lee had the nerve to strike her as though she was some drifting animal, since she had catered to his sick needs for almost two years now. She knew for sure that she would leave him for good after this fight. She'd move right back in with Henry and Minnie. Lee didn't know whether to believe her or not. He thought of all the reasons he could for why she might be lying. He easily dodged her flying legs and feet. His eyes scanned the room for the nearest object he could throw at her. Nothing seemed hard enough. Finally, he settled for the box with his clothes folded neatly inside. The box missed her head but bruised her flaring arms that she used as a shield. All the clothes tumbled to the floor and on top of Vivian. Something hard that was buried under the clothes fell to the floor with a clicking thump. Lee could see the edge of the leather holster sticking out of the pillowcase that Casey had given him containing the "gift." Lee felt that same sense of power that he felt when Casey had first given him the knife. He seized the weapon and pulled the bright blade from its shaft.

Mary stared at the dazzling toy with an eerie feeling. She searched the faces of her parents— hardly recognizing them for their contorted demeanor. Mary was even more petrified when she witnessed her mother laughing at the toy and swinging her arms and legs violently in the air. Vivian laughed mercilessly at her powerless husband. He did not have the influence to control her any longer, she decided. She was sick of his threats. No fear that he could place her in would keep her with him—even if it meant going away with Henry, she would afford herself the opportunity to leave Lee.

He stood triumphantly over her, flaunting the knife in a daring way. Lee tasted satisfaction by the mere fact that Vivian was obviously surprised he owned such a splendid weapon that she'd never seen. Vivian wasn't through fighting, either. She had never fought him like this before. Tonight, she decreed to give him the rumble of his life. He wanted to accuse her when he was the guilty party! She would show him that a pocketknife couldn't frighten her into submission. Vivian wanted him to know what his role was in the detriment of their marriage.

"You have all these women, and you'd dare question *me*?" Lee was like a block of ice, cold and unable to move. "It's easy for you to go do it to somebody, but you can't even stand the *idea* of a man touching me..." she smiled and looked thoughtfully at the ceiling, "and holding me." She waited for his reaction. None came. She rested assured, knowing she would elicit a response from him eventually. Ever more, it became important for her to share with him how she ached inside over her conclusion that he was driving their relationship to ruins. Lee was visibly sweating, yet he couldn't move even to wipe the water beads from his forehead.

"All the times I begged you to love me, you were too busy loving everyone else. You brought Maybelle up in my house, you hang out all kinds of nights with your friends--you do whatever you damn please, while I stay home with the baby. But you put a baby up in Maybelle when you were supposed to be marrying me! Then you have the nerves to beat me. Henry tried to help me that night when you left me all beat up like that. You whipped me like I was a man, then went on out in the night like nothing took place. You have no right to blame me for anything I have done." Vivian desperately hoped he was paying attention to her pleas. Her words meant so much. If only he could understand her heart-rending turmoil.

Lee simply waited for her to deny that she had been with Henry. Nothing else she said mattered to him. He waited for her to verbalize her meaning. When she said nothing more, Lee knew he needed the truth, whether he liked it or not.

"How many times?"

"How many times, what?"

"Don't make me say it, okay?" Looking away, she blushed. He followed her eyes to Mary, noticing her thick, dark cherry lips, and rounded eyes, recognizing for the first time that she did not get them from him. "How many times, Vivian?" She didn't answer. She was tired of this Russian Roulette where she took a shot at him, and he took one at her. "You're tainted! You was spoiled before I married you, right? You's a damn slut."

That did it! She balled her fist tightly, until the blood shot rapidly up to her head. The rush prevented her from remaining calm. And Lee was compelling himself to become enraged by the words he suggested.

"I am not a slut!" He had to know, she thought. She had given him all the clues in the world. Still, she couldn't tell him about Mary because she believed he would harm her seriously. She wanted so badly to say it out right. Lee wanted it out right, too, or not at all. No more games with her would he play.

"He spoiled you down South, didn't he?"

"Hell no!"

"Yeah, he did. When I left you at my house after we were supposed to be getting engaged. Did you give him a baby?"

"What? Who?" Vivian asked, gingerly surprised.

"The man you swore you ain't have nothing to do with. You looked me dead in my eye and told me he was too black and ugly for you to like. That's who I'm talking about, slut. Henry. Did you give Henry a baby and play like it was mine?"

Crawling, she backed up and stood, heading after Mary who was silently whimpering. He grabbed her by her shoulder with his free hand, pulling her backward and spun her around. Then, he let her go and smacked her back to the ground. "Did he *ruin* you, whore? And you *let* him? He turned around and married your *sister,* but you let him knock you up, first?" He looked at her with disbelief. "I'm asking as a friend, you stupid bitch! Truly, you don't care about yourself—you or your mama. In fact, all y'all jezebels are from the same sorry lot. Who the hell gonna say I'm not good enough for your whoring family?" She looked up at him, blood dripping from her nose, and emitted a delirious laugh to finally injure him like he'd injured her so many times in the past. He swarmed down and smacked her again. This time, his knuckles scalded her lips, sending a spree of saliva in small particles in the air. Lee heard his voice crack from deep within.

"How many times," he asked calmly, still clutching the knife by his side.

"You're crazy!" Her screams at him weren't quite as shrill as Mary's protest.

"Shut-up! Both of you," Lee yelled back, looking back and forth from Mary to Vivian. Mary became immediately still upon seeing his contorted face aimed at her. He moved in on Vivian and kicked her in the leg. She grabbed herself with both arms and drew away. All these last weeks with her since Casey had told him was spent dismissing Casey's words. But now, when he looked at her, he didn't see the sweet princess he had married. Instead, before him was an unwholesome con artist who had deceived him. This was a conniving harlot who lied to get him to marry her, and once he was misled, she continued to cheat on him behind his back as though the first slap wasn't enough. He felt no connection anymore to her or Mary, although he still loved both of them. He hated Vivian because he loved her so deeply.

"It doesn't matter, Lee, because I'm leaving you, anyway. You ain't no good no more. See how you like to beat on me?" She was sobbing, getting more anxious by the second, soothed by the remembrance of what tears did to ease his frenzy.

"Where are you gonna go?" He asked in a scratchy voice.

"I'm going back to my sister's house," she yelled. "Least it was some peace there, and bigger than this dump." His ego took a nosedive when her words criticized what he worked hard to provide for her.

"You mean you're going back to Henry." He drove his fist in her shoulder, crouching down a bit. Then he stood back, crossing his arms. Vivian wanted to physically conquer him most of all, but he proved she could never subdue him. Her face burned with scrapes and bruises. So she attacked more ferociously with her words since he insisted on fighting.

"And you're not welcome there. You can walk your yellow bastard ass back to Florida for all I care."

"You can't wait to get back to Henry!"

"It's my sister's house."

"Don't try it, Vivian."

"Yes! Yes! Is that what you want to hear so badly? I'm going to Minnie… and Henry. But that's not why I'm going. Henry helped me. Yes, I cried in his arms, Lee, but I always loved you . . . but you were too busy plowing with all your heifers down South, and up here, too. Henry was the one to see me cry over you down South and up here, too. You are the one who made me cry so somebody else could be there to dry my eyes. Henry was that someone else." She noticed that for the first time, she had his complete attention. She was in command once and for all.

"You lied to me, Vivian." Lee was sobering up very rapidly. Vivian felt like he was missing the point.

"How did you expect me to deal with your ways all the time? Even about what Floyd did. I can never tell you or have you to be there for me because you and your friends are the ones causing the pain!"

"This ain't got nothing to do with Floyd. Why would you bring him up? This is about Henry."

"Most of the time you were wrong about Henry and me, anyway! I brought Floyd up because of hurt that you refused to see. I'm not a whore, Lee. I was just confused.

"Henry is the one…"

"It happened only one time down South, and that was after you beat me senseless and just left me there. Ain't nobody planned it to be like it was—it just happened. But you are so hateful minded that it's hard for me to repent it! And how can we be talking about this when you have cheated and cheated on me, Lee? You deserve what you get, and then some!"

She regretted her stingy words immediately, but it was too late. Lee was now almost completely unfrozen—the only thing that remained iced was his heart. Vivian could tell by his eyes that she had lost control, and that she had lost him. Getting the truth out once and for all had seemed exceedingly important to her. A rush of relief flooded her being as she expressed the burden that had lain on her heart for so long.

"You cried in *his arms*?"

"Yes! *Henry's arms*! Okay?"

"This is bullshit. First, you tell me he was holding your hand 'cause you was crying over some silly shit, now you say you was in his arms. That's a big damn difference, you li'l slut."

"Why do you always forget your part, Lee? That time he held my hand was when you knocked me out. There's nothing silly about that, except why you put your hands on me in the first place."

"I can't believe you. You lie too damn much."

"And you love to call me a slut. Henry would never call me ugly names like that," she taunted.

"Of course he wouldn't call you a slut—he was too busy making you one…so what's worse?"

"It just shows how you be disrespecting me…"

"Slut, you disrespected yourself—you can't blame me for calling a spade a spade."

"Lee, you don't know what shape you left me in that night." She tried to get rid of her angry demons and resort back into sweet Princess Vivian. It was important that he see her like a princess and not a slut. "I couldn't even walk. How could you beat me and not know how badly it hurts me? Just like now, I'm trying to get us to talk, but you can't talk without balling up your fists at me." It was as though she was asking if it were all right for her to finally let go of her secret. "And yes, it *was* when we broke up after you beat me. Just leave me alone about it. You're the one who's been cheating on me! How did the focus get to be on me suddenly, and what I did to poor you? It doesn't matter. It's over between me and you." Lee was stuck on her words, *"Henry's arms."* Had she worked with a harsher description of her intercourse with Henry, Lee would have been less befuddled. She instantly recognized that her heightened passion caused her to utter words she had previously vowed never to reveal. She remembered how out of control he had been that first, crisp day in the woods at the rock when he'd slapped her and twisted her arm when he'd suspected that she was flirting with Henry.

He clutched the knife frantically, looking on at her with hatred. As he swung his arm fiercely, he saw the image of Henry, big Henry with his delicate Vivian. Vivian screamed. The knife had cut her arm, and he was coming back down with it. The splendid, sharp blade was covered with the warm blood from her left arm, and now her right hand, as she sought to shield her face and chest areas from his crazed advances. Lee was blinded by rage. She had just as much stated that she was leaving him to go back to Henry. Never. It was to his dismay that in his mind he possessed none of her. His attempts to lock her up in the bedroom were futile. The leash he thought clasped her heart to his palm was covered with the fleas of deceit. All the months during their marriage, he had thought she was his bride, a soft virgin. He felt now that she was worse than a dog, because a dog is unable to willfully deceive a man with a vicious motive. He had to stop her. Lee felt trapped. This was his *wife* making these statements. There was no way he could let her go back to Henry! At that moment, Lee didn't want her anymore, but he wanted no one else to have her since he still considered her his wife.

"What? You wanna leave me alone in Pontiac after it was your idea that I quit my job down South? Bitch, you gone mad. You destroyed my life!" He was mad enough to kill her. "I would send you back down South, but then you'd end up with some other man between your legs. After all I done for you, wench. I supported you and your baby which probably ain't even mine, and you gonna be an ungrateful brat and repay me with shame and humiliation? And if that's Henry's baby, you was too stupid to get rid of it? Your own mama could have told you how to do *that*!"

He didn't want to force the issue about the true paternity of Mary. The expression on her face when he suggested that he was not the father gave him all the distress he could swallow. He lifted his arm that held the knife again, and brought it down clumsily, blindly, just enough, he hoped, to give her the scare of her life. It swept across her throat. She had been sitting against the wall, and now he saw her try to disappear into the wall as the blade came down on her. Lee wanted her dead at that moment, but he didn't have the guts to kill her. He stood there watching the frightened look in her eyes. Ah! So much more comforting than the wild, challenging look she'd offered earlier. Lee was well pleased that he had gained control again.

He knew she was spoiled, but he hadn't fathomed losing her forever. Maybe a beating like this would get their relationship back on track if it was salvageable at all. One thing was certain; he would make true on his plan to move somewhere else, preferably out west, if the marriage would have any chance. It should be clear to her that he meant business, and that she should correct her behavior. Her eyes looked so sad and empty. He could see thick bubbles oozing up from underneath the red sea that covered her throat. He decided on the spot that he'd have to forgive her if he didn't want to lose her. It was Henry who took advantage of her weaknesses. Henry saw her in a state of disrepair and moved on her, Lee guessed. He let his mind roam back to the night he beat her bloody and senseless in Florida, and how he had left her on the floor in his house. Certainly, if Henry, with his blazing flame saw her like *that*, he would seize the opportunity to pose as her knight.

Why had she mentioned Floyd, whom she despised, though? Suddenly, he remembered how Floyd had the same burning blaze for Vivian, only he repulsed her and Henry didn't, *and* Henry evidentially was persistent and she was weak…*and* Floyd had always been persistent *and* vengeful! And Vivian was weak, weak, weak. He could see that, now. Then, he recalled how distant Floyd became whenever he would see him after he left him alone in his house with Vivian. The whole series of events were now replayed in Lee's mind.

"Oh, God, Vivian! I was a boy, then, but now I'm a man! You hafta forgive me for not protecting you and leaving you in harm's way because I was a fool! Did Floyd hurt you?"

Vivian tried to speak to him, but her voice was too faint for him to make out her words. She tried to look around for Mary, but the excruciating pain she felt at attempting to turn her head made her pass out.

"Vivian!" Weeping, he fell prostrate in her lap. "Don't you know I love you? I always thought I had something to prove out there. I didn't know how to be your husband, but now I know. Please don't say it's too late for me." He hoped she would at least whimper. Nothing. He grew more frightened and felt more alone than he'd ever felt in his life. "Jesus died for our sins, right? Don't I deserve another chance? Nobody or nothing matters but you…"

When she came to, Lee was on his knees beside her, looking on with fear. It slowly registered to him how badly he'd cut her. He was peering through the fluid, as though trying to figure out exactly what had happened to her.

"Henri-Anna," she whispered, "get my baby . . . Henri-Anna . . . where is she?" Lee was so shocked at her condition that his heart was not troubled by the announcement of Mary's middle name that he never knew. He looked around to find Mary cowered under the bed, watching it all. Not knowing what else to do, he went to retrieve the baby, and brought her back to Vivian. She was too listless to even hold out her arms for the child. Instead, she smiled at Henri-Anna, forming her mouth in a kiss at her.

"Vivian!" Lee gasped. Her eyes were closing, but the blood continued to flow. Lee surveyed the room for something that would stop the blood. He deposited Mary on the floor besides her mother, and fetched the blanket from their bed. When he returned, Vivian's head was slumped unnaturally over her chest, as she remained sitting upright against the wall. From that moment on, everything was a blur. Lee felt himself grab Mary, who was sitting in a pool of blood, trying to climb in her mother's lap. He grabbed Mary and hugged her hard, smashing her face into his chest, finally conscious that she was seeing all this drama. Lee didn't want Mary to see him trying to get her mother back awake. He knew nothing about how to check a pulse, so he knelt close to her to listen for her breath.

She couldn't be dead.

Lee carried Mary to the far corner of the room, sorry now that he had refused to take the crib to their new home because of his pride. Mary worked her way back to the threshold of the horror scene, comforted by the feeling of warmth coming from her father. He wanted mommy, and so did she. Mary saw her father straighten the blanket out around her mother, keeping her covered up to her chin. She wanted to be with the two of them, but she didn't understand the strangeness of the circumstances.

Eleven minutes passed before Lee was psychologically able to gather Mary again and go for help. He wrapped Mary in his arms and proceeded to his doorway. He stood there for a long moment before moving out into the September air. Still in a daze, covered with blood, he walked outside and down the street. He couldn't tell just anyone, like the other boarders in the house because this was a personal matter. The coldness of the evening only served to freeze Lee's emotions while he moved quickly through the streets.

He never considered Robeena as any special kind of friend, but for some reason, she was the only person with whom he felt he could share this disaster. Lee thought these thoughts as he became conscious that he was making his way toward her house. He half wanted to turn back and go to his own house to see if Vivian had gotten any better or worse. She couldn't be dead. He gagged when the hot, tart smell of blood at last registered past his shock to his sensory receptors. He picked up his pace, hardly noticing the child in his arms.

Robeena recognized Lee coming up the street from her position outside in her yard. She was standing with Bruno, engaged in a departure dramatization. She knew Casey would come by later, and she didn't want him to see Bruno. Nowadays, since Casey visited so few and far between, Robeena didn't want to chance infuriating him, which could cause him to stay away from her for too long a while. Casey treated her in a way that no other man ever had. Robeena was surprised that not seeing him would be this difficult.

As Lee neared, Bruno noticed the blood first. It wasn't until Robeena saw that Bruno was aghast that she, too, saw the blood all over Lee, and then all over Mary. She screamed mechanically and dashed out into the street to meet them. Bruno was on her heels, making sure she didn't enter what could prove to be a very dangerous association. He reached for her arm just as she came within inches of Lee and the young child. Lee stopped in his tracks, not assimilating until Robeena approached him that he had already reached her house.

"Where's Viv?" Robeena asked instinctively. It was nearing 7:00 p.m. Robeena knew Vivian could be nowhere except at home. The mention of Vivian's name caused a stir of fear in all of them. Bruno remembered the sweet girl at the party, and how she begrudgingly had gone home that night to an obviously problematic relationship. That night, he thought Robeena was tough compared to Vivian's softness. But that was a long time ago. Robeena wasn't so tough at all, simply scared of true love. Now, Bruno wouldn't dream of trading Robeena for anyone else. He just had to make her see that she was the sweetest princess; she was a princess hidden from the world because she chose to hide behind the tough exterior she tried to construct. He had to make her see that Casey was no good for her. Robeena often talked to Bruno about Lee being a rotten husband to Vivian, yet Bruno deemed Casey to be a far worse example. Bruno easily concluded that this must be Vivian's family standing before him, now.

A surge rushed through Lee when he heard his wife's name. He couldn't answer the question because it was too confusing to him. As soon as Robeena mouthed her sister's name, she immediately knew something was dreadfully wrong. Lee had only been to her house one time, and that was to get Vivian. Robeena screamed again, this time, her proximity to Lee, coupled with the shrill sound of her voice jarred him.

"Oh, God," Lee managed, "we got in a fight. I gotta go back and see if she's okay." Suddenly, Lee felt as if he knew what to do. Vivian needed him. She was all alone on the cold floor. Lee shuddered at the image of the blanket slipping down, leaving her exposed. "Keep Mary. I gotta go back." Before Robeena could protest, Lee shoved Mary in her arms, and quickly retreated up the street.

It was a nightmare for Robeena. She stood immobilized, standing asleep until she heard Bruno's voice creep urgently into her horror. He was nudging her, saying that they should do something. As though in a trance, she took Mary inside, and knocked on Connie's room door to ask her to keep Mary for a spell. Connie had been looking out of her window when all the drama was unfolding. She couldn't recognize the dark colors as blood, but she could feel the danger through the loud voices and screams. She flung her door open on Robeena's first knock, ready and willing to take the child from Robeena's hand. She didn't see the blood on the baby until Mary was in her arms.

Robeena and Bruno were right on Lee's trail in the rush to Vivian's aid. When the former two reached the scene, Lee was bawling like a two-year-old child sitting crouched next to Vivian. Robeena saw Lee, and then her eyes quickly jumped to the massive lump of a bloody figure that had Vivian's shape. It was a smelly, frightful creature. Robeena had never seen such a ghastly sight. Gummy, white foam was bubbling out of the creature's chapped lip mouth. Vivian's hair was disarrayed and caked with crusty blood. Her neck was twisted in a strained position. She had fallen all the way onto the floor.

"Oooohhh! Lee, you done killed her!" Lee looked at her sheepishly, not knowing how to respond to the accusation. Those were such strong words Robeena had selected. Bruno got down on his knees, checked Vivian's pulse, and listened for her breath. He stood up slowly, brushing his trousers back straight, staring at the floor. He shook his head, then glanced at Lee and lowered his gaze again. At last, he lifted his head once more, looking directly at Robeena.

"Your sister is gone for sure. She's dead, and there's no bringing her back." Robeena went into a hysterical fit, flinging her arms in the air, and twisting her body in wild jerks. Bruno grabbed her around her waist and swayed his upper torso about with hers, allowing her some movement, yet preventing her from thrashing about too frantically. Lee was still pondering the seriousness of the indictment Robeena had charged him with. He couldn't think of Vivian as "dead," even though he was conscious of the fact that there was always that possibility.

Still holding Robeena steadily, Bruno glanced backward and saw that a small crowd of onlookers had gathered in their doorway. Lee was staring at Vivian and did not notice the spectators until he heard Bruno speaking to them over Robeena's cries. Bruno told two young men to send word quickly to Henry Raison that Vivian was dead. Lee thought that this friend of Robeena's certainly wasn't an expert on life and death. What did he know? And who made Henry her guardian that should be the first to know?

Lee hadn't really believed she was dead until Bruno said it again. He heard Bruno send someone else to call the police. "A woman is laying up here choked to death in her own blood. Get the police over here!"

"Nooooo!" Lee chimed in with Robeena's shrill scream. The record player emitted an enormously annoying screech, but the angry needle was not enough to drown out Robeena's horror. Everything else was more of the same blur for Lee. Six Caucasian police officers were at the scene in no time, followed by a rescue squad team. Lee squeezed his eyes closed, trying to wish the reality away. He decided he had not *really* been mad enough to kill her. They could have worked it out. The blood pounded in Lee's head. He took his hands and covered his face area, not stopping his fingernails from digging heavily into his scalp. He threw himself on the floor across the room from where Vivian lay, only hearing murmurs of what was taking place around him.

After hearing bits and pieces of the account about what happened, two of the policemen grabbed Lee, not too roughly, cuffed his hands behind his back, and pushed him out of the door in front of them. Two other officers followed, shaking their heads in disgust. Robeena shook violently, still needing the support of Bruno as she watched solemnly, wishing the men in their deathly uniforms would hurry and remove the body from her sight. Her next thought was how she was going to tell their mother about the tragedy.

"My mother never wanted us to come up here all together no way. I'm the one who told Viv she should come . . ."

"Shhh," Bruno hushed her, rocking her closer. Her eyes blinked as she tried to focus in on Lee. "Let me wrap your sister up, Robeena. At least I can pack her wounds." He glared at a few officers standing around, not really doing anything. With authority, Bruno took over by ordering people to provide him with items he needed. One neighbor ran to get scissors, and another brought back some rags. The officers were happy that someone knew what to do. Bruno patched Vivian's neck with the rags and covered her up with another one of Mary's clean blankets. He cleaned her up as best he could. He said to Robeena, "No since in her looking like this. It's just not decent. What's taking the medics so long to get in here? Aren't they outside?" He heard an onlooker mumble that the medics were outside as a formality, but they typically didn't get too involved whenever the victim was a Negro.

"This is the 20's! Black people have rights! Get me some help in here!" Bruno shouted vainly. With Bruno losing his patience, Robeena followed two of the officers outside to see what the medics were doing. Other officers were pushing Lee's head down in the backseat of a police car. Lee was yelling at everyone to forgive him. He blurted to the crowd that he had lost control because his brother-in-law had been sleeping with his wife, and he blacked out from sanity, and thus slew her. When they got him securely in the wagon, the officers told him they'd record all that he had to say once they made it to the station.

More than being irate, Robeena inwardly sought answers for the destruction of the young life of her sister. Never had she contemplated that anything like this would ever take place. Even after Casey asserted his aim to discuss Henry with Lee, she did not dream that Casey would utter a word to Lee about the confidential conversation she had with him concerning Henry and any relationship with Vivian. She didn't realize the full extent of how her gossip to Casey was instrumental in setting the stage for Lee's uncontrolled vehemence. However, it was abundantly clear to her how her sister's reckless life and involvement in such an abusive relationship led from one tragic episode to another.

Vivian's role in the destruction of her own life went unnoticed by many since she had become the final apparent victim. No one had yet considered the ultimate, life-long effect all this would have on Mary.

Robeena saw Gancy race through the growing crowd anxiously and start to question folk. He dropped his head, after gathering the facts. She looked away because his concerned and pained expression only brought her more grief. Somehow, she felt that they all had let him down. Gancy didn't need this sort of news about a family he had bent over backward to mentor. He was a respectable man, and he tried to help their family become respectable, too.

Henry arose abruptly from his catnap when he heard someone outside. Minnie was awakened when she felt the warm arms of her husband leave her. "Go back to sleep, honey. Somebody's knocking on the door. I'll see about it." He rubbed her back with the palm of his hands until she relaxed.

"Henry Raison?" The two men knocked again. "It's John Cook and my brother, William. We got some bad news for you. Come on and open up." Henry stood up straight, his body tensing everywhere. Minnie jumped up with him. He and Minnie rushed for their trousers and dress respectively when they heard the pressing announcement. Henry tried tying his pants together on his way down the stairs, leaving Minnie a minute behind as she struggled with her buttons. After Henry dashed out of the room, Minnie started wringing her hands, full of worry. She thought first of all the tools and wood Henry had "borrowed" from his job. She forced herself to follow Henry, using the banister for support as she descended the stairs. Minnie made it downstairs just in time to hear the dreaded ending of the message to her husband.

"Somebody already done called the ambulance and the police. I doubt if the body is still there."

"Who?" Minnie asked fearfully. "Whose body?" She envisioned the wicked lifestyle of Robeena, and assumed she had gotten herself injured.

"They say her husband killed her," the man concluded. The two messengers rushed down the walkway, with Henry and Minnie on their heels.

CHAPTER TWENTY-THREE
1930

Detroit was a cold place in 1930. Henry recalled confessing to Vivian the need to escape the racist South, yet it disturbed him to witness Black on Black assault, especially in relationships. Henry was despondent about all the Klansmen inspired lynching reports constantly in the news. The murder of thousands of Black people did not move him like Lee's assault on one woman, one princess. Henry sat numbly every time Minnie, in her attempts to discuss politics, but not really being in tune with the issues, raced to point out an article about white violence, while she never spoke of Vivian's tragedy. Minnie tried to inform Henry about events in the country, hoping she could get him to talk to her. He already knew about it, but she relayed information about Dr. Sweet. In 1925, a riot broke out when Ossian Sweet, a Black doctor, moved into a Caucasian neighborhood. During the confusion, a shot was fired from his house, killing a Caucasian man. The famous lawyer, Clarence Darrow protected Sweet on the grounds that any man, regardless of race, had the right to defend himself and his own home. Although the all-Caucasian jury acquitted Sweet, the trouble made the entire city more prone to racial injustice for the next 75 years and still today.

Sweet received his freedom, but the Black residents of the city did not gain better treatment. The Sweet trial had allowed the liberal segment of the city's government to mistakenly believe the situation had improved for Black residents in Detroit. However, housing segregation and discrimination continued, leading to larger racial disturbances in 1943 and 1967, and hundreds of other undocumented adversities.

The most noted act of Klan-inspired violence during this time was in Rosewood, Florida, which would later be chronicled in a heart wrenching film. Though far away from Detroit, the tremors of Rosewood and other killing grounds for Black people were felt from coast to coast. In January of 1923, an out-of-control Caucasian mob harassed the modest town of Rosewood. The mob was incited by a report of a Caucasian woman having been assaulted by a Black man in the nearby town of Sumner. The riot resulted in several residents of Rosewood being brutally murdered, and the Black portion of town being burnt to the ground. Fearing for their lives, many Black residents fled into the close at hand swamps and relocated as soon as they were able to escape. Never were charges filed against the perpetrators, which the mob was reported to have had several Klansmen from outside the area.

Being the most talked about race riot of the 20's versus being the bloodiest are two different things, and Rosewood took a distant second on being the bloodiest. The credit for the most gruesome and horrific annihilation goes to the American west side murderers of Black people. In Tulsa, Oklahoma, a mob of over 10,000 hostile, carnivorous Caucasians, some sporting machine guns, attacked the Black section of the city, devastating thirty-five square blocks, and leaving north of 400 innocent people dead. The mob used at least eight airplanes to spy on the Black residents and may have even used the planes to bomb some areas. The listing of all the race riots and lynching of the 1920s would fill several volumes. Many, such as Rosewood, were reported nationally.

The nation reported that *"The good citizens of the State of Florida are not unconcerned about the fate of Negroes, but it is a problem no one can solve. Indeed, Rosewood was awful, but when you stick your feet in hot water, expect to get burned. Our Klansmen have a hard job --place yourselves in their shoes. The Tampa Times newspaper writers have told the truth: Blacks "are anything but a Christian and civilized people." The Gainesville Sun writers are sharing the sentiment of most of us when they reported that lynching would exist as long as scandalous nigger assaults continued on innocent Caucasian women. The Gainesville Times paper had in print that the Rosewood massacre is likened to "the death of a dog."*

To add insult to injury, America had slipped into the Great Depression with the stock market crash of 1929. Every household was affected in some way. Casey's brother was laid-off from his job at Ford Motors. Outside Detroit, near Ford plants in Highland Park and Dearborn, strikes and marches were taking place back-to-back. Even though it was the Communists who led a march right outside the Ford Motor plant, which engaged some 3,000 unemployed men, Casey's brother, Tim, was involved. Casey summoned his girls to participate in the rally on his brother's behalf.

Out of control mobs were in the streets, yelling and cursing about things that couldn't be changed. Fearful policemen used tear gas, water hoses, and machine guns against the demonstrators who were unarmed. The demonstrators forcefully answered with rocks and sticks lying nearby. The executive committee of the Detroit American Civil Liberties League directed attention to the injustices being done, but there was no remedy for America's crumbling society.

Daily, Robeena rallied with Casey, albeit she wasn't fully aware of what was taking place. Robeena had been bitter for years. When she finally accepted Bruno's advice early in 1930 to look for decent gains, she was successful enough to convince a young Caucasian, love struck executive at Pontiac Motors, with whom she had been creeping with, to give her a job sweeping the auto plant. He was the nephew of the company's vice-president. This employment was short-lived because there was not a Black woman in any auto plant anywhere in the 20's working in any position. Her mere presence in the personnel office caused great racial resentment, and hiring her obstructed the establishment of the organized labor movement. The sight of her sex and blackness almost caused a riot on her first day at work. There were no Black women who could work in most areas in the 20's. Robeena could not expect to even get a secretarial job with her aboriginal face during that era. White men were the secretaries. Women stayed at home unless they were Black, and then if they were working, it was as a wet nurse, or a cleaner, or a cook in a white family's house. Period. It really wasn't much better for Black men. They were merely used as replacement laborers during strikes at auto plants in the early 1920s and mid-1930s.

Unfortunately, the Great Depression was not the time for a woman, particularly with Robeena's attitude to be hired in front of starving men, regardless of their ethnicity, and regardless of if it was just a sweeping job. A sweeping job in the auto factory meant handling a large shovel and about a ton of debris. The love-struck executive knew he couldn't pull those types of strings, but it was worth a try if he could promise it and get Robeena to spend another night with him. As such, he escorted her through the angry mob to the personnel office. Paperwork was rushed through; the white men working at the desks eyed the strange couple suspiciously, and within moments, the love-struck executive's uncle came in to possibly have his nephew committed if he was crazy enough to bring Robeena in past the gates with a straight face. Within twenty minutes, she was fired, and the son of her would-be supervisor was hired in her spot after he lost his executive position at the Pontiac Press Newspaper.

Bars were closing, men were losing their jobs, Black people were being lynched---it was a mess. Robeena relished the days when she could waltz into a bar penniless, and by the next morning have enough money to pay her rent. The Great Depression put an end to her carefree ways. Shortly after Vivian's accident, Robeena sought refuge in the employment Casey offered her. He promised her he would see to it that she ate and received shelter in sunshine or rain.

Notwithstanding, it was Bruno who represented a picture of sunshine on a stormy day, even if Robeena wouldn't look at him. Though personally unaffected by the Depression, he saw the world around him in despair. The love of his life, Robeena had been saving money to lease or buy a cabaret, but she had to dip into her pot many, many times. He watched her make a halfwit decision to rely on Casey for sustenance. Crestfallen, Bruno tried to convince her that he would take care of her, and that she didn't need Casey. Quick money was all she would listen to, unfortunately. Bruno consistently replaced the money in her pot and begrudgingly assisted her in pursuing her dream. To his sadness, once she had control of a run-down bar, she still refused to chisel the thread of Casey's presence.

Meanwhile, Casey was very vocal during the strikes and marches. No one had the right to work his brother to the bone and then throw him in the streets like spoiled meat after Tim had given Ford Motors almost twenty years of his life. If he had to burn the plant to the ground, Casey would see to it that someone paid for his brother's losses. Seen as a troublemaker, Casey's picture was taken, and he became a target for the local police. They arrested his girls at every opportunity, and followed him for the sake of harassment. Soon, Casey recognized that he wasn't the big bad fellow who possessed the clout to stop the Depression, regardless of how much it upset him. Tail between his legs, he continued to march, but not with as much fervor.

Then, during one of the communist protests, four marchers were killed, including Tim, and several more were wounded. Casey hid inside of his grief, retreating to his mother's home for almost two weeks. He was having a grim time facing the fact that he was powerless. His reputation was on the line. He didn't want his girls to lose faith that he could protect them, when, obviously, he couldn't protect himself or his own family. It was during this time of Casey's retreat that Robeena allowed herself to spend lost time with Bruno, Henry, and Minnie. Like Casey, she ran and ran, until she ended up at the doors of home. At home, she was faced with stowed away memories filled with grief, regret, and deceit. Her own guilt convicted her of the role she may have played in Vivian's demise, all because she kept secrets from Minnie.

Minnie was not clueless concerning Mary's paternity, although she had never discussed this with a soul. She knew it long before Robeena and Casey suggested it to her whenever Henry was at work one afternoon following Vivian's accident. For their efforts, all they got in return was a blank stare from Minnie. She didn't ever say a word to anyone concerning this horrifying affair, she never intended to deliberate about it, and would have fought tooth and nail with anyone who tried to pursue it. She swept it under the rug and went on with her life.

Nonetheless, she believed it was only natural that she should keep Mary and rear her as though she had given birth to her. Robeena certainly wasn't mature enough to handle the responsibility of a child, and their mother was too torn apart over her loss to be considered. Carol didn't make it up for Vivian's funeral. She wasn't psychologically able to come up and get Mary and care for her forever. Henry insisted that the baby stay right there with them. Minnie knew that she couldn't dare argue with Henry about something so important to him. She knew that if she ever would express her concern with him over Mary's living arrangements and her true paternity, her husband just might confess the truth about how Mary was conceived, and then he would put his foot down and demand that Mary stay with them, anyway. As it was, he rarely called her "Mary," and Minnie thought she heard him emphasize the "Henri" in the first part of her middle name a time or two.

Henry had become a quiet man, consuming himself with building things, church, and his job. He built a shed in the backyard of his house, and he built a den for Bruno one summer. He took loving care of Henri-Anna, who doted after him as well. Henry wasn't sure if she knew about her real mama or not. He knew she must grieve over her mama if she remembered anything at all. He was certainly brokenhearted still, after eight years. When she was younger, Henry often squeezed Henri-Anna to his heart and cried over her mother.

Robeena got everyone started calling her Mary Henri-Anna. Mary Henri-Anna was an outgoing girl who loved to go to church with her parents and boss all her friends around on Sunday. Her favorite headpiece was a washed-out bonnet that her father had given her on her seventh birthday. He told her that her mother used to wear it to church a long time ago. When Mary became an adult, she took a long rest from church that lasted for years and years, but she kept the bonnet in her boutique forever.

Minnie became a reverend at her church. All the extra energy and love she wanted to give Henry went into her religious mission, which became her main source of sanity and true happiness. Mary Henri-Anna spent a lot of time in the children's room whenever she went with her mother. When her father took her to his church, the two of them sat together in one of the back rows of chairs. After eight years of never discussing the tragic stabbing of Vivian, the congregations still only whispered about the illicit affair that had been uncovered because of that episode. As much as Mrs. Brown from down the block loved Henry, she found it necessary to confirm the rumors being spread amongst the congregation.

~~~

Carol was happy to see Wali Eli, as usual, as he did not visit the area much anymore. She prepared coffee in the unique way he taught her, and served it with honey and lemon. Wali Eli spread the books he carried in his sack on her end table, waiting to share with her and the other guests. After Carol set all the condiments before everyone, she peeped over to examine the literature, hoping he'd brought additional books of scriptures or another copy of the Lincoln-Douglas debate. Sometimes, he would be away on business for months at a time. He told everyone he was going away. They didn't know where he meant. Perhaps back to his brothers out east? Maybe Detroit for a while? Carol couldn't explain it, but she hoped he would spend a few years in Detroit. Eight years after her daughter's death only proved to cause a dull ache in Carol's heart. She couldn't go there, but at the same time, she wanted a kindred spirit to be there as a guardian over her family. She was just beginning to forgive herself of the blame she claimed over Vivian's death.

"I knew that boy was no good for her, Mistuh Eli!" He closed the book of scriptures he'd been reading to them. Everyone hummed in musical unison, soothing Carol.

"No one dies except by God's permission."

"I didn't even go to my own daughter's funeral."

"I know, I know." He gave her a handkerchief. "Just keep on living, Sister Carol." She nodded her head. "I've been traveling in and out of this place called Detroit. Black Bottom. I have visited Pontiac. I want to help your family and all our lost brothers and sisters in the wilderness of North America. Senseless killings, hopelessness, and mental slavery must be addressed. Look at how you suffer because of it!"

"You're going back to Detroit, Brother Eli?" Mr. Anderson asked.

"Yes. I'm going to continue seeking out our people. I'm going to visit the ground where your daughter's blood was spilled, and I will try to soak up every drop with the love I have."

"How will you meet the people that need you? Do you think you can check on Robeena and Minnie?

"I met you, didn't I? And I have these leaflets." He gave her a professional looking brochure for inspection. She was impressed with all the colors, but didn't want to embarrass herself by attempting to read any of the words.

"I wish God would snap his fingers and make everything okay."

"It doesn't work like that, Sister Carol. God gave man a free will. The devil is here as a temptation. You cannot resist the devil until you know who he is, though."

"Oh, yeah...I know who he is, alright. Him and that darn pitchfork, working his way up from underground to hurt people. That red devil Satan has attacked my family!" Everyone hummed again.

"The Devil isn't some red monster with a tail living under the ground. The Devil is that side of us that buries the voice of God within when we hear it. Devil is that part of us that knows right from wrong and still chooses wrong in pursuit of our low desires. See, we rationalize the truth and make right seem wrong and wrong seem right. We use deceptive intelligence to make evil seem like a fair choice."

"Well, if you put it like that, Lee Hiram was the devil himself!"

"Don't look for a Devil outside of yourself, Sister Carol. We can talk about that another time."

"Oh!" Ms. Esther said.

"Amen!" Mr. Anderson piped.

"I know. Or at least I'm beginning to know. I really don't know what to say except thank you." He took the last sip of his coffee and then gathered his books in his arms.

~~~

Sometimes, Mary Henri-Anna called Minnie "Big Mama," and she called Henry "daddy." The rumor of her adoption finally crushed her ears in the summer of 1930 when she attended a party Big Mama was having in their backyard. Mary Henri-Anna didn't mind large crowds at all. She was old enough to really help with the preparation of the food, and feel important while doing so. Floods of friends milled around talking about old times, laughing, and eating heartily. Mary liked having the opportunity to talk to her two cousins. Big Mama was very lively during these family gatherings, too. Henry's cousin Rufus had moved up from Florida a few years ago with his family, and the wife hit it off perfectly with Minnie since the time they arrived.

When everyone had been served, and after she covered all the food, Mary Henri-Anna stepped a few feet away from the table. She had been the one to help her daddy set the cardboard table up as a serving area for their guests. Standing over by the grape vine that represented a median between the next-door neighbor's house, Cousin Dorothy was waving two roasted hotdogs at her, and nodding her chin down at the ground where there were two plastic cups filled with something to drink. Mary Henri-Anna took a quick glance into the crowd to make sure everyone seemed content before she finally would walk away to have some real fun of her own with her cousin. There were more friends from their church than family members, although the original idea was to have a family affair.

She recalled that everyone had wanted her grandmother, Carol Johnson to make it up for the gathering. Mary Henri-Anna was disappointed when Carol Johnson didn't show up because she really wanted to get the chance to finally meet her mother's mother from down South, especially since her daddy didn't do too much talking about his own mama. "Grandma Carol said she ain't setting foot on this soil up North 'cause it's the soil that holds her daughter's blood," Dorothy, Robeena's seven-year-old daughter said, prancing in front of Henri- Anna. "She said this land up here is cursed by Satan himself." Both girls shuddered.

"Who said that's what Grandma Carol said?"

"My mama told me all about it," Dorothy said proudly. Mary Henri-Anna had a lot of respect for her wise and crafty Aunt Robeena. She always knew everything that was going on, although she never went to church where a lot of information was passed.

"What's Grandma Carol's daughter's name that has blood on this soil?"

"Believe it be Vivian. That's who they say is *your real* mama." Mary Henri-Anna forced herself to remain steady. She took another drink from her soda, staring Dorothy right in her eyes. After one more bite of her hotdog, and one last sip, she decided she wasn't thirsty or hungry anymore. She threw the half-eaten hotdog with incredible strength over the fence into the neighbor's yard. It hit the house, sticking at first, and then the mustard on the hotdog aided its slippery path to the ground. With a mouth full of food, Dorothy laughed, losing some of the mushy swine to her chin. Then Mary Henri-Anna tossed the rest of her drink into Dorothy's face, causing her to cough as some of the soda caught the back of her throat.

"Hey! What'd you do that for, Henri-Anna?" Mary Henri-Anna ran around to the front of the house, through the door, and up to her room. It was the same room that Lee and Vivian shared with her so long ago. She threw herself on the bed, raging mad at Dorothy. Abruptly, she sat up again. She *knew* there was another woman in her life besides Big Mama. Mary Henri-Anna tried to close her eyes and see this other person. She tried to crush her ears closed when all she could recall at first were angry voices. She could see herself cuddled on a familiar lap, getting her hair combed, listening to a soft song. "*Swing low, sweet chariot, coming for to carry me home, swing low...*"

The voice rang clearly to her now. It was not Minnie's stern, rich voice. This voice was chirpy and delicate. Henri-Anna slumped back on the bed with her eyes closed, gaining peace from the song in her heart.

Outside, Dorothy ran screaming to her Aunt Minnie. Very seldom would she go to her mother for affection and tenderness when her shielding aunt was around. "Henri-Anna poured her drink all over me, Aunt Minnie!" Looking on at them, Robeena sipped from her punch (which was spiked with the whiskey she kept in a pouch hidden in her purse), thrilled that she could relax without being bothered by the worrisome cries of ill-behaved children.

"Well, Mary will just hafta give you one of her dresses to wear, 'cause you certainly can't run around like that. Look at you!" She led her niece by the hand through the back door of the house. On the way, Dorothy told her aunt how mad Mary Henri-Anna had gotten when she mentioned her real mama. Minnie spun around at the bottom of the stairs and grabbed Dorothy by the neck.

"That's nonsense, child!"

"But my mama said that . . ."

"Your mama ain't got no business talking to you like that. Don't ever say nothing like that ever again!" Dorothy became frightened at this demeanor of her tender aunt. Minnie was hissing at her, and her eyes were rolling about wildly. Just as quickly as she turned to correct her niece, she turned back around again to rush up the stairs with Dorothy right behind her. Minnie went into Mary Henri-Anna's room without knocking. The girl was staring at the ceiling with her arms folded across her chest. She rolled her eyes over at her visitors, then back up at the chipped paint.

"Shame on you, heifer," Minnie fussed at Mary Henri-Anna, "that ain't no way to act."

"But she started it, Big Mama! She said mean things to me 'bout you not being my real moth-"

"Hush your mouth, Mary! How many times have I told you not to call me 'Big Mama'? That's for ev'ryone else to do, but not you. I'm your mama. You get your lazy butt out of that bed and find a clean dress for Dotty. I *swear* I don't wanna hear no more talk like that coming from either of you." They both knew she was serious to swear like that because Minnie never swore. She used to tell them that God would strike a person down with lightning for swearing. When she left the room, Mary Henri-Anna and Dorothy hugged each other and cried, praying together that lightning wouldn't strike Minnie down to her death. Then Dorothy tore her dress off while Mary Henri-Anna flung another one out of the closet at her. Dorothy jumped into her older cousin's two sizes too big clothing without checking her hair or washing her face. Eager to escape what had just transpired, they raced each other back outside.

Minnie refused to discuss it. As far as she was concerned, Mary *was* her child. In her home, she discouraged any kind of talk about what took place so many years ago. Many people started adding to Mary's beloved name, Henri-

Anna, but Minnie never would.

She even knew the night her husband was intimate with Vivian down South. She had known it before it happened. She never wanted Henry to go looking for Vivian that night so long ago after Lee had dragged her out of the church and disappeared with her, being that she didn't want to lose him to her. Minnie always imagined that if Vivian could convince Henry to be with her, he would, considering her view, that he preferred Vivian. The fact that he would never give her his heart fully became clear to Minnie after they moved to Pontiac where there was no Vivian. Henry was kind to her, and that's all. Minnie grew to love him for his kindness, giving up hopes of the butterfly hops in her abdomen. The tingling of toes when he said something dear disappeared. His hairs didn't stand up on his arms when she batted her eyes at him anymore, but whenever Vivian's name was mentioned, his whole being perked like a baby chicken seeing the sun for the first time.

At first, Minnie thought Vivian's marriage with Lee would change things. That's why it didn't bother her when they moved with them in Pontiac. One year between them seemed to change a lot of things, notably for Vivian. Her middle sister was a mature young woman with a husband and a child. And for a long time, Minnie didn't see any hints of the flames that burned in Florida. She couldn't catch Henry's eyes staring into Vivian's flesh. Vivian didn't regularly prance in front of him, forcing his attention. Henry didn't look back at Vivian while he talked with her. After several weeks passed, Minnie knew something was still strange, although she couldn't place her finger on it.

Then, she realized it was Lee's attitude that caused her discomfort. It didn't appear he was doing enough to keep Vivian focused on growing together as a family with him and Mary. Minnie resented the street life that kept Lee out at unthinkable hours, and sometimes all night long. She knew this activity concerned her husband, and not simply because he was a church-going man, either. Whenever Lee stayed out extra late, at first, Minnie refused to go to bed and leave Vivian and Henry downstairs together. Even if she was dead tired, she'd find some reason not to retire. Vivian would be sitting in the living room sewing, and Henry would be in the dining room reading the newspaper. Once or twice, Henry tried to tell her to go on to bed and that he'd be up in a minute, but Minnie knew he wanted the chance to be alone with Vivian. Minnie began to feel if she allowed him to be alone with Vivian sometimes, then perhaps he would be happy, and she would do anything to make him happy if it would keep him with her. It made her miserable to share her husband with her sister, but she didn't want to lose him, so she played along like she didn't see what was taking place right under her nose. Even that time when she went to the bridal show in Detroit with Robeena, she felt it was a sacrifice that she had to make to save her marriage. To assuage her ruffled feathers and to bury the heavy weight hatchet, she could always disassemble the facts to create a camouflaged reality. Minnie liked to play the pretend game and sweep the truth under the rug. It made her feel secure—it was the only way she could survive what Henry was doing to her.

She noticed that Henry's mood seemed to change with the weather of Vivian's marital problems. Minnie understood that Lee's jealousy kept Vivian locked in her bedroom, and she never invited her sister to join the rest of the family, particularly during Lee's absence. Privately, she granted that it made her happy when Lee used to lock Vivian in their bedroom like an animal because that's what she acted like, Minnie thought.

Minnie took up fussing about the lack of income Lee was bringing to their household. She hinted her disdain for Lee to Vivian and made snide comments to Lee. Her intentions were to shame them into finding a place of their own. One evening, she expressed her concerns about the money issue to Henry in attempts to gain his support. She knew Henry wanted Lee to be a better provider for his family. Well then, shouldn't they try striking it out on their own? Lee was nothing more than a two-bit hustler, smooching off their hard work when Gancy had practically thrown a job in his lap.

Her worst nightmare came to pass when Henry capitulated that he wouldn't mind seeing Lee off, but stipulated that Vivian and Mary should stay, given that Lee was obviously not fit to care for them by himself. Crestfallen, Minnie was forced to reassemble the reality of the circumstances. She knew that Henry knew there was no way Lee would leave without Vivian. Minnie knew Lee could keep a job. He was working when Vivian met him, and he provided for her then...what was wrong with him finding a job in Michigan? Henry told her to be patient with Lee. Minnie wanted to argue about it further, but Henry wanted no part in the discussion after the first two minutes. He picked up his newspaper while she ranted and raved until she walked away dispirited. She never did know why he married her in the first place instead of Vivian. She remembered painfully how Vivian had dressed in her best dresses for Henry on the Sundays they went to church together down South. Her shame and embarrassment stopped her from ever confronting Henry with her suspicions.

Now, she apperceived with all the slack talk that went on in the town, Mary was bound to hear the truth about her real mother. Yet, to discuss it would mean to talk about the fact that she was barren. She swept that under the rug, too, as she clung to Mary Henri-Anna as proof of her fertility. If ever

Mary Henri-Anna *would* hear the truth, Minnie would rather that she kept it to herself. This was fine for Mary Henri-Anna in as much as she didn't want to remember the blood she saw when she was not yet two years old. Nonetheless, she couldn't stop the assorted images from sprouting to the surface from time to time. Alas, nor did her denial stop the emptiness she felt somewhere deep in her soul.

At one point, Mary Henri-Anna didn't think she'd ever find out the truth. Hadn't her mother denied that there was another mother somewhere? She understood some people were mean and told vicious lies. People sometimes took the partial truth, and turned it into what they called the "real" story. Mary Henri-Anna tried to keep her memories and questions about the past buried, although she continued to hear bits and pieces of the rumors from different family members over the years, mostly when they got drunk. Her Uncle Bruno was helpful in keeping her Aunt Robeena quiet about it, but because their marriage was failing, Bruno was not present during some major episodes.

Bruno was fond of Mary Henri-Anna from the start. The day he saw her dripping in blood and orphaned, he would personally adopt her if there was a need to do such a thing. He was the one who'd checked her mother's pulse and sent for help. He was the one who arranged the funeral services for Vivian when her family collapsed at the seams: Henry went into a silent shock, unable to utter a word for nearly a month, Robeena lived her life on the continual verge of a nervous breakdown, and Minnie was busy trying to figure out what to do about Henry. Henry was cognizant of people thinking he was going crazy when his shock drove him to absolute silence after Vivian's death, but he just didn't have anything to say to anyone. For half an hour he stared at the spot of blood that had been left where Vivian was slain. Then, he turned to Minnie who was running back and forth, and told her to see to it that Mary got home with them to stay. After that, he kept quiet. At his job, everything was fine as long as he continued to do the work required of him; they left him alone, which is what he wished everyone else would do.

Bruno commissioned Yetta to sing "Swing Low, Sweet Chariot" at the services, while he agreed with Gancy that young David Foster was mature enough to play the piano. Bruno made the decision to have the funeral at Minnie's church.

Even though Robeena was dead set against marrying him, Bruno would still adopt Mary Henri-Anna. He understood that Robeena despised him simply because he was of the male persuasion. He knew of all the men in her life that had abused her; her father didn't claim her, nor did he support her, her brother-in-law cheated on her sister, her other brother-in-law stabbed her other sister, her grandmother's former slave master used her grandmother like she was a piece of meat, then he threw her away, and her grandfather was an alcoholic. Bruno witnessed her psychological torment in her everyday behavior and decided to save her if he could. He would show her that though it appeared that the Black man was destroyed, this wasn't so. Bruno had read in one of the pamphlets he'd been given by the brothers in the Allah Temple that the Black man was a strong warrior, likened unto a king, with the bravery and courage of a lion. However, it seemed like his greatness had been suppressed--like the Biblical sleeping lion in Genesis. The sleeping lion in Judah could be awakened, Bruno thought, and this Black man would one day take his rightful place.

The glimmer of hope was evident when Robeena's eyes twinkled as she told him of Mr. Anderson, Uncle Jack, Rufus Raison, and the kind friend named Wali Eli who protected and tutored her mother down South. It became clear to Bruno that Robeena would let herself love and live again if only she could see the godliness she saw in Wali Eli in another man. Well, then. They could no longer be intimate. He would protect and befriend Robeena in the most decent way. He would try to honor Robeena so that her eyes would sparkle whenever she said *his* name.

Bruno was patient with her through and through. He stood in the back at Vivian's closed casket funeral and waited until all the guests left before ushering Robeena from the gravesite. It took Bruno over a year of hanging around after that before Robeena accepted his hand in marriage. He listened to her bitter stories about her applications being rejected for dance school. He urged her not to drink so much alcohol because it was not only detrimental to her business, but to her health, as well.

She threw things at him when he told her he wanted to go and she wanted him to go because he didn't want to sleep with her. Robeena danced in front of him, shredding her clothes until he looked away. But she came back around in front of his eyes and danced some more. They were intimate while he hated himself for falling weak after he'd said he wouldn't dishonor her. As soon as it was over she told him that she was a prostitute and that she wanted to be a prostitute because all men were dogs, including him. He said, "Don't you mean Casey?" and she slapped him. And Casey walked in and out of her life.

Bruno stopped going to nightclubs, but Robeena kept going and working at them until she made enough money to lease one herself. Bruno told her he disapproved of the line of profession she'd chosen as it wasn't good for any future children to be brought up in that atmosphere. She told him to shut-up and be thankful that she only worked for Casey part time, now.

Bruno said she should realize she was finally admitting she was still Casey's girl, despite his advice that she didn't have to work for Casey. He grabbed her wrists when she tried to scratch his eyes out. She started crying and screaming at him that he couldn't take her dreams away of being a dancer. He didn't tell her that she wasn't ever going to be a dancer because she had chosen to be a drunk and a prostitute, instead. He waited until she calmed down and then he held her and rocked her until the tears came again. He paid her personal bills when her business lost hundreds of dollars from one fiscal year to the next.

Casey smacked her around and he set fire to her bar. Each time, Robeena said if he ever hit her again, she would leave him. Bruno never said, "I told you so" when Robeena fell on her face. The bar was salvaged because Bruno had been paying the insurance for months on it when Robeena decided to let the policy lapse.

He kept at her about drinking so much until she cried that she couldn't help it. She said she needed the alcohol to get her through each passing moment. She said her sister was dead because she'd told Casey about Henry. Bruno held her and she reached for another drink, but he didn't let go. Then Casey told Bruno he was going to kill him but Bruno didn't leave. Just like the first day Casey met Bruno, he'd stayed in the house with Robeena while Casey went for a walk. Bruno regretted leaving that first day because he knew Casey would come back after he was gone. Then, every time Casey came around, he tried to get Bruno to leave by walking around the block, threatening to come back. Bruno never left even though Robeena wanted him to sometimes. Bruno asked Robeena to marry him and she said no. The day after he proposed for the fifth time, Casey came over and took Robeena back to Detroit with him, while Bruno waited. When she got back two nights later, she wouldn't look him in the eye, but he asked her again to marry him and she said no again.

Four Caucasian officers beat Casey nearly to death one evening after they stopped him for speeding. He had two of his girls with him, including the half-breed one. Robeena went to the hospital to see him but they wouldn't let her in because she wasn't his family. Chelsea claimed to be his wife and Sandra claimed to be his only sister, and Sandra shot daggers at Robeena in the waiting area until Robeena picked up and left. Bruno had waited outside for her and drove her home.

Robeena got pregnant with Bruno's child and she finally considered marrying him. She could only imagine how rough it would be to be a single woman with a child. He married her like he promised he would and he tried to love her, but Robeena wanted to get back at men, so she took her frustrations out on Bruno. He told her he loved her and she told him she hated him, and that she only agreed to marry him because he had begged her for so long. He bought her new shoes and she hid his shoes when he got too aggravated to stay home with her sometimes. One December, he walked off with socks on in the snow because she dared him to hit her- but he wouldn't- so she hid his shoes so he couldn't leave.

Bruno began to spend more time with his brothers and parents, and less time with his wife and child, and child on the way. Robeena asked for a divorce. Bruno told her that they should try to make their marriage work and that he wouldn't give her a divorce. Bruno's brother told him that Casey was back out there in the streets. He didn't have to tell Bruno, though, because Robeena had picked Casey up from the hospital in Bruno's new car.

Rufus and another brother in a suit and bow tie handed Bruno a professional looking multi-colored pamphlet while he stood outside of the jailhouse in Detroit. He had just made bond for Robeena who had been arrested the night before for prostitution, and he was waiting on her release. The pamphlet contained information about "Islam in the West" and an invitation to attend a religious meeting. Three days later he joined the Nation of Islam and changed his name to Bruno X. Robeena told him he was crazy and that she couldn't tell her family she was married to a Muslim. She took his bow ties and smeared the light ones with lipstick and washed the dark ones with bleach. She charged at him, daring him to hit her, but he didn't.

He opened an accounting firm in Romeo, Michigan, five miles away from her bar and she swore he was having an affair with his secretary, but she was wrong. She insisted that she was right because "all men cheated" and she had her whole family as proof. Bruno stopped defending himself against her accusations, but continued to spend more and more time with his brothers and parents. They were proud that despite the Depression, he was able to be a successful accountant. Bruno laughed and said people needed accountants more than ever.

Robeena drove to his firm one morning after she came home at 3:00 a.m. to find him absent. She never got as far as the kitchen to see his note on the table explaining that his father had taken ill, and that he would be at his mother's house until morning. At the firm, she didn't see his car, but she broke his office window with a rock because she thought he might've been hiding inside with the secretary. Police officers caught her before she could make it home and they took her to jail. She told them that her husband owned the firm but they took her to jail anyway-they said a coon had no business trying to have something nice like that.

Bruno tried to shield Mary Henri-Anna from the madness going on in his household whenever she visited. He took her to the park with his daughter, or just Mary Henri-Anna would go with him. Bruno told Mary Henri-Anna she was special and she believed him. He tried to build her self-esteem considering the tragedy she experienced. Whenever Mary Henri-Anna would spend weekends with her cousins, sometimes her Aunt Robeena got drunk and cried over her sister that had been murdered. One night, Henry went over to his sister-in-law's house to pick up Mary Henri-Anna, only to find Robeena drunk again, and filled with misery over the past. Bruno was visiting his brothers that evening. Mary Henri-Anna stood behind the hallway wall, waiting to be called out by her father. She saw her Aunt Robeena's fingernails polished in red paint as they grasped the curtains. Then she saw her run away from the window to put her whiskey back under the cabinet and to wipe her eyes. Robeena respected Henry and the way he looked after Mary. Sometimes, he would come all the way over in the rain, simply to walk Mary home if she tarried too long, or if he knew she hadn't taken an umbrella with her.

Henry knocked once and then tried the door. When he came through the screen, Robeena rushed him. Automatically, he held her tightly. Henri-Anna peeped around the corner at them. "Hey, hey, hey, Robeena," he said calmly. "What's the matter?" She doubled over in anguish.

"Oh Henry! I know you loved her! I miss her! How could we have let that monster do that to our family? Least you got Mary, but I ain't got no parts of my sister left in this world." Henry quieted her, choking back his own sobs.

"Don't talk like that, Beena. We both gotta go on. Ain't no sense in causing no more pain to nobody. Henri-Anna belongs to all of us, including Minnie." Mary Henri-Anna turned away at this, convinced now of the truth that Minnie indeed wasn't her real mother. She had no one to tell. Those who knew feigned like they didn't know, or simply refused to talk about it. She was more comfortable wondering if it were true or not. Henri-Anna felt as though she had no choice but to push it as far back in her mind as possible. Later in life, she came to think of any mention of it as an intrusion—a direct assault against her person.

"It's your fault, Henry! He killed her over you. He murdered my sister on account of you. She tried to hide the fact that you were her lover!"

"Whatchu trying to do to me, Beena? You want me to die right now? Huh? You think I sleep well at night? Hell naw. I toss and turn wishing I'd never met her. I should've been like Zachariah with her, but I…I fell short, Beena. I can't help wondering what her life would've been like if I hadn't broken it all to pieces. Then I wonder if I had spent that first day with her instead of…." His voice trailed off.

"I don't see how Minnie could've ever forgiven you. I hate her! She could've stopped this whole thing…"

"There was no way she could've stopped it, and you know it." Robeena still hung on to him frantically. "I loved her more than any of y'all knew. Nobody could've stopped what I felt for her.

"*I* could've stopped it."

"How?"

"Deep down, I knew he would kill her if those ugly rumors ever got to him about her and you. But I told it, Henry."

"You didn't know any such thing, Beena." He shook his head. "Besides, you don't know what happened in that house. They could've been fighting about anything from apples to zebras."

She snickered. "You are so naive, Henry. They always fought about you. He blackened her eyes and slapped her on account of you. Lee told it to everyone—that's what he said happened at the trial." Frowning, he turned her loose. "You is crazy if you think your affair with her was a secret. Ev'rybody knew it." He thought of Minnie. "Minnie refuses to talk to me about it. I don't have nobody. This whole thing is swallowing me up, Henry. The entire town knows about it, but all people like to do is whisper. Ain't nobody willing to say nothing to my face."

"Shhh."

"The whole town is laughing at Minnie 'cause she wanna make believe she had a baby come out of her when ev'rybody knows she didn't. She won't even accept that Mary was her sister's child. Sooner or later that girl is gonna find out, Henry, if she don't already know."

"She's heard enough from you to know the truth by now, Beena. I reckon that's what you wanted, anyhow."

"She has the right to know."

"Yeah, I used to think the same thing. But does she *need* to know? I mean, how's that gonna make things easier?"

"Ain't for you to say what she be needing. They say Black folk don't need to vote, but shouldn't we have that right, since we's free and all?"

"Okay, Robeena. Point made."

"So?"

"I'll talk to her about this whole thing—when the time is right."

"The time ain't never gonna be right. Not in this lifetime."

It was a challenge all over again for Henry to repress the diary of what he shared with Vivian when Lee was released from prison that next year, in 1931. The only way Henry thought he could survive was by pushing her face totally out of his mind. Nonetheless, the sight of his daughter, who was the perfect likeness to her mother, often caused a deep surge of grief to rush through his heart. Yet, her big brown eyes and high cheekbones brought him the same intensity in joy. Mary's presence helped to bring him back to normalcy. Every time he looked at her, he grew stronger.

However, the presence of Henri-Anna could never replace Vivian's innocent smile and warm eyes. Certainly, not Minnie in her own grieving could shelter him from the loss of Vivian. Henri-Anna did fill a void that was so deep within him that he could have died had she not been there. He took walks with her, talked, and sang to her. One early Saturday morning, they walked together to the store right up the block on the corner of Franklin Road and California Street. Henry wanted to get a loaf of bread to make toast with for breakfast. Henri-Anna enjoyed cutting fat slices for her mother as she'd watched her father do so many times before. They would take toast and coffee to her in bed sometimes on Saturday and Sunday mornings. Minnie indeed had become quite spoiled with Henry's guilty, pampering ways.

Henry felt something burning on his back as he stepped one foot into the store. He turned to see a scraggly man across the dirt road under the streetlight smoking a pipe. Slowly, he retreated and stood on the grassy sidewalk to get a better look at this familiar face. The man was in dire need of a shave, hair wash, and cut. Henry barely recognized the man as the two now stood staring at each other for the first time since the accident. After the last box was moved away from the bedroom Lee once occupied in Henry's home, Henry saw very little of her. Whenever Lee came by after that to drop off or pick up Mary, Henry stayed out of sight because he couldn't face Lee after Lee took her away from him. The afternoon of Vivian's demise, the troubled couple stopped by to pick up Mary, only Vivian stayed in the car. Lee made it a point to brag about spending the day in Detroit with Vivian, knowing Henry did not want to hear the drunken accounts. Three hours later, Vivian was dead.

Henry steadied himself by backing closer to the store wall, and placing one extended arm up against the building for support. He tried focusing on Gethsemane Church and its gray brick fixture. He wanted to hate him. He had cast in his mind thousands of times how he would kill Lee if he ever saw him again. Yet, he hadn't prepared himself for the wretched sight haunting him from across Franklin Road. There was no expression of hate on Lee's face, only mourning was written in the depth of his pores. Lee had been in prison for over eight years. Henry opened his eyes wide, and then squinted them, never once taking them from Lee. This was the man who had murdered Vivian in cold blood, yet, he had only been charged and convicted of manslaughter in the second degree. And now he was lurking around the neighborhood, spying on what was left of his family. The vacant stare Lee returned was proof of his destitution, which made Henry appreciate that his long-lost enemy was now living in a hell worse than anything imaginable.

The need to overpower Lee quickly vanished from Henry. They both had lost. They both had lost the precious treasure, the hidden princess named Vivian. Equipped now only with her memories, both men recognized that each was too emotionally frail to continue the fight. Reluctantly, Henry faced the hell where he, too, lived. This is because the warmth that he once shared with Vivian caused a permanent distancing between himself and Minnie. Henri-Anna's very presence was a reminder of his adultery, and all the toast and coffee on earth couldn't change that sad reality. Thus, there were some similarities to their hell, although Lee was further down in the pits, as far as Henry could see.

Mary Henri-Anna hardly noticed Lee at all. She didn't observe the defeated look in his eyes, nor did she notice her father gawking at the man. She went on into the store without Henry, hurrying to pick out some of the five-for-a penny pieces of candy that were in the glass case. The eager Caucasian man behind the counter knew she wanted to have the candy all selected before her daddy got inside, and he wanted to help her get as many items as he estimated her daddy would buy.

He had played this game with her many times. He knew this family as one who tremendously supported his enterprise. It was a lucrative business to set up shop where Black people lived. On the south side of Pontiac, most Black residents felt fortunate to be able to buy and rent property, and spend their money with those who came into the community with services and goods. Mr. Alex peered outside at Henry impatiently after Mary Henri-Anna had selected what she anticipated to be her limit.

Eventually, Henry struggled to shorten his gaze with very mixed emotions. He tore his arm from the supporting structure that held his body firmly to the ground and followed his daughter into the store to purchase the bread, and all twenty pieces of candy she'd selected. After receiving the money, Mr. Alex almost reached under the counter for a sack, when he remembered that they had not asked for one, and the girl wore nice pockets on her blue dress. He shoved the bread and candy toward them, accidentally pushing the loaf onto the floor when Henry's arms didn't reach out quick enough. Freeman Price entered the store as the bread hit the floor. He grinned from ear to ear at Alex, who did not acknowledge his new customer.

"Oops! I'm sorry. Henry, is it?"

Glancing at Henry, Mary swiped the candy in one motion. "Yeah, my daddy's name is Mr. Henry Raison." Alex smiled at her as she bent over to get the bread while she made little patches inside of each pocket with her candy. On her way down, a flash of hotness rushed over Henry's temples as he looked over at Freeman Price. He suddenly remembered his mother and the disrespectful treatment they received from the grocer, Lucifix Hopkins and his son roughly thirty years ago.

"Thank you, Henry," Mr. Alex said. Henry stood erect, pulling Mary up, too, leaving the bread on the dusty floor.

"Hi, ya, Henry," Freeman beamed.

"How's it going Freeman?"

"Pretty darn good. I'm glad to be off today. You?"

Henry said to Mr. Alex, "It's Mr. Raison."

"What's that?"

"I just can't recall giving you permission to call me by my first name. Freeman and I work together, and we've been on a first name basis for a while, and it's understood. But not you. And, if you want me to purchase that bread, then you'd best hop over that counter, run to the back, and fetch me a clean loaf…"

"For Christ's sake! That bread ain't dirty—only the outer fixings…"

"I reckon you'd better be mindful of your treatment of your customers. Seems like you are kinda out of your place a tad bit, Mr. Alex. I mean, you got one of your hands outstretched to take my money, while your other hand is shoving my family's food on the floor." When he felt Mary move closer to him, he took her hand in his and squeezed, and then he let it go. Freeman stood shuffling his feet, wishing Henry didn't have to act uppity in his presence. He didn't want Mr. Alex to think that all niggers were bad.

"Now, Henry, I don't see why you're acting all like that." He looked at Mary. "Gal, go on through that there aisle," he pointed, "and grab a new pack of bread, will ya?" She started away where he directed her. Henry stretched his arm out, catching her at the waist.

"Mary, don't ever let any old man send you on some errand without checking with your daddy, you hear?" She nodded. "Now, empty that candy out of your pocket, sweet girl, and drop it on the floor right next to that stale bread, and let's get the hell out of here." Alex licked his lips, wondering what had come over Henry, but he was too afraid to ask. Mary took the candy out one by one, and played a game of dropping them, and then trying to hit the ones she'd dropped with the remaining pieces. Henry was relieved that she didn't pout.

"Henry, if you're angry about something…"

"Look, y'all," Freeman butted. "I don't mind getting that bread for you, Mr. Alex. I knows you is trying to help Henry. I don't know why he…"

"No. I'm not. "I'm *very* concerned, not angry. I've had some tough times, Mr. Alex, and then I've had some good times. This is my daughter. I want her to grow up right. I want her chil'ren to grow up with self-respect and dignity. And if this world can't supply her with the support she needs for that to happen, then I want her chil'ren's chil'ren to grow up with it. I never feared God before, because I wasn't aware of his wrath. I'm living proof that the wrath of God exists. Well, I've gone far enough in life to know a li'l bit about right and wrong, justice and injustice. So, I can't let you treat me like I'm a lesser man than you are, even if it's by accident that you behave the way you do." He wiped his brow and glanced back outside at Lee.

"A whole lot of people have suffered in this life, Mr. Alex. See, the way I figure it, is if we all just stand up and be men, some of this suffering can stop. If we stop lying to ourselves and others about our feelings, then maybe we won't end up all tied up like a knot inside. But before I knot myself up due to injustice again, I might take someone's head off."

"I understand."

"I reckon you don't understand at all, Mr. Alex. That's why you was just about to be the one to get your head knocked off by me—a man that keeps mostly to himself."

"Yes, sir, Mr. Raison."

"Well, I best be on my way—just as soon as you would politely drop my money back on the counter, I'll be out of your way." Alex stared at Henry square in the eyes until Henry's blaze caused a burning in Alex's retina. Filled with animosity, he looked away from Henry. Reluctantly, Alex placed the money on the counter as he was instructed. He wanted to frown, but he thought better of it. Immediately, his thoughts went to how much Freeman came to spend, and whether he was apologetic enough for Henry's attitude to make up the loss with a heaping purchase.

"Daddy, can I have that money for me some new hair bows and a bonnet?"

"Come on, Mary. Have a good day, gentlemen."

Lee had taken a seat on a bench at the adjacent corner. He got back up when they came outside of the store. The street was quiet except for the wind whistling a quiet song and a few birds chirping along to the melody. Lee swigged something hidden in a brown paper bag, turning his back on them as his eyes rolled back at Henry, pretending not to notice Mary. "Who is that, daddy?"

"No one, dear. No one," he mumbled. "Just a stranger." Henry forced himself to turn away.

Lee, turning to steal another glance, stood under the streetlight for a few minutes longer, hoping Mary would turn and see him, too. He watched them walk the short distance home, and he saw Henry drape his arm around the child's shoulder protectively, as though he could still feel Lee's eyes sizzling on his back. The two went on inside the house without either of them looking back.

The disdain Lee once felt for Henry changed to appreciation now that he witnessed that Mary would be cared for properly. He walked closer to the house for a better look. Lee wished some miracle would take place to cause Mary to know that he was sorry for killing her mother. He wanted her to know that he loved her regardless of whether he had fathered her. These thoughts at least gave him peace, for he knew he could never utter them to Mary.

Henry felt almost certain Lee was not going to bother them. After monitoring his presence for several months, there was an implied deal that Lee would forgive Henry for destroying his family if Henry would forgive him for doing the same. Henry felt that Lee was in such bad shape that he needed a glimpse of what was in order to continue functioning. Lee had no one. Henry wanted so much to urge Lee to go back down South where his family lived.

Lee knew in his heart that he would be happier back in Florida, but first, he wanted Mary to know who he was, and that he was sorry. He couldn't let her know that from down South—he couldn't see her down South. He wanted to always see Mary, who was proof of his dear, lost Vivian. In Florida lived a past that might not welcome him. How could he face Leland and Maybelle? He'd left that family to run off with a girl he thought was better than Maybelle, and he left his son without ever tossing him a bone or a birthday wish. And he had dogged Liz out too much to even say her name out loud. Could he really go back to Florida and seek solace in the arms of Maybelle? Would she accept him? In all the years of his running, alas, Maybelle represented the only home for him that he desired. Somehow, she became someone he longed for.

It came to pass that mostly the whole town knew who Lee was, as the scandal of what happened between him and his wife was a rare occasion. Lee didn't care. He thought that most of the town thought he was Mary's daddy, and not Henry, since he was married to Vivian all that time. When the rumor got to Mary through her cousin Dorothy that this drunken loiterer was her be-grieved mother's husband, and allegedly her father—the one who killed her mother, she responded with silent tears. She spent her life without ever acknowledging the validity of it. The sight of him tarnished the image of what she imagined her mother to be. How could that sweet voice she remembered singing to her be wrapped up with this foul looking mortal, this murderer? She clung to the Raison's as her real parents, pushing the horrible rumors away.

Minnie prayed for his soul when she heard he'd been released. She prayed for her soul when he was imprisoned. The months she'd spent wishing Vivian and Lee gone crept into her nightmares. Since she believed herself to be a woman of God, Minnie concluded that God granted her wish by eliminating Vivian from her life. But more than anything, it exasperated her to admit that if Henry learned of her role in Vivian's demise, she judged that he'd never forgive her. He wouldn't consider her emotional predicament that he himself contributed to with his infidelities. Minnie felt that she was her husband's leftovers—that he wished she had died instead of Vivian.

"I was a fool for ever inviting her to stay with us at all. Oh, my dear sister! I should've known you would behave that way. And Lee. Obviously, I gave him too much credit," she deliberated to herself.

Minnie scarcely recognized who Lee was when she saw him. This is because she hardly looked at him. She looked through him as though he was a lowly beast occupying space in her neighborhood. She weighed him by his tattered clothes, broken shoes, and scraggly beard. She'd seen him, this bum lurking about before she learned that Lee had been released. It was hard for her to fathom that the parasite down the block was a part of her family that had been discarded. And they could do that? Through an unspoken, make-believe family meeting, there was a vote and Lee was kicked out of the family, but Henry would go free, unharmed, chastised not.

Then sadly, Minnie collided with a newly formed estimation that Henry didn't go free at all--*she* was Henry's nightmare. She was his punishment. Henry couldn't have Vivian; he was stuck with *her*, and Vivian was dead and Lee came back as a reminder to her. One thing was absolute in Minnie's mind; she would never allow Lee the opportunity to contaminate Mary's mind or to expose the lie they all were living.

She watched him from her window, becoming obsessed with his presence. She waited to see if he would walk by their house on the other side of the street, which he did quite often, purposefully whenever Henry wasn't home. His presence was harassment to her.

It was a feverish Tuesday. No rain offered consolation to the scarred browning leaves sinking in the dry branches. She was convinced that Henry's hair under his safety hat was musky by now, as he was probably halfway to work. Minnie poured herself a steaming cup of coffee to go with the weather and her mood, and then took her seat in the chair by the door. The house was stuffy from the outside humidity. The wind was fast and quick as it passed every house except hers. She could almost smell that he was out there. When she couldn't stand it any longer, Minnie hazarded outside early that Tuesday morning while Mary was still asleep and after Henry had gone to work. There he was, sitting a block away with another low-life shooting dice. They were turning her neighborhood to ruins. She tightened the strings on her cotton frock and patted her braids down.

"Hey, you!" She wasn't speaking loudly enough, and she knew it. She needed to test her voice against the vicious Michigan wind a second time. "Hey, you!" Lee saw her standing in the middle of the road, motioning to him. Surely not. "Come here." She took a few strides in his direction and then stopped, while Lee watched her.

"You talking to me, woman?" He stood slowly to see if she would continue to advance.

"Meet you half-way," she suggested as she inched further. Lee didn't meet her halfway. He stood stark still until she prodded to near where he stood. The other man ignored them and continued tossing the dice around. She was looking past him. "Let's talk over there." She was pointing to the trees in the field across the street from Gethsemane Church and behind Alex's store. Lee nodded his head reluctantly. In silence, they ducked out of sight to where grasshoppers were tempted to jump on her stockingless legs. She looked deeply at him when they were alone as if to make sure it was really Lee.

"Why are you here, Lee?"

"This is where I live." He wouldn't look at her. He remembered that she never liked him. Even in Florida, Minnie tried to keep him from her.

"Where's your house? That bench? Or is there a hole under that bench that you crawl under with the rest of the bugs?"

Stubbornly, he repeated, "I live here."

"You don't live here." He said nothing. "What you did was murder somebody. You trying to rub it in? You here to threaten my husband? You wanna cut him, too? Or is it me you wanna smack? Or is it Mary?"

"Why are you asking if I wanna hurt Henry? Why would I?"

"Then why are you here?"

"Seems like *you* would wanna cut Henry more than I would."

"I doubt that, killer."

"Your husband caused all of this, not me."

"How could they let you out of prison if you's still the same old bum you was when they locked you up? Don't seem like you is rehabilitated, niggah."

"Now you listen to me!" He was livid. Lee held his finger up and pointed sharply at her. The fingers of his other hand were fanned wide. Minnie was frightened for a moment. These were the rusty hands that had snatched life away from a human being. His was the deceitfully smooth voice that surrounded her sister's ears with insincere murmurs of love. "Vivian was my wife. I hate what happened."

"Then you must hate yourself."

"I certainly don't *love* myself, and I certainly don't love you, neither. You hated me from the beginning, but you didn't even know me."

"I knew you were trash and that you wanted to trash up my sister. That's all I needed to know."

"I *married* her! Which I never would've done if I would've known that your husband had already trashed her up, not me."

"That's a lie."

"Well, maybe I still would've married her. In fact, I know I would've. I loved her, Minnie. She never knew that I loved her no matter what Henry made her do. All she had to do was tell me. I would've been blind with anger. I might have even left for a minute, but that's about as long as I used to could stay away from her. She was just a young girl, a virgin girl and I was her boyfriend, and I never—not 'til I married her. Henry ain't have no business messing around with her like that and then leaving her all alone. She was only sixteen, for Christ's sake, and he was nearly thirty and engaged to you."

"I didn't know you knew Henry's age and horoscope and what be on his mind. Are you a male witch or something?"

"What kinda man would do that to a sweet girl like Vivian? She didn't deserve that."

"This is the part where your lies keep on coming. Who was that stinking cow that wagged her wide ass down to the church when you knocked her up and then left *her* alone trying to marry Vivian? Do you know what a lying hypocrite is, and what the Lord does with your kind? And keep my husband out of your snares. Henry ain't never done nothing to her."

"Did your husband tell you it was a lie?" She shook her head, her eyes fixated on the grime buried in his too long fingernails. "He *wanted* me to kill her because he felt that if he couldn't have her, he ain't want nobody else to have her—including her own husband. Your husband was always up in my face letting me know what he wanted, daring me to put a stop to it. I did put a stop to it, Minnie. You were too pathetic. Somebody had to stop them. They were making a fool outta all of us, but you were the biggest fool because you made out like it wasn't happening. I took care of your problem, didn't I?" Minnie refused to let the tears behind her eyelids humble her.

"What kinda a monster are you, Lee?"

"You wanted her dead, Minnie. That makes you the monster. Henry wanted her dead, too. I was a fool back then. Henry knew I was whipping on her, and he didn't mind me doing it because it gave him the chance he needed to act like he was consoling her. As long as I was messing up, Henry was running to my woman, making it seem like he was better than me. See, that's when he got her pregnant down South. Me and her got in a fight, and he knew she was confused, but still, he took advantage of my woman. Did he tell you he spoiled her?"

"You hafta take the blame for this, Lee. Suppose they were all rumors? The whole bit of it. Suppose you murdered her thinking she was like you and the whole thing was a lie?"

"It was an accident."

"*You* was an accident. You killed her because you knew she never loved you. How could she love a filthy thing like you? You were way outta your league when you came over to mess with her, and you knew it. That's how come you used to beat her like you did—because you knew slime like you would never be good enough for her. You couldn't deal with her. She was the princess and you were the frog. They said you had a cute face." She sucked her teeth. "Brown skinned don't make you cute. You look like a lizard. What you needed was a niggah tramp slave, like that oversized whore you got pregnant in Florida. Vivian was always too good for you. You tried to force her to love you." He believed her.

"Has Henry fallen in love with you, yet? Or is he still grieving over my wife?" He took a cigarette out of his pants pocket and lit it. "Vivian *told* me that Henry made love to her. It wasn't a lie."

"She never told you that."

"The hell she didn't."

"She made it up. All to trick you, she made it up, and you were too ignorant to see through her games, so you killed her. You killed her because the lie you were living couldn't blind her no more. She saw you for what you was, and she pinpointed that you was a piece of horse manure."

"You have always lived a lie, Minnie. Not me." He dropped his smoke to the ground and crushed the blaze out with his shoe. Patent leather shoes with the soles almost gone. So faded they looked gray when they were black. Shoes the prison kept for him all the years he was there. "Henry never wanted you. You were too stupid to see that, so you begged him to marry you, even though he slept with your sister and you knew it." He spit in the grass. "You *knew* he had her, but you also knew ain't no 'nother man alive that would've married you—an ugly, too tall girl with those big ole manly hands."

"He didn't sleep with her. I see now why Vivian could never love you.

You's a horrible liar." Again, Minnie gorged back unwanted tears.

"He took her virginity and got her pregnant. I can deal with it now. Vivian did love me, Minnie. We...it just didn't work. All your interference paid off. Maybe if you had left us alone, none of this ever would've happened. You tried to control her relationship 'til you found out that you couldn't control your own. You wanted her dead." Minnie lost the tear gorging battle. Her cheeks soaked in the heated waterfall.

"You's bitter because I still have Henry and Mary and you have no one but your wretched, lowly, dirty self." He took another cigarette out of his pants pocket and lit it. Minnie waved the smoke away dramatically.

"I don't have my wife, nor do you have your sister. Seems like you would be bitter 'bout that, too, unless you planned it this way." He took a long drag. "Maybe that's okay with you. Maybe you felt Vivian was in the way of things, huh? Since you seem to know it was a lie, maybe you started the lie to get rid of her, thinking that would make Henry interested in you again."

"Maybe you killed her because you knew you was unfit. Viv told me several times that she was gonna leave you. She hated you. She wanted to get rid of you. She told me that marrying you was a mistake."

"I saved her by marrying her. Even if she didn't love me, I saved her reputation because somebody had ruined her. Henry spoiled her and left her alone like a tramp. Then you married him after he dogged her."

"Stop lying! Stop your mothafucking lies!" She reached out to claw his face. He grabbed her arms and threw her to the ground. She didn't move. Lee grew frightened that perhaps he'd bruised her. Instantly, he regretted touching her at all. Kneeling, he tried to help her up.

"Minnie? Is you okay?" She jumped to her feet with overwhelming strength.

"Don't touch me, you black bastard motha fucka! Don't ever put your perverted paws on me!"

"I've never met such a royal bitch." He rose quickly.

"You're a murderer!" She couldn't stop the tears.

"Where do you get off so high and mighty? I served my time, and this is where I wanna be right now. I don't have no other place to go, Minnie. Can't you see I'm without anything?" He felt like crying, too, but he knew she wouldn't appreciate his tears, just as he didn't appreciate hers.

"Seems like you got money to buy that whiskey."

"I ain't had nothing to drink in four days."

"You know what I think? I think you's hanging around here on account of you trying to get to Mary. Well, let me tell you something. She's off limits to you, Lee. Mary doesn't know nothing about what you did to us. We're taking care of her, got her in church, and ev'rything." She stood back, dropping her head slightly. "I'm begging you not to try to take that away from us by trying to bring up the past."

"That's what you're doing, Minnie. Bringing up the past. I'm not here to tell Mary nothing. Besides, I guess she ain't my relative no how. She's your daughter and your niece all at the same time because your husband fathered her. Ain't that the truth?"

"No, it's not the truth, Lee."

"Well, then. If Mary is my daughter, you ain't got no right to tell me to stay away."

"Just stay away. Okay?"

"Yeah, yeah, yeah. I reckon I'll stay away from your niece and your daughter."

"Look. I can't be seen around here talking to you all afternoon."

"Yeah. If that's all you wanted, I reckon you can go on. Leave me to myself." He really wanted to hold her, and have her hold him. Let the tears fall. Ask her about Robeena. He felt empty when she started away, but at least she'd taken the opportunity to give him the time of day.

"I said what I had to say. My concern is for Mary. You stay away from her, Lee. Ev'rybody was cheerful 'til you started creeping around. Just stay away from us!" She turned from him and trotted all the way back inside of her house, hoping that he'd gotten her message. When she got inside, she threw herself on the couch and sobbed.

"How can y'all be *cheerful* when Vivian is dead? How..." Lee was whispering to the grasshoppers, which were tittering louder than his mumble. Lee hated her. He wished he had ignored her when she first beckoned him, but he knew that would've been impossible. The past was too unanswered. He declared that he wanted as much of it as they would allow him to have, even if it meant being spit on, like Minnie had just done. He wasn't ready to let go of Vivian. These were the closest people who held on to pieces of the puzzle. He had to confront them. Maybe not with words, but they would have to let him see Vivian in them.

CHAPTER TWENTY-FOUR
The Furthest Star

 For twenty more years Lee sauntered through the neighborhood, not talking to anyone except other drunkards. He never came too close to the family. He wanted to be near them, and he didn't want to be near them. How could they ever accept him again after he destroyed their precious Vivian? She didn't belong to him anymore. It was like she belonged to him for a short while, and yet he thought she was his always, but after her death, he realized he was just borrowing her from *them*. In fact, even though he had been borrowing her against their will, now, they wouldn't allow him into their lives a second time. He couldn't even walk down their street to steal a memory without the family going into an uproar. It took a long time for him to surmise Vivian did not belong to anyone, except God. Lee felt that she was a real-life princess, a hidden princess; an angel who had been masked in the debris of societal conditions. Vivian stood out--everyone knew she was different. Spending hours upon hours on the corner doing nothing all day, and having no place to go, Lee spied a variety of women over the years. It happened that there was something special about each of them, yet their goodness was not visible to common people. The chemistry that could ignite royal characteristics buried in each of them was pivotal to discovering all the hidden princesses. For sure, each one was an angel, a beacon of light. He had not been skillful enough to notice or mine out the precious gems buried inside of Maybelle, or Liz for that matter. It slowly was unveiled to Lee that Vivian was only one hidden princess in the sea of princesses.

 For the twenty years that Lee hung around, Mary Henri-Anna never looked him in the eyes. She pretended he did not exist. One day, she monitored that she had not seen him walking around in several weeks, which turned to months, then years. Never once did she discuss her mother or Lee with anyone. Her cousin Dorothy learned a long time ago that the subject was taboo around her. Mary Henri-Anna tried to make the memories go away with Lee when she stopped seeing him. She hoped if it were not talked about, it would go away. The Raison's were her parents. Henry was her father.

 When she was eighteen, she met Harvey Billings. He was an escape for her from the perfect life she was pretending to have, with her perfect parents who never fought with each other. Harvey liked to drink plenty of liquor, and he did not try to hide this fact. His lack of sobriety was not of major concern because even as a young child, Mary Henri-Anna often found occasions to steal a shot of whiskey here and there from her Aunt Robeena's stow away cabinets in her dining room. Whenever she helped her aunt clean up in the bar, Mary Henri-Anna was constantly testing the goods to be sold later in the evening. Although she never let her aunt catch her in the stash, Mary Henri-Anna was convinced that much of her hiding was simply routine, for surely Robeena could smell the strong drink coming from her nostrils at times. There was no hiding with Harvey. She let the poisonous fluid ooze down her throat whenever she was with him without a care in the world.

Mary Henri-Anna learned that she could be free now, with Harvey. He held her whenever she let herself suffer from the memories of her sordid past. There were no questions, no accusations, he simply held her. He drank with her to help her repress the past. Harvey promised to take her away from the lie she was living with her parents. Although she never told him about her real mother, it was understood that he knew. The whole town knew. Mary Henri-Anna felt he loved her enough to not talk with her about it. Mary couldn't wait to stop going to her parent's churches where she was suffocating. Harvey let her know right away that he wasn't an attendee of any church, even though he assured her that he believed in God.

She hid him from her parents until the absolute last minute of their courtship. This is because she didn't ever want her father to think a young man was taking advantage of her. There was a time when she was fifteen that she met a boy named Elroy. Her father didn't give him a chance before he hinted loudly that the boy wasn't welcome. Then there was Thaddeus whom Mary Henri-Anna really liked, but her father found it fit to scare him off as well. With Harvey's drinking and carrying on, she knew not to bring him within two blocks of her father, until it was safe. In October, after four months of unchaperoned courting, Mary Henri-Anna came home with a bombshell.

"Mama, Daddy, y'all busy?" She charged into the house, running past them, and having to double back. They both knew that whenever she came like that, whatever business they were attending to needed to wait until she said what was on her mind. Henry was sitting on the sofa reading the newspaper, and Minnie was sitting under him on the floor, stitching something. He put the paper down when she came into the house well past the time they were expecting her. She had left two hours ago to see if Dorothy wanted to spend the night with her.

"What's wrong, honey? You alright?" Minnie sat erect against the sofa, knowing Henry would be managing whatever it was.

"Yes, daddy, everything is fine." Mary Henri-Anna paused to take his emotional pulse. He remained calm, although signs of agitation were visible in his clenched fists. Once she could see his fingertips emerge from the cup of his palm, she continued. "There's a good man outside who says he wants to marry me, and I want to marry him, too. Please, Daddy!" Henry stood, letting the newspaper slip from his lap. "Daddy, you at least gotta meet him. You don't never give nobody a chance before you go running somebody off! Harvey is a decent man."

"Oh yeah? Who is his parents? What church home he belongs to?"

"His parents be from North Carolina. Father's name is Tom, and his mama is Lula." She turned to Minnie. "Mama, I love him!" Henry rushed past his daughter to go outside where this stranger was waiting. Mary Henri-Anna slid outside after her father and stood several yards away.

Harvey was the most elegant looking man Henry had seen in a long time. His beige pants were creased and clean, matching his checkered wool jacket. The velvety green hat Harvey wore was free from lint or dust particles, and his shoes matched his hat. His smile showed even polished teeth. He wasn't the least bit disarmed that Henry had rushed out to meet him, even considering the things Mary Henri-Anna had told him about her father. His ebony hair was straight as an arrow, and cut short. He looked like a Carolina Geechie, Henry thought. He was definitely good looking. Somehow, Henry knew Mary Henri-Anna was serious about this one, and he was serious about her as well.

"What's your intention toward my daughter, boy?" Harvey took off his hat, fumbling moderately to gain his composure. "You hear me talking, boy? I say what is your intentions?"

"I 'tend on marrying her, sir.

"She in trouble?" Mary ran to Harvey's defense.

"Daddy!" Harvey remained steady and calm. He didn't take his eyes off Henry to look at Mary, who was now clutching his hand.

"Naw, Mr. Raison, she ain't in no trouble at all. My parents raised me decently. I love her and want to marry her is why I'm here."

Henry stared off at the furthest star, marveling at how the years had sped away. Vivian would love to behold her beautiful daughter. He had tried to give Mary Henri-Anna a sheltered upbringing. Henri-Anna was so special to him as his only child. Now Henry felt he could no longer screen her. After all, she had hid this current romance from him and Minnie. He remembered how she used to ask for his opinion on important matters. Henry recognized that if he did not say yes to their marriage request, they would continue to see each other behind his back.

Henry was afraid that this man couldn't take care of her because Henri-Anna had problems. She had witnessed her mother being murdered by her father. She had seen the entire thing, and she wore the blood of it on her clothes that night and in her spirit for the years to come. Although she was sweet, she was a sneaky, rebellious, bossy girl. She hadn't developed to handle critical issues in a mature way at all. She writhed in pain at the least heartrending discomfort. Henry knew that Henri-Anna would crumble if any major ailment would befall her. Henry learned from Robeena several years ago that Henri-Anna did know the truth about her real mother. Therefore, Henry had decided to explain things to her once and for all one quiet afternoon while they were alone in the house, about six years ago.

"Henri-Anna, come sit with me," he had said, signaling her to join him at the dining room table. She was out on the front porch braiding her hair. She went in at the sound of her father's voice and sat down joyously, smiling at her daddy. She continued to braid her hair at the table, even though Minnie had warned her not to do that sort of thing.

"I need to discuss something with you, darling. Listen carefully to me, you hear?"

"Sure, daddy." Henry started to say something about her hair strands but decided against it.

"Honey, your Aunt Robeena told me that you do know some things that I should've told you years ago." She twisted in her seat.

"Daddy, I don't want to talk about nothing like that. I know things, and then I don't know things. And what I don't know, I reckon I don't want to know." She scooted back in her chair, ready to stand. He touched her shoulder.

"I insist, Henri-Anna. It ain't no sense in you knowing any half-truths." He saw her begin to shake. He let her stand, standing with her.

"You trembling, child!" He held onto her arms when she resisted his hold.

"No, daddy. Let me be." She again tried to turn away from him, but he wouldn't let her. He *had* to speak to her about this.

"Honey, your real mother died when you were just a baby." She broke away from him at last. He pressed on. "You gotta listen to me!"

"No I ain't, neither. You always be trying to upset me, daddy. Why?"

"There's no way I would try to hurt you on purpose…and I never wanted to hurt your mother," he said soothingly. "There ain't nothing you can do about the truth except try to understand things."

"I'll kill you if you say that to me! Liar!" Mary Henri-Anna broke loose.

"Wait just a minute, girl. Slow it down! Just slow it down!" She tuned him out.

She dashed out of the room and out of the house, her hair in half braided plaits, leaving her father speechless in the middle of the floor. She returned home about an hour later, and acted like nothing had ever happened.

Now here stood this man, Harvey, who knew nothing about her past, claiming he wanted to marry her, take care of her forever. Henry surveyed that Harvey was just a boy himself. What could he have possibly learned that could equip him for the long journey ahead? One thing Harvey and Henri-Anna both had was determination. They wanted to be together and there was little Henry could do to stop it.

"Minnie," he called, "come on over here!" Smiling, Minnie emerged from behind the shadow of the door, where she had been listening to every word. "I reckon there's someone out here you need to meet."

Henri-Anna screamed with excitement and jumped in Harvey's arms, just the way Minnie had done with Henry so many years ago.

CHAPTER TWENTY-FIVE
Gancy's Treasure

Gancy heard the commotion just like every other Black person on the south side of Pontiac. He was at his sister's house when a crowd of people rushed past to the place where they heard a murder was taking place. He wasted no time in following the crowd, and he knew where they were going before they turned the corner of Vivian's street. He, too, was disillusioned when Lee moved her away from her family, because the fact that Lee was unstable was made clear to him from the time they met. He felt sorry for Vivian from the beginning. Gancy made it a point to spend more time in Pontiac so he would have an excuse to see Vivian more. He noticed that Henry tried to guard her, but still, Vivian was an emotional wreck whenever he saw her. She always tried to appear leveled during her trips to the urban league, but he knew those trips were often an escape from her nightmarish life. On some occasions, after Lee left for work, Gancy would deliberate about knocking on her door, but he never did. What would the neighbors think?

He saw Lee smack her just a few hours earlier outside the urban league, and he knew he had to do something. Vivian had waited for hours for Lee at the Fox Theater, and only went to the urban league after it was obvious that Lee stood her up. Gancy had told Vivian the truth when he said he was on his way to visit his sister in Pontiac. What he didn't tell her was that he was going with the intention of being close to her, not his sister. His sister was a convenience because she lived only minutes away from Vivian.

That day, if he would notice Lee's car gone whenever he strolled by their house (and he had planned to take a nice walk later that evening), he was prepared to knock on her door and make her face herself. Once it was dark, he planned, no one would know who he was at her door. He hoped she would let him in so they could have privacy, and then he would leave in a reasonable amount of time just in case someone saw him enter. Shaking himself from thoughts of what could have been, Gancy swallowed hard as the onlookers continued to exclaim that a man had just murdered his wife in cold blood while their baby watched.

"Get back! Get back!" The medics made their way through the crowd. It was their turn to behave with importance. Bruno had just finished cleaning

Vivian up. "Can anyone tell us what happened here?"

"The police already arrested the man, sir," Bruno stated.

"You the one who is looking after her?"

"Yes, sir." The two medics nodded their heads approvingly at the wound wrapping.

"Good job, boy." They gathered Vivian up, and left the room toting her on a gurney and boarded her into the back of their wagon. They removed Bruno's work to examine her wounds and determine the cause of death. Henry arrived around the same time as Gancy, but he couldn't look as he saw them rolling Vivian into the wagon. He would never see her again. Henry's vision became blurry as he leaned forward and vomited where he stood in the street. Tears welled up in Bruno's eyes when he saw Henry drop to his knees after vomiting. Bruno thought Henry should be the one to be the family's leader, but that was not happening. Therefore, Bruno dumped Robeena into the care of Minnie so he could assist in the procedures as best as he could. Gancy saw Bruno climb in the back of the wagon with a medic. He followed.

"I'll ride to the hospital with you all."

"We ain't going to no hospital, boy. We're gonna do our examination right here." The medic called Billy went up front to finish his sandwich. There was no need for two people to hover over a dead body. "We got a vet on the way to declare the time of death. We don't do nothing with niggers except to find out if they are dead. Only some reason this ambulance company answered the call is because the police called us about a murder." He also wanted to get back to his sandwich, but Billy had pulled a fast one on him. "Did you check her pulse, Billy?"

Billy put his sandwich down and got off the wagon bench to see about Vivian. "Naw." He looked at Bruno. "Ain't you the nigger who checked her pulse?" He put his instruments by Vivian's chest, and did a quick examination.

"Yes, I'm the man."

"She got her a slight pulse, but she'll probably be dead by the time we get to the morgue." Gancy's heart raced, and so did Bruno's.

"Sweet Jesus!" Gancy breathed.

"Sweet is right, Gancy! Holy Allah!" Bruno and Gancy could not believe what they were hearing. The thought of it was melodic.

"What y'all niggers getting happy about? Her pulse is so weak, I can't hardly detect it, even with my scope.

"A pulse...did you hear that, Bruno?" They both tuned out everything else the medics said. It was as though they could hear Vivian's pulse over any other words the medics said.

"Ain't no nigger hospitals. She's just as good as gone, boys. She won't last more than an hour." The medics regretted allowing the Black men inside of the wagon. They were trying to respect the family, but they didn't need any trouble. Bruno read their thoughts.

"Good thing we are here. I have a feeling you would have dropped her off at the morgue even with a pulse because she's colored.

"We have to save her!" Gancy panicked. "Bruno, your brother…"

"Now look…" Billy started,

"My brother is a doctor," Bruno stated with authority. He got a clinic right on Telegraph Road. What will it take for you all to wheel this wagon down where I tell you?" Both medics laughed. Bruno looked at Gancy and Gancy nodded at him. Bruno pulled out his wallet and dropped two twenty-dollar bills into Jim Bob's lap. They stopped laughing and called out to the driver.

"Watkins! Start her up." The motor began to drum. "Now, that's a start, but it ain't enough to get us moving nowhere. You hear me, boy?" Bruno stood and reached for his wallet again. Gancy put his hand out to stop him. He reached in his wallet and withdrew another twenty. Billy snatched it.

"The next thing coming out of my wallet won't be for the ride. It'll be for you to do some of your medical stuff to keep this lady breathing. And then I'm gonna ask my brother here to come out of his wallet and dig really deep, and that will be so you all can say you gave us the body to bury, you hear? We don't want nobody—including your driver -- to know she still got her a pulse." The medics nodded, already beginning to clean her wound and give her oxygen. The blood on her neck had caked, stopping her from bleeding to death. Jim Bob took the address down and told the driver where the clinic was.

Once they were rolling steadily, Bruno whispered to Gancy, "What are we doing?"

"We gotta save her."

"I know! But why are we lying about saving her? How come we didn't let everyone know she still is alive?" Bruno asked, trying to remain levelheaded.

"Didn't you hear them? They weren't gonna do nothing to help her 'til some animal doctor made his way over here. But with our money, they fixed her wounds like she's a human being. They were gonna let her die and they already had this wagon fixed toward the morgue!

"I know, but…"

"Look. You know me. I'm the co-director of the Detroit Urban League. I ain't no crook. I know a lot about this family."

"Me, too."

"Well, if you know half as much as I know, then it shouldn't be a surprise to you that they let this happen to her. They're irresponsible. We can't give her back to them—not now. If she lives, I'm asking that you tell your brother to release her to me, and I'll take care of this lady and nurse her back to health."

"I don't know about all that, Mr. Gancy."

"What kind of plans do you have?" Bruno didn't say anything. "I'm gonna save her life, in many ways. Don't try to stop me from doing that."

"I won't."

"Nobody's gonna stop me from helping her. I've waited too long not doing something. My work at the Urban League—this is the real work in dealing with our people."

"I just don't want you to get yourself too involved. You know…unnecessarily involved and then get caught up with the law and catch a case over something that could've been prevented."

"I know, man. But there just ain't no other way. Besides, I'm already too involved."

"I sort of figured that much."

"Best piece of advice I can offer you is to help me get her to your brother, and then forget you ever saw her. You want a job? See about Mary. She's gonna need you after this, and Vivian is gonna need me."

July 1930

Dear Lee,

I reckon you'll be getting out of prison here for long. A gentleman from the parole board sent a letter asking me to vouch for your living situation once you got out. Said they was gonna give you a bus ticket so you could come on home, Lee.

Now, I knowed what you say in your letters, that you ain't wanting to come home when you get out, but I reckon it would be best for all if you'd just come on back. Seems to me I got some explaining to do. Can't explain nothing in a letter. It was always my style to look a man square in the eyes when things of important nature come about. And you is a man, now, Lee. I never told you that you were a man, don't think. Your mama was decent folk. She was head strong like Vivian. Lee, if I thought you would hurt that girl I would've done something. 'Course I should have known since accidents are what happens when you get too emotional 'bout situations. Now hear me out. Charmin is writing this letter for me just how

I am saying things to you. My words may not come out right, but I gots to speak to you from my heart, son. I swear if you come home, I will sit you down and tell you about your mama.

Maybelle ain't got herself nobody. She comes around and asks about you from time to time. She's kind enough to let me spend time with my grandson. You should see your boy! Leeland is just a youngster, but he helps Floyd run one of those gambling houses, and he is really slick. He looks just like you, Lee. It's like having you here when I got that boy with me.

Please think about coming home, son. It'd kill me if you stay up there where you ain't wanted. Ain't nothing up there for you. Your house will still be here, and it's half in your name. I love you with my whole heart, son.

Love,

Pops

ABOUT THE AUTHOR

Dedra Lori Muhammad

Dear Reader,

Thank you for your indulgence. Please honor me by submitting your honest review of my work:

https://www.amazon.com/author/dedra_muhammad

https://www.goodreads.com/book/show/60293504-hidden-princess

I don't describe myself by my degrees and awards because I am a lifelong student. All Glory belongs to God. I grew up on the south side of Pontiac, Michigan, and I graduated from Pontiac Central High School. As a child, I liked to climb trees, ride my sled, and steal green apples from the neighborhood trees. Today, I love writing about those warm, youthful feelings; I am thrilled to make black words dance on white paper. The sequel to Hidden Princess: The Rebirth of Making Mary is on the horizon, God-Willing. In fact, I pray to complete the trilogy.

As a child, I can recall staring at the tall bookshelves in our library, imagining each book as a jeweled piece of fruit I could pluck at will. Nothing was off-limits.
Once, I was in K-Mart with my mom whenever I spotted a book called "How to be the Perfect Liar" or something like that. I thumbed through it filled with amazement since it was absolutely creative and hilarious. My mother refused to purchase the likes of it. Later, she went back without me to buy it. She stated she had promised herself that if any of her children ever took an interest in reading, she would support them.

As a member of my high school's track team, I would huddle in the back seats of buses reading Black romance magazines with my friends. Things were innocent in those days. I read everything from entire encyclopedia sets to the Falconhurst and Mandingo series...all the way to everything by Donald Goins, Charlotte Bronte, John Grisham, Richard Wright, Ralph Ellison, Toni Morrison, and more. However, my idea to write was because I merely wanted to get a hidden story told. The only way to do that would be if I wrote that story. The story you just read is based on true accounts of my family, with a lot of fiction added to fill in the gaps.

Please stay connected by following me on GoodReads and here: dedramuhammad.com.